TRISTRAM SHANDY

S. Sterne

From the first portrait of Sterne painted by Reynolds (1760). This portrait is in the Lansdowne Collection.

LAURENCE STERNE

THE LIFE AND OPINIONS
OF
TRISTRAM SHANDY,
GENTLEMAN

Edited by JAMES AIKEN WORK

THE ODYSSEY PRESS
New York

PREFACE

When Sterne first offered the manuscript of *Tristram Shandy* to Dodsley he observed that his local readers wished him to send the work into the world *"cum Notis Variorum,"* and added that "there is great Room for it." Today there is even greater room, for many of Sterne's allusions to men and books well known in his century are no longer recognized, and a considerable number of his words and even many of the ideas they express are no longer in general circulation.

In this edition I have attempted to place at the disposal of the modern reader some of the information which Sterne assumed his intelligent contemporaries to possess, that he may read it with the same understanding and therefore with the same relish as did they. In the Introduction I have discussed Sterne's life and art with a view to illuminating certain aspects of the novel which present difficulties to many readers, and in the notes I have translated all foreign words, defined unusual and obsolete words, identified as far as possible actual persons and books and events to which Sterne refers, and explained the more significant of the allusions which the passage of time has rendered obscure. I have referred to the vexed subject of Sterne's sources only when he has quoted (with or without quotation marks) or paraphrased material which he surely expected his well-read contemporaries to recognize as borrowed, and when a reference to his source would clarify his meaning for the reader.

It is with pleasure that I here record my debt to many friends who have graciously assisted me in my work. I am grateful to Professor Chauncey B. Tinker of Yale, who suggested and directed my initial study of Sterne and whose stimulating interest and wise counsel have contributed much to this volume; to Professor Lewis P. Curtis of Yale, the editor of Sterne's letters, and to Professor Edward H. Weatherly of the University of Missouri, who have read the Introduction and have offered generous suggestions concerning the notes; and to Professor Edward Bensly of St. Albans, England, who in spite of illness came to my aid in explaining passages in *Shandy* which were dark to me. For assistance in divers notes I again thank Professor R. H. Griffith of the University of Texas, Professor H. V. Velten of the State College of Washington, Mr. John H. Jacobson of Yale; and Professor V. B. Heltzel, Professor W. C. Holbrook, Dr. Clark Kuebler, Professor M. E. Prior, Professor J. W. Spargo, Miss Viola Dunbar, and Miss Wilda Miessner, all of Northwestern. I am indebted to Professor Arthur E. Case of Northwestern for permission to reproduce the Hogarth engravings in his copy of *Tristram Shandy,* and to E. P. Dutton and Co. for permission to reproduce the text of "Lillibulero" from *A Book of Songs* by Ernest Macmillan. I gratefully acknowledge the generous assistance and endless patience of Professor Robert Shafer, the General Editor of this Series. Greatest of all, however, is my debt to my wife, without whose constant criticism my work would have been done in half the time and not half so well.

J. A. W.

CONTENTS

	PAGE
INTRODUCTION	
I. The Reception of *Tristram Shandy*	ix
II. The Author of *Tristram Shandy*	xiv
III. *Tristram Shandy*	xlv
Structure	xlvi
Humour: Characters and Bawdy	li
Didacticism: Satire and Philanthropy	lxii
Sensibility: Humour and Sentiment	lxvii
SELECTED BIBLIOGRAPHY	lxxii
NOTE ON THE TEXT	lxxv

THE LIFE AND OPINIONS OF TRISTRAM SHANDY, GENTLEMAN

Volume I	Published December, 1759	3
Volume II		81
Volume III	Published January, 1761	157
Volume IV		244
Volume V	Published December, 1761	341
Volume VI		408
Volume VII	Published January, 1765	479
Volume VIII		539
Volume IX	Published January, 1767	597

INTRODUCTION

I. THE RECEPTION OF *TRISTRAM SHANDY*

During the early days of January in 1760 David Garrick received from Miss Catherine Fourmantel, a professional singer who was spending the winter season at York, a sprightly letter bespeaking his countenance not of a new play nor of a new actor nor of herself, but of a new book.

There are two Volumes just published here which have made a great noise, and have had a prodigious Run; for in two Days after they came out, the Bookseller sold two hundred——and continues selling them very fast. It is The Life and Opinions of Tristram Shandy . . . If you have not seen it, pray get it and read it, because it has a great Character as a witty smart Book, and if You think it is so, your good word in Town will do the Author, I am sure, great Service . . . His name is Sterne, a gentleman of great Preferment and a Prebendary of the Church of York, [who] has a great Character in these Parts as a man of Learning and wit.——The Graver People, however, say 'tis not fit for young Ladies to read his Book, so perhaps you'll think it not fit for a young Lady to recommend it. However, the Nobility and great Folks stand up mightily for it, and say 'tis a good Book tho' a little tawdry in some places . . .

Had the great actor known that his correspondent was but transcribing the lines of another, and that the author of *Tristram Shandy* was himself the author of the note which the disingenuous singer copied and signed, he might have been tickled at the conceit or annoyed at the deception of the enterprising novelist. Ignorant of the ruse, however, when he received a copy of the work recommended, Garrick read it and at once advertised its merit among his friends. With the

acknowledged regulator of public taste its champion, the novel
took at once, and soon all the fashionables of London were
talking of the new book.

And there was much to talk of, in those initial volumes.
"Tristram Shandy" signified, to those versed in the dialect of
Yorkshire, "a sad, crack-brained fellow," and the contents of
the work appeared of a piece with the title. A glance at the
volumes revealed an unconventional sprinkling of italics and
black letter type, passages in large capitals and small, brackets
and hands, series of long dashes and asterisks, and one leaf
solidly besmirched on both sides with printer's ink. Closer
examination disclosed long passages in French and shorter
ones in Latin and Greek, erudite-looking footnotes, a dedication in the middle of the eighth chapter (a mock one at that),
one chapter running to sixty pages in length and another to
four lines, an invocation to the moon, a formidable-seeming
legal document which turned out to be a burlesque, a grave
pronouncement in French by three learned doctors of the
Sorbonne, and a much-interrupted sermon on the abuses of
conscience. And as a crowning anomaly, the "gentleman"
whose life and opinions the title-page had announced proved
to be but an embryo! The brilliant topsyturviness of the
volumes—the variety of their subject-matter and the daring
of their digressions; the chronological confusion; the shocking
juxtaposition of bawdy *double entendres* and affecting sentiments, of impious jests and pious moralizing; the subtle characterizations, the odd talk, the wayward wit, and the lively,
sensitive style in which they were presented—made *Shandy*
the book of the hour.

Even the critics liked it. "Oh rare Tristram Shandy!"
apostrophized the *London Magazine,* "——Thou very sensible
—— humorous—— pathetick —— humane —— unaccountable!
——what shall we call thee?——Rabelais, Cervantes, What?
. . . If thou publishest fifty volumes, all abounding with the
profitable and pleasant like these, we will venture to say thou
wilt be read and admir'd." Less Shandean but no less sincere
in its commendation was the *Monthly Review,* which feared

only that in his multiplicity of digressions Tristram would leave the work before his story was finished, and which ventured "to recommend Mr. Tristram Shandy, as a writer infinitely more ingenious and entertaining than any other of the present race of novelists. His characters are striking and singular, his observations shrewd and pertinent; and, making a few exceptions, his humour is easy and genuine." Other reviewers were similarly commendatory, and the fame and sale of the book increased.

And as the book was read, curiosity grew about its author. Various journals reproduced from the opening volume the description of Yorick, that fellow of infinite jest, "as a specimen of the work; and the rather as it is by some supposed to be the character of the author, as he chuses it should be exhibited." Interest in the author, which but increased as meagre rumours of the country parson drifted in from Yorkshire, had become widespread by the first week of March, when Sterne, who had written "not to be *fed* but to be *famous,*" presented himself in London, only too eager to satisfy all curiosity about himself and to relish the tribute his labours had won him.

The story of this visit to London reads, as Wilbur L. Cross, Sterne's biographer, has remarked, like romance rather than sober history. At the onset of the winter Sterne had left under the care of a curate his vicarages of Sutton and Stillington where the first volumes of *Shandy* had been written, and had taken a small house in the Minster Yard at York, where he could better care for his wife, who was suffering from a mental disorder, better educate his twelve-year-old daughter, who was taking up dancing, and more conveniently carry on a wanton flirtation with Miss Fourmantel. Here he chanced one morning early in March to meet his good friend Squire Stephen Croft, who was setting out on a journey to London and who offered to take him along for the sake of his company, paying all his expenses. Having been allowed "an hour's law to go home to pack up his best breeches," Sterne joined his friend in the York coach and with him arrived in

London, unheralded and unknown, the evening of March fourth.

After spending the night with Croft's son-in-law, Sterne sallied forth the following morning, too impatient to wait for breakfast, and made for the bookshop of the Dodsley brothers, his London agents, where his vanity was flattered when on asking for the works of Tristram Shandy he was told that "there was not such a Book to be had in London either for Love or money." Later in the morning he was cordially re-received by James Dodsley, who, though he had refused the manuscript of *Shandy* before its publication at York, now purchased the copyright on the initial volumes for 250 pounds, and that on the partly-written third and fourth volumes for 380 pounds more. To him Sterne "mortgaged his brains" to continue *Shandy* indefinitely, in annual instalments, and to prepare for immediate publication a batch of sermons which he had prudently carried with him up to London. Then the novelist returned to his wondering friends, "and came skipping into the room, and said that he was the richest man in Europe."

The following morning Sterne called upon "dear Mr. Garrick," who at once took him up, introduced him to almost everyone in London of wit or distinction, and left "nothing undone that can do me either Service or Credit." "My Lodgings," he wrote a few days later to his "dear, enchanting Slut," Catherine Fourmantel,

is every hour full of your great People of the first Rank who strive who shall most honour me——even all the Bishops have sent their Compliments to me, and I set out on Munday morning to pay my Visits to them all.——I am to dine with Lord Chesterfield, this week &c &c——and next Sunday Lord Rockingham takes me to Court——I have snatch'd this single Moment, tho' there is Company in my rooms to tell my dear dear dear Kitty this, and that I am hers for ever and ever.

But more substantial honours were soon showered upon the lucky novelist. William Warburton, Bishop of Gloucester, who had "warmly recommended 'Tristram Shandy' to all the

best company in town" as "the English Rabelais," gave him a
purse of guineas, and Earl Fauconberg presented him with the
curacy of Coxwold, a choice preferment in the diocese of York.
"From morning to night," he scribbled to his "dear Love" a
week or so later, "my Lodgings, which by the by, are the genteelest in Town, are full of the greatest Company——I dined
these two Days with two Ladies of the Bedchamber——then
with Lord Rockingham, Lord Edgecomb——Lord Winchil-
sea, Lord Littleton, a Bishop——&c &c——I assure you, my
Kitty, that Tristram is the Fashion."

On the first of April, the day before the second edition[1]
of *Shandy* was published with its felicitous dedication to Pitt
and its engraving by Hogarth, Sterne crowed over an invitation from Lord Rockingham to join his suit when he went
to Windsor to be installed Knight of the Garter, and as the
month sped on, he found himself almost literally hurried off
his legs "by going to great People." According to the poet
Gray, the company was invited to dinner, where Sterne was
to dine, a fortnight beforehand; according to John Croft,
Sterne "frequently had cards of Invitation from the Nobility
and People of the first Fashion, for a month to come, [so]
that it allmost amounted to a Parliamentary Interest to have
his company at any rate."

Among his literary associations Sterne was pleased, as we
have seen, at the attention of the Earl of Chesterfield, Bishop
Warburton, and Lord Lyttleton. He may have been pleased
at meeting, probably in the company of Prince Edward from
whom he was at this time receiving great notice, a "curious
cub" from Scotland, one James Boswell, who thought him the
best companion he had ever known, and at once dashed off a
set of bad verses in praise of the "lousy prebendary" who had
overnight become the most sought-after man in London:

> By Fashion's hands compleatly drest,
> He's everywhere a wellcome Guest:

---

[1]That is, the first London edition, on which the present text is based.
There were two further editions published by Dodsley, as well as several
pirated editions, before the end of the year.

He runs about from place to place,
Now with my Lord, then with his Grace,
And, mixing with the brilliant throng,
He straight commences *Beau Garcon*.
In Ranelagh's delightfull round
Squire Tristram oft is flaunting found;
A buzzing whisper flys about;
Where'er he comes they point him out;
Each Waiter with an eager eye
Observes him as he passes by;
'That there is he, do, Thomas! look,
Who's wrote such a damn'd clever book.'

But most pleased was he by the unique distinction paid him
by the famous old Lord Bathurst, who had been the friend of
Pope and Swift, of Addison and Prior and Congreve. "He
came up to me, one day," Sterne wrote long afterward,

as I was at the Princess of Wales's court. 'I want to know you,
Mr. Sterne; but it is fit you should know, also, who it is that wishes
this pleasure. You have heard,' continued he, 'of an old Lord
Bathurst, of whom your Popes, and Swifts, have sung and spoken
so much: I have lived my life with geniuses of that cast; but have
survived them; and, despairing ever to find their equals, it is some
years since I have closed my accounts, and shut up my books, with
thoughts of never opening them again: but you have kindled a desire in me of opening them once more before I die; which I now
do; so go home and dine with me.'

II. THE AUTHOR OF *TRISTRAM SHANDY*

While during these days of lionizing Sterne was learning
much about the world of fashion in London, the world was
likewise learning much about Sterne. All who had laid eyes
on him knew that, like Parson Yorick in his book, he was
straight and tall but lean as a skeleton, and that the large nose
and full lips, and the luminous, deep-set eyes which shone
from a bloodless face lent a satyric inscrutability to the lively
features wherein united intelligence and humour. But not
until the April (1760) number of the *Royal Female Magazine*

carried a brief biographical sketch, which was at once copied by most of the London newspapers, was it generally known that the country parson, whose adroit manner and varied wit had charmed all who had met him, was a gentleman born, the son of an army officer, the nephew of an Archdeacon and Precentor of York, the great-grandson of an Archbishop of York, and himself a churchman of parts and a graduate of the University of Cambridge.

Sterne had been born in 1713 in Ireland, whither the 34th Regiment of Foot, in which his father was an ensign, had been withdrawn after the peace of Utrecht. For the first ten years of his life, his had been the hazardous fortunes of a camp-follower. In the pathetic account he later wrote of these early years with their dozen distressful "decampings" to new barracks (scarcely reached before "all [was] unhing'd" and the family was on the move again), and with their half-dozen successive babies, each "of a fine delicate frame, not made to last long" (four of which "left us behind in this weary journey"), Sterne drew a picture of a drifting existence, filled with struggle and disquietude. Yet to the boy, this life with its frequently shifting scenes, its easy and promiscuous friendships, and its agreeable notoriety, must have been a not unpleasant one. And to the artist who was later to depict with quiet authority the campaigns and reminiscences of my uncle Toby and corporal Trim, a childhood spent in friendly intimacy with men who had fought in Flanders under William and Marlborough was singularly fortunate. But such a vagrant, undisciplined existence was scarcely fit for a growing boy, by nature impressionable and unsteady, and in 1723 or 1724 his father placed him in school under the eye of his relatives in Yorkshire.

While his family continued to follow the drum, Laurence picked up the pieces of a scattered education near Halifax where, tradition has it, he studied but when he liked and "had more whippings than lessons," but where he nevertheless laid the foundation for what his writings show to have been a ready knowledge of French and the classical literatures.

And from his observation of the cloth-making industry in Halifax came the effective metaphors dealing with clues and skeins and webs, which frequently appear in *Tristram Shandy*. Study at grammar school ended, Sterne was in 1733 enrolled a sizar at Jesus College, Cambridge. In 1737 he received the B.A. and in 1740 the M.A. from this university, which, as members of Jesus College, his cousin Richard, his uncle Jaques, and his great-grandfather Richard, the Archbishop, had attended before him.

Details of Sterne's career at the university are wanting—it was said that he "read a little, laugh'd a great deal, and sometimes took the diversion of puzzling his tutors," and that he "left Cambridge with the character of an odd man, that had no harm in him; and who had parts if he would use them"— but a few significant facts are clear. He continued his study of the classics, and was introduced by his friend John Hall (later John Hall-Stevenson) to Rabelais and other French wits on whose facetious stories he was later to draw in *Tristram Shandy*. He developed a derisive contempt for the pedantic rules of formal logic, which seemed to him but a meaningless juggling of words, and which he later satirized in the theories of my father and the tale of Slawkenbergius and the argument of the visitation dinner. He formed a deep admiration for the philosophy and writings of "the sagacious Locke," in whose doctrine of ideas he found an explanation of his own sensibility, and whose influence on his thinking and writing he later declared might be traced "in all his pages, in all his lines, in all his expressions." And he awoke one morning to find that from a broken vessel in his lungs he had "bled the bed full," and to realize that Death, having once found out his lodgings, might at any moment return to conduct him to the uncertain beatitude of the next world before he would willingly relinquish the certain joys of this—a realization which prompted him to take a hedonistic delight in whatever experiences and sensations, however great or small, he might thereafter crowd into his fugitive days.

Cambridge behind him, Sterne entered the church, not because of any peculiar piety but because his pleasures at the university had left him badly in debt and because his uncle Jaques, a worldly-wise pluralist who was both Archdeacon of Cleveland and Precentor of York, now deigned to notice the youth and decided that he might be made useful in furthering his own designs. In these motives Sterne was neither better nor worse than many of his fellows, for at this time the ministry was commonly a secular profession like the law or medicine, not a divine "calling," and many a greater pagan than Sterne complacently wore clericals. Consequently, in 1738 he was inducted into the vicarage of Sutton on the Forest, a village within his uncle's archdeaconry; in 1741 he received a prebendal stall in York Minster; and in 1744 he secured the living of Stillington, two miles to the north of Sutton.

It is doubtful whether Sterne intended ever to live in the wilderness to which his induction called him. Certainly for the next two years he made but infrequent visits to Sutton, which he left to the ministrations of an assistant, while he lived near the centre of gaiety and fashion and church politics in York. For York was in those days the capital of the north in fact as in location. Throughout the year it was the residence of many families of wealth and fashion; others came in for the winter season with its assemblies and music-meetings, theatres and balls; and still others poured in during May and August for the cock-fighting and the great horse-races held on the Knavesmire. And it is easy to picture Sterne, the free and easy manners of the barracks refined by his residence in Cambridge, taking his place with a bachelor's competence among the gay throngs at the Assembly Rooms and the playhouse, the coffee houses and the races, exchanging greetings and jests, mixing with lords spiritual and temporal, disporting himself in flirtations and intrigues, but with an eye ever alert for the main chance.

It was during this period of agreeable activity that Sterne met and wooed and finally wed Miss Elizabeth Lumley, the daughter of a Yorkshire clergyman, who though but "a homely woman," according to John Croft, had been reared "in stile," and "had many Admirers, as she was reported to have a Fortune." For two years his tender courtship continued until, moved by the lachrymose sensibility which was to find its ultimate expression in *A Sentimental Journey,* Miss Lumley became his bride in March, 1741. But even the sentiment of a bridegroom was unable to repress Sterne's overmastering love of the ludicrous, and the following Sunday he shocked his parishioners, according to a contemporary account, by discoursing upon the fifth verse of the fifth chapter of Luke: "We have toiled all the night, and have taken nothing."

The marriage amused Miss Lumley's cousin Elizabeth Robinson, who was later to achieve fame as Mrs. Montagu, the celebrated bluestocking, when she heard of it in a letter from her brother, who was taking the waters at Bath. "Our cousin Betty Lumley," he wrote, "is married to a Parson who once delighted in debauchery, who is possessed of about £100 a year in preferment, and has a good prospect of more. What hopes our relation may have of settling the affections of a light and fickle man I know not, but I imagine she will set about it not by means of beauty but of the arm of flesh."

Almost from the beginning, indeed, "Sterne and his Wife," as Croft phrased it, "did not *gee* well together." Temperamentally mismated—it is questionable whether Sterne's volatile nature could have settled into jog-trot matrimony with anyone—they failed to live in perfect harmony "chiefly owing to his infidelity to the Marriage Bed." One of the tales of their troubles related how Mrs. Sterne caught her husband with the serving-maid, handled him roughly with "the arm of flesh," and then went out of her mind and "fancied herself the Queen of Bohemia." Another tells how she, discovering him rifling the strong box in which they were saving their daughter's dowry, fell into a faint from which she recovered to quarrel roundly with him and to spread the story maliciously abroad. But the whole fault must not be laid to Sterne's charge. Long years of matrimony with Mrs. Sterne, who was rarely happy and never satisfied, would have tried the temper of a less mercurial philosopher than he. Even Mrs. Montagu,

who could not imagine him "of a sort to make a good husband," described her cousin as *"si tracassiere,* she puts every
Town into a combustion in a month." "Mrs. Sterne," she
wrote on another occasion, "is a woman of great integrity
and has many virtues, but they stand like quills upon the fret-
full porcupine, ready to go forth in sharp arrows on the least
supposed offence; she would not do a wrong thing, but she
does right things in a very unpleasing manner, and the only
way to avoid a quarrel with her is to keep a due distance."

Sterne himself, in spite of his serious deficiencies, was on
occasion most tender with his wife; he was solicitous for her
creature comforts, he ministered to her during her frequent
sicknesses, and he never blamed her, though he had cause sufficient, for her financial extravagance.   And not every day was
turbulent.   We have occasional glimpses of husband and wife
managing their affairs, visiting their neighbours, shopping in
York, and driving out together in their carriage in cheerful
amity. When Mrs. Sterne fancied herself the Queen of
Bohemia, her husband's sense of the ludicrous combined with
his good nature in moving him to treat her "as such, with all
the supposed respect due to a crowned head."   "To induce
her to take the air," the account continues, Sterne, who loved
hunting, "proposed coursing in the way practised in Bohemia.
For that purpose he procured bladders and filled them with
beans and tied them to the wheels of a single horse-chair,
when he drove madam into a stubble field.   With the motion
of the carriage and the bladders' rattle it alarmed the hares,
and the greyhounds were ready to take them."   And John
Croft, who knew the pair better than anyone else who has
written of them, recorded that though Mrs. Sterne "used to
say herself, that the largest House in England cou'd not contain them both, on account of their Turmoils and Disputes,
they were [yet] every day writing and addressing Love Letters
to one another."

* * * * * * *

With his marriage came a change in the place as well as the
manner of Sterne's life. Lacking the means, and perhaps at

first the desire, to settle with his bride in York, he at once removed to Sutton, eight miles north of the metropolis, where he entered upon the retired life of a country parson and landed squire which he was to follow, with but occasional interruptions, for twenty years.

With two parishes under his direction he preached Sunday mornings at Sutton, and afternoons, using doubtless the same sermon, at Stillington; and he cared for his parishioners, though without denying himself incidental rural pleasures, with surprising scrupulosity. Croft has left us "Idle tales," it is true, to the contrary: walking over the fields one Sunday to preach at Stillington, and his pointer springing a covey of partridges, Sterne, according to the report, "went directly home for his Gun and left his Flock that was waiting for him in the Church, in the lurch"; once, while he was skating, "the Ice broke in with him in the middle of the Pond, and none of the Parishioners wou'd assist to extricate him, as they were at variance"; because of his temperamental instability, his solid, rustic neighbours "generally considered him as crazy, or crackbrained." Like parson Yorick's, "the brisk gale of [Sterne's] spirits" may have run him "foul ten times in a day of some body's tackling." Yet the records of his ministrations reveal an unusual zeal in caring for his communicants. And save for occasional outbursts such as those Croft has recorded, he seems to have got on amicably enough with his parishioners.

As a prebendary of York, Sterne was active in diocesan politics; he took his turns and frequently those of others in preaching in the Cathedral; before he was thirty he was selected to preach the first sermon in the Minster before a newly installed archbishop; and two of his sermons delivered at York on special occasions were printed and sold in pamphlet form —one of which, *The Abuses of Conscience,* published at "the unanimous Request" of "many Gentlemen of Worth and Character," he liked well enough to present to a larger public as a sermon of parson Yorick's in the second volume of *Tristram Shandy.* As a preacher, indeed, Sterne seems to have been

generally successful, in spite of a vocal weakness which resulted from his haemorrhages. And from his training in
delivery, as well as from his interest in drama and art, proceeded his awareness of the significance of posture and gesture which was to make *Tristram Shandy* unique in its minute
delineation of suggestive bodily attitudes.

Along with his clerical activities, Sterne ambitiously
branched out into general farming. Year after year he added
to his holdings, and while Mrs. Sterne busied her fretful self
with managing her household and her "gooses," he was occupied with improving his lands and raising extensive crops of
barley and oats, rape, wheat, and potatoes. But he overshot
himself, and in the end reaped little but sorrow from his
seeming increase in property and wealth. Indeed, the finest
fruit of his farming is the passage in *Shandy* where my father's
"calculating the simple expence of paring and burning, and
fencing in the *Ox-moor*," appears to be a gentle satire on
Sterne's own over-exuberant ambitions. One can well understand why Sterne was relieved to turn, in 1760, from the pursuit of husbandry to the more pleasant and more remunera-
tive pursuit of literature.

In the yearly rounds of sowing and reaping, confirming and
preaching, Sterne did not neglect his amusements. To the
vigorous sports of hunting and skating, in which we have
glimpsed him taking pleasure, he added calmer recreations
and became, like Tristram Shandy, "at certain intervals and
changes of the Moon . . . both fiddler and painter." "He
was not steady to his Pastimes," recorded Croft in partial explanation of his local reputation for being crack-brained. "At
one time he wou'd take up the Gun and follow shooting till
he became a good shott, then he wou'd take up the Pencil and
paint Pictures." At first his artistic ideal was Hogarth, whose
style he imitated and whose *Analysis of Beauty* he recommended to readers of *Shandy;* later his style became more
idealized, owing, perhaps, to a brief association with Christopher Steele and his apprentice, George Romney. Of Sterne's
knowledge of the theory and history of painting, sufficient

evidence is found in *Tristram Shandy,* which abounds in allusions to the technical terms and critical tenets of the art, to its masters and their works. In his detailed descriptions of Trim's and my father's oratorical attitudes, in his elaborate analysis according to De Piles's "painter's scale" of his mock-dedication, in his impatience with the canting connoisseur's "rules and compasses" of criticism, in his rhapsody on "the *Poco piu* and the *Poco meno* of the *Italian* artists;—the insensible MORE or LESS [which determines] the precise line of beauty in the sentence, as well as in the statue," Sterne reveals his familiarity with and his enthusiasm for art. Indeed, a writer, he concludes, is much like a painter: each must learn what parts of his subject "he is to cast into shade,——and whereabouts he is to throw his light"; and each, forced to choose between two evils, deems it "more pardonable to trespass against truth, than beauty."

When he laid down the brush and took up the bow, Sterne played both the violin and the cello at least well enough to entertain festive gatherings of his friends; and *Tristram Shandy* bears witness to his knowledge of music no less than to his knowledge of painting. Famous are the story of poor Maria who piped "the sweetest notes I ever heard," the singular musical "characters" with which Yorick passed judgement upon his sermons, and the *entr'acte* concert upon his out-of-tune Cremona with which Tristram punished the ears of his sensitive hearers. Frequently Sterne discriminates shades of emotion by describing in precisely which of the "infinitude of notes, tunes, cants, chants, airs, . . . and accents" a word or phrase is pronounced. How pallid, for example, would be my father's pedantic arguments, did he not enforce them with "his hand upon your breast, . . . and in that soft and irresistible *piano* of voice, which the nature of the *argumentum ad hominem* absolutely requires." Again and again the nuances of Sterne's style, in passages vigorous as well as delicate, evidence an ear sensitive to and practised in musical harmony. And again he reveals how closely associated in his mind were the various arts, by concluding that writing a book "is for all

the world like humming a song——be but in tune with yourself, madam, 'tis no matter how high or how low you take it."

Most important of the amusements of the future author of
Tristram Shandy, however, was his reading. During the long
winter days and evenings when the weather or his constitution
held him prisoner in the vicarage, Sterne recreated and stored
his facile mind with a wide assortment of books. Most vivid
in his memory (and sometimes nearest to his hand) as he
wrote his own book were Rabelais, and Cervantes, and Burton's *Anatomy of Melancholy,* whose thoughts and phrases and
tricks of style he reworked as his own. Next to these in his
affections and in their contribution to *Shandy* may be placed
Montaigne and Erasmus and Horace, Bacon and Swift and
Hall. But he was familiar with general literature, both ancient
and modern, and with special subjects of all sorts, from medicine to biography and history and political science. He was
acquainted with the important literature of theology and
philosophy; he knew well the followers of Rabelais in France
and the wits of the Augustan age in England; and he appears
to have had first-hand experience of most of the long list of
volumes on military science over which my uncle Toby sat
up "whole nights baking [his] blood with hectic watchings."
And throughout his writings may be traced the pervasive influence, in thought and style, of Locke, and in cadence and
phrase, of Shakespeare and the Bible.

But though a great reader, Sterne was not a great thinker.
His mind was alert and facile, and he displayed at times an
intuitive logic, but he lacked the power of deep and sustained
thought. His intellect was at the mercy of his sensibility,
and he created no ideas of significance. He was not even, in
the best sense of the word, a learned man: nine-tenths of the
"erudition" of *Shandy* he took second-hand from compilers,
notably from Burton and Bayle and Chambers. Rather, he
had a scrap-book mind that collected diverting information
regardless of its importance or its source. And such was the
reading—the great literature of the world zestfully interlarded
with quaint erudition, frank nonsense, and facetious quibbles,

and with specialized scientific and philosophical and theological works—with which the scrap-book was filled year after year in the quiet parsonage at Sutton, and which was to reappear, refined and transmuted and sometimes strangely joined, in the pages of *Tristram Shandy*.

But Sterne's amusements were not confined, during his rustication at Sutton, to his own fireside. He and Mrs. Sterne constantly visited their "cordial friends" the Crofts, at Stillington Hall, for supper and an evening of music and stories and jests. Occasionally they dined and played quadrille with Lord Fauconberg and his lady at Newburgh Priory. Every week or two, roads and health permitting, Sterne would drive in to York to maintain his social and professional fences. Frequently Mrs. Sterne would accompany him, marketing, and visiting her friends, while he made the rounds of his own friends, or attended a concert in the Assembly Rooms, or gossiped and caught up on the news of the world in the coffee-room of the George, "the principal inn, where those who drank little wine, and did not choose too much expence, might read the news-papers." Then there were drives to visit friends and take the waters at Scarborough, the fashionable seaside resort some thirty-five miles to the east of Sutton.

Most memorable of these jaunts abroad, however, were Sterne's gay visits with his Cambridge friend, Hall-Stevenson, who after travelling abroad had married and retired to his family seat, Skelton Castle, a fantastic heap of buttressed terraces and turrets rising lugubriously above a stagnant moat, two and a half miles from Saltburn-by-the-Sea, which he characteristically re-christened "Crazy Castle." Here Sterne spent an occasional week or two with his convivial "cousins" the Demoniacs, an impious, roistering, madbrained group of a dozen Yorkshire parsons and squires who, in comparatively mild imitation of the notorious "monks" of Medmenham Abbey, assembled at Skelton to spend their days in riding, shooting, and fishing, and their nights in singing, jesting, and "joyous deliriums" over the burgundy. On fine days Sterne and his host would ride over to Guisborough where they visited a widow and her daughter, or to Saltburn where they spent many an exhilarating afternoon racing their chariots along the level beach, as much as five miles at a stretch, "with one wheel in the Sea." Perhaps these visits to Crazy Castle had as much to do as anything in Sterne's life with the crack-brained humour of *Tristram Shandy*. Hall-Stevenson possessed "a fine library" in which, tradition has it, Sterne found many a curious volume that contributed to the out-of-the-way lore of his own book. The extravagant stories, salacious jests, and Rabelaisian plays upon Latin words with which the "cousins" shortened the long winter evenings doubtless provided many a jest and quibble and bawdy *double entendre* for *Tristram Shandy*. Hall-Stevenson actually appears in the book, ironically enough, as the discreet and admonitory Eugenius; and from the odd group of humorists who gathered around his burgundy may have come traits which, fused with observations of other men and with memories of books, Sterne translated to immortality in Trim and my father and my uncle Toby.

The writing of *Tristram Shandy* was the result, however, of Sterne's activity in church politics. Jaques Sterne had first aided his nephew, as has been said, in the hope that he might prove of use to him, and at the outset he found his patronage of the young man well repaid. For several years the vicar wrote political pamphlets and "villainous letters" to the newspapers in successful support of Sir Robert Walpole and local Whig campaigners; and although records of the time are wanting, it is probable that during the turbulent months of the Forty-five, when the line between Tory and Whig, Catholic and Protestant, assumed perilous significance, Sterne again supported his uncle's party with his pen. Certainly his strong prejudice against the Church of Rome dates from this period, when his uncle overzealously hunted out all Jacobites and Catholics, real and imaginary. Of one of the Tory suspects, Dr. John Burton, author, antiquary, and obstetrician of note, Sterne conceived such dislike that in later years he caricatured him in *Tristram Shandy* as Dr. Slop, the "little, squat, uncourtly" Papist and man-midwife. And against the Catholic Church, "a pecuniary system, well contrived to operate upon men's passions and weakness, whilst their pockets are o'picking," whose history has ever been accompanied by "scenes of cruelty, murders, rapines, blood-shed," he poured forth conventional invective until residence in France and Italy revealed to him that Catholics could, after all, be both humane and happy.

Sometime during those years, however, a coolness arose between the Precentor and his nephew which by the end of the decade had developed into open and bitter animosity. According to Sterne, the quarrel started "because I would not write [political] paragraphs in the newspapers"; according to local gossip, the two men "fell out about a favourite Mistress of the Precentor's, who proved with child by Laury." Whatever the cause, Jaques Sterne became more zealous to break his nephew than he had ever been to advance him, and from small beginnings he contrived a master-stroke by which to discredit the younger man forever: he had Sterne's widowed mother and sister, who had long been harassing the vicar for more money than in justice to his wife and infant daughter he dared allow them, lodged in some charitable institution, probably a debtors' prison—the "Very place," expostulated Sterne, "where a hard report might do me (as a Clergyman) the most real Disservice"—and then spread the word that they were there through Sterne's neglect. The stratagem was successful. There is evidence that the quarrel with his mother was eventually made up and that Sterne continued to contribute money toward her support; but he was never able wholly to put down the gossip which quickly spread abroad and which was later given epigrammatic perpetuity by Byron's sneer at "that dog Sterne, who preferred whining over a dead ass to relieving a living mother." "The whole plan of the attack," Sterne wrote in *Shandy,* "was put in execution all at once,——with so little mercy on the side of the allies,——and so little suspicion in *Yorick,* of what was carrying on against him,——that when he thought, good easy man! full surely preferment was o'ripening,——they had smote his root, and then he fell, as many a worthy man had fallen before him."

For a number of years after this defeat, the humiliated vicar appears to have withdrawn from active participation in capitular politics. But in 1758 there came to a head a quarrel between John Fountayne, Dean of the Cathedral, and Francis Topham, a Yorkshire attorney who over years of pushing and intriguing had obtained for himself a majority of the legal offices connected with the Diocese of York. Of the long struggle between the two men and their satellites the climax and conclusion was a devastating satire on Dr. Topham written by Sterne in the manner of Swift and entitled *A Political Romance*. This pamphlet, which was later called *The History of a Good Warm Watch-Coat,* was printed early in 1759, and "what all the serious arguments in the world could not effect," said the London papers of the following year, "this brought about." Although the witty performance exploded Dr. Topham's pretensions in a burst of ridicule, its circulation would have harmed the dignity of the chapter as a whole, and Sterne was finally persuaded to allow all save a few copies to be burnt. But the amusement the work had afforded his friends fired him to attempt another and no middle flight in satirico-humorous writing. "Till he had finished his Watchcoat," it was said, "he hardly knew that he could write at all, much less with Humour, so as to make his Reader laugh." Now, encouraged by the success of this *jeu d'esprit,* in which his later satirical technique and the hobby-horses of my father and my uncle Toby were prefigured, Sterne set himself seriously to literary work, and from the ashes of the *Political Romance* arose *Tristram Shandy*.

Starting late in January, 1759, Sterne wrote as fast as he "possibly could," and by June had completed the first draft of the opening volumes. For all his enthusiasm, there were moments of depression. Once, when he was reading some loose sheets of the work to a company at Stillington Hall, his hearers fell asleep, "at which Sterne was so nettled that he threw the Manuscript into the fire, and had not luckily Mr

Croft rescued the scorched papers from the flames, the work wou'd have been consigned to oblivion." More than once his friends protested against the grossness of portions of the work as unbefitting a clergyman. To one he replied that "an Attention to his Character would damp his Fire and check the Flow of his Humour, and that if he went on, and hoped to be read, he must not look at his Band or his Cassock." To another he inveighed against "this understrapping Virtue of Prudence," and in defending himself coupled his name with those with which he loved best to see it: "I deny I have gone as farr as Swift——He keeps a due distance from Rabelais——and I keep a due distance from him——Swift has said a hundred things I durst Not Say——Unless I was Dean of St. Patricks." Then there were financial difficulties, for both the local booksellers and the Dodsleys in London refused to risk publishing so unprecedented and topsyturvy a work. But Sterne pruned and revised his book——"I have Burn'd More wit," he wrote, "than I have publish'd"; a generous friend loaned him "One hundred pounds towards the Printing"; late in December the two volumes were published; and in March, April, and May of 1760 their gleeful author was disporting himself, as we have seen, the man of the moment in London.

* * * * * *

During the last week of May, Sterne, riding in his own carriage and driving his own horses, returned in triumph to Yorkshire. Less than three months before, an obscure country parson, unable to pay his expenses to London, he was now perhaps the most famous man in England. A group of his friends in the capital wagered that a letter addressed to "Tristram Shandy, Europe," would reach him: the letter, recorded Croft, "came down into Yorkshire and the Post Boy meeting Sterne on the road to Sutton pulled off his hatt and gave it him." Looking back on Sterne's stay in London, Croft declared "that his Vanity mounted on his slowest Hobby Horse ran away with him beyond all bounds, and he boasted of Favours that he never received, and . . . flattered himself

that his Person was very much admired by the Ladies, so that
he turned his mind intirely to Galantry." There is no question that Sterne, who was accustomed to accepting whatever
pleasures came his way, enjoyed his triumph to the full.
Nevertheless, he realized the precariousness of fame such as
his, and compared himself to "a fashionable mistress, whom
every body solicits, because 'tis the fashion, but who may walk
the street [in] a fortnight, and in vain solicit corporal Stare
for a dinner."

And indeed, even before he left London, a darkling under-
current of disapprobation of him and his works had begun
to make itself felt. Many readers who had praised *Tristram
Shandy* as the work of an unknown author tightened their lips
when they learned that it was written by a clergyman who had
deserted his band and cassock for the cap and bells of a jester.
Certain men of letters condemned the book: Walpole, as
insipid and tedious; Goldsmith, as bawdy and pert and vain;
Richardson, as wild, incoherent, and indecent. Some time
later the Bishop of Sodor and Man "accidentally read" a
portion of the book and re-named it "Shameless-Shandy."
The press, ever on the side of the vociferous, took up the
attack and a flood of hostile articles began to appear in the
papers and magazines, some soberly censuring, but more
rowdily ridiculing Sterne's obscenity. One of a number of
satirical poems, an epistle presumably written by Shandy to
the students of divinity at Oxford, exhorts them to apply
themselves for advancement to the study, not of divinity, but
of bawdy, and to follow, in that course, his own example. A
prose attack, which was characteristic of many, breaks into a
sarcastic encomium on the novel and its author:

A fine work it is, full of laughs and strokes and jests. But the best
of all is——may be you do not know it——*Tristy*'s a clergyman of
the church of *England* [no conformist, thank goodness!]——
smoke the parson!——Did you ever know such a jolly dog of a
divine?——He has the finest knack of talking bawdy!——and he
makes such a joke of religion!——What do you think of his introducing a sermon in the midst of a smutty tale, and making the

preacher curse and swear by way of parenthesis? . . . There is nothing STERN in this doctrine——*Nomini nulla fides.*

Much of the abuse heaped upon the head of "the indelicately witty Yorick" should more justly have been directed, however, against the spawn of crude and common catch-penny pamphlets written about and in feeble imitation of *Shandy*. When the sensitive Citizen of the World asked his bookseller why such works as Sterne's were written, he was told, "The book was published in order to be sold; and no book sold better, except the criticisms upon it, which came out soon after." But in the litter of "imitations," many of which were the shoddiest of mere jest-books, the beauties of Sterne were never approached and his suggestiveness was ever coarsened and vulgarized. "There is a shilling pamphlet wrote against Tristram," Sterne crowed on reading the first of the lot; "I wish they would write a hundred such." But though these works of "profligate scribblers," the bathos of Grub Street, puffed his fame, their breath was malodorous; and long before the hundredth had been counted, "God forgive me," he cried, "for the Volumes of Ribaldry I've been the cause of."

The dissidence over Sterne but increased when a few days before leaving London he sought to "balance" his character by publishing in two volumes, and with an impressive list of subscribers which included almost every man of distinction in England, the long awaited *Sermons of Mr. Yorick*. The title of the volumes was generally censured as in bad taste, its most violent critic angrily declaring, in the *Monthly Review* for May, that it was

the greatest outrage against sense and decency, that has been offered since the first establishment of Christianity——an outrage which would scarce have been tolerated even in the days of paganism. . . . For who is this *Yorick?* We have heard of one of that name who was a *Jester*——we have read of a *Yorick* likewise, in an obscene romance.——But are the solemn dictates of religion fit to be conveyed from the mouths of buffoons and ludicrous romancers? Would any man believe that a preacher was in earnest, who should mount the pulpit in a Harlequin's coat?

But the sermons themselves, which turned, as Sterne had prefaced, "chiefly upon philanthropy, and those kindred virtues to it, upon which hang all the Law and the Prophets," and which proceeded "more from the heart than the head," were almost universally praised. The Monthly Reviewer just quoted, his spleen against the use of Yorick's name vented, declared of the sermons that "no compositions of this kind in the English language . . . are written with more ease, purity, and elegance; and tho' there is not much of the pathetic or devotional to be found in them, yet there are many fine and delicate touches of the human heart and passions, which, abstractedly considered, shew marks of great benevolence and sensibility of mind. If we consider them as moral essays, they are, indeed, highly commendable, and equally calculated for the entertainment and instruction of the attentive reader." Most critics and readers of taste approved this judgement. The sermons deal generally and comfortably with the temporal advantages of religion and the pleasures of philanthropy; they are enlivened by vividly dramatic episodes and character-sketches drawn from sacred and secular history; and they are cast in the most flowing of styles, which follows to a miracle the idiomatic flexibility of the spoken word. But to Dr. Johnson, who had little use for "the man, Sterne," they were mere "froth from the surface" of the cup of salvation, read only to beguile the tedium of a journey by stagecoach: "I should not have even deigned to look at them," he grunted, "had I been at large."

* * * * * * *

Sterne, meanwhile, having provided a curate for Sutton and Stillington, and adjusted mortgages and leases on his farms, had moved his family to Coxwold, "a sweet retirement in comparison of Sutton," some eight miles to the north of Stillington. Here, in the low, rambling, gabled dwelling which he named Shandy Hall, he proceeded at once with volumes three and four of his book. The Bishop of Gloucester, who along with the purse of guineas had given him in London "books to improve his Stile," now wrote Sterne admonishing him to make his work "useful," and to avoid "any violations of decency and good manners." The humorist cheerfully replied that "willingly and knowingly" he would "give no offence to any mortal," but that he feared he might "find it very hard, in writing such a book as 'Tristram Shandy,' to mutilate everything in it down to the prudish humour of every particular." He would do his best, "though laugh, my lord, I will, and as loud as I can, too." Laughing over his hero's broken nose and perverted name, over his oblique stroke at Catholicism in reproducing Ernulf's appalling anathema, over his merry satire on scholasticism in philosophy and religion in Slawkenbergius's Tale and in the account of the visitation dinner, over his attack on pedantic critics in general and those of the *Monthly Review* in particular, and over his misplaced preface, his missing chapter, and his bawdily suggestive "nose," Sterne wrote on—though seeking occasional relaxation in "pruneing, or digging or trenching, or weeding, or hacking up old roots, or wheeling away Rubbish"—until December, when, the week before Christmas, he went up to London to see his new volumes through the press.

Sterne's second visit to the capital was even more festive than his first. "I never dined at home once since I arrived," he wrote to Stephen Croft (as for "my dear dear dear Kitty," she had been forgotten long ago); "where I had one friend last year, who did me honour, I have three now." But when *Shandy* was published, on January 28, 1761, all the reviewers but one, resentful at his pert refusal to accept their censures of his having published his sermons under Yorick's name and at his telling satire on the "rules and compasses" of their trade, denounced the work as dull, insipid, and humourless. This was patently unfair, for though the third volume was but tolerably good reading the fourth was as brilliant as anything Sterne had yet done; and the book sold, in spite of the critics. "One half of the town abuse my book as bitterly, as the other half cry it up to the skies," Sterne wrote to Croft in February; "——the best is, they abuse and buy it, and at such a rate, that we are going on with a second edition, as fast as possible." And a month later the continued upbraiding afforded him an opportunity to relate himself again to his two great predecessors in satire. "If my enemies knew that by this rage of abuse, and ill will, they were effectually serving the interests both of myself, and works," he declared, "they would be more quiet——but it has been the fate of my betters, who have found, that the way to fame, is like the way to heaven—— through much tribulation——and till I shall have the honour to be as much mal-treated as Rabelais, and Swift were, I must continue humble; for I have not filled up the measure of half their *persecutions*."

The season drew to its close, and by the latter part of June Sterne was posting back to Yorkshire, where he soon set about his parish duties with unaccustomed zeal. He preached regularly, cared well for his communicants, and on the day of the King's coronation entertained the whole countryside with "a large Ox . . . roasted whole, with his Head on and Horns gilt." Meanwhile his domestic life flowed smoothly, and work on the fifth and sixth volumes of *Shandy* progressed. " 'Tis a very agreeable ride out in the chaise I purchased for my wife," he wrote to a friend early that fall. "Lyd has a poney which she delights in.——Whilst they take these diversions, I am scribbling away at my Tristram. These two volumes are, I think, the best.——I shall write as long as I live, 'tis, in fact, my hobby-horse: and so much am I delighted with my uncle Toby's imaginary character, that I am become an enthusiast.——My Lydia helps to copy for me——and my wife knits and listens as I read her chapters."

The requisite number of chapters finished, Sterne was again in London by the end of November. At this time occurred at the home of Sir Joshua Reynolds the only known meeting between him and Dr. Johnson. "In a company where I lately was," the lexicographer was said to have related, "Tristram Shandy introduced himself; and Tristram Shandy had scarcely sat down, when he informed us that he had been writing a Dedication to Lord Spencer; and *sponte suâ* he pulled it out of his pocket; and *sponte suâ,* for nobody desired him, he began to read it; and before he had read half a dozen lines, *sponte meâ,* sir, I told him it was not English, sir." During the evening, it was said, Sterne passed about "a drawing too indecently gross to have delighted a brothel," at which Dr. Johnson left the room; later he told Miss Reynolds that he "would rather give up the pleasure of her brother's society than meet such a contemptible priest as Sterne."

When the critics, who had been awaiting the appearance of the latest instalment of *Shandy* to renew their attacks on Sterne's indecencies, read the volumes, they were amazed and delighted at the new and rich vein of whimsical humour and touching sentiment which they revealed. Trim's animadversions on death, my uncle Toby's campaigns, and the death of Le Fever were admired on all hands; my uncle Toby's oath was pronounced "a conceit of genius"; and the story of Le Fever was reprinted in nearly every magazine and newspaper in the kingdom. Never before had Sterne and his works been in such good repute.

But the novelist had come to London in weakened health, and his strenuous round of engagements in the city induced the most serious haemorrhage he had yet suffered. It was imperative that he take a long rest in a climate more grateful to his lungs than that of England; so, after putting his affairs in order in case he should die abroad, he set off early in January, 1762, on his famous race with that "long-striding scoundrel of a scare-sinner," Death. His "spider legs" were scarce able to support him, his voice was sunk to a whisper, and his face was as colourless, he said, as a dishclout. But his spirits, as he was to hail them in the next volume of *Shandy,* never

once deserted me, or tinged the objects which came in my way, either with sable, or with a sickly green . . . and when DEATH himself knocked at my door——ye bad him come again; and in so gay a tone of careless indifference, did ye do it, that he doubted of his commission——

'——There must certainly be some mistake in this matter,' quoth he. . . . By heaven! I will lead him a dance he little thinks of——for I will gallop, quoth I, without looking once behind me to the banks of the Garonne . . . *Allons!* said I; the post boy gave a crack with his whip——off I went like a cannon, and in half a dozen bounds got into Dover.

Unexpectedly stimulated by the air of Paris, "clear always and Elastick," and by the "unexpected honours" which he received on arriving there, the pale man clad in black improved so rapidly that he spent half a year in the French capital before proceeding south. "Tristram was almost as much known here as in London," he reported to Garrick, "at least among your men of condition and learning, and has got me introduced into so many circles ('tis comme a Londres.) . . . [I] have converted many unto Shandeism—for be it known I Shandy it away fifty times more than I was ever wont, [and] talk more nonsense than ever you heard me talk in your days." M. Tollot, a friend of Hall-Stevenson who met Sterne at this time, wrote:

I sometimes envy the happy disposition of our friend Mr. Sterne; all objects are rose coloured to that lucky mortal, and what to others appears sad and gloomy, to his eyes presents an aspect gay and smiling. His sole pursuit is pleasure; but he is not like other men who when they have attained their desire usually know not how to enjoy it, for he drains the bowl to the last drop and still has not begun to quench his thirst.

But during the spring, while affectionately arranging for Mrs. Sterne and Lydia to join him abroad, he suffered serious reverses in health, and thenceforth his chief concern was with comfortably moving his family and himself to Toulouse.

Of the journey south, which was accomplished during three weeks of weather "hot as *Nebuchadnezzar's oven*," Sterne gave the world an idealized account in the seventh volume of *Shandy*. Settled pleasantly in Toulouse, he sat him down, his face turned for inspiration toward Crazy Castle, and commenced "playing the fool with my uncle Toby, who I have got soused over head and ears in love." But even "in these sportive plains, and under this genial sun," he found himself

unable to make much headway with his work. Perturbed by
financial worries, by a mental ennui which he attributed to
"the eternal platitude of the French characters," and by "a
continual warfare with agues, fevers, and physicians," he left
Toulouse in the spring, moved ever hopefully from one place
to another, and spent the following winter in Montpelier.
But his heart was in England, whither, after settling his wife
and daughter comfortably in France as they desired, he set out
early in the spring of 1764. *En route,* however, he stopped in
Paris where, meeting his friend John Wilkes, recently expelled
from the House of Commons, and other English bloods—
"good and generous souls," he enthusiastically called them—
he was seduced to live with them, "shag rag and bobtail . . .
a most jolly nonsensical life of it [in] this city of seductions"
until late in May, when he left "foutre-land" and recrossed the
channel to "go and visit my wife the church in Yorkshire."

His wife the church languished without him yet a little
longer, however, while he spent a few weeks visiting friends
in London, a couple of months enjoying the festivities of the
summer season in York, and a fortnight "playing the good
fellow" at Scarborough, the most fashionable watering-place
on the northern coast. Settling finally in Coxwold the last of
September, Sterne left his curate in charge of his flock—his
lungs, he averred, would never permit him to preach more—
and sat down in his "Philosophical Hut" where, my uncle
Toby's amours still progressing but slowly, he conceived the
expedient of turning a penny from his wanderings abroad.
Facilely he composed "as odd a Tour thro' france, as ever
was projected or executed by traveller or travell Writer, since
the world began"; which, after an introduction to explain the
miscarriage of his customary volumes the preceding years,
he placed in volume seven, reserving the amours of my uncle
Toby and widow Wadman for volume eight, that the instalment might leave the reader on the main thread of his puzzled
skein. Publishing the new volumes in London in January,
1765, he was rallied on their slightness, on the padding of his
travels from guide-books, and on the vulgarity of the story

of the Abbess of Andouillets; but their clever episodes and gentle humour recommended them to the public, and they sold well.

Toward the end of his London season which, though as festive as ever, had been interrupted by illness, Sterne repaired to Bath where he spent a month resting, sitting to Gainsborough for a portrait, and "playing the devil" with a bevy of fair widows and maidens. For his unnumbered philanderings, Bagehot called Sterne "an old flirt [who] dawdled about pretty women," and the unnecessarily scandalized Thackeray denounced him as a "wretched worn-out old scamp." His own apologia, probably sincere, was: "I myself must ever have some dulcinea in my head——it harmonises the soul . . . but I carry on my affairs quite in the French way, sentimentally—— '*l'amour*' (say they) *'n'est rien sans sentiment.'*" But though he described himself to one of the dulcineas of Bath as "totally spiritualized out of all form for conubial purposes," there was at least one other on whom he would have "rejoice[d] to batten the rest of my days . . . if I had not a piece of legal meadow of my own."

The summer of 1765 Sterne spent in Yorkshire, pushing, whenever his frequent haemorrhages would allow, the subscription list to the third and fourth volumes of his sermons, which were published the ensuing winter. "Have you seen my seventh and eighth graceless Children"? he enquired of one of his friends, alluding, of course, to the latest instalment of *Shandy*.

But I am doing penance for them, in begetting a couple of more ecclesiastick ones——which are to stand penance (again) in their turns——in Sheets[1] about the middle of September——they will appear in the Shape of the third and fourth Volumes of Yorick. These you must know are to keep up a kind of balance, in my shandaic character, and are push'd into the world for that reason by my friends with as splendid and numerous a List of Nobility &c——

---

[1] A punning allusion to the old custom of requiring those guilty of adultery to do penance by standing in a public place, barelegged and bareheaded, and wrapped in a white sheet.

as ever pranced before a book, since subscriptions came into fashion
——I should grieve not to have your name amongst those of my
friends——and in so much good company as it has a right to be
in——so tell me to set it down.

Requests so disarming as this could not go unheeded, and
when the list of subscribers, nearly seven hundred in all, was
published, it included practically every name worth knowing
in Britain, and from France such famous ones as Crébillon,
Diderot, d'Holbach, and Voltaire.

Pausing in London only to leave his sermons with Becket,
who published them in January, Sterne took himself as rapidly
as possible to the Continent where he spent a "joyous" winter
in France and Italy, frolicking with friends old and new, visiting Mrs. Sterne and Lydia, and gathering material which,
fused with reminiscences of his former trip, he was later to
refashion for the artful pages of *A Sentimental Journey*. By
July, 1766, he had returned to his "peaceful retreat" at Coxwold and set himself at the next instalment of *Shandy*. It proceeded but slowly, however, for his spirits were clouded by
worry. He was again having frequent haemorrhages; he was
fretted by parish duties which he found himself no longer
able to perform; and he was alarmed, though he made no complaint to her, by his wife's extravagant expenses—nearly double the sum agreed upon—in France. Only once that summer, so far as is known, did he make a public appearance; the
once, however, was appropriate to his fame. The races that
season were greater and gayer than ever before, owing to the
presence of the Duke of York, and as a fitting conclusion to
the week's festivities Sterne, who had come to know His Royal
Highness well, was called upon to preach before him the following Sunday in the minster. The "excellent discourse"
reported in the London newspapers was Sterne's valediction
in St. Peter's, where he had first gained honour nearly thirty
years before.

Posting to London the first of January, 1767, "to ly in of another child"—the last, as it proved—"of the Shandaick procreation," Sterne soon found himself in the customary whirl

of dinners, theatre parties, and assemblies. By the end of the
month the lone volume of *Shandy,* with its graceful dedication
to Pitt, now the Earl of Chatham, had made its appearance
and, to his joy, was "liked the best of all." Upon the shocking conclusion of my uncle Toby's amours, with its—to use
Coleridge's phrase—"dallying with the devil," he was severely
reprobated; indeed, a number of scandalized persons wrote to
his good friend, the Archbishop of York, hinting that the
heteroclite vicar be unfrocked. But most of the critics now
accepted Sterne as the English Rabelais and praised his latest
performance. "We wish," wrote the Critical Reviewer, "that
it had been a little better accommodated to the ear of innocence, *virginibus puerisque;* but, perhaps, of all the authors
who have existed since the days of Rabelais, none can with
more justice than Tristram put his arms a-kimbo, strut through
his room and say, 'None but myself can be my parallel.' " My
uncle Toby's courtship and the misarranged chapters were
thought diverting; but the affecting apostrophe to time, "flying over our heads like light clouds of a windy day, never to
return more," the cadenced invocation to the "Gentle Spirit
of sweetest humour, who erst didst sit upon the easy pen of
my beloved Cervantes," and the tender idyl of poor Maria,
"sitting upon a bank playing her vespers upon her pipe, with
her little goat beside her,"—these were the purple passages
which were reprinted by newspapers and magazines throughout the land and which took their places along with the story
of Le Fever and the incident of my uncle Toby and the fly,
in the regard of Sterne's sentimental contemporaries, as the
finest creations of their author's genius.

* * * * * * *

It was during the round of dinner parties this winter in
London that Sterne met and wooed Eliza—Elizabeth Draper,
the twenty-two-year-old wife of an official at Bombay of the
East India Company—his one great passion in a life of petty
philanderings. An attractive person, with bright eyes and a
face "the most perfect oval I ever saw," her vivacious conver-

sation and profuse sentiment held a strong attraction for the lonely, fifty-three-year-old invalid. There can be no question of the Platonic nature of Sterne's affection for Mrs. Draper. A chronic valetudinarian who had "not an ounce and a half of carnality" about him, he made no secret of his infatuation, and addressed her as father to daughter no less than as suitor to sweetheart. Yet he was soon writing,

My wife cannot live long . . . I know not the woman I should like so well for her substitute as yourself. . . . what I want in youth, I will make up in wit and good humour.——Not Swift so loved his Stella, Scarron his Maintenon, or Waller his Sacharissa, as I will love, and sing thee, my wife elect! All those names, eminent as they were, shall give place to thine, Eliza.

When her husband commanded that she sail for Bombay in April, Sterne felt their parting to be "the Separation of Soul and Body—and equal to nothing but what passes on that tremendous Moment"; and after she had gone he wrote: "in ten minutes after I dispatched my letter, this poor, fine-spun frame of Yorick's gave way, and I broke a vessel in my breast, and could not stop the loss of blood till four this morning. I have filled all thy India handkerchiefs with it.——It came, I think, from my heart!"

Before they parted, each had agreed to keep for the other a journal of his movements and emotions. In the portion of Sterne's which alone is preserved, he painted for her an affecting picture of his melancholy condition during his remaining weeks in London, and during his summer's work on *A Sentimental Journey* in retirement at Coxwold. For as he wrote the *Journey* and continued daily entries in the *Journal,* so constantly did the sick man think on his Eliza that occasionally something very like hallucination came upon him. While yet in London he had begun to "feel a pleasure in this kind of resigned Misery arising from this Situation, of heart unsupported by aught but its own tenderness"; at Coxwold this sentimental pleasure combined with his constant hunger for Eliza to bring her form beside him again and again, with moving reality. "Dear Enthusiasm!" he cried to her in joy, "thou bringst things forwards in a moment, which Time keeps for Ages back——I have you ten times a day besides me——I talk to You Eliza, for hours together——I take your Council——I hear your reasons . . . ——to this magic of a warm Mind, I owe all that's worth living for, during this State of our Trial." Such was the very mood and temper—the desire of a sick mind to find solace in its own fond fancies (which was itself but the pathological manifestation of Sterne's normal inability "to think two moments upon any grave subject")—from which sprang the famous apostrophe in *A Sentimental Journey* to the

Sweet pliability of man's spirit, that can at once surrender itself to illusions, which cheat expectation and sorrow of their weary moments!——Long——long since had ye number'd out my days, had I not trod so great a part of them upon this enchanted ground; when my way is too rough for my feet, or too steep for my strength, I get off it, to some smooth velvet path which fancy has scattered over with rose-buds of delights; and having taken a few turns in it, come back strengthen'd and refresh'd.

Indeed, the great significance of the *Journal to Eliza* lies, as Cross has observed, in the fact that it "reveals the pathological state of the emotions . . . whence sprang the *Sentimental Journey,* during the composition of which Sterne was fast dying of consumption . . . Each work is the counterpart of the other. In the journal, we have the crude expression of the maudlin sentiment which often accompanies a wasting disease; in the *Sentimental Journey,* we have sentiment refined to an art so exquisite as to place the author among the first masters of English prose."

A dreaded event of the summer was a visitation from Mrs. Sterne and Lydia who, wishing to reside permanently in France, desired to force a final separation and settlement. But Sterne took the situation philosophically, and the encounter proved far milder than had been feared. "All, my dearest Eliza, has turned out more favourable than my hopes," Sterne wrote with satisfaction the first of November; "Mrs. S and my dear Girl have been two Months with me and they have this day left me . . . after having settled every thing to their hearts content. . . . I have conquerd her, as I would every one else, by humanity and Generosity——and she leaves me, more than half in Love with me."

During the summer Sterne's health had improved, but late in the season he again commenced spitting blood; and after labouring steadily throughout November to complete *A Sentimental Journey* he quite collapsed and was for three weeks confined to his room. "Yorick," he wrote to a friend, "has worn out both his spirits and body with the Sentimental Journey——'tis true that an author must feel himself, or his reader will not——but I have torn my whole frame into pieces by my feelings." But though he heard the footsteps of Death hard upon him, he hazarded his customary trip to London. He wished to see his host of friends there, he hoped that once again a change in surroundings would work a miracle upon him, and he desired to be in the metropolis when his new volumes presented him to his readers in a new character. "I am going to ly-in; being at Christmas at my full reckoning," he jested, "and unless what I shall bring forth is . . . *press'd* to death by these devils of printers, I shall have the honour of presenting to you a *couple of as clean brats* as ever chaste brain conceiv'd——they are frolicksome too, *mais cela n'empeche pas.*" Designing in *Tristram Shandy* to amuse his readers, he had not always been scrupulous as to how he tickled them to make them laugh; designing in *A Sentimental Journey,* however, "to teach us to love the world and our fellow creatures better than we do," he portrayed mostly "those gentler passions and affections" which contribute to man's humanity. "The world has imagined, because I wrote Tristram Shandy," he declared, "that I was myself more Shandean than I really ever was"; and the man who wrote not to be fed but to be famous was eager to be present at his public metamorphosis. Those who had read *Tristram* in the bedroom, would read his *Journey,* he forecast, in the parlour.

Published late in February of 1768, *A Sentimental Journey* proved to be everything Sterne and his friends had hoped. The first edition was sold out within a month, and no review save the *Critical,* whose former editor Sterne had satirized as "Smelfungus," the splenetic traveller, had for it aught but praise. Even Walpole, who had found in *Shandy* but "the dregs of nonsense," pronounced the new book "very pleasing, though too much dilated," and praised its "great good nature and strokes of delicacy." Sterne's friendly critics had long urged him to exploit the talent for sentiment with which he had occasionally illumined the pages of *Shandy;* and here, in a series of exquisitely wrought vignettes delineated in delicate colours and voiced in faultlessly limpid yet lively prose, he depicted the moving incidents and sweet emotions of his journeys through France. The sincerity of its sentiment and the chastity of its wit have with justice been questioned: among its scenes of touching pathos are others so palpably artificial that Sterne appears to be posturing before the reader, imploring him to see and weep with his sensibility; behind its apparent innocence one may glimpse, in Thackeray's phrase, the "Satyr's eyes leer[ing] out of the leaves." It is less broad in its scope, less varied in its characterizations, and less rich in its humanity and humour than is *Tristram Shandy,* yet during its brief length and within its narrow limits, *A Sentimental Journey* is as near perfection as any piece of English prose.

But Sterne did not live to enjoy the full measure of his final triumph. An attack of influenza developed into pleurisy, of which he died on the eighteenth of March. A footman, sent by a group of the sick man's friends to inquire for him, brought the report: "I went to Mr. Sterne's lodging; the mistress opened the door; I inquired how he did. She told me to go up to the nurse. I went into the room, and he was just a-dying. I waited ten minutes; but in five he said: *'Now it is come.'* He put up his hand as if to stop a blow, and died in a minute." The newspapers soon printed the notice of his death, some adding Hamlet's lament, "Alas, poor Yorick . . .

a fellow of infinite jest." The *London Magazine,* aware of illiberal gossip about him, declared, paraphrasing the most famous lines, perhaps, he ever wrote, "If the accusing spirit flies up to heaven's chancery with his indiscretions, it will blush to give them in," or "the recording angel in writing them down will drop a tear upon each and wash it away forever." And Lessing, the German critic and dramatist, on hearing of Sterne's death declared, "I would have given ten years of my own life if I had been able to lengthen Sterne's by one year."

* * * * * * *

Of Sterne's character each reader will form his own judgement. Few today will denounce him with Thackeray as a cowardly, hypocritical Joseph Surface, a "wretched worn-out old scamp . . . vain . . . wicked . . . witty . . . false"; yet all, even in this conscientiously tolerant age, may not agree with Lewis P. Curtis, the editor of his letters, that "his faults, once set down to the score of wickedness," seem now "little more than foibles." With justice it may be said that he was unstable, impious, unchaste both in body and in mind—a trying husband and a heteroclite priest. But it may with equal justice, if not in extenuation, be replied that in these matters he fell little if any below the average of his contemporaries, and that clergymen reached in the mid-eighteenth century a nadir in sanctity. His rational faculties, as has been said, were not strong; indeed, though he loved the Pythagoreans for their "getting out of the body, in order to think well," to him "Reason [was], half of it, sense";[1] and he more frequently acted, accordingly, "from the first impulse . . . according as the fly stings," than from intelligent forethought. But though his actions may at times have produced harmful effects, and though in his pursuit of pleasurable emotions he may have confused right feeling with right doing, he was not himself either vicious or hypocritical. Mrs. Montagu, whose praise was ever measured and who knew her cousin's husband well, admitted

---

[1] *I.e.,* based on and drawn from sensation.

that "he erred from levity, not malice," and declared that "whatever he may want in seriousness he makes up in good nature."

From the casual life of a camp-follower during his childhood, from the uncertainty of his family's attention and support during his youth, and from the constant dread, after his haemorrhage at Cambridge, that he "must be cut short in the midst of [his] days, and taste no more of 'em than what [he may] borrow from [his] imagination," Sterne developed, perhaps unconsciously, a hedonism which led him to embrace life zestfully as it came, accepting as inevitable both its pleasures and its pains. And from this fatalistic attitude toward his own life developed his philosophy—if it may be dignified by the name—of humanitarian laughter. His life was lived, as *Tristram Shandy* was written, "in a constant endeavour to fence against the infirmities of ill health, and other evils of life, by mirth"; and without much questioning the ethical implications or the social effects of such a course, he Shandied it away, converting himself and others to the spirit of "true *Shandeism* [which], think what you will against it, opens the heart and lungs, and like all those affections which partake of its nature, . . . forces the blood and other vital fluids of the body to run freely thro' its channels, and makes the wheel of life run long and chearfully round."

III. *TRISTRAM SHANDY*

When *Tristram Shandy* was still moist from the press, readers were asking each other what the book meant, whither the seeming confusion was tending, what the incongruous combination of wit and wisdom, sentiment and bawdy might signify. Sterne's whimsicality, his sudden starts and stops, his jests and impertinences, and his rapid, idiomatic, conversational style puzzled readers accustomed to the smooth lucidity of a Richardson or the easy vigour of a Fielding. "Perhaps if the Book has any fault at all," wrote a friend of Hall-Stevenson's after the opening volumes had been published, "it is, that some of [Sterne's] touches are too refined to be perceived in their full force and extent by every Reader." And the passing of the years has not rendered these touches more perceptible, or made more obvious the sophisticated structure, humour, didacticism, and sensibility of the book.

STRUCTURE

The most immediate source of confusion to a reader of *Shandy* is the apparent confusion of the book itself. Although it begins, as Sterne points out, *ab ovo,* it thereafter appears to wander in all directions—at times, indeed, in all directions at once—without form or plan. A recent critic, who echoes the general opinion, writes of "the absolute disorder of *Tristram Shandy* . . . an indefinite theme, worked out by a verve that has not the slightest concern for order, unity, or logic." But the book was planned and written, for the most part, slowly and with care; and though no one would attempt or wish to reduce it to complete regularity, a just consideration of Sterne's purposes and of the work itself will remove the impression that it is compounded of naught but caprice.

Sterne's first plan for his book, according to the recollection of Stephen Croft, "was to travell his Hero Tristram Shandy all over Europe and after making his remarks on the different Courts, proceed with making strictures and reflections on the different Governments . . . and at length to return Tristram well informed and a compleat English Gentleman." But this design, influenced by the structure of travelogue-satires such as those of Rabelais and Swift which were Sterne's earliest models, and by the renaissance courtesy-books which he recurrently satirizes, became uncongenial to the novelist as with increasing experience and sureness he felt his own genius develop. From politics and education his interest turned to men and manners, and *The Life and Opinions of Tristram Shandy* became, in consequence, the lives and opinions of the adult members of the Shandy family, their servants, and their companions.

Not, let it be remembered, "lives and adventures." Of
them Sterne's generation had had no end. Defoe had narrated the life and strange, surprising adventures of Robinson
Crusoe and of Moll Flanders and of Roxanna in innumerable
details ordered in temporal sequence; like beads on a string,
the incidents were held together only by the single character
who experienced them all, and were ended only when the
fertility of their creator was exhausted. Richardson had with
rare psychological insight delineated the histories of Pamela
and of Clarissa; but for all the finesse of his analyses and the
dramatic inevitability of his closing scenes, his incidents had
been likewise largely strung upon the thread of the ever-
present leading character, whose long endurance seems the
only measure of their number. Fielding had portrayed, in the
adventures of Joseph Andrews and of Tom Jones and of
Amelia, a masterly composed three-dimensional world
crowded with life, in which the hero was but one of many
characters who abundantly bid for the reader's attention, and
in which the *dénouement* was reached in inevitable, dramatic
fashion; yet the materials of which those works had been
wrought were the lustiest of overt, physical adventures,
arranged, as far as the development of the different threads of
the action allowed, in temporal sequence. And Smollett had
narrated the barbarous adventures of Roderick Random and
of Peregrine Pickle most vividly, but in the crudely chronological, linear structure of the earlier picaresque romance. Of
"life and adventures," the components are shipwrecks and
mutinies, rapes and murders, drubbings and abductions and
amours, and they are of necessity arranged in chronological
order.

But in "life and opinions" action ceases to be the great
or even an essential desideratum; and in the relation and interplay of opinions, actual chronology becomes invalid. Neither
the arrangement of the scenes nor the development of any
individual scene need be chronological. One may have
opinions—or at least, one may record those of one's adult relatives—before one is born. And those opinions, expressed in

all the freedom of friendly conversation, may run an illimit-
able gamut in theme and time, from love to politics or from
Marlborough to Moses and back again. But this does not
mean that "life and opinions" necessarily have no form.
Amorphous as at first glance *Tristram Shandy* may appear, it
actually employs several structural devices of importance
(aside from the "continuity of the characters" which Coleridge has noted), and in the development of its matter is frequently quite as logical as are the apparently more rational
"lives and adventures."

¶The most obvious structural device in *Shandy* is the simple
one of veritable chronology. The book abounds in allusions
to historic events and frequently provides the reader with
actual dates to which he may hitch the action. My uncle
Toby was wounded during the siege of Namur in 1695; five
or six years later he posted down to the country to start campaigning on his bowling-green; at once widow Wadman
fell in love with him, but until the demolition of Dunkirk
late in 1713 he had no leisure to attend her brief but enlighten-
ing warfare. My father, who had begun business in London
about the year his brother was invalided home, retired to his
country-house in 1713 (seven years after the siege of Dendermond); Tristram was "begot in the night, betwixt the first
Sunday and the first *Monday* in the month of *March,* in the
year of our Lord one thousand seven hundred and eighteen";
when he was five years old he experienced the accident of the
window sash; in 1741 he led Mr. Noddy's son·through Europe. And so on. The datable events are not arranged in
chronological order, of course, but anyone who chooses may
search out a complete time-scheme extending with but one or
two negligible inconsistencies from 1689, when Trim joined
the army, to "this 12th day of August, 1766," when Tristram
sat down to write the first chapter of the final volume of his
life and opinions.

And the leading overt actions of the story, developed
through two overlapping sequences, are arranged within each
sequence in perfectly chronological order. In the first se-

quence, which deals primarily with my father and his household, Tristram is begot, born, and baptized; my father attends the visitation dinner, receives his aunt Dinah's legacy, and learns of Bobby's death; he writes the *Tristra-pædia,* decides to engage a tutor, and puts Tristram—at the end of this sequence, in the middle of volume six—in breeches. The scene then changes to the bowling-green whence, in the second sequence, already begun, we follow to the end of the book the fortunes of my uncle Toby, first in war and then in love and finally in disillusionment.

And though certain passages such as the account of the journey through France and the story of poor Maria are obviously inserted episodically, and though Sterne may occasionally have written the first sentence and trusted to Almighty God for the second, as he facetiously declared was his wont, there is yet evidence of his foresighted planning of many of the incidents of his story. My father's theory of geniture, for example, was clearly in his mind when he wrote the opening chapter of the book. My father's theory of names, developed in the first volume, demands the complementary incident of Tristram's unfortunate christening in the fourth; and his theory of noses, first hinted in volume two, makes imperative the catastrophe in volume three and the exposition of the theory which follows in volume four. My uncle Toby's hobby horse is ridden a well-planned course throughout the whole of the book; and his unfortunate amours, with which the unfinished work closes, are frequently alluded to in earlier volumes and were clear in Sterne's mind at the outset of his work.

But the most important structural device is the principle of the association of ideas upon which the whole progression of the book is based. Save for the new departures made when he has a strong propensity to begin nonsensically and will not balk his fancy, Sterne's development of the work, even in its seemingly wildest digressions, is based upon the theory of "the sagacious *Locke"* that certain ideas come to be associated in a man's mind, either by their natural correspondence or by chance or by custom, and that such associated ideas "always keep in company, and the one no sooner at any time comes into the understanding, but its associate appears with it; and if they are more than two which are thus united, the whole gang, always inseparable, show themselves together."[1]

It was to my mother's unfortunate association of ideas, as all the world knows, that Tristram owed his miserable conception; and similarly eccentric associations of ideas, sometimes comic, sometimes incongruous, motivate and direct the conversation in all the great scenes of the book. Dr. Slop's unexpected entrance into my father's back parlour in volume two, for example, brings Stevinus into my uncle Toby's head; my father, scenting the approach of his brother's hobby, fulminates against curtains and hornworks; Slop, interpreting these terms according to his own coarse usage, laughs immoderately; my uncle Toby, to set the doctor straight, explains these and a number of other military terms; at this my father, angered by Slop's puns and piqued at my uncle Toby for allowing his hobby to run away with him, insults his brother; but my uncle Toby, being of a kindly disposition (which reminds Tristram of his humane treatment, ten years later, of a fly), refuses to take offence and, to show that he harbours no resentment, continues his original discourse on Stevinus and his sailing-chariot; Dr. Slop expresses enthusiasm for such a mode of conveyance, since it would bring speedy relief to women in labour and since wind costs nothing; my father objects at once to anything that is free, and is launching into a dissertation on the principles of trade when the entrance of the corporal gives a new turn to the conversation. And when Trim starts in volume eight to tell the story of the King of Bohemia and his seven castles, before he has finished the first sentence he has been interrupted—through my uncle Toby's and his own associations of ideas—by discussions of mutability, of military history, of geography, of chronology, of the Duke of Marlborough's marches, of the origin of gunpowder, of the power and compassion of the Deity, of contingency and

---

[1] Locke, John, *An Essay Concerning Human Understanding* 2.33.5.

free will, and, finally, of his own early love affair with "a popish clergy-woman." Such is the unpredictable (but irrefutable) logic of conversation.

Sterne frequently complicates matters, as in the digression on my uncle Toby and the fly, by interpolating his own associated ideas amongst those of his characters. Such is the origin of many of his digressions, which are always planned, which as their author boasts are digressive and progressive too, and which are frequently interpolated to heighten or throw side lights on the characters. Making the most of the free and easy conversational manner he adopts toward his reader, Sterne mischievously tries to trick him, and not infrequently, to his obvious glee, he succeeds. Amusing but precarious, as a consequence, is the reader's pursuit of the devious but almost unexceptionably logical sequence—by association—of ideas in *Tristram Shandy*.

HUMOUR: CHARACTERS AND BAWDY

As Sterne was above all else a humorist—"the most complete example in modern literature," Cross has called him, "of a man whose other faculties are overpowered by a sense of humor"—so *Tristram Shandy* is above all else a humorous book. Sterne's avowed purpose in writing it was to do the world good "by ridiculing what I thought deserving of it" as well as by making his readers laugh—for laughter "adds something to this Fragment of Life." But for all its instructiveness, for all its ridicule of pretence and pedantry, for all its famed sentiment even, the book is fundamentally and finally humorous. No subject is too serious and none too trivial to rouse Sterne's mirthful sense of the incongruous: birth and baptism and death; a cut thumb, a hot chestnut, a chamber-pot—all are grist for his risibilities. And the best of his humour and satire as well is unfolded through conversations. Instead of sending Tristram abroad, after Pantagruel and Gulliver, in search of ludicrous and satirical adventures, he merely chose a group of crack-brained characters—of whom Tristram was not one—set the stage, and allowed them to talk. Or, to use his own figure, he mounted them each upon his hobby, and allowed them to canter away as merrily and to jostle and over throw each other as frequently as they would.

For Sterne conceived his characters according to the doctrine of ruling passions, the eighteenth century's equivalent of what Jonson had termed the doctrine of humours. A "humorous" character was one whose mind was biased by a peculiar humour or passion (Sterne uses the terms interchangeably) which coloured his vision and perverted his judgement of every aspect of life: "When a man gives himself up to the government of a ruling passion,——or, in other words, when his HOBBY-HORSE grows head-strong,——farewell cool reason and fair discretion!" Yet Sterne's creations are far more than the incarnated oddities of Jonson and Smollett. Though based on the accepted theory of humours, my uncle Toby and my father and the rest emerge from the sensitive mind of their author as characters, not as caricatures. As in the great humorous characters of Cervantes and Shakespeare, their ruling passions are cunningly overlaid and softened by other and subtler qualities of mind and heart which transform them from mere eccentrics into human folk of flesh and blood.

The hobby on which my uncle Toby gallops full tilt is his absorption in military history and manœuvres. During the four years he was confined by the wound in his groin which he had received during the attack upon Namur, he collected as many maps, plans of fortification, and books on military history and science "as Don *Quixote* was found to have of chivalry, when the curate and barber invaded his library." The constant perusal of these led him, like his illustrious predecessor, not only to the overt practice of his hobby in prosecuting campaigns in miniature—"for the good of the nation"—on his bowling-green, but also to an inability to think or speak out of it. A train of ideas suggests to him only a train of artillery; Yorick's figurative use of the word "point-blank" moves him to discourse upon projectiles; my father's awkward thrusting of his left hand into his right pocket reminds him of the "transverse zig-zaggery" in which he had been wounded, whereupon, forgetting the conversation in progress, he starts to send for a map of Namur to measure the returning angles of the traverses of the attack; and his brother's auxiliary verbs remind him of the Danish auxiliaries at Limerick—though he conceives them to have been different things.

But unlike the knight of La Mancha, my uncle Toby is not mad. And unlike his hobbyhorsical precursor, Smollett's Commodore Trunnion, he is at all points a human being, not a caricature. Dismounted from his hobby, he stands a plain, unassuming man, mild yet valiant, amazingly naïve yet wise in the intuitive wisdom of the heart, modest as a maiden, benign, infinitely kind. Somewhat romantic, indeed, is Sterne's exaltation of him as a "natural" man, the personification of native, untutored goodness. "Man as fashioned by his Maker," declared Sterne in another place, is "innocent and upright— full of the tenderest dispositions—with a heart inclining him to kindness, and the love and protection of his species." As such a man he has drawn my uncle Toby, who in describing Tristram's governor characterizes himself: "free, and generous, and bountiful, and brave."

In matters alien to his hobby, however, my uncle Toby's brain is like wet tinder in which no spark can possibly take hold, and his charming naïveté more than once approaches stupidity. His romantic simplicity is pushed until it becomes a very unromantic lack of acuteness which is in truth the groundwork of his humour, blinding him to the triviality of his mimic warfare on the green and rendering him a perfect foil to my father's extravagant theorizing. Inconsistent, indeed, in a man who cannot follow the simplest chain of reasoning or understand the commonest metaphors, is his ability to read Italian and Latin treatises on physics and higher mathematics, and occasionally to quote and translate Latin from memory; and the shrewd cynicism with which he suggested to his brother the all-important article of compensation in my mother's marriage contract is strangely out of character with the artless soul whose innocence widow Wadman shocks. In general,

however, his character as a good man of singularly circumscribed understanding is consistently drawn. When he cannot make head or tail of the wordy warfare in the back-
parlour of Shandy Hall, or when a proposition unusually offensive to his common sense is offered, he is content to sit
quietly puffing at his pipe or eloquently whistling *Lillibullero*.
He has become, as Traill observed, "as much the archetype of
guileless good nature, of affectionate simplicity, as Hamlet is
of irresolution, or Iago of cunning, or Shylock of race-hatred."
Compounded of pure good nature, he is, in Hazlitt's famous
phrase, "one of the finest compliments ever paid to human
nature."

In dramatic contrast to my uncle Toby, whose humour is
based on his simplicity and naïveté, stands my father, whose
humorous excesses spring from his passion for ingenious and
tortuous speculation. As simply conceived as his younger
brother, my father seems a more complex character than he because of the restlessness of his mind and the variety of his
intellectual ventures. He had "the oddest way of thinking,
that ever man in [the universe] was bless'd with," writes Tristram, explaining his particular humour. "The truth was, his
road lay so very far on one side, from that wherein most men
travelled,——that every object before him presented a face and
section of itself to his eye, altogether different from the plan
and elevation of it seen by the rest of mankind.——In other
words, 'twas a different object,——and in course was differently
considered." While my uncle Toby lives in reminiscence and
simply guides his life by warm-hearted considerations of circumstances, my father looks to the future and pedantically
seeks to regulate his own conduct and that of others by *a priori*
principles of action. A philosopher in grain, it is his humour
to take up odd notions half in jest and to speculate upon them,
with a sublime disregard for reality and common sense, until
he formulates them into hypotheses. And for him, hypotheses
have sanctity and power in themselves. "What is the character of a family," he cries, "to an hypothesis? . . . Nay, if you
come to that——what is the life of a family?" Like Cornelius

Scriblerus before him and Sir Austin Feverel after, he would regulate the life of his household, and particularly that of his son, by pedantic and abstract theories.   He does not want wit and intelligence of a sort; but as Pope had written of the ruling passion that, once in control of a mind,

> Wit, Spirit, Faculties, but make it worse;
> Reason itself but gives it edge and pow'r,

so my father's "judgement, at length, became the dupe of his wit," and he "would move both heaven and earth, and twist and torture every thing in nature to support his hypothesis. . . . By which means," Sterne adds, "never man crucified TRUTH at the rate he did."

My father's most famous hypotheses are those of names and of noses.   The former holds that one's Christian name is of utmost importance in determining one's character and life; that a great name such as Archimedes or Trismegistus will perforce make its bearer great, while a mean name such as Nyky or Simkin—or, most pitiful of all, Tristram—will inevitably degrade its bearer.   The latter hypothesis postulates a direct relationship between the length of a man's nose and the strength of his body, mind, and character; my father can "not conceive how the greatest family in *England* could stand it out against an uninterrupted succession of six or seven short noses," whereas "the same number of long and jolly noses following one another in a direct line, [would] raise and hoist it up into the best vacancies in the kingdom."   But there are others.   One, illustrated and perhaps suggested to him by widow Wadman's stratagems to gain my uncle Toby, is that love, in such cases as theirs, is not so much a sentiment as a situation; another, also illustrated by the widow, maintains that every evil and disorder in the world from the fall of Adam on, has been owing to the lust of women; another, concerning political science, embraces complicated theories of migration and government, of trade and population.   And yet another, concerning the seat of the soul, illustrates the assimilative nature of a healthy hypothesis by attracting to itself subordinate hypotheses on the importance of the vigorous conception and easy delivery of infants.

Normally my father, like my uncle Toby, is a mild and courteous—but never naïve—man, amiable to his family, to his friends, to his servants. But it is his misfortune to be constantly crossed and harassed, and as a result he frequently displays the peevish, subacid drollery which, after his genius for hypothesizing, is his most prominent characteristic. When his great theories for Tristram's welfare—those of his geniture, his nose, and his name—are one by one violated by actuality, when their futility is made apparent, he is bitterly aware of the irony of his situation. And when his lesser speculations strike impediments, he is whimsically annoyed. Next to developing a hypothesis, he loves most to bring other men to his beliefs; but never a convert can he make. For the unique feature of the Shandy household, and one in which Sterne's dramatic genius shines forth, is that while each member is spurring his peculiar hobby as hard as it will bear, each acts as a check-rein, vexing yet sanatory, upon the others. My father thinks his brother's hobby "the most ridiculous horse that ever gentleman mounted," laughing at it when he is in good humour and fulminating against it when in bad. But he is paid off in his own coin. Parson Yorick, who alone understands his arguments, will never accept them; my uncle Toby, who hears them with all the good will in the world, can never understand them; and my mother, who prefers knitting at home to travelling abroad, neither understands nor desires to understand. "Cursed luck!——said he to himself, one afternoon, as he walk'd out of the room, after he had been stating [an argument] for an hour and a half to her, to no manner of purpose;——cursed luck! said he, biting his lip as he shut the door,——for a man to be master of one of the finest chains of reasoning in nature,——and have a wife at the same time with such a head-piece, that he cannot hang up a single inference within side of it, to save his soul from destruction."

My mother indeed, though she appears rarely, says little, and has "no character at all," is one of the most delightful of

Sterne's creations. A fine example of his tact in characterization, she is chiefly notable for her inability—or lack of desire—
to say anything for herself. And in her placid, vegetal existence, which is itself a bathetic commentary on the practical
value of his fine theorizing, she too acts as a foil to my father.
To him, who delights in explaining almost as much as in arguing, her consistent refusal not merely to debate but even to ask
questions on any subject, is a second source of vexation.
"That she is not a woman of science, my father would say——
is her misfortune——but she might ask a question." But she
never did, and as a consequence "a discourse seldom went on
much further betwixt them, than a proposition,——a reply, and
a rejoinder; at the end of which, it generally took breath for
a few minutes . . . and then went on again."

Of the servants in the Shandy household, none save Corporal Trim, the loquacious but deferential follower of my uncle
Toby, evidences any qualities unusual to his position; yet
each is delineated, down to the fat, foolish scullion, with striking individuality. Nowhere in the book is Sterne's economy
in characterization more happily displayed than in the dramatic use made of Locke's theory of the association of ideas in
the famous kitchen scene, in which Trim, hat and stick in
hand, surrounded by the other servants, and with Susannah's
hand on his shoulder, delivers his moving oration on .mor-
tality. The report of Bobby's death calls forth associated
thoughts which reveal the characters of the whole crew. To
the vain Susannah's mind it brings the joyful prospect of receiving her mistress's wardrobe when my mother goes into
mourning. To the scullion, who had long been struggling with
the dropsy, it brings only the complacent observation that
she herself is yet alive. To Obadiah, the out-of-door man, who
knows that only the cost of Bobby's education has cramped my
father's agricultural projects, it brings a premonition of the
terrible piece of work he will have stubbing the Ox-moor.
To Jonathan, the dull-witted coachman, it brings only a recollection of the last time he saw the boy. And to Trim it brings
a golden opportunity to make a speech. "In battle, I value

death not this . . . He's nothing, *Obadiah,* at all in the field.
——But he's very frightful in a house, quoth *Obadiah.*——I
never mind it myself, said *Jonathan,* upon a coach-box.——It
must, in my opinion, be most natural in bed, replied *Susannah.*——And could I escape him by creeping into the worst
calf's skin that ever was made into a knapsack, I would do it
there——said *Trim*——but that is nature."

Parson Yorick is, of course, a sublimated, idealized Sterne
—Sterne as he wished himself known to the world; but however effective as a bit of special pleading for the author, he is
too self-consciously drawn for perfect credibility as a character. Tristram, who flits ubiquitously through the pages of the
book as another adumbration of the author, of whose personality he is a projection and for whom he is a convenient
mouthpiece, has, as a consequence, much in common with
poor Yorick. Both are mercurial creatures with an insurmountable aversion to affected gravity ("a mysterious carriage
of the body to cover the defects of the mind"); both are light-
hearted jesters, careless of fame; and both have little use for
"that understrapping virtue of discretion." Concerning himself, Sterne was not reticent. In Yorick he depicted his own
appearance, his heteroclite gaiety, his lack of worldly cunning,
and his whimsicality, even hinting at his relations with his
parishioners; in Tristram he revealed much concerning his ill
health and distresses, his clothing, complexion, and voice, his
skill as fiddler and painter, his carelessness, impulsiveness, and
good nature, and his sentimentalism, amorousness, and love
of activity. Eugenius, Yorick's cautious adviser and friend, is
a compliment (surely ironical) to Hall-Stevenson, but never
rises to the stature of a living character. The only actual
caricature in the book, Dr. Slop, the huffy and stolid man-
midwife and Papist, is, as has been said, a heavy-handed satire
on Sterne's old Tory enemy, Dr. John Burton; whether the
two men were ever reconciled is not recorded, but it is worthy
of note that after Sterne's trips abroad, which did much to
ameliorate his antipathy toward both Jacobites and Catholics,
Dr. Slop drops almost entirely from the book. And as for

widow Wadman—"A daughter of Eve . . . was widow Wadman, and 'tis all the character I intend to give of her."

* * * * * *

One phase of the manifold mirth of *Tristram Shandy* in which many readers consider Sterne's good taste to be peculiarly lacking, but which nevertheless moved his boisterous contemporaries to quenchless laughter, is its bawdiness. This feature of his work the Victorian critics deplored as inartistic because indecent; with a greater tolerance today we may yet regret it as ineffective because so much of it is no longer understood. For as such wit depends to a considerable degree upon ephemeral usage, slang, and *double entendre* couched in terms whose secondary meanings are evanescent, the modern reader frequently misses Sterne's point and finds merely meaningless what once was ribald. The obvious symbolism of noses and whiskers and spouts, of plackets and crevices and button-holes, and of fosses and covered-ways and cuvettes is dateless; but when Sterne asks his reader the difference between *"an old hat cock'd——*and *a cock'd old hat,"* or challenges him to discover "who was *Tickletoby*'s mare," or reiterates Susannah's desire for a green gown, or makes passing references to buttered buns, the modern reader who lacks considerable knowledge of the post-restoration wits (or an acquaintance with works such as Eric Partridge's *Dictionary of Slang and Unconventional English*) is likely to take for dullness what the novelist's contemporaries recognized as a form, however questionable, of wit. And even the most perspicacious reader who is yet unfamiliar with Latin will miss the humour of many of Sterne's Rabelaisian coinages. Sometimes he slanders a character with an unsavoury Latin name phonetically spelt, as *Phutatorius;* sometimes he forms hybrid compounds of Latin and English syllables, as *Kunastrokius;* sometimes he transliterates English words into bogus Latin spellings, as *Kysarcius.* There are many others; dubious significance may be found even in *Saint Boogar* and *Hafen*

Slawkenbergius and *Mynheer Vander Blonederdondergewden-stronke.*

Not all the bawdy in the book, of course, is so esoteric. Like Cervantes and Rabelais and Swift, Sterne finds the bodily functions amusing; like the latter two he finds merriment in contemplating the processes of generation and birth. And with a curiously perverse and possibly self-revelatory sense of the incongruous he grins again and again over sexual impotence, the suspicion of which hovers like a dubious halo over the head of every Shandy male, including the bull. In none of these matters is he so outspoken as most of his humorous predecessors or as some of his contemporaries. His bawdy, like himself, lacked the lusty, natural vigour of Aristophanes and Rabelais and Swift and Fielding; he but sniggers where they roared aloud. He "sidles up," as Thackeray charged, "and whispers a nasty story."

Unlike many humorists, however, Sterne does not dabble in filth for its own sake, and infrequently does he talk bawdy merely for the sake of the jest. Such passages as the reference to the "drole foible" of Dr. Kunastrokius and the tale of the abbess of Andouillets (taken, said his critics, from the common Parisian jest-books) appear to reflect either personal dislike or unfortunate lapses in artistic judgement on Sterne's part, and are comparatively rare. Usually his bawdy is skilfully adapted to the actors in his comedy, to the characterization of whom it adds heightening touches. Nearly all the equivocal passages in which my uncle Toby figures deal either with his ignorance of "the right end of a woman" or with the doubtful effect of the wound in his groin, and become, ironically enough, the bases for most of Sterne's delineation of the good man's unparalleled innocence and modesty. Similarly, the scene in which my father's dissertation on the precocious composition of Lipsius is cut short by my uncle Toby's uncomprehending comment, adds a heightening stroke to the simplicity of his mind. The equivocal passages in which my father is the chief figure usually elaborate or ironically underscore the futility of his remarkable theories on the necessity that a child have a vigorous generation, a pressureless delivery, a fortunate name, and a prominent nose. Over Tristram's head hangs, as has been said, the suspicion of impotence, to the heightening of which nearly all the equivocal jests concerning him contribute. The bawdy occasioned by widow Wadman's activities colours the picture Sterne paints us of a daughter of Eve determined to acquire in her second husband what she unhappily lacked in her first, and heightens by contrast my uncle Toby's "naked and defenceless" innocence; that relating to my mother accentuates both her own woeful want of desires of any sort and my father's physical and mental frustration; that connected with Bridget and Trim and Susannah contributes to their portrayal as not wholly Platonic lovers and therefore intensifies the contrast between their normality and the strange passionlessness of the Shandys. And even the ludicrous incident of the hot chestnut, which at first sight appears to be dragged in gratuitously, notably heightens, in the interplay of recrimination and conversation which it induces, the characterizations of the eccentric and witty individuals at the visitation dinner assembled.

This is not to say that Sterne never delighted in a dubious jest or a shocking story for its own sake. All that we know of him reveals his uncontrollable love of the ludicrous, in whatever circumstances it presented itself. But in his dextrous use of bawdy for the oblique development of character and situation, he is perhaps unique. Of most of his equivocal passages it could be said, as he boasts of his digressions, that by them "some familiar strokes and faint designations" of his characters are touched in, by which the reader is much better acquainted with them than he was before.

And though Sterne's innuendo may yet be disliked by some readers, it is not in any case of the sort to do them much harm. To Sterne himself the charge that *Shandy* might debauch its readers seemed droll enough: "Heaven forbid the stock of chastity should be lessen'd by the life and opinions of Tristram Shandy," he cried; "God take [all female readers] under his protection in this fiery trial, and send us plenty of

Duenas to watch the workings of their humours, 'till they have safely got thro' the whole work." Sir Walter Scott answered such charges once for all when he declared that "the licentious humour of *Tristram Shandy* is [not] of the kind which applies itself to the passions, or is calculated to corrupt society." To Thomas Jefferson, indeed, "The writings of Sterne . . . form the best course of morality that ever was written." And Goethe had for him naught but praise. "Yorick Sterne," he declared, "is the finest type of wit that ever exerted an influence in literature. Whoever reads him feels himself lifted above the petty cares of the world. His humour is inimitable, and it is not every kind of humour that leaves the soul calm and serene."

DIDACTICISM: SATIRE AND PHILANTHROPY

In "doing the world good by ridiculing what I thought deserving of it——or of disservice to sound learning," Sterne designed, it was said, "to take in all Ranks and Professions, and to laugh them out of their Absurdities." As a consequence, his book abounds in satire. Not since Rabelais had any writer so thoroughly ridiculed the dead lumber of speculative philosophy; not since Swift had any writer turned so penetrating an eye and so ludicrous a pen on the follies and weaknesses of mankind. "Every thing in this world, said my father, is big with jest,——and has wit in it, and instruction too,——if we can but find it out."

The first profession to be satirized was the novelist's own, for in opening his book nine months before Tristram's birth and in pirouetting upon all subjects and at all times and places, Sterne was ridiculing his conventional fellows who began their novels with the birth of their hero and tamely developed them in chronological order and regular style through his childhood and amours to his marriage or death. Sterne was the freest spirit of his century, said Goethe; the freest writer of all time, said Nietzsche. And through his freedom —his eccentric technique, his skipping at will (though not always capriciously) from one scene to another, his insertion of extraneous material of all sorts, his recurring informal essays on sundry subjects, and his heterodox syntax—he loosened the English novel in structure and in style and in content, damaging its form perhaps but liberating its spirit and potentialities, and preparing the way for the psychological novelists, his spiritual and aesthetic descendants, of our own day.

Still attending his own profession, Sterne satirized literary boot-lickers who praised their patrons in fulsome dedications, by writing one of his own and coolly offering it to any patron who would pay him fifty guineas for it. And the account of his travels through France was a satire against travelling "as puppies travel" and as Tobias Smollett travelled, and against guide books which give all the dead facts and none of the living spirit of one's journey.

Affected gravity, however, was the chief of the ogres against which Sterne set his merry lance, the narrow-headed, cheerless gravity of pedantry and affectation which falsifies and distorts all images from their true perspective. And this gravity—which had bubbled wise men into accepting that "*Magna Charta* of stupidity," the distinction between wit and judgement, and had deceived my father into too high an opinion of his bull, and had been all along confounded with candour and integrity—he attacked in whatever disguise it presented itself to gull mankind. "Tall, opaque words," which are but the mystery-making cloak worn by gravity to cover its defects, he satirized, ridiculing the ordained terminology of the theologians and scholastic philosophers, of the rhetoricians and geometricians, of the critics and connoisseurs, of the physicians and the lawyers. Pretentiousness, and the cant and pomposity which go with it, were ever Sterne's game. He satirized the minute theorizing of the historians and political scientists, and the "*scaffold work* of INSTRUCTION" of the professional educators. He burlesqued the pedantic marshalling of weighty quotations and learned authorities to prove the self-evident. And like Rabelais and Swift before him he parodied at times the very style and manner of speculative philosophers and grave authoritarians.

The satiric technique by which Sterne took the wind from bellying sails is frequently the commonplace and humorous one of contrast and bathos. My father's pedantic learning is effectively set off by my uncle Toby's naïve queries or his quietly indignant *Lillibullero;* the commentary on my father's oration on death, learnedly patched together from famous sayings of antiquity, is Trim's simple discourse which, like Sterne's own sermons, proceeded "more from the heart than the head"; the foil to my father's eloquent theorizing is, as we have seen, the helpless taciturnity of my uncle Toby who, had his name been Alexander, could have done no more at Namur than his duty. When Dr. Slop, carried away by his enthusiasm for the new improvements in obstetrics, wondered how the world had got on so long without them, "I wish, quoth my uncle *Toby,* you had seen what prodigious armies we had in *Flanders."* The final lesson of Slawkenbergius's Tale—a brilliantly ludicrous work, packed with satire on philosophical and theological pedantry, and with undercurrents of a different sort: one of the very few imitations of Rabelais that would do credit to the master himself—appears to be that the city of Strasburg was taken by the French and has decayed ever since, because of a man's nose. And my father's elaborate researches into the nature of the radical heat and moisture, in which he quotes Van Helmont and Aristotle and confutes Hippocrates and Bacon, end in a *reductio ad absurdum:* "If a child, as he grows up, can but be taught to avoid running into fire or water, . . . 'twill be all that is needful to be done upon that head." Here Sterne has achieved what Coleridge termed the "one humorific point common to all that can be called humorous": "The little is made great, and the great little in order to destroy both; because all is equal in contrast with the infinite."

Of this didacticism in his book, Sterne was sincerely proud. Fancying himself as the successor to Rabelais and Swift, he alluded again and again to the serious purpose behind his satire. Throughout the work, however, Sterne excoriates no one, urges no reform. He appears merely to be giving his risible mind a loose, playing with incongruous and nonsensical ideas for their own sake—the absurd, the ridiculous are made ends in themselves. Indeed, the word "satire" is perhaps too strong to be applied to his amiable foolery. Certainly he had neither the powerful intellect nor the high seriousness of the great satirists. Unlike Swift, his greatest English predecessor and in some degree his model, Sterne never touches any of the momentous intellectual or moral or social abuses upon which a satirist cannot but be in deadly earnest. Much of his jesting, indeed, is directed against scholastic modes of thought that were obsolete in his own day. And unlike Swift and Smollett, whose satire had been directed largely against personal enemies or at least grew out of personal experience, Sterne never rages or hates. His abuse of Dr. Slop is as ludicrous as rancorous, his attacks on Popery are largely conventional, even his rebukes to his critics are temperate. He has, he confesses, neither anger nor zeal; he reverences truth, but he hates disputes and bad smells, and is resolved never to be a martyr.

Sterne's satire sprang, indeed, not from a contempt of the world or from any great desire to root out evil, but from his sense of the ridiculous, his awareness of the farcical in life. And as a consequence he toys with his satire in a kindly, almost affectionate manner, and makes it less a stricture on anything external to himself than an unconscious revelation of the triviality of his own mind. For he himself delighted in quaint lore and much enjoyed, as long as it was not taken seriously, the very sort of intellectual humbuggery he ridicules in *Shandy*. Swift's sardonic *"Vive la bagatelle!"* Sterne adopted, literally, as his own rallying-cry until, warmed by the southern sun, he altered it to "VIVA LA JOIA!"

If his satire has any constructive value it lies in his impatience with received forms and *a priori* principles, and his somewhat romantic plea for a renaissance of faith in individual judgement based (particularly in the arts) not on reason alone but upon feeling as well. Such an aesthetic is but what one would expect from a man who lived and wrote (in the eighteenth century) as freely as Sterne; and though in the growing romanticism of his century it was of less force, as dogma, than were his philanthropic sentimentalism and his exaltation of the "natural" man, as examples, it yet assures him of a niche among the early apologists of the movement in which his writings hold a significant place. Nevertheless, the constructive note in *Shandy* is not strong. If he was emotionally a sentimentalist, Sterne was intellectually, in the last analysis, an amiable dilettante.

* * * * * * *

But the ridicule of "learned blockheads" was only a part of the serious merit Sterne claimed for *Shandy*. When, in the Advertisement to the 1766 edition of "The Abuses of Conscience," he referred to the novel as "a moral work, more read than understood," he was thinking of his benevolent philosophy—the teaching of Shaftesbury and Hutcheson, which had wide Latitudinarian as well as philosophical sanction—which lay behind it and which he hoped to disseminate through it. Although he was not a crusader, he would do the world what good he might in his own way; and he was altruistic enough to desire his revelation of the pompous and the absurd to restore to his readers their sense of proportion in life. Unlike Swift, he never sobers his readers by an attack on serious evils; like Shaftesbury, he would laugh them out of wrong-headedness and folly.

Though the book was written primarily to promote laughter, Sterne would have his readers "as WISE as they [are] MERRY," for "a habit of virtue" must combine with mirth to make them "the happiest people under heaven." But this habit of virtue, the vicar of Sutton knew, can best be inculcated indirectly. "Lessons of wisdom," he observed, "have never such a power over us, as when they are wrought into the heart, through the ground-work of a story which engages the passions: . . . we are like iron, and must first be heated before we can be wrought upon." Through engaging the passions of his reader, then, Sterne designed in *Tristram Shandy* as in *A Sentimental Journey* and, indeed, as in his sermons, "to teach us to love the world and our fellow creatures better than we do," and as a consequence he wrote "a careless kind of a civil, nonsensical, good humoured *Shandean* book, which will do all your hearts good—— ——And all your heads too, ——provided you understand it."

SENSIBILITY: HUMOUR AND SENTIMENT

The quality which distinguishes Sterne's humour and didacticism, like his sentiment, from the ordinary, and which raises them at their finest to the level of absolute genius, is his essential and almost unique sensibility.

No writer has surpassed Sterne in the vividness of his brief scenes, in his attention to suggestive sensory details, in his catching the dramatic undercurrents and ironic antitheses of a situation. This faculty for particularizing and dramatizing, for seizing and vividly portraying the emotional elements, the humour or pathos of a situation, which was the distinguishing quality of his genius,—this "bringing forward into distinct consciousness those minutiæ of thought and feeling which appear trifles, yet have an importance for the moment," the propensity to notice which constitutes, according to Coleridge's analysis, the humorist—this is the mark of a mind delicately attuned and peculiarly sensitive to external impressions and influences. That Sterne possessed such a mind he was himself aware. He attributed his ideas, after Locke, not to innate principles but to sensation and reflection—the very Deity he addressed in *A Sentimental Journey* as "great SENSORIUM of the world!"—and he recognized that his originality proceeded from "one of those delicate organizations in which predominates the sacred informing principle of the soul, that immortal flame which nourishes life and devours it at the same time, and which exalts and varies, in sudden and unexpected ways, all sensations." And it is this sharpened receptive faculty, which he called "imagination or sensibility, according as it expresses itself, under the pen of a writer, in depicting scenes or in portraying the passions," which is responsible for the ineffable touches of humour and sentiment in Sterne's writings.

* * * * * *

At its best, Sterne's mirth derives from sheer comedy of humours which at moments reaches heights of purity and delicacy unsurpassed by any other writer save perhaps his master Cervantes. Amusing as are Slop's fall and the incident of the chestnut, the most delightful scenes in the book are free alike from slap-stick, physical grotesquerie, and comic stage-settings, and from the Shandean clowning in style and typography—the Rabelaisian catalogues of nouns and adjectives, and the excessive use of stars and dashes—which seemed so amusing to Sterne's earliest readers. The humour of the great scenes is, as Traill has observed, of "that deepest and most penetrative kind which springs from the eternal incongruities of human nature, the ever-recurring cross-purposes of human lives." Simplicity itself is the setting of Trim's oration on death, of the disquisitions on the radical heat and moisture, of the conference in which Trim and my uncle Toby proceed from deprecating my father's theory of names to pantomiming a military attack, of Trim's report to my uncle Toby of his visit to the bedside of Le Fever, of Tristram's encounter with the ass, of the Gascoigne roundelay. The exquisite humour of such scenes derives from no adventitious trappings but from the essential expression and dramatic interplay of character and personality, heightened, when the Shandy brothers take the stage, by the unexpressed irony and pathos of their mutual sympathy and mutual incomprehensibility. And these fine shades of character are commonly revealed by a word or a gesture or a tone of voice so slight that only Sterne's senses, preternaturally alert to external influences, could catch them, and only his pen, preternaturally sharpened to depict scintillæ of thought and feeling, could set them down.

Nor is a whole scene necessary to the revelation of the sensibility of Sterne's humour. Coleridge has called attention to the great humour in my father's remark, "Learned men, brother *Toby,* don't write dialogues upon long noses for nothing"; similarly, there is more humour in my uncle Toby's one query, "And what said the Duchess of *Suffolk* to it?" than in the whole of the ludicrous conversation that called it forth. Although Sterne satirizes "the minutiæ of philosophy, which should always turn the balance [of] the scientific steel-yard," he apostrophizes "the *Pocu più* and the *Poco meno* of the *Italian* artists;——the insensible MORE or LESS, [which determines] the precise line of beauty in the sentence, as well as in the statue! . . . the slight touches of the chisel, the pencil, the pen, the fiddle-stick, *et cætera,* [which] give the true swell, which gives the true pleasure!" Such sensitivity to slight touches was the genius of Sterne's art. And nowhere does his economy in humorific drawing reach a finer mark than in the pin-point passages in which the play of a shadow over a man's face or the intonation of a voice or the movement of a muscle is infinitely suggestive: "Humph!——said my uncle *Toby;*—— tho' not accented as a note of acquiescence,——but as an interjection of that particular species of surprize, when a man, in looking into a drawer, finds more of a thing than he expected. . . . Dr. *Slop,* who had an ear, understood my uncle Toby as well as if he had wrote a whole volume against the seven sacraments." Scarcely less concentrated are two of the most purely humorous incidents in the book. One is played in my father's bedroom: "I have left *Trim* my bowling-green, cried my uncle *Toby*——My father smiled——I have left him moreover a pension, continued my uncle *Toby*——My father looked grave." The other takes place in the kitchen: "What is the finest face that ever man looked at! [cried Trim] . . . what is it! (*Susannah* laid her hand upon *Trim's* shoulder)—— but corruption?——*Susannah* took it off."

* * * * * * *

As one turns the pages of *Tristram Shandy* he becomes aware of Sterne's increasing devotion of his sensibility to arousing the tender emotions of his reader rather than the risible. This is not to say that pathos overcame him; to the day of his death he remained a humorist, and the final episode of *Shandy* is as coarsely mirthful as any in the book. But after the episodes of my uncle Toby and the fly and of Le Fever's death had been published, the English public, nurtured on the tenderness of Steele and the tears of Richardson, had demanded more incidents in the sentimental vein, and Sterne was not the man to resist so congenial a call. Nor was the transition (never, be it repeated, complete) difficult to him. So fine was the line in his own frame between smiles and tears that one frequently shaded into and called forth the other. "I laugh 'till I cry," he once said, "and in the same tender moments *cry 'till I laugh.*"

Basing his sentiment on a fusion of Locke's theory of ideas with Shaftesbury's and Hutcheson's doctrine of benevolence (which held that philanthropy produces the highest form of pleasurable self-satisfaction, which is largely its own reward), Sterne dropped a social tear not only for the sake of suffering humanity but also for the delicious sensation which the action produced within his own breast. With him, indeed, the self-satisfaction became more important than the philanthropy which theoretically called it forth. The tenderness of my uncle Toby to the fly "instantly set my whole frame into one vibration of most pleasurable sensation." In the famous apostrophe in *A Sentimental Journey* to "Dear sensibility! source inexhausted of all that's precious in our joys, or costly in our sorrows!" Sterne feels "some generous joys and generous cares beyond [him]self," but the emphasis lies throughout upon the pleasurable rather than upon the ethical aspect of his benevolence. Even his melancholy on the departure of his Eliza shortly became sublimated, as we have seen, to the degree that he could "begin to feel a pleasure in this kind of resigned Misery arising from this Situation, of heart unsupported by aught but its own tenderness." This epicureanism in emotion is Sterne's significant contribution to the development of sentimentalism in the eighteenth century, a development which reached its culmination in *A Sentimental Journey*.

The emotions with which Sterne loved to philander were those of pity and compassion, but his sense of humour combined with the luxury of his feelings to prevent his sentimentalism from becoming the muse of the woeful countenance. In most of the sentimental passages in *Shandy* he managed to keep his balance between pathos and mirth. The incident of the ass and the macaroons, Trim's report of Le Fever's sickness, the Gascoigne roundelay, and a dozen scenes in which my uncle Toby's gentle nature is displayed without fault. But occasionally Sterne's artistic instinct was not sufficiently sure and strong to restrain either his great love of sentiment or his greater love of laughter from marring a tender passage at its close. In *Shandy* two such scenes are worthy of note. Over the dying Le Fever and over poor Maria and her little pet, Sterne the sentimentalist weeps; but he weeps a moment too long, until Sterne the humorist suspects that there is developing a certain affectation, an incongruity between the object and his emotion (the one is, after all, but a soldier whose work is done; the other, a crazed peasant and her goat), and breaks into laughter—laughter at both himself and his reader for having allowed themselves to be humbugged by their overly-tender feelings. As Spenser had destroyed his lovingly fashioned Bower of Bliss, so Sterne (on very different principles) destroyed these scenes; dull indeed would be the reader who fails to feel a tender pathos as they are drawn, but much duller is he who does not see at their close Sterne's moist eyes gleaming in merriment.

Many times, indeed, the reader feels those lustrous eyes of Sterne's upon him. And this is as it should be. In matter and manner there is no more insinuatingly intimate work in fiction. The door that is shut in the fourth chapter is never opened; the whole book is a conversation between Sterne and his reader, a drama in which they two play the principal parts. Sterne is constantly present, smiling at the reader and mocking, beckoning and obstructing, revealing and concealing, leading and misleading, intriguing and irritating and delighting him—sometimes in clericals, more frequently in

motley; sometimes weeping, more frequently grinning; sometimes clear, more frequently inscrutable—but eternally there.
Indeed, the book and he are indivisible, indistinguishable.
" 'Tis a picture of myself," he once declared. And he wrote
it because he loved a jest in his heart.

SELECTED BIBLIOGRAPHY

Bagehot, Walter, "Sterne and Thackeray," in his *Literary Studies* (various editions).

A sane but hardly inspired and somewhat unsympathetic essay on Sterne's life and writings, invalidated in part by incomplete biographical knowledge.

Carlyle, Thomas, "Jean Paul Friedrich Richter," in his *Critical and Miscellaneous Essays* (many editions).

Contains a thoughtful two-page analysis, three-fourths of the way through the essay, of the interrelationship of humour, satire, and sensibility, citing Sterne and other humorists as examples.

Coleridge, Samuel Taylor, "Lecture IX. On the Distinctions of the Witty, the Droll, the Odd, and the Humorous," in his *Works,* edited by Shedd (New York, 1871), 4.275 ff.

Brief but profoundly significant analysis of the metaphysical basis of humour in general and of Sterne's in particular.

Cross, Wilbur L., "Laurence Sterne in the Twentieth Century," in *The Yale Review,* N. S. 15 (1925–1926). 99 ff.

A graceful essay on Sterne as a literary artist.

——, *The Life and Times of Laurence Sterne* (third edition, New Haven, 1929).

The latest and most important full-dress biography of Sterne. Contains, in addition to the detailed biography, a wise and penetrating analysis of Sterne's character; attempts no elaborate commentary on his art.

Elwin, Whitwell, "Sterne," in *The Quarterly Review,* March, 1854; reprinted in his *Some Eighteenth Century Men of Letters* (London, 1902), 2.3 ff.

Following the biographical sketch, now superseded, is a lengthy and wise discussion of Sterne's works.

Hazlitt, William, "On the English Novelists," in his *English Comic Writers* (various editions).

Contains a single paragraph of panegyric on Sterne's style, sentiment, and characters.

Maack, Rudolf, *Laurence Sterne im Lichte seiner Zeit* (Hamburg, 1936).

A detailed and suggestive analysis of Sterne's relation to the contemporary theory and practice of philosophy and the arts. The most extended study yet published of Sterne as thinker and artist.

More, Paul Elmer, "Laurence Sterne," in his *Shelburne Essays,* Third Series (New York, 1905), pp. 177 ff.

Judicious comment on various aspects of Sterne's life and writings and art.

Morley, Christopher, Introduction to *Tristram Shandy,* The Limited Editions Club (New York, 1935).

A brief but zestful and appreciative essay.

Priestley, J. B., Introduction to *Tristram Shandy* (London, 1928).

A brief comment, suggesting significant likenesses and differences between Sterne and some modern novelists.

Read, Herbert, "Sterne," in the *Times Literary Supplement,* May 26, 1927; reprinted in his *Sense of Glory* (New York, 1930).

An admirable study of Sterne's humour and morality and art; one of the most important essays yet published on Sterne as a writer.

Saintsbury, George, Introduction to *Tristram Shandy,* Everyman's Library Edition (London, 1912).

A salty and valuable essay on Sterne's chief work.

Scherer, Edmond, "Laurence Sterne, or the Humorist," in his *Essays on English Literature* (translated by George Saintsbury, New York, 1891), pp. 150 ff.

Discusses the nature of humour and of Sterne's humour.

Sterne, Laurence, *Letters of Laurence Sterne,* edited by Lewis Perry Curtis (Oxford, 1935).

The definitive edition of Sterne's extant correspondence, richly annotated, and preceded by an illuminating Introduction on Sterne as man and writer.

——, *The Works and Life of Laurence Sterne,* edited by Wilbur L. Cross, 12 vols. (New York, 1904).

An appreciative essay by the editor precedes each of the works, the life (by Percy Fitzgerald), and a collection of biographical anecdotes.

Thackeray, William Makepeace, "Sterne and Goldsmith," in his *The English Humorists* (various editions).

A vitriolic attack on Sterne as man and writer, vitiated to a considerable extent by incomplete biographical information. The classic example of the "Victorian" attitude toward Sterne.

Traill, H. D., *Sterne,* in English Men of Letters series (London, 1882).

The biographical material has been superseded by Cross, but the final chapters on Sterne's humour, sentiment, and dramatic power remain among the best treatments of those topics.

Vaughan, C. E., "Sterne and the Novel of his Times," in *The Cambridge History of English Literature* (Cambridge, 1913), 10.46 ff.

A brief but valuable essay on Sterne's humour.

Watts-Dunton, Theodore, Review of Traill's *Sterne,* in the
  Athenaeum for 1882, 2.655 ff.

An important essay on humorists and humour in general and
Sterne and Sterne's humour in particular.

NOTE ON THE TEXT

Not since Sterne's lifetime has an authentic text of *Tristram
Shandy* been published. Of the editions available today but
two or three make any claim to textual accuracy. Those are
reprints of the text of the unknown editor who in 1780, twelve
years after Sterne's death, published the first collected edition
of his works. But that edition of *Shandy* contained innumerable differences of all sorts from the text which Sterne had
himself corrected for the press: in many places the style was
marred, in some the wit was dulled, and in not a few the very
sense was spoiled.

The present text is a reprint of the first London edition of
each of the nine volumes of the work—the latest edition of
each volume which Sterne himself is known to have seen
through the presses, and therefore the only edition which can
safely be called authoritative. The reprint is verbatim, even
to the preserving of Sterne's strange punctuation[1] and his inconsistent spellings of many words, save that in the infrequent
cases of indubitable errors and in the inconsistent use of
italics in Volumes VII–IX I have made silent corrections, using
as the basis of my correction the edition of 1780.

---

[1] The punctuation is oral rather than syntactical; Sterne was a talker,
not a grammarian.

THE

LIFE

AND

OPINIONS

OF

TRISTRAM SHANDY,
GENTLEMAN.

Ταράσσει τὰς Ἀνθρώπες ὒ τὰ ΠράΓμαΐα,
ἀλλὰ τὰ περὶ τῶν ΠραΓμάτων, ΔοΓμάτα.

VOL. I.

The SECOND EDITION.

LONDON:

Printed for R. and J. DODSLEY in *Pall-Mall*.
M.DCC.LX.

Facsimile of the title page to the first London edition of Volumes I and II. The motto, from Chapter V of the *Encheiridion* of Epictetus (c.60–c.120), the Roman Stoic philosopher, may be translated: "It is not actions, but opinions concerning actions, which disturb men."

TRISTRAM SHANDY

VOLUME I.

To the Right Honourable

M r . P I T T .[1]

SIR,

NEVER poor Wight of a Dedicator had less hopes from his Dedication, than I have from this of mine; for it is written in a bye corner of the kingdom, and in a retired thatch'd house, where I live in a constant endeavour to fence against the infirmities of ill health, and other evils of life, by mirth; being firmly persuaded that every time a man smiles, ——but much more so, when he laughs, that it adds something to this Fragment of Life.

I humbly beg, Sir, that you will honour this book by taking it——(not under your Protection,——it must protect itself, but)——into the country with you; where, if I am ever told, it has made you smile, or can conceive it has beguiled you of one moment's pain——I shall think myself as happy as a minister of state;———perhaps much happier than any one (one only excepted) that I have ever read or heard of.

I am, great Sir,
(and what is more to your Honour,)
I am, good Sir,
Your Well-wisher,
and most humble Fellow-Subject,

THE AUTHOR.

[1]According to his friend John Croft, Sterne wished when first writing *Tristram Shandy* to dedicate it to William Pitt (1708–1778), the great Whig statesman and orator who was then Secretary of State and for whom he had deep admiration. Fearing perhaps that a dedication from an unknown clergyman might seem presumptuous, Sterne published the first edition without it; on March 28, 1760, however, when the book and its author had taken London by storm, Sterne sent a note to Pitt half asking but more than half assuming his consent to this dedication, which first appeared in the second edition of volumes 1 and 2, on April 2.

CHAP. I.

I Wish either my father or my mother, or indeed both of them, as they were in duty both equally bound to it, had minded what they were about when they begot me; had they duly consider'd how much depended upon what they were then doing;—that not only the production of a rational Being was concern'd in it, but that possibly the happy formation and temperature of his body, perhaps his genius and the very cast of his mind;—and, for aught they knew to the contrary, even the fortunes of his whole house might take their turn from the humours[1] and dispositions which were then uppermost:——Had they duly weighed and considered all this, and proceeded accordingly,——I am verily persuaded I should have made a quite different figure in the world, from that, in which the reader is likely to see me.——Believe me, good folks, this is not so inconsiderable a thing as many of you may think it;—— you have all, I dare say, heard of the animal spirits,[2] as how they are transfused from father to son, &c. &c.——and a great deal to that purpose:——Well, you may take my word, that nine parts in ten of a man's sense or his nonsense, his successes and miscarriages in this world depend upon their motions and activity, and the different tracks and trains you put them into, so that when they are once set a-going, whether right or wrong, 'tis not a halfpenny matter,——away they go

---

[1]The bodily fluids (blood, phlegm, yellow bile, and black bile), a proper balance of which was thought by ancient physicians to be requisite to health of body and mind. By extension, one's special condition of mind; disposition, mental state, mood.

[2]According to Descartes's modification of Galen's doctrine, the animal spirits were subtle and almost incorporeal particles of the living body which pass through the nerves (which were regarded as tubular vessels) between the brain and the periphery, acting as the agents of volition and sensation, and responsible, in Sterne's use of the term, for the nervous force, buoyancy, and animation of mind and body.

cluttering like hey-go-mad; and by treading the same steps over and over again, they presently make a road of it, as plain and as smooth as a garden-walk, which, when they are once used to, the Devil himself sometimes shall not be able to drive them off it.

Pray, my dear, quoth my mother, *have you not forgot to wind up the clock?*———*Good G—!* cried my father, making an exclamation, but taking care to moderate his voice at the same time,———*Did ever woman, since the creation of the world, interrupt a man with such a silly question?* Pray, what was your father saying?———Nothing.

CHAP. II.

———Then, positively, there is nothing in the question, that I can see, either good or bad.———Then let me tell you, Sir, it was a very unseasonable question at least,———because it scattered and dispersed the animal spirits, whose business it was to have escorted and gone hand-in-hand with the *HOMUNCULUS*,[1] and conducted him safe to the place destined for his reception.

The Homunculus, Sir, in how-ever low and ludicrous a light he may appear, in this age of levity, to the eye of folly or prejudice:———to the eye of reason in scientifick research, he stands confess'd———a Being guarded and circumscribed with rights:———The minutest philosophers, who, by the bye, have the most enlarged understandings, (their souls being inversely as their enquiries) shew us incontestably, That the Homunculus is created by the same hand,———engender'd in the same course of nature,———endowed with the same loco-motive powers and faculties with us:———That he consists, as we do, of skin, hair, fat, flesh, veins, arteries, ligaments, nerves, cartilages, bones, marrow, brains, glands, genitals, humours, and articulations;———is a Being of as much activity,———and, in all senses of the word, as much and as truly our fellow-creature as my Lord Chancellor of England.———He may be benefited,

---

[1] Little man; in this instance, spermatazoön.

he may be injured,——he may obtain redress;——in a word, he has all the claims and rights of humanity, which *Tully*,[2] *Puffendorff*, or the best ethick writers allow to arise out of that state and relation.

Now, dear Sir, what if any accident had befallen him in his way alone?——or that, thro' terror of it, natural to so young a traveller, my little gentleman had got to his journey's end miserably spent;——his muscular strength and virility worn down to a thread;——his own animal spirits ruffled beyond description,——and that in this sad disorder'd state of nerves, he had laid down a prey to sudden starts, or a series of melancholy dreams and fancies for nine long, long months together. ——I tremble to think what a foundation had been laid for a thousand weaknesses both of body and mind, which no skill of the physician or the philosopher could ever afterwards have set thoroughly to rights.

CHAP. III.

TO my uncle Mr. *Toby Shandy* do I stand indebted for the preceding anecdote, to whom my father, who was an excellent natural philosopher, and much given to close reasoning upon the smallest matters, had oft, and heavily, complain'd of the injury; but once more particularly, as my uncle *Toby* well remember'd, upon his observing a most unaccountable obliquity, (as he call'd it) in my manner of setting up my top, and justifying the principles upon which I had done it,——the old gentleman shook his head, and in a tone more expressive by half of sorrow than reproach,——he said his heart all along foreboded, and he saw it verified in this, and from a thousand other observations he had made upon me, That I should neither think nor act like any other man's child:——*But alas!* continued he, shaking his head a second time, and wiping away a tear which was trickling down his cheeks, *My Tris-*

---

[2]Marcus Tullius Cicero (106–43 B.C.), the Roman orator and statesman; the allusion here is to his *De Legibus*. Samuel Pufendorf (1632–1694), a German jurist, historian, and philosopher, whose chief work, alluded to here, is *De Jure Naturae et Gentium*.

tram's misfortunes began nine months before ever he came into the world.

——My mother, who was sitting by, look'd up,——but she knew no more than her backside what my father meant, ——but my uncle, Mr. *Toby Shandy,* who had been often informed of the affair,——understood him very well.

CHAP. IV.

I Know there are readers in the world, as well as many other good people in it, who are no readers at all,——who find themselves ill at ease, unless they are let into the whole secret from first to last, of every thing which concerns you.

It is in pure compliance with this humour of theirs, and from a backwardness in my nature to disappoint any one soul living, that I have been so very particular already. As my life and opinions are likely to make some noise in the world, and, if I conjecture right, will take in all ranks, professions, and denominations of men whatever,——be no less read than the *Pilgrim's Progress* itself——and, in the end, prove the very thing which *Montaigne* dreaded his essays should turn out, that is, a book for a parlour-window;[1] I find it necessary to consult every one a little in his turn; and therefore must beg pardon for going on a little further in the same way: For which cause, right glad I am, that I have begun the history of myself in the way I have done; and that I am able to go on tracing every thing in it, as *Horace* says, *ab Ovo.*[2]

Horace, I know, does not recommend this fashion alto-

---

[1]"I am vex'd that my *Essays* only serve the *Ladies* for a common moveable, a Book to lye in the Parlour Window; this Chapter shall prefer me to the Closet . . ."——"Upon Some Verses of Virgil" (Cotton's translation), by Michel de Montaigne (1533–1592), the French essayist, who was one of Sterne's favourite authors and an important source of ideas in *Tristram Shandy.*

[2]From the egg; i.e., from the beginning. In his *Ars Poetica,* 146 ff., Quintus Horatius Flaccus (65–8 B.C.), the Roman poet and critic, commends Homer for not tracing the rise of the Trojan war from the egg of Leda (*i.e.,* from the birth of Helen), but rushing his reader into the midst of his story.

gether: But that gentleman is speaking only of an epic poem or a tragedy;——(I forget which)——besides, if it was not so, I should beg Mr. *Horace's* pardon;——for in writing what I have set about, I shall confine myself neither to his rules, nor to any man's rules that ever lived.

To such, however, as do not choose to go so far back into these things, I can give no better advice, than that they skip over the remaining part of this Chapter; for I declare before hand, 'tis wrote only for the curious and inquisitive.

————————————————Shut the door.————————————

I was begot in the night, betwixt the first *Sunday* and the first *Monday* in the month of *March,* in the year of our Lord one thousand seven hundred and eighteen. I am positive I was.——But how I came to be so very particular in my account of a thing which happened before I was born, is owing to another small anecdote known only in our own family, but now made publick for the better clearing up this point.

My father, you must know, who was originally a *Turkey* merchant, but had left off business for some years, in order to retire to, and die upon, his paternal estate in the county of ————, was, I believe, one of the most regular men in every thing he did, whether 'twas matter of business, or matter of amusement, that ever lived. As a small specimen of this extreme exactness of his, to which he was in truth a slave,——he had made it a rule for many years of his life,——on the first *Sunday night* of every month throughout the whole year,—— as certain as ever the *Sunday night* came,——to wind up a large house-clock which we had standing upon the back-stairs head, with his own hands:——And being somewhere between fifty and sixty years of age, at the time I have been speaking of,——he had likewise gradually brought some other little family concernments to the same period, in order, as he would often say to my uncle *Toby,* to get them all out of the way at one time, and be no more plagued and pester'd with them the rest of the month.

It was attended but with one misfortune, which, in a great measure, fell upon myself, and the effects of which I fear I

shall carry with me to my grave; namely, that, from an unhappy association of ideas which have no connection in nature,
it so fell out at length, that my poor mother could never hear
the said clock wound up,——but the thoughts of some other
things unavoidably popp'd into her head,——& vice versâ:——
which strange combination of ideas, the sagacious *Locke*,[3] who
certainly understood the nature of these things better than
most men, affirms to have produced more wry actions than all
other sources of prejudice whatsoever.

But this by the bye.

Now it appears, by a memorandum in my father's pocket-
book, which now lies upon the table, "That on *Lady-Day*,
which was on the 25th of the same month in which I date my
geniture,——my father set out upon his journey to *London*
with my eldest brother *Bobby,* to fix him at *Westminster*
school;" and, as it appears from the same authority, "That he
did not get down to his wife and family till the *second week*
in *May* following,"——it brings the thing almost to a certainty.
However, what follows in the beginning of the next chapter
puts it beyond all possibility of doubt.

——But pray, Sir, What was your father doing all *December,—January,* and *February?*——Why, Madam,——he was
all that time afflicted with a Sciatica.[4]

CHAP. V.

ON the fifth day of *November,* 1718, which to the æra fixed
on, was as near nine kalendar months as any husband
could in reason have expected,——was I *Tristram Shandy,*

---

[3]In his *Essay Concerning Human Understanding* John Locke (1632–
1704), the English philosopher, who profoundly influenced all Sterne's
thinking and writing, observed: "This wrong connexion in our minds
of ideas, in themselves loose and independent of one another, has such
an influence, and is of so great force to set us awry in our actions, as well
moral as natural, passions, reasonings, and notions themselves, that perhaps there is not any one thing that deserves more to be looked after"
(2.33.9).   See the Introduction, pp. xlix–l.

[4]Neuralgia of hip and thigh.

Gentleman, brought forth into this scurvy and disasterous world of ours.——I wish I had been born in the Moon, or in any of the planets, (except *Jupiter* or *Saturn,* because I never could bear cold weather) for it could not well have fared worse with me in any of them (tho' I will not answer for *Venus*) than it has in this vile, dirty planet of ours,——which o' my conscience, with reverence be it spoken, I take to be made up of the shreds and clippings of the rest;——not but the planet is well enough, provided a man could be born in it to a great title or to a great estate; or could any how contrive to be called up to publick charges, and employments of dignity or power;—— but that is not my case;——and therefore every man will speak of the fair as his own market has gone in it;——for which cause I affirm it over again to be one of the vilest worlds that ever was made;——for I can truly say, that from the first hour I drew my breath in it, to this, that I can now scarce draw it at all, for an asthma I got in scating against the wind in *Flanders;*——I have been the continual sport of what the world calls fortune; and though I will not wrong her by saying, She has ever made me feel the weight of any great or signal evil; ——yet with all the good temper in the world, I affirm it of her, that in every stage of my life, and at every turn and corner where she could get fairly at me, the ungracious Duchess has pelted me with a set of as pitiful misadventures and cross accidents as ever small HERO sustained.

CHAP. VI.

IN the beginning of the last chapter, I inform'd you exactly *when* I was born;——but I did not inform you, *how. No;* that particular was reserved entirely for a chapter by itself; ——besides, Sir, as you and I are in a manner perfect strangers to each other, it would not have been proper to have let you into too many circumstances relating to myself all at once.—— You must have a little patience. I have undertaken, you see, to write not only my life, but my opinions also; hoping and

expecting that your knowledge of my character, and of what
kind of a mortal I am, by the one, would give you a better
relish for the other: As you proceed further with me, the
slight acquaintance which is now beginning betwixt us, will
grow into familiarity; and that, unless one of us is in fault,
will terminate in friendship.——*O diem præclarum!*[1]——then
nothing which has touched me will be thought trifling in its
nature, or tedious in its telling. Therefore, my dear friend
and companion, if you should think me somewhat sparing of
my narrative on my first setting out,——bear with me,——
and let me go on, and tell my story my own way:——or if I
should seem now and then to trifle upon the road,——or
should sometimes put on a fool's cap with a bell to it, for a
moment or two as we pass along,——don't fly off,——but
rather courteously give me credit for a little more wisdom than
appears upon my outside;——and as we jogg on, either laugh
with me, or at me, or in short, do any thing,——only keep your
temper.

CHAP. VII.

IN the same village where my father and my mother dwelt,
  dwelt also a thin, upright, motherly, notable, good old body
of a midwife, who, with the help of a little plain good sense,
and some years full employment in her business, in which she
had all along trusted little to her own efforts, and a great deal
to those of dame nature,——had acquired, in her way, no small
degree of reputation in the world;——by which word *world,*
need I in this place inform your worship, that I would be understood to mean no more of it, than a small circle described
upon the circle of the great world, of four *English* miles
diameter, or thereabouts, of which the cottage where the good
old woman lived, is supposed to be the centre.——She had
been left, it seems, a widow in great distress, with three or
four small children, in her forty-seventh year; and as she was
at that time a person of decent carriage,——grave deportment,

---

[1] O splendid day!

——a woman moreover of few words, and withall an object
of compassion, whose distress and silence under it call'd out
the louder for a friendly lift: the wife of the parson of the
parish was touch'd with pity; and having often lamented an
inconvenience, to which her husband's flock had for many
years been exposed, inasmuch, as there was no such thing as a
midwife, of any kind or degree to be got at, let the case have
been never so urgent, within less than six or seven long miles
riding; which said seven long miles in dark nights and dismal
roads, the country thereabouts being nothing but a deep clay,
was almost equal to fourteen; and that in effect was sometimes
next to having no midwife at all; it came into her head, that
it would be doing as seasonable a kindness to the whole parish,
as to the poor creature herself, to get her a little instructed in
some of the plain principles of the business, in order to set
her up in it.   As no woman thereabouts was better qualified
to execute the plan she had formed than herself, the Gentlewoman very charitably undertook it; and having great influence over the female part of the parish, she found no difficulty
in effecting it to the utmost of her wishes.   In truth, the
parson join'd his interest with his wife's in the whole affair; and
in order to do things as they should be, and give the poor soul
as good a title by law to practise, as his wife had given by institution,——he chearfully paid the fees for the ordinary's
licence himself, amounting, in the whole, to the sum of eighteen
shillings and fourpence; so that, betwixt them both, the good
woman was fully invested in the real and corporal possession
of her office, together with all its *rights, members, and appur-
tenances whatsoever.*

These last words, you must know, were not according to the
old form in which such licences, faculties, and powers usually
ran, which in like cases had heretofore been granted to the
sisterhood.   But it was according to a neat *Formula* of *Didius*[1]

---

[1]Didius, who appears at intervals throughout the book as "the great
church lawyer," is a satirical representation of Dr. Francis Topham, an
able Yorkshire lawyer who, over years of pushing and intriguing in
which he was frequently opposed by Sterne, had obtained for himself a
majority of the legal offices connected with the Diocese of York, and

his own devising, who having a particular turn for taking to
pieces, and new framing over again, all kind of instruments in
that way, not only hit upon this dainty amendment, but coax'd
many of the old licensed matrons in the neighbourhood, to
open their faculties afresh, in order to have this whim-wham
of his inserted.

I own I never could envy *Didius* in these kinds of fancies of
his:——But every man to his own taste.——Did not Dr. *Kunastrokius*,[2] that great man, at his leisure hours, take the greatest
delight imaginable in combing of asses tails, and plucking the
dead hairs out with his teeth, though he had tweezers always
in his pocket?   Nay, if you come to that, Sir, have not the
wisest of men in all ages, not excepting *Solomon* himself,——
have they not had their HOBBY-HORSES;[3]——their running
horses,——their coins and their cockle-shells, their drums and
their trumpets, their fiddles, their pallets,——their maggots
and their butterflies?——and so long as a man rides his
HOBBY-HORSE peaceably and quietly along the King's highway,
and neither compels you or me to get up behind him,——
pray, Sir, what have either you or I to do with it?

CHAP. VIII.

——*De gustibus non est disputandum;*[1]——that is, there is
no disputing against HOBBY-HORSES; and, for my part, I seldom
do; nor could I with any sort of grace, had I been an enemy to
them at the bottom; for happening, at certain intervals and

who had been the object of Sterne's ridicule in *A Political Romance*.
(See the Introduction, p. xxvii.)   In the name, Sterne may have extended
an allusion to Julianus Severus Didius who in A.D. 193 purchased the
Roman Empire from the praetorian guards, to the indignation of the
people whose subsequent revolt forced the senate to condemn and execute him.

   [2]A portmanteau-word of Sterne's invention, alluding to a "very volup-
tuous" infirmity of Dr. Richard Mead (1673–1754), an eminent London
physician.

   [3]Hobbies.

   [1]There is no disputing about tastes; a proverbial observation.

changes of the Moon, to be both fiddler and painter, according as the fly stings:——Be it known to you, that I keep a couple of pads myself, upon which, in their turns, (nor do I care who knows it) I frequently ride out and take the air;——tho' sometimes, to my shame be it spoken, I take somewhat longer journies than what a wise man would think altogether right.—— But the truth is,——I am not a wise man;——and besides am a mortal of so little consequence in the world, it is not much matter what I do; so I seldom fret or fume at all about it: Nor does it much disturb my rest when I see such great Lords and tall Personages as hereafter follow;——such, for instance, as my Lord A, B, C, D, E, F, G, H, I, K, L, M, N, O, P, Q, and so on, all of a row, mounted upon their several horses; ——some with large stirrups, getting on in a more grave and sober pace;——others on the contrary, tuck'd up to their very chins, with whips across their mouths, scouring and scampering it away like so many little party-colour'd devils astride a mortgage,——and as if some of them were resolved to break their necks.——So much the better——say I to myself;——for in case the worst should happen, the world will make a shift to do excellently well without them;——and for the rest,——why,——God speed them,——e'en let them ride on without opposition from me; for were their lordships unhorsed this very night,——'tis ten to one but that many of them would be worse mounted by one half before tomorrow morning.

Not one of these instances therefore can be said to break in upon my rest.——But there is an instance, which I own puts me off my guard, and that is, when I see one born for great actions, and, what is still more for his honour, whose nature ever inclines him to good ones;——when I behold such a one, my Lord, like yourself, whose principles and conduct are as generous and noble as his blood, and whom, for that reason, a corrupt world cannot spare one moment;——when I see such a one, my Lord, mounted, though it is but for a minute beyond the time which my love to my country has prescribed to him, and my zeal for his glory wishes,—then, my Lord, I

cease to be a philosopher, and in the first transport of an
honest impatience, I wish the HOBBY-HORSE, with all his fra-
ternity, at the Devil.

My Lord,
"I Maintain this to be a dedication, notwithstanding its singularity in the three great essentials of matter, form and
place: I beg, therefore, you will accept it as such, and that
you will permit me to lay it, with the most respectful humility,
at your Lordship's feet,——when you are upon them,——which
you can be when you please;——and that is, my Lord, when
ever there is occasion for it, and I will add, to the best purposes too.   I have the honour to be,

My Lord,
Your Lordship's most obedient,
and most devoted,
and most humble servant,
TRISTRAM SHANDY.

CHAP. IX.

I Solemnly declare to all mankind, that the above dedication
was made for no one Prince, Prelate, Pope, or Potentate,
——Duke, Marquis, Earl, Viscount, or Baron of this, or any
other Realm in Christendom;——nor has it yet been hawk'd
about, or offered publickly or privately, directly or indirectly,
to any one person or personage, great or small; but is honestly
a true Virgin-Dedication untried on, upon any soul living.

I labour this point so particularly, merely to remove any
offence or objection which might arise against it, from the
manner in which I propose to make the most of it;——which
is the putting it up fairly to publick sale; which I now do.

——Every author has a way of his own, in bringing his
points to bear;——for my own part, as I hate chaffering and
higgling for a few guineas in a dark entry;——I resolved
within myself, from the very beginning, to deal squarely and

openly with your Great Folks in this affair, and try whether I should not come off the better by it.

If therefore there is any one Duke, Marquis, Earl, Viscount, or Baron, in these his Majesty's dominions, who stands in need of a tight, genteel dedication, and whom the above will suit, (for by the bye, unless it suits in some degree, I will not part with it)——it is much at his service for fifty guineas;—— which I am positive is twenty guineas less than it ought to be afforded for, by any man of genius.

My Lord, if you examine it over again, it is far from being a gross piece of daubing, as some dedications are. The design, your Lordship sees, is good, the colouring transparent, ——the drawing not amiss;——or to speak more like a man of science,——and measure my piece in the painter's scale, divided into 20,——I believe, my Lord, the out-lines will turn out as 12,——the composition as 9,——the colouring as 6,—— the expression 13 and a half,——and the design,——if I may be allowed, my Lord, to understand my own *design,* and sup- posing absolute perfection in designing, to be as 20,——I think it cannot well fall short of 19. Besides all this,——there is keeping in it, and the dark strokes in the HOBBY-HORSE, (which is a secondary figure, and a kind of back-ground to the whole) give great force to the principal lights in your own figure, and make it come off wonderfully;——and besides, there is an air of originality in the *tout ensemble.*[1]

Be pleased, my good Lord, to order the sum to be paid into the hands of Mr. *Dodsley,*[2] for the benefit of the author; and in the next edition care shall be taken that this chapter be ex- punged, and your Lordship's titles, distinctions, arms and good actions, be placed at the front of the preceding chapter: All which, from the words, *De gustibus non est disputandum,* and whatever else in this book relates to HOBBY-HORSES, but no more, shall stand dedicated to your Lordship.——The rest I dedicate to the MOON, who, by the bye, of all the PATRONS

---

[1] All together; whole composition.

[2] James Dodsley who, with his brother Robert, was Sterne's first Lon- don publisher and bookseller.

or MATRONS I can think of, has most power to set my book a-going, and make the world run mad after it.

Bright Goddess,
If thou art not too busy with CANDID[3] and Miss CUNEGUND's affairs,——take *Tristram Shandy*'s under thy protection also.

CHAP. X.

WHatever degree of small merit, the act of benignity in favour of the midwife, might justly claim, or in whom that claim truly rested,——at first sight seems not very material to this history;——certain however it was, that the gentlewoman, the parson's wife, did run away at that time with the whole of it: And yet, for my life, I cannot help thinking but that the parson himself,[1] tho' he had not the good fortune to hit upon the design first,——yet, as he heartily concurred in it the moment it was laid before him, and as heartily parted with his money to carry it into execution, had a claim to some share of it,——if not to a full half of whatever honour was due to it.

The world at that time was pleased to determine the matter otherwise.

Lay down the book, and I will allow you half a day to give a probable guess at the grounds of this procedure.

Be it known then, that, for about five years before the date of the midwife's licence, of which you have had so circumstantial an account,——the parson we have to do with, had made himself a country-talk by a breach of all decorum, which he had committed against himself, his station, and his office; ——and that was, in never appearing better, or otherwise

---

[3]Characters in Voltaire's *Candide,* published and translated into English in 1759.

[1]From its first publication, the following account of the parson was generally understood "to be the character of the author, as he chuses it should be exhibited." See the Introduction, p. lviii.

mounted, than upon a lean, sorry, jack-ass of a horse, value about one pound fifteen shillings; who, to shorten all description of him, was full brother to *Rosinante*,[2] as far as similitude congenial could make him; for he answered his description to a hair-breadth in every thing,——except that I do not remember 'tis any where said, that *Rosinante* was broken winded; and that, moreover, *Rosinante,* as is the happiness of most *Spanish* horses, fat or lean,——was undoubtedly a horse at all points.

I know very well that the HERO's horse was a horse of chaste deportment, which may have given grounds for a contrary opinion: But it is as certain at the same time, that *Rosinante's* continency (as may be demonstrated from the adventure of the *Yanguesian* carriers[3]) proceeded from no bodily defect or cause whatsoever, but from the temperance and orderly current of his blood.——And let me tell you, Madam, there is a great deal of very good chastity in the world, in behalf of which you could not say more for your life.

Let that be as it may, as my purpose is to do exact justice to every creature brought upon the stage of this dramatic work, ——I could not stifle this distinction in favour of Don *Quixote's* horse;——in all other points the parson's horse, I say, was just such another,——for he was as lean, and as lank, and as sorry a jade, as HUMILITY herself could have bestrided.

In the estimation of here and there a man of weak judgment, it was greatly in the parson's power to have helped the figure of this horse of his,——for he was master of a very handsome demi-peak'd saddle, quilted on the seat with green plush, garnished with a double row of silver-headed studs, and a noble pair of shining brass stirrups, with a housing altogether suitable, of grey superfine cloth, with an edging of black lace,

---

[2] Don Quixote's horse, "whose bones stuck out like the corners of a Spanish Real, being a worse jade than Gonela's, *qui tantum pellis et ossa fuit* [who was but so much skin and bones]." (*Don Quixote* [the Motteux-Ozell translation], 1.1.1.)

[3] Though "all the mares in the pastures of Cordova could not have rais'd [Rozinante] to attempt an indecent thing," a number of Galician mares, belonging to some Yanguesian carriers, proved him (to his own undoing) to be but flesh and blood after all. See *Don Quixote,* 1.3.1.

terminating in a deep, black, silk fringe, *poudré d'or*,[4]——all
which he had purchased in the pride and prime of his life,
together with a grand embossed bridle, ornamented at all
points as it should be.——But not caring to banter his beast,
he had hung all these up behind his study door;——and, in
lieu of them, had seriously befitted him with just such a bridle
and such a saddle, as the figure and value of such a steed might
well and truly deserve.

In the several sallies about his parish, and in the neighbour-
ing visits to the gentry who lived around him,——you will
easily comprehend, that the parson, so appointed, would both
hear and see enough to keep his philosophy from rusting.   To
speak the truth, he never could enter a village, but he caught
the attention of both old and young.——Labour stood still as
he pass'd,——the bucket hung suspended in the middle of the
well,——the spinning-wheel forgot its round,——even chuck-
farthing and shuffle-cap[5] themselves stood gaping till he had
got out of sight; and as his movement was not of the quickest,
he had generally time enough upon his hands to make his
observations,——to hear the groans of the serious,——and the
laughter of the light-hearted;——all which he bore with excellent tranquility.——His character was,——he loved a jest in
his heart——and as he saw himself in the true point of ridicule, he would say, he could not be angry with others for
seeing him in a light, in which he so strongly saw himself:
So that to his friends, who knew his foible was not the love
of money, and who therefore made the less scruple in banter-
ing the extravagance of his humour,——instead of giving the
true cause,——he chose rather to join in the laugh against himself; and as he never carried one single ounce of flesh upon his
own bones, being altogether as spare a figure as his beast,——
he would sometimes insist upon it, that the horse was as good
as the rider deserved;——that they were, centaur-like,——both
of a piece.   At other times, and in other moods, when his

---

[4]Powdered with gold.

[5]Games in which farthings are tossed or chucked into a hole; in which
money is shaken in a hat or cap.

spirits were above the temptation of false wit,——he would
say, he found himself going off fast in a consumption; and,
with great gravity, would pretend, he could not bear the sight
of a fat horse without a dejection of heart, and a sensible
alteration in his pulse; and that he had made choice of the
lean one he rode upon, not only to keep himself in countenance,
but in spirits.

At different times he would give fifty humorous and opposite reasons for riding a meek-spirited jade of a broken-winded
horse, preferably to one of mettle;——for on such a one he
could sit mechanically, and meditate as delightfully *de vanitate
mundi et fugâ sæculi,*[6] as with the advantage of a death's head
before him;——that, in all other exercitations, he could spend
his time, as he rode slowly along,——to as much account as
in his study;——that he could draw up an argument in his
sermon,——or a hole in his breeches, as steadily on the one as
in the other;——that brisk trotting and slow argumentation,
like wit and judgment, were two incompatible movements.——
But that upon his steed——he could unite and reconcile every
thing,——he could compose his sermon,——he could compose
his cough,——and, in case nature gave a call that way, he
could likewise compose himself to sleep.——In short, the parson upon such encounters would assign any cause, but the true
cause,——and he with-held the true one, only out of a nicety
of temper, because he thought it did honour to him.

But the truth of the story was as follows: In the first years
of this gentleman's life, and about the time when the superb
saddle and bridle were purchased by him, it had been his manner, or vanity, or call it what you will,——to run into the
opposite extream.——In the language of the county where he
dwelt, he was said to have loved a good horse, and generally
had one of the best in the whole parish standing in his stable
always ready for saddling; and as the nearest midwife, as I
told you, did not live nearer to the village than seven miles,
and in a vile country,——it so fell out that the poor gentleman
was scarce a whole week together without some piteous ap-

[6]On the vanity of the world and the swift passing of time.

plication for his beast; and as he was not an unkind-hearted man, and every case was more pressing and more distressful than the last,——as much as he loved his beast, he had never a heart to refuse him; the upshot of which was generally this, that his horse was either clapp'd,[7] or spavin'd, or greaz'd;—— or he was twitter-bon'd, or broken-winded, or something, in short, or other had befallen him which would let him carry no flesh;——so that he had every nine or ten months a bad horse to get rid of,——and a good horse to purchase in his stead.

What the loss in such a balance might amount to, *communibus annis*,[8] I would leave to a special jury of sufferers in the same traffic, to determine;——but let it be what it would, the honest gentleman bore it for many years without a murmur, till at length, by repeated ill accidents of the kind, he found it necessary to take the thing under consideration; and upon weighing the whole, and summing it up in his mind, he found it not only disproportion'd to his other expences, but withall so heavy an article in itself, as to disable him from any other act of generosity in his parish: Besides this he considered, that with half the sum thus galloped away, he could do ten times as much good;——and what still weighed more with him than all other considerations put together, was this, that it confined all his charity into one particular channel, and where, as he fancied, it was the least wanted, namely, to the child-bearing and child-getting part of his parish; reserving nothing for the impotent,——nothing for the aged,——nothing for the many comfortless scenes he was hourly called forth to visit, where poverty, and sickness, and affliction dwelt together.

For these reasons he resolved to discontinue the expence; and there appeared but two possible ways to extricate him clearly out of it;——and these were, either to make it an irrev-

---

[7]Clapp'd: affected with a swelling in the legs. Spavin'd: diseased in the hock-joint. Greaz'd: affected with the grease, an inflammation in the heels attended with the secretion of oily matter. Twitter-bon'd: affected with twitter-bone, an excrescence on a hoof, hence shaky. Broken-winded: incapacitated by ruptured air-cells.

[8]In ordinary years.

ocable law never more to lend his steed upon any application whatever,——or else be content to ride the last poor devil, such as they had made him, with all his aches and infirmities, to the very end of the chapter.

As he dreaded his own constancy in the first,——he very chearfully betook himself to the second; and tho' he could very well have explain'd it, as I said, to his honour,——yet, for that very reason, he had a spirit above it; choosing rather to bear the contempt of his enemies, and the laughter of his friends, than undergo the pain of telling a story, which might seem a panegyric upon himself.

I have the highest idea of the spiritual and refined sentiments of this reverend gentleman, from this single stroke in his character, which I think comes up to any of the honest refinements of the peerless knight of *La Mancha*,[9] whom, by the bye, with all his follies, I love more, and would actually have gone further to have paid a visit to, than the greatest hero of antiquity.

But this is not the moral of my story: The thing I had in view was to shew the temper of the world in the whole of this affair.——For you must know, that so long as this explanation would have done the parson credit,——the devil a soul could find it out,——I suppose his enemies would not, and that his friends could not.——But no sooner did he bestir himself in behalf of the midwife, and pay the expences of the ordinary's licence to set her up,——but the whole secret came out; every horse he had lost, and two horses more than ever he had lost, with all the circumstances of their destruction, were known and distinctly remembered.——The story ran like wild-fire. ——"The parson had a returning fit of pride which had just seized him; and he was going to be well mounted once again in his life; and if it was so, 'twas plain as the sun at noon-day, he would pocket the expence of the licence, ten times told the very first year:——so that every body was left to judge what were his views in this act of charity."

What were his views in this, and in every other action of his

[9]Don Quixote.

life,——or rather what were the opinions which floated in the brains of other people concerning it, was a thought which too much floated in his own, and too often broke in upon his rest, when he should have been sound asleep.

About ten years ago this gentleman had the good fortune to be made entirely easy upon that score,——it being just so long since he left his parish,——and the whole world at the same time behind him,——and stands accountable to a judge of whom he will have no cause to complain.

But there is a fatality attends the actions of some men: Order them as they will, they pass thro' a certain medium which so twists and refracts them from their true directions ——that, with all the titles to praise which a rectitude of heart can give, the doers of them are nevertheless forced to live and die without it.

Of the truth of which this gentleman was a painful example. ——But to know by what means this came to pass,——and to make that knowledge of use to you, I insist upon it that you read the two following chapters, which contain such a sketch of his life and conversation, as will carry its moral along with it.——When this is done, if nothing stops us in our way, we will go on with the midwife.

CHAP. XI.

YORICK was this parson's name, and, what is very remarkable in it, (as appears from a most antient account of the family, wrote upon strong vellum, and now in perfect preservation) it had been exactly so spelt for near,——I was within an ace of saying nine hundred years;——but I would not shake my credit in telling an improbable truth, however indisputable in itself;——and therefore I shall content myself with only saying,——It had been exactly so spelt, without the least variation or transposition of a single letter, for I do not know how long; which is more than I would venture to say of one half of the best surnames in the kingdom; which, in a course of years, have generally undergone as many chops and changes as their owners.——Has this been owing to the pride, or to the shame of the respective proprietors?——In honest truth, I think, sometimes to the one, and sometimes to the other, just as the temptation has wrought. But a villainous affair it is, and will one day so blend and confound us all together, that no one shall be able to stand up and swear, "That his own great grand father was the man who did either this or that."

This evil had been sufficiently fenced against by the prudent care of the *Yorick*'s family, and their religious preservation of these records I quote, which do further inform us, That the family was originally of *Danish* extraction, and had been transplanted into *England* as early as in the reign of *Horwendillus,* king of *Denmark*,[1] in whose court it seems, an ancestor of this Mr. *Yorick*'s, and from whom he was lineally descended, held a considerable post to the day of his death. Of what nature this considerable post was, this record saith not;——it only adds, That, for near two centuries, it had been totally abolished as altogether unnecessary, not only in that court, but in every other court of the Christian world.

It has often come into my head, that this post could be no other than that of the king's chief Jester;——and that *Hamlet*'s *Yorick,* in our *Shakespear,* many of whose plays, you know, are founded upon authenticated facts,——was certainly the very man.

I have not the time to look into *Saxo-Grammaticus*'s *Danish* history, to know the certainty of this;——but if you have leisure, and can easily get at the book, you may do it full as well yourself.

I had just time, in my travels through *Denmark* with Mr. *Noddy*'s eldest son, whom, in the year 1741, I accompanied as governor, riding along with him at a prodigious rate thro' most parts of *Europe,* and of which original journey perform'd by us two, a most delectable narrative will be given in the

---

[1] In Book 3 of the great *Historia Danica* of Saxo Grammaticus (fl. c. 1200), Horwendillus, King of Denmark, is the father of Amlethus, from whose story Shakespeare's *Hamlet* is derived.

progress of this work. I had just time, I say, and that was all,
to prove the truth of an observation made by a long sojourner
in that country;——namely, "That nature was neither very
lavish, nor was she very stingy in her gifts of genius and
capacity to its inhabitants;——but, like a discreet parent, was
moderately kind to them all; observing such an equal tenor in
the distribution of her favours, as to bring them, in those
points, pretty near to a level with each other; so that you will
meet with few instances in that kingdom of refin'd parts; but
a great deal of good plain houshold understanding amongst
all ranks of people, of which every body has a share;" which is,
I think, very right.

With us, you see, the case is quite different;——we are all
ups and downs in this matter;——you are a great genius;——
or 'tis fifty to one, Sir, you are a great dunce and a blockhead;
——-not that there is a total want of intermediate steps,——no,
——we are not so irregular as that comes to;——but the two
extremes are more common, and in a greater degree in this
unsettled island, where nature, in her gifts and dispositions of
this kind, is most whimsical and capricious; fortune herself
not being more so in the bequest of her goods and chattels
than she.

This is all that ever stagger'd my faith in regard to *Yorick*'s
extraction, who, by what I can remember of him, and by all
the accounts I could ever get of him, seem'd not to have had
one single drop of *Danish* blood in his whole crasis; in nine
hundred years, it might possibly have all run out:——I will
not philosophize one moment with you about it; for happen
how it would, the fact was this:——That instead of that cold
phlegm and exact regularity of sense and humours, you would
have look'd for, in one so extracted;——he was, on the contrary, as mercurial and sublimated a composition,——as
heteroclite a creature in all his declensions;——with as much
life and whim, and *gaité de cœur*[2] about him, as the kindliest
climate could have engendered and put together. With all
this sail, poor *Yorick* carried not one ounce of ballast; he was

---

[2]Gaiety of heart.

utterly unpractised in the world; and, at the age of twenty-six, knew just about as well how to steer his course in it, as a romping, unsuspicious girl of thirteen: So that upon his first setting out, the brisk gale of his spirits, as you will imagine, ran him foul ten times in a day of some body's tackling; and as the grave and more slow-paced were oftenest in his way, ——you may likewise imagine, 'twas with such he had generally the ill luck to get the most entangled. For aught I know there might be some mixture of unlucky wit at the bottom of such *Fracas:*——For, to speak the truth, *Yorick* had an invincible dislike and opposition in his nature to gravity; ——not to gravity as such;——for where gravity was wanted, he would be the most grave or serious of mortal men for days and weeks together;——but he was an enemy to the affectation of it, and declared open war against it, only as it appeared a cloak for ignorance, or for folly; and then, whenever it fell in his way, however sheltered and protected, he seldom gave it much quarter.

Sometimes, in his wild way of talking, he would say, That gravity was an errant scoundrel; and he would add,——of the most dangerous kind too,——because a sly one; and that, he verily believed, more honest, well-meaning people were bubbled out of their goods and money by it in one twelve-month, than by pocket-picking and shop-lifting in seven. In the naked temper which a merry heart discovered, he would say, There was no danger,——but to itself:——whereas the very essence of gravity was design, and consequently deceit;—— 'twas a taught trick to gain credit of the world for more sense and knowledge than a man was worth; and that, with all its pretensions,——it was no better, but often worse, than what a *French* wit had long ago defined it,——*viz. A mysterious carriage of the body to cover the defects of the mind;*[3]—— which definition of gravity, *Yorick,* with great imprudence, would say, deserved to be wrote in letters of gold.

But, in plain truth, he was a man unhackneyed and unprac-

---

[3]One of the *Maxims* of François de la Rochefoucauld (1613–1680), the French philanthropist and moralist.

tised in the world, and was altogether as indiscreet and foolish on every other subject of discourse where policy is wont
to impress restraint. *Yorick* had no impression but one, and
that was what arose from the nature of the deed spoken of;
which impression he would usually translate into plain *English* without any periphrasis,——and too oft without much distinction of either personage, time, or place;——so that when
mention was made of a pitiful or an ungenerous proceeding,
——he never gave himself a moment's time to reflect who was
the Hero of the piece,——what his station,——or how far
he had power to hurt him hereafter;——but if it was a dirty
action,——without more ado,——The man was a dirty fellow,——and so on:——And as his comments had usually the
ill fate to be terminated either in a *bon mot*,[4] or to be enliven'd
throughout with some drollery or humour of expression, it
gave wings to *Yorick*'s indiscretion. In a word, tho' he never
sought, yet, at the same time, as he seldom shun'd occasions
of saying what came uppermost, and without much ceremony;
——he had but too many temptations in life, of scattering his
wit and his humour,——his gibes and his jests about him.——
They were not lost for want of gathering.

What were the consequences, and what was *Yorick*'s catastrophe thereupon, you will read in the next chapter.

CHAP. XII.

THE *Mortgager* and *Mortgagée* differ the one from the
other, not more in length of purse, than the *Jester* and
Jestée do, in that of memory. But in this the comparison between them runs, as the scholiasts call it, upon all-four; which,
by the bye, is upon one or two legs more, than some of the
best of *Homer's* can pretend to;——namely, That the one
raises a sum and the other a laugh at your expence, and think
no more about it. Interest, however, still runs on in both
cases;——the periodical or accidental payments of it, just serv-

---

[4] Witty expression.

ing to keep the memory of the affair alive; till, at length, in
some evil hour,——pop comes the creditor upon each, and by
demanding principal upon the spot, together with full interest to the very day, makes them both feel the full extent of
their obligations.

As the reader (for I hate your *ifs*) has a thorough knowledge
of human nature, I need not say more to satisfy him, that my
Hero could not go on at this rate without some slight experience of these incidental mementos. To speak the truth, he
had wantonly involved himself in a multitude of small book-
debts of this stamp, which, notwithstanding *Eugenius's*[1] frequent advice, he too much disregarded; thinking, that as not
one of them was contracted thro' any malignancy;——but, on
the contrary, from an honesty of mind, and a mere jocundity
of humour, they would all of them be cross'd out in course.

Eugenius would never admit this; and would often tell him,
that one day or other he would certainly be reckoned with;
and he would often add, in an accent of sorrowful apprehension,——to the uttermost mite. To which *Yorick,* with his
usual carelessness of heart, would as often answer with a
pshaw!——and if the subject was started in the fields,——with
a hop, skip, and a jump, at the end of it; but if close pent up
in the social chimney corner, where the culprit was barricado'd
in, with a table and a couple of arm chairs, and could not so
readily fly off in a tangent,——*Eugenius* would then go on
with his lecture upon discretion, in words to this purpose,
though somewhat better put together.

Trust me, dear *Yorick,* this unwary pleasantry of thine will
sooner or later bring thee into scrapes and difficulties, which
no after-wit can extricate thee out of.——In these sallies, too
oft, I see, it happens, that a person laugh'd at, considers him-

---

[1]Eugenius, who appears throughout the book as the friend and discreet
adviser of Yorick, is an idealized depiction of John Hall-Stevenson, the
eccentric master of Skelton Castle in Yorkshire, whom Sterne had met
when they were students together at Cambridge and with whom he
maintained a warm friendship throughout his life. See the Introduction,
pp. xvi, xxiv–xxv. Sterne probably chose the name Eugenius because of
its Latin signification: well-born, noble, generous.

self in the light of a person injured, with all the rights of such a situation belonging to him; and when thou viewest him in that light too, and reckons up his friends, his family, his kindred and allies,——and musters up with them the many recruits which will list under him from a sense of common danger;——'tis no extravagant arithmetic to say, that for every ten jokes,——thou hast got a hundred enemies; and till thou hast gone on, and raised a swarm of wasps about thy ears, and art half stung to death by them, thou wilt never be convinced it is so.

I cannot suspect it in the man whom I esteem, that there is the least spur from spleen or malevolence of intent in these sallies.——I believe and know them to be truly honest and sportive:——But consider, my dear lad, that fools cannot distinguish this,——and that knaves will not; and thou knowest not what it is, either to provoke the one, or to make merry with the other,——whenever they associate for mutual defence, depend upon it, they will carry on the war in such a manner against thee, my dear friend, as to make thee heartily sick of it, and of thy life too.

REVENGE from some baneful corner shall level a tale of dishonour at thee, which no innocence of heart or integrity of conduct shall set right.——The fortunes of thy house shall totter,——thy character, which led the way to them, shall bleed on every side of it,——thy faith questioned,——thy works belied,——thy wit forgotten,——thy learning trampled on. To wind up the last scene of thy tragedy, CRUELTY and COWARDICE, twin ruffians, hired and set on by MALICE in the dark, shall strike together at all thy infirmities and mistakes:——the best of us, my dear lad, lye open there,——and trust me,—— trust me, *Yorick, When to gratify a private appetite, it is once resolved upon, that an innocent and an helpless creature shall be sacrificed, 'tis an easy matter to pick up sticks enew from any thicket where it has strayed, to make a fire to offer it up with.*[2]

---

[2]Paraphrased from the "Discourse by Way of Introduction," by Thomas Tenison (1636–1715), Archbishop of Canterbury, to *Baconiana, or Certain Genuine Remains of Sr. Francis Bacon* (London, 1679), p. 16.

Yorick scarce ever heard this sad vaticination of his destiny read over to him, but with a tear stealing from his eye, and a promissory look attending it, that he was resolved, for the time to come, to ride his tit with more sobriety.——But, alas, too late!——a grand confederacy, with ***** and ***** at the head of it, was form'd before the first prediction of it.——The whole plan of the attack, just as *Eugenius* had foreboded, was put in execution all at once,——with so little mercy on the side of the allies,——and so little suspicion in *Yorick,* of what was carrying on against him,——that when he thought, good easy man! full surely preferment was o' ripening,——they had smote his root, and then he fell, as many a worthy man had fallen before him.[3]

Yorick, however, fought it out with all imaginable gallantry for some time; till, over-power'd by numbers, and worn out at length by the calamities of the war,——but more so, by the ungenerous manner in which it was carried on,——he threw down the sword; and though he kept up his spirits in appearance to the last,——he died, nevertheless, as was generally thought, quite broken hearted.

What inclined *Eugenius* to the same opinion, was as follows:

A few hours before *Yorick* breath'd his last, *Eugenius* stept in with an intent to take his last sight and last farewell of him: Upon his drawing *Yorick*'s curtain, and asking how he felt himself, *Yorick,* looking up in his face, took hold of his hand, ——and, after thanking him for the many tokens of his friendship to him, for which, he said, if it was their fate to meet hereafter,——he would thank him again and again,——he told him, he was within a few hours of giving his enemies the slip for ever.——I hope not, answered *Eugenius,* with tears trickling down his cheeks, and with the tenderest tone that ever man spoke,——I hope not, *Yorick,* said he.——*Yorick* replied, with a look up, and a gentle squeeze of *Eugenius*'s hand, and that was all,——but it cut *Eugenius* to his heart.

---

[3] See the Introduction, pp. xxvi–xxvii.

——Come,——come, *Yorick,* quoth *Eugenius,* wiping his eyes, and summoning up the man within him,——my dear lad, be comforted,——let not all thy spirits and fortitude forsake thee at this crisis when thou most wants them;——who knows what resources are in store, and what the power of God may yet do for thee?——*Yorick* laid his hand upon his heart, and gently shook his head;——for my part, continued *Eugenius,* crying bitterly as he uttered the words,——I declare I know not, *Yorick,* how to part with thee,——and would gladly flatter my hopes, added *Eugenius,* chearing up his voice, that there is still enough left of thee to make a bishop,——and that I may live to see it.——I beseech thee, *Eugenius,* quoth *Yorick,* taking off his night-cap as well as he could with his left hand, ——his right being still grasped close in that of *Eugenius,*—— I beseech thee to take a view of my head.——I see nothing that ails it, replied *Eugenius.* Then, alas! my friend, said *Yorick,* let me tell you, that 'tis so bruised and mis-shapen'd with the blows which ***** and *****, and some others have so unhandsomely given me in the dark, that I might say with *Sancho Pança,*[4] that should I recover, and "Mitres thereupon be suffer'd to rain down from heaven as thick as hail, not one of 'em would fit it."——*Yorick*'s last breath was hanging upon his trembling lips ready to depart as he uttered this;——yet still it was utter'd with something of a *cervantick*[5] tone;—— and as he spoke it, *Eugenius* could perceive a stream of lambent fire lighted up for a moment in his eyes;——faint picture of those flashes of his spirit, which (as *Shakespear* said of his ancestor) were wont to set the table in a roar!

Eugenius was convinced from this, that the heart of his friend was broke; he squeez'd his hand,——and then walk'd softly out of the room, weeping as he walk'd. *Yorick* fol-

---

[4]Assured by his master Don Quixote that when he becomes a king his wife will be a queen, "I doubt of it, reply'd Sancho Pança; for I can't help believing, that though it should rain kingdoms down upon the face of the earth, not one of them would sit well upon Mary Gutierez's head." (*Don Quixote,* 1.1.7.) Sterne probably mistook the long "s" of "sit," in his duodecimo copy of the Motteux-Ozell translation, for an "f."

[5]Satirical, such as that of Cervantes in *Don Quixote.*

lowed *Eugenius* with his eyes to the door,——he then closed them,——and never opened them more.

He lies buried in a corner of his church-yard, in the parish of ———, under a plain marble slabb, which his friend *Eugenius,* by leave of his executors, laid upon his grave, with no more than these three words of inscription serving both for his epitaph and elegy.[6]

Alas, poor YORICK!

Ten times in a day has *Yorick's* ghost the consolation to hear his monumental inscription read over with such a variety of plaintive tones, as denote a general pity and esteem for him; ——a foot-way crossing the church-yard close by the side of his grave,——not a passenger goes by without stopping to cast a look upon it,——and sighing as he walks on,

Alas, poor Y O R I C K !

---

[6]See Shakespeare, *Hamlet,* 5.1.201.

CHAP. XIII.

IT is so long since the reader of this rhapsodical work has been parted from the midwife, that it is high time to mention her again to him, merely to put him in mind that there is such a body still in the world, and whom, upon the best judgment I can form upon my own plan at present,——I am going to introduce to him for good and all: But as fresh matter may be started, and much unexpected business fall out betwixt the reader and myself, which may require immediate dispatch; ——'twas right to take care that the poor woman should not be lost in the mean time;——because when she is wanted, we can no way do without her.

I think I told you that this good woman was a person of no small note and consequence throughout our whole village and township;——that her fame had spread itself to the very outedge and circumference of that circle of importance, of which kind every soul living, whether he has a shirt to his back or no,——has one surrounding him;——which said circle, by the way, whenever 'tis said that such a one is of great weight and importance in the *world*,——I desire may be enlarged or contracted in your worship's fancy, in a compound-ratio of the station, profession, knowledge, abilities, height and depth (measuring both ways) of the personage brought before you.

In the present case, if I remember, I fixed it at about four or five miles, which not only comprehended the whole parish, but extended itself to two or three of the adjacent hamlets in the skirts of the next parish; which made a considerable thing of it. I must add, That she was, moreover, very well looked on at one large grange-house and some other odd houses and farms within two or three miles, as I said, from the smoke of her own chimney:——But I must here, once for all, inform you, that all this will be more exactly delineated and explain'd in a map, now in the hands of the engraver, which, with many other pieces and developments to this work, will be added

to the end of the twentieth volume,——not to swell the work,
——I detest the thought of such a thing;——but by way of
commentary, scholium, illustration, and key to such passages,
incidents, or inuendos as shall be thought to be either of private interpretation, or of dark or doubtful meaning after my
life and my opinions shall have been read over, (now don't forget the meaning of the word) by all the *world;*——which, betwixt you and me, and in spight of all the gentlemen reviewers
in *Great-Britain,* and of all that their worships shall undertake to write or say to the contrary,——I am determined shall
be the case.——I need not tell your worship, that all this is
spoke in confidence.

CHAP. XIV.

UPON looking into my mother's marriage settlement, in
order to satisfy myself and reader in a point necessary to
be clear'd up, before we could proceed any further in this
history;——I had the good fortune to pop upon the very thing
I wanted before I had read a day and a half straight forwards,
——it might have taken me up a month;——which shews
plainly, that when a man sits down to write a history,——tho'
it be but the history of *Jack Hickathrift*[1] or *Tom Thumb,* he
knows no more than his heels what lets and confounded hin-
derances he is to meet with in his way,——or what a dance
he may be led, by one excursion or another, before all is over.
Could a historiographer drive on his history, as a muleteer
drives on his mule,——straight forward;——for instance, from
Rome all the way to *Loretto,* without ever once turning his
head aside either to the right hand or to the left,——he might
venture to foretell you to an hour when he should get to his
journey's end;——but the thing is, morally speaking, impossible: For, if he is a man of the least spirit, he will have fifty
deviations from a straight line to make with this or that party

---

[1]Probably a slip for *Tom Hickathrift,* a mythical strong man whose
story, an old popular romance, belongs to the same series as that of Jack
the Giant-killer. *Tom Thumb* is an old popular nursery tale.

as he goes along, which he can no ways avoid. He will have views and prospects to himself perpetually solliciting his eye, which he can no more help standing still to look at than he can fly; he will moreover have various

　　Accounts to reconcile:

　　Anecdotes to pick up:

　　Inscriptions to make out:

　　Stories to weave in:

　　Traditions to sift:

　　Personages to call upon:

　　Panegyricks to paste up at this door:

　　Pasquinades at that:——All which both the man and his mule are quite exempt from. To sum up all; there are archives at every stage to be look'd into, and rolls, records, documents, and endless genealogies, which justice ever and anon calls him back to stay the reading of:——In short, there is no end of it;——for my own part, I declare I have been at it these six weeks, making all the speed I possibly could,——and am not yet born:——I have just been able, and that's all, to tell you *when* it happen'd, but not *how;*——so that you see the thing is yet far from being accomplished.

These unforeseen stoppages, which I own I had no conception of when I first set out;——but which, I am convinced now, will rather increase than diminish as I advance,——have struck out a hint which I am resolved to follow;——and that is,—— not to be in a hurry;——but to go on leisurely, writing and publishing two volumes of my life every year;——which, if I am suffered to go on quietly, and can make a tolerable bargain with my bookseller, I shall continue to do as long as I live.

CHAP. XV.

THE article in my mother's marriage settlement, which I told the reader I was at the pains to search for, and which, now that I have found it, I think proper to lay before him,——is so much more fully express'd in the deed itself, than ever I can pretend to do it, that it would be barbarity to take it out of the lawyer's hand:——It is as follows.

"**And this Indenture further witnesseth,** That the said *Walter Shandy,* merchant, in consideration of the said intended marriage to be had, and, by God's blessing, to be well and truly solemnized and consummated between the said *Walter Shandy* and *Elizabeth Mollineux* aforesaid, and divers other good and valuable causes and considerations him thereunto specially moving,——doth grant, covenant, condescend, consent, conclude, bargain, and fully agree to and with *John Dixon* and *James Turner,* Esqrs. the above-named trustees, *&c. &c.*—— **to wit,**——That in case it should hereafter so fall out, chance, happen, or otherwise come to pass,——That the said *Walter Shandy,* merchant, shall have left off business before the time or times, that the said *Elizabeth Mollineux* shall, according to the course of nature, or otherwise, have left off bearing and bringing forth children;——and that, in consequence of the said *Walter Shandy* having so left off business, he shall, in despight, and against the free-will, consent, and good-liking of the said *Elizabeth Mollineux,*——make a departure from the city of *London,* in order to retire to, and dwell upon, his estate at *Shandy-Hall,* in the county of ——, or at any other country seat, castle, hall, mansion-house, messuage, or grainge-house, now purchased, or hereafter to be purchased, or upon any part or parcel thereof:——That then, and as often as the said *Elizabeth Mollineux* shall happen to be enceint with child or children severally and lawfully begot, or to be begotten, upon the body of the said *Elizabeth Mollineux* during her said coverture,——he the said *Walter Shandy* shall, at his own proper cost and charges, and out of his own proper monies, upon good and reasonable notice, which is hereby agreed to be within six weeks of her the said *Elizabeth Mollineux's* full reckoning, or time of supposed and computed delivery,—— pay, or cause to be paid, the sum of one hundred and twenty pounds of good and lawful money, to *John Dixon* and *James Turner,* Esqrs. or assigns,——upon TRUST and confidence, and for and unto the use and uses, intent, end, and purpose following:——**That is to say,**——That the said sum of one hundred and twenty pounds shall be paid into the hands of the said *Elizabeth Mollineux,* or to be otherwise applied by them the said trustees, for the well and truly hiring of one coach, with able and sufficient horses, to carry and convey the body of the said *Elizabeth Mollineux* and the child or children which she shall be then and there enceint and pregnant with,——unto the city of *London;* and for the further paying and defraying of all other incidental costs, charges, and expences whatsoever,—— in and about, and for, and relating to her said intended delivery and lying-in, in the said city or suburbs thereof. And that the said *Elizabeth Mollineux* shall and may, from time to time, and at all such time and times as are here covenanted and agreed upon,——peaceably and quietly hire the said coach and horses, and have free ingress, egress, and regress throughout her journey, in and from the said coach, according to the tenor, true intent, and meaning of these presents, without any let, suit, trouble, disturbance, molestation, discharge, hinderance, forfeiture, eviction, vexation, interruption, or incumberance whatsoever.——And that it shall moreover be lawful to and for the said *Elizabeth Mollineux,* from time to time, and as oft or often as she shall well and truly be advanced in her said pregnancy, to the time heretofore stipulated and agreed upon, ——to live and reside in such place or places, and in such family or families, and with such relations, friends, and other persons within the said city of *London,* as she, at her own will and pleasure, notwithstanding her present coverture, and as if she was a *femme sole*[1] and unmarried,——shall think fit.——**And this Indenture further witnesseth,** That for the more effectually carrying of the said covenant into execution, the said *Walter Shandy,* merchant, doth hereby grant, bargain, sell, release, and confirm unto the said *John Dixon,* and *James Turner,* Esqrs. their heirs, executors, and assigns, in their actual possession now being, by virtue of an indenture of bargain and sale for a year to them the said *John Dixon* and *James*

---

[1]Single woman.

Turner, Esqrs. by him the said *Walter Shandy,* merchant,
thereof made; which said bargain and sale for a year, bears
date the day next before the date of these presents, and by
force and virtue of the statute for transferring of uses into possession,——**All** that the manor and lordship of *Shandy* in the
county of ———, with all the rights, members, and appurte-
nances thereof; and all and every the messuages, houses, build-
ings, barns, stables, orchards, gardens, backsides, tofts, crofts,
garths, cottages, lands, meadows, feedings, pastures, marshes,
commons, woods, underwoods, drains, fisheries, waters, and
water-courses;——together with all rents, reversions, services,
annuities, fee-farms, knights fees, views of frank-pledge,[2]
escheats, reliefs, mines, quarries, goods and chattels of felons
and fugitives, felons of themselves, and put in exigent,
deodands, free warrens, and all other royalties and seignories,
rights and jurisdictions, privileges and hereditaments whatsoever.——**And also** the advowson, donation, presentation and
free disposition of the rectory or parsonage of *Shandy* aforesaid,
and all and every the tenths, tythes, glebe-lands"——In three
words,——"My mother was to lay in, (if she chose it) in
London."

But in order to put a stop to the practice of any unfair play
on the part of my mother, which a marriage article of this
nature too manifestly opened a door to, and which indeed had
never been thought of at all, but for my·uncle *Toby Shandy;*
——a clause was added in security of my father, which was
this:——"That in case my mother hereafter should, at any
time, put my father to the trouble and expence of a *London*
journey upon false cries and tokens;——that for every such
instance she should forfeit all the right and title which the
covenant gave her to the next turn;——but to no more,——
and so on, *toties quoties,*[3] in as effectual a manner, as if such
a covenant betwixt them had not been made."——This, by the
way, was no more than what was reasonable;——and yet, as

---

[2]Courts held periodically for the gathering and inspection of the members of a frankpledge or mutually responsible local group.

[3]Every time.

reasonable as it was, I have ever thought it hard that the whole weight of the article should have fallen entirely, as it did, upon myself.

But I was begot and born to misfortunes;——for my poor mother, whether it was wind or water,——or a compound of both,——or neither;——or whether it was simply the mere swell of imagination and fancy in her;——or how far a strong wish and desire to have it so, might mislead her judgment;——in short, whether she was deceived or deceiving in this matter, it no way becomes me to decide. The fact was this, That, in the latter end of *September, 1717*, which was the year before I was born, my mother having carried my father up to town much against the grain,——he peremptorily insisted upon the clause;——so that I was doom'd, by marriage articles, to have my nose squeez'd as flat to my face, as if the destinies had actually spun me without one.

How this event came about,——and what a train of vexatious disappointments, in one stage or other of my life, have pursued me from the mere loss, or rather compression, of this one single member,——shall be laid before the reader all in due time.

CHAP. XVI.

MY father, as any body may naturally imagine, came down with my mother into the country, in but a pettish kind of a humour. The first twenty or five-and-twenty miles he did nothing in the world but fret and teaze himself, and indeed my mother too, about the cursed expence, which he said might every shilling of it have been saved;——then what vexed him more than every thing else was the provoking time of the year,——which, as I told you, was towards the end of *September,* when his wall-fruit, and green gages especially, in which he was very curious, were just ready for pulling:——"Had he been whistled up to *London,* upon a *Tom Fool's* errand in any other month of the whole year, he should not have said three words about it."

For the next two whole stages, no subject would go down, but the heavy blow he had sustain'd from the loss of a son, whom it seems he had fully reckon'd upon in his mind, and register'd down in his pocket-book, as a second staff for his old age, in case *Bobby* should fail him. "The disappointment of this, he said, was ten times more to a wise man than all the money which the journey, *&c.* had cost him, put together,——rot the hundred and twenty pounds,——he did not mind it a rush."

From *Stilton,* all the way to *Grantham,* nothing in the whole affair provoked him so much as the condolences of his friends, and the foolish figure they should both make at church the first *Sunday;*——of which, in the satirical vehemence of his wit, now sharpen'd a little by vexation, he would give so many humorous and provoking descriptions,——and place his rib and self in so many tormenting lights and attitudes in the face of the whole congregation;——that my mother declared, these two stages were so truly tragi-comical, that she did nothing but laugh and cry in a breath, from one end to the other of them all the way.

From *Grantham,* till they had cross'd the *Trent,* my father was out of all kind of patience at the vile trick and imposition which he fancied my mother had put upon him in this affair.——"Certainly," he would say to himself, over and over again, "the woman could not be deceived herself;——if she could,——what weakness!"——tormenting word! which led his imagination a thorny dance, and, before all was over, play'd the duce and all with him;——for sure as ever the word *weakness* was uttered, and struck full upon his brain,——so sure it set him upon running divisions upon how many kinds of weaknesses there were;——that there was such a thing as weakness of the body,——as well as weakness of the mind,——and then he would do nothing but syllogize within himself for a stage or two together, How far the cause of all these vexations might, or might not, have arisen out of himself.

In short, he had so many little subjects of disquietude spring-ing out of this one affair, all fretting successively in his mind

as they rose up in it, that my mother, whatever was her journey up, had but an uneasy journey of it down.——In a word,
as she complained to my uncle *Toby,* he would have tired out
the patience of any flesh alive.

CHAP. XVII.

THough my father travelled homewards, as I told you, in
none of the best of moods,——pshaw-ing and pish-ing all
the way down,——yet he had the complaisance to keep the
worst part of the story still to himself;——which was the resolution he had taken of doing himself the justice, which my
uncle *Toby*'s clause in the marriage settlement empowered him;
nor was it till the very night in which I was begot, which was
thirteen months after, that she had the least intimation of his
design; when my father, happening, as you remember, to be a
little chagrin'd and out of temper,——took occasion as they
lay chatting gravely in bed afterwards, talking over what was
to come,——to let her know that she must accommodate herself as well as she could to the bargain made between them in
their marriage deeds; which was to lye-in of her next child in
the country to balance the last year's journey.

My father was a gentleman of many virtues,——but he had
a strong spice of that in his temper which might, or might
not, add to the number.——'Tis known by the name of perse-
verance in a good cause,——and of obstinacy in a bad one:
Of this my mother had so much knowledge, that she knew
'twas to no purpose to make any remonstrance,——so she e'en
resolved to sit down quietly, and make the most of it.

CHAP. XVIII.

AS the point was that night agreed, or rather determin'd,
that my mother should lye-in of me in the country, she
took her measures accordingly; for which purpose, when she

was three days, or thereabouts, gone with child, she began to
cast her eyes upon the midwife, whom you have so often heard
me mention; and before the week was well got round, as the
famous Dr. *Maningham*[1] was not to be had, she had come to a
final determination in her mind,——notwithstanding there
was a scientifick operator[2] within so near a call as eight miles
of us, and who, moreover, had expressly wrote a five shillings
book upon the subject of midwifery, in which he had exposed,
not only the blunders of the sisterhood itself,——but had likewise superadded many curious improvements for the quicker
extraction of the fœtus in cross births, and some other cases
of danger which belay us in getting into the world; notwithstanding all this, my mother, I say, was absolutely determined
to trust her life and mine with it, into no soul's hand but this
old woman's only.——Now this I like;——when we cannot get
at the very thing we wish,——never to take up with the next
best in degree to it;——no; that's pitiful beyond description;
——it is no more than a week from this very day, in which
I am now writing this book for the edification of the world,
——which is *March 9, 1759,*——that my dear, dear *Jenny*[3]
observing I look'd a little grave, as she stood cheapening a
silk of five-and-twenty shillings a yard,——told the mercer,
she was sorry she had given him so much trouble;——and immediately went and bought herself a yard-wide stuff of ten-
pence a yard.——'Tis the duplication of one and the same
greatness of soul; only what lessen'd the honour of it somewhat, in my mother's case, was, that she could not heroine it

---

[1] Sir Richard Manningham, M.D., F.R.S. (1690–1759), the leading English
man-midwife of his day; his fame was yet to be made, however, at the
time of Tristram's birth.

[2] An allusion to John Burton, M.D. (1710–1771), antiquary and physician
of York, and author of "a most learned and masterly" *Essay on Midwifery* (1751). See p. 104, n. 1.

[3] In the earlier portions of the book, "Jenny" represents Catherine Fourmantel, a professional singer with whom, while she appeared at the
Assembly Rooms in York during the season of 1759–60, Sterne carried
on an open and perhaps Platonic sentimental flirtation. See the Introduction, pp. ix, xi–xiii, xxxii. Later in the book "Jenny" is probably
merely a symbol for any woman beloved by any man.

into so violent and hazardous an extream, as one in her situation might have wish'd, because the old midwife had really some little claim to be depended upon,——as much, at least, as success could give her; having, in the course of her practice of near twenty years in the parish, brought every mother's son of them into the world without any one slip or accident which could fairly be laid to her account.

These facts, tho' they had their weight, yet did not altogether satisfy some few scruples and uneasinesses which hung upon my father's spirits in relation to this choice.——To say nothing of the natural workings of humanity and justice,——or of the yearnings of parental and connubial love, all which prompted him to leave as little to hazard as possible in a case of this kind;——he felt himself concern'd in a particular manner, that all should go right in the present case;——from the accumulated sorrow he lay open to, should any evil betide his wife and child in lying-in at *Shandy-Hall.*——He knew the world judged by events, and would add to his afflictions in such a misfortune, by loading him with the whole blame of it.—— "Alas o'day;——had Mrs. *Shandy,* poor gentlewoman! had but her wish in going up to town just to lye-in and come down again;——which, they say, she begg'd and pray'd for upon her bare knees,——and which, in my opinion, considering the fortune which Mr. *Shandy* got with her,——was no such mighty matter to have complied with, the lady and her babe might both of 'em have been alive at this hour."

This exclamation, my father knew was unanswerable;—— and yet, it was not merely to shelter himself,——nor was it altogether for the care of his offspring and wife that he seem'd so extremely anxious about this point;——my father had extensive views of things,——and stood, moreover, as he thought, deeply concern'd in it for the publick good, from the dread he entertained of the bad uses an ill-fated instance might be put to.

He was very sensible that all political writers upon the subject had unanimously agreed and lamented, from the beginning of Queen *Elizabeth*'s reign down to his own time, that the current of men and money towards the metropolis, upon one frivolous errand or another,——set in so strong,——as to become dangerous to our civil rights;——tho', by the bye,——a *current* was not the image he took most delight in,——a *distemper* was here his favourite metaphor, and he would run it down into a perfect allegory, by maintaining it was identically the same in the body national as in the body natural, where blood and spirits were driven up into the head faster than they could find their ways down;——a stoppage of circulation must ensue, which was death in both cases.

There was little danger, he would say, of losing our liberties by *French* politicks or *French* invasions;——nor was he so much in pain of a consumption from the mass of corrupted matter and ulcerated humours in our constitution,——which he hoped was not so bad as it was imagined;——but he verily feared, that in some violent push, we should go off, all at once, in a state-apoplexy;——and then he would say, *The Lord have mercy upon us all.*

My father was never able to give the history of this distemper,——without the remedy along with it.

"Was I an absolute prince," he would say, pulling up his breeches with both his hands, as he rose from his arm-chair, "I would appoint able judges, at every avenue of my metropolis, who should take cognizance of every fool's business who came there;——and if, upon a fair and candid hearing, it appeared not of weight sufficient to leave his own home, and come up, bag and baggage, with his wife and children, farmers sons, &c. &c. at his backside, they should be all sent back, from constable to constable, like vagrants as they were, to the place of their legal settlements.   By this means I shall take care, that my metropolis totter'd not thro' its own weight;——that the head be no longer too big for the body;——that the extreams, now wasted and pin'd in, be restored to their due share of nourishment, and regain, with it, their natural strength and beauty:——I would effectually provide, That the meadows and corn-fields, of my dominions, should laugh and sing;——that good chear and hospitality flourish once more;——and that such weight and influence be put thereby into the hands of the Squirality[4] of my kingdom, as should counterpoise what I perceive my Nobility are now taking from them.

"Why are there so few palaces and gentlemen's seats," he would ask, with some emotion, as he walked a-cross the room, "throughout so many delicious provinces in *France?*   Whence is it that the few remaining *Chateaus* amongst them are so dismantled,——so unfurnished, and in so ruinous and desolate a condition?——Because, Sir," (he would say) "in that kingdom no man has any country-interest to support;——the little interest of any kind, which any man has any where in it, is concentrated in the court, and the looks of the Grand Monarch;[5] by the sun-shine of whose countenance, or the clouds which pass a-cross it, every *French* man lives or dies."

Another political reason which prompted my father so strongly to guard against the least evil accident in my mother's lying-in in the country,——was, That any such instance would infallibly throw a balance of power, too great already, into the weaker vessels of the gentry, in his own, or higher stations; ——which, with the many other usurped rights which that part of the constitution was hourly establishing,——would, in the end, prove fatal to the monarchical system of domestick government established in the first creation of things by God.

In this point he was entirely of Sir *Robert Filmer's*[6] opinion, That the plans and institutions of the greatest monarchies in the eastern parts of the world, were, originally, all stolen from that admirable pattern and prototype of this household and paternal power;——which, for a century, he said, and more, had gradually been degenerating away into a mix'd government; ——the form of which, however desirable in great combinations of the species,——was very troublesome in small ones,

---

Squirearchy; the class of landed proprietors.

[5]Louis XIV.

[6]Sir Robert Filmer (d. 1653), an English political writer, based his defence of the divine right of kings on the theory that the government of a family by its father is the true original and model of all government, and that kings rule by natural right as the supreme fathers of their people.

————and seldom produced any thing, that he saw, but sorrow and confusion.

For all these reasons, private and publick, put together,——my father was for having the man-midwife by all means,——my mother by no means. My father begg'd and intreated, she would for once recede from her prerogative in this matter, and suffer him to choose for her;——my mother, on the contrary, insisted upon her privilege in this matter, to choose for herself,——and have no mortal's help but the old woman's.—— What could my father do? He was almost at his wit's end; ——talked it over with her in all moods;——placed his arguments in all lights;——argued the matter with her like a christian,——like a heathen,——like a husband,——like a father,——like a patriot,——like a man:——My mother answered every thing only like a woman; which was a little hard upon her;——for as she could not assume and fight it out behind such a variety of characters,——'twas no fair match;—— 'twas seven to one.——What could my mother do?——She had the advantage (otherwise she had been certainly overpowered) of a small reinforcement of chagrin personal at the bottom which bore her up, and enabled her to dispute the affair with my father with so equal an advantage,——that both sides sung *Te Deum*.[7] In a word, my mother was to have the old woman,——and the operator was to have licence to drink a bottle of wine with my father and my uncle *Toby Shandy* in the back parlour,——for which he was to be paid five guineas.

I must beg leave, before I finish this chapter, to enter a caveat in the breast of my fair reader;——and it is this:—— Not to take it absolutely for granted from an unguarded word or two which I have dropp'd in it,——"That I am a married man."——I own the tender appellation of my dear, dear *Jenny,* ——with some other strokes of conjugal knowledge, interspersed here and there, might, naturally enough, have misled the most candid judge in the world into such a determination

---

[7]The title of an ancient hymn of thanksgiving (from the opening words, *Te Deum laudamus:* We praise thee, God), which has come to signify exultation over a victory.

against me.——All I plead for, in this case, Madam, is strict
justice, and that you do so much of it, to me as well as to
yourself,——as not to prejudge or receive such an impression
of me, till you have better evidence, than I am positive, at present, can be produced against me:——Not that I can be so vain
or unreasonable, Madam, as to desire you should therefore
think, that my dear, dear *Jenny* is my kept mistress;——no,
——that would be flattering my character in the other extream,
and giving it an air of freedom, which, perhaps, it has no
kind of right to. All I contend for, is the utter impossibility
for some volumes, that you, or the most penetrating spirit upon
earth, should know how this matter really stands.——It is not
impossible, but that my dear, dear *Jenny*! tender as the appellation is, may be my child.[8]——Consider,——I was born in the
year eighteen.——Nor is there any thing unnatural or extravagant in the supposition, that my dear *Jenny* may be my friend.
——Friend!——My friend.——Surely, Madam, a friendship
between the two sexes may subsist, and be supported without
——Fy! Mr. *Shandy:*——Without any thing, Madam, but
that tender and delicious sentiment, which ever mixes in
friendship, where there is a difference of sex. Let me intreat
you to study the pure and sentimental parts of the best *French*
Romances;——it will really, Madam, astonish you to see with
what a variety of chaste expression this delicious sentiment,
which I have the honour to speak of, is dress'd out.

CHAP. XIX.

I Would sooner undertake to explain the hardest problem in
Geometry, than pretend to account for it, that a gentleman
of my father's great good sense,——knowing, as the reader
must have observed him, and curious too, in philosophy,——
wise also in political reasoning,——and in polemical (as he will
find) no way ignorant,——could be capable of entertaining a
notion in his head, so out of the common track,——that I fear

[8]See p. 44, n. 3.

the reader, when I come to mention it to him, if he is the least
of a cholerick temper, will immediately throw the book by;
if mercurial, he will laugh most heartily at it;——and if he is
of a grave and saturnine cast, he will, at first sight, absolutely
condemn as fanciful and extravagant; and that was in respect
to the choice and imposition of Christian names, on which he
thought a great deal more depended than what superficial
minds were capable of conceiving.

His opinion, in this matter, was, That there was a strange
kind of magick bias, which good or bad names, as he called
them, irresistibly impress'd upon our characters and conduct.

The Hero of *Cervantes*[1] argued not the point with more seriousness,——nor had he more faith,——or more to say on the
powers of Necromancy in dishonouring his deeds,——or on
Dulcinea's name, in shedding lustre upon them, than my father
had on those of Trismegistus[2] or Archimedes, on the one hand,
——or of Nyky and Simkin on the other.   How many Cæsars
and Pompeys, he would say, by mere inspiration of the names,
have been render'd worthy of them?   And how many, he
would add, are there who might have done exceeding well in
the world, had not their characters and spirits been totally depress'd and Nicodemus'd[3] into nothing.

I see plainly, Sir, by your looks, (or as the case happen'd) my
father would say,——that you do not heartily subscribe to this
opinion of mine,——which, to those, he would add, who have
not carefully sifted it to the bottom,——I own has an air more
of fancy than of solid reasoning in it;——and yet, my dear Sir,

[1]For the frequent miscarriages of his enterprises, Don Quixote was wont
to blame the superior power of hostile magicians; his occasional successes were rendered the more sweet to him because they were undertaken in and glorified by the name of his imaginary mistress, "the empress
of La Mancha, the peerless Dulcinea del Toboso."

[2]For Trismegistus, see p. 207, n. 2.   Archimedes was the famous Greek
mathematician and inventor (c. 287–212 B.C.); Nyky and Simkin are of
course nicknames for Nicholas (or Nicodemus!) and Simeon.

[3]Suggesting the character of Nicodemus, a Pharisee and a member of
the Sanhedrin who, according to John, 3.1–13 and 7.45–53, in a cautious
visit to Christ by night had become at heart a believer but before the
Sanhedrin was afraid to avow his faith or to defend Christ; pusillanimous,
weak-spirited, faint-hearted.

if I may presume to know your character, I am morally assured,
I should hazard little in stating a case to you,——not as a party
in the dispute,——but as a judge, and trusting my appeal upon
it to your own good sense and candid disquisition in this matter;——you are a person free from as many narrow prejudices
of education as most men;——and, if I may presume to penetrate further into you,——of a liberality of genius above bearing down an opinion, merely because it wants friends.   Your
son!——your dear son,——from whose sweet and open temper
you have so much to expect.——Your BILLY, Sir!——would
you, for the world, have called him JUDAS?——Would you, my
dear Sir, he would say, laying his hand upon your breast, with
the genteelest address,——and in that soft and irresistible
piano[4] of voice, which the nature of the *argumentum ad
hominem*[5] absolutely requires,——Would you, Sir, if a *Jew*
of a godfather had proposed the name for your child, and offered you his purse along with it, would you have consented
to such a desecration of him?——O my God! he would say,
looking up, if I know your temper right, Sir,——you are incapable of it;——you would have trampled upon the offer;
——you would have thrown the temptation at the tempter's
head with abhorrence.

Your greatness of mind in this action, which I admire, with
that generous contempt of money which you shew me in the
whole transaction, is really noble;——and what renders it more
so, is the principle of it;——the workings of a parent's love
upon the truth and conviction of this very hypothesis, namely,
That was your son called JUDAS,——the sordid and treacherous
idea, so inseparable from the name, would have accompanied
him thro' life like his shadow, and, in the end, made a miser
and a rascal of him, in spite, Sir, of your example.

I never knew a man able to answer this argument.——But,
indeed, to speak of my father as he was;——he was certainly
irresistible, both in his orations and disputations;——he was

---

[4]Softness.

[5]Argument to the individual man; an appeal to one's personal prejudices or interests.

born an orator;——Θεοδίδακτος.[6]——Persuasion hung upon his lips, and the elements of Logick and Rhetorick were so blended up in him,——and, withall, he had so shrewd a guess at the weaknesses and passions of his respondent,——that NATURE might have stood up and said,——"This man is eloquent." In short, whether he was on the weak or the strong side of the question, 'twas hazardous in either case to attack him:—— And yet, 'tis strange, he had never read *Cicero*[7] nor *Quintilian de Oratore*, nor *Isocrates*, nor *Aristotle*, nor *Longinus* amongst the antients;——nor *Vossius*, nor *Skioppius*, nor *Ramus*, nor *Farnaby* amongst the moderns;——and what is more astonishing, he had never in his whole life the least light or spark of subtilty struck into his mind, by one single lecture upon *Crackenthorp* or *Burgersdicius*, or any *Dutch* logician or commentator;——he knew not so much as in what the difference of an argument *ad ignorantiam*,[8] and an argument *ad hominem* consisted; so that I well remember, when he went up along

---

[6]Taught of God.

[7]Cicero's treatises *De Oratore*, *Brutus*, and *Orator* develop a complete system of rhetorical training. Marcus Fabius Quintilianus (c.35–c.95) was a Roman rhetorician whose most celebrated work, the *Institutio Oratoria*, is a detailed treatise on the training of the orator. Isocrates (436–338 B.C.) was an Attic orator and distinguished teacher of eloquence. Aristotle (384–322 B.C.), the most famous and influential of Greek philosophers, was the founder of the Peripatetic school; the reference here is to his *Rhetoric*, a treatise on "the faculty of discerning in every case the available means of persuasion." Cassius Longinus (c.210–273), a celebrated Greek rhetorician and philosopher surnamed "Philologus," is the reputed author of *On the Sublime*, a famous study of impressiveness in literary style. Gerhard Johann Voss (1577–1649) was a Dutch classical scholar, grammarian, and theologian of note; the reference is to his *Ars Rhetorica* and *Commentariorum Rhetoricorum Libri VI*. Caspar Schoppe (1576–1649) was a German controversialist and scholar whose chief work was his *Grammatica Philosophica*. Petrus Ramus (1515–1572) was a French logician noted for his writings against Aristotelianism. Thomas Farnaby (c.1575–1647) was an English humanist whose *Systema Grammaticum*, written at the request of Charles I for use in the public schools, was published in 1641. Richard Crakanthorpe (1567–1624) was an eloquent Puritan divine, famous for his powers as a logician and a disputant. Francis Burgersdyk (1590–1629) was a Dutch logician famed for his *Institutionum Logicarum Libri Duo*.

[8]Argument to ignorance; an argument which presumes upon an adversary's ignorance of the facts disputed. For *ad hominem*, see p. 50, n. 5.

with me to enter my name at *Jesus College* in ****,[9]——it was
a matter of just wonder with my worthy tutor, and two or
three fellows of that learned society,——that a man who knew
not so much as the names of his tools, should be able to work
after that fashion with 'em.

To work with them in the best manner he could, was what
my father was, however, perpetually forced upon;——for he
had a thousand little sceptical notions of the comick kind to
defend,——most of which notions, I verily believe, at first
enter'd upon the footing of mere whims, and of a *vive la Bagatelle;*[10] and as such he would make merry with them for half
an hour or so, and having sharpen'd his wit upon 'em, dismiss
them till another day.

I mention this, not only as matter of hypothesis or conjecture
upon the progress and establishment of my father's many odd
opinions,——but as a warning to the learned reader against the
indiscreet reception of such guests, who, after a free and undisturbed enterance, for some years, into our brains,——at
length claim a kind of settlement there,——working sometimes
like yeast;——but more generally after the manner of the
gentle passion, beginning in jest,——but ending in downright
earnest.

Whether this was the case of the singularity of my father's
notions,——or that his judgment, at length, became the dupe
of his wit;——or how far, in many of his notions, he might,
tho' odd, be absolutely right;——the reader, as he comes at
them, shall decide. All that I maintain here, is, that in this
one, of the influence of Christian names, however it gain'd
footing, he was serious;——he was all uniformity;——he was
systematical, and, like all systematick reasoners, he would move
both heaven and earth, and twist and torture every thing in
nature to support his hypothesis. In a word, I repeat it over
again;——he was serious;——and, in consequence of it, he
would lose all kind of patience whenever he saw people, espe-

---

[9]Sterne himself was a graduate of Jesus College, Cambridge. See Introduction, p. xvi.

[10]Long live trifles; hurrah for frivolity!

cially of condition, who should have known better,——as careless and as indifferent about the name they imposed upon their
child,——or more so, than in the choice of *Ponto* or *Cupid* for
their puppy dog.

This, he would say, look'd ill;——and had, moreover, this
particular aggravation in it, *viz.* That when once a vile name
was wrongfully or injudiciously given, 'twas not like the case
of a man's character, which, when wrong'd, might hereafter be
clear'd;——and, possibly, sometime or other, if not in the
man's life, at least after his death,——be, somehow or other,
set to rights with the world: But the injury of this, he would
say, could never be undone;——nay, he doubted even whether
an act of parliament could reach it:——He knew as well as
you, that the legislature assum'd a power over surnames;——
but for very strong reasons, which he could give, it had never
yet adventured, he would say, to go a step further.

It was observable, that tho' my father, in consequence of
this opinion, had, as I have told you, the strongest likings and
dislikings towards certain names;——that there were still numbers of names which hung so equally in the balance before
him, that they were absolutely indifferent to him. *Jack, Dick,*
and *Tom* were of this class: These my father call'd neutral
names;——affirming of them, without a satyr, That there had
been as many knaves and fools, at least, as wise and good men,
since the world began, who had indifferently borne them;——
so that, like equal forces acting against each other in contrary
directions, he thought they mutually destroyed each others
effects; for which reason, he would often declare, He would
not give a cherry-stone to choose amongst them. *Bob,* which
was my brother's name, was another of these neutral kinds of
Christian names, which operated very little either way; and as
my father happen'd to be at *Epsom,* when it was given him,
——he would oft times thank Heaven it was no worse.
Andrew was something like a negative quantity in Algebra
with him;——'twas worse, he said, than nothing.——*William*
stood pretty high:——*Numps* again was low with him;——
and *Nick,* he said, was the DEVIL.

But, of all the names in the universe, he had the most unconquerable aversion for TRISTRAM;[11]——he had the lowest and
most contemptible opinion of it of any thing in the world,——
thinking it could possibly produce nothing in *rerum naturâ,*[12]
but what was extreamly mean and pitiful: So that in the midst
of a dispute on the subject, in which, by the bye, he was frequently involved,——he would sometimes break off in a sudden and spirited EPIPHONEMA,[13] or rather EROTESIS, raised a
third, and sometimes a full fifth, above the key of the discourse,——and demand it categorically of his antagonist,
Whether he would take upon him to say, he had ever remember'd,——whether he had ever read,——or even whether he
had ever heard tell of a man, call'd *Tristram,* performing any
thing great or worth recording?——No——, he would say,
——TRISTRAM!——The thing is impossible.

What could be wanting in my father but to have wrote a
book to publish this notion of his to the world?   Little boots
it to the subtle speculatist to stand single in his opinions,——
unless he gives them proper vent:——It was the identical thing
which my father did;——for in the year sixteen, which was two
years before I was born, he was at the pains of writing an
express DISSERTATION simply upon the word *Tristram,*——
shewing the world, with great candour and modesty, the
grounds of his great abhorrence to the name.

When this story is compared with the title-page,——Will
not the gentle reader pity my father from his soul?——to see
an orderly and well-disposed gentleman, who tho' singular,
——yet inoffensive in his notions,——so played upon in them
by cross purposes;——to look down upon the stage, and see
him baffled and overthrown in all his little systems and wishes;
to behold a train of events perpetually falling out against him,
and in so critical and cruel a way, as if they had purposedly
been plann'd and pointed against him, merely to insult his

---

[11]Based on Latin *tristis,* Tristram means "sorrowful."

[12]The nature of things.

[13]A confirming, summing, or concluding sentence.   Erotesis is a rhetorical question.

speculations.——In a word, to behold such a one, in his old age, ill-fitted for troubles, ten times in a day suffering sorrow; ——ten times in a day calling the child of his prayers TRIS-TRAM!——Melancholy dissyllable of sound! which, to his ears, was unison to *Nicompoop,* and every name vituperative under heaven.——By his ashes! I swear it,——if ever malignant spirit took pleasure, or busied itself in traversing the purposes of mortal man,——it must have been here;——and if it was not necessary I should be born before I was christened, I would this moment give the reader an account of it.

CHAP. XX.

——How could you, Madam, be so inattentive in reading the last chapter? I told you in it, *That my mother was not a papist.*——Papist! You told me no such thing, Sir. Madam, I beg leave to repeat it over again, That I told you as plain, at least, as words, by direct inference, could tell you such a thing.——Then, Sir, I must have miss'd a page. ——No, Madam,——you have not miss'd a word.——Then I was asleep, Sir.——My pride, Madam, cannot allow you that refuge.——Then, I declare, I know nothing at all about the matter.——That, Madam, is the very fault I lay to your charge; and as a punishment for it, I do insist upon it, that you immediately turn back, that is, as soon as you get to the next full stop, and read the whole chapter over again.

I have imposed this penance upon the lady, neither out of wantonness or cruelty, but from the best of motives; and therefore shall make her no apology for it when she returns back:——'Tis to rebuke a vicious taste which has crept into thousands besides herself,——of reading straight forwards, more in quest of the adventures, than of the deep erudition and knowledge which a book of this cast, if read over as it should be, would infallibly impart with them.——The mind should be accustomed to make wise reflections, and draw curious conclusions as it goes along; the habitude of which made

Pliny the younger[1] affirm, "That he never read a book so bad, but he drew some profit from it."   The stories of *Greece* and *Rome,* run over without this turn and application,——do less service, I affirm it, than the history of *Parismus* and *Parismenus,*[2] or of the Seven Champions of *England,* read with it.

——But here comes my fair Lady.   Have you read over again the chapter, Madam, as I desired you?——You have: And did you not observe the passage, upon the second reading, which admits the inference?——Not a word like it!   Then, Madam, be pleased to ponder well the last line but one of the chapter, where I take upon me to say, "It was *necessary* I should be born before I was christen'd."   Had my mother, Madam, been a Papist, that consequence did not follow.*

It is a terrible misfortune for this same book of mine, but more so to the Republick of Letters;——so that my own is quite swallowed up in the consideration of it,——that this self-same vile pruriency for fresh adventures in all things, has got so strongly into our habit and humours,——and so wholly intent are we upon satisfying the impatience of our concupiscence that way,——that nothing but the gross and more carnal parts of a composition will go down:——The subtle hints and sly communications of science fly off, like spirits, upwards;——the heavy moral escapes downwards; and both the one and the other are as much lost to the world, as if they were still left in the bottom of the ink-horn.

I wish the male-reader has not pass'd by many a one, as quaint and curious as this one, in which the female-reader has been detected.   I wish it may have its effects;——and that all good people, both male and female, from her example, may be taught to think as well as read.

---

[1]Caius Plinius Caecilius Secundus (62–113), Roman author, did write "He read nothing without making extracts, for he used to say that no book was so bad but that some part of it was useful" (*Epistolae,* 3.5); "he," however, was Pliny the Elder (23–79), the Roman naturalist, of whom his nephew was here writing.

[2]See p. 460, n. 1.

*The *Romish* Rituals direct the baptizing of the child, in cases of danger, *before* it is born;——but upon this proviso, That some part or

MÉMOIRE presenté à Messieurs les Docteurs de SORBONNE*.[3]

*U*N *Chirurgien Accoucheur, represente à Messieurs les Doctueurs de* Sorbonne, *qu'il y a des cas, quoique trés rares, où une mere ne sçauroit accoucher, & même où l'enfant est tellement renfermé dans le sein de sa mere, qu'il ne fait paroître aucune partie de son corps, ce qui seroit un cas, suivant les Rituels, de lui conférer, du moins sous condition,*

other of the child's body be seen by the baptizer:——But the Doctors of the *Sorbonne,* by a deliberation held amongst them, *April* 10, 1733,—— have enlarged the powers of the midwives, by determining, That tho' no part of the child's body should appear,——that baptism shall, never-theless, be administered to it by injection,——*par le moyen d'une petite Canulle,*——Anglicè *a squirt.*[a]——'Tis very strange that St. *Thomas Aquinas,*[b] who had so good a mechanical head, both for tying and untying the knots of school divinity,——should, after so much pains bestowed upon this,——give up the point at last, as a second *La chose impossible,*[c] ——"Infantes in maternis uteris existentes (quoth St. *Thomas*) baptizari possunt *nullo modo.*"[d]——O *Thomas! Thomas!*

If the reader has the curiosity to see the question upon baptism, *by injection,* as presented to the Doctors of the *Sorbonne,* with their consul-tation thereupon, it is as follows. [Sterne's note. The reference is to the "Memoire" and "Reponse" above, which Sterne incorporated in the main text of the chapter.]

[a]By means of a little injection-pipe,—in English, by a squirt.

[b]St. Thomas Aquinas (c. 1227–1274), the Italian theologian and scholastic philosopher, whose chief work, the *Summa Theologiæ,* is here referred to.

[c]Impossible thing.

[d]Infants yet in maternal wombs cannot be baptized by any means.

*Vide Deventer, Paris edit., 4to, 1734, p. 366. [Sterne's note, added in the second edition after the authenticity of the quotation had been questioned.]

[3]This passage, as Sterne's note indicates, is taken almost verbatim from the *Observations importantes sur le manuel des accouchemens* of Hein-rich van Deventer (1651–1724), a famous Dutch physician and obste-trician. It may be translated as follows:
    "*Memorandum* presented to the Doctors of the *Sorbonne*
    "An obstetrical surgeon declares to the Doctors of the *Sorbonne* that there are sometimes cases, although they are very rare, in which a mother cannot deliver her child, and in which the child is held in its mother's womb in such a way that it cannot make any part of its body appear, which latter would be a case, according to the Rituals, to bap-tize it, at least conditionally. The surgeon who raises the question as-

le baptême. Le Chirurgien, qui consulte, prétend, par le moyen d'une petite canulle, *de pouvoir baptiser immediatement l'enfant, sans faire aucun tort à la mere.——Il demande si ce moyen, qu'il vient de proposer, est permis & légitime, et s'il peut s'en servir dans le cas qu'il vient d'exposer.*

REPONSE

*L*E *Conseil estime, que la question proposée souffre de grandes difficultés. Les Théologiens posent d'un côté pour principe, que le baptême, qui est une naissance spirituelle, suppose une premiere naissance; il faut être né dans le monde, pour renaître en* Jesus Christ, *comme ils l'enseignent.* S. Thomas, 3 part. quæst. 68. artic. 11. *suit cette doctrine comme une verité constante; l'on ne peut, dit ce S. Docteur, baptiser les enfans qui sont renfermés dans le sein de leurs Meres, et S.* Thomas *est fondé sur ce, que les enfans ne sont point nés, & ne peuvent être comptés parmi les autres hommes; d'où il conclud, qu'ils ne peuvent être l'object d'une action extérieure, pour recevoir par leur ministére, les sacremens nécessaires au salut:* Pueri in maternis uteris existentes nondum prodierunt in lucem ut cum aliis hominibus vitam ducant; unde

---

serts that by means of a *little injection-pipe* he can baptize the child directly, without doing any harm to the mother. He asks whether this means which he proposes is permissible and lawful, and whether it may be employed in such cases as he has described.

"REPLY

"The Council observes that the question proposed presents great difficulties. The Theologians assume the hypothesis that baptism, which is a spiritual birth, supposes a former birth; as they teach it, it is necessary to be born into the world to be reborn in Jesus Christ. Saint *Thomas* [Aquinas], in *part 3, question 68, article 11,* follows this doctrine as an accepted truth; one cannot, says this Holy Doctor, baptize children who are yet held in their mothers' wombs, and Saint *Thomas* bases his opinion on the fact that such children are not born and cannot be counted among other men; from this he concludes that they cannot be the object of an external action in receiving through the ministry of men the sacraments necessary to salvation: *Children remaining in maternal wombs have not yet come forth into the light that they may lead*

non possunt subjici actioni humanæ, ut per eorum ministerium
sacramenta recipiant ad salutem. *Les rituels ordonnent dans
la pratique ce que les théologiens ont établi sur les mêmes
matiéres, & ils deffendent tous d'une maniére uniforme de baptiser les enfans qui sont renfermés dans le sein de leurs meres,
s'ils ne font paroître quelque partie de leurs corps. Le concours
des théologiens, & des rituels, qui sont les règles des diocéses,
paroît former une autorité qui termine la question presente;
cependant le conseil de conscience considerant d'un côté, que
le raisonnement des théologiens est uniquement fondé sur
une raison de convenance, & que la deffense des rituels, suppose que l'on ne peut baptiser immediatement les enfans
ainsi renfermés dans le sein de leurs meres, ce qui est contre la
supposition presente; & d'un autre côté, considerant que les
mêmes théologiens enseignent, que l'on peut risquer les sacremens qu'* Jesus Christ *a établis comme des moyens faciles,
mais nécessaires pour sanctifier les hommes; & d'ailleurs estimant, que les enfans renfermés dans le sein de leurs meres,
pourroient être capables de salut, parce qu'ils sont capables de
damnation;——pour ces considerations, & en égard à l'exposé,
suivant lequel on assure avoir trouvé un moyen certain de
baptiser ces enfans ainsi renfermés, sans faire aucun tort à*

their life among other men; therefore they cannot be the objects of human
action that they may receive through the ministry of men the sacraments
necessary to salvation. The rituals follow in practice what the theologians have ordained in these matters, and in a uniform manner they
prohibit the baptism of infants who are retained in their mothers'
wombs, if no part of their bodies appears. The agreement of the
theologians and of the rituals, which are the rules of the dioceses, appears to establish an authority which settles the present question; however, the council conscientiously considering, on the one hand, that the
reasoning of the theologians is founded merely upon a matter of expediency, and that the maintenance of the rituals assumes that one cannot directly baptize infants thus retained in their mothers' wombs, the
which is contrary to the present supposition; and considering, on the
other hand, that the same theologians teach that one may risk adminis-
tering the sacraments which *Jesus Christ* has established as the easy but
necessary means for the salvation of men; and deeming, furthermore,
that children retained in their mothers' wombs are capable of salvation
even as they are capable of damnation;—for these considerations, and in
regard of the statement which affirms that a certain means has been
found of baptizing children thus retained, without doing any harm to

*la mere, le Conseil estime que l'on pourroit se servir du moyen
proposé, dans la confiance qu'il a, que Dieu n'a point laissé ces
sortes d'enfans sans aucuns secours, & supposant, comme il
est exposé, que le moyen dont il s'agit est propre à leur procurer
le baptême; cependant comme il s'agiroit, en autorisant la
pratique proposée, de changer une règle universellement
établie, le Conseil croit que celui qui consulte doit s'addresser
à son évêque, & à qui il appartient de juger de l'utilité, &
du danger du moyen proposé, & comme, sous le bon plaisir de
l'évêque, le conseil estime qu'il faudroit recourir au Pape, qui
a le droit d'expliquer les règles de l'église, et d'y déroger
dans le cas, où la loi ne sçauroit obliger, quelque sage &
quelque utile que paroisse la maniére de baptiser dont il
s'agit, le conseil ne pourroit l'approuver sans le concours de
ces deux autorités. On conseille au moins à celui qui consulte,
de s'addresser à son évêque, & de lui faire part de la presente
décision, afin que, si le prelat entre dans les raisons sur
lesquelles les docteurs soussignés s'appuyent, il puisse être
autorisé dans le cas de nécessité, où il risqueroit trop d'at-
tendre que la permission fût demandée & accordée d'em-
ployer le moyen qu'il propose si avantageux au salut de
l'enfant. Au reste le conseil, en estimant que l'on pourroit*

the mother, the Council deems that one may take advantage of the proposed expedient, in the faith which it has that God would never leave
this sort of infants without any succour, and supposing, as is asserted,
that the means under discussion is proper to procure their baptism.
However, since in authorizing the proposed practice it would be proceeding to change a rule universally established, the Council believes that
he who consults it ought to address himself to his bishop and to whom-
soever it appertains to judge the utility and the danger of the proposed
means, and since, with submission to the pleasure of the bishop,
the Council deems that it would be necessary to appeal to the Pope, who
has the authority to. interpret the rules of the church and to derogate
them in case the law cannot accommodate whatever wisdom and utility
may appear in the manner of baptizing here considered, the Council cannot approve the practice without the confirmation of these two authorities. The consulter is advised at least to address himself to his bishop
and to apprise him of the present decision, in order that, if the prelate
agrees with the reasons upon which the undersigned doctors base their
opinion, in case of necessity in which he might risk too much to wait
while the permission was asked and granted, he can be authorized to
employ the means which he proposes, so advantageous to the salva-

*s'en servir croit cependant, que si les enfans dont il s'agit,
venoient au monde, contre l'esperance de ceux qui se seroient
servis du même moyen, il seroit nécessaire de les baptiser*
sous condition, *& en cela le conseil se conforme à tous les
rituels, qui en autorisant le baptême d'un enfant qui fait
paroître quelque partie de son corps, enjoignent néantmoins,
& ordonnent de le baptiser* sous condition, *s'il vient heureuse-
ment au monde.*

Déliberé en *Sorbonne,* le 10 *Avril,* 1733.

A. LE MOYNE,
L. DE ROMIGNY,
DE MARCILLY.

Mr. *Tristram Shandy's* compliments to Messrs. *Le Moyne, De
Romigny,* and *De Marcilly,* hopes they all rested well the night
after so tiresome a consultation.——He begs to know, whether,
after the ceremony of marriage, and before that of consumma-
tion, the baptizing all the HOMUNCULI[4] at once, slap-dash, by
injection, would not be a shorter and safer cut still; on condition, as above, That if the HOMUNCULI do well and come safe
into the world after this, That each and every of them shall
be baptized again (*sous condition.*[5])——And provided, in the
second place, That the thing can be done, which Mr. *Shandy*
apprehends it may, *par le moyen d'une* petite canulle, and *sans
faire aucun tort au pere.*[6]

---

tion of the infant. In decreeing that one may avail himself of this manner of baptism, the Council nevertheless believes that if the infants in
question should come into the world, against the expectation of those
who had availed themselves of this expedient, it would be necessary to
baptize them *conditionally;* and in this the Council is in conformity with
all the rituals which, in authorizing the baptism of an infant any portion
of whose body appears, nevertheless enjoin and ordain that it be baptized
conditionally if it comes happily into the world.
    Determined in the Sorbonne, *10 April, 1733.*

*A. Le Moyne,
L. De Romigny,
De Marcilly."*

[4]Plural of *homunculus;* see p. 5, n. 1.
[5]Conditionally.
[6]By means of a little injection-pipe, and without doing any harm to
the father.

CHAP. XXI.

——I wonder what's all that noise, and running backwards
and forwards for, above stairs, quoth my father, addressing
himself, after an hour and a half's silence, to my uncle *Toby,*
——who you must know, was sitting on the opposite side of
the fire, smoking his social pipe all the time, in mute contemplation of a new pair of black-plush-breeches which he had
got on;——What can they be doing brother? quoth my father,
——we can scarce hear ourselves talk.

I think, replied my uncle *Toby,* taking his pipe from his
mouth, and striking the head of it two or three times upon the
nail of his left thumb, as he began his sentence,——I think,
says he:——But to enter rightly into my uncle *Toby's* sentiments upon this matter, you must be made to enter first a little
into his character, the out-lines of which I shall just give you,
and then the dialogue between him and my father will go on
as well again.

——Pray what was that man's name,——for I write in such a
hurry, I have no time to recollect or look for it,——who first
made the observation, "That there was great inconstancy in
our air and climate?"   Whoever he was, 'twas a just and good
observation in him.——But the corollary drawn from it,
namely, "That it is this which has furnished us with such a
variety of odd and whimsical characters;"——that was not
his;——it was found out by another man, at least a century
and a half after him:——Then again,——that this copious
store-house of original materials, is the true and natural cause
that our Comedies are so much better than those of *France,* or
any others that either have, or can be wrote upon the Continent;——that discovery was not fully made till about the middle of king *William's* reign,——when the great *Dryden,* in
writing one of his long prefaces, (if I mistake not) most for-
tunately hit upon it.   Indeed towards the latter end of queen
Anne, the great *Addison* began to patronize the notion, and

more fully explained it to the world in one or two of his Spec-
tators;——but the discovery was not his.[1]——Then, fourthly
and lastly, that this strange irregularity in our climate, producing so strange an irregularity in our characters,——doth thereby, in some sort, make us amends, by giving us somewhat to
make us merry with when the weather will not suffer us to go
out of doors,——that observation is my own;——and was
struck out by me this very rainy day, *March* 26, 1759, and betwixt the hours of nine and ten in the morning.

Thus,——thus my fellow labourers and associates in this
great harvest of our learning, now ripening before our eyes;
thus it is, by slow steps of casual increase, that our knowledge
physical, metaphysical, physiological, polemical, nautical,
mathematical, ænigmatical, technical, biographical, romantical,
chemical, and obstetrical, with fifty other branches of it, (most
of 'em ending, as these do, in *ical*) have, for these two last centuries and more, gradually been creeping upwards towards that
Ακμή[2] of their perfections, from which, if we may form a
conjecture from the advances of these last seven years, we cannot possibly be far off.

When that happens, it is to be hoped, it will put an end to
all kind of writings whatsoever;——the want of all kind of
writing will put an end to all kind of reading;——and that
in time, *As war begets poverty, poverty peace,*——must, in
course, put an end to all kind of knowledge,——and then
——we shall have all to begin over again; or, in other words,
be exactly where we started.

——Happy! thrice happy Times! I only wish that the æra

---

[1]The first "observation" and its corollary—that the English climate is
varied and that from this climate results the variety of English characters
—had long been accepted as commonplaces by English writers and natural philosophers, and Addison and Dryden were far from being the sole
patrons of the conclusion that to the variety of native characters was due
the superiority of English comedy to continental. The "long preface" is
Dryden's *Essay of Dramatick Poesie,* which develops and illustrates the
idea at some length; Addison made frequent reference to the effect of
climate on men's dispositions, but he connected English humours with
the drama in only one *Spectator,* the 371st.

[2]Acme, peak.

of my begetting, as well as the mode and manner of it, had been a little alter'd,——or that it could have been put off with any convenience to my father or mother, for some twenty or five-and-twenty years longer, when a man in the literary world might have stood some chance.——

But I forget my uncle *Toby,* whom all this while we have left knocking the ashes out of his tobacco pipe.

His humour was of that particular species, which does honour to our atmosphere; and I should have made no scruple of ranking him amongst one of the first-rate productions of it, had not there appear'd too many strong lines in it of a family-likeness, which shewed that he derived the singularity of his temper more from blood, than either wind or water, or any modifications or combinations of them whatever: And I have, therefore, oft times wondered, that my father, tho' I believe he had his reasons for it, upon his observing some tokens of excentricity in my course when I was a boy,——should never once endeavour to account for them in this way; for all the SHANDY FAMILY were of an original character throughout;—— I mean the males,——the females had no character at all,—— except, indeed, my great aunt DINAH, who, about sixty years ago, was married and got with child by the coachman, for which my father, according to his hypothesis of Christian names, would often say, She might thank her godfathers and godmothers.

It will seem very strange,——and I would as soon think of dropping a riddle in the reader's way, which is not my interest to do, as set him upon guessing how it could come to pass, that an event of this kind, so many years after it had happened, should be reserved for the interruption of the peace and unity, which otherwise so cordially subsisted, between my father and my uncle *Toby.* One would have thought, that the whole force of the misfortune should have spent and wasted itself in the family at first,——as is generally the case:——But nothing ever wrought with our family after the ordinary way. Possibly at the very time this happened, it might have something else to afflict it; and as afflictions are sent down for our

good, and that as this had never done the SHANDY FAMILY any
good at all, it might lye waiting till apt times and circumstances should give it an opportunity to discharge its office.
——Observe, I determine nothing upon this.——My way is
ever to point out to the curious, different tracts of investigation, to come at the first springs of the events I tell;——not
with a pedantic *Fescue*,[3]——or in the decisive Manner of
Tacitus,[4] who outwits himself and his reader;——but with the
officious humility of a heart devoted to the assistance merely
of the inquisitive;——to them I write,——and by them I shall
be read,——if any such reading as this could be supposed to
hold out so long, to the very end of the world.

Why this cause of sorrow, therefore, was thus reserved for
my father and uncle, is undetermined by me. But how and
in what direction it exerted itself, so as to become the cause
of dissatisfaction between them, after it began to operate, is
what I am able to explain with great exactness, and is as follows:

My uncle TOBY SHANDY, Madam, was a gentleman, who, with
the virtues which usually constitute the character of a man of
honour and rectitude,——possessed one in a very eminent
degree, which is seldom or never put into the catalogue; and
that was a most extream and unparallel'd modesty of nature;
——tho' I correct the word nature, for this reason, that I may
not prejudge a point which must shortly come to a hearing;
and that is, Whether this modesty of his was natural or ac-
quir'd.——Which ever way my uncle *Toby* came by it, 'twas
nevertheless modesty in the truest sense of it; and that is,
Madam, not in regard to words, for he was so unhappy as to
have very little choice in them,——but to things;——and this
kind of modesty so possess'd him, and it arose to such a height
in him, as almost to equal, if such a thing could be, even the
modesty of a woman: That female nicety, Madam, and inward

---

[3] A straw or slender rod; a teacher's pointer.

[4] Cornelius Tacitus (c. 55–c. 120), a Roman historian, whose style, proverbial for its brevity, is occasionally obscure and affected, and whose
interpretation of actions appears sometimes to be over-subtilized.

cleanliness of mind and fancy, in your sex, which makes you
so much the awe of ours.

You will imagine, Madam, that my uncle *Toby* had contracted all this from this very source;——that he had spent a
great part of his time in converse with your sex; and that,
from a thorough knowledge of you, and the force of imitation
which such fair examples render irresistable,——he had acquired this amiable turn of mind.

I wish I could say so,——for unless it was with his sister-in-
law, my father's wife and my mother,——my uncle *Toby* scarce
exchanged three words with the sex in as many years;——no,
he got it, Madam, by a blow.——A blow!——Yes, Madam, it
was owing to a blow from a stone, broke off by a ball from the
parapet of a horn-work[5] at the siege of *Namur*,[6] which struck
full upon my uncle *Toby*'s groin.—Which way could that
effect it?   The story of that, Madam, is long and interesting;
——but it would be running my history all upon heaps to give
it you here.——'Tis for an episode hereafter; and every circumstance relating to it in its proper place, shall be faithfully
laid before you:——'Till then, it is not in my power to give
further light into this matter, or say more than what I have
said already,——That my uncle *Toby* was a gentleman of unparallel'd modesty, which happening to be somewhat sub-
tilized and rarified by the constant heat of a little family-pride,
——they both so wrought together within him, that he could
never bear to hear the affair of my aunt DINAH touch'd upon,
but with the greatest emotion.——The least hint of it was
enough to make the blood fly into his face;——but when my
father enlarged upon the story in mixed companies, which
the illustration of his hypothesis frequently obliged him to
do,——the unfortunate blight of one of the fairest branches
of the family, would set my uncle *Toby*'s honour and modesty
o'bleeding; and he would often take my father aside, in the

---

[5] A military work with but one front, consisting of two demi-bastions,
thrown out beyond the glacis for the protection of any weak point.

[6] After a stubborn resistance of sixty-seven days, Namur capitulated to
the Allies on August 30, 1695.

greatest concern imaginable, to expostulate and tell him, he would give him any thing in the world, only to let the story rest.

My father, I believe, had the truest love and tenderness for my uncle *Toby,* that ever one brother bore towards another, and would have done any thing in nature, which one brother in reason could have desir'd of another, to have made my uncle *Toby's* heart easy in this, or any other point.　But this lay out of his power.

——My father, as I told you, was a philosopher in grain,—— speculative,——systematical;——and my aunt *Dinah's* affair was a matter of as much consequence to him, as the retrogradation of the planets[7] to *Copernicus:*——The backslidings of *Venus* in her orbit fortified the *Copernican* system, call'd so after his name; and the backslidings of my aunt *Dinah* in her orbit, did the same service in establishing my father's system, which, I trust, will for ever hereafter be call'd the *Shandean System,* after his.

In any other family dishonour, my father, I believe, had as nice a sense of shame as any man whatever;——and neither he, nor, I dare say, *Copernicus,* would have divulged the affair in either case, or have taken the least notice of it to the world, but for the obligations they owed, as they thought, to truth. ——*Amicus Plato,* my father would say, construing the words to my uncle *Toby,* as he went along, *Amicus Plato;* that is, DINAH was my aunt;——*sed magis amica veritas*[8]——but TRUTH is my sister.

This contrariety of humours betwixt my father and my uncle, was the source of many a fraternal squabble.　The one could not bear to hear the tale of family disgrace recorded, ——and the other would scarce ever let a day pass to an end without some hint at it.

For God's sake, my uncle *Toby* would cry,——and for my

---

[7]Backward motion, apparent or real, of a planet in the zodiac.

[8]Plato is my friend, but truth is a greater friend.　A proverbial expression, developed from Socrates's saying, "And I would ask you to be thinking of the truth and not of Socrates," recorded in Plato's *Phædo,* 91.

sake, and for all our sakes, my dear brother *Shandy,*——do let
this story of our aunt's and her ashes sleep in peace;——how
can you,——how can you have so little feeling and compassion
for the character of our family:——What is the character of a
family to an hypothesis? my father would reply.——Nay, if
you come to that——what is the life of a family:——The life
of a family!——my uncle *Toby* would say, throwing himself
back in his arm-chair, and lifting up his hands, his eyes, and
one leg.——Yes the life,——my father would say, maintaining
his point. How many thousands of 'em are there every year
that come cast away, (in all civilized countries at least)——
and consider'd as nothing but common air, in competition of
an hypothesis. In my plain sense of things, my uncle *Toby*
would answer,——every such instance is downright MURDER,
let who will commit it.——There lies your mistake, my father
would reply;——for, in *Foro Scientiæ*[9] there is no such thing
as MURDER,——'tis only DEATH, brother.

My uncle *Toby* would never offer to answer this by any other
kind of argument, than that of whistling half a dozen bars of
Lillabullero.[10]——You must know it was the usual channel
thro' which his passions got vent, when any thing shocked or
surprised him;——but especially when any thing, which he
deem'd very absurd, was offered.

As not one of our logical writers, nor any of the commentators upon them, that I remember, have thought proper to
give a name to this particular species of argument,——I here
take the liberty to do it myself, for two reasons. First, That,

----

[9]The forum or tribunal of science.

[10]*Lillabullero* (variously spelt) was said to have been the watchword of
the Irish Roman Catholics during their massacre of the Protestants in
1641; later it became the name of a nonsense song ridiculing the Irish
Papists, which was extremely popular in England and which, according
to Bishop Percy, "slight and insignificant as [it] may now seem, had once
a more powerful effect than either the Philippics of Demosthenes, or
Cicero; and contributed not a little towards the great revolution in
1688" (*Reliques of Ancient English Poetry,* fourth edition (1794), 2.373).
Bishop Burnet testified that the "foolish ballad . . . made an impression
on the [English] army, that cannot be well imagined by those who saw
it not. The whole army, and at last all people both in city and country,

LILLIBURLERO

Lord Wharton
(1648-1715)

Henry Purcell
(1658-1695)

were singing it perpetually. And perhaps never had so slight a thing so great an effect" (*History of His Own Time,* 4.792). The words, presumably written by Lord Wharton, were set to one of Purcell's exercises for the harpsichord; the text, which follows, was not included in early editions of *Shandy.*

in order to prevent all confusion in disputes, it may stand as
much distinguished for ever, from every other species of argument,———as the *Argumentum ad Verecundiam*,[11] *ex Absurdo, ex Fortiori,* or any other argument whatsoever:———
And, secondly, That it may be said by my children's children,
when my head is laid to rest,———that their learned grandfather's head had been busied to as much purpose once, as
other people's:———That he had invented a name,———and generously thrown it into the TREASURY of the *Ars Logica*,[12] for
one of the most unanswerable arguments in the whole science.
And if the end of disputation is more to silence than convince,
———they may add, if they please, to one of the best arguments
too.

I do therefore, by these presents, strictly order and command,
That it be known and distinguished by the name and title of
the *Argumentum Fistulatorium*,[13] and no other;———and that
it rank hereafter with the *Argumentum Baculinum,* and the
Argumentum ad Crumenam, and for ever hereafter be treated
of in the same chapter.

As for the *Argumentum Tripodium*,[14] which is never used
but by the woman against the man;———and the *Argumentum
ad Rem,* which, contrarywise, is made use of by the man only
against the woman:———As these two are enough in conscience
for one lecture;———and, moreover, as the one is the best answer to the other,———let them likewise be kept apart, and be
treated of in a place by themselves.

---

[11]Argument addressed to modesty; an appeal to one's reverence for
authority. *Ex Absurdo:* disproof of a proposition by showing the absurdity or impossibility of one or more of its consequences. *Ex Fortiori:*
with a stronger reason; hence, more conclusive. All these are orthodox
terms of logic.

[12]Art of logic.

[13]Literally, the argument of one who plays upon a shepherd's pipe; the
argument of a whistler (not an orthodox term). *Argumentum Baculinum:* literally, the argument of a stick; an appeal to one's sense of fear.
Argumentum ad Crumenam: an argument to the purse; an appeal to one's
thrift or avarice.

[14]Argument addressed to the third leg. *Argumentum ad Rem:* Argument addressed to the thing.

CHAP. XXII.

THE learned Bishop *Hall*,[1] I mean the famous Dr. *Joseph Hall*, who was Bishop of *Exeter* in King *James* the First's reign, tells us in one of his *Decads,* at the end of his divine art of meditation, imprinted at *London,* in the year 1610, by *John Beal,* dwelling in *Aldersgate-street,* "That it is an abominable thing for a man to commend himself;"——and I really think it is so.

And yet, on the other hand, when a thing is executed in a masterly kind of a fashion, which thing is not likely to be found out;——I think it is full as abominable, that a man should lose the honour of it, and go out of the world with the conceit of it rotting in his head.

This is precisely my situation.

For in this long digression which I was accidentally led into, as in all my digressions (one only excepted) there is a master-stroke of digressive skill, the merit of which has all along, I fear, been overlooked by my reader,——not for want of pene-tration in him,——but because 'tis an excellence seldom looked for, or expected indeed, in a digression;——and it is this: That tho' my digressions are all fair, as you observe,——and that I fly off from what I am about, as far and as often too as any writer in *Great-Britain;* yet I constantly take care to order affairs so, that my main business does not stand still in my absence.

I was just going, for example, to have given you the great out-lines of my uncle *Toby's* most whimsical character;—— when my aunt *Dinah* and the coachman came a-cross us, and led us a vagary some millions of miles into the very heart of the planetary system: Notwithstanding all this you perceive that the drawing of my uncle *Toby's* character went on gently

---

[1]Joseph Hall (1574–1656), bishop, successively, of Exeter and Norwich, satirist and polemist. Hall frequently inveighs against vanity, but I have been unable to find this particular sentence in any of his works.

all the time;——not the great contours of it,——that was impossible,——but some familiar strokes and faint designations
of it, were here and there touch'd in, as we went along, so
that you are much better acquainted with my uncle *Toby* now
than you was before.

By this contrivance the machinery of my work is of a species
by itself; two contrary motions are introduced into it, and
reconciled, which were thought to be at variance with each
other. In a word, my work is digressive, and it is progressive
too,——and at the same time.

This, Sir, is a very different story from that of the earth's
moving round her axis, in her diurnal rotation, with her
progress in her elliptick orbit which brings about the year,
and constitutes that variety and vicissitude of seasons we enjoy;——though I own it suggested the thought,——as I believe
the greatest of our boasted improvements and discoveries have
come from some such trifling hints.

Digressions, incontestably, are the sunshine;——they are the
life, the soul of reading;——take them out of this book for
instance,——you might as well take the book along with them;
——one cold eternal winter would reign in every page of it;
restore them to the writer;——he steps forth like a bridegroom,——bids All hail; brings in variety, and forbids the
appetite to fail.

All the dexterity is in the good cookery and management of
them, so as to be not only for the advantage of the reader, but
also of the author, whose distress, in this matter, is truely
pitiable: For, if he begins a digression,——from that moment,
I observe, his whole work stands stock-still;——and if he goes
on with his main work,——then there is an end of his digression.

——This is vile work.——For which reason, from the beginning of this, you see, I have constructed the main work and
the adventitious parts of it with such intersections, and have
so complicated and involved the digressive and progressive
movements, one wheel within another, that the whole machine,
in general, has been kept a-going;——and, what's more, it

shall be kept a-going these forty years, if it pleases the fountain of health to bless me so long with life and good spirits.

CHAP. XXIII.

I Have a strong propensity in me to begin this chapter very nonsensically, and I will not balk my fancy.——Accordingly I set off thus.

If the fixure of *Momus's* glass,[1] in the human breast, according to the proposed emendation of that arch-critick, had taken place,——first, This foolish consequence would certainly have followed,——That the very wisest and the very gravest of us all, in one coin or other, must have paid window-money[2] every day of our lives.

And, secondly, That had the said glass been there set up, nothing more would have been wanting, in order to have taken a man's character, but to have taken a chair and gone softly, as you would to a dioptrical bee-hive, and look'd in,—— view'd the soul stark naked;——observ'd all her motions,—— her machinations;——traced all her maggots from their first engendering to their crawling forth;——watched her loose in her frisks, her gambols, her capricios; and after some notice of her more solemn deportment, consequent upon such frisks, *&c.*——then taken your pen and ink and set down nothing but what you had seen, and could have sworn to:——But this is an advantage not to be had by the biographer in this planet, ——in the planet *Mercury* (belike) it may be so, if not better still for him;——for there the intense heat of the country, which is proved by computators, from its vicinity to the sun, to be more than equal to that of red hot iron,——must, I think, long ago have vitrified the bodies of the inhabitants, (as the

---

[1]Momus, Greek god of mockery and censoriousness, expressed dissatisfaction with man because there was no window in his breast through which the secrets of his heart could be seen.

[2]A tax formerly levied on windows of houses.

efficient cause[3]) to suit them for the climate (which is the
final cause); so that, betwixt them both, all the tenements of
their souls, from top to bottom, may be nothing else, for
aught the soundest philosophy can shew to the contrary, but
one fine transparent body of clear glass (bating the umbilical
knot);——so, that till the inhabitants grow old and tolerably
wrinkled, whereby the rays of light, in passing through them,
become so monstrously refracted,——or return reflected
from their surfaces in such transverse lines to the eye, that
a man cannot be seen thro';——his soul might as well,
unless, for more ceremony,——or the trifling advantage
which the umbilical point gave her,——might, upon all other
accounts, I say, as well play the fool out o'doors as in her own
house.

But this, as I said above, is not the case of the inhabitants of
this earth;——our minds shine not through the body, but are
wrapt up here in a dark covering of uncrystalized flesh and
blood; so that if we would come to the specifick characters
of them, we must go some other way to work.

Many, in good truth, are the ways which human wit has
been forced to take to do this thing with exactness.

Some, for instance, draw all their characters with wind
instruments.——*Virgil* takes notice of that way in the affair of
Dido and *Æneas;*[4]——but it is as fallacious as the breath of
fame;——and, moreover, bespeaks a narrow genius. I am not
ignorant that the *Italians* pretend to a mathematical exactness
in their designations of one particular sort of character among
them, from the *forte* or *piano*[5] of a certain wind instrument
they use,——which they say is infallible.——I dare not mention
the name of the instrument in this place;——'tis sufficient we
have it amongst us,——but never think of making a drawing
by it;——this is ænigmatical, and intended to be so, at least,

----

[3]Efficient cause: producing force. Final cause: purpose.

[4]An allusion to the voices (elsewhere spoken of as trumpets) of *Fama*
or Rumour, which spread abroad the ill report of Dido's passion for
Aeneas in the *Aeneid*, 4.173ff.

[5]Loud or soft.

ad populum:[6]——And therefore I beg, Madam, when you come here, that you read on as fast as you can, and never stop to make any inquiry about it.[7]

There are others again, who will draw a man's character from no other helps in the world, but merely from his evacuations;——but this often gives a very incorrect out-line,—— unless, indeed, you take a sketch of his repletions too; and by correcting one drawing from the other, compound one good figure out of them both.

I should have no objection to this method, but that I think it must smell too strong of the lamp,——and be render'd still more operose, by forcing you to have an eye to the rest of his *Non-Naturals*.[8]——Why the most natural actions of a man's life should be call'd his Non-Naturals,——is another question.

There are others, fourthly, who disdain every one of these expedients;——not from any fertility of their own, but from the various ways of doing it, which they have borrowed from the honourable devices which the Pentagraphic Brethren* of the brush have shewn in taking copies.——These, you must know, are your great historians.

One of these you will see drawing a full-length character *against the light;*——that's illiberal,——dishonest,——and hard upon the character of the man who sits.

Others, to mend the matter, will make a drawing of you in

---

[6]To the populace.

[7]This passage probably alludes, with purposed equivocation, to the Italian *castrati*, some of whom had been imported into England, in the face of considerable popular opposition, to aid in the presentation of operas.

[8]A term formerly used by physicians to indicate the six things which because they do not enter into the composition of the body are not "natural" yet which are essential to animal life and health and which by accident or abuse often cause disease: air, meat and drink, excretion and retention, sleep and waking, motion and rest, and the affections of the mind. This is perhaps an oblique glance at Sterne's enemy Dr. John Burton, who in 1738 had published a *Treatise of the Non-naturals;* the term, however, was in universal use.

*Pentagraph, an instrument to copy prints and pictures mechanichally, and in any proportion. [Sterne's note.]

the *Camera;*[9]——that is most unfair of all,——because, *there*
you are sure to be represented in some of your most ridiculous
attitudes.

To avoid all and every one of these errors, in giving you my
uncle *Toby's* character, I am determin'd to draw it by no
mechanical help whatever;——nor shall my pencil be guided
by any one wind instrument which ever was blown upon, either
on this, or on the other side of the *Alps;*——nor will I consider
either his repletions or his discharges,——or touch upon his
Non-Naturals;——but, in a word, I will draw my uncle *Toby's*
character from his HOBBY-HORSE.

CHAP. XXIV.

IF I was not morally sure that the reader must be out of all
patience for my uncle *Toby's* character,——I would here
previously have convinced him, that there is no instrument so
fit to draw such a thing with, as that which I have pitch'd
upon.

A man and his HOBBY-HORSE, tho' I cannot say that they
act and re-act exactly after the same manner in which the soul
and body do upon each other: Yet doubtless there is a communication between them of some kind, and my opinion
rather is, that there is something in it more of the manner of
electrified bodies,——and that by means of the heated parts of
the rider, which come immediately into contact with the back
of the HOBBY-HORSE.——By long journies and much friction,
it so happens that the body of the rider is at length fill'd as
full of HOBBY-HORSICAL matter as it can hold;——so that if you
are able to give but a clear description of the nature of the
one, you may form a pretty exact notion of the genius and
character of the other.

Now the HOBBY-HORSE which my uncle *Toby* always rode

[9]Private chamber, closet; possibly, however, a reference to the *camera
obscura,* a periscope-like contrivance widely used by inept artists, the
simple form of which produced an inverted and reversed image of the
object.

upon, was, in my opinion, an HOBBY-HORSE well worth giving
a description of, if it was only upon the score of his great
singularity; for you might have travelled from *York* to *Dover,*
——from *Dover* to *Penzance* in *Cornwall,* and from *Penzance* to *York* back again, and not have seen such another
upon the road; or if you had seen such a one, whatever haste
you had been in, you must infallibly have stopp'd to have
taken a view of him.   Indeed, the gait and figure of him was
so strange, and so utterly unlike was he, from his head to his
tail, to any one of the whole species, that it was now and then
made a matter of dispute,——whether he was really a HOBBY-
HORSE or no: But as the Philosopher would use no other argument to the sceptic, who disputed with him against the reality
of motion, save that of rising up upon his legs, and walking
a-cross the room;[1]——so would my uncle *Toby* use no other
argument to prove his HOBBY-HORSE was a HOBBY-HORSE indeed, but by getting upon his back and riding him about;——
leaving the world after that to determine the point as it
thought fit.

In good truth, my uncle *Toby* mounted him with so much
pleasure, and he carried my uncle *Toby* so well,——that he
troubled his head very little with what the world either said
or thought about it.

It is now high time, however, that I give you a description
of him:——But to go on regularly, I only beg you will give me
leave to acquaint you first, how my uncle *Toby* came by him.

CHAP. XXV.

THE wound in my uncle *Toby*'s groin, which he received
at the siege of *Namur,* rendering him unfit for the service,
it was thought expedient he should return to *England,* in
order, if possible, to be set to rights.

---

[1]To refute the arguments of Zeno of Elea (fl. 5th C. B.C.) against motion, Diogenes of Sinope (c. 412–323 B.C.), the eccentric Cynic philosopher, is said to have risen and walked. The proverbial reply to Zeno
is *Solvitur ambulando: it is settled by walking.*

He was four years totally confined,——part of it to his bed, and all of it to his room; and in the course of his cure, which was all that time in hand, suffer'd unspeakable miseries,—— owing to a succession of exfoliations from the *os pubis*,[1] and the outward edge of that part of the *coxendix* called the *os ilium*,——both which bones were dismally crush'd, as much by the irregularity of the stone, which I told you was broke off the parapet,——as by its size,——(though it was pretty large) which inclined the surgeon all along to think, that the great injury which it had done my uncle *Toby*'s groin, was more owing to the gravity of the stone itself, than to the projectile force of it,——which he would often tell him was a great happiness.

My father at that time was just beginning business in *London*, and had taken a house;——and as the truest friendship and cordiality subsisted between the two brothers,——and that my father thought my uncle *Toby* could no where be so well nursed and taken care of as in his own house,——he assign'd him the very best apartment in it.——And what was a much more sincere mark of his affection still, he would never suffer a friend or an acquaintance to step into the house on any occasion, but he would take him by the hand, and lead him up stairs to see his brother *Toby*, and chat an hour by his bed side.

The history of a soldier's wound beguiles the pain of it; ——my uncle's visiters at least thought so, and in their daily calls upon him, from the courtesy arising out of that belief, they would frequently turn the discourse to that subject,—— and from that subject the discourse would generally roll on to the siege itself.

These conversations were infinitely kind; and my uncle *Toby* received great relief from them, and would have received much more, but that they brought him into some unforeseen perplexities, which, for three months together, retarded his cure greatly; and if he had not hit upon an expedient to extri-

---

[1]The pubis; a *Coxendix:* the hip-bone. *Os ilium:* the ilium.

cate himself out of them, I verily believe they would have laid him in his grave.

What these perplexities of my uncle *Toby* were,——'tis impossible for you to guess;——if you could,——I should blush; not as a relation,——not as a man,——nor even as a woman, ——but I should blush as an author; inasmuch as I set no small store by myself upon this very account, that my reader has never yet been able to guess at any thing. And in this, Sir, I am of so nice and singular a humour, that if I thought you was able to form the least judgment or probable conjecture to yourself, of what was to come in the next page,——I would tear it out of my book.

END of the FIRST VOLUME.

VOLUME II.[1]

CHAP. I.

I Have begun a new book, on purpose that I might have room enough to explain the nature of the perplexities in which my uncle *Toby* was involved, from the many discourses and interrogations about the siege of *Namur,* where he received his wound.

I must remind the reader, in case he has read the history of King *William's* wars,——but if he has not,——I then inform him, that one of the most memorable attacks in that siege, was that which was made by the *English* and *Dutch* upon the point of the advanced counterscarp,[2] before the gate of *St. Nicolas,* which inclosed the great sluice or water-stop, where the *English* were terribly exposed to the shot of the counter-guard and demi-bastion of *St. Roch:* The issue of which hot dispute, in three words, was this; That the *Dutch* lodged themselves upon the counter-guard,——and that the *English* made themselves masters of the covered way before *St. Nicolas's* gate, notwithstanding the gallantry of the *French* officers, who exposed themselves upon the glacis sword in hand.

As this was the principal attack of which my uncle *Toby*

---

[1]Published, with Volume 1, in December, 1759.

[2]Counterscarp: outer side of the ditch, supporting the covered way. Counter-guard: small rampart raised before the salient angle of a bastion, its two faces parallel to those of the bastion. Demi-bastion: a bastion having but one face and one flank. Covered-way: a continuous open corridor bordering the ditch and ranging round the outworks, masked by an embankment or glacis. Scarp: inner side of the ditch at the foot of the rampart. Glacis: a sloping earthen embankment, serving as parapet to the covered way, on which attackers are exposed to fire. Half-moon: outwork of two faces forming a salient angle, placed outside the main ditch of a fortification and before a bastion. Ravelin: outwork of two faces forming a salient angle, placed outside the main ditch of a fortification and before a curtain.

was an eye-witness at *Namur,*——the army of the besiegers being cut off, by the confluence of the *Maes* and *Sambre,* from seeing much of each other's operations,——my uncle *Toby* was generally more eloquent and particular in his account of it; and the many perplexities he was in, arose out of the almost insurmountable difficulties he found in telling his story intelligibly, and giving such clear ideas of the differences and distinctions between the scarp and counterscarp,——the glacis and covered way,——the half-moon and ravelin,——as to make his company fully comprehend where and what he was about.

Writers themselves are too apt to confound these terms; ——so that you will the less wonder, if in his endeavours to explain them, and in opposition to many misconceptions, that my uncle *Toby* did oft times puzzle his visiters, and sometimes himself too.

To speak the truth, unless the company my father led up stairs were tolerably clear-headed, or my uncle *Toby* was in one of his best explanatory moods, 'twas a difficult thing, do what he could, to keep the discourse free from obscurity.

What rendered the account of this affair the more intricate to my uncle *Toby,* was this,——that in the attack of the counterscarp before the gate of *St. Nicolas,* extending itself from the bank of the *Maes,* quite up to the great water-stop;——the ground was cut and cross-cut with such a multitude of dykes, drains, rivulets, and sluices, on all sides,——and he would get so sadly bewilder'd and set fast amongst them, that frequently he could neither get backwards or forwards to save his life; and was oft times obliged to give up the attack upon that very account only.

These perplexing rebuffs gave my uncle *Toby Shandy* more perturbations than you would imagine; and as my father's kindness to him was continually dragging up fresh friends and fresh inquirers,——he had but a very uneasy task of it.

No doubt my uncle *Toby* had great command of himself, ——and could guard appearances, I believe, as well as most men;——yet any one may imagine, that when he could not retreat out of the ravelin without getting into the half-moon,

or get out of the covered way without falling down the counterscarp, nor cross the dyke without danger of slipping into
the ditch, but that he must have fretted and fumed inwardly:
——He did so;——and these little and hourly vexations, which
may seem trifling and of no account to the man who has not
read *Hippocrates*,[3] yet, whoever has read *Hippocrates,* or Dr.
James Mackenzie,[4] and has considered well the effects which
the passions and affections of the mind have upon the digestion,——(Why not of a wound as well as of a dinner?)——
may easily conceive what sharp paroxisms and exacerbations
of his wound my uncle *Toby* must have undergone upon that
score only.

——My uncle *Toby* could not philosophize upon it;——
'twas enough he felt it was so,——and having sustained the
pain and sorrows of it for three months together, he was
resolved some way or other to extricate himself.

He was one morning lying upon his back in his bed, the
anguish and nature of the wound upon his groin suffering him
to lye in no other position, when a thought came into his
head, that if he could purchase such a thing, and have it pasted
down upon a board, as a large map of the fortifications of
the town and citadel of *Namur,* with its environs, it might be
a means of giving him ease.——I take notice of his desire to
have the environs along with the town and citadel, for this
reason,——because my uncle *Toby*'s wound was got in one of
the traverses, about thirty toises[5] from the returning angle[6]

---

[3]Hippocrates (c. 460–c. 377 B.C.), a Greek philosopher and writer, surnamed "The Father of Medicine."   The reference is to his *De Morbis
Vulgaribus* 6 (now considered spurious).   5, probably *via* Mackenzie (for
whom, see the following note), the *History of Health,* 1.6.

[4]Dr. James Mackenzie (1680?–1761), noted Scottish physician and
author of the *History of Health and the Art of Preserving It* wherein,
under the heading "Of the Passions and Affections of the Mind," he urges
those who would preserve their health to keep their passions in absolute subjection to their reason (2.2).

[5]Old French measure of length equivalent to 6.395 English feet.

[6]Returning angle: an angle whose vertex points inward, its sides opening toward the field.   Salient angle: the acute angle formed by the faces
of a bastion.   Demi-bastion: see p. 81, n. 2.

of the trench, opposite to the salient angle of the demi-bastion of *St. Roch;*——so that he was pretty confident he could stick a pin upon the identical spot of ground where he was standing in when the stone struck him.

All this succeeded to his wishes, and not only freed him from a world of sad explanations, but, in the end, it prov'd the happy means, as you will read, of procuring my uncle *Toby* his HOBBY-HORSE.

CHAP. II.

THERE is nothing so foolish, when you are at the expence of making an entertainment of this kind, as to order things so badly, as to let your criticks and gentry of refined taste run it down: Nor is there any thing so likely to make them do it, as that of leaving them out of the party, or, what is full as offensive, of bestowing your attention upon the rest of your guests in so particular a way, as if there was no such thing as a critick (by occupation) at table.

——I guard against both; for, in the first place, I have left half a dozen places purposely open for them;——and, in the next place, I pay them all court,——Gentlemen, I kiss your hands,——I protest no company could give me half the pleasure,——by my soul I am glad to see you,——I beg only you will make no strangers of yourselves, but sit down without any ceremony, and fall on heartily.

I said I had left six places, and I was upon the point of carrying my complaisance so far, as to have left a seventh open for them,——and in this very spot I stand on;——but being told by a critick, (tho' not by occupation,——but by nature) that I had acquitted myself well enough, I shall fill it up directly, hoping, in the mean time, that I shall be able to make a great deal of more room next year.

——How, in the name of wonder! could your uncle *Toby,* who, it seems, was a military man, and whom you have represented as no fool,——be at the same time such a confused, pudding-headed, muddle-headed fellow, as——Go look.

So, Sir Critick, I could have replied; but I scorn it.——'Tis language unurbane,——and only befitting the man who cannot give clear and satisfactory accounts of things, or dive deep enough into the first causes of human ignorance and confusion. It is moreover the reply valiant,——and therefore I reject it; for tho' it might have suited my uncle *Toby*'s character as a soldier excellently well,——and had he not accustomed himself, in such attacks, to whistle the *Lillabullero*,——as he wanted no courage, 'tis the very answer he would have given; yet it would by no means have done for me. You see as plain as can be, that I write as a man of erudition;——that even my similies, my allusions, my illustrations, my metaphors, are erudite,——and that I must sustain my character properly, and contrast it properly too,——else what would become of me? Why, Sir, I should be undone;——at this very moment that I am going here to fill up one place against a critick,——I should have made an opening for a couple.

——Therefore I answer thus:

Pray, Sir, in all the reading which you have ever read, did you ever read such a book as *Locke*'s Essay upon the Human Understanding?[1]——Don't answer me rashly,——because many, I know, quote the book, who have not read it,——and many have read it who understand it not:——If either of these is your case, as I write to instruct, I will tell you in three words what the book is.——It is a history.——A history! of who? what? where? when? Don't hurry yourself.——It is a history-book, Sir, (which may possibly recommend it to the world) of what passes in a man's own mind; and if you will say so much of the book, and no more, believe me, you will cut no contemptible figure in a metaphysic circle.

But this by the way.

Now if you will venture to go along with me, and look down into the bottom of this matter, it will be found that the

[1]See p. 9, n. 3. The following passage is a paraphrase and dramatic elaboration of Locke's *Essay Concerning Human Understanding*, 2.29.3.

cause of obscurity and confusion, in the mind of man, is three-fold.

Dull organs, dear Sir, in the first place. Secondly, slight and transient impressions made by objects when the said organs are not dull. And, thirdly, a memory like unto a sieve, not able to retain what it has received.——Call down *Dolly* your chamber-maid, and I will give you my cap and bell along with it, if I make not this matter so plain that *Dolly* herself shall understand it as well as *Malbranch*.[2]——When *Dolly* has indited her epistle to *Robin,* and has thrust her arm into the bottom of her pocket hanging by her right-side;——take that opportunity to recollect that the organs and faculties of perception, can, by nothing in this world, be so aptly typified and explained as by that one thing which *Dolly*'s hand is in search of.——Your organs are not so dull that I should inform you, ——'tis an inch, Sir, of red seal-wax.

When this is melted and dropped upon the letter, if *Dolly* fumbles too long for her thimble, till the wax is over harden'd, it will not receive the mark of her thimble from the usual impulse which was wont to imprint it. Very well: If *Dolly*'s wax, for want of better, is bees-wax, or of a temper too soft, ——tho' it may receive,——it will not hold the impression, how hard soever *Dolly* thrusts against it; and last of all, supposing the wax good, and eke the thimble, but applied thereto in careless haste, as her Mistress rings the bell;——in any one of these three cases, the print, left by the thimble, will be as unlike the prototype as a brass-jack.

Now you must understand that not one of these was the true cause of the confusion in my uncle *Toby*'s discourse; and it is for that very reason I enlarge upon them so long, after the manner of great physiologists,——to shew the world what it did *not* arise from.

What it did arise from, I have hinted above, and a fertile source of obscurity it is,——and ever will be,——and that is the unsteady uses of words which have perplexed the clearest and most exalted understandings.

---

[2]Nicholas Malebranch (1638–1715), a French philosopher.

It is ten to one (at *Arthur's*[3]) whether you have ever read the literary histories of past ages;——if you have,——what terrible battles, 'yclept logomachies, have they occasioned and perpetuated with so much gall and ink-shed,——that a good natured man cannot read the accounts of them without tears in his eyes.

Gentle critick! when thou hast weigh'd all this, and consider'd within thyself how much of thy own knowledge, discourse, and conversation has been pestered and disordered, at one time or other, by this, and this only:——What a pudder and racket in COUNCILS about οὐσία and ὑπόστασις;[4] and in the SCHOOLS of the learned about power and about spirit;—— about essences, and about quintessences;——about substances, and about space.——What confusion in greater THEATRES from words of little meaning, and as indeterminate a sense;—— when thou considers this, thou wilt not wonder at my uncle *Toby's* perplexities,——thou wilt drop a tear of pity upon his scarp and his counterscarp;——his glacis and his covered-way; ——his ravelin and his half-moon: 'Twas not by ideas,——by heaven! his life was put in jeopardy by words.

CHAP. III.

WHEN my uncle *Toby* got his map of *Namur* to his mind, he began immediately to apply himself, and with the utmost diligence, to the study of it; for nothing being of more importance to him than his recovery, and his recovery depending, as you have read, upon the passions and affections of his mind, it behoved him to take the nicest care to make himself so far master of his subject, as to be able to talk upon it without emotion.

In a fortnight's close and painful application, which, by the bye, did my uncle *Toby's* wound, upon his groin, no good,

---

[3] A reputable London club.

[4] Essence (substance) and substance (essence), *i.e.,* a "distinction without a difference."

——he was enabled, by the help of some marginal documents at the feet of the elephant,[1] together with *Gobesius's* military architecture and pyroballogy,[2] translated from the *Flemish,* to form his discourse with passable perspicuity; and before he was two full months gone,——he was right eloquent upon it, and could make not only the attack of the advanced counter-scarp with great order;——but having, by that time, gone much deeper into the art, than what his first motive made necessary,——my uncle *Toby* was able to cross the *Maes* and *Sambre;* make diversions as far as *Vauban's* line, the abbey of *Salsines, &c.* and give his visiters as distinct a history of each of their attacks, as of that of the gate of *St. Nicolas,* where he had the honour to receive his wound.

But the desire of knowledge, like the thirst of riches, increases ever with the acquisition of it. The more my uncle *Toby* pored over his map, the more he took a liking to it;—— by the same process and electrical assimilation, as I told you, thro' which I ween the souls of connoisseurs themselves, by long friction and incumbition, have the happiness, at length, to get all be-virtu'd,——be-pictur'd,——be-butterflied, and be-fiddled.

The more my uncle *Toby* drank of this sweet fountain of science, the greater was the heat and impatience of his thirst, so that, before the first year of his confinement had well gone round, there was scarce a fortified town in *Italy* or *Flanders,* of which, by one means or other, he had not procured a plan, reading over as he got them, and carefully collating therewith the histories of their sieges, their demolitions, their improvements, and new works, all which he would read with that intense application and delight, that he would forget himself, his wound, his confinement, his dinner.

In the second year my uncle *Toby* purchased *Ramelli*[3] and

---

[1]Possibly elephant-paper, drawing paper 28 x 23 inches on which maps were printed; it is more likely, however, that the cartouche of my uncle Toby's map included among its decorations the figure of an elephant.

[2]Possibly the *Descriptio Belli Ivoniae* of Leonhard Gorecius (fl. c. 1577).

[3]Agostino Ramelli (1531?–1590?), Italian engineer, author of *Le Diverse ed artificiose machine;* Girolamo Cataneo, author of *Opera nuova di*

Cataneo, translated from the *Italian;*——likewise *Stevinus, Marolis,* the Chevalier *de Ville, Lorini, Coehorn, Sheeter,* the Count *de Pagan,* the Marshal *Vauban,* Mons. *Blondel,* with almost as many more books of military architecture, as Don *Quixote* was found to have of chivalry, when the curate and barber invaded his library.[4]

Towards the beginning of the third year, which was in *August,* ninety-nine,[5] my uncle *Toby* found it necessary to understand a little of projectiles:——And having judged it best to draw his knowledge from the fountain-head, he began with *N. Tartaglia,*[6] who it seems was the first man who detected the imposition of a canon-ball's doing all that mischief under the notion of a right line.——This *N. Tartaglia* proved to my uncle *Toby* to be an impossible thing.

---

fortificare, offendere et difendere (1564) and many other works on military science; Simon Stevinus (1548–1620), Dutch mathematician, author of *Nieuwe Maniere van Sterctebou door Spilshuysen;* Samuel Marolois (fl. early 17th C.), French mathematician, author of *Fortification, ou architecture militaire;* Antoine de Ville (1596–c. 1656), a French engineer and mathematician, author of *Les Fortifications;* Buonajute Lorini (c. 1540– c. 1611), Italian engineer highly reputed for his knowledge of fortifications, author of *Delle fortificationi;* Baron Menno van Coehoorn (1641– 1704), Dutch soldier and military engineer, author of *Nieuwe Vestingbouw;* Johann Bernhard von Scheither (fl. 17th C.), author of *Novissima Praxis Militaris* and other military books; Count Blaise-François de Pagan (1604–1665), soldier and author of the great *Traité des fortifications;* Sébastien le Prestre de Vauban (1633–1707), marshal of France and the most celebrated of military engineers, author of numerous treatises on all phases of the attack on and defence of fortifications; François Blondel (1617–1686), mathematician and architect, author of several works on military science, including *L'Art de jetter les bombes* and *Nouvelle manière de fortifier les places.*

[4] In Don Quixote's library the curate and the barber "found above an hundred large volumes neatly bound, and a good number of small ones . . ." (*Don Quixote,* 1.1.6). Not unlike my uncle Toby, as he is described in the following paragraphs, was the Don, who "gave himself up so wholly to the reading . . . that a-nights he would pore on till 'twas day, and a-days he would read on till 'twas night; and thus by sleeping little, and reading much, the moisture of his brain was exhausted to that degree, that at last he lost the use of his reason." (*Don Quixote,* 1.1.1.)

[5] *I.e.,* 1699.

[6] Niccolò Tartaglia (c. 1499–1557), Italian mathematician who treats problems of artillery in his *Questi et inventioni diverse,* and who claimed the invention of the gunner's quadrant.

——Endless is the Search of Truth!

No sooner was my uncle *Toby* satisfied which road the cannon-ball did not go, but he was insensibly led on, and resolved in his mind to enquire and find out which road the ball did go: For which purpose he was obliged to set off afresh with old *Maltus*,[7] and studied him devoutly.——He proceeded next to *Gallileo* and *Torricellius,* wherein, by certain geometrical rules, infallibly laid down, he found the precise path to be a PARABOLA,——or else an HYPERBOLA,——and that the parameter, or *latus rectum,* of the conic section of the said path, was to the quantity and amplitude in a direct *ratio,* as the whole line to the sine of double the angle of incidence, form'd by the breech upon an horizontal plane;——and that the semi-parameter,——stop! my dear uncle *Toby,*——stop!——go not one foot further into this thorny and bewilder'd track,—— intricate are the steps! intricate are the mases[8] of this labyrinth! intricate are the troubles which the pursuit of this bewitching phantom, KNOWLEDGE, will bring upon thee.——O my uncle! fly—fly—fly from it as from a serpent.——Is it fit, good-natur'd man! thou should'st sit up, with the wound upon thy groin, whole nights baking thy blood with hectic watchings?——Alas! 'twill exasperate thy symptoms,——check thy perspirations,——evaporate thy spirits,——waste thy animal strength,——dry up thy radical moisture,[9]——bring thee into a costive habit of body, impair thy health,——and hasten all the infirmities of thy old age.——O my uncle! my uncle *Toby!*

---

[7] François Malthus (d. 1658), *"commissaire ordinaire de l'artillerie"* in France, whose most important work was *Pratique de la guerre;* Galileo Galilei (1564–1642), the Italian astronomer and experimental scientist, who demonstrated in the fourth of his dialogues on mechanics that the path described by a projectile is, save for the resistance of the air, a parabola; Evangelista Torricelli (1608–1647), Italian physicist and mathematician, whose treatise *De Motu* reports his discoveries concerning the path of projectiles.

[8] Mazes.

[9] Fundamental or natural moisture of the body.

CHAP. IV.

I Would not give a groat for that man's knowledge in pen-
craft, who does not understand this,——That the best plain
narrative in the world, tack'd very close to the last spirited
apostrophe to my uncle *Toby*,——would have felt both cold
and vapid upon the reader's palate;——therefore I forthwith
put an end to the chapter,——though I was in the middle of
my story.

——Writers of my stamp have one principle in common
with painters.——Where an exact copying makes our pictures
less striking, we choose the less evil; deeming it even more
pardonable to trespass against truth, than beauty.——This is
to be understood *cum grano salis;*[1] but be it as it will,——as
the parallel is made more for the sake of letting the apostrophe
cool, than any thing else,——'tis not very material whether
upon any other score the reader approves of it or not.

In the latter end of the third year, my uncle *Toby* perceiving
that the parameter and semi-parameter of the conic section,
angered his wound, he left off the study of projectiles in a kind
of a huff, and betook himself to the practical part of fortification only; the pleasure of which, like a spring held back, returned upon him with redoubled force.

It was in this year that my uncle began to break in upon the
daily regularity of a clean shirt,——to dismiss his barber un-
shaven,——and to allow his surgeon scarce time sufficient to
dress his wound, concerning himself so little about it, as not
to ask him once in seven times dressing how it went on:
When, lo!——all of a sudden, for the change was as quick as
lightening, he began to sigh heavily for his recovery;——complain'd to my father, grew impatient with the surgeon;——and
one morning as he heard his foot coming up stairs, he shut up
his books, and thrust aside his instruments, in order to expostulate with him upon the protraction of his cure, which, he

---

[1]With a grain of salt.

told him, might surely have been accomplished at least by that
time:——He dwelt long upon the miseries he had undergone, and the sorrows of his four years melancholy imprisonment;——adding, that had it not been for the kind looks, and
fraternal chearings of the best of brothers,——he had long
since sunk under his misfortunes.——My father was by: My
uncle *Toby*'s eloquence brought tears into his eyes;——'twas
unexpected.——My uncle *Toby,* by nature, was not eloquent;
——it had the greater effect.——The surgeon was confounded;
——not that there wanted grounds for such, or greater, marks
of impatience,——but 'twas unexpected too; in the four years
he had attended him, he had never seen any thing like it in
my uncle *Toby*'s carriage; he had never once dropp'd one fretful or discontented word;——he had been all patience,——all
submission.

——We lose the right of complaining sometimes by for-
bearing it;——but we oftner treble the force:——The surgeon
was astonished;——but much more so, when he heard my
uncle *Toby* go on, and peremptorily insist upon his healing up
the wound directly,——or sending for Monsieur *Ronjat,*[2] the
King's Serjeant-Surgeon, to do it for him.

The desire of life and health is implanted in man's nature;
——the love of liberty and enlargement is a sister-passion to it:
These my uncle *Toby* had in common with his species;——
and either of them had been sufficient to account for his
earnest desire to get well and out of doors;——but I have told
you before that nothing wrought with our family after the
common way;——and from the time and manner in which this
eager desire shew'd itself in the present case, the penetrating
reader will suspect there was some other cause or crotchet for
it in my uncle *Toby*'s head:——There was so, and 'tis the subject of the next chapter to set forth what that cause and
crotchet was. I own, when that's done, 'twill be time to return back to the parlour fire-side, where we left my uncle
Toby in the middle of his sentence.

---

[2]Etienne Ronjat, First Surgeon to William III.

CHAP. V.

WHEN a man gives himself up to the government of a
ruling passion,——or, in other words, when his HOBBY-
HORSE grows head-strong,——farewell cool reason and fair discretion!

My uncle *Toby*'s wound was near well, and as soon as the
surgeon recovered his surprize, and could get leave to say as
much——he told him, 'twas just beginning to incarnate; and
that if no fresh exfoliation happen'd, which there was no signs
of,——it would be dried up in five or six weeks. The sound
of as many olympiads twelve hours before, would have convey'd an idea of shorter duration to my uncle *Toby*'s mind.
——The succession of his ideas was now rapid,——he broil'd
with impatience to put his design in execution;——and so,
without consulting further with any soul living,——which, by
the bye, I think is right, when you are predetermined to take
no one soul's advice,——he privately ordered *Trim,* his man,
to pack up a bundle of lint and dressings, and hire a chariot
and four to be at the door exactly by twelve o'clock that day,
when he knew my father would be upon 'Change.[1]——So leaving a bank-note upon the table for the surgeon's care of him,
and a letter of tender thanks for his brother's,——he pack'd
up his maps, his books of fortification, his instruments, *&c.*
——and, by the help of a crutch on one side, and *Trim* on the
other,——my uncle *Toby* embark'd for *Shandy-Hall.*

The reason, or rather the rise, of this sudden demigration,[2]
was as follows:

The table in my uncle *Toby*'s room, and at which, the night
before this change happened, he was sitting with his maps,
&c. about him,——being somewhat of the smallest, for that
infinity of great and small instruments of knowledge which

---

[1] Exchange, Bourse; a building in London where the merchants met
daily to transact business with each other.

[2] Emigration.

usually lay crouded upon it;——he had the accident, in reaching over for his tobacco-box, to throw down his compasses, and in stooping to take the compasses up, with his sleeve he threw down his case of instruments and snuffers;——and as the dice took a run against him, in his endeavouring to catch the snuffers in falling,——he thrust Monsieur *Blondel* off the table and Count *de Pagan* o'top of him.

'Twas to no purpose for a man, lame as my uncle *Toby* was, to think of redressing all these evils by himself,——he rung his bell for his man *Trim;——Trim!* quoth my uncle *Toby,* pri'thee see what confusion I have here been making.——I must have some better contrivance, *Trim.*——Can'st not thou take my rule and measure the length and breadth of this table, and then go and bespeak me one as big again?——Yes, an' please your Honour, replied *Trim,* making a bow;——but I hope your Honour will be soon well enough to get down to your country seat, where,——as your Honour takes so much pleasure in fortification, we could manage this matter to a T.

I must here inform you, that this servant of my uncle *Toby's,* who went by the name of *Trim,* had been a Corporal in my uncle's own company,——his real name was *James Butler,*—— but having got the nick-name of *Trim* in the regiment, my uncle *Toby,* unless when he happened to be very angry with him, would never call him by any other name.

The poor fellow had been disabled for the service, by a wound on his left knee by a musket-bullet, at the battle of *Landen,* which was two years before the affair of *Namur;*—— and as the fellow was well beloved in the regiment, and a handy fellow into the bargain, my uncle *Toby* took him for his servant, and of excellent use was he, attending my uncle *Toby* in the camp and in his quarters as valet, groom, barber, cook, sempster,[3] and nurse; and indeed, from first to last, waited upon him and served him with great fidelity and affection.

My uncle *Toby* loved the man in return, and what attached him more to him still, was the similitude of their knowledge:

---

[3]Seamster; man or woman employed in sewing.

——For Corporal *Trim,* (for so, for the future, I shall call him) by four years occasional attention to his Master's discourse upon fortified towns, and the advantage of prying and peeping continually into his Master's plans, &c. exclusive and besides what he gained Hobby-Horsically, as a body-servant, *Non Hobby-Horsical per se;*[4]——had become no mean proficient in the science; and was thought, by the cook and chamber-maid, to know as much of the nature of strong-holds as my uncle *Toby* himself.

I have but one more stroke to give to finish Corporal *Trim's* character,——and it is the only dark line in it.——The fellow lov'd to advise,——or rather to hear himself talk; his carriage, however, was so perfectly respectful, 'twas easy to keep him silent when you had him so; but set his tongue a-going,—— you had no hold of him;——he was voluble;——the eternal interlardings of *your Honour,* with the respectfulness of Corporal *Trim's* manner, interceding so strong in behalf of his elocution,——that tho' you might have been incommoded,—— you could not well be angry. My uncle *Toby* was seldom either the one or the other with him,——or, at least, this fault, in *Trim,* broke no squares[5] with 'em. My uncle *Toby,* as I said, loved the man;——and besides, as he ever looked upon a faithful servant,——but as a humble friend,——he could not bear to stop his mouth.——Such was Corporal *Trim.*

If I durst presume, continued *Trim,* to give your Honour my advice, and speak my opinion in this matter.——Thou art welcome, *Trim,* quoth my uncle *Toby,*——speak,——speak what thou thinkest upon the subject, man, without fear. Why then, replied *Trim,* (not hanging his ears and scratching his head like a country lout, but) stroking his hair back from his forehead, and standing erect as before his division.——I think, quoth *Trim,* advancing his left, which was his lame leg, a little forwards,——and pointing with his right hand open towards a map of *Dunkirk,* which was pinn'd against the hangings,——I think, quoth Corporal *Trim,* with humble sub-

[4]Not Hobby-Horsical in himself.
[5]Made no difference.

mission to your Honour's better judgment,——that these ravelins, bastions,[6] curtins, and hornworks make but a poor, contemptible, fiddle faddle piece of work of it here upon paper,
compared to what your Honour and I could make of it, were
we in the country by ourselves, and had but a rood, or a rood
and a half of ground to do what we pleased with: As summer
is coming on, continued *Trim,* your Honour might sit out of
doors, and give me the nography——(call it ichnography,
quoth my uncle)——of the town or citadel, your Honour was
pleased to sit down before,——and I will be shot by your Honour upon the glacis of it, if I did not fortify it to your Honour's
mind.——I dare say thou would'st, *Trim,* quoth my uncle.——
For if your Honour, continued the Corporal, could but mark
me the polygon,[7] with its exact lines and angles.——That I
could do very well, quoth my uncle.——I would begin with
the fossé, and if your Honour could tell me the proper depth
and breadth,——I can to a hair's breadth, *Trim,* replied my
uncle,——I would throw out the earth upon this hand towards
the town for the scarp,——and on that hand towards the campaign for the counterscarp.——Very right, *Trim;* quoth my
uncle *Toby.*——And when I had sloped them to your mind,
——an' please your Honour, I would face the glacis, as the
finest fortifications are done in *Flanders,* with sods,——and as
your Honour knows they should be,——and I would make the
walls and parapets with sods too;——The best engineers call
them gazons, *Trim,* said my uncle *Toby;*——Whether they are
gazons or sods, is not much matter, replied *Trim,* your Honour knows they are ten times beyond a facing either of brick
or stone;——I know they are, *Trim,* in some respects,——
quoth my uncle *Toby,* nodding his head;——for a cannon-ball

---

[6]Bastions: projecting portions of fortifications built in the form of
irregular pentagons with their bases in the line of the main works. Curtins: those portions of the main wall of a fortification which lie between
and join bastions. For the other military terms, see pp. 67, n. 5, and 81,
n. 2.

[7]A polygon, the vertices of which are the bastion-centers of the enclos-
ing fortification. Campaign: champaign, open country. The other terms
have been defined on p. 81, n. 2.

enters into the gazon right onwards, without bringing any
rubbish down with it, which might fill the fossé, (as was the
case at *St. Nicolas's Gate*) and facilitate the passage over it.

Your Honour understands these matters, replied Corporal
Trim, better than any officer in his Majesty's service;——but
would your Honour please to let the bespeaking of the table
alone, and let us but go into the country, I would work under
your Honour's directions like a horse, and make fortifications
for you something like a tansy,[8] with all their batteries, saps,
ditches, and palisadoes, that it should be worth all the world's
riding twenty miles to go and see it.

My uncle *Toby* blushed as red as scarlet as *Trim* went on;
——but it was not a blush of guilt,——of modesty,——or of
anger;——it was a blush of joy;——he was fired with Corporal
Trim's project and description.——*Trim!* said my uncle *Toby,*
thou hast said enough.——We might begin the campaign, continued *Trim,* on the very day that his Majesty[9] and the Allies
take the field, and demolish them town by town as fast as——
Trim, quoth my uncle *Toby,* say no more.——Your Honour,
continued *Trim,* might sit in your arm-chair (pointing to it)
this fine weather, giving me your orders, and I would——Say
no more, *Trim,* quoth my uncle *Toby.*——Besides, your Honour would get not only pleasure and good pastime,——but
good air, and good exercise, and good health,——and your
Honour's wound would be well in a month. Thou hast said
enough, *Trim,*——quoth my uncle *Toby* (putting his hand
into his breeches-pocket)——I like thy project mightily;——
And if your Honour pleases, I'll, this moment, go and buy a

---

[8]Perfect, thorough, with nothing lacking; probably in allusion to the
many ingredients of a tansy pudding. Saps: covered trenches by which
besiegers approach a fortification when within range of fire. Palisadoes:
palisades, defensive enclosures made of a fence of stakes set in the
ground.

[9]William III (1650–1702), King of England. In the War of the Spanish Succession (1701–1713) Louis XIV, supported by Spain, Bavaria,
and Cologne, was opposed by a coalition which had grown naturally
out of the Grand Alliance and which consisted of Austria, Prussia and
others of the German states, Denmark, Portugal, Savoy, the Netherlands,
and England.

pioneer's spade to take down with us, and I'll bespeak a shovel and a pick-ax, and a couple of——Say no more, *Trim*, quoth my uncle *Toby*, leaping up upon one leg, quite overcome with rapture,——and thrusting a guinea into *Trim*'s hand,—*Trim*, said my uncle *Toby*, say no more;——but go down, *Trim*, this moment, my lad, and bring up my supper this instant.

Trim ran down and brought up his master's supper,——to no purpose:——*Trim*'s plan of operation ran so in my uncle *Toby*'s head, he could not taste it.——*Trim*, quoth my uncle *Toby*, get me to-bed;——'twas all one.——Corporal *Trim*'s description had fired his imagination,——my uncle *Toby* could not shut his eyes.——The more he consider'd it, the more bewitching the scene appeared to him;——so that, two full hours before day-light, he had come to a final determination, and had concerted the whole plan of his and Corporal *Trim*'s decampment.

My uncle *Toby* had a little neat country-house of his own, in the village where my father's estate lay at *Shandy*, which had been left him by an old uncle, with a small estate of about one hundred pounds a year. Behind this house, and contiguous to it, was a kitchen-garden of about half an acre;——and at the bottom of the garden, and cut off from it by a tall yew hedge, was a bowling-green, containing just about as much ground as Corporal *Trim* wished for;——so that as Trim uttered the words, "A rood and a half of ground to do what they would with:"——this identical bowling-green instantly presented itself, and became curiously painted, all at once, upon the retina of my uncle *Toby*'s fancy;——which was the physical cause of making him change colour, or at least, of heightening his blush to that immoderate degree I spoke of.

Never did lover post down to a belov'd mistress with more heat and expectation, than my uncle *Toby* did, to enjoy this self-same thing in private;——I say in private;——for it was sheltered from a house, as I told you, by a tall yew hedge, and was covered on the other three sides, from mortal sight, by rough holly and thickset flowering shrubs;——so that the idea of not being seen, did not a little contribute to the idea of pleasure pre-conceived in my uncle *Toby*'s mind.——Vain thought! however thick it was planted about,——or private so-ever it might seem,——to think, dear uncle *Toby,* of enjoying a thing which took up a whole rood and a half of ground,—— and not have it known!

How my uncle *Toby* and Corporal *Trim* managed this mat-ter,——with the history of their campaigns, which were no way barren of events,——may make no uninteresting under-plot in the epitasis[10] and working up of this drama.——At present the scene must drop,——and change for the parlour fire-side.

CHAP. VI.

——What can they be doing, brother? said my father.——I think, replied my uncle *Toby,*——taking, as I told you, his pipe from his mouth, and striking the ashes out of it as he be-gan his sentence;——I think, replied he,——it would not be amiss, brother, if we rung the bell.

Pray, what's all that racket over our heads, *Obadiah?*—— quoth my father;——my brother and I can scarce hear our-selves speak.

Sir, answer'd *Obadiah,* making a bow towards his left-shoul-der,——my Mistress is taken very badly;——and where's *Su-sannah* running down the garden there, as if they were going to ravish her?——Sir, she is running the shortest cut into the town, replied *Obadiah,* to fetch the old midwife.——Then saddle a horse, quoth my father, and do you go directly for Dr. *Slop,* the man-midwife, with all our services,——and let him know your Mistress is fallen into labour,——and that I desire he will return with you with all speed.

It is very strange, says my father, addressing himself to my uncle *Toby,* as *Obadiah* shut the door,——as there is so expert an operator as Dr. *Slop* so near——that my wife should persist

[10]That portion of a drama which presents the main action of the play and leads to the catastrophe.

to the very last in this obstinate humour of hers, in trusting the life of my child, who has had one misfortune already, to the ignorance of an old woman;——and not only the life of my child, brother,——but her own life, and with it the lives of all the children I might, peradventure, have begot out of her hereafter.

Mayhap, brother, replied my uncle *Toby,* my sister does it to save the expence:——A pudding's end,——replied my father, ——the doctor must be paid the same for inaction as action, ——if not better,——to keep him in temper.

——Then it can be out of nothing in the whole world, quoth my uncle *Toby,* in the simplicity of his heart,——but Modesty: ——My sister, I dare say, added he, does not care to let a man come so near her ****. I will not say whether my uncle *Toby* had completed the sentence or not;——'tis for his advantage to suppose he had,——as, I think, he could have added no One Word which would have improved it.

If, on the contrary, my uncle *Toby* had not fully arrived at his period's end,——then the world stands indebted to the sudden snapping of my father's tobacco-pipe, for one of the neatest examples of that ornamental figure in oratory, which Rhetoricians stile the *Aposiopesis.*[1]——Just heaven! how does the *Poco più* and the *Poco meno* of the *Italian* artists;——the insensible MORE or LESS, determine the precise line of beauty in the sentence, as well as in the statue! How do the slight touches of the chisel, the pencil, the pen, the fiddle-stick, *et cætera,*——give the true swell, which gives the true pleasure! ——O my countrymen!——be nice;——be cautious of your language;——and never, O! never let it be forgotten upon what small particles your eloquence and your fame depend.

——"My sister, mayhap," quoth my uncle *Toby,* "does not choose to let a man come so near her ****." Make this dash, ——'tis an Aposiopesis.——Take the dash away, and write *Backside,*——'tis Bawdy.——Scratch Backside out, and put *Cover'd-way* in,——'tis a Metaphor;——and, I dare say, as for-

---

[1] The suppression by a speaker or writer of what he had seemed to be about to say.

tification ran so much in my uncle *Toby*'s head, that if he had been left to have added one word to the sentence,——that word was it.

But whether that was the case or not the case;——or whether the snapping of my father's tobacco-pipe so critically, happened thro' accident or anger,——will be seen in due time.

CHAP. VII.

THO' my father was a good natural philosopher,——yet he was something of a moral philosopher too; for which reason, when his tobacco-pipe snapp'd short in the middle,—— he had nothing to do,——as such,——but to have taken hold of the two pieces, and thrown them gently upon the back of the fire.——He did no such thing;——he threw them with all the violence in the world;——and, to give the action still more emphasis,——he started up upon both his legs to do it.

This look'd something like heat;——and the manner of his reply to what my uncle *Toby* was saying, prov'd it was so.

——"Not choose," quoth my father, (repeating my uncle *Toby*'s words) "to let a man come so near her."——By heaven, brother *Toby!* you would try the patience of a *Job;*——and I think I have the plagues of one already, without it.——Why? ——Where?——Wherein?——Wherefore?——Upon what account, replied my uncle *Toby,* in the utmost astonishment.—— To think, said my father, of a man living to your age, brother, and knowing so little about women!——I know nothing at all about them,——replied my uncle *Toby;* and I think, continued he, that the shock I received the year after the demolition of *Dunkirk,* in my affair with widow *Wadman;*——which shock you know I should not have received, but from my total ignorance of the sex,——has given me just cause to say, That I neither know, nor do pretend to know, any thing about 'em, or their concerns either.——Methinks, brother, replied my father, you might, at least, know so much as the right end of a woman from the wrong.

It is said in *Aristotle's Master-Piece,* "That when a man do think of any thing which is past,——he looketh down upon the ground;——but that when he thinketh of something which is to come, he looketh up towards the heavens."[1]

My uncle *Toby,* I suppose, thought of neither,——for he look'd horizontally.——Right end,——quoth my uncle *Toby,* muttering the two words low to himself, and fixing his two eyes insensibly as he muttered them, upon a small crevice, form'd by a bad joint in the chimney-piece.——Right end of a woman!——I declare, quoth my uncle, I know no more which it is, than the man in the moon;——and if I was to think, continued my uncle *Toby,* (keeping his eye still fix'd upon the bad joint) this month together, I am sure I should not be able to find it out.

Then brother *Toby,* replied my father, I will tell you.

Every thing in this world, continued my father (filling a fresh pipe)——every thing in this earthly world, my dear brother *Toby,* has two handles.——Not always, quoth my uncle *Toby.*——At least, replied my father, every one has two hands,——which comes to the same thing.——Now, if a man was to sit down coolly, and consider within himself the make, the shape, the construction, com-at-ability, and convenience of all the parts which constitute the whole of that animal, call'd Woman, and compare them analogically.——I never understood rightly the meaning of that word,——quoth my uncle *Toby.*——ANALOGY, replied my father, is the certain relation and agreement, which different——Here a devil of a rap at the door snapp'd my father's definition (like his tobacco-pipe) in two,——and, at the same time, crushed the head of as notable and curious a dissertation as ever was engendered in the womb

---

[1]Not in *Aristotle's Masterpiece: or, the Secrets of Generation Displayed in all the Parts Thereof,* but in *Aristotle's Book of Problems, with other Astronomers, Astrologers, Physicians, and Philosophers,* which was sometimes published with it as the third part of *Aristotle's Works Compleated,* are answers to the questions: "Why doth a man lift up his Head towards the Heavens, when he doth imagine?" and "Why doth a man when he museth, or thinketh on things past, look down towards the earth?" (*Problems,* 25th edition (London, n. d, (?1733)), pp. 9–10.)

of speculation;——it was some months before my father could get an opportunity to be safely deliver'd of it:——And, at this hour, it is a thing full as problematical as the subject of the dissertation itself,——(considering the confusion and distresses of our domestic misadventures, which are now coming thick one upon the back of another) whether I shall be able to find a place for it in the third volume or not.

CHAP. VIII.

IT is about an hour and a half's tolerable good reading since my uncle *Toby* rung the bell, when *Obadiah* was order'd to saddle a horse, and go for Dr. *Slop* the man-midwife;——so that no one can say, with reason, that I have not allowed *Obadiah* time enough, poetically speaking, and considering the emergency too, both to go and come;——tho', morally and truly speaking, the man, perhaps, has scarce had time to get on his boots.

If the hypercritic will go upon this; and is resolved after all to take a pendulum, and measure the true distance betwixt the ringing of the bell, and the rap at the door;——and, after finding it to be no more than two minutes, thirteen seconds, and three fifths,——should take upon him to insult over me for such a breach in the unity, or rather probability, of time;——I would remind him, that the idea of duration and of its simple modes, is got merely from the train and succession of our ideas,——and is the true scholastic pendulum,——and by which, as a scholar, I will be tried in this matter,——abjuring and detesting the jurisdiction of all other pendulums whatever.

I would, therefore, desire him to consider that it is but poor eight miles from *Shandy-Hall* to Dr. *Slop,* the man midwife's house;——and that whilst *Obadiah* has been going those said miles and back, I have brought my uncle *Toby* from *Namur,* quite across all *Flanders,* into *England:*——That I have had him ill upon my hands near four years;——and have since travelled him and Corporal *Trim,* in a chariot and four,

a journey of near two hundred miles down into *Yorkshire;*
——all which put together, must have prepared the reader's
imagination for the entrance of Dr. *Slop* upon the stage,——
as much, at least (I hope) as a dance, a song, or a concerto
between the acts.

If my hypercritic is intractable, alledging, that two minutes
and thirteen seconds are no more than two minutes and
thirteen seconds,——when I have said all I can about them;
——and that this plea, tho' it might save me dramatically, will
damn me biographically, rendering my book, from this very
moment, a profess'd ROMANCE, which, before, was a book
apocryphal:——If I am thus pressed——I then put an end to
the whole objection and controversy about it all at once,——
by acquainting him, that *Obadiah* had not got above three-
score yards from the stable-yard before he met with Dr. *Slop;*
——and indeed he gave a dirty proof that he had met with
him,——and was within an ace of giving a tragical one too.

Imagine to yourself;——but this had better begin a new
chapter.

CHAP. IX.

IMagine to yourself a little, squat, uncourtly figure of a Doctor *Slop*,[1] of about four feet and a half perpendicular
height, with a breadth of back, and a sesquipedality[2] of belly,
which might have done honour to a serjeant in the horse-
guards.

Such were the out-lines of Dr. *Slop*'s figure, which,——if
you have read *Hogarth*'s analysis of beauty,[3] and if you have

[1]A caricature of Dr. John Burton, an able physician, obstetrician, author,
and antiquary of York, whose vigorous Toryism had rendered him suspect of Jacobitism and aroused the animosity of Sterne who ridicules him
as an ignorant man-midwife and Papist. See the Introduction, pp. xxv,
lviii; and p. 44, n. 2.

[2]Foot-and-a-half-ness.

[3]A graceful compliment to William Hogarth (1697–1764), English
painter and engraver, whose style in caricaturing Sterne had imitated.
His *Analysis of Beauty,* a treatise written "to fix the fluctuating ideas of

not, I wish you would;——you must know, may as certainly be
caracatur'd, and convey'd to the mind by three strokes as three
hundred.

Imagine such a one,——for such, I say, were the out-lines of
Dr. *Slop*'s figure, coming slowly along, foot by foot, waddling
thro' the dirt upon the vertebræ of a little diminutive pony, of
a pretty colour;——but of strength,——alack!——scarce able
to have made an amble of it, under such a fardel, had the
roads been in an ambling condition.——They were not.——
Imagine to yourself, *Obadiah* mounted upon a strong monster
of a coach-horse, prick'd into a full gallop, and making all
practicable speed the adverse way.

Pray, Sir, let me interest you a moment in this description.
Had Dr. *Slop* beheld *Obadiah* a mile off, posting in a narrow lane directly towards him, at that monstrous rate,——
splashing and plunging like a devil thro' thick and thin, as he
approach'd, would not such a phænomenon, with such a vortex of mud and water moving along with it, round its axis,
——have been a subject of juster apprehension to Dr. *Slop* in
his situation, than the *worst* of *Whiston*'s comets?[4]——To say
nothing of the NUCLEUS; that is, of *Obadiah* and the coach-
horse.——In my idea, the vortex alone of 'em was enough to
have involved and carried, if not the doctor, at least the doctor's pony quite away with it.   What then do you think must
the terror and hydrophobia of Dr. *Slop* have been, when you
read (which you are just going to do) that he was advancing
thus warily along towards *Shandy-Hall,* and had approach'd to
within sixty yards of it, and within five yards of a sudden turn,
made by an acute angle of the garden wall,——and in the dirti-
est part of a dirty lane,——when *Obadiah* and his coach-horse
turn'd the corner, rapid, furious,——pop,——full upon him!

Taste," had appeared in 1753; following the publication of the above
passage Hogarth obliged Sterne with the two illustrations of *Shandy*
which are reproduced in this edition.

[4]William Whiston (1667–1752), an English theologian and mathematician who, in his *New Theory of the Earth,* had explained all temp-
ests and predicted the final conflagration of the earth by the approach to
the earth of comets.

——Nothing, I think, in nature, can be supposed more terrible, than such a Rencounter,——so imprompt! so ill prepared to stand the shock of it as Dr. *Slop* was!

What could Dr. *Slop* do?——He cross'd himself $+$ —— Pugh!——but the doctor, Sir, was a Papist.——No matter; he had better have kept hold of the pummel.——He had so;—— nay, as it happened, he had better have done nothing at all; ——for in crossing himself he let go his whip,——and in attempting to save his whip betwixt his knee and his saddle's skirt, as it slipp'd, he lost his stirrup,——in losing which, he lost his seat;——and in the multitude of all these losses (which, by the bye, shews what little advantage there is in crossing) the unfortunate doctor lost his presence of mind. So that, without waiting for *Obadiah's* onset, he left his pony to its destiny, tumbling off it diagonally, something in the stile and manner of a pack of wool, and without any other consequence from the fall, save that of being left (as it would have been) with the broadest part of him sunk about twelve inches deep in the mire.

Obadiah pull'd off his cap twice to Dr. *Slop;*——once as he was falling,——and then again when he saw him seated.—— Ill-timed complaisance!——had not the fellow better have stopp'd his horse, and got off and help'd him?——Sir, he did all that his situation would allow;——but the MOMENTUM of the coach-horse was so great, that *Obadiah* could not do it all at once;——he rode in a circle three times round Dr. *Slop,* before he could fully accomplish it any how;——and at the last, when he did stop his beast, 'twas done with such an explosion of mud, that *Obadiah* had better have been a league off. In short, never was a Dr. *Slop* so beluted,[5] and so transubstantiated, since that affair came into fashion.

[5]Covered with lute, or clay. "Transubstantiated" alludes to Slop's papistry and the disagreement of the churches of Rome and England on the nature of the Eucharist.

CHAP. X.

WHEN Dr. *Slop* entered the back-parlour, where my
father and my uncle *Toby* were discoursing upon the
nature of women,——it was hard to determine whether Dr.
Slop's figure, or Dr. *Slop's* presence, occasioned more surprize
to them; for as the accident happened so near the house, as not
to make it worth while for *Obadiah* to remount him,——*Obadiah* had led him in as he was, *unwiped, unappointed, un-
anealed,*[1] with all his stains and blotches on him.——He stood
like *Hamlet's* ghost,[2] motionless and speechless, for a full minute and a half, at the parlour door (*Obadiah* still holding his
hand) with all the majesty of mud. His hinder parts, upon
which he had received his fall, totally besmear'd,——and in
every other part of him, blotched over in such a manner with
Obadiah's explosion, that you would have sworn (without
mental reservation[3]) that every grain of it had taken effect.

Here was a fair opportunity for my uncle *Toby* to have triumph'd over my father in his turn;——for no mortal, who
had beheld Dr. *Slop* in that pickle, could have dissented from
so much, at least, of my uncle *Toby's* opinion, "That mayhap
his sister might not care to let such a Dr. *Slop* come so near

---

[1] Not having received extreme unction.

[2] In *Hamlet*, 1.1.41–49 and 1.4.38–57 the ghost stands motionless and
speechless; in 1.5.76–79 the ghost complains that he was

        Cut off even in the blossoms of my sin,
        Unhousel'd, disappointed, unanel'd,
        No reckoning made, but sent to my account
        With all my imperfections on my head . . .

[3] Another allusion to Slop's papistry and to the practice of Jacobites and
Romish sympathizers of swearing to support the government and church
of England, but "with mental reservations." "All Catholic writers were,
and are, agreed that when there is good reason, [equivocations with mental reservations] may be made use of, and that they are not lies. Those
who hear them may understand them in a sense which is not true, but
their self-deception may be permitted by the speaker for a good reason."
—"Mental Reservation," in *The Catholic Encyclopedia* (N. Y., 1907–14),
10.195b.

her ****" But it was the *Argumentum ad hominem*;[4] and if
my uncle *Toby* was not very expert at it, you may think, he
might not care to use it.——No; the reason was,——'twas not
his nature to insult.

Dr. *Slop*'s presence, at that time, was no less problematical
than the mode of it; tho', it is certain, one moment's reflection
in my father might have solved it; for he had apprized Dr.
Slop but the week before, that my mother was at her full
reckoning; and as the doctor had heard nothing since, 'twas
natural and very political too in him, to have taken a ride to
Shandy-Hall, as he did, merely to see how matters went on.

But my father's mind took unfortunately a wrong turn in
the investigation; running, like the hypercritic's, altogether
upon the ringing of the bell and the rap upon the door,——
measuring their distance,——and keeping his mind so intent
upon the operation, as to have power to think of nothing else,
——common-place infirmity of the greatest mathematicians!
working with might and main at the demonstration, and so
wasting all their strength upon it, that they have none left in
them to draw the corollary, to do good with.

The ringing of the bell and the rap upon the door, struck
likewise strong upon the sensorium of my uncle *Toby,*——
but it excited a very different train of thoughts;——the two
irreconcileable pulsations instantly brought *Stevinus,* the great
engineer,[5] along with them, into my uncle *Toby*'s mind:——
What business *Stevinus* had in this affair,——is the greatest
problem of all;——it shall be solved,——but not in the next
chapter.

CHAP. XI.

WRiting, when properly managed, (as you may be sure
I think mine is) is but a different name for conversation: As no one, who knows what he is about in good com-

[4]See p. 51, n. 5.
[5]See p. 89, n. 3.

pany, would venture to talk all;——so no author, who understands the just boundaries of decorum and good breeding,
would presume to think all: The truest respect which you can
pay to the reader's understanding, is to halve this matter
amicably, and leave him something to imagine, in his turn, as
well as yourself.

For my own part, I am eternally paying him compliments of
this kind, and do all that lies in my power to keep his imagination as busy as my own.

'Tis his turn now;——I have given an ample description of
Dr. *Slop*'s sad overthrow, and of his sad appearance in the
back parlour;——his imagination must now go on with it for
a while.

Let the reader imagine then, that Dr. *Slop* has told his tale;
——and in what words, and with what aggravations his fancy
chooses:——Let him suppose, that *Obadiah* has told his tale
also, and with such rueful looks of affected concern, as he
thinks will best contrast the two figures as they stand by each
other:——Let him imagine, that my father has stepp'd up
stairs to see my mother:——And, to conclude this work of
imagination,——let him imagine the doctor wash'd,——rubb'd
down,——condoled with,——felicitated,——got into a pair
of *Obadiah*'s pumps, stepping forwards towards the door, upon
the very point of entring upon action.

Truce!——truce, good Dr. *Slop*!——stay thy obstetric hand;
——return it safe into thy bosom to keep it warm;——little
dost thou know what obstacles;——little dost thou think
what hidden causes retard its operation!——Hast thou, Dr.
Slop,——hast thou been intrusted with the secret articles of
this solemn treaty which has brought thee into this place?
——Art thou aware that, at this instant, a daughter of *Lucina*[1]
is put obstetrically over thy head? Alas! 'tis too true.——
Besides, great son of *Pilumnus!*[2] what canst thou do?——Thou

---

[1]"She who brings to light"; in Roman mythology, the goddess who presided over childbirth.

[2]Ancient rustic Roman god of matrimony, regarded as guardian of
women in childbed and of new-born infants.

hast come forth unarm'd;——thou hast left thy *tire tête*,[3]——
thy new-invented *forceps*,——thy *crotchet*,——thy *squirt*, and
all thy instruments of salvation and deliverance behind thee.
——By heaven! at this moment they are hanging up in a green
bays[4] bag, betwixt thy two pistols, at thy bed's head!——Ring;
——call;——send *Obadiah* back upon the coach-horse to bring
them with all speed.

——Make great haste, *Obadiah*, quoth my father, and I'll
give thee a crown;——and, quoth my uncle *Toby*, I'll give him
another.

CHAP. XII.

YOUR sudden and unexpected arrival, quoth my uncle
Toby, addressing himself to Dr. *Slop* (all three of them
sitting down to the fire together, as my uncle *Toby* began to
speak)——instantly brought the great *Stevinus* into my head,
who, you must know, is a favourite author with me.——Then,
added my father, making use of the argument *Ad Crumenam*,[1]
——I will lay twenty guineas to a single crown piece, (which
will serve to give away to *Obadiah* when he gets back) that this
same *Stevinus* was some engineer or other,——or has wrote
something or other, either directly or indirectly, upon the
science of fortification.

He has so,——replied my uncle *Toby*.——I knew it, said my
father;——tho', for the soul of me, I cannot see what kind of
connection there can be betwixt Dr. *Slop*'s sudden coming,
and a discourse upon fortification;——yet I fear'd it.——Talk
of what we will, brother,——or let the occasion be never so
foreign or unfit for the subject,——you are sure to bring it in:
I would not, brother *Toby*, continued my father,——I declare I would not have my head so full of curtins and horn-

---

[3]"Head-drawer," extracting forceps used in childbirth. Crotchet:
hooked surgical instrument used in embryotomy.

[4]Baize.

[1]See p. 71, n. 13.

works.——That, I dare say, you would not, quoth Dr. *Slop,* interrupting him, and laughing most immoderately at his pun.

Dennis the critic[2] could not detest and abhor a pun, or the insinuation of a pun, more cordially than my father;——he would grow testy upon it at any time;——but to be broke in upon by one, in a serious discourse, was as bad, he would say, as a fillip upon the nose;——he saw no difference.

Sir, quoth my uncle *Toby,* addressing himself to Dr. *Slop,* ——the curtins my brother *Shandy* mentions here, have nothing to do with bed-steads;——tho', I know, *Du Cange*[3] says, "That bed-curtains, in all probability, have taken their name from them;"——nor have the horn-works, he speaks of, any thing in the world to do with the horn-works of cuckoldom:[4] ——But the *curtin,* Sir, is the word we use in fortification, for that part of the wall or rampart which lies between the two bastions and joins them.——Besiegers seldom offer to carry on their attacks directly against the curtin, for this reason, because they are so well *flanked.* ('Tis the case of other curtins, quoth Dr. *Slop,* laughing). However, continued my uncle *Toby,* to make them sure, we generally choose to place ravelins before them, taking care only to extend them beyond the fossé or ditch:——The common men, who know very little of fortification, confound the ravelin and the half-moon together, ——tho' they are very different things;——not in their figure

---

[2]John Dennis (1657–1734), the English critic, poet, and playwright, fulminated to the dramatist Wycherly, who had sent him a *Panegyrick upon Puns,* "I will no more believe nauseous Equivocals to be Wit, because some Sots have admir'd them, than I will believe Garlick to be God, because the Ægyptians ador'd it. Nay, it is a more damnable Sign of Stupidity in an *Englishman* to make Wit of a Quibble, than it was in the Ægyptians to make a God of their Garlick." To Dennis is attributed the remark, "He who will make a pun will pick a pocket."

[3]Charles du Fresne du Cange (1610–1688), a learned French philologist and historian; the quotation is a paraphrase of a passage under *"Cortina"* in his great *Glossarium ad Scriptores Mediæ et Infimæ Latinitatis,* which, with the two following sentences, Sterne paraphrased from the article "Curtin" in Ephraim Chambers's *Cyclopædia: or, an Universal Dictionary of Arts and Sciences.*

[4]The imaginary horns jocularly supposed to be worn by a cuckold.

or construction, for we make them exactly alike in all points;
——for they always consist of two faces, making a salient
angle, with the gorges, not straight, but in form of a crescent.
——Where then lies the difference? (quoth my father, a little
testily.)——In their situations, answered my uncle *Toby*:——
For when a ravelin, brother, stands before the curtin, it is a
ravelin; and when a ravelin stands before a bastion, then the
ravelin is not a ravelin;——it is a half-moon;——a half-moon
likewise is a half-moon, and no more, so long as it stands before its bastion;——but was it to change place, and get before
the curtin,——'twould be no longer a half-moon; a half-moon,
in that case, is not a half-moon;——'tis no more than a ravelin.
——I think, quoth my father, that the noble science of defence has its weak sides,——as well as others.

——As for the horn-works (high! ho! sigh'd my father)
which, continued my uncle *Toby,* my brother was speaking of,
they are a very considerable part of an outwork;——they are
called by the *French* engineers, *Ouvrage à corne,* and we generally make them to cover such places as we suspect to be
weaker than the rest;——'tis form'd by two epaulments[5] or
demi-bastions,——they are very pretty, and if you will take a
walk, I'll engage to shew you one well worth your trouble.——
I own, continued my uncle *Toby,* when we crown them,——
they are much stronger, but then they are very expensive, and
take up a great deal of ground; so that, in my opinion, they
are most of use to cover or defend the head of a camp; otherwise the double tenaille——By the mother who bore us!——
brother *Toby,* quoth my father, not able to hold out any
longer,——you would provoke a saint;——here have you got
us, I know not how, not only souse into the middle of the old
subject again:——But so full is your head of these confounded
works, that.tho' my wife is this moment in the pains of labour,
——and you hear her cry out,——yet nothing will serve you

---

[5]Earthworks raised to protect extremities of lines or batteries from
the enemy's fire. For demi-bastions see p. 81, n. 2. Double tenaille:
outwork of three faces forming two re-entering angles, located in the main
ditch in front of the curtain and between two bastions.

but to carry off the man-midwife.——*Accoucheur*,[6]——if you please, quoth Dr. *Slop*.——With all my heart, replied my father, I don't care what they call you,——but I wish the whole science of fortification, with all its inventors, at the devil;—— it has been the death of thousands,——and it will be mine, in the end.——I would not, I would not, brother *Toby*, have my brains so full of saps, mines, blinds,[7] gabions, palisadoes, ravelins, half-moons, and such trumpery, to be proprietor of *Namur*, and of all the towns in *Flanders* with it.

My uncle *Toby* was a man patient of injuries;——not from want of courage,——I have told you in the fifth[8] chapter of this second book, "That he was a man of courage:"——And will add here, that where just occasions presented, or called it forth,——I know no man under whose arm I would sooner have taken shelter; nor did this arise from any insensi- bility or obtuseness of his intellectual parts;——for he felt this insult of my father's as feelingly as a man could do;——but he was of a peaceful, placid nature,——no jarring element in it,——all was mix'd up so kindly within him; my uncle *Toby* had scarce a heart to retaliate upon a fly.

——Go——says he, one day at dinner, to an over-grown one which had buzz'd about his nose, and tormented him cruelly all dinner-time,——and which, after infinite attempts, he had caught at last, as it flew by him;——I'll not hurt thee, says my uncle *Toby*, rising from his chair, and going a-cross the room, with the fly in his hand,——I'll not hurt a hair of thy head: ——Go, says he, lifting up the sash, and opening his hand as he spoke, to let it escape;——go poor devil, get thee gone, why should I hurt thee?——This world surely is wide enough to hold both thee and me.

I was but ten years old when this happened; but whether it was, that the action itself was more in unison to my nerves at

---

[6]The French (and hence polite) term for obstetrician.

[7]Blindage, screen or shelter for troops. Gabions: wicker cylinders filled with earth serving to shelter men from an enemy's fire. The other terms have been defined on p. 81, n. 2, and p. 97, n. 8.

[8]Second?

that age of pity, which instantly set my whole frame into one vibration of most pleasurable sensation;——or how far the manner and expression of it might go towards it;——or in what degree, or by what secret magic,——a tone of voice and harmony of movement, attuned by mercy, might find a passage to my heart, I know not;——this I know, that the lesson of universal good-will then taught and imprinted by my uncle *Toby,* has never since been worn out of my mind: And tho' I would not depreciate what the study of the *Literæ humaniores,*[9] at the university, have done for me in that respect, or discredit the other helps of an expensive education bestowed upon me, both at home and abroad since;——yet I often think that I owe one half of my philanthropy to that one accidental impression.

☞ This is to serve for parents and governors instead of a whole volume upon the subject.

I could not give the reader this stroke in my uncle *Toby*'s picture, by the instrument with which I drew the other parts of it,——that taking in no more than the mere HOBBY-HORSICAL likeness;——this is a part of his moral character. My father, in this patient endurance of wrongs, which I mention, was very different, as the reader must long ago have noted; he had a much more acute and quick sensibility of nature, attended with a little soreness of temper; tho' this never transported him to any thing which looked like malignancy;——yet, in the little rubs and vexations of life, 'twas apt to shew itself in a drollish and witty kind of peevishness:—— He was, however, frank and generous in his nature;——at all times open to conviction; and in the little ebullitions of this subacid humour towards others, but particularly towards my uncle *Toby,* whom he truly loved;——he would feel more pain, ten times told (except in the affair of my aunt *Dinah,* or where an hypothesis was concerned) than what he ever gave.

The characters of the two brothers, in this view of them, reflected light upon each other, and appear'd with great advantage in this affair which arose about *Stevinus.*

---

[9]Humane letters, the humanities.

I need not tell the reader, if he keeps a Hobby-Horse,——
that a man's Hobby-Horse is as tender a part as he has about
him; and that these unprovoked strokes, at my uncle *Toby*'s
could not be unfelt by him.——No;——as I said above, my
uncle *Toby* did feel them, and very sensibly too.

Pray, Sir, what said he?——How did he behave?——O, Sir!
——it was great: For as soon as my father had done insulting
his Hobby-Horse,——he turned his head, without the least
emotion, from Dr. *Slop,* to whom he was addressing his discourse, and look'd up into my father's face, with a countenance spread over with so much good nature;——so placid;
——so fraternal;——so inexpressibly tender towards him;——
it penetrated my father to his heart: He rose up hastily from
his chair, and seizing hold of both my uncle *Toby*'s hands as
he spoke:——Brother *Toby,* said he,——I beg thy pardon;——
forgive, I pray thee, this rash humour which my mother gave
me.——My dear, dear brother, answer'd my uncle *Toby,* rising
up by my father's help, say no more about it;——you are
heartily welcome, had it been ten times as much, brother.
But 'tis ungenerous, replied my father, to hurt any man;——
a brother worse;——but to hurt a brother of such gentle manners,——so unprovoking,——and so unresenting;——'tis base:
——By heaven, 'tis cowardly.——You are heartily welcome,
brother, quoth my uncle *Toby,*——had it been fifty times as
much.——Besides, what have I to do, my dear *Toby,* cried my
father, either with your amusements or your pleasures, unless
it was in my power (which it is not) to increase their measure?

——Brother *Shandy,* answer'd my uncle *Toby,* looking wistfully in his face,——you are much mistaken in this point;——
for you do increase my pleasure very much, in begetting children for the *Shandy* family at your time of life.——But, by
that, Sir, quoth Dr. *Slop,* Mr. *Shandy* increases his own.——
Not a jot, quoth my father.

CHAP. XIII.

MY brother does it, quoth my uncle *Toby,* out of *princi-*
ple.——In a family-way, I suppose, quoth Dr. *Slop.*——
Pshaw!——said my father,——'tis not worth talking of.

CHAP. XIV.

AT the end of the last chapter, my father and my uncle *Toby*
were left both standing, like *Brutus* and *Cassius* at the
close of the scene making up their accounts.[1]

As my father spoke the three last words,——he sat down;
——my uncle *Toby* exactly followed his example, only, that
before he took his chair, he rung the bell, to order Corporal
Trim, who was in waiting, to step home for *Stevinus;*——my
uncle *Toby's* house being no further off than the opposite side
of the way.

Some men would have dropp'd the subject of *Stevinus;*——
but my uncle *Toby* had no resentment in his heart, and he
went on with the subject, to shew my father that he had none.

Your sudden appearance,. Dr. *Slop,* quoth my uncle, resuming the discourse, instantly brought *Stevinus* into my head.
(My father, you may be sure, did not offer to lay any more
wagers upon *Stevinus's* head)——Because, continued my uncle
Toby, the celebrated sailing chariot, which belonged to Prince
Maurice,[2] and was of such wonderful contrivance and velocity,
as to carry half a dozen people thirty *German* miles, in I don't

---

[1] See Shakespeare's *Julius Cæsar,* 4.2.52, at which point, according to
eighteenth century stage directions, all save Brutus and Cassius *exeunt.*

[2] The most famous invention of Stevinus (see p. 89, n. 3) was a carriage with sails, which, about 1600, was used on the seashore between
Petten and Scheveningen (Schevling) by Maurice of Nassau, Prince of
Orange. The carriage, which was propelled solely by wind power, was
said to have carried twenty-eight passengers at a speed exceeding that of
horses.

know how few minutes,——was invented by *Stevinus,* that great mathematician and engineer.

You might have spared your servant the trouble, quoth Dr. *Slop* (as the fellow is lame) of going for *Stevinus's* account of it, because, in my return from *Leyden* thro' the *Hague,* I walked as far as *Schevling,* which is two long miles, on purpose to take a view of it.

——That's nothing, replied my uncle *Toby,* to what the learned *Peireskius*[3] did, who walked a matter of five hundred miles, reckoning from *Paris* to *Schevling,* and from *Schevling* to *Paris* back again, in order to see it,——and nothing else.

Some men cannot bear to be out-gone.

The more fool *Peireskius,* replied Dr. *Slop.* But mark, 'twas out of no contempt of *Peireskius* at all;——but that *Peireskius's* indefatigable labour in trudging so far on foot out of love for the sciences, reduced the exploit of Dr. *Slop,* in that affair, to nothing;——the more fool *Peireskius,* said he again: ——Why so?——replied my father, taking his brother's part, not only to make reparation as fast as he could for the insult he had given him, which sat still upon my father's mind;—— but partly, that my father began really to interest himself in the discourse.——Why so?——said he. Why is *Peireskius,* or any man else, to be abused for an appetite for that, or any other morsel of sound knowledge? For, notwithstanding I know nothing of the chariot in question, continued he, the inventor of it must have had a very mechanical head; and tho' I cannot guess upon what principles of philosophy he has atchiev'd it; ——yet certainly his machine has been constructed upon solid ones, be they what they will, or it could not have answer'd at the rate my brother mentions.

It answered, replied my uncle *Toby,* as well, if not better; for, as *Peireskius* elegantly expresses it, speaking of the velocity of its motion, *Tam citus erat, quam erat ventus;* which, unless I have forgot my Latin, is, *that it was as swift as the wind itself.*

---

[3]Nicholas Claude Fabri de Peiresc (1580–1637), senator of Aix, an eminent antiquary, scholar, and patron of learning.

But pray, Dr. *Slop*, quoth my father, interrupting my uncle (tho' not without begging pardon for it, at the same time) upon what principles was this self-same chariot set a-going? ——Upon very pretty principles to be sure, replied Dr. *Slop;* ——and I have often wondered, continued he, evading the question, why none of our gentry, who live upon large plains like this of ours,——(especially they whose wives are not past child-bearing) attempt nothing of this kind; for it would not only be infinitely expeditious upon sudden calls, to which the sex is subject,——if the wind only served,——but would be excellent good husbandry to make use of the winds, which cost nothing, and which eat nothing, rather than horses, which (the devil take 'em) both cost and eat a great deal.

For that very reason, replied my father, "Because they cost nothing, and because they eat nothing,"——the scheme is bad; ——it is the consumption of our products, as well as the manufactures of them, which gives bread to the hungry, circulates trade,——brings in money, and supports the value of our lands;——and tho', I own, if I was a prince, I would generously recompense the scientific head which brought forth such contrivances;——yet I would as peremptorily suppress the use of them.

My father here had got into his element,——and was going on as prosperously with his dissertation upon trade, as my uncle *Toby* had before, upon his of fortification;——but, to the loss of much sound knowledge, the destinies in the morning had decreed that no dissertation of any kind should be spun by my father that day;——for as he opened his mouth to begin the next sentence,

CHAP. XV.

IN popp'd Corporal *Trim* with *Stevinus:*——But 'twas too late,——all the discourse had been exhausted without him, and was running into a new channel.

——You may take the book home again, *Trim,* said my uncle *Toby,* nodding to him.

But pri'thee, Corporal, quoth my father, drolling,——look first into it, and see if thou canst spy aught of a sailing chariot in it.

Corporal *Trim,* by being in the service, had learned to obey, ——and not to remonstrate;——so taking the book to a side-table, and running over the leaves; an' please your Honour, said *Trim,* I can see no such thing;——however, continued the Corporal, drolling a little in his turn, I'll make sure work of it, an' please your Honour;——so taking hold of the two covers of the book, one in each hand, and letting the leaves fall down, as he bent the covers back, he gave the book a good sound shake.

There is something fallen out, however, said *Trim,* an' please your Honour; but it is not a chariot, or any thing like one:——Pri'thee Corporal, said my father, smiling, what is it then?——I think, answered *Trim,* stooping to take it up, ——'tis more like a sermon,——for it begins, with a text of scripture, and the chapter and verse;—and then goes on, not as a chariot,——but like a sermon directly.

The company smiled.

I cannot conceive how it is possible, quoth my uncle *Toby,* for such a thing as a sermon to have got into my *Stevinus.*

I think 'tis a sermon, replied *Trim;*——but if it please your Honours, as it is a fair hand, I will read you a page;——for *Trim,* you must know, loved to hear himself read almost as well as talk.

I have ever a strong propensity, said my father, to look into things which cross my way, by such strange fatalities as these; ——and as we have nothing better to do, at least till *Obadiah* gets back, I should be obliged to you, brother, if Dr. *Slop* has no objection to it, to order the Corporal to give us a page or two of it,——if he is as able to do it, as he seems willing. An' please your Honour, quoth *Trim,* I officiated two whole campaigns in *Flanders,* as clerk to the chaplain of the regiment.——He can read it, quoth my uncle *Toby,* as well as I can.——*Trim,* I assure you, was the best scholar in my company, and should have had the next halberd, but for the poor fellow's misfortune. Corporal *Trim* laid his hand upon his heart, and made an humble bow to his master;——then laying down his hat upon the floor, and taking up the sermon in his left-hand, in order to have his right at liberty,——he advanced, nothing doubting, into the middle of the room, where he could best see, and be best seen by, his audience.

CHAP. XVI.

——If you have any objection,——said my father, addressing himself to Dr. *Slop*. Not in the least, replied Dr. *Slop;*—— for it does not appear on which side of the question it is wrote; ——it may be a composition of a divine of our church, as well as yours;——so that we run equal risks.——'Tis wrote upon neither side, quoth *Trim,* for 'tis only upon *Conscience,* an' please your Honours.

*Trim'*s reason put his audience into good humour,——all but Dr. *Slop,* who, turning his head about towards *Trim,* look'd a little angry.

Begin, *Trim,*——and read distinctly, quoth my father;——I will, an' please your Honour, replied the Corporal, making a bow, and bespeaking attention with a slight movement of his right-hand.

CHAP. XVII.

——But before the Corporal begins, I must first give you a description of his attitude;[1]——otherwise he will naturally stand represented, by your imagination, in an uneasy posture, ——stiff,——perpendicular,——dividing the weight of his

[1]Early in March, 1760, when Sterne was in London preparing to publish the second edition of the initial volumes of his book, he wrote "most Shandaically" to his friend Richard Berenger, "I would give both my Ears . . . for no more than ten Strokes of *Howgarth's* witty Chissel, to clap at the Front of my next Edition of *Shandy.* . . . The loosest Sketch in Nature, of Trim's reading the Sermon to my Father &c., would do the Business . . ." The following illustration, drawn by Hogarth and engraved by Ravenet, was the result.

W. Hogarth inv.ᵗ   S. Ravenet Sculp.ᵗ

121

body equally upon both legs;——his eye fix'd, as if on duty;
——his look determined,——clinching the sermon in his left-
hand, like his firelock:——In a word, you would be apt to
paint *Trim,* as if he was standing in his platoon ready for
action:——His attitude was as unlike all this as you can conceive.

He stood before them with his body swayed, and bent forwards just so far, as to make an angle of 85 degrees and a half
upon the plain of the horizon;——which sound orators, to
whom I address this, know very well, to be the true persuasive
angle of incidence;——in any other angle you may talk and
preach;——'tis certain,——and it is done every day;——but
with what effect,——I leave the world to judge!

The necessity of this precise angle of 85 degrees and a half
to a mathematical exactness,——does it not shew us, by the
way,——how the arts and sciences mutually befriend each
other?

How the duce Corporal *Trim,* who knew not so much as an
acute angle from an obtuse one, came to hit it so exactly;——
or whether it was chance or nature, or good sense or imitation, *&c.* shall be commented upon in that part of this cyclopædia of arts and sciences, where the instrumental parts of the
eloquence of the senate, the pulpit, the bar, the coffee-
house, the bed-chamber, and fire-side, fall under consideration.

He stood,——for I repeat it, to take the picture of him in at
one view, with his body sway'd, and somewhat bent forwards,
——his right-leg firm under him, sustaining seven-eighths of
his whole weight,——the foot of his left-leg, the defect of
which was no disadvantage to his attitude, advanced a little,
——not laterally, nor forwards, but in a line betwixt them;
——his knee bent, but that not violently,——but so as to fall
within the limits of the line of beauty;[2]——and I add, of the
line of science too;——for consider, it had one eighth part of
his body to bear up;——so that in this case the position of the

---

[2]A line of undulating curvature, generally resembling a slender, elon-
gated letter S, which some critics maintain to be an essential factor in all
graceful combinations of line and form.

leg is determined,——because the foot could be no further
advanced, or the knee more bent, than what would allow him
mechanically, to receive an eighth part of his whole weight
under it,——and to carry it too.

☞ This I recommend to painters:——need I add,——to
orators?——I think not; for, unless they practise it,——they
must fall upon their noses.

So much for Corporal *Trim's* body and legs.——He held the
sermon loosely,——not carelessly, in his left-hand, raised
something above his stomach, and detach'd a little from his
breast;——his right-arm falling negligently by his side, as
nature and the laws of gravity ordered it,——but with the
palm of it open and turned towards his audience, ready to aid
the sentiment, in case it stood in need.

Corporal *Trim's* eyes and the muscles of his face were in full
harmony with the other parts of him;——he look'd frank,
——unconstrained,——something assured,——but not bordering upon assurance.

Let not the critic ask how Corporal *Trim* could come by all
this; I've told him it shall be explained;——but so he stood
before my father, my uncle *Toby,* and Dr. *Slop,*——so swayed
his body, so contrasted his limbs, and with such an oratorical
sweep throughout the whole figure,——a statuary might have
modell'd from it;——nay, I doubt whether the oldest Fellow
of a College,——or the *Hebrew* Professor himself, could have
much mended it.

Trim made a bow, and read as follows:

The SERMON.[1]

HEBREWS xiii. 18.

——*For we* trust *we have a good Conscience.*——

"TRust!——Trust we have a good conscience!"
    [Certainly, *Trim,* quoth my father, interrupting him,
you give that sentence a very improper accent; for you curl up

---

[1]See p. 142, n. 18.

your nose, man, and read it with such a sneering tone, as if the
Parson was going to abuse the Apostle.

He is, an' please your Honour, replied *Trim*. Pugh! said
my father, smiling.

Sir, quoth Dr. *Slop*, *Trim* is certainly in the right; for the
writer (who I perceive is a Protestant) by the snappish manner in which he takes up the Apostle, is certainly going to
abuse him,——if this treatment of him has not done it already.
But from whence, replied my father, have you concluded so
soon, Dr. *Slop*, that the writer is of our Church?——for aught
I can see yet,——he may be of any Church:——Because, answered Dr. *Slop*, if he was of ours,——he durst no more take
such a licence,——than a bear by his beard:——If, in our com-
munion, Sir, a man was to insult an Apostle,——a saint,——
or even the paring of a saint's nail,——he would have his eyes
scratched out.——What, by the saint, quoth my uncle *Toby*.
No, replied Dr. *Slop*,——he would have an old house over his
head.[2]   Pray is the Inquisition an antient building, answered
my uncle *Toby*, or is it a modern one?——I know nothing of
architecture, replied Dr. *Slop*.——An' please your Honours,
quoth *Trim*, the Inquisition is the vilest——Pri'thee spare thy
description, *Trim*, I hate the very name of it, said my father.
——No matter for that, answered Dr. *Slop*,——it has its uses;
for tho' I'm no great advocate for it, yet in such a case as this,
he would soon be taught better manners; and I can tell him, if
he went on at that rate, would be flung into the Inquisition for
his pains.   God help him then, quoth my uncle *Toby*.   Amen,
added *Trim;* for, heaven above knows, I have a poor brother
who has been fourteen years a captive in it.——I never heard
one word of it before, said my uncle *Toby*, hastily:——How
came he there, *Trim?*——O, Sir! the story will make your heart
bleed,——as it has made mine a thousand times;——but it is
too long to be told now;——your Honour shall hear it from
first to last some day when I am working beside you in our
fortifications;——but the short of the story is this:——That
my brother *Tom* went over a servant to *Lisbon*,——and then

---

[2]A proverbial expression meaning to get into trouble.

married a *Jew's* widow, who kept a small shop, and sold
sausages, which, some how or other, was the cause of his
being taken in the middle of the night out of his bed, where
he was lying with his wife and two small children, and carried
directly to the Inquisition, where, God help him, continued
Trim, fetching a sigh from the bottom of his heart,——the
poor honest lad lies confined at this hour;——he was as honest
a soul, added *Trim,* (pulling out his handkerchief) as ever
blood warm'd.——

——The tears trickled down *Trim's* cheeks faster than he
could well wipe them away.——A dead silence in the room ensued for some minutes.——Certain proof of pity!

Come, *Trim,* quoth my father, after he saw the poor fellow's grief had got a little vent,——read on,——and put this
melancholy story out of thy head:——I grieve that I interrupted thee;——but pri'thee begin the sermon again;——for if
the first sentence in it is matter of abuse, as thou sayest, I have
a great desire to know what kind of provocation the Apostle
has given.

Corporal *Trim* wiped his face, and returning his handkerchief into his pocket, and, making a bow as he did it,——he
began again.]

The SERMON.

HEBREWS xiii. 18.

——*For we* trust *we have a good Conscience.*——

"TRust! trust we have a good conscience! Surely if there
is any thing in this life which a man may depend upon,
and to the knowledge of which he is capable of arriving upon
the most indisputable evidence, it must be this very thing,——
whether he has a good conscience or no."

[I am positive I am right, quoth Dr. *Slop.*]

"If a man thinks at all, he cannot well be a stranger to the
true state of this account;——he must be privy to his own
thoughts and desires;——he must remember his past pursuits,

and know certainly the true springs and motives, which, in general, have governed the actions of his life."

[I defy him, without an assistant, quoth Dr. *Slop*.]

"In other matters we may be deceived by false appearances; and, as the wise man complains, *hardly do we guess aright at the things that are upon the earth, and with labour do we find the things that are before us.*[3] But here the mind has all the evidence and facts within herself;——is conscious of the web she has wove;——knows its texture and fineness, and the exact share which every passion has had in working upon the several designs which virtue or vice had plann'd before her."

[The language is good, and I declare *Trim* reads very well, quoth my father.]

"Now,——as conscience is nothing else but the knowledge which the mind has within herself of this; and the judgment, either of approbation or censure, which it unavoidably makes upon the successive actions of our lives; 'tis plain you will say, from the very terms of the proposition,——whenever this inward testimony goes against a man, and he stands self-accused, ——that he must necessarily be a guilty man.——And, on the contrary, when the report is favourable on his side, and his heart condemns him not;——that it is not a matter of *trust,* as the Apostle intimates,——but a matter of *certainty* and fact, that the conscience is good, and that the man must be good also."

[Then the Apostle is altogether in the wrong, I suppose, quoth Dr. *Slop,* and the Protestant divine is in the right. Sir, have patience, replied my father, for I think it will presently appear that *St. Paul* and the Protestant divine are both of an opinion.——As nearly so, quoth Dr. *Slop,* as east is to west; ——but this, continued he, lifting both hands, comes from the liberty of the press.

It is no more, at the worst, replied my uncle *Toby,* than the liberty of the pulpit; for it does not appear that the sermon is printed, or ever likely to be.

---

[3]Paraphrase of Ecclesiastes, 8.17.

Go on, *Trim,* quoth my father.]

"At first sight this may seem to be a true state of the case; and I make no doubt but the knowledge of right and wrong is so truly impressed upon the mind of man,——that did no such thing ever happen, as that the conscience of a man, by long habits of sin, might (as the scripture assures it may) insensibly become hard;——and, like some tender parts of his body, by much stress and continual hard usage, lose, by degrees, that nice sense and perception with which God and nature endow'd it:——Did this never happen;——or was it certain that self-love could never hang the least bias upon the judgment; ——or that the little interests below, could rise up and perplex the faculties of our upper regions, and encompass them about with clouds and thick darkness:——Could no such thing as favour and affection enter this sacred COURT:——Did WIT disdain to take a bribe in it;——or was asham'd to shew its face as an advocate for an unwarrantable enjoyment:——Or, lastly, were we assured, that INTEREST stood always unconcern'd whilst the cause was hearing,——and that passion never got into the judgment-seat, and pronounc'd sentence in the stead of reason, which is supposed always to preside and determine upon the case:——Was this truly so, as the objection must suppose;——no doubt then, the religious and moral state of a man would be exactly what he himself esteem'd it;——and the guilt or innocence of every man's life could be known, in general, by no better measure, than the degrees of his own approbation and censure.

"I own, in one case, whenever a man's conscience does accuse him (as it seldom errs on that side) that he is guilty; and, unless in melancholy and hypocondriac cases, we may safely pronounce upon it, that there is always sufficient grounds for the accusation.

"But the converse of the proposition will not hold true;—— namely, that whenever there is guilt, the conscience must accuse; and if it does not, that a man is therefore innocent. ——This is not fact:——So that the common consolation which some good christian or other is hourly administring to himself,——that he thanks God his mind does not misgive him; and that, consequently, he has a good conscience, because he has a quiet one,——is fallacious;——and as current as the inference is, and as infallible as the rule appears at first sight, yet, when you look nearer to it, and try the truth of this rule upon plain facts,——you see it liable to so much error from a false application;——the principle upon which it goes so often perverted;——the whole force of it lost, and sometimes so vilely cast away, that it is painful to produce the common examples from human life which confirm the account.

"A man shall be vicious and utterly debauched in his principles;——exceptionable in his conduct to the world; shall live shameless, in the open commission of a sin which no reason or pretence can justify;——a sin, by which contrary to all the workings of humanity, he shall ruin for ever the deluded partner of his guilt;——rob her of her best dowry; and not only cover her own head with dishonour,——but involve a whole virtuous family in shame and sorrow for her sake.—— Surely, you will think conscience must lead such a man a troublesome life;——he can have no rest night or day from its reproaches.

"Alas! Conscience had something else to do, all this time, than break in upon him; as *Elijah* reproached the god *Baal,* ——this domestic God *was either talking, or pursuing, or was in a journey, or peradventure he slept and could not be awoke.*[4]

"Perhaps HE was gone out in company with HONOUR to fight a duel; to pay off some debt at play;——or dirty annuity, the bargain of his lust: Perhaps CONSCIENCE all this time was engaged at home, talking loud against petty larceny, and executing vengeance upon some such puny crimes as his fortune and rank in life secured him against all temptation of committing; so that he lives as merrily," [If he was of our church tho', quoth Dr. *Slop,* he could not]——"sleeps as soundly in his bed;——and at last meets death as unconcernedly;——perhaps much more so than a much better man."

[All this is impossible with us, quoth Dr. *Slop,* turning to my

---

[4]Paraphrase of 1 Kings, 18.27.

father,——the case could not happen in our church.——It happens in ours, however, replied my father, but too often.——I
own, quoth Dr. *Slop* (struck a little with my father's frank
acknowledgment)——that a man in the *Romish* church may
live as badly;——but then he cannot easily die so.——'Tis
little matter, replied my father, with an air of indifference,
——how a rascal dies.——I mean, answer'd Dr. *Slop,* he would
be denied the benefits of the last sacraments.——Pray how
many have you in all, said my uncle *Toby,*——for I always forget?——Seven, answered Dr. *Slop.*——Humph!——said my
uncle *Toby;* tho' not accented as a note of acquiescence,——
but as an interjection of that particular species of surprize,
when a man, in looking into a drawer, finds more of a thing
than he expected.——Humph! replied my uncle *Toby.* Dr.
Slop, who had an ear, understood my uncle *Toby* as well as if
he had wrote a whole volume against the seven sacraments.
——Humph! replied Dr. *Slop,* (stating my uncle *Toby*'s argument over again to him)——Why, Sir, are there not seven
cardinal virtues?——Seven mortal sins?——Seven golden can-
dlesticks?——Seven heavens?——'Tis more than I know, replied my uncle *Toby.*———Are there not seven wonders of the
world?——Seven days of the creation?——Seven planets?——
Seven plagues?——That there are, quoth my father, with a
most affected gravity. But pri'thee, continued he, go on with
the rest of thy characters, *Trim.*]

"Another is sordid, unmerciful," (here *Trim* waved his right-
hand) "a strait-hearted, selfish wretch, incapable either of
private friendship or public spirit. Take notice how he passes
by the widow and orphan in their distress, and sees all the
miseries incident to human life without a sigh or a prayer."
[And please your Honours, cried *Trim,* I think this a viler man
than the other.]

"Shall not conscience rise up and sting him on such occasions?——No; thank God there is no occasion; *I pay every
man his own;——I have no fornication to answer to my conscience;——no faithless vows or promises to make up;——I
have debauched no man's wife or child; thank God, I am not*

as other men, adulterers, unjust, or even as this libertine, who
stands before me.

"A third is crafty and designing in his nature. View his whole life;——'tis nothing but a cunning contexture of dark arts and unequitable subterfuges, basely to defeat the true intent of all laws,——plain dealing and the safe enjoyment of our several properties.——You will see such a one working out a frame of little designs upon the ignorance and perplexities of the poor and needy man;——shall raise a fortune upon the inexperience of a youth, or the unsuspecting temper of his friend, who would have trusted him with his life.

"When old age comes on, and repentance calls him to look back upon this black account, and state it over again with his conscience,——CONSCIENCE looks into the STATUTES at LARGE;——finds no express law broken by what he has done;——perceives no penalty or forfeiture of goods and chattels incurred;——sees no scourge waving over his head, or prison opening his gates upon him:——What is there to affright his conscience?——Conscience has got safely entrenched behind the Letter of the Law; sits there invulnerable, fortified with 𝕮𝖆𝖘𝖊𝖘 and 𝕽𝖊𝖕𝖔𝖗𝖙𝖘 so strongly on all sides;——that it is not preaching can dispossess it of its hold."

[Here Corporal *Trim* and my uncle *Toby* exchanged looks with each other.——Aye,——aye, *Trim!* quoth my uncle *Toby*, shaking his head,——these are but sorry fortifications, *Trim.*——O! very poor work, answered *Trim*, to what your Honour and I make of it.——The character of this last man, said Dr. *Slop*, interrupting *Trim*, is more detestable than all the rest;——and seems to have been taken from some pettifogging Lawyer amongst you:——Amongst us, a man's conscience could not possibly continue so long *blinded;*——three times in a year, at least, he must go to confession. Will that restore it to sight? quoth my uncle *Toby*.——Go on, *Trim*, quoth my father, or *Obadiah* will have got back before thou hast got to the end of thy sermon;——'tis a very short one, replied *Trim*.——I wish it was longer, quoth my uncle *Toby*, for I like it hugely.——*Trim* went on.]

"A fourth man shall want even this refuge;——shall break through all this ceremony of slow chicane;——scorns the doubtful workings of secret plots and cautious trains to bring about his purpose:——See the bare-faced villain, how he cheats, lies, perjures, robs, murders.——Horrid!——But indeed much better was not to be expected, in the present case,——the poor man was in the dark!———his priest had got the keeping of his conscience;——and all he would let him know of it, was, That he must believe in the Pope;——go to Mass;——cross himself;——tell his beads;——be a good Catholic, and that this, in all conscience, was enough to carry him to heaven. What;——if he perjures!——Why;——he had a mental reservation in it.——But if he is so wicked and abandoned a wretch as you represent him;——if he robs,——if he stabs,——will not conscience, on every such act, receive a wound itself? Aye, ——but the man has carried it to confession;——the wound digests there, and will do well enough, and in a short time be quite healed up by absolution. O Popery! what hast thou to answer for?——when, not content with the too many natural and fatal ways, thro' which the heart of man is every day thus treacherous to itself above all things;——thou hast wilfully set open this wide gate of deceit before the face of this unwary traveller, too apt, God knows, to go astray of himself; and confidently speak peace to himself, when there is no peace.

"Of this the common instances which I have drawn out of life, are too notorious to require much evidence. If any man doubts the reality of them, or thinks it impossible for a man to be such a bubble to himself,——I must refer him a moment to his own reflections, and will then venture to trust my appeal with his own heart.

"Let him consider in how different a degree of detestation, numbers of wicked actions stand *there,* tho' equally bad and vicious in their own natures;——he will soon find that such of them, as strong inclination and custom have prompted him to commit, are generally dress'd out and painted with all the false beauties, which a soft and a flattering hand can give them;——and that the others, to which he feels no propensity, appear, at once, naked and deformed, surrounded with all the true circumstances of folly and dishonour.

"When *David* surprized *Saul* sleeping in the cave, and cut off the skirt of his robe,[5]——we read his heart smote him for what he had done:——But in the matter of *Uriah*,[6] where a faithful and gallant servant, whom he ought to have loved and honoured, fell to make way for his lust,——where conscience had so much greater reason to take the alarm, his heart smote him not. A whole year had almost passed from the first commission of that crime, to the time *Nathan* was sent to reprove him; and we read not once of the least sorrow or compunction of heart which he testified, during all that time, for what he had done.

"Thus conscience, this once able monitor,——placed on high as a judge within us, and intended by our maker as a just and equitable one too,——by an unhappy train of causes and impediments, takes often such imperfect cognizance of what passes,——does its office so negligently,——sometimes so corruptly,——that it is not to be trusted alone; and therefore we find there is a necessity, an absolute necessity of joining another principle with it to aid, if not govern, its determinations.

"So that if you would form a just judgment of what is of infinite importance to you not to be misled in,——namely, in what degree of real merit you stand either as an honest man, an useful citizen, a faithful subject to your king, or a good servant to your God,——call in religion and morality.—— Look,——What is written in the law of God?——How readest thou?——Consult calm reason and the unchangeable obligations of justice and truth;——what say they?

"Let Conscience determine the matter upon these reports; ——and then if thy heart condemns thee not, which is the case

---

[5] 1 Samuel, 24.4–5.

[6] Because Uriah refused to accommodate David in his lust after his wife, Bathsheba, David caused him to be slain. Some time after David's first child by Bathsheba was born, Nathan reproved him through the parable of the ewe lamb. See 2 Samuel, 11.2–12.14.

the Apostle supposes,——the rule will be infallible;" [Here
Dr. *Slop* fell asleep] *"thou wilt have confidence towards God;*[7]
——that is, have just grounds to believe the judgment thou
hast past upon thyself, is the judgment of God; and nothing
else but an anticipation of that righteous sentence which will
be pronounced upon thee hereafter by that Being, to whom
thou art finally to give an account of thy actions.

"Blessed is the man, indeed then, as the author of the book
of *Ecclesiasticus* expresses it, *who is not prick'd with the multitude of his sins: Blessed is the man whose heart hath not
condemn'd him; whether he be rich, or whether he be poor, if
he have a good heart* (a heart thus guided and informed) *he
shall at all times rejoice in a chearful countenance; his mind
shall tell him more than seven watch-men that sit above upon
a tower on high."*[8]——[A tower has no strength, quoth my
uncle *Toby,* unless 'tis flank'd.] "In the darkest doubts it shall
conduct him safer than a thousand casuists, and give the state
he lives in a better security for his behaviour than all the
clauses and restrictions put together, which law-makers are
forced to multiply:——*Forced,* I say, as things stand; human
laws not being a matter of original choice, but of pure necessity, brought in to fence against the mischievous effects of
those consciences which are no law unto themselves; well intending, by the many provisions made,——that in all such
corrupt and misguided cases, where principles and the checks
of conscience will not make us upright,——to supply their
force, and, by the terrors of goals[9] and halters, oblige us to
it."

[I see plainly, said my father, that this sermon has been composed to be preached at the Temple,[10]——or at some Assize.
——I like the reasoning,——and am sorry that Dr. *Slop* has

---

[7]Paraphrase of 1 John, 3.21.

[8]A loose paraphrase of Ecclesiasticus, 14.1–2, 13.25–26.

[9]Gaols (jails).

[10]The Temple Church, in London, where many barristers connected
with the Inns of Court attended divine services. Assize: court of justice.

fallen asleep before the time of his conviction;——for it is now clear, that the Parson, as I thought at first, never insulted St. *Paul* in the least;——nor has there been, brother, the least difference between them.——A great matter, if they had differed, replied my uncle *Toby,*——the best friends in the world may differ sometimes.——True,——brother *Toby,* quoth my father, shaking hands with him,——we'll fill our pipes, brother, and then *Trim* shall go on.

Well,——what dost thou think of it? said my father, speaking to Corporal *Trim,* as he reach'd his tobacco-box.

I think, answer'd the Corporal, that the seven watch-men upon the tower, who, I suppose, are all centinels there,——are more, an' please your Honour, than were necessary;——and, to go on at that rate, would harrass a regiment all to pieces, which a commanding officer, who loves his men, will never do, if he can help it; because two centinels, added the Corporal, are as good as twenty.——I have been a commanding officer myself in the *Corps de Garde* a hundred times, continued *Trim,* rising an inch higher in his figure, as he spoke,——and all the time I had the honour to serve his Majesty King *William,* in relieving the most considerable posts, I never left more than two in my life.——Very right, *Trim,* quoth my uncle *Toby,* ——but you do not consider, *Trim,* that the towers, in *Solomon's* days, were not such things as our bastions, flank'd and defended by other works;——this, *Trim,* was an invention since *Solomon's* death; nor had they horn-works, or ravelins before the curtin, in his time;——or such a fossé as we make with a cuvette[11] in the middle of it, and with cover'd-ways and counterscarps pallisadoed along it, to guard against a *Coup de main:*[12]——So that the seven men upon the tower were a party, I dare say, from the *Corps de Garde,* set there, not only to look out, but to defend it.——They could be no more, an' please your Honour, than a Corporal's Guard.—— My father smiled inwardly,——but not outwardly;——the subject between my uncle *Toby* and Corporal *Trim* being rather

[11]Trench dug in the middle of a large ditch.
[12]Sudden attack.

too serious, considering what had happened, to make a jest of:
——So putting his pipe into his mouth, which he had just
lighted,——he contented himself with ordering *Trim* to read
on. He read on as follows:]

"To have the fear of God before our eyes, and, in our mutual
dealings with each other, to govern our actions by the eternal
measures of right and wrong:——The first of these will comprehend the duties of religion;——the second, those of morality, which are so inseparably connected together, that you
cannot divide these two *tables*,[13] even in imagination (tho' the
attempt is often made in practice) without breaking and mutually destroying them both.

"I said the attempt is often made, and so it is;——there
being nothing more common than to see a man who has no
sense at all of religion,——and indeed has so much honesty
as to pretend to none, who would take it as the bitterest
affront, should you but hint at a suspicion of his moral character,——or imagine he was not conscientiously just and scrupulous to the uttermost mite.

"When there is some appearance that it is so,——tho' one is
unwilling even to suspect the appearance of so amiable a
virtue as moral honesty, yet were we to look into the grounds
of it, in the present case, I am persuaded we should find little
reason to envy such a one the honour of his motive.

"Let him declaim as pompously as he chooses upon the subject, it will be found to rest upon no better foundation than
either his interest, his pride, his ease, or some such little and
changeable passion as will give us but small dependance upon
his actions in matters of great stress.

"I will illustrate this by an example.

"I know the banker I deal with, or the physician I usually
call in," [There is no need, cried Dr. *Slop,* (waking) to call in
any physician in this case] "to be neither of them men of much
religion: I hear them make a jest of it every day, and treat
all its sanctions with so much scorn, as to put the matter past

---

[13]An allusion to the tables of stone given by the Lord to Moses, who
broke them.   See Exodus, 32.15 ff.

doubt.   Well;——notwithstanding this, I put my fortune into
the hands of the one;——and what is dearer still to me, I trust
my life to the honest skill of the other.

"Now, let me examine what is my reason for this great confidence.——Why, in the first place, I believe there is no probability that either of them will employ the power I put into
their hands to my disadvantage;——I consider that honesty
serves the purposes of this life:——I know their success in the
world depends upon the fairness of their characters.——In a
word,——I'm persuaded that they cannot hurt me, without
hurting themselves more.

"But put it otherwise, namely, that interest lay, for once,
on the other side; that a case should happen, wherein the one,
without stain to his reputation, could secrete my fortune, and
leave me naked in the world;——or that the other could send
me out of it, and enjoy an estate by my death, without dishonour to himself or his art:——In this case, what hold have I
of either of them?——Religion, the strongest of all motives, is
out of the question:——Interest, the next most powerful
motive in the world, is strongly against me:——What have
I left to cast into the opposite scale to balance this temptation?
——Alas! I have nothing,——nothing but what is lighter
than a bubble——I must lay at the mercy of Honour, or
some such capricious principle.——Strait security for two of
my most valuable blessings!——my property and my life.

"As, therefore, we can have no dependence upon morality
without religion;——so, on the other hand, there is nothing
better to be expected from religion without morality; nevertheless, 'tis no prodigy to see a man whose real moral character stands very low, who yet entertains the highest notion of
himself, in the light of a religious man.

"He shall not only be covetous, revengeful, implacable,——
but even wanting·in points of common honesty; yet, inasmuch
as he talks aloud against the infidelity of the age,——is zealous
for some points of religion,——goes twice a day to church,
——attends the sacraments,——and amuses himself with a
few instrumental parts of religion,——shall cheat his con-

science into a judgment that, for this, he is a religious man,
and has discharged truly his duty to God: And you will find
that such a man, through force of this delusion, generally looks
down with spiritual pride upon every other man who has
less affectation of piety,——though, perhaps, ten times more
moral honesty than himself.

"*This likewise is a sore evil under the sun;*[14] and, I believe
there is no one mistaken principle, which, for its time, has
wrought more serious mischiefs.———For a general proof of
this,——examine the history of the *Romish* church;"——
[Well, what can you make of that? cried Dr. *Slop*]——"see
what scenes of cruelty, murders, rapines, blood-shed," [They
may thank their own obstinacy, cried Dr. *Slop*] "have all been
sanctified by a religion not strictly governed by morality.

"In how many kingdoms of the world," [Here *Trim* kept
waving his right-hand from the sermon to the extent of his
arm, returning it backwards and forwards to the conclusion
of the paragraph.]

"In how many kingdoms of the world has the crusading
sword of this misguided saint-errant spared neither age, or
merit, or sex, or condition?——and, as he fought under the
banners of a religion which set him loose from justice and
humanity, he shew'd none; mercilessly trampled upon both,
——heard neither the cries of the unfortunate, nor pitied their
distresses."

[I have been in many a battle, an' please your Honour, quoth
Trim, sighing, but never in so melancholy a one as this.——I
would not have drawn a tricker[15] in it, against these poor souls,
——to have been made a general officer.——Why? what do
you understand of the affair? said Dr. *Slop,* looking towards
Trim with something more of contempt than the Corporal's
honest heart deserved.——What do you know, friend, about
this battle you talk of?——I know, replied *Trim,* that I never
refused quarter in my life to any man who cried out for it;
——but to a woman or a child, continued *Trim,* before I would

---

[14]Paraphrase of Ecclesiastes, 5.13.

[15]Trigger.

level my musket at them, I would lose my life a thousand times.——Here's a crown for thee, *Trim,* to drink with *Obadiah* to-night, quoth my uncle *Toby,* and I'll give *Obadiah* another too.——God bless your Honour, replied *Trim,*——I had rather these poor women and children had it.——Thou art an honest fellow, quoth my uncle *Toby.*——My father nodded his head,——as much as to say,——and so he is.——

But pri'thee *Trim,* said my father, make an end,——for I see thou hast but a leaf or two left.]

Corporal *Trim* read on.

"If the testimony of past centuries in this matter is not sufficient,——consider at this instant, how the votaries of that religion are every day thinking to do service and honour to God, by actions which are a dishonour and scandal to themselves.

"To be convinced of this, go with me for a moment into the prisons of the inquisition."——[God help my poor brother *Tom.*]——"Behold *Religion,* with *Mercy* and *Justice* chained down under her feet,——there sitting ghastly upon a black tribunal, propp'd up with racks and instruments of torment. Hark!——hark! what a piteous groan!" [Here *Trim's* face turned as pale as ashes.]   "See the melancholy wretch who utter'd it,"——[Here the tears began to trickle down] "just brought forth to undergo the anguish of a mock trial, and endure the utmost pains that a studied system of cruelty has been able to invent."——[D—n them all, quoth *Trim,* his colour returning into his face as red as blood.]——"Behold this helpless victim delivered up to his tormentors,——his body so wasted with sorrow and confinement."——[Oh! 'tis my brother, cried poor *Trim* in a most passionate exclamation, dropping the sermon upon the ground, and clapping his hands together——I fear 'tis poor *Tom.*   My father's and my uncle *Toby's* hearts yearn'd with sympathy for the poor fellow's distress,——even *Slop* himself acknowledged pity for him.——Why, *Trim,* said my father, this is not a history,—— 'tis a sermon thou art reading;——pri'thee begin the sentence again.]——"Behold this helpless victim deliver'd up to his

tormentors,——his body so wasted with sorrow and confinement, you will see every nerve and muscle as it suffers.

"Observe the last movement of that horrid engine!" [I
would rather face a cannon, quoth *Trim,* stamping.]——"See
what convulsions it has thrown him into!——Consider the
nature of the posture in which he now lies stretched——what
exquisite tortures he endures by it!"——[I hope 'tis not in
Portugal.]——" 'Tis all nature can bear! Good God! see how
it keeps his weary soul hanging upon his trembling lips!" [I
would not read another line of it, quoth *Trim,* for all this
world;——I fear, an' please your Honours, all this is in *Portu-*
gal, where my poor brother *Tom* is. I tell thee, *Trim,* again,
quoth my father, 'tis not an historical account,——'tis a
description.——'Tis only a description, honest man, quoth
Slop, there's not a word of truth in it.——That's another story,
replied my father.——However, as *Trim* reads it with so much
concern,——'tis cruelty to force him to go on with it.——Give
me hold of the sermon, *Trim,*——I'll finish it for thee, and
thou mayst go. I must stay and hear it too, replied *Trim,* if
your Honour will allow me;——tho' I would not read it myself for a Colonel's pay.——Poor *Trim!* quoth my uncle
Toby. My father went on.]

"——Consider the nature of the posture in which he now
lies stretch'd,——what exquisite torture he endures by it!——
'Tis all nature can bear!——Good God! See how it keeps his
weary soul hanging upon his trembling lips,——willing to
take its leave,——but not suffered to depart!——Behold the
unhappy wretch led back to his cell!" [Then, thank God, however, quoth *Trim,* they have not killed him]——"See him
dragg'd out of it again to meet the flames, and the insults in
his last agonies, which this principle,——this principle, that
there can be religion without mercy, has prepared for him."
[Then, thank God,——he is dead, quoth *Trim,*——he is out
of his pain,——and they have done their worst at him.——O
Sirs!——Hold your peace, *Trim,* said my father, going on with
the sermon, lest *Trim* should incense Dr. *Slop,*——we shall
never have done at this rate.]

"The surest way to try the merit of any disputed notion is, to trace down the consequences such a notion has produced, and compare them with the spirit of Christianity;——'tis the short and decisive rule which our Saviour hath left us, for these and such-like cases, and it is worth a thousand arguments,——*By their fruits ye shall know them.*[16]

"I will add no further to the length of this sermon, than, by two or three short and independent rules deducible from it.

"*First,* Whenever a man talks loudly against religion,—— always suspect that it is not his reason, but his passions which have got the better of his CREED. A bad life and a good belief are disagreeable and troublesome neighbours, and where they separate, depend upon it, 'tis for no other cause but quietness sake.

"*Secondly,* When a man, thus represented, tells you in any particular instance,——That such a thing goes *against* his conscience,——always believe he means exactly the same thing, as when he tells you such a thing goes *against* his stomach; ——a present want of appetite being generally the true cause of both.

"In a word,——trust that man in nothing, who has not a CONSCIENCE in every thing.

"And, in your own case, remember this plain distinction, a mistake in which has ruined thousands,——that your conscience is not a law:——No, God and reason made the law, and have placed conscience within you to determine;——not like an *Asiatic* Cadi, according to the ebbs and flows of his own passions,——but like a *British* judge in this land of liberty and good sense, who makes no new law, but faithfully declares that law which he knows already written."

F I N I S

Thou hast read the sermon extremely well, *Trim,* quoth my father.——If he had spared his comments, replied Dr. *Slop,* he would have read it much better. I should have read it ten

[16]Matthew, 7.20.

times better, Sir, answered *Trim,* but that my heart was so full.——That was the very reason, *Trim,* replied my father, which has made thee read the sermon as well as thou hast done; and if the clergy of our church, continued my father, addressing himself to Dr. *Slop,* would take part in what they deliver, as deeply as this poor fellow has done,——as their compositions are fine; (I deny it, quoth Dr. *Slop*)—I maintain it, that the eloquence of our pulpits, with such subjects to inflame it,——would be a model for the whole world:—— But, alas! continued my father, and I own it, Sir, with sorrow, that, like *French* politicians in this respect, what they gain in the cabinet they lose in the field.——'Twere a pity, quoth my uncle, that this should be lost. I like the sermon well, replied my father,——'tis dramatic,——and there is something in that way of writing, when skilfully managed, which catches the attention.——We preach much in that way with us, said Dr. *Slop.*——I know that very well, said my father,——but in a tone and manner which disgusted Dr. *Slop,* full as much as his assent, simply, could have pleased him.——But in this, added Dr. *Slop,* a little piqued,——our sermons have greatly the advantage, that we never introduce any character into them below a patriarch or a patriarch's wife, or a martyr or a saint. ——There are some very bad characters in this, however, said my father, and I do not think the sermon a jot the worse for 'em.——But pray, quoth my uncle *Toby,*——who's can this be?——How could it get into my *Stevinus?* A man must be as great a conjurer as *Stevinus,* said my father, to resolve the second question:——The first, I think, is not so difficult;—— for unless my judgment greatly deceives me,——I know the author, for 'tis wrote, certainly, by the parson of the parish.

The similitude of the stile and manner of it, with those my father constantly had heard preach'd in his parish-church, was the ground of his conjecture,——proving it as strongly, as an argument *à priori*[1] could prove such a thing to a philosophic mind, That it was *Yorick's* and no one's else:——It was proved

---

[1]From prior information, by deductive reasoning; *A posteriori:* from subsequent information, inductive reasoning.

to be so *à posteriori,* the day after, when *Yorick* sent a servant
to my uncle *Toby's* house to enquire after it.

It seems that *Yorick,* who was inquisitive after all kinds of
knowledge, had borrowed *Stevinus* of my uncle *Toby,* and had
carelessly popp'd his sermon, as soon as he had made it, into
the middle of *Stevinus;* and, by an act of forgetfulness, to
which he was ever subject, he had sent *Stevinus* home, and his
sermon to keep him company.

Ill-fated sermon! Thou wast lost, after this recovery of
thee, a second time, dropp'd thro' an unsuspected fissure in
thy master's pocket, down into a treacherous and a tatter'd lining,——trod deep into the dirt by the left hind foot of his
Rosinante, inhumanly stepping upon thee as thou falledst;
——buried ten days in the mire,——raised up out of it by a
beggar, sold for a halfpenny to a parish-clerk,——transferred
to his parson,——lost for ever to thy own, the remainder of his
days,——nor restored to his restless MANES till this very moment, that I tell the world the story.

Can the reader believe, that this sermon of *Yorick's* was
preach'd at an assize, in the cathedral of *York,* before a thousand witnesses, ready to give oath of it, by a certain prebendary
of that church, and actually printed by him when he had
done,[2]——and within so short a space as two years and three
months after *Yorick's* death.——*Yorick,* indeed, was never better served in his life!——but it was a little hard to male-
treat him before, and plunder him after he was laid in his
grave.

However, as the gentleman who did it, was in perfect
charity with *Yorick,*——and, in conscious justice, printed but
a few copies to give away;——and that, I am told, he could
moreover have made as good a one himself, had he thought
fit,——I declare I would not have published this anecdote to

---

[2]Sterne, a prebendary of York, preached the sermon in the cathedral
at the close of the summer assizes on July 29, 1750; it was published by
him, "at the Request of the High Sheriff and Grand Jury," on August 7
of the same year. He published it yet a third time, as the last sermon
in the fourth volume of *The Sermons of Mr. Yorick,* in 1766. See the
Introduction, pp. xx, lxvi.

the world;——nor do I publish it with an intent to hurt his character and advancement in the church;——I leave that to others;——but I find myself impelled by two reasons, which I cannot withstand.

The first is, That, in doing justice, I may give rest to *Yorick's* ghost;——which, as the country people,——and some others, believe,——*still walks.*

The second reason is, That, by laying open this story to the world, I gain an opportunity of informing it,——That in case the character of parson *Yorick,* and this sample of his sermons is liked,——that there are now in the possession of the *Shandy* family, as many as will make a handsome volume, at the world's service,——and much good may they do it.

CHAP. XVIII.

OBADIAH gain'd the two crowns without dispute; for he came in jingling, with all the instruments in the green bays bag we spoke of, slung across his body, just as Corporal *Trim* went out of the room.

It is now proper, I think, quoth Dr. *Slop* (clearing up his looks) as we are in a condition to be of some service to Mrs. *Shandy,* to send up stairs to know how she goes on.

I have ordered, answered my father, the old midwife to come down to us upon the least difficulty;——for you must know, Dr. *Slop,* continued my father, with a perplexed kind of a smile upon his countenance, that by express treaty, solemnly ratified between me and my wife, you are no more than an auxiliary in this affair,——and not so much as that, ——unless the lean old mother of a midwife above stairs cannot do without you.——Women have their particular fancies, and in points of this nature, continued my father, where they bear the whole burden, and suffer so much acute pain for the advantage of our families, and the good of the species,——

they claim a right of deciding, *en Soveraines*,[1] in whose hands, and in what fashion, they chuse to undergo it.

They are in the right of it,——quoth my uncle *Toby*. But, Sir, replied Dr. *Slop,* not taking notice of my uncle *Toby's* opinion, but turning to my father,——they had better govern in other points;——and a father of a family, who wished its perpetuity, in my opinion, had better exchange this prerogative with them, and give up some other rights in lieu of it.—— I know not, quoth my father, answering a little too testily, to be quite dispassionate in what he said,——I know not, quoth he, what we have left to give up, in lieu of who shall bring our children into the world,——unless that,——of who shall beget them.———One would almost give up any thing, replied Dr. *Slop.*——I beg your pardon,——answered my uncle *Toby*. ——Sir, replied Dr. *Slop,* it would astonish you to know what Improvements we have made of late years in all branches of obstetrical knowledge, but particularly in that one single point of the safe and expeditious extraction of the *fœtus,*—— which has received such lights, that, for my part (holding up his hands) I declare I wonder how the world has——I wish, quoth my uncle *Toby,* you had seen what prodigious armies we had in *Flanders*.

CHAP. XIX.

I Have dropp'd the curtain over this scene for a minute,—— to remind you of one thing,——and to inform you of another.

What I have to inform you, comes, I own, a little out of its due course;——for it should have been told a hundred and fifty pages ago, but that I foresaw then 'twould come in pat hereafter, and be of more advantage here than elsewhere.—— Writers had need look before them to keep up the spirit and connection of what they have in hand.

When these two things are done,——the curtain shall be

[1]As sovereigns.

drawn up again, and my uncle *Toby,* my father, and Dr. *Slop* shall go on with their discourse, without any more interruption.

First, then, the matter which I have to remind you of, is this;——that from the specimens of singularity in my father's notions in the point of Christian-names, and that other point previous thereto,——you was led, I think, into an opinion, (and I am sure I said as much) that my father was a gentleman altogether as odd and whimsical in fifty other opinions. In truth, there was not a stage in the life of man, from the very first act of his begetting,——down to the lean and slipper'd pantaloon in his second childishness, but he had some favourite notion to himself, springing out of it, as sceptical, and as far out of the high-way of thinking, as these two which have been explained.

——Mr. *Shandy,* my father, Sir, would see nothing in the light in which others placed it;——he placed things in his own light;——he would weigh nothing in common scales;——no, ——he was too refined a researcher to lay open to so gross an imposition.——To come at the exact weight of things in the scientific steel-yard, the fulcrum, he would say, should be almost invisible, to avoid all friction from popular tenets;—— without this the minutiæ of philosophy, which should always turn the balance, will have no weight at all.——Knowledge, like matter, he would affirm, was divisible *in infinitum;*[1]—— that the grains and scruples were as much a part of it, as the gravitation of the whole world.——In a word, he would say, error was error,——no matter where it fell,——whether in a fraction,——or a pound,——'twas alike fatal to truth, and she was kept down at the bottom of her well as inevitably by a mistake in the dust of a butterfly's wing,——as in the disk of the sun, the moon, and all the stars of heaven put together.

He would often lament that it was for want of considering this properly, and of applying it skilfully to civil matters, as well as to speculative truths, that so many things in this world were out of joint;——that the political arch was giving way;

[1]Into infinite parts.

——and that the very foundations of our excellent constitution in church and state, were so sapp'd as estimators had
reported.

You cry out, he would say, we are a ruined, undone people.
——Why? he would ask, making use of the sorites or syllogism
of *Zeno* and *Chrysippus,*[2] without knowing it belonged to
them.——Why? why are we a ruined people?——Because we
are corrupted.——Whence is it, dear Sir, that we are corrupted?——Because we are needy;——our poverty, and not
our wills, consent.——And wherefore, he would add, are we
needy?——From the neglect, he would answer, of our pence
and our halfpence:——Our bank-notes, Sir, our guineas,——
nay our shillings, take care of themselves.

'Tis the same, he would say, throughout the whole circle of
the sciences;——the great, the established points of them, are
not to be broke in upon.——The laws of nature will defend
themselves;——but error——(he would add, looking earnestly
at my mother)——error, Sir, creeps in thro' the minute holes,
and small crevices, which human nature leaves unguarded.

This turn of thinking in my father, is what I had to remind
you of:——The point you are to be informed of, and which
I have reserved for this place, is as follows:

Amongst the many and excellent reasons, with which my
father had urged my mother to accept of Dr. *Slop*'s assistance
preferably to that of the old woman,——there was one of a
very singular nature; which, when he had done arguing the
matter with her as a Christian, and came to argue it over
again with her as a philosopher, he had put his whole strength
to, depending indeed upon it as his sheet .anchor.——It failed
him; tho' from no defect in the argument itself; but that, do

---

[2]Zeno of Citium (c. 360–c. 264 B.C.) was the founder of the Stoic
school of philosophers; Chrysippus (c. 280–c. 206 B.C.), possibly a student of Zeno and next to him the most eminent member of the sect, was
famous for his dialectic and logical skill. The latter attempted to solve
a puzzling sophism called *sorites,* a chain of syllogisms in which the conclusion of each becomes the premise of the next, and in which the reasoner is seduced, by accepting gradual changes from a true proposition,
into drawing a false inference.

what he could, he was not able for his soul to make her comprehend the drift of it.——Cursed luck!——said he to himself,
one afternoon, as he walk'd out of the room, after he had been
stating it for an hour and a half to her, to no manner of purpose;——cursed luck! said he, biting his lip as he shut the
door,——for a man to be master of one of the finest chains
of reasoning in nature,——and have a wife at the same time
with such a head-piece, that he cannot hang up a single inference within side of it, to save his soul from destruction.

This argument, tho' it was intirely lost upon my mother,
——had more weight with him, than all his other arguments
joined together:——I will therefore endeavour to do it justice,
——and set it forth with all the perspicuity I am master of.

My father set out upon the strength of these two following
axioms:

First, That an ounce of a man's own wit, was worth a tun
of other peoples; and,

Secondly, (Which, by the bye, was the ground-work of the
first axiom,——tho' it comes last) That every man's wit must
come from every man's own soul,——and no other body's.

Now, as it was plain to my father, that all souls were by
nature equal,——and that the great difference between the
most acute and the most obtuse understanding,——was from
no original sharpness or bluntness of one thinking substance
above or below another,——but arose merely from the lucky
or unlucky organization of the body, in that part where the
soul principally took up her residence,——he had made it
the subject of his enquiry to find out the identical place.

Now, from the best accounts he had been able to get of this
matter, he was satisfied it could not be where *Des Cartes*[3] had
fixed it, upon the top of the *pineal* gland of the brain; which,
as he philosophised, formed a cushion for her about the size
of a marrow pea; tho' to speak the truth, as so many nerves

---

[3] René Descartes (1596–1650), a French philosopher, reasoned that because the pineal gland is located midway in the brain, at the supposed
meeting-place of the mind and the vital spirits, it must be the seat of the
soul.

did terminate all in that one place,——'twas no bad conjecture;——and my father had certainly fallen with that great
philosopher plumb into the centre of the mistake, had it not
been for my uncle *Toby,* who rescued him out of it, by a story
he told him of a *Walloon* officer at the battle of *Landen,* who
had one part of his brain shot away by a musket-ball,——and
another part of it taken out after by a *French* surgeon; and,
after all, recovered, and did his duty very well without it.

If death, said my father, reasoning with himself, is nothing
but the separation of the soul from the body;——and if it is
true that people can walk about and do their business without
brains,——then certes the soul does not inhabit there.
Q. E. D.[4]

As for that certain, very thin, subtle, and very fragrant juice
which *Coglionissimo Borri,* the great *Milaneze* physician,[5]
affirms, in a letter to *Bartholine,* to have discovered in the
cellulæ of the occipital parts of the cerebellum, and which he
likewise affirms to be the principal seat of the reasonable soul
(for, you must know, in these latter and more enlightened
ages, there are two souls in every man living,——the one,
according to the great *Metheglingius,* being called the *Animus,*[6] the other the *Anima*);——as for this opinion, I say, of
Borri,——my father could never subscribe to it by any means;
the very idea of so noble, so refined, so immaterial, and so
exalted a being as the *Anima,* or even the *Animus,* taking up
her residence, and sitting dabbling, like a tad-pole, all day

---

[4]*Quod erat demonstrandum:* which was to be demonstrated; formula
used in geometrical proofs.

[5]Joseph Francis Borri (1627–1695), a famous chemist, empiric, and
heretic. The letter referred to is *De Ortu Cerebri et Usu Medico,* written, to Thomas Bartholine (1616–1680), an eminent Danish physician.
"Coglionissimo" is Sterne's formation on *coglione,* meaning, with an obscene implication, "greatest dolt," "complete fool."

[6]The rational soul or spiritual principle of life (masculine); *anima:* the
animal spirit or vital principle of life (feminine). "The great *Metheglingius"* I have been unable to identify; one is tempted to suggest that
Sterne may have coined the name on *metheglin* (a beverage of fermented
honey and water, mead) by way of intimating that such a theory must
have been conceived when the philosopher was in his cups.

long, both summer and winter, in a puddle,——or in a liquid of any kind, how thick or thin soever, he would say, shock'd his imagination; he would scarce give the doctrine a hearing.

What, therefore, seem'd the least liable to objections of any, was, that the chief sensorium, or head-quarters of the soul, and to which place all intelligences were referred, and from whence all her mandates were issued,——was in, or near, the cerebellum,——or rather some-where about the *medulla oblongata,* wherein it was generally agreed by *Dutch* anatomists, that all the minute nerves from all the organs of the seven senses concentered, like streets and winding alleys, into a square.

So far there was nothing singular in my father's opinion, ——he had the best of philosophers, of all ages and climates, to go along with him.——But here he took a road of his own, setting up another *Shandean* hypothesis upon these corner-stones they had laid for him;——and which said hypothesis equally stood its ground; whether the subtilty and fineness of the soul depended upon the temperature and clearness of the said liquor, or of the finer net-work and texture in the cerebellum itself; which opinion he favoured.

He maintained, that next to the due care to be taken in the act of propagation of each individual, which required all the thought in the world, as it laid the foundation of this incomprehensible contexture in which wit, memory, fancy, eloquence, and what is usually meant by the name of good natural parts, do consist;——that next to this and his Christian-name, which were the two original and most efficacious causes of all; ——that the third cause, or rather what logicians call the *Causa sine quâ non,*[7] and without which all that was done was of no manner of significance,——was the preservation of this delicate and fine-spun web, from the havock which was generally made in it by the violent compression and crush which the head was made to undergo, by the nonsensical method of bringing us into the world by that part foremost.

---

[7] Cause without which he would have had no case; indispensable argument.

——This requires explanation.

My father, who dipp'd into all kinds of books, upon looking into *Lithopædus Senonesis de Partu difficili**, published by *Adrianus Smelvgot,* had found out, That the lax and pliable state of a child's head in parturition, the bones of the cranium having no sutures at that time, was such,——that by force of the woman's efforts, which, in strong labour-pains, was equal, upon an average, to a weight of 470 pounds averdupoise acting perpendicularly upon it;——it so happened that, in 49 instances out of 50, the said head was compressed and moulded into the shape of an oblong conical piece of dough, such as a pastry-cook generally rolls up in order to make a pye of.—— Good God! cried my father, what havock and destruction must this make in the infinitely fine and tender texture of the cerebellum!——Or if there is such a juice as *Borri* pretends,——is it not enough to make the clearest liquor in the world both feculent and mothery?

But how great was his apprehension, when he further understood, that this force, acting upon the very vertex of the head, not only injured the brain itself or cerebrum,——but that it

*The author is here twice mistaken;——for *Lithopædus* should be wrote thus, *Lithopædii Senonensis Icon.* The second mistake is, that this *Lithopædus* is not an author, but a drawing of a petrified child. The account of this, published by *Albosius,* 1580, may be seen at the end of *Cordæus's* works in *Spachius.* Mr. *Tristram Shandy* has been led into this error, either from seeing *Lithopædus's* name of late in a catalogue of learned writers in Dr. ——, or by mistaking *Lithopædus* for *Trinecavellius,*——from the too great similitude of the names. [Sterne's note. This nonsense is a burlesque of an attack made by Dr. Burton (Dr. Slop) on Dr. William Smellie (Adrianus Smelvgot), a noted obstetrician of Glasgow, accusing him of having mistaken, in his *Treatise on the Theory and Practice of Midwifery,* the title of a print of a drawing of a petrified child for the name of an author: "The seventeenth Author . . . is *Lithopedus Senonensis,* which instead of being an Author, is only the Drawing of a petrefied Child, when taken from its Mother, after she was opened; and this is evident from the Title, *Lithopædii Senonensis Icon,* which, with the Explanation, is contained in one single Page only. The Account of it, as published by *Albosius,* in 1582, in Octavo, may be seen at the End of *Cordæus's* Works in *Spachius,* whence again, I think, it is evident you must have taken your Extracts from some bad Copier."—*Letter to William Smellie, M.D.* (London, 1753), p. 21. *De Partu difficili: Of Difficult Parturition.*]

necessarily squeez'd and propell'd the cerebrum towards the cerebellum, which was the immediate seat of the understanding.——Angels and Ministers of grace defend us! cried my father,——can any soul withstand this shock?——No wonder the intellectual web is so rent and tatter'd as we see it; and that so many of our best heads are no better than a puzzled skein of silk,——all perplexity,——all confusion within side.

But when my father read on, and was let into the secret, that when a child was turn'd topsy-turvy, which was easy for an operator to do, and was extracted by the feet;——that instead of the cerebrum being propell'd towards the cerebellum, the cerebellum, on the contrary, was propell'd simply towards the cerebrum where it could do no manner of hurt:——By heavens! cried he, the world is in a conspiracy to drive out what little wit God has given us,——and the professors of the obstetric art are listed into the same conspiracy.——What is it to me which end of my son comes foremost into the world, provided all goes right after, and his cerebellum escapes uncrushed?

It is the nature of an hypothesis, when once a man has conceived it, that it assimilates every thing to itself as proper nourishment; and, from the first moment of your begetting it, it generally grows the stronger by every thing you see, hear, read, or understand. This is of great use.

When my father was gone with this about a month, there was scarce a phænomenon of stupidity or of genius, which he could not readily solve by it;——it accounted for the eldest son being the greatest blockhead in the family.——Poor devil, he would say,——he made way for the capacity of his younger brothers.——It unriddled the observations of drivellers and monstrous heads,——shewing, *à priori,* it could not be otherwise,——unless ✳ ✳ ✳ ✳ I don't know what. It wonderfully explain'd and accounted for the acumen of the *Asiatic* genius, and that sprightlier turn, and a more penetrating intuition of minds, in warmer climates; not from the loose and common-place solution of a clearer sky, and a more perpetual sunshine, *&c.*——which, for aught he knew, might as well rarify

and dilute the faculties of the soul into nothing, by one extreme,——as they are condensed in colder climates by the
other;——but he traced the affair up to its spring-head;——
shew'd that, in warmer climates, nature had laid a lighter tax
upon the fairest parts of the creation;——their pleasures more;
——the necessity of their pains less, insomuch that the pressure and resistance upon the vertex was so slight, that the
whole organization of the cerebellum was preserved;——nay,
he did not believe, in natural births, that so much as a single
thread of the net-work was broke or displaced,——so that the
soul might just act as she liked.

When my father had got so far,——what a blaze of light
did the accounts of the *Cæsarian* section,[8] and of the towering
geniuses who had come safe into the world by it, cast upon
this hypothesis? Here you see, he would say, there was no
injury done to the sensorium;——no pressure of the head
against the pelvis;——no propulsion of the cerebrum towards
the cerebellum, either by the *os pubis*[9] on this side, or the *os
coxcygis* on that;——and, pray, what were the happy consequences? Why, Sir, your *Julius Cæsar,* who gave the operation a name;——and your *Hermes Trismegistus,*[10] who was
born so before ever the operation had a name;——your *Scipio
Africanus;* your *Manlius Torquatus;* our *Edward* the Sixth,
——who, had he lived, would have done the same honour to
the hypothesis:——These, and many more, who figur'd high

---

[8]An operation in which a child is delivered by an incision of the abdomen and uterus, so called from a legend of its employment at the birth
of Julius Caesar. But although this procedure has been practiced on a
dead mother since early times, the first authenticated instance of its
being performed on a living woman occurred about 1500.

[9]See p. 79, n. 1. *Os coxcygis: coccyx,* the last four bones of the spinal
column.

[10]See p. 279, n. 2. According to Pliny, who may have been Sterne's
source here, Scipio Africanus Major (c. 234–183 B.C.) and "Manilius . . .
who entered Carthage with his army" were born in this manner (*Naturalis Historia,* 7.7[9]. Mr. Tristram Shandy may again have been led into
error "from the too great similitude of the names." The death of Jane
Seymour of puerperal fever twelve days after she had given birth to
Edward gave rise to the probably baseless story that her life had been
deliberately sacrificed by the performance of a Caesarean section.

in the annals of fame,——all came *side-way,* Sir, into the world.

This incision of the *abdomen* and *uterus,* ran for six weeks together in my father's head;——he had read, and was satisfied, that wounds in the *epigastrium,* and those in the *matrix,* were not mortal;——so that the belly of the mother might be opened extremely well to give a passage to the child.——He mentioned the thing one afternoon to my mother,——merely as a matter of fact;——but seeing her turn as pale as ashes at the very mention of it,[11] as much as the operation flattered his hopes,——he thought it as well to say no more of it,——contenting himself with admiring——what he thought was to no purpose to propose.

This was my father Mr. *Shandy's* hypothesis; concerning which I have only to add, that my brother *Bobby* did as great honour to it (whatever he did to the family) as any one of the great heroes we spoke of:——For happening not only to be christen'd, as I told you, but to be born too, when my father was at *Epsom,*——being moreover my mother's *first* child,—— coming into the world with his head *foremost,*——and turning out afterwards a lad of wonderful slow parts,——my father spelt all these together into his opinion; and as he had failed at one end,——he was determined to try the other.

This was not to be expected from one of the sisterhood, who are not easily to be put out of their way,——and was therefore one of my father's great reasons in favour of a man of science, whom he could better deal with.

Of all men in the world, Dr. *Slop* was the fittest for my father's purpose;——for though his new-invented forceps was the armour he had proved, and what he maintained, to be the safest instrument of deliverance,——yet, it seems, he had scattered a word or two in his book, in favour of the very thing which ran in my father's fancy;——tho' not with a view to the

---

[11]Anaesthetics were not used in surgical operations until 1846, and until about the same time the recorded mortality of mothers in Caesarean sections was over fifty per cent.

soul's good in extracting by the feet, as was my father's sys-tem,——but for reasons merely obstetrical.

This will account for the coalition betwixt my father and Dr. *Slop,* in the ensuing discourse, which went a little hard against my uncle *Toby.*——In what manner a plain man, with nothing but common sense, could bear up against two such allies in science,——is hard to conceive.——You may conjec-ture upon it, if you please,——and whilst your imagination is in motion, you may encourage it to go on, and discover by what causes and effects in nature it could come to pass, that my uncle *Toby* got his modesty by the wound he received upon his groin.——You may raise a system to account for the loss of my nose by marriage articles,——and shew the world how it could happen, that I should have the misfortune to be called TRISTRAM, in opposition to my father's hypothesis, and the wish of the whole family, God-fathers and God-mothers not excepted.——These, with fifty other points left yet un-raveled, you may endeavour to solve if you have time;——but I tell you before-hand it will be in vain, for not the sage *Alquife,* the magician in Don *Belianis* of *Greece,*[12] nor the no less famous *Urganda,* the sorceress his wife, (were they alive) could pretend to come within a league of the truth.

The reader will be content to wait for a full explanation of these matters till the next year,——when a series of things will be laid open which he little expects.

END of the SECOND VOLUME.

---

[12] A famous 16th C. Spanish romance of chivalry.

THE
LIFE
AND
OPINIONS
OF
TRISTRAM SHANDY,
GENTLEMAN.

Multitudinis imperitæ non formido judicia; meis
tamen, rogo, parcant opusculis —— in quibus
fuit propositi semper, a jocis ad seria, a seriis
vicissim ad jocos transire.

JOAN. SARESBERIENSIS,
Episcopus Lugdun.

VOL. III.

LONDON:

Printed for R. and J. DODSLEY in *Pall-Mall.*
M.DCC.LXI.

Facsimile of the title page to the first edition of Volumes III and IV.
The motto is from the *Policraticus* of John of Salisbury (c.1115–1180), a
noted English churchman and scholar who became bishop, not of Leiden,
but of Chartres. Sterne has elaborated the latter part of the sentence,
[over]

which he probably found quoted in the Preface to Ozell's translation of Rabelais (edition of 1694, p. clv), to read as follows: "I do not fear the opinions of the ignorant crowd; nevertheless I pray that they spare my little work, in which it has ever been my purpose to pass from the gay to the serious and from the serious again to the gay." The sentence originally ended: "... *in quibus fuit propositi semper à nugis ad bona transire seria*" ("... in which it has ever been my purpose to pass from jests to worthy seriousness").

VOLUME III.

CHAP. I.

——" *I* Wish, Dr. *Slop*," quoth my uncle *Toby* (repeating his wish for Dr. *Slop* a second time, and with a degree of more zeal and earnestness in his manner of wishing, than he had wished it at first*)——"*I wish*, Dr. *Slop*," quoth my uncle *Toby*, "*you had seen what prodigious armies we had in Flanders.*"

My uncle *Toby*'s wish did Dr. *Slop* a disservice which his heart never intended any man,——Sir, it confounded him—— and thereby putting his ideas first into confusion, and then to flight, he could not rally them again for the soul of him.

In all disputes,——male or female,——whether for honour, for profit or for love,——it makes no difference in the case; ——nothing is more dangerous, madam, than a wish coming sideways in this unexpected manner upon a man: the safest way in general to take off the force of the wish, is, for the party wished at, instantly to get up upon his legs——and wish the *wisher* something in return, of pretty near the same value, ——so balancing the account upon the spot, you stand as you were——nay sometimes gain the advantage of the attack by it.

This will be fully illustrated to the world in my chapter of wishes.——

Dr. *Slop* did not understand the nature of this defence;—— he was puzzled with it, and it put an entire stop to the dispute for four minutes and half;——five had been fatal to it: ——my father saw the danger——the dispute was one of the most interesting disputes in the world, "Whether the child of his prayers and endeavours should be born without a head or

---

*Vid. Vol. II. p. 159.   [Sterne's note; the reference is to p. 144 in the present edition.]

with one:"——he waited to the last moment to allow Dr. *Slop,* in whose behalf the wish was made, his right of returning it; but perceiving, I say, that he was confounded, and continued looking with that perplexed vacuity of eye which puzzled souls generally stare with,——first in my uncle *Toby*'s face——then in his——then up——then down——then east ——east and by east, and so on,——coasting it along by the plinth of the wainscot till he had got to the opposite point of the compass,——and that he had actually begun to count the brass nails upon the arm of his chair——my father thought there was no time to be lost with my uncle *Toby,* so took up the discourse as follows.

CHAP. II.

"——WHAT prodigious armies you had in *Flanders!*"—— Brother *Toby,* replied my father, taking his wig from off his head with his right hand, and with his *left* pulling out a striped *India* handkerchief from his right coat pocket, in order to rub his head, as he argued the point with my uncle *Toby.*——

——Now, in this I think my father was much to blame; and I will give you my reasons for it.

Matters of no more seeming consequence in themselves than, *"Whether my father should have taken off his wig with his right hand or with his left,"*——have divided the greatest kingdoms, and made the crowns of the monarchs who governed them, to totter upon their heads.——But need I tell you, Sir, that the circumstances with which every thing in this world is begirt, give every thing in this world its size and shape;——and by tightening it, or relaxing it, this way or that, make the thing to be, what it is——great——little——good ——bad——indifferent or not indifferent, just as the case happens.

As my father's *India* handkerchief was in his right coat pocket, he should by no means have suffered his right hand to have got engaged: on the contrary, instead of taking off his wig with it, as he did, he ought to have committed that entirely to the left; and then, when the natural exigency my father was under of rubbing his head, call'd out for his handkerchief, he would have had nothing in the world to have done, but to have put his right hand into his right coat pocket and taken it out;——which he might have done without any violence, or the least ungraceful twist in any one tendon or muscle of his whole body.

In this case, (unless indeed, my father had been resolved to make a fool of himself by holding the wig stiff in his left hand ——or by making some nonsensical angle or other at his elbow joint, or arm-pit)——his whole attitude had been easy—— natural——unforced: *Reynolds*[1] himself, as great and gracefully as he paints, might have painted him as he sat.

Now, as my father managed this matter,——consider what a devil of a figure my father made of himself.

——In the latter end of Queen *Anne*'s reign, and in the beginning of the reign of King *George* the first——*"Coat pockets were cut very low down in the skirt."*——I need say no more ——the father of mischief, had he been hammering at it a month, could not have contrived a worse fashion for one in my father's situation.

CHAP. III.

IT was not an easy matter in any king's reign, (unless you were as lean a subject as myself) to have forced your hand diagonally, quite across your whole body, so as to gain the bottom of your opposite coat-pocket.——In the year, one thousand seven hundred and eighteen, when this happened, it was extremely difficult; so that when my uncle *Toby* discovered the

---

[1] Sir Joshua Reynolds (1723–1792), the English portrait-painter, had painted during March and April of 1760 the portrait of Sterne which is reproduced as the frontispiece to this volume; he was to paint another in 1764 and a third (which, because of Sterne's illness, remained unfinished) in 1768.

transverse zig-zaggery of my father's approaches towards it, it instantly brought into his mind those he had done duty in, before the gate of St. *Nicholas;*——the idea of which drew off his attention so entirely from the subject in debate, that he had got his right hand to the bell to ring up *Trim,* to go and fetch his map of *Namur,* and his compasses and sector along with it, to measure the returning angles of the traverses of that attack,——but particularly of that one, where he received his wound upon his groin.

My father knit his brows, and as he knit them, all the blood in his body seemed to rush up into his face——my uncle *Toby* dismounted immediately.

——I did not apprehend your uncle *Toby* was o' horse-back.——

CHAP. IV.

A Man's body and his mind, with the utmost reverence to both I speak it, are exactly like a jerkin, and a jerkin's lining;——rumple the one——you rumple the other. There is one certain exception however in this case, and that is, when you are so fortunate a fellow, as to have had your jerkin made of a gum-taffeta, and the body-lining to it, of a sarcenet or thin persian.

Zeno,[1] *Cleanthes, Diogenes Babylonius, Dyonisius Heracleotes, Antipater, Panætius* and *Possidonius* amongst the

---

[1]Half burlesque, half serious is this catalogue of eminent men, all of whom were Stoics by profession or in deed. Zeno (see p. 146, n. 2) founded, about 308 B.C., the sect of Stoics, who maintain that men should be free from passion, unmoved by joy or grief, and resigned without complaint to unavoidable necessity. Cleanthes (c. 301–c. 220 B.C.) was a Stoic whose power of patient endurance earned him the epithet "the Ass," but who was so greatly esteemed for his high moral qualities that on the death of Zeno he became the leader of the school. Diogenes the Babylonian (fl. 155 B.C.), a philosopher of great reputation, was at one time head of the Stoic school in Seleucia; Seneca relates (*De Ira,* 3.38) that when, while he was discoursing on anger, an insolent young fellow spat in his face, he bore the affront patiently, saying, "I am not angry; but yet I doubt whether I ought not to be angry." Dionysius of Heraclea (fl. 3rd C., B.C.) was a Stoic, praised for his moderation, until the pains of disease led him to join the Eleatics. Antipater of Tarsus (fl. 2nd C., B.C.)

Greeks;——*Cato* and *Varro* and *Seneca* amongst the *Romans;*
——*Pantenus* and *Clemens Alexandrinus* and *Montaigne*
amongst the Christians; and a score and a half of good honest,
unthinking, *Shandean* people as ever lived, whose names I
can't recollect,——all pretended that their jerkins were made
after this fashion,——you might have rumpled and crumpled,
and doubled and creased, and fretted and fridged the outsides
of them all to pieces;——in short, you might have played the
very devil with them, and at the same time, not one of the
insides of 'em would have been one button the worse, for all
you had done to them.

I believe in my conscience that mine is made up somewhat
after this sort:——for never poor jerkin has been tickled off, at
such a rate as it has been these last nine months together,[2]

---

was the successor of Diogenes the Babylonian as leader of the Stoics.
Panætius (c. 185–c. 110 B.C.), who had studied under Diogenes the
Babylonian, became head of the Stoic school in Athens and wrote important works on ethics. Posidonius of Apamea (c. 130–50 B.C.), a
Stoic philosopher, studied under Panætius and became the most learned
man of his time. Marcus Porcius Cato Uticensis (95–46 B.C.), the Roman
patriot, was a Stoic philosopher. Marcus Terentius Varro (116–27 B.C.),
a learned Roman scholar and man of letters, was a "stoicizing Platonist,"
erroneously supposed to have been a professed Stoic. Lucius Annæus
Seneca (c. 3 B.C.–65 A.D.) was a celebrated Roman Stoic and statesman.
Pantænus (fl. 200), head of the catechetical school at Alexandria, was
originally a Stoic. Clemens Alexandrinus (fl. 200), Greek Father of the
Church, was an eclectic philosopher who adopted the moral doctrine of
the Stoics and regarded Christianity as the revelation of perfect philosophical truth. Montaigne (see p. 7, n. 1), who was inclined to scepti-
cism and to musing on the vanity of human life, warned his reader, in
the Preface to his *Essays:* "I have had no regard in [publishing my
book], either to thy service, or my own glory . . . Had I been to court
the favour of the public, I should have adorned myself with borrowed
beauties: but I am desirous to appear in my plain, natural, ordinary dress,
without study or artifice . . . Thus, Reader, I am myself the subject of
my own book; a subject too vain and frivolous to take up even thy spare
time. Adieu therefore."

[2] On May 22, 1760, Sterne had published two volumes of his sermons
under the title *The Sermons of Mr. Yorick.* The appearance of sermons
under the name of a professional jester (whether Sterne's or Shakespeare's) aroused indignation among many readers and reviewers, the
most violently abusive of whom was the critic for the *Monthly Review*
to whom Sterne refers in the following paragraph. See the Introduction, pp. xxix–xxxi.

——and yet I declare the lining to it,——as far as I am a judge of the matter, it is not a three-penny piece the worse;—— pell mell, helter skelter, ding dong, cut and thrust, back stroke and fore stroke, side way and long way, have they been trimming it for me:——had there been the least gumminess in my lining,——by heaven! it had all of it long ago been fray'd and fretted to a thread.

——You Messrs. the monthly Reviewers!——how could you cut and slash my jerkin as you did?——how did you know, but you would cut my lining too?

Heartily and from my soul, to the protection of that Being who will injure none of us, do I recommend you and your affairs,——so God bless you;——only next month, if any one of you should gnash his teeth, and storm and rage at me, as some of you did last MAY, (in which I remember the weather was very hot)——don't be exasperated, if I pass it by again with good temper,——being determined as long as I live or write (which in my case means the same thing) never to give the honest gentleman a worse word or a worse wish, than my uncle *Toby* gave the fly which buzz'd about his nose all *dinner time,*——"Go,——go poor devil," quoth he, "——get thee gone,——why should I hurt thee?   This world is surely wide enough to hold both thee and me."

CHAP. V.

ANY man, madam, reasoning upwards, and observing the prodigious suffusion of blood in my father's countenance, ——by means of which, (as all the blood in his body seemed to rush up into his face, as I told you) he must have redden'd, pictorically and scientintically speaking, six whole tints and a half, if not a full octave above his natural colour:——any man, madam, but my uncle *Toby,* who had observed this, together with the violent knitting of my father's brows, and the extravagant contortion of his body during the whole affair,——would have concluded my father in a rage; and taking that for

granted,——had he been a lover of such kind of concord as
arises from two such instruments being put into exact tune,
——he would instantly have skrew'd up his, to the same pitch;
——and then the devil and all had broke loose——the whole
piece, madam, must have been played off like the sixth of
Avison Scarlatti[1]——*con furia*,——like mad.——Grant me patience!——What has *con furia*,——*con strepito*,[2]——or any
other hurlyburly word whatever to do with harmony?

Any man, I say, madam, but my uncle *Toby,* the benignity
of whose heart interpreted every motion of the body in the
kindest sense the motion would admit of, would have concluded my father angry and blamed him too. My uncle *Toby*
blamed nothing but the taylor who cut the pocket-hole;——
so sitting still, till my father had got his handkerchief out of
it, and looking all the time up in his face with inexpressible
good will——my father at length went on as follows.

CHAP. VI.

——"WHAT prodigious armies you had in *Flanders!*"
——Brother *Toby,* quoth my father, I do believe
thee to be as honest a man, and with as good and as upright a
heart as ever God created;——nor is it thy fault, if all the children which have been, may, can, shall, will or ought to be begotten, come with their heads foremost into the world:——but
believe me, dear *Toby,* the accidents which unavoidably way-
lay them, not only in the article of our begetting 'em,——
though these in my opinion, are well worth considering,——

[1]Apparently a misprint for "Avison's Scarlatti." The reference is to
the second movement of the sixth concerto in the collection of *Twelve
Concerto's in Seven Parts for Four Violins, One Alto Viola, a Violincello,
and a Thorough Bass, Done from Two Books of Lessons for the Harpsichord Composed by Sig. Domenico Scarlatti. . . . by C[harles] Avison*
(London, 1744). Scarlatti (1685–1757) was an Italian harpsichord player
and composer of great excellence; Avison (c. 1710–1770) was an English
composer and writer on music with whose best-known work, *An Essay
on Musical Expression,* Sterne was probably familiar.
[2]With great noise.

but the dangers and difficulties our children are beset with, after they are got forth into the world, are enow,——little need is there to expose them to unnecessary ones in their passage to it.——Are these dangers, quoth my uncle *Toby,* laying his hand upon my father's knee, and looking up seriously in his face for an answer,——are these dangers greater now o' days, brother, than in times past?   Brother *Toby,* answered my father, if a child was but fairly begot, and born alive, and healthy, and the mother did well after it,——our forefathers never looked further.——My uncle *Toby* instantly withdrew his hand from off my father's knee, reclined his body gently back in his chair, raised his head till he could just see the cornish[1] of the room, and then directing the buccinatory muscles along his cheeks, and the orbicular muscles around his lips to do their duty——he whistled *Lillabullero.*

CHAP. VII.

WHILST my uncle *Toby* was whistling Lillabullero to my father,——Dr. *Slop* was stamping, and cursing and damning at *Obadiah* at a most dreadful rate;——it would have done your heart good, and cured you, Sir, for ever, of the vile sin of swearing to have heard him.——I am determined therefore to relate the whole affair to you.

When Dr. *Slop's* maid delivered the green bays bag, with her master's instruments in it, to *Obadiah,* she very sensibly exhorted him to put his head and one arm through the strings, and ride with it slung across his body: so undoing the bow-knot, to lengthen the strings for him, without any more ado, she helped him on with it.   However, as this, in some measure, unguarded the mouth of the bag, lest any thing should bolt out in galloping back at the speed *Obadiah* threatened, they consulted to take it off again; and in the great care and caution of their hearts, they had taken the two strings and tied them close (pursing up the mouth of the bag first) with

---

[1]Cornice.

half a dozen hard knots, each of which, *Obadiah,* to make all safe, had twitched and drawn together with all the strength of his body.

This answered all that *Obadiah* and the maid intended; but was no remedy against some evils which neither he or she foresaw.   The instruments, it seems, as tight as the bag was tied above, had so much room to play in it, towards the bottom, (the shape of the bag being conical) that *Obadiah* could not make a trot of it, but with such a terrible jingle, what with the *tire-tête, forceps* and *squirt,* as would have been enough, had *Hymen*[1] been taking a jaunt that way, to have frightened him out of the country; but when *Obadiah* accelerated this motion, and from a plain trot assayed to prick his coach-horse into a full gallop——by heaven! Sir,——the jingle was incredible.

As *Obadiah* had a wife and three children——the turpitude of fornication, and the many other political ill consequences of this jingling, never once entered his brain,——he had however his objection, which came home to himself, and weighed with him, as it has oft-times done with the greatest patriots.——*"The poor fellow, Sir, was not able to hear himself whistle."*

CHAP. VIII.

AS *Obadiah* loved wind musick preferably to all the instrumental musick he carried with him,——he very considerately set his imagination to work, to contrive and to invent by what means he should put himself in a condition of enjoying it.

In all distresses (except musical) where small cords are wanted,——nothing is so apt to enter a man's head, as his hatband:——the philosophy of this is so near the surface——I scorn to enter into it.

As *Obadiah's* was a mix'd case,——mark, Sirs,——I say, a

---

[1]Greek god of marriage.

mix'd case; for it was obstetrical,——*scrip*-tical, squirtical,
papistical,——and as far as the coach-horse was concerned in
it,——caball-istical[1]——and only partly musical;——*Obadiah*
made no scruple of availing himself of the first expedient which
offered;——so taking hold of the bag and instruments, and
gripeing them hard together with one hand, and with the finger and thumb of the other, putting the end of the hat-band
betwixt his teeth, and then slipping his hand down to the middle of it,——he tied and cross-tied them all fast together from
one end to the other (as you would cord a trunk) with such
a multiplicity of round-abouts and intricate cross turns, with a
hard knot at every intersection or point where the strings
met,——that Dr. *Slop* must have had three fifths of *Job*'s
patience at least to have unloosed them.——I think in my
conscience, that had NATURE been in one of her nimble moods,
and in humour for such a contest——and she and Dr. *Slop*
both fairly started together——there is no man living who had
seen the bag with all that *Obadiah* had done to it,——and
known likewise, the great speed the goddess can make when
she thinks proper, who would have had the least doubt remaining in his mind——which of the two would have carried
off the prize.   My mother, madam, had been delivered sooner
than the green bag infallibly——at least by twenty *knots*.——
Sport of small accidents, *Tristram Shandy!* that thou art, and
ever will be! had that trial been made for thee, and it was fifty
to one but it had,——thy affairs had not been so depress'd——
(at least by the depression of thy nose) as they have been; nor
had the fortunes of thy house and the occasions of making
them, which have so often presented themselves in the course
of thy life, to thee, been so often, so vexatiously, so tamely, so
irrecoverably abandoned——as thou hast been forced to leave
them!——but 'tis over,——all but the account of 'em, which
cannot be given to the curious till I am got out into the world.

---

[1] A play on *cabalistic* (occult, esoteric), and *caballus,* the Latin word
for horse.

CHAP. IX.

GREAT wits jump: for the moment Dr. *Slop* cast his eyes upon his bag (which he had not done till the dispute with my uncle *Toby* about midwifery put him in mind of it) ——the very same thought occurred.——'Tis God's mercy, quoth he, (to himself) that Mrs. *Shandy* has had so bad a time of it,——else she might have been brought to bed seven times told, before one half of these knots could have got untied.——But here, you must distinguish——the thought floated only in Dr. *Slop's* mind, without sail or ballast to it, as a simple proposition; millions of which, as your worship knows, are every day swimming quietly in the middle of the thin juice of a man's understanding, without being carried backwards or forwards, till some little gusts of passion or interest drive them to one side.

A sudden trampling in the room above, near my mother's bed, did the proposition the very service I am speaking of.   By all that's unfortunate, quoth Dr. *Slop,* unless I make haste, the thing will actually befall me as it is.

CHAP. X.

IN the case of *knots*,——by which, in the first place, I would not be understood to mean slip-knots,——because in the course of my life and opinions,——my opinions concerning them will come in more properly when I mention the catastrophe of my great uncle Mr. *Hammond Shandy*,——a little man,——but of high fancy:——he rushed into the duke of *Monmouth's* affair:[1]——nor, secondly, in this place, do I mean that particular species of knots, called bow-knots;——there is

---

[1] The abortive rebellion, in 1685, of James Scott, Duke of Monmouth (1649–1685), against James II.

so little address, or skill, or patience, required in the unloosing
them, that they are below my giving any opinion at all about
them.——But by the knots I am speaking of, may it please
your reverences to believe, that I mean good, honest, devilish
tight, hard knots, made *bona fide*,[2] as *Obadiah* made his;——
in which there is no quibbling provision made by the duplication and return of the two ends of the strings through the an-
nulus or noose made by the second *implication* of them——to
get them slipp'd and undone by——I hope you apprehend me.

In the case of these *knots* then, and of the several obstructions, which, may it please your reverences, such knots cast in
our way in getting through life——every hasty man can whip
out his penknife and cut through them.——'Tis wrong. Believe me, Sirs, the most virtuous way, and which both reason
and conscience dictate——is to take our teeth or our fingers
to them.——Dr. *Slop* had lost his teeth—his favourite instrument, by extracting in a wrong direction, or by some misap-
plication of it, unfortunately slipping, he had formerly in a
hard labour, knock'd out three of the best of them, with the
handle of it:——he tried his fingers——alas! the nails of his
fingers and thumbs were cut close.——The deuce take it! I
can make nothing of it either way, cried Dr. *Slop*.——The
trampling over head near my mother's bed side increased.——
Pox take the fellow! I shall never get the knots untied as
long as I live.——My mother gave a groan——Lend me your
penknife——I must e'en cut the knots at last - - - - - pugh! - - -
psha! - - - Lord! I have cut my thumb quite across to the very
bone——curse the fellow——if there was not another man
midwife within fifty miles——I am undone for this bout——
I wish the scoundrel hang'd——I wish he was shot——I wish
all the devils in hell had him for a blockhead———

My father had a great respect for *Obadiah*, and could not
bear to hear him disposed of in such a manner——he had
moreover some little respect for himself——and could as ill
bear with the indignity offer'd to himself in it.

Had Dr. *Slop* cut any part about him, but his thumb——my

---

[2] In good faith.

father had pass'd it by——his prudence had triumphed: as it was, he was determined to have his revenge.

Small curses, Dr. *Slop,* upon great occasions, quoth my father, (condoling with him first upon the accident) are but so much waste of our strength and soul's health to no manner of purpose.——I own it, replied Dr. *Slop.*——They are like sparrow shot, quoth my uncle *Toby,* (suspending his whistling) fired against a bastion.——They serve, continued my father, to stir the humours——but carry off none of their acrimony:——for my own part, I seldom swear or curse at all ——I hold it bad——but if I fall into it, by surprize, I generally retain so much presence of mind (right, quoth my uncle *Toby*) as to make it answer my purpose——that is, I swear on, till I find myself easy.   A wise and a just man however would always endeavour to proportion the vent given to these humours, not only to the degree of them stirring within himself ——but to the size and ill intent of the offence upon which they are to fall.——*"Injuries come only from the heart,"*—— quoth my uncle *Toby.*   For this reason, continued my father, with the most *Cervantick*[3] gravity, I have the greatest veneration in the world for that gentleman, who, in distrust of his own discretion in this point, sat down and composed (that is at his leisure) fit forms of swearing suitable to all cases, from the lowest to the highest provocations which could possibly happen to him,——which forms being well consider'd by him, and such moreover as he could stand to, he kept them ever by him on the chimney piece, within his reach, ready for use. ——I never apprehended, replied Dr. *Slop,* that such a thing was ever thought of,——much less executed.   I beg your pardon——answered my father; I was reading, though not using, one of them to my brother *Toby* this morning, whilst he pour'd out the tea——'tis here upon the shelf over my head;——but if I remember right, 'tis too violent for a cut of the thumb. ——Not at all, quoth Dr. *Slop*——the devil take the fellow. ——Then answered my father, 'Tis much at your service, Dr. *Slop*——on condition you will read it aloud;——so rising up

[3]Unsmilingly satirical, as was Cervantes.

and reaching down a form of excommunication of the church of *Rome,* a copy of which, my father (who was curious in his collections) had procured out of the leger-book of the church of *Rochester,* writ by ERNULPHUS the bishop——with a most affected seriousness of look and voice, which might have cajoled ERNULPHUS himself,——he put it into Dr. *Slop's* hands. ——Dr. *Slop* wrapt his thumb up in the corner of his hand-kerchief, and with a wry face, though without any suspicion, read aloud, as follows,——my uncle *Toby* whistling *Lilla-bullero,* as loud as he could, all the time.

Textus de Ecclesiâ Roffensi, per Ernulfum Episcopum.[4]

CAP. XXV.

EXCOMMUNICATIO.*

EX auctoritate Dei omnipotentis, Patris, et Filij, et Spiritus Sancti, et sanctorum canonum, sanctæque et intemeratæ Virginis Dei genetricis Mariæ,

---

[4]*Text of the Church of Rochester,* by Ernulf the Bishop. As the prac-tice of anathematizing or excommunicating offenders against the church spread during the early centuries of Christianity, individual prelates de-veloped various forms of the cùrse, of which this of Ernulf (1040–1124), who was Bishop of Rochester from 1114 to 1124, is one of the more elaborate now extant. Sterne's transcription is close to that of the *Textus Roffensis* published at Oxford in 1720 by Thomas Hearnius.

*As the genuineness of the consultation of the *Sorbonne* upon the ques-tion of baptism, was doubted by some, and denied by others,——'twas thought proper to print the original of this excommunication; for the copy of which Mr. *Shandy* returns thanks to the chapter clerk of the dean and chapter of *Rochester.* [Sterne's note.]

CHAP. XI.

"BY the authority of God Almighty, the Father, Son, and
Holy Ghost, and of the holy canons, and of the undefiled Virgin *Mary,* mother and patroness of our Saviour." I
think there is no necessity, quoth Dr. *Slop,* dropping the paper
down to his knee, and addressing himself to my father,——as
you have read it over, Sir, so lately, to read it aloud;——and
as Captain *Shandy* seems to have no great inclination to hear
it,——I may as well read it to myself. That's contrary to
treaty, replied my father,——besides, there is something so
whimsical, especially in the latter part of it, I should grieve
to lose the pleasure of a second reading. Dr. *Slop* did not altogether like it,——but my uncle *Toby* offering at that instant to give over whistling, and read it himself to them;——
Dr. *Slop* thought he might as well read it under the cover of
my uncle *Toby*'s whistling,——as suffer my uncle *Toby* to
read it alone;——so raising up the paper to his face, and holding it quite parallel to it, in order to hide his chagrin,——
he read it aloud as follows,——my uncle *Toby* whistling
Lillabullero, though not quite so loud as before.

————Atque omnium cœlestium virtutum, angelorum, arch-
angelorum, thronorum, dominationum, potestatuum, cherubin
ac seraphin, & sanctorum patriarchum, prophetarum, & omnium
apostolorum et evangelistarum, & sanctorum innocentum, qui
in conspectu Agni soli digni inventi sunt canticum cantare
novum, et sanctorum martyrum, et sanctorum confessorum, et
sanctarum virginum, atque omnium simul sanctorum et elec-
                                             vel os
torum Dei,————Excommunicamus, et anathematizamus hunc
       s   *vel* os   s
furem, vel hunc malefactorem, N. N. et a liminibus sanctæ Dei
                                   vel i
ecclesiæ sequestramus et æternis suppliciis excruciandus, manci-
   n
petur, cum Dathan et Abiram, et cum his qui dixerunt Domino
Deo, Recede à nobis, scientiam viarum tuarum nolumus: et
                                             vel eorum
sicut aquâ ignis extinguitur, sic extinguatur lucerna ejus in
           n   n
secula seculorum nisi respuerit, et ad satisfactionem venerit.
Amen.

             os
    Maledicat illum Deus Pater qui hominem creavit.   Maledicat
os   os
illum Dei Filius qui pro homine passus est.   Maledicat illum
                                             os
Spiritus Sanctus qui in baptismo effusus est.   Maledicat illum
sancta crux, quam Christus pro nostrâ salute hostem tri-
umphans, ascendit.

             os
    Maledicat illum sancta Dei genetrix et perpetua Virgo Maria.
          os
Maledicat illum sanctus Michael, animarum susceptor sacrarum.
          os
Maledicant illum omnes angeli et archangeli, principatus et
potestates, omnisque militia cœlestis.

"By the authority of God Almighty, the Father, Son, and Holy Ghost, and of the undefiled Virgin *Mary,* mother and patroness of our Saviour, and of all the celestial virtues, angels, archangels, thrones, dominions, powers, cherubins and seraphins, and of all the holy patriarchs, prophets, and of all the apostles and evangelists, and of the holy innocents, who in the sight of the holy Lamb, are found worthy to sing the new song of the holy martyrs and holy confessors, and of the holy virgins, and of all the saints together, with the holy and elect of God.——May he," (*Obadiah*) "be damn'd," (for tying these knots.)——"We excommunicate, and anathematise him, and from the thresholds of the holy church of God Almighty we sequester him, that he may be tormented, disposed and delivered over with *Dathan* and *Abiram,*[1] and with those who say unto the Lord God, Depart from us, we desire none of thy ways. And as fire is quenched with water, so let the light of him be put out for evermore, unless it shall repent him" (*Obadiah,* of the knots which he has tied) "and make satisfaction" (for them.)   Amen.

"May the Father who created man, curse him.——May the Son who suffered for us, curse him.——May the Holy Ghost who was given to us in baptism, curse him (*Obadiah.*)—— May the holy cross which Christ for our salvation triumphing over his enemies, ascended,——curse him.

"May the holy and eternal *Virgin Mary,* mother of God, curse him.——May St. *Michael* the advocate of holy souls, curse him.——May all the angels and archangels, principalities and powers, and all the heavenly armies, curse him." [Our

---

[1]Israelites who were punished for their rebellion against the leadership of Moses and Aaron by being swallowed alive in an earthquake. See Numbers, 16.1–35 and Psalms, 106.17.

        os
Maledicat illum patriarcharum et prophetarum laudabilis
      os
numerus. Maledicat illum sanctus Johannes præcursor et
Baptista Christi, et sanctus Petrus, et sanctus Paulus, atque
sanctus Andreas, omnesque Christi apostoli, simul et cæteri
discipuli, quatuor quoque evangelistæ, qui sua prædicatione
                          os
mundum universum converterunt. Maledicat illum cuneus
martyrum et confessorum mirificus, qui Deo bonis operibus
placitus inventus est.

       os
Maledicant illum sacrarum virginum chori, quæ mundi vana
causa honoris Christi respuenda contempserunt. Maledicant
  os
illum omnes sancti qui ab initio mundi usque in finem seculi
Deo dilecti inveniuntur.

       os
Maledicant illum cœli et terra, et omnia sancta in eis
manentia.

     i n   n
Maledictus sit ubicunque fuerit, sive in domo, sive in agro,
sive in viâ, sive in semitâ, sive in silvâ, sive in aquâ, sive in
ecclesiâ.

     i n
Maledictus sit vivendo, moriendo,————————————
——   ——   ——   ——   ——   ——
——   ——   ——   ——   ——   ——
——   ——   ——   ——   ——   ——
——   ——   ——   ——   ——   ——

manducando, bibendo, esuriendo, sitiendo, jejunando, dormi-

armies swore terribly in *Flanders,* cried my uncle *Toby,*——
but nothing to this.——For my own part, I could not have
a heart to curse my dog so.]

May St. John the præ-cursor, and St. John the Baptist,[2]
and St. Peter and St. Paul, and St. Andrew, and all other
Christ's apostles, together curse him.   And may the rest of his
disciples and four evangelists, who by their preaching converted the universal world,——and may the holy and wonderful company of martyrs and confessors, who by their holy
works are found pleasing to God Almighty, curse him (*Obadiah.*)

"May the holy choir of the holy virgins, who for the honour
of Christ have despised the things of the world, damn him.
——May all the saints who from the beginning of the world to
everlasting ages are found to be beloved of God, damn him.
——May the heavens and earth, and all the holy things remaining therein, damn him," (*Obadiah*) "or her," (or whoever else had a hand in tying these knots.)

"May he (*Obadiah*) be damn'd wherever he be,——whether
in the house or the stables, the garden or the field, or the high-
way, or in the path, or in the wood, or in the water, or in the
church.——May he be cursed in living, in dying." [Here my
uncle *Toby* taking the advantage of a *minim*[3] in the second
barr of his tune, kept whistling one continual note to the end
of the sentence——Dr. *Slop* with his division of curses moving
under him, like a running bass all the way.] "May he be
cursed in eating and drinking, in being hungry, in being

---

[2]The same person; the translation should read: "May St. John, the
Præcursor and Baptizer of Christ, . . ."

[3]A half-note; "taking the advantage of" is used in the sense of "overreaching," or "imposing upon."

tando, dormiendo, vigilando, ambulando, stando, sedendo, jacendo, operando, quiescendo, mingendo, cacando, flebotomando.

     i   n
Maledictus sit in totis viribus corporis.

     i   n
Maledictus sit intus et exterius.

     i n   i n
Maledictus sit in capillis; maledictus sit in cerebro. Male-
  i n
dictus sit in vertice, in temporibus, in fronte, in auriculis, in superciliis, in oculis, in genis, in maxillis, in naribus, in dentibus, mordacibus sive molaribus, in labiis, in guttere, in humeris, in harnis, in brachiis, in manubus, in digitis, in pectore, in corde, et in omnibus interioribus stomacho tenus, in renibus, in inguinibus, in femore, in genitalibus, in coxis, in genubus, in cruribus, in pedibus, et in unguibus.

Maledictus sit in totis compagibus membrorum, a vertice capitis, usque ad plantam pedis——non sit in eo sanitas.

Maledicat illum Christus Filius Dei vivi toto suæ majestatis imperio thirsty, in fasting, in sleeping, in slumbering, in walking, in standing, in sitting, in lying, in working, in resting, in pissing, in shitting, and in blood-letting."

"May he (*Obadiah*) be cursed in all the faculties of his body.

"May he be cursed inwardly and outwardly.——May he be cursed in the hair of his head.——May he be cursed in his brains, and in his vertex," (that is a sad curse, quoth my father) "in his temples, in his forehead, in his ears, in his eye-brows, in his cheeks, in his jaw-bones, in his nostrils, in his foreteeth and grinders, in his lips, in his throat, in his shoulders, in his wrists, in his arms, in his hands, in his fingers.

"May he be damn'd in his mouth, in his breast, in his heart and purtenance, down to the very stomach.

"May he be cursed in his reins, and in his groin," (God in heaven forbid, quoth my uncle *Toby*)——"in his thighs, in his genitals," (my father shook his head) "and in his hips, and in his knees, his legs, and feet, and toe-nails.

"May he be cursed in all the joints and articulations of his members, from the top of his head to the soal of his foot, may there be no soundness in him.

"May the Son of the living God, with all the glory of his Majesty"——[Here my uncle *Toby* throwing back his head, gave a monstrous, long, loud Whew——w——w——something betwixt the interjectional whistle of *Hey day!* and the word itself.——

——By the golden beard of *Jupiter*——and of *Juno,* (if her majesty wore one), and by the beards of the rest of your heathen worships, which by the bye was no small number, since what with the beards of your celestial gods, and gods aerial and aquatick,——to say nothing of the beards of town-gods and country-gods, or of the celestial goddesses your wives, or of the infernal goddesses your whores and concu-

——et insurgat adversus illum cœlum cum omnibus virtuti-
bus quæ in eo moventur ad *damnandum* eum, nisi penituerit
et ad satisfactionem venerit.   Amen.   Fiat, fiat.   Amen.

bines, (that is in case they wore 'em)——all which beards, as
Varro[4] tells me, upon his word and honour, when mustered
up together, made no less than thirty thousand effective beards
upon the pagan establishment;——every beard of which
claimed the rights and privileges of being stroked and sworn
by,——by all these beards together then,——I vow and protest, that of the two bad cassocks I am worth in the world, I
would have given the better of them, as freely as ever *Cid
Hamet*[5] offered his,——only to have stood by, and heard my
uncle *Toby*'s accompanyment.]

——"Curse him," continued Dr. *Slop*,——"and may heaven
with all the powers which move therein, rise up against him,
curse and damn him (*Obadiah*) unless he repent and make
satisfaction. Amen. So be it,——so be it. Amen."

I declare, quoth my uncle *Toby*, my heart would not let me
curse the devil himself with so much bitterness.——He is the
father of curses, replied Dr. *Slop*.——So am not I, replied my
uncle.——But he is cursed, and damn'd already, to all eternity,
——replied Dr. *Slop*.

I am sorry for it, quoth my uncle *Toby*.

Dr. *Slop* drew up his mouth, and was just beginning to return my uncle *Toby* the compliment of his Whu——u——u
——or interjectional whistle,——when the door hastily opening in the next chapter but one——put an end to the affair.

[4]Marcus Terentius Varro (116–27 B.C.) was the most learned scholar
and author among the Romans; the reference would appear to be to his
Antiquitates Rerum Divinarum, but actually Sterne has miscopied it from
The Anatomy of Melancholy, 3.4.1.3, which he is here paraphrasing: "The
Romans borrowed from all, besides their own gods, which were *majorum*
and *minorum gentium* . . . some celestial select and great ones . . .
some for the Land, some for Sea; some for Heaven, some for Hell: . . .
beastly women, and arrant whores, amongst the rest . . . male and female gods, of all ages, sexes, and dimensions, with beards, without
beards, married, unmarried . . . *Hesiodus* reckons up at least 30,000
gods, *Varro* 300 *Jupiters.*"

[5]"Cid Hamet Benengeli, an Arabian historiographer," the imaginary
chronicler from whom Cervantes pretended to have translated many of
the adventures of Don Quixote, swore "by Mahomet, he would have
given the best coat of two that he had, only to have seen the knight and
the matron walk thus hand in hand from the chamber-door to the bed-
side." (*Don Quixote,* 2.4.48.)

CHAP. XII.

NOW don't let us give ourselves a parcel of airs, and pretend that the oaths we make free with in this land of liberty of ours are our own; and because we have the spirit to swear them,——imagine that we have had the wit to invent them too.

I'll undertake this moment to prove it to any man in the world, except to a connoisseur;——though I declare I object only to a connoisseur in swearing,——as I would do to a connoisseur in painting, &c. &c. the whole set of 'em are so hung round and *befetish'd* with the bobs and trinkets of criticism, ——or to drop my metaphor, which by the bye is a pity,—— for I have fetch'd it as far as from the coast of *Guinea;*—— their heads, Sir, are stuck so full of rules and compasses, and have that eternal propensity to apply them upon all occasions, that a work of genius had better go to the devil at once, than stand to be prick'd and tortured to death by 'em.

——And how did *Garrick*[1] speak the soliloquy last night? ——Oh, against all rule, my Lord,——most ungrammatically! betwixt the substantive and the adjective, which should agree together in *number, case* and *gender,* he made a breach thus, ——stopping, as if the point wanted settling;——and betwixt the nominative case, which your lordship knows should govern the verb, he suspended his voice in the epilogue a dozen times, three seconds and three fifths by a stop-watch, my Lord, each time.——Admirable grammarian!——But in suspending his voice——was the sense suspended likewise? Did no expression of attitude or countenance fill up the chasm?——Was the eye silent? Did you narrowly look?——I look'd only at the stop-watch, my Lord.——Excellent observer!

And what of this new book the whole world makes such

---

[1]David Garrick (1717–1779), the actor-manager, had been the earliest sponsor in London of *Tristram Shandy* and, from their first meeting in 1760, a good and useful friend to Sterne.   See the Introduction, pp. ix, xii.

a rout about?——Oh! 'tis out of all plumb, my Lord,——quite
an irregular thing!——not one of the angles at the four corners
was a right angle.——I had my rule and compasses, &c. my
Lord, in my pocket.——Excellent critic!

——And for the epick poem, your lordship bid me look at;
——upon taking the length, breadth, height, and depth of it,
and trying them at home upon an exact scale of *Bossu*'s,[2]——
'tis out, my Lord, in every one of its dimensions.——Admirable connoisseur!

——And did you step in, to take a look at the grand picture,
in your way back.——'Tis a melancholy daub! my Lord; not
one principle of the *pyramid* in any one group!——and what
a price!——for there is nothing of the colouring of *Titian*,[3]
——the expression of *Rubens*,——the grace of *Raphael*,——the
purity of *Dominichino*,——the *corregiescity* of *Corregio*,——

---

[2]René le Bossu (1631–1680), a respected French critic whose *Traité du
poème épique* had set forth definite rules, founded on classical examples,
for the writing of epics.

[3]In this satire on the jargon of critics, Sterne has in most cases tritely
hit off the most obvious qualities of the artists listed. Tiziano Vecelli
(c. 1477–1576), a Venetian painter, was perhaps the greatest of all
painters in his use of colour, tone, richness, and harmony, and in his
production of a dignified and beautiful pictorial whole. Peter Paul
Rubens (1577–1640), a Flemish painter, produced vast canvases famous
for their vigour of design, their pictorial skill, their breadth of touch, and,
above all, their rich and brilliant colouring. Raphael Sanzio (1483–
1520), an Italian painter, was a master of draughtmanship, colouring,
and graceful composition. Domenico Zampieri (1581–1641), an Italian
painter, was noted for his correctness of design, truth of colouring and
expression, and natural elegance. Antonio Allegri of Correggio (1494–
1534), a painter of the Lombard school, was celebrated for his skill in
chiaroscuro and foreshortening, and for the grace of both the expression
and the technical execution of his works; "corregiescity" is Sterne's
coinage. Nicolas Poussin (1594–1665), a French historical and land-
scape painter, was noted for his intimate knowledge of classical art.
Guido Reni (1575–1642) was a painter of the Bolognese school, whose
best works are famous for their suave dignity and graceful amenity of
sentiment and form. Lodovico Carracci (1555–1619) was the founder,
and his cousins and pupils, Agostino (1558–1602) and Annibale (1560–
1609), were members of the eclectic school of Bologna, who sought to
unite in their works the excellencies of each of the great masters of painting. Michelangelo Buonarroti (1475–1564), the most famous artist of
the Italian renaissance, produced paintings famous for their physical and
intellectual strength, boldness of design, and technical mastery.

the learning of *Poussin*,——the airs of *Guido*,——the taste of
the *Carrachi*'s,——or the grand contour of *Angelo*.——Grant
me patience, just heaven!——Of all the cants which are canted
in this canting world,——though the cant of hypocrites may
be the worst,——the cant of criticism is the most tormenting!

I would go fifty miles on foot, for I have not a horse worth
riding on, to kiss the hand of that man whose generous heart
will give up the reins of his imagination into his author's
hands,——be pleased he knows not why, and cares not wherefore.

Great *Apollo!* if thou art in a giving humour,——give me,
——I ask no more, but one stroke of native humour, with a
single spark of thy own fire along with it,——and send *Mercury,* with the *rules and compasses,* if he can be spared, with
my compliments to——no matter.

Now to any one else, I will undertake to prove, that all the
oaths and imprecations, which we have been puffing off upon
the world for these two hundred and fifty years last past, as
originals,——except St. *Paul*'s *thumb*,——*God's flesh and God's
fish,* which were oaths monarchical,[4] and, considering who
made them, not much amiss; and as kings oaths, 'tis not much
matter whether they were fish or flesh;——else, I say, there is
not an oath, or at least a curse amongst them, which has not
been copied over and over again out of *Ernulphus,* a thousand
times: but, like all other copies, how infinitely short of the
force and spirit of the original!——It is thought to be no bad
oath,——and by itself passes very well——*"G—d damn
you."*——Set it beside *Ernulphus's*——"God Almighty the
Father damn you,——God the Son damn you,——God the
Holy Ghost damn you,"——you see 'tis nothing.——There is
an orientality in his, we cannot rise up to: besides, he is more
copious in his invention,——possess'd more of the excellencies
of a swearer,——had such a thorough knowledge of the hu-

---

[4]Sterne may be thinking of Richard III, who frequently swore by St.
Paul, and Charles II, who swore by " 'Od's fish." "God's fish" is presumably a euphemism for "God's flesh." To swear by some part of the
body of the deity or of a saint was formerly, of course, very common.

man frame, its membranes, nerves, ligaments, knittings of the joints, and articulations,——that when *Ernulphus* cursed,—— no part escaped him.——'Tis true, there is something of a *hardness* in his manner,——and, as in *Michael Angelo,* a want of *grace,*——but then there is such a greatness of *gusto!*——

My father, who generally look'd upon every thing in a light very different from all mankind,——would, after all, never allow this to be an original.——He consider'd rather *Ernulphus's* anathema, as an institute of swearing, in which, as he suspected, upon the decline of *swearing* in some milder pontificate, *Ernulphus,* by order of the succeeding pope, had with great learning and diligence collected together all the laws of it;——for the same reason that *Justinian,* in the decline of the empire, had ordered his chancellor *Tribonian* to collect the *Roman* or civil laws all together into one code or digest,[5]—— lest through the rust of time,——and the fatality of all things committed to oral tradition, they should be lost to the world for ever.

For this reason my father would oft-times affirm, there was not an oath, from the great and tremendous oath of *William* the Conqueror, (*By the splendour of God*)[6] down to the lowest oath of a scavenger, (*Damn your eyes*) which was not to be found in *Ernulphus.*——In short, he would add,——I defy a man to swear *out* of it.

The hypothesis is, like most of my father's, singular and ingenious too;——nor have I any objection to it, but that it overturns my own.

---

[5]Flavius Anicius Justinianus (483–565), surnamed the Great, the most famous of the emperors of the Eastern Roman Empire, directed a commission, headed by Tribonian, in consolidating and annotating the body of Roman law in his great *Corpus Juris Civilis,* the most important of all monuments of jurisprudence.

[6]William's special oath was "by the splendour and resurrection of God."

CHAP. XIII.

——BLESS my soul!——my poor mistress is ready to faint,
——and her pains are gone,——and the drops are
done,——and the bottle of julap[1] is broke,——and the nurse
has cut her arm,——(and I, my thumb, cried Dr. *Slop*) and
the child is where it was, continued *Susannah*,——and the
midwife has fallen backwards upon the edge of the fender, and
bruised her hip as black as your hat.——I'll look at it, quoth
Dr. *Slop*.——There is no need of that, replied *Susannah*,——
you had better look at my mistress,——but the midwife would
gladly first give you an account how things are, so desires you
would go up stairs and speak to her this moment.

Human nature is the same in all professions.

The midwife had just before been put over Dr. *Slop's* head.
——He had not digested it.——No, replied Dr. *Slop*, 'twould
be full as proper, if the midwife came down to me.——I like
subordination, quoth my uncle *Toby*,——and but for it, after
the reduction of *Lisle*, I know not what might have become
of the garrison of *Ghent*, in the mutiny for bread, in the year
Ten.[2]——Nor, replied Dr. *Slop*, (parodying my uncle *Toby's*
hobby-horsical reflection, though full as hobby-horsically himself)——do I know, Captain *Shandy*, what might have become of the garrison above stairs, in the mutiny and confusion
I find all things are in at present, but for the subordination of
fingers and thumbs to ******—— the application of which,
Sir, under this accident of mine, comes in so *a propos,* that
without it, the cut upon my thumb might have been felt by
the *Shandy* family, as long as the *Shandy* family had a name.

---

[1]Julep.
[2]A confused reference. Lille surrendered in December, 1708, and during the severe winter of 1709–1710 people in many provinces perished of
famine and revolts broke out in every direction, but neither Lille nor
Ghent was particularly concerned in the campaign of 1710.

CHAP. XIV.

LET us go back to the ******——in the last chapter.

It is a singular stroke of eloquence (at least it was so, when eloquence flourished at *Athens* and *Rome,* and would be so now, did orators wear mantles) not to mention the name of a thing, when you had the thing about you, *in petto*,[1] ready to produce, pop, in the place you want it. A scar, an axe, a sword, a pink'd-doublet, a rusty helmet, a pound and a half of pot-ashes in an urn, or a three-halfpenny pickle pot, ——but above all, a tender infant royally accoutred.——Tho' if it was too young, and the oration as long as *Tully's* second *Philippick,*[2]——it must certainly have beshit the orator's mantle.——And then again, if too old,——it must have been unwieldy and incommodious to his action,——so as to make him lose by his child almost as much as he could gain by it.—— Otherwise, when a state orator has hit the precise age to a minute,——hid his BAMBINO in his mantle so cunningly that no mortal could smell it,——and produced it so critically, that no soul could say, it came in by head and shoulders,—— Oh, Sirs! it has done wonders.——It has open'd the sluices, and turn'd the brains, and shook the principles, and unhinged the politicks of half a nation.

These feats however are not to be done, except in those states and times, I say, where orators wore mantles,——and pretty large ones too, my brethren, with some twenty or five and twenty yards of good purple, superfine, marketable cloth in them,——with large flowing folds and doubles, and in a great stile of design.——All which plainly shews, may it please your worships, that the decay of eloquence, and the little good service it does at present, both within, and without

---

[1] In one's breast, in secret.

[2] The second and longest of Cicero's fourteen orations against Mark Antony, which though published was not delivered, is approximately fifty pages in length.

doors, is owing to nothing else in the world, but short coats, and the disuse of *trunk-hose*.[3]——We can conceal nothing under ours, Madam, worth shewing.

CHAP. XV.

D R. *Slop* was within an ace of being an exception to all this argumentation: for happening to have his green bays bag upon his knees, when he began to parody my uncle *Toby*, ——'twas as good as the best mantle in the world to him: for which purpose, when he foresaw the sentence would end in his new invented *forceps,* he thrust his hand into the bag in order to have them ready to clap in, where your reverences took so much notice of the******, which had he managed,—— my uncle *Toby* had certainly been overthrown: the sentence and the argument in that case jumping closely in one point, so like the two lines which form the salient angle of a raveline,—— Dr. *Slop* would never have given them up;——and my uncle *Toby* would as soon have thought of flying, as taking them by force: but Dr. *Slop* fumbled so vilely in pulling them out, it took off the whole effect, and what was a ten times worse evil (for they seldom come alone in this life) in pulling out his *forceps,* his *forceps* unfortunately drew out the *squirt* along with it.

When a proposition can be taken in two senses,——'tis a law in disputation That the respondent may reply to which of the two he pleases, or finds most convenient for him.——This threw the advantage of the argument quite on my uncle *Toby*'s side.——"Good God!" cried my uncle *Toby, "are children brought into the world with a squirt?"*

---

[3]Full, puffy, bag-like breeches covering the body from the waist to the middle of the thigh, worn by men during the 16th and 17th centuries. During the 18th century tight knee-breeches were in style.

CHAP. XVI.

——UPON my honour, Sir, you have tore every bit of the
skin quite off the back of both my hands with your
forceps, cried my uncle *Toby*,——and you have crush'd all my
knuckles into the bargain with them, to a jelly. 'Tis your
own fault, said Dr. *Slop*,——you should have clinch'd your
two fists together into the form of a child's head, as I told you,
and sat firm.——I did so, answered my uncle *Toby*.——Then
the points of my forceps have not been sufficiently arm'd, or
the rivet wants closing——or else the cut on my thumb has
made me a little aukward,——or possibly——'Tis well, quoth
my father, interrupting the detail of possibilities,——that the
experiment was not first made upon my child's head piece.
——It would not have been a cherry stone the worse, answered Dr. *Slop*. I maintain it, said my uncle *Toby*, it would
have broke the cerebellum, (unless indeed the skull had been
as hard as a granado[1]) and turned it all into a perfect posset.
Pshaw! replied Dr. *Slop*, a child's head is naturally as soft
as the pap of an apple;——the sutures give way,——and
besides, I could have extracted by the feet after.——Not you,
said she.——I rather wish you would begin that way, quoth my
father.

Pray do, added my uncle *Toby*.

CHAP. XVII.

—— AND pray, good woman, after all, will you take upon
you to say, it may not be the child's hip, as well as
the child's head?——'Tis most certainly the head, replied
the midwife. Because, continued Dr. *Slop*, (turning to my
father) as positive as these old ladies generally are,——'tis a

[1]Grenade.

point very difficult to know,——and yet of the greatest consequence to be known;——because, Sir, if the hip is mistaken
for the head,——there is a possibility (if it is a boy) that the
forceps * * * * * * * * * * * * * * * * *
* * * * * * * * * * * * * * * * *

——What the possibility was, Dr. *Slop* whispered very low
to my father, and then to my uncle *Toby*.——There is no such
danger, continued he, with the head.——No, in truth, quoth
my father,——but when your possibility has taken place at
the hip,——you may as well take off the head too.

——It is morally impossible the reader should understand
this,——'tis enough Dr. *Slop* understood it;——so taking the
green bays bag in his hand, with the help of *Obadiah*'s pumps,
he tripp'd pretty nimbly, for a man of his size, across the room
to the door,——and from the door was shewn the way, by
the good old midwife, to my mother's apartment.

CHAP. XVIII.

IT is two hours, and ten minutes,——and no more,——cried
my father, looking at his watch, since Dr. *Slop* and *Obadiah*
arrived,——and I know not how it happens, brother *Toby,*
——but to my imagination it seems almost an age.

——Here——pray, Sir, take hold of my cap,——nay, take the
bell along with it, and my pantoufles[1] too.——

Now, Sir, they are all at your service; and I freely make you
a present of 'em, on condition, you give me all your attention
to this chapter.

Though my father said, *"he knew not how it happen'd,"*
——yet he knew very well, how it happen'd;——and at the
instant he spoke it, was pre-determined in his mind, to give
my uncle *Toby* a clear account of the matter by a metaphysical
dissertation upon the subject of *duration and its simple modes,*
in order to shew my uncle *Toby,* by what mechanism and men-

---

[1]Pantofles, slippers.

surations in the brain it came to pass, that the rapid succession of their ideas, and the eternal scampering of discourse from one thing to another, since Dr. *Slop* had come into the room, had lengthened out so short a period, to so inconceivable an extent.——"I know not how it happens,——cried my father, ——but it seems an age."

——'Tis owing, entirely, quoth my uncle *Toby,* to the succession of our ideas.

My father, who had an itch in common with all philosophers, of reasoning upon every thing which happened, and accounting for it too,——proposed infinite pleasure to himself in this, of the succession of ideas, and had not the least apprehension of having it snatch'd out of his hands by my uncle *Toby,* who (honest man!) generally took every thing as it happened;——and who, of all men in the world, troubled his brain the least with abstruse thinking;——the ideas of time and space,——or how we came by those ideas,——or of what stuff they were made,——or whether they were born with us, ——or we pick'd them up afterwards as we went along,—— or whether we did it in frocks,——or not till we had got into breeches,——with a thousand other inquiries and disputes about INFINITY, PRESCIENCE, LIBERTY, NECESSITY, and so forth, upon whose desperate and unconquerable theories, so many fine heads have been turned and crack'd,——never did my uncle *Toby*'s the least injury at all; my father knew it,——and was no less surprised, than he was disappointed with my uncle's fortuitous solution.

Do you understand the theory of that affair? replied my father.

Not I, quoth my uncle.

——But you have some ideas, said my father, of what you talk about.——

No more than my horse, replied my uncle *Toby.*

Gracious heaven! cried my father, looking upwards, and clasping his two hands together,——there is a worth in thy honest ignorance, brother *Toby,*——'twere almost a pity to exchange it for a knowledge.——But I'll tell thee.——

To understand what *time* is aright, without which we never
can comprehend *infinity,* insomuch as one is a portion of the
other,——we ought seriously to sit down and consider what
idea it is, we have of *duration,* so as to give a satisfactory account, how we came by it.——What is that to any body?
quoth my uncle *Toby.* * *For if you will turn your eyes inwards upon your mind,* continued my father, *and observe attentively, you will perceive, brother, that whilst you and I are
talking together, and thinking and smoaking our pipes: or
whilst we receive successively ideas in our minds, we know
that we do exist, and so we estimate the existence, or the con-
tinuation of the existence of ourselves, or any thing else com-
mensurate to the succession of any ideas in our minds, the
duration of ourselves, or any such other thing co existing with
our thinking,——and so according to that preconceived——*
You puzzle me to death, cried my uncle *Toby.*——

——'Tis owing to this, replied my father, that in our com-
putations of *time,* we are so used to minutes, hours, weeks,
and months,——and of clocks (I wish there was not a clock in
the kingdom[2]) to measure out their several portions to us, and
to those who belong to us,——that 'twill be well, if in time to
come, the *succession of our ideas* be of any use or service to us
at all.

Now, whether we observe it or no, continued my father, in
every sound man's head, there is a regular succession of ideas
of one sort or other, which follow each other in train just like

*Vid. Locke. [Sterne's note. This and the two following paragraphs
are dramatically paraphrased from *An Essay Concerning Human Understanding,* 2.14.3,4,19,9.]

[2]An allusion to *The Clockmaker's Outcry against the Author of the Life
and Opinions of Tristram Shandy,* a catch-penny pamphlet which had
been published on May 9, 1760, the whimsical writer of which had made
capital of the notorious clock scene at the opening of Sterne's work,
which, he declared, had ruined his trade. "The directions I had for
making several clocks for the country," he complained, "are now countermanded; because no modest Lady now dares to mention a word
about *winding-up a clock,* without exposing herself to the sly leers and
jokes of the family. . . . Alas, reputable, hoary clocks, that have
flourished for ages, are ordered to be taken down by virtuous Matrons,
and disposed of as obscene lumber, exciting to acts of carnality!"

———A train of artillery? said my uncle *Toby*.———A train of a fiddle stick!———quoth my father,———which follow and succeed one another in our minds at certain distances, just like the images in the inside of a lanthorn turned round by the heat of a candle.———I declare, quoth my uncle *Toby, mine are like a smoak-jack.*[3]———Then, brother *Toby,* I have nothing more to say to you upon the subject, said my father.

CHAP. XIX.

———WHAT a conjuncture was here lost!———My father in one of his best explanatory moods,———in eager pursuit of a metaphysic point into the very regions where clouds and thick darkness would soon have encompassed it about; ———my uncle *Toby* in one of the finest dispositions for it in the world;———his head like a smoak-jack;———the funnel unswept, and the ideas whirling round and round about in it, all obfuscated and darkened over with fuliginous matter!——— By the tomb stone of *Lucian*[1]———if it is in being,———if not, why then, by his ashes! by the ashes of my dear *Rabelais,*[2] and dearer *Cervantes,*———my father and my uncle *Toby's* discourse upon TIME and ETERNITY,———was a discourse devoutly to be wished for! and the petulancy of my father's humour in putting a stop to it, as he did, was a robbery of the *Ontologic treasury,*[3] of such a jewel, as no coalition of great occasions and great men, are ever likely to restore to it again.

---

[3]A machine placed in a chimney to turn a roasting-spit by use of the current of ascending air.

[1]Lucian (c. 120–c. 180), Greek satirist and humorist.

[2]François Rabelais (c. 1495–1553), the French humorist whose *Gargantua* and *Pantagruel* strongly influenced both the humour and the style of *Tristram Shandy*.

[3]*I.e.,* the treasury of ontology, the branch of metaphysics which deals with the nature or essential properties of things in the abstract.

CHAP. XX.

THO' my father persisted in not going on with the discourse,——yet he could not get my uncle *Toby's* smoak-
jack out of his head,——piqued as he was at first with it;——
there was something in the comparison at the bottom, which
hit his fancy; for which purpose resting his elbow upon the
table, and reclining the right side of his head upon the palm
of his hand,——but looking first stedfastly in the fire,——he
began to commune with himself and philosophize about it:
but his spirits being wore out with the fatigues of investigat-
ing new tracts, and the constant exertion of his faculties upon
that variety of subjects which had taken their turn in the discourse,——the idea of the smoak-jack soon turned all his ideas
upside down,——so that he fell asleep almost before he knew
what he was about.

As for my uncle *Toby,* his smoak-jack had not made a dozen
revolutions, before he fell asleep also.——Peace be with them
both.——Dr. *Slop* is engaged with the midwife, and my
mother above stairs.——*Trim* is busy in turning an old pair
of jack-boots into a couple of mortars to be employed in the
siege of *Messina* next summer,——and is this instant boring
the touch holes with the point of a hot poker.——All my
heroes are off my hands;——'tis the first time I have had a
moment to spare,——and I'll make use of it, and write my
preface.

THE

Author's PREFACE.

NO, I'll not say a word about it,——here it is;——in publishing it,——I have appealed to the world,——and to
the world I leave it;——it must speak for itself.

All I know of the matter is,——when I sat down, my intent

was to write a good book; and as far as the tenuity of my understanding would hold out,——a wise, aye, and a discreet,
——taking care only, as I went along, to put into it all the wit
and the judgment (be it more or less) which the great author
and bestower of them had thought fit originally to give me,
——so that, as your worships see,——'tis just as God pleases.

Now, *Agelastes*[1] (speaking dispraisingly) sayeth, That there
may be some wit in it, for aught he knows,——but no judgment at all. And *Triptolemus* and *Phutatorius* agreeing thereto, ask, How is it possible there should? for that wit and judgment in this world never go together; inasmuch as they are
two operations differing from each other as wide as east is
from west.——So, says *Locke*,[2]——so are farting and hickup-
ing, say I. But in answer to this, *Didius* the great church
lawyer, in his code *de fartandi et illustrandi fallaciis*,[3] doth
maintain and make fully appear, That an illustration is no
argument,——nor do I maintain the wiping of a looking-glass
clean, to be a syllogism;——but you all, may it please your
worships, see the better for it,——so that the main good these
things do, is only to clarify the understanding, previous to
the application of the argument itself, in order to free it from
any little motes, or specks of opacular matter, which if left
swimming therein, might hinder a conception and spoil all.

Now, my dear Anti-Shandeans, and thrice able critics, and

---

[1]"One who never laughs"; probably a locally recognizable satire on one
of Sterne's acquaintance who disapproved of his sportive vein. *Triptolemus:* probably taken from the Triptolemus of Greek mythology who
was the inventor of agriculture and a giver of laws, and, subsequently, a
judge in the infernal regions. *Phutatorius:* copulator, lecher.

[2]In distinguishing between wit and judgment, Locke had written:
"Wit [lies] most in the assemblage of ideas, and putting those together
with quickness and variety, wherein can be found any resemblance or
congruity, thereby to make up pleasant pictures and agreeable visions in
the fancy; judgment, on the contrary, lies quite on the other side, in
separating carefully, one from another, ideas wherein can be found the
least difference, thereby to avoid being misled by similitude and by
affinity to take one thing for another." (*An Essay Concerning Human
Understanding,* 2.11.2.)

[3]*Of farting, and the explaining of deceptions.* For Didius, see p. 12,
n. 1.

fellow-labourers, (for to you I write this Preface)[4]——and to
you, most subtle statesmen and discreet doctors (do——pull
off your beards) renowned for gravity and wisdom;——*Mono-
polus*[5] my politician,——*Didius,* my counsel; *Kysarcius,* my
friend;——*Phutatorius,* my guide;——*Gastripheres,* the pre-
server of my life; *Somnolentius,* the balm and repose of it,
——not forgetting all others as well sleeping as waking,——
ecclesiastical as civil, whom for brevity, but out of no resentment to you, I lump all together.——Believe me, right worthy,

My most zealous wish and fervent prayer in your behalf,
and in my own too, in case the thing is not done already for
us,——is, that the great gifts and endowments both of wit
and judgment, with every thing which usually goes along with
them,——such as memory, fancy, genius, eloquence, quick
parts, and what not, may this precious moment without stint
or measure, let or hinderance, be poured down warm as each
of us could bear it,——scum and sediment an' all; (for I would
not have a drop lost) into the several receptacles, cells, cellules,
domiciles, dormitories, refectories, and spare places of our
brains,——in such sort, that they might continue to be in-
jected and tunn'd[6] into, according to the true intent and meaning of my wish, until every vessel of them, both great and
small, be so replenished, saturated and fill'd up therewith, that
no more, would it save a man's life, could possibly be got
either in or out.

Bless us!——what noble work we should make!——how
should I tickle it off!——and what spirits should I find my-

---

[4]A paraphrase of the opening sentence of the Author's Prologue to the
First Book of Rabelais: "Most noble and illustrious drinkers, and you
thrice-precious pockified blades (for to you and none else do I dedicate
my writings) . . ." (the Urquehart-Motteux translation). Of course
Sterne expected the paraphrase to be recognized and himself to be compared with Rabelais.

[5]"A monopolist"; probably locally recognizable satire. *Kysarcius:* a
portmanteau-word, probably Sterne's translation of *Baise-cul,* a "great
lord" in Rabelais, 2.10–13. *Gastripheres:* another portmanteau-word,
"Paunch-carrier," or "Big-belly." *Somnolentius:* one who sleeps; probably local satire on an acquaintance too dull to understand or applaud
Sterne's wit.

[6]Poured, as liquor into a tun or cask.

self in, to be writing away for such readers!——and you,——
just heaven!——with what raptures would you sit and read,
——but oh!——'tis too much,——I am sick,——I faint away
deliciously at the thoughts of it!——'tis more than nature can
bear!——lay hold of me,——I am giddy,——I am stone blind,
——I'm dying,——I am gone.——Help! Help! Help!——
But hold,——I grow something better again, for I am beginning to foresee, when this is over, that as we shall all of us
continue to be great wits,——we should never agree amongst
ourselves, one day to an end:——there would be so much
satire and sarcasm,——scoffing and flouting, with raillying and
reparteeing of it,——thrusting and parrying in one corner or
another,——there would be nothing but mischief amongst us.
——Chaste stars! what biting and scratching, and what a
racket and a clatter we should make, what with breaking of
heads, and rapping of knuckles, and hitting of sore places,——
there would be no such thing as living for us.

But then again, as we should all of us be men of great judgment, we should make up matters as fast as ever they went
wrong; and though we should abominate each other, ten times
worse than so many devils or devilesses, we should nevertheless, my dear creatures, be all courtesy and kindness,——milk
and honey,——'twould be a second land of promise,——a paradise upon earth, if there was such a thing to be had,——so that
upon the whole we should have done well enough.

All I fret and fume at, and what most distresses my invention at present, is how to bring the point itself to bear; for as
your worships well know, that of these heavenly emanations
of *wit* and *judgment,* which I have so bountifully wished both
for your worships and myself,——there is but a certain *quantum* stored up for us all, for the use and behoof of the whole
race of mankind; and such small *modicums* of 'em are only
sent forth into this wide world, circulating here and there in
one by corner or another,——and in such narrow streams, and
at such prodigious intervals from each other, that one would
wonder how it holds out, or could be sufficient for the wants
and emergencies of so many great states, and populous empires.

Indeed there is one thing to be considered, that in *Nova Zembla,*[7] *North Lapland,* and in all those cold and dreary tracts of the globe, which lie more directly under the arctick and antarctick circles,——where the whole province of a man's concernments lies for near nine months together, within the narrow compass of his cave,——where the spirits are compressed almost to nothing,——and where the passions of a man, with every thing which belongs to them, are as frigid as the zone itself;——there the least quantity of *judgment* imaginable does the business,——and of *wit,*——there is a total and an absolute saving,——for as not one spark is wanted, ——so not one spark is given.   Angels and ministers of grace defend us!   What a dismal thing would it have been to have governed a kingdom, to have fought a battle, or made a treaty, or run a match, or wrote a book, or got a child, or held a provincial chapter[8] there, with so *plentiful a lack* of wit and judgment about us! for mercy's sake! let us think no more about it, but travel on as fast as we can southwards into *Norway,*—— crossing over *Swedeland,* if you please, through the small triangular province of *Angermania*[9] to the lake of *Bothnia;*[10] coasting along it through east and west *Bothnia,*[11] down to *Carelia,*[12] and so on, through all those states and provinces which border upon the far side of the *Gulf* of *Finland,* and the north east of the *Baltick,* up to *Petersbourg,*[13] and just stepping into *Ingria;*[14]——then stretching over directly from thence through the north parts of the *Russian* empire——leaving *Siberia* a little upon the left hand till we get into the very heart of *Russian* and *Asiatick Tartary.*

---

[7]An uninhabited island in the Arctic Ocean north of Russia and northwest of Siberia.

[8]The chapter or council of a provincial bishop.

[9]Angermanland, a district in northern Sweden.

[10]The Gulf of Bothnia, the northern extension of the Baltic Sea.

[11]The territory lying to the east and west of the Gulf of Bothnia.

[12]Karelia, a district east of the Gulf of Bothnia.

[13]St. Petersburg, the former name of Leningrad.

[14]Ingermanland, a territory lying east of Esthonia on the south-eastern shore of the Gulf of Finland.

Now throughout this long tour which I have led you, you observe the good people are better off by far, than in the polar countries which we have just left:——for if you hold your hand over your eyes, and look very attentively, you may perceive some small glimmerings (as it were) of wit, with a comfortable provision of good plain *houshold* judgment, which taking the quality and quantity of it together, they make a very good shift with,——and had they more of either the one or the other, it would destroy the proper ballance betwixt them, and I am satisfied moreover they would want occasions to put them to use.

Now, Sir, if I conduct you home again into this warmer and more luxuriant island, where you perceive the spring tide of our blood and humours runs high,——where we have more ambition, and pride, and envy, and lechery, and other whoreson passions upon our hands to govern and subject to reason,——the *height* of our wit and the *depth* of our judgment, you see, are exactly proportioned to the *length* and *breadth* of our necessities,——and accordingly, we have them sent down amongst us in such a flowing kind of decent and creditable plenty, that no one thinks he has any cause to complain.

It must however be confessed on this head, that, as our air blows hot and cold,——wet and dry, ten times in a day, we have them in no regular and settled way;——so that sometimes for near half a century together, there shall be very little wit or judgment, either to be seen or heard of amongst us:—— the small channels of them shall seem quite dried up,——then all of a sudden the sluices shall break out, and take a fit of running again like fury,——you would think they would never stop:——and then it is, that in writing and fighting, and twenty other gallant things, we drive all the world before us.

It is by these observations, and a wary reasoning by analogy in that kind of argumentative process, which *Suidas*[15] calls *dialectick induction,*——that I draw and set up this position as most true and veritable.

---

[15]Suidas (probably fl. 10th or 11th C. A.D.) was a Byzantine lexicographer, author of a famous encyclopaedic Greek lexicon.

That of these two luminaries, so much of their irradiations are suffered from time to time to shine down upon us; as he, whose infinite wisdom which dispenses every thing in exact weight and measure, knows will just serve to light us on our way in this night of our obscurity; so that your reverences and worships now find out, nor is it a moment longer in my power to conceal it from you, That the fervent wish in your behalf with which I set out, was no more than the first insinuating *How d'ye* of a caressing prefacer stifling his reader, as a lover sometimes does a coy mistress into silence. For alas! could this effusion of light have been as easily procured, as the exordium wished it——I tremble to think how many thousands for it, of benighted travellers (in the learned sciences at least) must have groped and blundered on in the dark, all the nights of their lives,——running their heads against posts, and knocking out their brains without ever getting to their journies end;——some falling with their noses perpendicularly into sinks,[16]——others horizontally with their tails into kennels. Here one half of a learned profession tilting full butt against the other half of it, and then tumbling and rolling one over the other in the dirt like hogs.——Here the brethren, of another profession, who should have run in opposition to each other, flying on the contrary like a flock of wild geese, all in a row the same way.——What confusion!——what mistakes!——fiddlers and painters judging by their eyes and ears, ——admirable!——trusting to the passions excited in an air sung, or a story painted to the heart,——instead of measuring them by a quadrant.

In the foreground of this picture, a *statesman* turning the political wheel, like a brute, the wrong way round——*against* the stream of corruption,——by heaven!——instead of *with* it.

In this corner, a son of the divine *Esculapius*,[17] writing a book against predestination; perhaps worse,——feeling his patient's pulse, instead of his apothecary's——a brother of the

---

[16]Sewers. Kennels: gutters.

[17]In Greek mythology, Aesculapius, the son of Apollo and Coronis, was a physician and the god of the arts of healing.

faculty in the back ground upon his knees in tears,——drawing the curtains[18] of a mangled victim to beg his forgiveness; ——offering a fee,——instead of taking one.

In that spacious HALL, a coalition of the gown,[19] from all the barrs of it, driving a damn'd, dirty, vexatious cause before them, with all their might and main, the wrong way;——kicking it *out* of the great doors, instead of, *in,*——and with such fury in their looks, and such a degree of inveteracy in their manner of kicking it, as if the laws had been originally made for the peace and preservation of mankind:——perhaps a more enormous mistake committed by them still,——a litigated point fairly hung up;——for instance, Whether *John o'Nokes*[20] his nose, could stand in *Tom o'Stiles* his face, without a trespass, or not,——rashly determined by them in five and twenty minutes, which, with the cautious pro's and con's required in so intricate a proceeding, might have taken up as many months,——and if carried on upon a military plan, as your honours know, an ACTION should be, with all the stratagems practicable therein,——such as feints,——forced marches,—— surprizes,——ambuscades,——mask-batteries, and a thousand other strokes of generalship which consist in catching at all advantages on both sides,——might reasonably have lasted them as many years, finding food and raiment all that term for a centumvirate[21] of the profession.

As for the clergy————No——If I say a word against them, I'll be shot.——I have no desire,——and besides, if I had,—— I durst not for my soul touch upon the subject,——with such weak nerves and spirits, and in the condition I am in at present, 'twould be as much as my life was worth, to deject and contrist[22] myself with so sad and melancholy an account,——

---

[18]Bed curtains.

[19]The costume of certain learned professions; by extension, members of such a profession, in this instance the legal.

[20]Jack Nokes and Tom Stiles were fictitious names formerly used in actions of ejectment as John Doe and Richard Roe are used.

[21]A body of one hundred men.

[22]Make sorrowful.

and therefore, 'tis safer to draw a curtain across, and hasten from it, as fast as I can, to the main and principal point I have undertaken to clear up,——and that is, How it comes to pass, that your men of least *wit* are reported to be men of most *judgment*.——But mark,——I say, *reported to be,*——for it is no more, my dear Sirs, than a report, and which like twenty others taken up every day upon trust, I maintain to be a vile and a malicious report into the bargain.

This by the help of the observations already premised, and I hope already weighed and perpended by your reverences and worships, I shall forthwith make appear.

I hate set dissertations,——and above all things in the world, 'tis one of the silliest things in one of them, to darken your hypothesis by placing a number of tall, opake words, one before another, in a right line, betwixt your own and your reader's conception,——when in all likelihood, if you had looked about, you might have seen something standing, or hanging up, which would have cleared the point at once,—— "for what hinderance, hurt or harm, doth the laudable desire of knowledge bring to any man, if even from a sot, a pot, a fool, a stool, a winter-mittain, a truckle for a pully, the lid of a goldsmith's crucible, an oyl bottle, an old slipper, or a cane chair?"[23]——I am this moment sitting upon one. Will you give me leave to illustrate this affair of wit and judgment, by the two knobs on the top of the back of it,——they are fasten'd on, you see, with two pegs stuck slightly into two gimlet-holes, and will place what I have to say in so clear a light, as to let you see through the drift and meaning of my whole preface, as plainly as if every point and particle of it was made up of sun beams.

I enter now directly upon the point.

——Here stands *wit,*——and there stands *judgment,* close beside it, just like the two knobbs I'm speaking of, upon the back of this self same chair on which I am sitting.

——You see, they are the highest and most ornamental parts

---

[23]The quoted passage, save the final phrase, is transcribed with slight alteration from Rabelais, 3.16.

of its *frame*,——as wit and judgment are of *ours*,——and like them too, indubitably both made and fitted to go together, in order as we say in all such cases of duplicated embellishments, ——*to answer one another.*

Now for the sake of an experiment, and for the clearer illustrating this matter,——let us for a moment, take off one of these two curious ornaments (I care not which) from the point or pinacle of the chair it now stands on;——nay, don't laugh at it.——But did you ever see in the whole course of your lives such a ridiculous business as this has made of it? ——Why, 'tis as miserable a sight as a sow with one ear; and there is just as much sense and symmetry in the one, as in the other:——do,——pray, get off your seats, only to take a view of it.——Now would any man who valued his character a straw, have turned a piece of work out of his hand in such a condition?——nay, lay your hands upon your hearts, and answer this plain question, Whether this one single knobb which now stands here like a blockhead by itself, can serve any purpose upon earth, but to put one in mind of the want of the other;——and let me further ask, in case the chair was your own, if you would not in your consciences think, rather than be as it is, that it would be ten times better without any knobb at all?

Now these two knobs——or top ornaments of the mind of man, which crown the whole entablature,——being, as I said, wit and judgment, which of all others, as I have proved it, are the most needful,——the most priz'd,——the most calamitous to be without, and consequently the hardest to come at,—— for all these reasons put together, there is not a mortal amongst us, so destitute of a love of good fame or feeding,——or so ignorant of what will do him good therein,——who does not wish and stedfastly resolve in his own mind, to be, or to be thought at least master of the one or the other, and indeed of both of them, if the thing seems any way feasible, or likely to be brought to pass.

Now your graver gentry having little or no kind of chance in aiming at the one,——unless they laid hold of the other,

——pray what do you think would become of them?——Why,
Sirs, in spite of all their *gravities,* they must e'en have been
contented to have gone with their insides naked:——this was
not to be borne, but by an effort of philosophy not to be supposed in the case we are upon,——so that no one could well
have been angry with them, had they been satisfied with what
little they could have snatched up and secreted under their
cloaks and great perrywigs, had they not raised a *hue* and *cry*
at the same time against the lawful owners.

I need not tell your worships, that this was done with so
much cunning and artifice,——that the great *Locke,* who was
seldom outwitted by false sounds,——was nevertheless bubbled here. The cry, it seems, was so deep and solemn a one,
and what with the help of great wigs, grave faces, and other
implements of deceit, was rendered so general a one against
the *poor wits* in this matter, that the philosopher himself was
deceived by it,——it was his glory to free the world from the
lumber of a thousand vulgar errors;——but this was not of
the number; so that instead of sitting down coolly, as such
a philosopher should have done, to have examined the matter
of fact before he philosophised upon it;——on the contrary, he
took the fact for granted, and so joined in with the cry, and
halloo'd it as boisterously as the rest.[24]

This has been made the *Magna Charta* of stupidity ever
since,——but your reverences plainly see, it has been obtained
in such a manner, that the title to it is not worth a groat;——
which by the bye is one of the many and vile impositions
which gravity and grave folks have to answer for hereafter.

As for great wigs, upon which I may be thought to have
spoken my mind too freely,——I beg leave to qualify whatever has been unguardedly said to their dispraise or prejudice,
by one general declaration——That I have no abhorrence whatever, nor do I detest and abjure either great wigs or long
beards,——any further than when I see they are bespoke and
let grow on purpose to carry on this self-same imposture——

---

[24]See p. 193, n. 2.

for any purpose,——peace be with them;—— ☞ mark only,
——I write not for them.

CHAP. XXI.

EVERY day for at least ten years together did my father
resolve to have it mended,——'tis not mended yet;——
no family but ours would have borne with it an hour,——and
what is most astonishing, there was not a subject in the world
upon which my father was so eloquent, as upon that of door-
hinges.——And yet at the same time, he was certainly one of
the greatest bubbles[1] to them, I think, that history can produce: his rhetoric and conduct were at perpetual handy-cuffs.[2]
——Never did the parlour-door open——but his philosophy or
his principles fell a victim to it;——three drops of oyl with
a feather, and a smart stroke of a hammer, had saved his honour for ever.

——Inconsistent soul that man is!——languishing under
wounds, which he has the power to heal!——his whole life a
contradiction to his knowledge!——his reason, that precious
gift of God to him——(instead of pouring in oyl) serving but
to sharpen his sensibilities,——to multiply his pains and render him more melancholy and uneasy under them!——poor
unhappy creature, that he should do so!——are not the necessary causes of misery in this life enow, but he must add vol-
untary ones to his stock of sorrow;——struggle against evils
which cannot be avoided, and submit to others, which a tenth
part of the trouble they create him, would remove from his
heart for ever?

By all that is good and virtuous! if there are three drops of
oyl to be got, and a hammer to be found within ten miles of
Shandy-Hall,——the parlour-door hinge shall be mended this
reign.

---

[1]Dupes.

[2]Handicuffs, blows with the hand.

CHAP. XXII.

WHEN corporal *Trim* had brought his two mortars to
bear, he was delighted with his handy-work above measure; and knowing what a pleasure it would be to his master
to see them, he was not able to resist the desire he had of
carrying them directly into his parlour.

Now next to the moral lesson I had in view in mentioning
the affair of *hinges,* I had a speculative consideration arising
out of it, and it is this.

Had the parlour-door open'd and turn'd upon its hinges, as
a door should do——

——Or for example, as cleverly as our government has been
turning upon its hinges,——(that is, in case things have all
along gone well with your worship,——otherwise I give up my
simile)——in this case, I say, there had been no danger either
to master or man, in corporal *Trim*'s peeping in: the moment,
he had beheld my father and my uncle *Toby* fast asleep,——
the respectfulness of his carriage was such, he would have retired as silent as death, and left them both in their arm-chairs,
dreaming as happy as he had found them: but the thing was
morally speaking so very impracticable, that for the many years
in which this hinge was suffered to be out of order, and
amongst the hourly grievances my father submitted to upon its
account,——this was one; that he never folded his arms to
take his nap after dinner, but the thoughts of being unavoidably awakened by the first person who should open the door,
was always uppermost in his imagination, and so incessantly
step'd in betwixt him and the first balmy presage of his repose,
as to rob him, as he often declared, of the whole sweets of it.

"*When things move upon bad hinges,* an' please your lordships, *how can it be otherwise?*"

Pray what's the matter?   Who is there? cried my father,
waking, the moment the door began to creak.——I wish the
smith would give a peep at that confounded hinge.——'Tis

nothing, an' please your honour, said *Trim,* but two mortars I am bringing in.——They shan't make a clatter with them here, cried my father hastily.——If Dr. *Slop* has any drugs to pound, let him do it in the kitchen.——May it please your honour, cried *Trim,*——they are two mortar-pieces for a siege next summer, which I have been making out of a pair of jack-boots, which *Obadiah* told me your honour had left off wearing.—— By heaven! cried my father, springing out of his chair, as he swore,——I have not one appointment belonging to me, which I set so much store by, as I do by these jack-boots,——they were our great-grandfather's, brother *Toby,*——they were *hereditary.* Then I fear, quoth my uncle *Toby, Trim* has cut off the entail.——I have only cut off the tops, an' please your honour, cried *Trim.*——I hate *perpetuities* as much as any man alive, cried my father,——but these jack-boots, continued he, (smiling, though very angry at the same time) have been in the family, brother, ever since the civil wars;——Sir *Roger Shandy* wore them at the battle of *Marston-Moor.*——I declare I would not have taken ten pounds for them.——I'll pay you the money, brother *Shandy,* quoth my uncle *Toby,* looking at the two mortars with infinite pleasure, and putting his hand into his breeches-pocket, as he viewed them.——I'll pay you the ten pounds this moment with all my heart and soul.——

Brother *Toby,* replied my father, altering his tone, you care not what money you dissipate and throw away, provided, continued he, 'tis but upon a SIEGE.——Have I not a hundred and twenty pounds a year, besides my half-pay? cried my uncle *Toby.*——What is that,——replied my father, hastily,——to ten pounds for a pair of jack-boots?——twelve guineas for your *pontoons;*——half as much for your *Dutch*-draw-bridge; ——to say nothing of the train of little brass-artillery you bespoke last week, with twenty other preparations for the siege of *Messina;* believe me, dear brother *Toby,* continued my father, taking him kindly by the hand,——these military operations of yours are above your strength;——you mean well, brother,——but they carry you into greater expences than you were first aware of,——and take my word,——dear *Toby,* they will in the end quite ruin your fortune, and make a beggar of you.——What signifies it if they do, brother, replied my uncle *Toby,* so long as we know 'tis for the good of the nation.——

My father could not help smiling for his soul;——his anger at the worst was never more than a spark,——and the zeal and simplicity of *Trim,*——and the generous (tho' hobby-horsical) gallantry of my uncle *Toby,* brought him into perfect good humour with them in an instant.

Generous souls!——God prosper you both, and your mortar-pieces too, quoth my father to himself.

CHAP. XXIII.

ALL is quiet and hush, cried my father, at least above stairs, ——I hear not one foot stirring.——Prithee, *Trim,* who is in the kitchen? There is no one soul in the kitchen, answered *Trim,* making a low bow as he spoke, except Dr. *Slop.* ——Confusion! cried my father, (getting up upon his legs a second time)——not one single thing has gone right this day! had I faith in astrology, brother, (which by the bye, my father had) I would have sworn some retrograde planet was hanging over this unfortunate house of mine, and turning every individual thing in it out of its place.——Why, I thought Dr. *Slop* had been above stairs with my wife, and so said you.——What can the fellow be puzzling about in the kitchen?——He is busy, an' please your honour, replied *Trim,* in making a bridge.——'Tis very obliging in him, quoth my uncle *Toby;* ——pray give my humble service to Dr. *Slop, Trim,* and tell him I thank him heartily.

You must know, my uncle *Toby* mistook the bridge as widely as my father mistook the mortars;——but to understand how my uncle *Toby* could mistake the bridge,——I fear I must give you an exact account of the road which led to it; ——or to drop my metaphor, (for there is nothing more dis-

honest in an historian, than the use of one,)——in order to
conceive the probability of this error in my uncle *Toby* aright,
I must give you some account of an adventure of *Trim's*,
though much against my will. I say much against my will,
only because the story, in one sense, is certainly out of its
place here; for by right it should come in, either amongst the
anecdotes of my uncle *Toby's* amours with widow *Wadman,* in
which corporal *Trim* was no mean actor,——or else in the
middle of his and my uncle *Toby's* campaigns on the bowling
green,——for it will do very well in either place;——but then
if I reserve it for either of those parts of my story,——I ruin
the story I'm upon,——and if I tell it here——I anticipate matters, and ruin it there.

——What would your worships have me to do in this case?
——Tell it, Mr. *Shandy,* by all means.——You are a fool,
Tristram, if you do.

O ye POWERS! (for powers ye are, and great ones too)——
which enable mortal man to tell a story worth the hearing,——
that kindly shew him, where he is to begin it,——and where
he is to end it,——what he is to put into it,——and what he is
to leave out,——how much of it he is to cast into shade,——
and whereabouts he is to throw his light!——Ye, who preside
over this vast empire of biographical freebooters, and see how
many scrapes and plunges your subjects hourly fall into;——
will you do one thing?

I beg and beseech you, (in case you will do nothing better
for us) that wherever, in any part of your dominions it so falls
out, that three several roads meet in one point, as they have
done just here,——that at least you set up a guide-post, in the
center of them, in mere charity to direct an uncertain devil,
which of the three he is to take.

CHAP. XXIV.

THO' the shock my uncle *Toby* received the year after the
demolition of *Dunkirk*,[1] in his affair with widow *Wadman,* had fixed him in a resolution, never more to think of the
sex,——or of aught which belonged to it;——yet corporal
Trim had made no such bargain with himself. Indeed in my
uncle *Toby's* case there was a strange and unaccountable concurrence of circumstances which insensibly drew him in, to
lay siege to that fair and strong citadel.——In *Trim's* case
there was a concurrence of nothing in the world, but of him
and *Bridget* in the kitchen;——though in truth, the love and
veneration he bore his master was such, and so fond was he
of imitating him in all he did, that had my uncle *Toby* employed his time and genius in tagging of points,[2]——I am persuaded the honest corporal would have laid down his arms,
and followed his example with pleasure. When therefore my
uncle *Toby* sat down before the mistress,——corporal *Trim*
incontinently took ground before the maid.

Now, my dear friend *Garrick,*[3] whom I have so much cause
to esteem and honour,——(why, or wherefore, 'tis no matter)
——can it escape your penetration,——I defy it,——that so
many play-wrights, and opificers[4] of chit chat have ever since
been working upon *Trim's* and my uncle *Toby's* pattern.——
I care not what *Aristotle,*[5] or *Pacuvius,* or *Bossu,* or *Ricaboni*

---

[1]Dunkirk was demolished, according to the Peace of Utrecht, during
September, October, and November of 1713.

[2]Fastening metal tags to laces; i.e., trivialities.

[3]See p. 180, n. 1.

[4]Fabricators, artificers.

[5]Alluding to Aristotle's *Poetics. Pacuvius* (c. 220–c. 130 B.C.) was a
Roman tragic poet. For *Bossu,* see p. 181, n. 2. *Ricaboni:* probably
Luigi Riccoboni (1675–1753), an Italian actor, playwright, and writer on
dramatic history and theory; Sterne may, however, have been thinking of
his son, Francesco (1707–1772), whose *L'Art du théâtre* had been published in 1750.

say,——(though I never read one of them)——there is not a
greater difference between a single-horse chair and madam
Pompadour's vis-à-vis,[6] than betwixt a single amour, and an
amour thus nobly doubled, and going upon all four, prancing
throughout a grand drama.——Sir, a simple, single, silly affair
of that kind,——is quite lost in five acts,——but that is neither
here or there.

After a series of attacks and repulses in a course of nine
months on my uncle *Toby's* quarter, a most minute account of
every particular of which shall be given in its proper place,
my uncle *Toby,* honest man! found it necessary to draw off his
forces, and raise the siege somewhat indignantly.

Corporal *Trim,* as I said, had made no such bargain either
with himself——or with any one else,——the fidelity however of his heart not suffering him to go into a house which
his master had forsaken with disgust,——he contented himself with turning his part of the siege into a blockade;——
that is, he kept others off,——for though he never after went
to the house, yet he never met *Bridget* in the village, but he
would either nod or wink, or smile, or look kindly at her,——
or (as circumstances directed), he would shake her by the hand,
——or ask her lovingly how she did,——or would give her a
ribban,——and now and then, though never but when it could
be done with decorum, would give *Bridget* a ———

Precisely in this situation, did these things stand for five
years; that is, from the demolition of *Dunkirk* in the year 13,
to the latter end of my uncle *Toby's* campaign in the year 18,
which was about six or seven weeks before the time I'm speaking of.——When *Trim,* as his custom was, after he had put
my uncle *Toby* to bed, going down one moon-shiny night to
see that every thing was right at his fortifications,——in the
lane separated from the bowling-green with flowering shrubs
and holly,——he espied his *Bridget.*

As the corporal thought there was nothing in the world so
well worth shewing as the glorious works which he and my
uncle *Toby* had made, *Trim* courteously and gallantly took her

———
[6]A carriage for two or four persons, seated face to face.

by the hand, and led her in: this was not done so privately,
but that the foul-mouth'd trumpet of Fame[7] carried it from
ear to ear, till at length it reached my father's, with this untoward circumstance along with it, that my uncle *Toby's* curious draw-bridge, constructed and painted after the *Dutch*
fashion, and which went quite across the ditch,——was broke
down, and some how or other crush'd all to pieces that very
night.

My father, as you have observed, had no great esteem for
my uncle *Toby's* hobby-horse,——he thought it the most ridiculous horse that ever gentleman mounted, and indeed unless
my uncle *Toby* vexed him about it, could never think of it
once, without smiling at it,——so that it never could get lame
or happen any mischance, but it tickled my father's imagination beyond measure; but this being an accident much more
to his humour than any one which had yet befall'n it, it
proved an inexhaustible fund of entertainment to him.——
Well,——but dear *Toby!* my father would say, do tell us
seriously how this affair of the bridge happened.——How
can you teaze me so much about it? my uncle *Toby* would
reply,——I have told it you twenty times, word for word as
Trim told it me.——Prithee, how was it then, corporal? my
father would cry, turning to *Trim*.——It was a mere misfortune, an' please your honour,——I was shewing Mrs.[8]
Bridget our fortifications, and in going too near the edge of
the fossé, I unfortunately slipp'd in.——Very well *Trim!* my
father would cry,——(smiling mysteriously, and giving a nod,
——but without interrupting him)——and being link'd fast,
an' please your honour, arm in arm with Mrs. *Bridget*, I
dragg'd her after me, by means of which she fell backwards
soss[9] against the bridge,——and *Trim's* foot, (my uncle *Toby*
would cry, taking the story out of his mouth) getting into the

---

[7]The trumpet through which the capricious goddess of Fame spreads
abroad all unpleasant rumours and unwelcome information.

[8]*Mistress,* a courtesy title formerly applied to both married and unmarried women.

[9]Directly, plump.

cuvette,[10] he tumbled full against the bridge too.——It was a thousand to one, my uncle *Toby* would add, that the poor fellow did not break his leg.———Ay truly! my father would say,——a limb is soon broke, brother *Toby,* in such encounters.——And so, an' please your honour, the bridge, which your honour knows was a very slight one, was broke down betwixt us, and splintered all to pieces.

At other times, but especially when my uncle *Toby* was so unfortunate as to say a syllable about cannons, bombs or petards,——my father would exhaust all the stores of his eloquence (which indeed were very great) in a panegyric upon the BATTERING-RAMS of the ancients,——the VINEA[11] which *Alexander* made use of at the siege of *Tyre.*——He would tell my uncle *Toby* of the CATAPULTÆ of the *Syrians* which threw such monstrous stones so many hundred feet, and shook the strongest bulwarks from their very foundation;——he would go on and describe the wonderful mechanism of the BALLISTA, which *Marcellinus* makes so much rout about,——the terrible effects of the PYRABOLI,——which cast fire,——the danger of the TEREBRA and SCORPIO, which cast javelins.——But what are these, he would say, to the destructive machinery of corporal *Trim?*——Believe me, brother *Toby,* no bridge, or bastion, or sally port[12] that ever was constructed in this world, can hold out against such artillery.

My uncle *Toby* would never attempt any defence against the force of this ridicule, but that of redoubling the vehemence of smoaking his pipe; in doing which, he raised so dense a vapour one night after supper, that it set my father, who was a little phthisical, into a suffocating fit of violent coughing: my uncle *Toby* leap'd up without feeling the pain upon his groin,——

----

[10]A trench dug in the middle of a large ditch to serve as a drain.

[11]A movable shed, serving to protect besiegers. Tyre fell to Alexander the Great in 332 B.C. *Catapultæ:* catapults. *Ballista:* ancient military engine for hurling great missiles. *Ammianus Marcellinus* (c. 330–c. 395) was a Greek historian of Rome; the reference is to his *Rerum Gestarum Libri,* 23.4.

[12]A postern gate leading from under the rampart into the ditch, by which a sally may be made through the covered-way.

and, with infinite pity, stood beside his brother's chair, tapping his back with one hand, and holding his head with the other, and from time to time, wiping his eyes with a clean cambrick handkerchief, which he pull'd out of his pocket.——
The affectionate and endearing manner in which my uncle *Toby* did these little offices,——cut my father thro' his reins, for the pain he had just been giving him.——May my brains be knock'd out with a battering ram or a catapulta, I care not which, quoth my father to himself,——if ever I insult this worthy soul more.

CHAP. XXV.

THE draw-bridge being held irreparable, *Trim* was ordered directly to set about another,——but not upon the same model; for cardinal *Alberoni's*[1] intrigues at that time being discovered, and my uncle *Toby* rightly foreseeing that a flame would inevitably break out betwixt *Spain* and the Empire, and that the operations of the ensuing campaign must in all likelihood be either in *Naples* or *Sicily,*——he determined upon an *Italian* bridge,——(my uncle *Toby,* by the bye, was not far out in his conjectures)——but my father, who was infinitely the better politician, and took the lead as far of my uncle *Toby* in the cabinet, as my uncle *Toby* took it of him in the field,——convinced him, that if the King of *Spain* and the Emperor went together by the ears, that *England* and *France* and *Holland* must, by force of their pre-engagements, all enter the lists too;——and if so, he would say, the combatants, brother *Toby,* as sure as we are alive, will fall to it again, pell-mell, upon the old prize-fighting stage of *Flanders;*——then what will you do with your *Italian* bridge?

——We will go on with it then, upon the old model, cried my uncle *Toby.*

[1]Giulio Alberoni (1664–1752), Spanish-Italian cardinal and statesman who, as prime minister of Philip V of Spain, pursued such an ambitious foreign policy that by 1718 Spain was involved in a disastrous war with England, France, Holland, and the Empire.

When Corporal *Trim* had about half finished it in that stile,
——my uncle *Toby* found out a capital defect in it, which he
had never thoroughly considered before. It turned, it seems,
upon hinges at both ends of it, opening in the middle, one half
of which turning to one side of the fossé, and the other, to the
other; the advantage of which was this, that by dividing the
weight of the bridge into two equal portions, it impowered
my uncle *Toby* to raise it up or let it down with the end of his
crutch, and with one hand, which, as his garrison was weak,
was as much as he could well spare,——but the disadvantages
of such a construction were insurmountable,——for by this
means, he would say, I leave one half of my bridge in my
enemy's possession,——and pray of what use is the other?

The natural remedy for this, was no doubt to have his
bridge fast only at one end with hinges, so that the whole
might be lifted up together, and stand bolt upright,——but
that was rejected for the reason given above.

For a whole week after he was determined in his mind to
have one of that particular construction which is made to draw
back horizontally, to hinder a passage; and to thrust forwards
again to gain a passage,——of which sorts your worships
might have seen three famous ones at *Spires* before its destruction,——and one now at *Brisac*,[2] if I mistake not;——but
my father advising my uncle *Toby,* with great earnestness, to
have nothing more to do with thrusting bridges,——and my
uncle foreseeing moreover that it would but perpetuate the
memory of the corporal's misfortune,——he changed his mind,
for that of the marquis *d'Hôpital*'s invention, which the
younger *Bernouilli* has so well and learnedly described, as your
worships may see,——*Act. Erud. Lips.* an. 1695,[3]——to these
a lead weight is an eternal ballance, and keeps watch as well as
a couple of centinels, inasmuch as the construction of them

---

[2] Alt-Breisach.

[3] *Acta Eruditorum,* Leipzig. Jacques Bernouilli (1654–1705), a famous
mathematician, presented his solution of the curve in the volume for
1695, pp. 65–66; but the reference, along with most of the discourse on
bridges in this chapter, Sterne took from the article "Bridge" in Chambers's *Cyclopædia*.

was a curve-line approximating to a cycloid,——if not a cycloid itself.

My uncle *Toby* understood the nature of a parabola as well as any man in *England*,——but was not quite such a master of the cycloid;——he talked however about it every day;——the bridge went not forwards.——We'll ask somebody about it, cried my uncle *Toby* to *Trim*.

CHAP. XXVI.

WHEN *Trim* came in and told my father, that Dr. *Slop* was in the kitchen, and busy in making a bridge,—— my uncle *Toby*,——the affair of the jack-boots having just then raised a train of military ideas in his brain,——took it instantly for granted that Dr. *Slop* was making a model of the marquis *d'Hôpital*'s bridge.——'Tis very obliging in him, quoth my uncle *Toby*;——pray give my humble service to Dr. *Slop, Trim,* and tell him I thank him heartily.

Had my uncle *Toby*'s head been a *Savoyard*'s box,[1] and my father peeping in all the time at one end of it,——it could not have given him a more distinct conception of the operations in my uncle *Toby*'s imagination, than what he had; so notwithstanding the catapulta and battering-ram, and his bitter imprecation about them, he was just beginning to triumph.——

When *Trim*'s answer, in an instant, tore the laurel from his brows, and twisted it to pieces.

CHAP. XXVII.

——THIS unfortunate draw-bridge of yours, quoth my father——God bless your honour, cried *Trim,* 'tis a bridge for master's nose.——In bringing him into the world with his vile instruments, he has crush'd his nose, *Susannah* says, as flat as a pancake to his face, and he is making a false

[1] A hurdy-gurdy.

bridge with a piece of cotton and a thin piece of whalebone out of *Susannah's* stays, to raise it up.

——Lead me, brother *Toby,* cried my father, to my room this instant.

CHAP. XXVIII.

FROM the first moment I sat down to write my life for the amusement of the world, and my opinions for its instruction, has a cloud insensibly been gathering over my father.——A tide of little evils and distresses has been setting in against him.——Not one thing, as he observed himself, has gone right: and now is the storm thicken'd, and going to break, and pour down full upon his head.

I enter upon this part of my story in the most pensive and melancholy frame of mind, that ever sympathetic breast was touched with.——My nerves relax as I tell it.——Every line I write, I feel an abatement of the quickness of my pulse, and of that careless alacrity with it, which every day of my life prompts me to say and write a thousand things I should not.——And this moment that I last dipp'd my pen into my ink, I could not help taking notice what a cautious air of sad composure and solemnity there appear'd in my manner of doing it.——Lord! how different from the rash jerks, and harebrain'd squirts thou art wont, *Tristram!* to transact it with in other humours,——dropping thy pen,——spurting thy ink about thy table and thy books,——as if thy pen and thy ink, thy books and thy furniture cost thee nothing.

CHAP. XXIX.

——I WON'T go about to argue the point with you,——'tis so,——and I am persuaded of it, madam, as much as can be, "That both man and woman bear pain or sorrow, (and, for aught I know, pleasure too) best in a horizontal position."

The moment my father got up into his chamber, he threw

himself prostrate across his bed in the wildest disorder imaginable, but at the same time, in the most lamentable attitude of a man borne down with sorrows, that ever the eye of pity dropp'd a tear for.——The palm of his right hand, as he fell upon the bed, receiving his forehead, and covering the greatest part of both his eyes, gently sunk down with his head (his elbow giving way backwards) till his nose touch'd the quilt;——his left arm hung insensible over the side of the bed, his knuckles reclining upon the handle of the chamber pot, which peep'd out beyond the valance,——his right leg (his left being drawn up towards his body) hung half over the side of the bed, the edge of it pressing upon his shin-bone. ——He felt it not. A fix'd, inflexible sorrow took possession of every line of his face.——He sigh'd once,——heaved his breast often,——but utter'd not a word.

An old set-stitch'd chair, valanced and fringed around with party-colour'd worsted bobs, stood at the bed's head, opposite to the side where my father's head reclined.——My uncle *Toby* sat him down in it.

Before an affliction is digested,——consolation ever comes too soon;——and after it is digested,——it comes too late: so that you see, madam, there is but a mark between these two, as fine almost as a hair, for a comforter to take aim at: my uncle *Toby* was always either on this side, or on that of it, and would often say, He believed in his heart, he could as soon hit the longitude;[1] for this reason, when he sat down in the chair, he drew the curtain a little forwards, and having a tear at every one's service,——he pull'd out a cambrick handkerchief,——gave a low sigh,——but held his peace.

CHAP. XXX.

——" *A* LL is not gain that is got into the purse."——So that notwithstanding my father had the happiness of reading the oddest books in the universe, and had more-

---

[1] A problem which seriously exercised astronomers and geodesists during the 17th and 18th centuries. See p. 588, n. 4.

over, in himself, the oddest way of thinking, that ever man in it was bless'd with, yet it had this drawback upon him after all,——that it laid him open to some of the oddest and most whimsical distresses; of which this particular one which he sunk under at present is as strong an example as can be given.

No doubt, the breaking down of the bridge of a child's nose, by the edge of a pair of forceps,——however scientifically applied,——would vex any man in the world, who was at so much pains in begetting a child, as my father was,——yet it will not account for the extravagance of his affliction, or will it justify the unchristian manner he abandoned and surrender'd himself up to it.

To explain this, I must leave him upon the bed for half an hour,——and my good uncle *Toby* in his old fringed chair sitting beside him.

CHAP. XXXI.

——I THINK it a very unreasonable demand,——cried my great grandfather, twisting up the paper, and throwing it upon the table.——By this account, madam, you have but two thousand pounds fortune, and not a shilling more,—— and you insist upon having three hundred pounds a year jointure for it.——

——"Because," replied my great grandmother, "you have little or no nose, Sir."——

Now, before I venture to make use of the word *Nose* a second time,——to avoid all confusion in what will be said upon it, in this interesting part of my story, it may not be amiss to explain my own meaning, and define, with all possible exactness and precision, what I would willingly be understood to mean by the term: being of opinion, that 'tis owing to the negligence and perverseness of writers, in despising this precaution, and to nothing else,——That all the polemical writings in divinity, are not as clear and demonstrative as those upon *a Will o' the Wisp,* or any other sound part of

philosophy, and natural pursuit; in order to which, what have
you to do, before you set out, unless you intend to go puzzling
on to the day of judgment,——but to give the world a good
definition, and stand to it, of the main word you have most
occasion for,——changing it, Sir, as you would a guinea, into
small coin?——which done,——let the father of confusion
puzzle you, if he can; or put a different idea either into your
head, or your reader's head, if he knows how.

In books of strict morality and close reasoning, such as this
I am engaged in,——the neglect is inexcusable; and heaven is
witness, how the world has revenged itself upon me for leaving so many openings to equivocal strictures,——and for depending so much as I have done, all along, upon the cleanliness of my reader's imaginations.

——Here are two senses, cried *Eugenius,* as we walk'd along,
pointing with the fore finger of his right hand to the word
Crevice, in the fifty-second page of the second volume of this
book of books,[1]——here are two senses,——quoth he.——
And here are two roads, replied I, turning short upon him,
——a dirty and a clean one,——which shall we take?——
The clean,——by all means, replied *Eugenius. Eugenius,* said
I, stepping before him, and laying my hand upon his breast,
——to define——is to distrust.——Thus I triumph'd over
Eugenius; but I triumph'd over him as I always do, like a fool.
——'Tis my comfort however, I am not an obstinate one;
therefore

I define a nose, as follows,——intreating only beforehand,
and beseeching my readers, both male and female, of what
age, complexion, and condition soever, for the love of God
and their own souls, to guard against the temptations and suggestions of the devil, and suffer him by no art or wile to put
any other ideas into their minds, than what I put into my
definition.——For by the word *Nose,* throughout all this long
chapter of noses, and in every other part of my work, where
the word *Nose* occurs,——I declare, by that word I mean a
Nose, and nothing more, or less.

[1] In the first edition; p. 102 in the present edition.

CHAP. XXXII.

——"BECAUSE," quoth my great grandmother, repeating the words again,——"you have little or no nose, Sir"——

S'death! cried my great grandfather, clapping his hand upon his nose,——'tis not so small as that comes to;——'tis a full inch longer than my father's.——Now, my great grandfather's nose was for all the world like unto the noses of all the men, women, and children, whom *Pantagruel* found dwelling upon the island of ENNASIN.——By the way, if you would know the strange way of getting a-kin amongst so flat-nosed a people,——you must read the book;——find it out yourself, you never can.[1]——

——'Twas shaped, Sir, like an ace of clubs.

——'Tis a full inch, continued my great grandfather, pressing up the ridge of his nose with his finger and thumb; and repeating his assertion,——'tis a full inch longer, madam, than my father's——. You must mean your uncle's, replied my great grandmother.

——My great grandfather was convinced.——He untwisted the paper, and signed the article.

CHAP. XXXIII.

——WHAT an unconscionable jointure, my dear, do we pay out of this small estate of ours, quoth my grandmother to my grandfather.

My father, replied my grandfather, had no more nose, my dear, saving the mark, than there is upon the back of my hand.——

——Now, you must know, that my great grandmother out-

---

[1] The "strange ways of being akin" in Ennasin, where the "men, women and children, have their noses shaped like an ace of clubs," are revealed in Rabelais, 4.9.

lived my grandfather twelve years; so that my father had the jointure to pay, a hundred and fifty pounds half yearly——(on *Michaelmas* and *Lady day*)——during all that time.

No man discharged pecuniary obligations with a better grace than my father.——And as far as the hundred pounds went, he would fling it upon the table, guinea by guinea, with that spirited jerk of an honest welcome, which generous souls, and generous souls only, are able to fling down money: but as soon as ever he enter'd upon the odd fifty,——he generally gave a loud *Hem!*——rubb'd the side of his nose leisurely with the flat part of his fore finger,——inserted his hand cautiously betwixt his head and the cawl[1] of his wig,——look'd at both sides of every guinea, as he parted with it,——and seldom could get to the end of the fifty pounds, without pulling out his handkerchief, and wiping his temples.

Defend me, gracious heaven! from those persecuting spirits who make no allowances for these workings within us.—— Never,——O never may I lay down in their tents, who cannot relax the engine, and feel pity for the force of education, and the prevalence of opinions long derived from ancestors!

For three generations at least, this *tenet* in favour of long noses had gradually been taking root in our family.—— Tradition was all along on its side, and Interest was every half year stepping in to strengthen it; so that the whimsicality of my father's brain was far from having the whole honour of this, as it had of almost all his other strange notions.——For in a great measure he might be said to have suck'd this in, with his mother's milk. He did his part however.——If education planted the mistake, (in case it was one) my father watered it, and ripened it to perfection.

He would often declare, in speaking his thoughts upon the subject, that he did not conceive how the greatest family in *England* could stand it out against an uninterrupted succession of six or seven short noses.——And for the contrary reason, he would generally add, That it must be one of the greatest problems in civil life, where the same number of long and

---

[1]Caul, netted substructure of a wig.

jolly noses following one another in a direct line, did not raise
and hoist it up into the best vacancies in the kingdom.———
He would often boast that the *Shandy* family rank'd very high
in king *Harry* the VIIIth's time, but owed its rise to no state
engine,——he would say,——but' to that only;——but that,
like other families, he would add,——it had felt the turn of
the wheel, and had never recovered the blow of my great
grandfather's nose.——It was an ace of clubs indeed, he would
cry, shaking his head,——and as vile a one for an unfortunate
family, as ever turn'd up trumps.[2]

———Fair and softly, gentle reader!———where is thy
fancy carrying thee?——If there is truth in man, by my great
grandfather's nose, I mean the external organ of smelling, or
that part of man which stands prominent in his face,——and
which painters say, in good jolly noses and well-proportioned
faces, should comprehend a full third,——that is, measuring
downwards from the setting on of the hair.——

——What a life of it has an author, at this pass!

CHAP. XXXIV.

IT is a singular blessing, that nature has form'd the mind of
man with the same happy backwardness and renitency
against conviction, which is observed in old dogs,——"of not
learning new tricks."

What a shuttlecock of a fellow would the greatest philosopher that ever existed, be whisk'd into at once, did he read
such books, and observe such facts, and think such thoughts,
as would eternally be making him change sides!

Now, my father, as I told you last year, detested all this.
——He pick'd up an opinion, Sir, as a man in a state of nature
picks up an apple.——It becomes his own,——and if he is a
man of spirit, he would lose his life rather than give it up.——

I am aware, that *Didius* the great civilian,[1] will contest

---

[2] In whist, the last card dealt, which is turned face up before the dealer,
sets the trump suit.

[1] One learned in civil law. For Didius, see p. 12, n. 1. *Ex confesso:*

this point; and cry out against me, Whence comes this man's
right to this apple? *ex confesso,* he will say,——things were in
a state of nature.——The apple, as much *Frank*'s apple, as
John's. Pray, Mr. *Shandy,* what patent has he to shew for it?
and how did it begin to be his? was it, when he set his heart
upon it? or when he gather'd it? or when he chew'd it? or
when he roasted it? or when he peel'd? or when he brought it
home? or when he digested?——or when he —— — ? ——.
For 'tis plain, Sir, if the first picking up of the apple, made it
not his,——that no subsequent act could.

Brother *Didius, Tribonius*[2] will answer,——(now *Tribonius*
the civilian and church lawyer's beard being three inches and
a half and three eighths longer than *Didius* his beard,——I'm
glad he takes up the cudgels for me, so I give myself no further trouble about the answer.)——Brother *Didius, Tribonius*
will say, it is a decreed case, as you may find it in the fragments of *Gregorius*[3] and *Hermogenes*'s codes, and in all the
codes from *Justinian*'s down to the codes of *Louis* and *Des*

---

from the acknowledged fact, confessedly. Sterne probably expected his
readers to recognize the following paragraphs as an amusing parody of
Locke's treatise *Of Civil Government,* 2.5.27 ff.

[2]The name may have been suggested by that of Tribonian, or Triboni-
anus (c. 475–545), the jurist and minister who under the direction of the
emperor Justinian was head of the commission for the codification of
Roman law in the great *Corpus Juris Civilis.*

[3]The Gregorian Code, of which but fragments are extant, was a collection of imperial constitutions made by a certain Gregorius, who may have
been a professor at the law school of Beirut, about 295 A.D. Hermogenes
(fl. 170 A.D.) was a Greek rhetorician whose rhetorical treatises include
sections on legal issues. It is possible that Sterne intended to write
Hermogenianus, whose Code, compiled about 324 A.D., was supplemen-
tary to the Gregorian Code. Before the time of Justinian (for whom,
see p. 183, n. 5), the codes of Gregorius and Hermogenianus had been
regarded as the only authoritative record of constitutions during the
periods they covered; from them Justinian obtained the constitutions contained in his Code for the period prior to Constantine. The codes of
Louis XIV (1638–1715), which have had a considerable influence on
modern law, were the latest great codes at the time Sterne wrote. *Des
Eaux* appears to be a confused reference to Louis XIV's *Ordonnance des
eaux et forêts* of 1669, a famous code designed to conserve and develop
French forests, of which numerous erudite interpretations were written.
This slip suggests that here, as in other known cases, Sterne derived his
"erudition" from marginalia rather than from the text.

Eaux,——That the sweat of a man's brows, and the exsudations[4] of a man's brains, are as much a man's own property, as
the breeches upon his backside;——which said exsudations,
&c. being dropp'd upon the said apple by the labour of finding
it, and picking it up; and being moreover indissolubly wasted,
and as indissolubly annex'd by the picker up, to the thing
pick'd up, carried home, roasted, peel'd, eaten, digested, and
so on;——'tis evident that the gatherer of the apple, in so
doing, has mix'd up something which was his own, with the
apple which was not his own, by which means he has acquired
a property;——or, in other words, the apple is *John*'s apple.

By the same learned chain of reasoning my father stood up
for all his opinions: he had spared no pains in picking them
up, and the more they lay out of the common way, the better
still was his title.——No mortal claim'd them: they had cost
him moreover as much labour in cooking and digesting as in
the case above, so that they might well and truely be said to
be of his own goods and chattles.——Accordingly he held fast
by 'em, both by teeth and claws,——would fly to whatever he
could lay his hands on,——and in a word, would intrench and
fortify them round with as many circumvallations and breast-
works, as my uncle *Toby* would a citadel.

There was one plaguy rub in the way of this,——the scarcity
of materials to make any thing of a defence with, in case of a
smart attack; inasmuch as few men of great genius had exercised their parts in writing books upon the subject of great
noses: by the trotting of my lean horse, the thing is incredible!
and I am quite lost in my understanding when I am considering what a treasure of precious time and talents together has
been wasted upon worse subjects,——and how many millions
of books in all languages, and in all possible types and bind-
ings, have been fabricated upon points not half so much tending to the unity and peace-making of the world. What was
to be had, however, he set the greater store by; and though
my father would oft-times sport with my uncle *Toby*'s library,
——which, by the bye, was ridiculous enough,——yet at the

[4]Exudations, oozings.

very same time he did it, he collected every book and treatise
which had been systematically wrote upon noses, with as
much care as my honest uncle *Toby* had done those upon
military architecture.——'Tis true, a much less table would
have held them,——but that was not thy transgression, my
dear uncle.——

Here,——but why here,——rather than in any other part of
my story,——I am not able to tell;——but here it is,——
my heart stops me to pay to thee, my dear uncle *Toby,* once
for all, the tribute I owe thy goodness.——Here let me thrust
my chair aside, and kneel down upon the ground, whilst I am
pouring forth the warmest sentiments of love for thee, and
veneration for the excellency of thy character, that ever virtue
and nature kindled in a nephew's bosom.——Peace and comfort rest for evermore upon thy head!——Thou envied'st no
man's comforts,——insulted'st no man's opinions.——Thou
blackened'st no man's character,——devoured'st no man's
bread: gently with faithful *Trim* behind thee, didst thou amble
round the little circle of thy pleasures, jostling no creature in
thy way;——for each one's sorrows, thou hadst a tear,——for
each man's need, thou hadst a shilling.

Whilst I am worth one, to pay a weeder,——thy path from
thy door to thy bowling green shall never be grown up.——
Whilst there is a rood and a half of land in the *Shandy* family,
thy fortifications, my dear uncle *Toby,* shall never be demolish'd.

CHAP. XXXV.

M Y father's collection was not great, but to make amends,
it was curious; and consequently, he was some time in
making it; he had the great good fortune however to set off
well, in getting *Bruscambille's*[1] prologue upon long noses, almost for nothing,——for he gave no more for *Bruscambille*

---

[1]The theatrical name of le Sieur Deslauriers, a comedian whose *Pro-
logues tant sérieux que facécieux,* facetious paradoxes and harangues on
a variety of topics, appeared in an authorized edition in 1610.

than three half crowns; owing indeed to the strong fancy which
the stall-man saw my father had for the book the moment he
laid his hands upon it.——There are not three *Bruscambilles*
in *Christendom,*——said the stall-man, except what are chain'd
up in the libraries of the curious. My father flung down the
money as quick as lightening,——took *Bruscambille* into his
bosom,——hyed home from *Piccadilly* to *Coleman*-street with
it, as he would have hyed home with a treasure, without taking his hand once off from *Bruscambille* all the way.

   To those who do not yet know of which gender *Bruscambille* is,——inasmuch as a prologue upon long noses might
easily be done by either,——'twill be no objection against
the simile,——to say, That when my father got home, he solaced himself with *Bruscambille* after the manner, in which, 'tis
ten to one, your worship solaced yourself with your first mistress,——that is, from morning even unto night: which by
the bye, how delightful soever it may prove to the inamorato,
——is of little, or no entertainment at all, to by-standers.——
Take notice, I go no farther with the simile,——my father's
eye was greater than his appetite,——his zeal greater than his
knowledge,——he cool'd——his affections became divided,
——he got hold of *Prignitz,*[2]——purchased *Scroderus, Andrea
Paræus, Bouchet's* Evening Conferences, and above all, the
great and learned *Hafen Slawkenbergius;* of which, as I shall
have much to say by and bye,——I will say nothing now.

CHAP. XXXVI.

OF all the tracts my father was at the pains to procure and
study in support of his hypothesis, there was not any one
wherein he felt a more cruel disappointment at first, than in

---

   [2]Prignitz and Scroderus have eluded me; the names sound suspicious
(particularly for Shandaic authorities on noses) and since they appear
to have been introduced merely for the jest on p. 233 it is at least possible that they, like Slawkenbergius, are Sterne's creations. Guillaume
Bouchet (1526–1606), of Poitiers, commenced publishing his *Sérées,* a
vivacious melange of wit, in 1584. For Paræus, see p. 233, n. 6; for
Slawkenbergius, see p. 230, n. 1.

the celebrated dialogue between *Pamphagus* and *Cocles*,[1] written by the chaste pen of the great and venerable *Erasmus,* upon the various uses and seasonable applications of long noses.————Now don't let Satan, my dear girl, in this chapter, take advantage of any one spot of rising-ground to get astride of your imagination, if you can any ways help it; or if he is so nimble as to slip on,————let me beg of you, like an unback'd filly, *to frisk it, to squirt it, to jump it, to rear it, to bound it, ————and to kick it, with long kicks and short kicks,* till like *Tickletoby's* mare, you break a strap or a crupper, and throw his worship into the dirt.————You need not kill him.————

————And pray who was *Tickletoby's* mare?————'tis just as discreditable and unscholar-like a question, Sir, as to have asked what year (*ab urb. con.*[2]) the second Punic war broke out.———— Who was *Tickletoby's* mare!————Read, read, read, read, my unlearned reader![3] read,————or by the knowledge of the great saint *Paraleipomenon*[4]————I tell you before-hand, you had better throw down the book at once; for without *much reading,* by which your reverence knows, I mean *much knowledge,* you will no more be able to penetrate the moral of the next marbled page (motly emblem of my work!) than the world with all its sagacity has been able to unravel the many opinions, transactions and truths which still lie mystically hid under the dark veil of the black one.

---

[1]"De Captandis Sacerdotiis," one of the *Colloquia Familiaria* of Desiderius Erasmus (1465–1536), the Dutch classicist, theologian, and satirist; see pp. 229–230.

[2]*Ab urbe condita:* from the founding of the city [of Rome]. Rome was founded about 753 B.C., the second Punic (or Carthaginian) War was begun in 218 B.C., *i.e.,* about 535 *ab urb. con.*

[3]If the "unlearned reader" will turn to *Rabelais,* 4.13, he will learn that Friar Tickletoby's filly, "a young mare that was never leaped yet," being alarmed, "began to start, to funk it, to squirt it, to trot it, to fart it, to bound it, to gallop it, to kick it, to spurn it, to calcitrate it, to wince it, to frisk it, to leap it, to curvet it, with double jerks and bum-motions; insomuch that she threw down Tickletoby, though he held fast by the tree of the pack-saddle with might and main." *Tickletoby:* English equivalent of Rabelais's *Tappecue,* cant term for penis.

[4]A Greek word meaning "things omitted," frequently applied to omitted writings; thus, a proper saint for the present invocation.

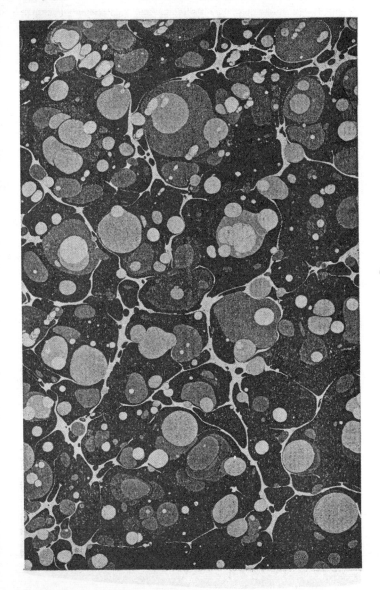

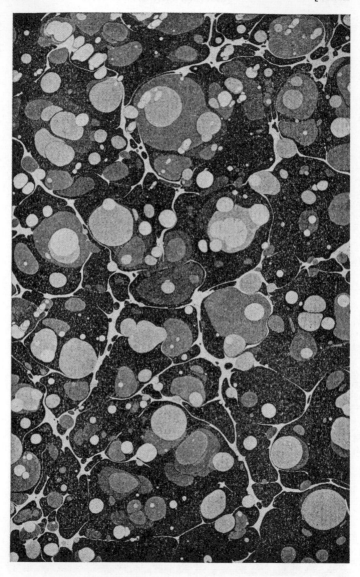

CHAP. XXXVII.

"*NIHIL me pœnitet hujus nasi,*"[1] quoth *Pamphagus;*——
that is,——"My nose has been the making of me."
——————"*Nec est cur pœniteat,*"[2] replies *Cocles;* that is,
"How the duce should such a nose fail?"

The doctrine, you see, was laid down by *Erasmus,* as my
father wished it, with the utmost plainness; but my father's
disappointment was, in finding nothing more from so able a
pen, but the bare fact itself; without any of that speculative
subtilty or ambidexterity of argumentation upon it, which
heaven had bestow'd upon man on purpose to investigate
truth and fight for her on all sides.——My father pish'd and
pugh'd at first most terribly,——'tis worth something to have
a good name. As the dialogue was of *Erasmus,* my father
soon came to himself, and read it over and over again with
great application, studying every word and every syllable of it
thro' and thro' in its most strict and literal interpretation,——
he could still make nothing of it, that way. Mayhaps there is
more meant, than is said in it, quoth my father.——Learned
men, brother *Toby,* don't write dialogues upon long noses for
nothing.——I'll study the mystic and the allegoric sense,——
here is some room to turn a man's self in, brother.

My father read on.——

Now, I find it needful to inform your reverences and worships, that besides the many nautical uses of long noses enu-
merated by *Erasmus,* the dialogist affirmeth that a long nose
is not without its domestic conveniences also, for that in a
case of distress,——and for want of a pair of bellows, it will
do excellently well, *ad excitandum focum,*[3] (to stir up the fire.)

[1]"This nose does not displease me."

[2]"Nor is there reason why it should displease you."

[3]All the texts of Erasmus accessible to me read *"Conducet excitando
foculo, si desuerit follis"* ("It will serve to blow the brazier, if bellows
are wanting"); it seems likely, therefore, that in preparing for the jest
which follows, Sterne was forced to wrench an instrument of blowing

Nature had been prodigal in her gifts to my father beyond measure, and had sown the seeds of verbal criticism as deep within him, as she had done the seeds of all other knowledge, ——so that he had got out his penknife, and was trying experiments upon the sentence, to see if he could not scratch some better sense into it.——I've got within a single letter, brother *Toby,* cried my father, of *Erasmus* his mystic meaning.—— You are near enough, brother, replied my uncle, in all conscience.——Pshaw! cried my father, scratching on,——I might as well be seven miles off.——I've done it,——said my father, snapping his fingers.——See, my dear brother *Toby,* how I have mended the sense.——But you have marr'd a word, replied my uncle *Toby.*[4]——My father put on his spectacles, ——bit his lip,——and tore out the leaf in a passion.

CHAP. XXXVIII.

O *Slawkenbergius!*[1] thou faithful analyzer of my *Disgrázias,*[2] ——thou sad foreteller of so many of the whips and short turns, which in one stage or other of my life have come slap upon me from the shortness of my nose, and no other cause, that I am conscious of.——Tell me, *Slawkenbergius!* what secret impulse was it? what intonation of voice? whence came it? how did it sound in thy ears?——art thou sure thou heard'st it?——which first cried out to thee,——go,——go, *Slawkenbergius!* dedicate the labours of thy life,——neglect thy pastimes,——call forth all the powers and faculties of thy

into one of stirring or poking, and to alter both the construction and the vocabulary of his original.

[4]My father's scratching could transform the original text into *ad excitandum ficum,* or into *ad excitandum locum,* either of which would serve Sterne's purpose.

[1]"Hafen Slawkenbergius" is, of course, Sterne's creation. *"Slawkenbergius"* (cf. German *Schlackenberg*) means "pile of slag," or "offal," or possibly "excrement," and *"Hafen"* is a colloquial German term for "chamber-pot"—a proper name for the writer of "a grand folio" on noses.

[2]Disgraces, misfortunes.

nature,——macerate thyself in the service of mankind, and write a grand FOLIO for them, upon the subject of their noses.

How the communication was conveyed into *Slawken-bergius*'s sensorium,——so that *Slawkenbergius* should know whose finger touch'd the key,——and whose hand it was that blew the bellows,——as *Hafen Slawkenbergius* has been dead and laid in his grave above fourscore and ten years,——we can only raise conjectures.

Slawkenbergius was play'd upon, for aught I know, like one of *Whitefield*'s disciples,[3]——that is, with such a distinct intelligence, Sir, of which of the two *masters* it was, that had been practising upon his *instrument*,——as to make all reasoning upon it needless.

——For in the account which *Hafen Slawkenbergius* gives the world of his motives and occasions for writing, and spending so many years of his life upon this one work——towards the end of his prolegomena, which by the bye should have come first,——but the bookbinder has most injudiciously placed it betwixt the analitical contents of the book, and the book itself,——he informs his reader, that ever since he had arrived at the age of discernment, and was able to sit down coolly, and consider within himself the true state and condition of man, and distinguish the main end and design of his being;——or,——to shorten my translation, for *Slawken-bergius*'s book is in *Latin,* and not a little prolix in this passage,——ever since I understood, quoth *Slawkenbergius,* any thing,——or rather *what was what,*——and could perceive that the point of long noses had been too loosely handled by all who had gone before;——have I, *Slawkenbergius,* felt a strong impulse, with a mighty and unresistible call within me, to gird up myself to this undertaking.

And to do justice to *Slawkenbergius,* he has entered the list with a stronger lance, and taken a much larger career in it,

---

[3]George Whitefield (1714–1770), one of the founders of Methodism and a moving pulpit orator, preached that without any rational thought the soul can feel whether its actions are motivated by the devil or by the spirit of God.

than any one man who had ever entered it before him,——
and indeed, in many respects, deserves to be *en-nich'd* as a
prototype for all writers, of voluminous works at least, to
model their books by,——for he has taken in, Sir, the whole
subject,——examined every part of it, *dialectically*,——then
brought it into full day; dilucidating[4] it with all the light
which either the collision of his own natural parts could strike,
——or the profoundest knowledge of the sciences had impowered him to cast upon it,——collating, collecting and com-
piling,——begging, borrowing, and stealing, as he went along,
all that had been wrote or wrangled thereupon in the schools
and porticos of the learned: so that *Slawkenbergius* his book
may properly be considered, not only as a model,——but as a
thorough-stitch'd DIGEST and regular institute of *noses;* com-
prehending in it, all that is, or can be needful to be known
about them.

For this cause it is, that I forebear to speak of so many
(otherwise) valuable books and treatises of my father's collecting, wrote either, plump upon noses,——or collaterally
touching them;——such for instance as *Prignitz,* now lying
upon the table before me, who with infinite learning, and
from the most candid and scholar-like examination of above
four thousand different skulls, in upwards of twenty charnel
houses in *Silesia,* which he had rummaged,——has informed
us, that the mensuration and configuration of the osseous or
boney parts of human noses, in any *given* tract of country, except *Crim Tartary,* where they are all crush'd down by the
thumb, so that no judgment can be formed upon them,——are
much nearer alike, than the world imagines;——the difference
amongst them, being, he says, a mere trifle, not worth taking
notice of,——but that the size and jollity of every individual
nose, and by which one nose ranks above another, and bears
a higher price, is owing to the cartilagenous and muscular
parts of it, into whose ducts and sinuses the blood and animal spirits being impell'd, and driven by the warmth and
force of the imagination, which is but a step from it, (bating

---

[4]Elucidating.

the case of ideots, whom *Prignitz,* who had lived many years
in *Turky,* supposes under the more immediate tutelage of
heaven)——it so happens, and ever must, says *Prignitz,* that
the excellency of the nose is in a direct arithmetical proportion to the excellency of the wearer's fancy.

It is for the same reason, that is, because 'tis all comprehended in *Slawkenbergius,* that I say nothing likewise of
Scroderus (Andrea) who all the world knows, set himself to
oppugn *Prignitz* with great violence,——proving it in his own
way, first, *logically* and then by a series of stubborn facts,
"That so far was *Prignitz* from the truth, in affirming that the
fancy begat the nose, that on the contrary,——the nose begat
the fancy."

——The learned suspected *Scroderus,* of an indecent sophism
in this,[5]——and *Prignitz* cried out aloud in the dispute, that
Scroderus had shifted the idea upon him,——but *Scroderus*
went on, maintaining his thesis.——

My father was just balancing within himself, which of the
two sides he should take in this affair; when *Ambrose Paræus*
decided it in a moment, and by overthrowing the systems,
both of *Prignitz* and *Scroderus,* drove my father out of both
sides of the controversy at once.

Be witness——

I don't acquaint the learned reader,——in saying it, I mention it only to shew the learned, I know the fact myself.——

That this *Ambrose Paræus*[6] was chief surgeon and nose-
mender to *Francis* the ninth of *France,* and in high credit with

---

[5] A play upon different meanings of the word *fancy:* "imagination" and
"love."

[6] Ambrose Paré (1510–1590), who first served as a military surgeon in
the army of Francis I, was chief surgeon to Henry II, Francis II, Charles
IX, and Henry III. Gaspar Tagliacozzi (1546–1599), an Italian surgeon
who was famed as a wonder-worker, devised a means of rhinoplasty by
which an injured nose might be patched with a flap of skin taken from
the patient's arm, the arm being fixed to the head until the flap had united
with the skin of the nose. Paré's "slip" would appear to be his description of the operation as a grafting of flesh or muscle, rather than of skin;
the account is found in his *Œuvres completes* (ed. J. F. Malgaigne, Paris,
1840–41), 17.2.

him and the two preceding, or succeeding kings (I know not which)———and that except in the slip he made in his story of *Taliacotius*'s noses, and his manner of setting them on,——— he was esteemed by the whole college of physicians at that time, as more knowing in matters of noses, than any one who had ever taken them in hand.

Now *Ambrose Paræus* convinced my father, that the true and efficient cause of what had engaged so much the attention of the world, and upon which *Prignitz* and *Scroderus* had wasted so much learning and fine parts,———was neither this nor that,———but that the length and goodness of the nose was owing simply to the softness and flaccidity in the nurse's breast,———as the flatness and shortness of *puisne*[7] noses was, to the firmness and elastic repulsion of the same organ of nutrition in the hale and lively,———which, tho' happy for the woman, was the undoing of the child, inasmuch as his nose was so snubb'd, so rebuff'd, so rebated, and so refrigerated thereby, as never to arrive *ad mensuram suam legitimam;*[8]——— but that in case of the flaccidity and softness of the nurse or mother's breast,———by sinking into it, quoth *Paræus,* as into so much butter, the nose was comforted, nourish'd, plump'd up, refresh'd, refocillated,[9] and set a growing for ever.[10]

I have but two things to observe of *Paræus;* first, that he proves and explains all this with the utmost chastity and decorum of expression:———for which may his soul for ever rest in peace!

And, secondly, that besides the systems of *Prignitz* and *Scroderus,* which *Ambrose Paræus* his hypothesis effectually overthrew,———it overthrew at the same time the system of peace and harmony of our family; and for three days together, not only embroiled matters between my father and my mother,

---

[7]Inferior (legal term).

[8]At its legitimate (proper) size.

[9]Revivified.

[10]This is the explanation of long and short noses given by Friar John in *Rabelais,* 1.40. The reference to Paré is to his *Œuvres* (Malgaigne's edition, 18.25), though Sterne may have taken it second-hand from Bouchet's *Sérées,* 24, or from Ozell's note to *Rabelais,* 1.40.

but turn'd likewise the whole house and every thing in it, except my uncle *Toby,* quite upside down.

Such a ridiculous tale of a dispute between a man and his wife, never surely in any age or country got vent through the key-hole of a street-door!

My mother, you must know,——but I have fifty things more necessary to let you know first,——I have a hundred difficulties which I have promised to clear up, and a thousand distresses and domestic misadventures crouding in upon me thick and three-fold, one upon the neck of another,——a cow broke in (to-morrow morning) to my uncle *Toby's* fortifications, and eat up two ratios[11] and half of dried grass, tearing up the sods with it, which faced his horn-work and covered way.——*Trim* insists upon being tried by a court-martial,——the cow to be shot,——*Slop* to be *crucifix'd,*——myself to be *tristram'd,* and at my very baptism made a martyr of;——poor unhappy devils that we all are!——I want swaddling,——but there is no time to be lost in exclamations.——I have left my father lying across his bed, and my uncle *Toby* in his old fringed chair, sitting beside him, and promised I would go back to them in half an hour, and five and thirty minutes are laps'd already.——Of all the perplexities a mortal author was ever seen in,——this certainly is the greatest,——for I have *Hafen Slawkenbergius's* folio, Sir, to finish——a dialogue between my father and my uncle *Toby,* upon the solution of *Prignitz, Scroderus, Ambrose Paræus, Ponocrates*[12] and *Grangousier* to relate,——a tale out of *Slawkenbergius* to translate, and all this in five minutes less, than no time at all;——such a head!—— would to heaven! my enemies only saw the inside of it!

---

[11]Rations.

[12]The tutor of Gargantua in Rabelais's book of that name; Grangousier was Gargantua's father.   See p. 240.

CHAP. XXXIX.

THERE was not any one scene more entertaining in our
family,——and to do it justice in this point;——and I
here put off my cap and lay it upon the table close beside my
ink-horn, on purpose to make my declaration to the world
concerning this one article, the more solemn,——that I believe in my soul, (unless my love and partiality to my understanding blinds me) the hand of the supreme Maker and first
Designer of all things, never made or put a family together,
(in that period at least of it, which I have sat down to write
the story of)——where the characters of it were cast or contrasted with so dramatic a felicity as ours was, for this end;
or in which the capacities of affording such exquisite scenes,
and the powers of shifting them perpetually from morning to
night, were lodged and intrusted with so unlimited a confidence, as in the SHANDY-FAMILY.

Not any one of these was more diverting, I say, in this
whimsical theatre of ours,——than what frequently arose out
of this self-same chapter of long noses,——especially when my
father's imagination was heated with the enquiry, and nothing would serve him but to heat my uncle *Toby*'s too.

My uncle *Toby* would give my father all possible fair play in
this attempt; and with infinite patience would sit smoking
his pipe for whole hours together, whilst my father was practising upon his head, and trying every accessible avenue to
drive *Prignitz* and *Scroderus*'s solutions into it.

Whether they were above my uncle *Toby*'s reason,——or
contrary to it,——or that his brain was like wet tinder, and
no spark could possibly take hold,——or that it was so full of
saps, mines, blinds, curtins, and such military disqualifica-
tions to his seeing clearly into *Prignitz* and *Scroderus*'s doctrines,——I say not,——let school-men——scullions, anatomists, and engineers, fight for it amongst themselves.——

'Twas some misfortune, I make no doubt, in this affair, that

my father had every word of it to translate for the benefit of
my uncle *Toby,* and render out of *Slawkenbergius's Latin,* of
which, as he was no great master, his translation was not always of the purest,——and generally least so where 'twas most
wanted,——this naturally open'd a door to a second misfortune;——that in the warmer paroxisms of his zeal to open my
uncle *Toby's* eyes——my father's ideas run on, as much faster
than the translation, as the translation outmoved my uncle
Toby's;——neither the one or the other added much to the
perspicuity of my father's lecture.

CHAP. XL.

THE gift of ratiocination and making syllogisms,——I
mean in man,——for in superior classes of beings, such as
angels and spirits,——'tis all done, may it please your worships, as they tell me, by INTUITION;——and beings inferior, as
your worships all know,——syllogize by their noses: though
there is an island swiming in the sea, though not altogether at
its ease, whose inhabitants, if my intelligence deceives me not,
are so wonderfully gifted, as to syllogize after the same
fashion, and oft-times to make very well out too:——but that's
neither here nor there——

The gift of doing it as it should be, amongst us,——or the
great and principal act of ratiocination in man, as logicians tell
us, is the finding out the agreement or disagreement of two
ideas one with another, by the intervention of a third; (called
the *medius terminus*[1]) just as a man, as *Locke* well observes,
by a yard,[2] finds two mens nine-pin-alleys to be of the same
length, which could not be brought together, to measure their
equality, by *juxta-position.*[3]

---

[1]Middle term.

[2]Yard-stick.

[3]Sterne improves on Locke, who had observed: "As a man, by a yard,
finds two houses to be of the same length, which could not be brought
together to measure their equality by juxta-position." (*An Essay Concerning Human Understanding,* 4.17.18.)

Had the same great reasoner looked on, as my father illustrated his systems of noses, and observed my uncle *Toby*'s deportment,——what great attention he gave to every word,—— and as oft as he took his pipe from his mouth, with what wonderful seriousness he contemplated the length of it,——surveying it transversely as he held it betwixt his finger and his thumb,——then foreright,——then this way, and then that, in all its possible directions and foreshortenings,——he would have concluded my uncle *Toby* had got hold of the *medius terminus;* and was syllogizing and measuring with it the truth of each hypothesis of long noses, in order as my father laid them before him. This by the bye, was more than my father wanted,——his aim in all the pains he was at in these philosophic lectures,——was to enable my uncle *Toby* not to *discuss,*——but *comprehend*——to *hold* the grains and scruples of learning,——not to *weigh* them.——My uncle *Toby,* as you will read in the next chapter, did neither the one or the other.

CHAP. XLI.

'TIS a pity, cried my father one winter's night, after a three hours painful translation of *Slawkenbergius,*—— 'tis a pity, cried my father, putting my mother's thread-paper into the book for a mark, as he spoke——that truth, brother *Toby,* should shut herself up in such impregnable fastnesses, and be so obstinate as not to surrender herself sometimes up upon the closest siege.——

Now it happened then, as indeed it had often done before, that my uncle *Toby*'s fancy, during the time of my father's explanation of *Prignitz* to him,——having nothing to stay it there, had taken a short flight to the bowling-green;——his body might as well have taken a turn there too,——so that with all the semblance of a deep school-man intent upon the *medius terminus,*——my uncle *Toby* was in fact as ignorant of the whole lecture, and all its pro's and con's, as if my father had been translating *Hafen Slawkenbergius* from the *Latin*

tongue into the *Cherokeè*. But the word *siege,* like a talis-
manic power, in my father's metaphor, wafting back my uncle
Toby's fancy, quick as a note could follow the touch,——he
open'd his ears,——and my father observing that he took his
pipe out of his mouth, and shuffled his chair nearer the table,
as with a desire to profit,——my father with great pleasure
began his sentence again,——changing only the plan, and
dropping the metaphor of the siege of it, to keep clear of some
dangers my father apprehended from it.

'Tis a pity, said my father, that truth can only be on one
side, brother *Toby,*——considering what ingenuity these
learned men have all shewn in their solutions of noses.——
Can noses be dissolved? replied my uncle *Toby.*——

——My father thrust back his chair,——rose up,——put on
his hat,——took four long strides to the door,——jerked it
open,——thrust his head half way out,——shut the door again,
——took no notice of the bad hinge,——returned to the table,
——pluck'd my mother's thread-paper out of *Slawkenbergius*'s
book,——went hastily to his bureau,——walk'd slowly back,
twisting my mother's thread-paper about his thumb,——unbutton'd his waistcoat,——threw my mother's thread-paper into
the fire,——bit her sattin pin-cushion in two, fill'd his mouth
with bran,——confounded it;——but mark!——the oath of
confusion was levell'd at my uncle *Toby*'s brain,——which was
e'en confused enough already,——the curse came charged only
with the bran,——the bran, may it please your honours,——
was no more than powder to the ball.

'Twas well my father's passions lasted not long; for so long
as they did last, they led him a busy life on't, and it is one
of the most unaccountable problems that ever I met with in
my observations of human nature, that nothing should prove
my father's mettle so much, or make his passions go off so
like gun-powder, as the unexpected strokes his science met
with from the quaint simplicity of my uncle *Toby*'s questions.
——Had ten dozen of hornets stung him behind in so many
different places all at one time,——he could not have exerted
more mechanical functions in fewer seconds,——or started half

so much, as with one single *quære*[1] of three words unseasonably popping in full upon him in his hobbyhorsical career.

'Twas all one to my uncle *Toby,*——he smoaked his pipe on, with unvaried composure,——his heart never intended offence to his brother,——and as his head could seldom find out where the sting of it lay,——he always gave my father the credit of cooling by himself.——He was five minutes and thirty-five seconds about it in the present case.

By all that's good! said my father, swearing, as he came to himself, and taking the oath out of *Ernulphus's* digest of curses,——(though to do my father justice it was a fault (as he told Dr. *Slop* in the affair of *Ernulphus*) which he as seldom committed as any man upon earth.)——By all that's good and great! brother *Toby,* said my father, if it was not for the aids of philosophy, which befriend one so much as they do, ——you would put a man beside all temper.——Why, by the *solutions* of noses, of which I was telling you, I meant as you might have known, had you favoured me with one grain of attention, the various accounts which learned men of different kinds of knowledge have given the world, of the causes of short and long noses.——There is no cause but one, replied my uncle *Toby,*——why one man's nose is longer than another's, but because that God pleases to have it so.——That is *Grangousier's* solution, said my father.[2]——'Tis he, continued my uncle *Toby,* looking up, and not regarding my father's interruption, who makes us all, and frames and puts us together in such forms and proportions, and for such ends, as is agreeable to his infinite wisdom.——'Tis a pious account, cried my father, but not philosophical,——there is more religion in it than sound science. 'Twas no inconsistent part of my uncle *Toby's* character,——that he feared God, and reverenced religion.——So the moment my father finished his remark,——

---

[1]Query.

[2]" 'What is the cause,' said Gargantua, 'that Friar John hath such a goodly nose?'

" 'Because,' said Grangousier, 'that God would have it so, who frameth us in such form, and for such end as is most agreeable to His divine will, even as a potter fashioneth his vessels.' " (*Rabelais,* 1.40.)

my uncle *Toby* fell a whistling *Lillabullero,* with more zeal
(though more out of tune) than usual.——

What is become of my wife's thread-paper?

CHAP. XLII.

NO matter,——as an appendage to seamstressy, the thread-
paper might be of some consequence to my mother,——
of none to my father, as a mark in *Slawkenbergius. Slawkenbergius* in every page of him was a rich treasury of inexhaustible knowledge to my father,——he could not open him amiss;
and he would often say in closing the book, that if all the arts
and sciences in the world, with the books which treated of
them, were lost,——should the wisdom and policies of governments, he would say, through disuse, ever happen to be forgot, and all that statesmen had wrote, or caused to be written,
upon the strong or the weak sides of courts and kingdoms,
should they be forgot also,——and *Slawkenbergius* only left,
——there would be enough in him in all conscience, he would
say, to set the world a-going again.   A treasure therefore was
he indeed! an institute of all that was necessary to be known
of noses, and every thing else,——at *matin,* noon, and vespers
was *Hafen Slawkenbergius* his recreation and delight: 'twas
for ever in his hands,——you would have sworn, Sir, it had
been a canon's prayer-book,——so worn, so glazed, so con-
trited and attrited was it with fingers and with thumbs in all
its parts, from one end even unto the other.

I am not such a bigot to *Slawkenbergius,* as my father;——
there is a fund in him, no doubt; but in my opinion, the best, I
don't say the most profitable, but the most amusing part of
Hafen Slawkenbergius, is his tales,——and, considering he was
a *German,* many of them told not without fancy:——these
take up his second book, containing nearly one half of his
folio, and are comprehended in ten decads, each decad containing ten tales.——Philosophy is not built upon tales; and
therefore 'twas certainly wrong in *Slawkenbergius* to send

them into the world by that name;——there are a few of them in his eighth, ninth, and tenth decads, which I own seem rather playful and sportive, than speculative,——but in general they are to be looked upon by the learned as a detail of so many independent facts, all of them turning round somehow or other upon the main hinges of his subject, and collected by him with great fidelity, and added to his work as so many illustrations upon the doctrines of noses.

As we have leisure enough upon our hands,——if you give me leave, madam, I'll tell you the ninth tale of his tenth decad.

THE END OF THE THIRD VOLUME.

VOLUME IV.[1]

SLAWKENBERGII
FABELLA*

*V*ESPERA *quâdâ frigidulâ, posteriori in parte mensis
Augusti, peregrinus, mulo fusco colore insidens, manticâ
a tergo, paucis indusijs, binis calceis, braccisque sericis coc-
cinejs repletâ,* Argentoratum *ingressus est.*

*Militi eum percontanti, quum portus intraret, dixit, se apud
Nasorum promontorium fuisse, Francofurtum proficisci, et
Argentoratum, transitu ad fines Sarmatiæ mensis intervallo,
reversurum.*

*Miles peregrini in faciem suspexit——Di boni, nova forma
nasi!*
*At multum mihi profuit, inquit peregrinus, carbum amento
extrahens, e quo pependit acinaces: Loculo manum inseruit;
& magnâ cum urbanitate, pilei parte anteriore tactâ manu
sinistrâ, ut extendit dextram, militi florinum dedit et processit.*

*Dolet mihi, ait miles, tympanistam nanum et valgum allo-
quens, virum adeo urbanum vaginam perdidisse; itinerari haud
poterit nudâ acinaci, neque vaginam toto* Argentorato, *habilem
inveniet.——Nullam unquam habui, respondit peregrinus*

[1]Published, with Volume 3, in January, 1761.

*As *Hafen Slawkenbergius de Nasis* is extremely scarce, it may not be
unacceptable to the learned reader to see the specimen of a few pages of
his original; I will make no reflection upon it, but that his story-telling
Latin is much more concise than his philosophic——and, I think, has
more of Latinity in it. [Sterne's note.]

VOLUME IV.

SLAWKENBERGIUS'S TALE

IT was one cool refreshing evening, at the close of a very sultry day, in the latter end of the month of *August,* when a stranger, mounted upon a dark mule, with a small cloak-bag behind him, containing a few shirts, a pair of shoes, and a crimson-sattin pair of breeches, entred the town of *Strasburg.*

He told the centinel, who questioned him as he entered the gates, that he had been at the promontory of NOSES——was going on to *Frankfort*——and should be back again at *Strasburg* that day month, in his way to the borders of *Crim-Tartary.*[2]

The centinel looked up into the stranger's face——never saw such a nose in his life!

——I have made a very good venture of it, quoth the stranger——so slipping his wrist out of the loop of a black ribban, to which a short scymetar was hung: He put his hand into his pocket, and with great courtesy touching the fore-part of his cap with his left-hand, as he extended his right—— he put a florin into the centinel's hand, and passed on.

It grieves me, said the centinel, speaking to a little dwarf-ish bandy-leg'd drummer, that so courteous a soul should have lost his scabbard——he cannot travel without one to his scymetar, and will not be able to get a scabbard to fit it in all *Strasburg.*——I never had one, replied the stranger, looking

---

[2]Crimea.

respiciens,——seque comiter inclinans——hoc more gesto,
nudam acinacem elevans, mulo lentò progrediente, ut nasum
tueri possim.

Non immerito, benigne peregrine, respondit miles.
Nihili æstimo, ait ille tympanista, e pergamenâ factitius est.

Prout christianus sum, inquit miles, nasus ille, ni sexties
major sit, meo esset conformis.
Crepitare audivi ait tympanista.
Mehercule! sanguinem emisit, respondit miles.
Miseret me, inquit tympanista, qui non ambo tetigimus!

Eodem temporis puncto, quo hæc res argumentata fuit inter
militem et tympanistam, disceptabatur ibidem tubicine &
uxore suâ, qui tunc accesserunt, et peregrino prætereunte, res-
titerunt.
Quantus nasus! æque longus est, ait tubicina, ac tuba.

Et ex eodem metallo, ait tubicen, velut sternutamento
audias.
Tantum abest, respondit illa, quod fistulam dulcedine vincit.
Æneus est, ait tubicen.
Nequaquam, respondit uxor.
Rursum affirmo, ait tubicen, quod æneus est.
Rem penitus explorabo; prius, enim digito tangam, ait uxor,
quam dormivero.
Mulus peregrini, gradu lento progressus est, ut unum-
quodque verbum controversiæ, non tantum inter militem et
tympanistam, verum etiam inter tubicinem et uxorem ejus,
audiret.
Nequaquam, ait ille, in muli collum fræna demittens, &
manibus ambabus in pectus positis, (mulo lentè progrediente)
nequaquam ait ille, respiciens, non necesse est ut res isthæc

back to the centinel, and putting his hand up to his cap as he spoke——I carry it, continued he, thus——holding up his naked scymetar, his mule moving on slowly all the time, on purpose to defend my nose.

It is well worth it, gentle stranger, replied the centinel.

——'Tis not worth a single stiver, said the bandy-leg'd drummer—'tis a nose of parchment.

As I am a true catholic——except that it is six times as big——'tis a nose, said the centinel, like my own.

——I heard it crackle, said the drummer.

By dunder, said the centinel, I saw it bleed.

What a pity, cried the bandy-legg'd drummer, we did not both touch it!

At the very time that this dispute was maintaining by the centinel and the drummer——was the same point debating betwixt a trumpeter and a trumpeter's wife, who were just then coming up, and had stopped to see the stranger pass by.

Benedicity![3]——What a nose! 'tis as long, said the trumpeter's wife, as a trumpet.

And of the same mettle, said the trumpeter, as you hear by its sneezing.

——'Tis as soft as a flute, said she.

——'Tis brass, said the trumpeter.

——'Tis a pudding's end——said his wife.

I tell thee again, said the trumpeter, 'tis a brazen nose.

I'll know the bottom of it, said the trumpeter's wife, for I will touch it with my finger before I sleep.

The stranger's mule moved on at so slow a rate, that he heard every word of the dispute, not only betwixt the centinel and the drummer; but betwixt the trumpeter and the trumpeter's wife.

No! said he, dropping his reins upon his mule s neck, and laying both his hands upon his breast, the one over the other in a saint-like position (his mule going on easily all the time) No! said he, looking up,——I am not such a debtor to the world——slandered and disappointed as I have been——as to

---

[3]Bless me!

dilucidata foret. Minime gentium! meus nasus nunquam tangetur, dum spiritus hos reget artus——ad quid agendum? ait uxor burgomagistri.

Peregrinus illi non respondit. Votum faciebat tunc temporis sancto Nicolao, quo facto, sinum dextram inserens, e quâ negligenter pependit acinaces, lento gradu processit per plateam Argentorati latam quæ ad diversorium templo ex adversum ducit.

Peregrinus mulo descendens stabulo includi, & manticam inferri jussit: quâ apertâ et coccineis sericis femoralibus extractis cum argenteo laciniato Περιζομaτὲ, his sese induit, statimque, acinaci in manu, ad forum deambulavit.

Quod ubi peregrinus esset ingressus, uxorem tubicinis obviam euntem aspicit; illico cursum flectit, metuens ne nasus suus exploraretur, atque ad diversorium regressus est——exuit se vestibus; braccas coccineas sericas manticæ imposuit mulumque educi jussit.

Francofurtum proficiscor, ait ille, et Argentoratum quatuor abhinc hebdomadis revertar.

Bene curasti hoc jumentum (ait) muli faciem manu demulcens——me, manticamque meam, plus sexcentis mille passibus portavit.

give it that conviction——no! said he, my nose shall never be touched whilst heaven gives me strength——To do what? said a burgomaster's wife.

The stranger took no notice of the burgomaster's wife—— he was making a vow to saint *Nicolas;*[4] which done, having uncrossed his arms with the same solemnity with which he crossed them, he took up the reins of his bridle with his left-hand, and putting his right-hand into his bosom, with his scymetar hanging loosely to the wrist of it, he rode on as slowly as one foot of the mule could follow another thro' the principal streets of *Strasburg,* till chance brought him to the great inn in the market-place over-against the church.

The moment the stranger alighted, he ordered his mule to be led into the stable, and his cloak-bag to be brought in; then opening, and taking out of it, his crimson-satin breeches, with a silver-fringed——(appendage to them, which I dare not translate)——he put his breeches, with his fringed cod-piece[5] on, and forthwith with his short scymetar in his hand, walked out to the grand parade.

The stranger had just taken three turns upon the parade, when he perceived the trumpeter's wife at the opposite side of it——so turning short, in pain lest his nose should be attempted, he instantly went back to his inn——undressed himself, packed up his crimson-sattin breeches, *&c.* in his cloak-bag, and called for his mule.

I am going forwards, said the stranger, for *Franckfort*—— and shall be back at *Strasburg* this day month.

I hope, continued the stranger, stroking down the face of his mule with his left-hand as he was going to mount it, that you have been kind to this faithful slave of mine——it has carried me and my cloak-bag, continued he, tapping the mule's back, above six hundred leagues.

---

[4]Saint Nicholas's patronage included, among others, wandering scholars, vagabonds, robbed persons, and travellers in general.

[5]A loose flaplike or baglike appendage formerly placed at the front of men's breeches at the separation of the legs; also, euphemistically, that portion of a man's body covered by a codpiece.

Longa via est! respondet hospes, nisi plurimum esset negoti.
——Enimvero ait peregrinus a nasorum promontorio redij,
et nasum speciosissimum, egregiosissimumque quem unquam
quisquam sortitus est, acquisivi!

Dum peregrinus hanc miram rationem, de seipso reddit,
hospes et uxor ejus, oculis intentis, peregrini nasum contem-
plantur——Per sanctos, sanctasque omnes, ait hospitis uxor,
nasis duodecim maximis, in toto Argentorato major est!——
estne ait illa mariti in aurem insusurrans, nonne est nasus
prægrandis?

Dolus inest, anime mi, ait hospes——nasus est falsus.——

Verus est, respondit uxor.——
Ex abiete factus est, ait ille, terebinthinum olet——

Carbunculus inest, ait uxor.
Mortuus est nasus, respondit hospes.
Vivus est, ait illa,——& si ipsa vivam tangam.

Votum feci sancto Nicolao, ait peregrinus, nasum meum in-
tactum fore usque ad——Quodnam tempus? illico respondit
illa.

Minime tangetur, inquit ille (manibus in pectus compositis)
usque ad illam horam——Quam horam? ait illa.——Nullam,
respondit peregrinus, donec pervenio, ad——Quem locum,
——obsecro? ait illa——Peregrinus nil respondens mulo con-
scenso discessit.

——'Tis a long journey, Sir, replied the master of the inn ——unless a man has great business.——Tut! tut! said the stranger, I have been at the promontory of Noses; and have got me one of the goodliest and jolliest, thank heaven, that ever fell to a single man's lot.

Whilst the stranger was giving this odd account of himself, the master of the inn and his wife kept both their eyes fixed full upon the stranger's nose——By saint *Radagunda*,[6] said the inn-keeper's wife to herself, there is more of it than in any dozen of the largest noses put together in all *Strasburg!* is it not, said she, whispering her husband in his ear, is it not a noble nose?

'Tis an imposture, my dear, said the master of the inn—— 'tis a false nose.——

'Tis a true nose, said his wife.——

'Tis made of fir-tree, said he,——I smell the turpen-tine.———

There's a pimple on it, said she.

'Tis a dead nose, replied the inn-keeper.

'Tis a live nose, and if I am alive myself, said the inn-keeper's wife, I will touch it.

I have made a vow to saint *Nicolas* this day, said the stranger, that my nose shall not be touched till——Here the stranger, suspending his voice, looked up——Till when? said she hastily.

It never shall be touched, said he, clasping his hands and bringing them close to his breast, till that hour.——What hour? cried the inn-keeper's wife.——Never!——never! said the stranger, never till I am got——For heaven sake into what place? said she.——The stranger rode away without saying a word.

The stranger had not got half a league on his way towards *Frankfort,* before all the city of *Strasburg* was in an uproar

---

[6] To Sterne, St. Radegunde (c.520–587), foundress at Poitiers of a double community of monks and nuns, and patroness of Jesus College, Cambridge (Sterne's college), was memorable chiefly for "the pricks which enter'd [her] flesh" when she mortified her body. See p. 557 and n. 1.

about his nose. The *Compline*-bells were just ringing to call
the *Strasburgers* to their devotions, and shut up the duties of
the day in prayer:——no soul in all *Strasburg* heard 'em——the
city was like a swarm of bees————men, women, and children
(the *Compline*-bells tinkling all the time) flying here and there
——in at one door, out at another——this way and that way
——long ways and cross ways——up one street, down another
street——in at this ally, out at that——did you see it? did
you see it? did you see it? O! did you see it?——who saw
it? who did see it? for mercy's sake, who saw it?

Alack o'day! I was at vespers!——I was washing, I was
starching, I was scouring, I was quilting——God help me! I
never saw it——I never touch'd it!——would I had been a
centinel, a bandy-leg'd drummer, a trumpeter, a trumpeter's
wife, was the general cry and lamentation in every street and
corner of *Strasburg*.

Whilst all this confusion and disorder triumphed throughout the great city of *Strasburg,* was the courteous stranger going on as gently upon his mule in his way to *Frankfort,* as if
he had had no concern at all in the affair——talking all the
way he rode in broken sentences, sometimes to his mule——
sometimes to himself——sometimes to his Julia.

O Julia, my lovely Julia!——nay I cannot stop to let thee bite
that thistle——that ever the suspected tongue of a rival should
have robbed me of enjoyment when I was upon the point of
tasting it.——

——Pugh!——'tis nothing but a thistle——never mind it
——thou shalt have a better supper at night.——

——Banish'd from my country——my friends——from
thee.——

Poor devil, thou'rt sadly tired with thy journey!——come
——get on a little faster——there's nothing in my cloak-bag
but two shirts——a crimson-sattin pair of breeches, and a
fringed——Dear Julia!

——But why to *Frankfort?*——is it that there is a hand unfelt, which secretly is conducting me through these meanders
and unsuspected tracts?——

——Stumbling! by saint *Nicolas!* every step——why at this
rate we shall be all night in getting in——

——To happiness——or am I to be the sport of fortune and
slander——destined to be driven forth unconvicted——un-
heard——untouched——if so, why did I not stay at *Strasburg,*
where justice——but I had sworn!——Come, thou shalt drink
——to *St. Nicolas*——O Julia!——What dost thou prick up
thy ears at?——'tis nothing but a man, *&c.*——

The stranger rode on communing in this manner with his
mule and Julia——till he arrived at his inn, where, as soon as
he arrived, he alighted——saw his mule, as he had promised it, taken good care of——took off his cloak bag, with his
crimson-sattin breeches, *&c.* in it——called for an omelet to
his supper, went to his bed about twelve o'clock, and in five
minutes fell fast asleep.

It was about the same hour when the tumult in *Strasburg*
being abated for that night,——the *Strasburgers* had all got
quietly into their beds——but not like the stranger, for the
rest either of their minds or bodies; queen *Mab,*[7] like an elf
as she was, had taken the stranger's nose, and without reduction of its bulk, had that night been at the pains of slitting
and dividing it into as many noses of different cuts and fash-
ions, as there were heads in *Strasburg* to hold them. The
abbess of *Quedlingberg,*[8] who, with the four great dignitaries
of her chapter, the prioress, the deaness, the sub-chantress, and
senior canoness, had that week come to *Strasburg* to consult the
university upon a case of conscience relating to their placket
holes——was ill all the night.

The courteous stranger's nose had got perched upon the top
of the pineal gland of her brain, and made such rousing work
in the fancies of the four great dignitaries of her chapter,
they could not get a wink of sleep the whole night thro' for it

---

[7]As Mercutio explains in the famous passage in *Romeo and Juliet,* 1.4,
Queen Mab is "the fairies' midwife" who brings men's secret hopes and
fancies to birth in their dreams.

[8]A town in Prussian Saxony, whose abbess long possessed unusual
ecclesiastical and political powers.

——there was no keeping a limb still amongst them——in short, they got up like so many ghosts.

The penitentiaries of the third order of saint *Francis*[9]—— the nuns of mount *Calvary*[10]——the *Præmonstratenses*[11]—— the *Clunienses**——the *Carthusians,*[12] and all the severer orders of nuns who lay that night in blankets or hair-cloth, were still in a worse condition than the abbess of *Quedlingberg* ——by tumbling and tossing, and tossing and tumbling from one side of their beds to the other the whole night long—— the several sisterhoods had scratch'd and mawl'd themselves all to death——they got out of their beds almost flead[13] alive—— every body thought saint *Antony* had visited them for proba- tion with his fire——they had never once, in short, shut their eyes the whole night long from vespers to matins.

The nuns of saint *Ursula*[14] acted the wisest——they never attempted to go to bed at all.

The dean of *Strasburg,* the prebendaries, the capitulars[15] and domiciliars[16] (capitularly assembled in the morning to

---

[9]The Tertiaries, or "Brothers and Sisters of Penance," were a wide- spread confraternity of lay men and women who tried to follow, without withdrawing from the world, Franciscan principles.

[10]The Bénédictines de Notre-Dame du Calvaire were an order founded at Poitiers early in the seventeenth century by Antoinette d'Orléans and the Capuchin Joseph Leclerc du Tremblay.

[11]An Augustinian order of canons regular.

**Hafen Slawkenbergius* means the Benedictine nuns of *Cluny,* founded in the year 940, by *Odo,* abbé de *Cluny.* [Sterne's note. Founded in 910 under the abbot Berno, the Cluniac Benedictines widely extended their numbers and their influence under Odo, the successor of Berno. But according to Joan Evans, *Monastic Life at Cluny* (London, 1931), p. 29, the first nunnery of the Cluniac order was founded at Marcigny in 1056.]

[12]An order of monks founded by St. Bruno in 1084 at Chartreuse.

[13]Flayed. "St. Anthony's fire": erysipelas.

[14]The Order of Ursulines, which was especially devoted to the educa- tion of young girls, was founded in 1535 by St. Angela de Merici; the Society of the Sisters of St. Ursula of the Blessed Virgin was founded in 1606 by the Venerable Anne de Xainctonge.

[15]Members of a cathedral chapter.

[16]Domiciliar canons; canons of a minor order, having no vote in a chapter.

consider the case of butter'd buns[17]) all wished they had followed the nuns of saint *Ursula*'s example.———In the hurry and confusion every thing had been in the night before, the bakers had all forgot to lay their leaven———there were no butter'd buns to be had for breakfast in all *Strasburg* ———the whole close of the cathedral was in one eternal commotion———such a cause of restlessness and disquietude, and such a zealous inquiry into the cause of that restlessness, had never happened in *Strasburg,* since *Martin Luther,* with his doctrines, had turned the city up-side down.

If the stranger's nose took this liberty of thrusting itself thus into the dishes* of religious orders, *&c.* what a carnival did his nose make of it, in those of the laity!———'tis more than my pen, worn to the stump as it is, has power to describe; tho' I acknowledge, (*cries* Slawkenbergius, *with more gaiety of thought than I could have expected from him*) that there is many a good simile now subsisting in the world which might give my countrymen some idea of it; but at the close of such a folio as this, wrote for their sakes, and in which I have spent the greatest part of my life———tho' I own to them the simile is in being, yet would it not be unreasonable in them to expect I should have either time or inclination to search for it? Let it suffice to say, that the riot and disorder it occasioned in the *Strasburgers* fantacies was so general———such an overpowering mastership had it got of all the faculties of the *Strasburgers* minds———so many strange things, with equal confidence on all sides, and with equal eloquence in all places, were spoken and sworn to concerning it, that turned the whole stream of all discourse and wonder towards it———every soul, good and bad ———rich and poor———learned and unlearned———doctor and student———mistress and maid———gentle and simple———nun's flesh and woman's flesh in *Strasburg* spent their time in hear-

---

[17]Cant term for women who have frequent sexual intercourse.

*Mr. *Shandy's* compliments to orators———is very sensible that *Slawkenbergius* has here changed his metaphor———which he is very guilty of; ———that as a translator, Mr. *Shandy* has all along done what he could to make him stick to it———but that here 'twas impossible. [Sterne's note.]

ing tidings about it——every eye in *Strasburg* languished to
see it——every finger——every thumb in *Strasburg* burned
to touch it.

Now what might add, if any thing may be thought necessary to add to so vehement a desire——was this, that the centinel, the bandy-legg'd drummer, the trumpeter, the trumpeter's
wife, the burgo-master's widow, the master of the inn, and the
master of the inn's wife, how widely soever they all differed
every one from another in their testimonies and descriptions
of the stranger's nose——they all agreed together in two points
——namely, that he was gone to *Frankfort,* and would not return to *Strasburg* till that day month; and secondly, whether
his nose was true or false, that the stranger himself was one
of the most perfect paragons of beauty——the finest made
man!——the most genteel!——the most generous of his purse
——the most courteous in his carriage that had ever entered
the gates of *Strasburg*——that as he rode, with his scymetar
slung loosely to his wrist, thro' the streets——and walked with
his crimson-sattin breeches across the parade——'twas with so
sweet an air of careless modesty, and so manly withal——as
would have put the heart in jeopardy (had his nose not stood
in his way) of every virgin who had cast her eyes upon him.

I call not upon that heart which is a stranger to the throbs
and yearnings of curiosity, so excited, to justify the abbess of
Quedlingberg, the prioress, the deaness and subchantress for
sending at noon-day for the trumpeter's wife: she went through
the streets of *Strasburg* with her husband's trumpet in her
hand;——the best apparatus the straitness of the time would
allow her, for the illustration of her theory——she staid no
longer than three days.

The centinel and the bandy-legg'd drummer!——nothing on
this side of old *Athens* could equal them! they read their lectures under the city gates to comers and goers, with all the
pomp of a *Chrysippus*[18] and a *Crantor* in their porticos.

The master of the inn, with his ostler on his left-hand, read

---

[18]See p. 146, n. 2.   Crantor (fl. c.300 B.C.) was a Greek philosopher of
the Old Academy, the first commentator on Plato.

his also in the same stile,——under the portico or gateway of his stable-yard——his wife, hers more privately in a back room: all flocked to their lectures; not promiscuously——but to this or that, as is ever the way, as faith and credulity marshal'd them——in a word, each *Strasburger* came crouding for intelligence——and every *Strasburger* had the intelligence he wanted.

'Tis worth remarking, for the benefit of all demonstrators in natural philosophy, *&c.* that as soon as the trumpeter's wife had finished the abbess of *Quedlinberg's* private lecture, and had begun to read in public, which she did upon a stool in the middle of the great parade——she incommoded the other demonstrators mainly, by gaining incontinently the most fashionable part of the city of *Strasburg* for her auditory——But when a demonstrator in philosophy (cries *Slawkenbergius*) has a *trumpet* for an apparatus, pray what rival in science can pretend to be heard besides him?

Whilst the unlearned, thro' these conduits of intelligence, were all busied in getting down to the bottom of the well, where TRUTH keeps her little court——were the learned in their way as busy in pumping her up thro' the conduits of dialect[19] induction——they concerned themselves not with facts——they reasoned——

Not one profession had thrown more light upon this subject than the faculty[20]——had not all their disputes about it run into the affair of *Wens* and œdematous swellings, they could not keep clear of them for their bloods and souls—— the stranger's nose had nothing to do either with wens or œdematous swellings.

It was demonstrated however very satisfactorily, that such a ponderous mass of heterogenious matter could not be congested and conglomerated to the nose, whilst the infant was *in Utero,*[21] without destroying the statical balance of the fœtus,

---

[19]Dialectic.

[20]Authorized members of a learned profession; in this instance, the medical.

[21]In the uterus.

and throwing it plump upon its head nine months before the time.———

———The opponents granted the theory———they denied the consequences.

And if a suitable provision of veins, arteries, &c. said they, was not laid in, for the due nourishment of such a nose, in the very first stamina and rudiments of its formation before it came into the world (bating the case of Wens) it could not regularly grow and be sustained afterwards.

This was all answered by a dissertation upon nutriment, and the effect which nutriment had in extending the vessels, and in the increase and prolongation of the muscular parts to the greatest growth and expansion imaginable———In the triumph of which theory, they went so far as to affirm, that there was no cause in nature, why a nose might not grow to the size of the man himself.

The respondents satisfied the world this event could never happen to them so long as a man had but one stomach and one pair of lungs———For the stomach, said they, being the only organ destined for the reception of food, and turning it into chyle,———and the lungs the only engine of sanguification——— it could possibly work off no more, than what the appetite brought it: or admitting the possibility of a man's overloading his stomach, nature had set bounds however to his lungs——— the engine was of a determined size and strength, and could elaborate but a certain quantity in a given time———that is, it could produce just as much blood as was sufficient for one single man, and no more; so that, if there was as much nose as man———they proved a mortification must necessarily ensue; and forasmuch as there could not be a support for both, that the nose must either fall off from the man, or the man inevitably fall off from his nose.

Nature accommodates herself to these emergencies, cried the opponents—else what do you say to the case of a whole stomach———a whole pair of lungs, and but *half* a man, when both his legs have been unfortunately shot off?———

He dies of a plethora, said they———or must spit blood,

and in a fortnight or three weeks go off in a consumption——

——It happens otherways——replied the opponents.——
It ought not, said they.

The more curious and intimate inquirers after nature and
her doings, though they went hand in hand a good way together, yet they all divided about the nose at last, almost as
much as the faculty itself.

They amicably laid it down, that there was a just and
geometrical arrangement and proportion of the several parts
of the human frame to its several destinations, offices, and
functions, which could not be transgressed but within certain
limits——that nature, though she sported——she sported
within a certain circle;——and they could not agree about the
diameter of it.

The logicians stuck much closer to the point before them
than any of the classes of the literati;——they began and ended
with the word nose; and had it not been for a *petitio prin-
cipii*,[22] which one of the ablest of them ran his head against in
the beginning of the combat, the whole controversy had been
settled at once.

A nose, argued the logician, cannot bleed without blood——
and not only blood——but blood circulating in it to supply
the phænomenon with a succession of drops——(a stream
being but a quicker succession of drops, that is included, said
he)——Now death, continued the logician, being nothing but
the stagnation of the blood——

I deny the definition——Death is the separation of the soul
from the body, said his antagonist——Then we don't agree
about our weapon, said the logician——Then there is an end
of the dispute, replied the antagonist.

The civilians[23] were still more concise; what they offered
being more in the nature of a decree——than a dispute.

——Such a monstrous nose, said they, had it been a true
nose, could not possibly have been suffered in civil society——

---

[22]Begging of the question.
[23]Practitioners of civil law.

and if false——to impose upon society with such false signs and tokens, was a still greater violation of its rights, and must have had still less mercy shewn it.

The only objection to this was, that if it proved any thing, it proved the stranger's nose was neither true nor false.

This left room for the controversy to go on. It was maintained by the advocates of the ecclesiastic court, that there was nothing to inhibit a decree, since the stranger *ex mero motu*[24] had confessed he had been at the Promontory of Noses, and had got one of the goodliest, *&c. &c.*——To this it was answered, it was impossible there should be such a place as the Promontory of Noses, and the learned be ignorant where it lay. The commissary of the bishop of *Strasburg* undertook the advocates, explained this matter in a treatise upon proverbial phrases, shewing them, that the Promontory of Noses was a mere allegoric expression, importing no more than that nature had given him a long nose: in proof of which, with great learning, he cited the underwritten authorities*, which had decided the point incontestably, had it not appeared that a dispute about some franchises of dean and chapter-lands had been determined by it nineteen years before.

It happened——I must not say unluckily for Truth, because they were giving her a lift another way in so doing; that the two universities of *Strasburg*——the *Lutheran,* founded in the year 1538 by *Jacobus Sturmius,*[25] counsellor of the senate,——

---

[24]From mere impulse, of his own accord.

*Nonnulli ex nostratibus eadem loquendi formulâ utun. Quinimo et Logistæ & Canonistæ——Vid. Parce Barne Jas in d. L. Provincial. Constitut. de conjec. vid. Vol. Lib. 4. Titul. 1. N. 7. quâ etiam in re conspir. Om. de Promontorio Nas. Tichmak. ff. d. tit. 3. fol. 189. passim. Vid. Glos. de contrahend. empt. *&c.* nec non J. Scrudr. in cap. §. refut. ff. per totum Cum his cons. Rever. J. Tubal, Sentent. & Prov. cap. 9. ff. 11, 12. obiter. V. et Librum, cui Tit. de Terris & Phras. Belg. ad finem, cum Comment. N. Bardy Belg. Vid. Scrip. Argentotarens. de Antiq. Ecc. in Episc. Archiv. fid. coll. per Von Jacobum Koinshoven Folio Argent. 1583, præcip. ad finem. Quibus add. Rebuff in L. obvenire de Signif. Nom. ff. fol. & de Jure, Gent. & Civil. de protib. aliena feud. per federa, test. Joha. Luxius in prolegom. quem velim videas, de Analy. Cap. 1, 2, 3. Vid Idea. [Sterne's note, a burlesque of pedantic authority-citing.]

[25]Johannes Sturmius.

and the *Popish*, founded by *Leopold*, arch-duke of *Austria*, were, during all this time, employing the whole depth of their knowledge (except just what the affair of the abbess of *Quedlinburg*'s placket-holes required)——in determining the point of *Martin Luther*'s damnation.

The *Popish* doctors had undertaken to demonstrate *a priori*; that from the necessary influence of the planets on the twenty-second day of *October* 1483——when the moon was in the twelfth house——*Jupiter, Mars,* and *Venus* in the third, the *Sun, Saturn,* and *Mercury* all got together in the fourth—— that he must in course, and unavoidably be a damn'd man—— and that his doctrines, by a direct corollary, must be damn'd doctrines too.

By inspection into his horoscope, where five planets were in coition all at once with scorpio* (in reading this my father would always shake his head) in the ninth house which the *Arabians* allotted to religion——it appeared that *Martin Luther* did not care one stiver about the matter——and that from the horoscope directed to the conjunction of *Mars*—— they made it plain likewise he must die cursing and blasphem-

---

*Hæc mira, satisque horrenda. [5] Planetarum coitio sub Scorpio Asterismo in nonâ cœli statione, quam Arabes religioni deputabant efficit *Martinum Lutherum* sacrilegum hereticum, christianæ religionis hostem acerrimum atque prophanum, ex horoscopi directione ad Martis coitum, [ir]religiosissimus obiit, ejus Anima scelestissima ad infernos navigavit ——ab Alecto, Tisiphone et Megaera flagellis igneis cruciata perenniter.
——Lucas Gauricus in Tractatu astrologico de præteritis multorum hominum accidentibus per genituras examinatis. [Sterne's note. This passage, taken from the article on Luther in Bayle's *Dictionary* (the 5-volume English edition of 1734–1738, here emended, within brackets, from the more correct 10-volume English edition of 1734–1741), may be literally translated as follows: "This is sufficiently wonderful and horrifying. The conjunction of five planets with Scorpio in the ninth house of the heavens, which the Arabians ascribe to religion, caused Luther to be a sacrilegious heretic, a most bitter and prophane enemy of the Christian religion. From the direction of the horoscope to the conjunction of Mars, it is evident that he died wholly irreligious. His most wicked soul sailed to hell, there to be scourged eternally with fiery whips by Allecto, Tisiphone, and Megaera.—Lucas Gauricus's *Astrological Treatise on the Past Accidents of Many Men, by Means of an Examination of Their Nativities.*" Gauricus (1476–1558) was Bishop of Civitate and a celebrated mathematician and astrologer.]

ing——with the blast of which his soul (being steep'd in
guilt) sailed before the wind, into the lake of hell fire.

The little objection of the *Lutheran* doctors to this, was, that
it must certainly be the soul of another man, born *Oct.* 22, 83,
which was forced to sail down before the wind in that manner
——inasmuch as it appeared from the register of *Islaben* in the
county of *Mansfelt,* that *Luther* was not born in the year 1483,
but in 84; and not on the 22d day of *October,* but on the 10th
of *November,* the eve of *Martinmas*-day, from whence he had
the name of *Martin.*

[——I must break off my translation for a moment; for if I
did not, I know I should no more be able to shut my eyes in
bed, than the abbess of *Quedlinburg*——It is to tell the reader,
that my father never read this passage of *Slawkenbergius* to my
uncle *Toby* but with triumph——not over my uncle *Toby,* for
he never opposed him in it——but over the whole world.

——Now you see, brother *Toby,* he would say, looking up,
"that christian names are not such indifferent things;"——had
Luther here been called by any other name but *Martin,* he
would have been damned to all eternity———Not that I look
upon *Martin,* he would add, as a good name——far from it
——'tis something better than a neutral, and but a little——
yet little as it is, you see it was of some service to him.

My father knew the weakness of this prop to his hypothesis,
as well as the best logician could shew him——yet so strange
is the weakness of man at the same time, as it fell in his way,
he could not for his life but make use of it; and it was certainly for this reason, that though there are many stories in
Hafen Slawkenbergius's Decads full as entertaining as this
I am translating, yet there is not one amongst them which my
father read over with half the delight——it flattered two of his
strangest hypotheses together——his NAMES and his NOSES——
I will be bold to say, he might have read all the books in the
Alexandrian library,[26] had not fate taken other care of them,

---

[26]The most important library of antiquity, formed at Alexandria during
the reign of the Ptolemies and said to have contained at one time about
half a million manuscript volumes.

and not have met with a book or a passage in one, which hit two such nails as these upon the head at one stroke.]

The two universities of *Strasburg* were hard tugging at this affair of *Luther's* navigation. The Protestant doctors had demonstrated, that he had not sailed right before the wind, as the Popish doctors had pretended; and as every one knew there was no sailing full in the teeth of it,——they were going to settle, in case he had sailed, how many points he was off; whether *Martin* had doubled the cape, or had fallen upon a lee-shore; and no doubt, as it was an enquiry of much edification, at least to those who understood this sort of NAVIGATION, they had gone on with it in spite of the size of the stranger's nose, had not the size of the stranger's nose drawn off the attention of the world from what they were about——it was their business to follow.——

The abbess of *Quedlinburg* and her four dignitaries was no stop; for the enormity of the stranger's nose running full as much in their fancies as their case of conscience——The affair of their placket-holes kept cold——In a word, the printers were ordered to distribute their types——all controversies dropp'd.

'Twas a square cap with a silk tassel upon the crown of it[27] ——to a nut shell——to have guessed on which side of the nose the two universities would split.

'Tis above reason, cried the doctors on one side.

'Tis below reason, cried the others.

'Tis faith, cried one.

'Tis a fiddle-stick, said the other.

'Tis possible, cried the one.

'Tis impossible, said the other.

God's power is infinite, cried the Nosarians, he can do any thing.

He can do nothing, replied the Antinosarians, which implies contradictions.

He can make matter think, said the Nosarians.

As certainly as you can make a velvet cap out of a sow's ear, replied the Antinosarians.

---

[27]*I.e.,* an academic cap.

He can make two and two five, replied the Popish doctors.——'Tis false, said their opponents.——

Infinite power is infinite power, said the doctors who maintained the *reality* of the nose.——It extends only to all possible things, replied the *Lutherans*.

By God in heaven, cried the Popish doctors, he can make a nose, if he thinks fit, as big as the steeple of *Strasburg*.

Now the steeple of *Strasburg* being the biggest and the tallest church-steeple to be seen in the whole world, the Antinosarians denied that a nose of 575 geometrical feet in length could be worn, at least by a middle-siz'd man——The Popish doctors swore it could——The *Lutheran* doctors said No;—— it could not.

This at once started a new dispute, which they pursued a great way upon the extent and limitation of the moral and natural attributes of God——That controversy led them naturally into *Thomas Aquinas*,[28] and *Thomas Aquinas* to the devil.

The stranger's nose was no more heard of in the dispute—— it just served as a frigate to launch them into the gulph of school-divinity,——and then they all sailed before the wind.

Heat is in proportion to the want of true knowledge.

The controversy about the attributes, *&c.* instead of cooling, on the contrary had inflamed the *Strasburgers* imaginations to a most inordinate degree——The less they understood of the matter, the greater was their wonder about it——they were left in all the distresses of desire unsatisfied——saw their doctors, the *Parchmentarians,* the *Brassarians,* the *Turpentarians,* on one side——the Popish doctors on the other, like *Pantagruel* and his companions in quest of the oracle of the bottle, all embarked and out of sight.[29]

——The poor *Strasburgers* left upon the beach!

——What was to be done?——No delay——the uproar increased——every one in disorder——the city gates set open.——

---

[28]See p. 58, n. 6.

[29]Pantagruel's embarkation "to visit the Oracle of Bacbuc, alias the Holy Bottle" occurs in *Rabelais,* 4.1.

Unfortunate *Strasburgers!* was there in the store-house of nature——was there in the lumber-rooms of learning——was there in the great arsenal of chance, one single engine left undrawn forth to torture your curiosities, and stretch your desires, which was not pointed by the hand of fate to play upon your hearts?——I dip not my pen into my ink to excuse the surrender of yourselves——'tis to write your panegyrick. Shew me a city so macerated with expectation——who neither eat, or drank, or slept, or prayed, or hearkned to the calls either of religion or nature for seven and twenty days together, who could have held out one day· longer.

On the twenty-eighth the courteous stranger had promised to return to *Strasburg.*

Seven thousand coaches (*Slawkenbergius* must certainly have made some mistake in his numerical characters) 7000 coaches——15000 single horse chairs——20000 waggons, crouded as full as they could all hold with senators, counsellors, syndicks——beguines,[30] widows, wives, virgins, canons, concubines, all in their coaches——The abbess of *Quedlinburg,* with the prioress, the deaness and sub-chantress leading the procession in one coach, and the dean of *Strasburg,* with the four great dignitaries of his chapter on her left-hand—— the rest following higglety-pigglety as they could; some on horseback——some on foot——some led——some driven—— some down the *Rhine*——some this way——some that——all set out at sun-rise to meet the courteous stranger on the road.

Haste we now towards the catastrophe of my tale——I say *Catastrophe* (cries *Slawkenbergius*) inasmuch as a tale, with parts rightly disposed, not only rejoiceth (*gaudet*) in the *Catastrophe* and *Peripetia* of a DRAMA, but rejoiceth moreover in all the essential and integrant parts of it——it has its *Protasis,*[31] *Epitasis, Catastasis,* its *Catastrophe* or *Peripetia* growing one out of the other in it, in the order *Aristotle* first

---

[30]Members of a lay sisterhood, not bound by vows, who went about reading the Scriptures and exhorting the people.

[31]Introduction. *Epitasis:* heightening. *Catastasis:* climax. *Peripetia:* dénouement, change in fortune. Most of the terms are post-Aristotelian.

planted them——without which a tale had better never be told at all, says *Slawkenbergius,* but be kept to a man's self.

In all my ten tales, in all my ten decads, have I, *Slawkenbergius,* tied down every tale of them as tightly to this rule, as I have done this of the stranger and his nose.

——From his first parley with the centinel, to his leaving the city of *Strasburg,* after pulling off his crimson-sattin pair of breeches, is the *Protasis* or first entrance——where the characters of the *Personæ Dramatis*[32] are just touched in, and the subject slightly begun.

The *Epitasis,* wherein the action is more fully entered upon and heightened, till it arrives at its state or height called the *Catastasis,* and which usually takes up the 2d and 3d act, is included within that busy period of my tale, betwixt the first night's uproar about the nose, to the conclusion of the trumpeter's wife's lectures upon it in the middle of the grand parade; and from the first embarking of the learned in the dispute——to the doctors finally sailing away, and leaving the *Strasburgers* upon the beach in distress, is the *Catastasis* or the ripening of the incidents and passions for their bursting forth in the fifth act.

This commences with the setting out of the *Strasburgers* in the *Frankfort* road, and terminates in unwinding the labyrinth and bringing the hero out of a state of agitation (as *Aristotle* calls it) to a state of rest and quietness.

This, says *Hafen Slawkenbergius,* constitutes the catastrophe or peripetia of my tale——and that is the part of it I am going to relate.

We left the stranger behind the curtain asleep——he enters now upon the stage.

——What dost thou prick up thy ears at?——'tis nothing but a man upon a horse——was the last word the stranger uttered to his mule. It was not proper then to tell the reader, that the mule took his master's word for it; and without any more *ifs* or *ands,* let the traveller and his horse pass by.

The traveller was hastening with all diligence to get to *Stras-*

---

[32]Persons in the drama.

burg that night——What a fool am I, said the traveller to himself, when he had rode about a league farther, to think of getting into *Strasburg* this night——*Strasburg!*——the great *Strasburg!*——*Strasburg,* the capital of all *Alsatia! Strasburg,* an imperial city! *Strasburg,* a sovereign state! *Strasburg,* garrisoned with five thousand of the best troops in all the world!——Alas! if I was at the gates of *Strasburg* this moment, I could not gain admittance into it for a ducat,——nay a ducat and half——'tis too much——better go back to the last inn I have passed——than lie I know not where——or give I know not what. The traveller, as he made these reflections in his mind, turned his horse's head about, and three minutes after the stranger had been conducted into his chamber, he arrived at the same inn.

——We have bacon in the house, said the host, and bread ——and till eleven o'clock this night had three eggs in it—— but a stranger, who arrived an hour ago, has had them dressed into an omlet, and we have nothing.——

——Alas! said the traveller, harrassed as I am, I want nothing but a bed——I have one as soft as is in *Alsatia,* said the host.

——The stranger, continued he, should have slept in it, for 'tis my best bed, but upon the score of his nose——He has got a defluxion,[33] said the traveller——Not that I know, cried the host——But 'tis a camp-bed, and *Jacinta,* said he, looking towards the maid, imagined there was not room in it to turn his nose in——Why so? cried the traveller starting back ——It is so long a nose, replied the host——The traveller fixed his eyes upon *Jacinta,* then upon the ground——kneeled upon his right knee——had just got his hand laid upon his breast——Trifle not with my anxiety, said he, rising up again ——'Tis no trifle, said *Jacinta,* 'tis the most glorious nose!—— The traveller fell upon his knee again——laid his hand upon his breast——then said he, looking up to heaven! thou hast conducted me to the end of my pilgrimage——'Tis *Diego!*

The traveller was the brother of the *Julia,* so often invoked

---

[33]Discharge of fluid matter.

that night by the stranger as he rode from *Strasburg* upon his mule; and was come, on her part, in quest of him. He had accompanied his sister from *Valadolid* across the *Pyrenean* mountains thro' *France,* and had many an entangled skein to wind off in pursuit of him thro' the many meanders and abrupt turnings of a lover's thorny tracks.

——*Julia* had sunk under it——and had not been able to go a step farther than to *Lyons,* where, with the many disquietudes of a tender heart, which all talk of——but few feel ——she sicken'd, but had just strength to write a letter to *Diego;* and having conjured her brother never to see her face till he had found him out, and put the letter into his hands, *Julia* took to her bed.

Fernandez (for that was her brother's name)——tho' the camp-bed was as soft as any one in *Alsace,* yet he could not shut his eyes in it.——As soon as it was day he rose, and hearing *Diego* was risen too, he enter'd his chamber, and discharged his sister's commission.

The letter was as follows:

"Seig. DIEGO.

"Whether my suspicions of your nose were justly excited or not——'tis not now to inquire——it is enough I have not had firmness to put them to farther tryal.

"How could I know so little of myself, when I sent my *Duena* to forbid your coming more under my lattice? or how could I know so little of you, *Diego,* as to imagine you would not have staid one day in *Valadolid* to have given ease to my doubts?——Was I to be abandoned, *Diego,* because I was deceived? or was it kind to take me at my word, whether my suspicions were just or no, and leave me, as you did, a prey to much uncertainty and sorrow?

"In what manner *Julia* has resented this——my brother, when he puts this letter into your hands, will tell you: He will tell you in how few moments she repented of the rash message she had sent you——in what frantic haste she flew to her lattice, and how many days and nights together she leaned immoveably upon her elbow, looking thro' it towards the way which *Diego* was wont to come.

"He will tell you, when she heard of your departure——how her spirits deserted her——how her heart sicken'd——how piteously she mourn'd——how low she hung her head. O *Diego!* how many weary steps has my brother's pity led me by the hand languishing to trace out yours! how far has desire carried me beyond strength——and how oft have I fainted by the way, and sunk into his arms, with only power to cry out ——O my *Diego!*

"If the gentleness of your carriage has not belied your heart, you will fly to me, almost as fast as you fled from me——haste as you will, you will arrive but to see me expire.——'Tis a bitter draught, *Diego,* but oh! 'tis embitter'd still more by dying *un*————."

She could proceed no farther.

Slawkenbergius supposes the word intended was *unconvinced,* but her strength would not enable her to finish her letter.

The heart of the courteous *Diego* overflowed as he read the letter——he ordered his mule forthwith and *Fernandez's* horse to be saddled; and as no vent in prose is equal to that of poetry in such conflicts——chance, which as often directs us to remedies as to *diseases,* having thrown a piece of charcoal into the window——*Diego* availed himself of it, and whilst the ostler was getting ready his mule, he eased his mind against the wall as follows.

ODE

Harsh and untuneful are the notes of love,
  Unless my Julia strikes the key,
Her hand alone can touch the part,
  Whose dulcet move-
    -ment charms the heart,
And governs all the man with sympathetic sway.

2d.

O Julia!

The lines were very natural——for they were nothing at all to the purpose, says *Slawkenbergius,* and 'tis a pity there were no more of them; but whether it was that Seig. *Diego* was slow in composing verses—or the ostler quick in saddling mules——is not averred; certain it was, that *Diego*'s mule and *Fernandez*'s horse were ready at the door of the inn, before *Diego* was ready for his second stanza; so without staying to finish his ode, they both mounted, sallied forth, passed the *Rhine,* traversed *Alsace,* shaped their course towards *Lyons,* and before the *Strasburgers* and the abbess of *Quedlinberg* had set out on their cavalcade, had *Fernandez, Diego,* and his *Julia,* crossed the *Pyrenean* mountains, and got safe to *Valadolid.*

'Tis needless to inform the geographical reader, that when *Diego* was in *Spain,* it was not possible to meet the courteous stranger in the *Frankfort* road; it is enough to say, that of all restless desires, curiosity being the strongest——the *Strasburgers* felt the full force of it; and that for three days and nights they were tossed to and fro in the *Frankfort* road, with the tempestuous fury of this passion, before they could submit to return home——When alas! an event was prepared for them, of all others the most grievous that could befal a free people.

As this revolution of the *Strasburgers* affairs is often spoken of, and little understood, I will, in ten words, says *Slawkenbergius,* give the world an explanation of it, and with it put an end to my tale.

Every body knows of the grand system of Universal Monarchy, wrote by order of Mons. *Colbert,* and put in manuscript into the hands of *Lewis* the fourteenth, in the year 1664.[34]

'Tis as well known, that one branch out of many of that system, was the getting possession of *Strasburg,* to favour an entrance at all times into *Suabia,* in order to disturb the quiet

---

[34]In this year Jean Baptiste Colbert (1619–1683), the great French statesman and minister of finance of Louis XIV, explained to his king how he could attain universal monarchy and endless glory by restricting the activities of his subjects to agriculture, commerce, and war by land and sea.

of *Germany*——and that in consequence of this plan, *Strasburg* unhappily fell at length into their hands.

It is the lot of few to trace out the true springs of this and such like revolutions——The vulgar look too high for them ——Statesmen look too low——Truth (for once) lies in the middle.

What a fatal thing is the popular pride of a free city! cries one historian——The *Strasburgers* deemed it a diminution of their freedom to receive an imperial garrison——and so fell a prey to a *French* one.

The fate, says another, of the *Strasburgers,* may be a warning to all free people to save their money———They anticipated their revenues——brought themselves under taxes, exhausted their strength, and in the end became so weak a people, they had not strength to keep their gates shut, and so the *French* pushed them open.

Alas! alas! cries *Slawkenbergius,* 'twas not the *French*—— 'twas CURIOSITY pushed them open———The *French* indeed, who are ever upon the catch, when they saw the *Strasburgers,* men, women, and children, all marched out to follow the stranger's nose——each man followed his own, and marched in.

Trade and manufactures have decayed and gradually grown down ever since——but not from any cause which commercial heads have assigned; for it is owing to this only, that Noses have ever so run in their heads, that the *Strasburgers* could not follow their business.

Alas! alas! cries *Slawkenbergius,* making an exclamation—— it is not the first——and I fear will not be the last fortress that has been either won——or lost by NOSES.

The END of

Slawkenbergius's TALE.

CHAP. I.

WITH all this learning upon Noses running perpetually in my father's fancy——with so many family prejudices ——and ten decads of such tales running on for ever along with them——how was it possible with such exquisite—— was it a true nose?——That a man with such exquisite feelings as my father had, could bear the shock at all below stairs ——or indeed above stairs, in any other posture, but the very posture I have described.

——Throw yourself down upon the bed, a dozen times—— taking care only to place a looking-glass first in a chair on one side of it, before you do it——But was the stranger's nose a true nose——or was it a false one?

To tell that before-hand, madam, would be to do injury to one of the best tales in the christian world; and that is the tenth of the tenth decad which immediately follows this.

This tale, crieth *Slawkenbergius* somewhat exultingly, has been reserved by me for the concluding tale of my whole work; knowing right well, that when I shall have told it, and my reader shall have read it thro'——'twould be even high time for both of us to shut up the book; inasmuch, continues *Slawkenbergius,* as I know of no tale which could possibly ever go down after it.

——'Tis a tale indeed!

This sets out with the first interview in the inn at *Lyons,* when *Fernandez* left the courteous stranger and his sister *Julia* alone in her chamber, and is overwritten,

The INTRICACIES

of

Diego and *Julia.*

Heavens! thou art a strange creature *Slawkenbergius!* what a whimsical view of the involutions of the heart of woman hast thou opened! how this can ever be translated, and yet if this specimen of *Slawkenbergius's* tales, and the exquisitiveness of his moral should please the world——translated shall a couple of volumes be.——Else, how this can ever be translated into good *English,* I have no sort of conception.——There seems in some passages to want a sixth sense to do it rightly.——What can he mean by the lambent pupilability of slow, low, dry chat, five notes below the natural tone,——which you know, madam, is little more than a whisper? The moment I pronounced the words, I could perceive an attempt towards a vibration in the strings, about the region of the heart.——The brain made no acknowledgment.——There's often no good understanding betwixt 'em.——I felt as if I understood it.——I had no ideas. ——The movement could not be without cause.——I'm lost. I can make nothing of it,——unless, may it please your worships, the voice, in that case being little more than a whisper, unavoidably forces the eyes to approach not only within six inches of each other——but to look into the pupils——is not that dangerous?——But it can't be avoided——for to look up to the cieling, in that case the two chins unavoidably meet ——and to look down into each others laps, the foreheads come into immediate contact, which at once puts an end to the conference——I mean to the sentimental part of it.——What is left, madam, is not worth stooping for.

CHAP. II.

MY father lay stretched across the bed as still as if the hand of death had pushed him down, for a full hour and a half, before he began to play upon the floor with the toe of that foot which hung over the bed-side; my uncle *Toby's* heart was a pound lighter for it.——In a few moments, his left-hand, the knuckles of which had all the time reclined upon the handle of the chamber-pot, came to its feeling——he thrust it a little more within the valance——drew up his hand, when he

had done, into his bosom——gave a hem!——My good uncle
Toby, with infinite pleasure, answered it; and full gladly
would have ingrafted a sentence of consolation upon the opening it afforded; but having no talents, as I said, that way, and
fearing moreover that he might set out with something which
might make a bad matter worse, he contented himself with
resting his chin placidly upon the cross of his crutch.

Now whether the compression shortened my uncle *Toby's*
face into a more pleasureable oval,——or that the philanthropy
of his heart, in seeing his brother beginning to emerge out of
the sea of his afflictions, had braced up his muscles,——so that
the compression upon his chin only doubled the benignity
which was there before, is not hard to decide.——My father,
in turning his eyes, was struck with such a gleam of sun-shine
in his face, as melted down the sullenness of his grief in a
moment.

He broke silence as follows.

CHAP. III.

D ID ever man, brother *Toby,* cried my father, raising himself up upon his elbow, and turning himself round to the
opposite side of the bed where my uncle *Toby* was sitting in
his old fringed chair, with his chin resting upon his crutch
——did ever a poor unfortunate man, brother *Toby,* cried my
father, receive so many lashes?——The most I ever saw given,
quoth my uncle *Toby,* (ringing the bell at the bed's head for
Trim) was to a grenadier, I think in *Makay's*[1] regiment.

——Had my uncle *Toby* shot a bullet thro' my father's
heart, he could not have fallen down with his nose upon the
quilt more suddenly.

Bless me! said my uncle *Toby.*

---

[1]Hugh Mackay (1640?–1692), a commander in the British division of
the grand army in Flanders during the War of the Grand Alliance.

CHAP. IV.

W AS it *Makay's* regiment, quoth my uncle *Toby,* where
the poor grenadier was so unmercifully whipp'd at
Bruges about the ducats?——O Christ! he was innocent! cried
Trim with a deep sigh.——And he was whipp'd, may it please
your honour, almost to death's door.——They had better have
shot him outright as he begg'd, and he had gone directly to
heaven, for he was as innocent as your honour.——I thank
thee, *Trim,* quoth my uncle *Toby.* I never think of his, continued *Trim,* and my poor brother *Tom's* misfortunes, for we
were all three school-fellows, but I cry like a coward.——Tears
are no proof of cowardice, *Trim.*——I drop them oft-times myself, cried my uncle *Toby.*——I know your honour does, replied *Trim,* and so am not ashamed of it myself.——But to
think, may it please your honour, continued *Trim,* a tear stealing into the corner of his eye as he spoke——to think of two
virtuous lads with hearts as warm in their bodies, and as honest as God could make them——the children of honest people,
going forth with gallant spirits to seek their fortunes in the
world——and fall into such evils!——poor *Tom!* to be tortured upon a rack for nothing——but marrying a *Jew's* widow
who sold sausages—honest *Dick Johnson's* soul to be scourged
out of his body, for the ducats another man put into his knapsack!——O!——these are misfortunes, cried *Trim,*——pulling
out his handkerchief——these are misfortunes, may it please
your honour, worth lying down and crying over.

——My father could not help blushing.

'Twould be a pity, *Trim,* quoth my uncle *Toby,* thou
shouldst ever feel sorrow of thy own——thou feelest it so
tenderly for others.——Alack-o-day, replied the corporal,
brightening up his face———your honour knows I have neither wife or child——I can have no sorrows in this world.——
My father could not help smiling.——As few as any man,
Trim, replied my uncle *Toby;* nor can I see how a fellow of

thy light heart can suffer, but from the distress of poverty in thy old age——when thou art passed all services, *Trim,*—— and hast out-lived thy friends——An' please your honour, never fear, replied *Trim* chearily——But I would have thee never fear, *Trim,* replied my uncle; and therefore, continued my uncle *Toby,* throwing down his crutch, and getting up upon his legs as he uttered the word *therefore*——in recom- pence, *Trim,* of thy long fidelity to me, and that goodness of thy heart I have had such proofs of——whilst thy master is worth a shilling——thou shalt never ask elsewhere, *Trim,* for a penny. *Trim* attempted to thank my uncle *Toby,*——but had not power——tears trickled down his cheeks faster than he could wipe them off——He laid his hands upon his breast ——made a bow to the ground, and shut the door.

——I have left *Trim* my bowling-green, cried my uncle *Toby*——My father smiled————I have left him moreover a pension, continued my uncle *Toby*——My father looked grave.

CHAP. V.

IS this a fit time, said my father to himself, to talk of PEN- SIONS and GRENADIERS?

CHAP. VI.

WHEN my uncle *Toby* first mentioned the grenadier, my father, I said, fell down with his nose flat to the quilt, and as suddenly as if my uncle *Toby* had shot him; but it was not added, that every other limb and member of my father instantly relapsed with his nose into the same precise attitude in which he lay first described; so that when corporal *Trim* left the room, and my father found himself disposed to rise off the bed,——he had all the little preparatory movements to run over again, before he could do it.——Attitudes are noth- ing, madam,——'tis the transition from one attitude to another——like the preparation and resolution of the discord into harmony, which is all in all.

For which reason my father played the same jig over again with his toe upon the floor——pushed the chamber-pot still a little farther within the valance——gave a hem——raised himself up upon his elbow——and was just beginning to address himself to my uncle *Toby*——when recollecting the unsuccessfulness of his first effort in that attitude,——he got upon his legs, and in making the third turn across the room, he stopped short before my uncle *Toby;* and laying the three first fingers of his right-hand in the palm of his left, and stooping a little, he addressed himself to my uncle *Toby* as follows.

CHAP. VII.

WHEN I reflect, brother *Toby,* upon MAN; and take a view of that dark side of him which represents his life as open to so many causes of trouble——when I consider, brother *Toby,* how oft we eat the bread of affliction, and that we are born to it, as to the portion of our inheritance——I was born to nothing, quoth my uncle *Toby,* interrupting my father——but my commission. Zooks![1] said my father, did not my uncle leave you a hundred and twenty pounds a year?——What could I have done without it? replied my uncle *Toby.*——That's another concern, said my father testily—— But I say, *Toby,* when one runs over the catalogue of all the cross reckonings and sorrowful *items* with which the heart of man is overcharged, 'tis wonderful by what hidden resources the mind is enabled to stand it out, and bear itself up, as it does against the impositions laid upon our nature.——'Tis by the assistance of Almighty God, cried my uncle *Toby,* looking up, and pressing the palms of his hands close together—— 'tis not from our own strength, brother *Shandy*——a sentinel in a wooden centry-box, might as well pretend to stand it out

---

[1] Gadzooks; a minced oath, a corruption of "God's hooks," referring to the nails with which Christ was fixed to the cross.

against a detachment of fifty men,——we are upheld by the grace and the assistance of the best of Beings.

——That is cutting the knot, said my father, instead of un-tying it.——But give me leave to lead you, brother *Toby,* a little deeper into this mystery.

With all my heart, replied my uncle *Toby.*

My father instantly exchanged the attitude he was in, for that in which *Socrates* is so finely painted by *Raffael* in his school of *Athens;*[2] which your connoisseurship knows is so ex-quisitely imagined, that even the particular manner of the reasoning of *Socrates* is expressed by it——for he holds the fore-finger of his left-hand between the fore-finger and the thumb of his right, and seems as if he was saying to the liber-tine he is reclaiming——*"You grant me* this——and this: and this, and this, I don't ask of you——they follow of them-selves in course."

So stood my father, holding fast his fore-finger betwixt his finger and his thumb, and reasoning with my uncle *Toby* as he sat in his old fringed chair, valanced around with party-coloured worsted bobs——O *Garrick!*[3] what a rich scene of this would thy exquisite powers make! and how gladly would I write such another to avail myself of thy immortality, and secure my own behind it.

CHAP. VIII.

THOUGH man is of all others the most curious vehicle, said my father, yet at the same time 'tis of so slight a frame and so totteringly put together, that the sudden jerks and hard jostlings it unavoidably meets with in this rugged jour-ney, would overset and tear it to pieces a dozen times a day ——was it not, brother *Toby,* that there is a secret spring within us——Which spring, said my uncle *Toby,* I take to be

---

[2] The famous fresco which decorates one of the walls of the Stanza della Segnatura in the Vatican.

[3] See p. 180, n. 1.

Religion.——Will that set my child's nose on? cried my father, letting go his finger, and striking one hand against the other ——It makes every thing straight for us, answered my uncle *Toby*——Figuratively speaking, dear *Toby,* it may, for aught I know, said my father; but the spring I am speaking of, is that great and elastic power within us of counterbalancing evil, which like a secret spring in a well-ordered machine, though it can't prevent the shock——at least it imposes upon our sense of it.

Now, my dear brother, said my father, replacing his fore-finger, as he was coming closer to the point,——had my child arrived safe into the world, unmartyr'd in that precious part of him——fanciful and extravagant as I may appear to the world in my opinion of christian names, and of that magic bias which good or bad names irresistably impress upon our characters and conducts——heaven is witness! that in the warmest transports of my wishes for the prosperity of my child, I never once wished to crown his head with more glory and honour, than what GEORGE or EDWARD would have spread around it.[1]

But alas! continued my father, as the greatest evil has be-fallen him——I must counteract and undo it with the greatest good.

He shall be christened *Trismegistus,*[2] brother.

I wish it may answer——replied my uncle *Toby,* rising up.

CHAP. IX.

WHAT a chapter of chances, said my father, turning him-self about upon the first landing, as he and my uncle *Toby* were going down stairs——what a long chapter of chances do the events of this world lay open to us! Take pen

---

[1]An oblique compliment to the young George III and his brother Ed-ward, Duke of York; during Sterne's visit to London the spring before this passage was written, he had been occasionally in the Duke's company.

[2]Hermes Trismegistus ("Hermes the thrice-greatest") was the Greek name of Thoth, the Egyptian god of wisdom, inventor of arts and

and ink in hand, brother *Toby,* and calculate it fairly——I know no more of calculations than this balluster, said my uncle *Toby,* (striking short of it with his crutch, and hitting my father a desperate blow souse upon his shin-bone)——'Twas a hundred to one——cried my uncle *Toby.*——I thought, quoth my father, (rubbing his shin) you had known nothing of calculations, brother *Toby.*——'Twas a meer chance, said my uncle *Toby*——Then it adds one to the chapter——replied my father.

The double success of my father's repartees tickled off the pain of his shin at once——it was well it so fell out—— (chance! again)——or the world to this day had never known the subject of my father's calculation——to guess it——there was no chance——What a lucky chapter of chances has this turned out! for it has saved me the trouble of writing one express, and in truth I have anew[1] already upon my hands without it——Have not I promised the world a chapter of knots? two chapters upon the right and the wrong end of a woman? a chapter upon whiskers? a chapter upon wishes? ——a chapter of noses?——No, I have done that——a chapter upon my uncle *Toby*'s modesty: to say nothing of a chapter upon chapters, which I will finish before I sleep——by my great grandfather's whiskers, I shall never get half of 'em through this year.

Take pen and ink in hand, and calculate it fairly, brother *Toby,* said my father, and it will turn out a million to one, that of all the parts of the body, the edge of the forceps should have the ill luck just to fall upon and break down that one part, which should break down the fortunes of our house with it.

It might have been worse, replied my uncle *Toby*——I don't comprehend, said my father——Suppose the hip had presented, replied my uncle *Toby,* as Dr. *Slop* foreboded.

---

sciences, and reputed author of the forty-two encyclopædic "Hermetic" sacred books of ancient Egypt, of which fragments treating of geography, astronomy, ritual, myths, and medicine are yet extant.

[1]Enough.

My father reflected half a minute——looked down——
touched the middle of his forehead slightly with his finger——

——True, said he.

CHAP. X.

IS it not a shame to make two chapters of what passed in
going down one pair of stairs? for we are got no farther
yet than to the first landing, and there are fifteen more steps
down to the bottom; and for aught I know, as my father and
my uncle *Toby* are in a talking humour, there may be as many
chapters as steps;——let that be as it will, Sir, I can no more
help it than my destiny:——A sudden impulse comes across
me——drop the curtain, *Shandy*——I drop it——Strike a line
here across the paper, *Tristram*——I strike it——and hey for
a new chapter!

The duce of any other rule have I to govern myself by in
this affair——and if I had one——as I do all things out of all
rule——I would twist it and tear it to pieces, and throw it
into the fire when I had done——Am I warm? I am, and the
cause demands it——a pretty story! is a man to follow rules
——or rules to follow him?

Now this, you must know, being my chapter upon chapters,
which I promised to write before I went to sleep, I thought it
meet to ease my conscience entirely before I lay'd down, by
telling the world all I knew about the matter at once: Is not
this ten times better than to set out dogmatically with a sen-
tentious parade of wisdom, and telling the world a story of a
roasted horse——that chapters relieve the mind——that they
assist——or impose upon the imagination——and that in a
work of this dramatic cast they are as necessary as the shifting
of scenes——with fifty other cold conceits, enough to extin-
guish the fire which roasted him.——O! but to understand

this, which is a puff at the fire of *Diana's*[1] temple——you must
read *Longinus*——read away——if you are not a jot the wiser
by reading him the first time over——never fear——read him
again——*Avicenna* and *Licetus,* read *Aristotle's* metaphysicks
forty times through a piece, and never understood a single
word.——But mark the consequence——*Avicenna*[2] turned out
a desperate writer at all kinds of writing——for he wrote books
de omni scribili; and for *Licetus (Fortunio)*[3] though all the
world knows he was born a fœtus*, of no more than five inches

[1]Apparently an allusion to the austerity of the virgin goddess. For
Longinus, see p. 52, n. 7. Sterne alludes here to *On the Sublime,* 3,
et passim, where are discussed the faults of tumidity and frigidity.

[2]Avicenna (980–1037), the most celebrated Arabian physician and
philosopher, was said to have read the *Metaphysics* forty times and even
to have memorized it, without understanding it, when the chance reading
of Al Farabius's treatise *Concerning the Objects of Metaphysics* at once
revealed Aristotle's meaning to him. *De omni scribili:* on all kinds of
writing.

[3]Licetus (1577–1657), named Fortunio because he had survived pre-
mature birth, was a celebrated Italian scholar and physician, one of whose
works, here referred to, was *De Ortu Animae Humanae.*

*Ce Fœtus n'étoit pas plus grand que la paume de la main; mais son
pere l'ayant éxaminé en qualité de Médecin, & ayant trouvé que c'étoit
quelque chose de plus qu'un Embryon, le fit transporter tout vivant à
Rapallo, où il le fit voir à Jerôme Bardi & à d'autres Médecins du lieu.
On trouva qu'il ne lui manquoit rien d'essentiel à la vie; & son pere pour
faire voir un essai de son expérience, entreprit d'achever l'ouvrage de la
Nature, & de travailler à la formation de l'Enfant avec le même artifice
que celui dont on se sert pour faire éclorre les Poulets en Egypte. Il
instruisit une Nourrice de tout ce qu'elle avoit à faire, & ayant fait mettre
son fils dans un four proprement accommodé, il reussit à l'élever et à lui
faire prendre ses accroissemens nécessaires, par l'uniformité d'une chaleur
étrangère mesurée éxactement sur les dégrés d'un Thermomètre, ou d'un
autre instrument équivalent. (Vide Mich. Giustinian, ne gli Scritt.
Liguri à Cart. 223.488.)
On auroit toujours été très satisfait de l'industrie d'un Pere si expéri-
menté dans l'Art de la Génération, quand il n'auroit pû prolonger la vie à
son fils que pour quelques mois, ou pour peu d'années.
Mais quand on se represente que l'Enfant a vécu pres de quatre-vingts
ans, & qu'il a composé quatre-vingts Ouvrages différents tous fruits d'une
longue lecture,——il faut convenir que tout ce qui est incroyable n'est pas
toujours faux, & que la *Vraisemblance n'est pas toujours du côté de la
Verité.*
Il n'avoit que dix-neuf ans lorsqu'il composa Gonopsychanthropologia
de Origine Animæ humanæ.
(Les Enfans celebres, revus & corrigés par M. De la Monnoye de

and a half in length, yet he grew to that astonishing height in
literature, as to write a book with a title as long as himself
————the learned know I mean his *Gonopsychanthropologia,*
upon the origin of the human soul.

So much for my chapter upon chapters, which I hold to
be the best chapter in my whole work; and take my word,
whoever reads it, is full as well employed, as in picking straws.[4]

CHAP. XI.

WE shall bring all things to rights, said my father, setting
his foot upon the first step from the landing————This
Trismegistus, continued my father, drawing his leg back, and
turning to my uncle *Toby*————was the greatest (*Toby*) of all
earthly beings————he was the greatest king————the greatest

l'Académie Françoise.)   [Sterne's note. This passage, taken with slight
alterations from Adrien Baillet's *Des Enfans devenus celebres par leurs
etudes et par leurs ecrits,* may be translated as follows: "The fœtus was
no larger than the palm of the hand; but his father having examined it in
his capacity of physician, and having found that it was something more
than an embryo, had it transported, all living, to Rapallo, where he
showed it to Jerome Bardi and other physicians of the place.   They
found that it lacked nothing essential to life, and the father, to make a
trial of his experience, undertook to complete the work of nature, and
to work at the formation of the infant with the same contrivance in
which chickens are hatched in Egypt.   He instructed a nurse in all that
she had to do, and having placed his son in an oven properly arranged
he succeeded in rearing him and in nurturing him to his necessary growth
by the uniformity of an artificial heat measured exactly by the degrees
of a thermometer or of an equivalent instrument.   (See Michael Giustinian, in the *Scrittori liguri,* 223.488.)

"People would have been quite satisfied with the industry of a father
experimenting similarly in the art of generation if he had been able to
prolong the life of his son for but a few months or for a few years.

"But when one recalls that this infant lived nearly eighty years, and
that he composed eighty different works, all fruits of long reading, it is
necessary to grant that everything which is incredible is not always un-
true, and that *appearance is not always on the side of truth.*

"He was but nineteen years of age when he composed *Gonopsychanthropologia concerning the Origin of the Human Soul.*

"(*Famous Children,* reviewed and corrected by M. de la Monnoye
of the French Academy.)"]

[4] *I.e.,* in worthless activity.

lawgiver——the greatest philosopher——and the greatest priest
———and engineer——said my uncle *Toby*.——
——In course, said my father.

CHAP. XII.

——AND how does your mistress? cried my father, taking
the same step over again from the landing, and calling to *Susannah,* whom he saw passing by the foot of the stairs
with a huge pin-cushion in her hand——how does your mistress?   As well, said *Susannah,* tripping by, but without looking up, as can be expected——What a fool am I! said my
father, drawing his leg back again——let things be as they
will, brother *Toby,* 'tis ever the precise answer——And how is
the child, pray?——No answer.   And where is doctor *Slop?*
added my father, raising his voice aloud, and looking over the
ballusters——*Susannah* was out of hearing.

Of all the riddles of a married life, said my father, crossing
the landing, in order to set his back against the wall, whilst he
propounded it to my uncle *Toby*——of all the puzzling riddles, said he, in a marriage state,——of which you may trust
me, brother *Toby,* there are more asses loads than all *Job's* stock
of asses could have carried[1]——there is not one that has more
intricacies in it than this——that from the very moment the
mistress of the house is brought to bed, every female in it,
from my lady's gentlewoman down to the cinder-wench, becomes an inch taller for it; and give themselves more airs upon
that single inch, than all their other inches put together.

I think rather, replied my uncle *Toby,* that 'tis we who sink
an inch lower.——If I meet but a woman with child——I do it
——'Tis a heavy tax upon that half of our fellow-creatures,
brother *Shandy,* said my uncle *Toby*——'Tis a piteous burden
upon 'em, continued he, shaking his head.——Yes, yes, 'tis a

---

[1]Before misfortune befell him, Job had "five hundred she asses"; after
misfortune had passed, he had a thousand.   (Job, 1.3; 42.12.)

painful thing——said my father, shaking his head too——but certainly since shaking of heads came into fashion, never did two heads shake together, in concert, from two such different springs.

God bless } 'em all————said my uncle *Toby* and my
Duce take } father, each to himself.

CHAP. XIII.

HOLLA!——you chairman![1]——here's sixpence——do step into that bookseller's shop, and call me a *day-tall*[2] critic. I am very willing to give any one of 'em a crown to help me with his tackling, to get my father and my uncle *Toby* off the stairs, and to put them to bed.——

——'Tis even high time; for except a short nap, which they both got whilst *Trim* was boring the jack-boots——and which, by the bye, did my father no sort of good upon the score of the bad hinge——they have not else shut their eyes, since nine hours before the time that doctor *Slop* was led into the back parlour in that dirty pickle by *Obadiah*.

Was every day of my life to be as busy a day as this,——and to take up,——truce——

I will not finish that sentence till I have made an observation upon the strange state of affairs between the reader and myself, just as things stand at present——an observation never applicable before to any one biographical writer since the creation of the world, but to myself——and I believe will never hold good to any other, until its final destruction——and therefore, for the very novelty of it alone, it must be worth your worships attending to.

I am this month one whole year older than I was this time twelve-month;[3] and having got, as you perceive, almost into the middle of my fourth volume——and no farther than to my

---

[1]One of the two carriers of a sedan-chair.

[2]Day-tale; a critic whose wages are reckoned by the day; *i.e.,* a hireling.

[3]When volumes one and two of *Shandy* had been composed.

first day's life——'tis demonstrative that I have three hundred
and sixty-four days more life to write just now, than when I
first set out; so that instead of advancing, as a common writer,
in my work with what I have been doing at it——on the contrary, I am just thrown so many volumes back——was every
day of my life to be as busy a day as this——And why not?
——and the transactions and opinions of it to take up as much
description——And for what reason should they be cut short?
as at this rate I should just live 364 times faster than I should
write——It must follow, an' please your worships, that the
more I write, the more I shall have to write——and consequently, the more your worships read, the more your worships will have to read.

Will this be good for your worships eyes?

It will do well for mine; and, was it not that my OPINIONS
will be the death of me, I perceive I shall lead a fine life of
it out of this self-same life of mine; or, in other words, shall
lead a couple of fine lives together.

As for the proposal of twelve volumes a year, or a volume a
month, it no way alters my prospect——write as I will, and
rush as I may into the middle of things, as *Horace* advises,[4]
——I shall never overtake myself——whipp'd and driven to
the last pinch, at the worst I shall have one day the start of my
pen——and one day is enough for two volumes——and two
volumes will be enough for one year.——

Heaven prosper the manufactures of paper under this pro-
pitious reign, which is now open'd to us,——as I trust its
providence will prosper every thing else in it that is taken in
hand.——

As for the propagation of Geese——I give myself no concern——Nature is all bountiful——I shall never want tools[5]
to work with.

——So then, friend! you have got my father and my uncle
Toby off the stairs, and seen them to bed?——And how did
you manage it?——You dropp'd a curtain at the stairs foot

[4]See p. 7, n. 2.

[5]*I.e.*, quill pens.

——I thought you had no other way for it——Here's a crown for your trouble.

CHAP. XIV.

——THEN reach me my breeches off the chair, said my father to *Susannah*——There is not a moment's time to dress you, Sir, cried *Susannah*——the child is as black in the face as my——As your, what? said my father, for like all orators, he was a dear searcher into comparisons——Bless me, Sir, said *Susannah,* the child's in a fit——And where's Mr. *Yorick*——Never where he should be, said *Susannah,* but his curate's in the dressing-room, with the child upon his arm, waiting for the name——and my mistress bid me run as fast as I could to know, as captain *Shandy* is the godfather, whether it should not be called after him.

Were one sure, said my father to himself, scratching his eye-brow, that the child was expiring, one might as well compliment my brother *Toby* as not——and 'twould be a pity, in such a case, to throw away so great a name as *Trismegistus* upon him——But he may recover.

No, no,——said my father to *Susannah,* I'll get up——There is no time, cried *Susannah,* the child's as black as my shoe. *Trismegistus,* said my father——But stay——thou art a leaky vessel, *Susannah,* added my father; canst thou carry *Trismegistus* in thy head, the length of the gallery without scattering——Can I? cried *Susannah,* shutting the door in a huff ——If she can, I'll be shot, said my father, bouncing out of bed in the dark, and groping for his breeches.

Susannah ran with all speed along the gallery.

My father made all possible speed to find his breeches.

Susannah got the start, and kept it——'Tis *Tris*——something, cried *Susannah*——There is no christian name in the world, said the curate, beginning with *Tris*——but *Tristram.* Then 'tis *Tristram-gistus,* quoth *Susannah.*

——There is no *gistus* to it, noodle!——'tis my own name,

replied the curate, dipping his hand as he spoke into the bason
——*Tristram!* said he, *&c. &c. &c. &c.* so *Tristram* was I called,
and *Tristram* shall I be to the day of my death.

My father followed *Susannah* with his night-gown across
his arm, with nothing more than his breeches on, fastened
through haste with but a single button, and that button
through haste thrust only half into the button-hole.

——She has not forgot the name, cried my father, half opening the door——No, no, said the curate, with a tone of intelligence——And the child is better, cried *Susannah*——And
how does your mistress? As well, said *Susannah*, as can be
expected——Pish! said my father, the button of his breeches
slipping out of the button-hole——So that whether the interjection was levelled at *Susannah,* or the button-hole,——
whether pish was an interjection of contempt or an interjection of modesty, is a doubt, and must be a doubt till I shall
have time to write the three following favorite chapters, that
is, my chapter of *chamber-maids*——my chapter of *pishes,* and
my chapter of *button-holes.*

All the light I am able to give the reader at present is this,
that the moment my father cried Pish! he whisk'd himself
about——and with his breeches held up by one hand, and his
night-gown thrown across the arm of the other, he returned
along the gallery to bed, something slower than he came.

CHAP. XV.

I Wish I could write a chapter upon sleep.
    A fitter occasion could never have presented itself, than
what this moment offers, when all the curtains of the family
are drawn——the candles put out——and no creature's eyes
are open but a single one, for the other has been shut these
twenty years, of my mother's nurse.

It is a fine subject!

And yet, as fine as it is, I would undertake to write a dozen

W Hogarth inv.   F. Ruvanet sculp.

289

chapters upon button-holes, both quicker and with more fame than a single chapter upon this.

Button-holes!——there is something lively in the very idea of 'em——and trust me, when I get amongst 'em——You gentry with great beards——look as grave as you will——I'll make merry work with my button-holes——I shall have 'em all to myself——'tis a maiden subject——I shall run foul of no man's wisdom or fine sayings in it.

But for sleep——I know I shall make nothing of it before I begin——I am no dab at your fine sayings in the first place ——and in the next, I cannot for my soul set a grave face upon a bad matter, and tell the world——'tis the refuge of the unfortunate——the enfranchisement of the prisoner——the downy lap of the hopeless, the weary and the broken-hearted; nor could I set out with a lye in my mouth, by affirming, that of all the soft and delicious functions of our nature, by which the great Author of it, in his bounty, has been pleased to recompence the sufferings wherewith his justice and his good pleasure has wearied us,——that this is the chiefest (I know pleasures worth ten of it) or what a happiness it is to man, when the anxieties and passions of the day are over, and he lays down upon his back, that his soul shall be so seated within him, that which ever way she turns her eyes, the heavens shall look calm and sweet above her——no desire——or fear ——or doubt that troubles the air, nor any difficulty pass'd, present, or to come, that the imagination may not pass over without offence, in that sweet secession.

——"God's blessing, said *Sancho Panca,* be upon the man who first invented this self-same thing called sleep——it covers a man all over like a cloak."[1]   Now there is more to me in this, and it speaks warmer to my heart and affections, than all the dissertations squeez'd out of the heads of the learned together upon the subject.

---

[1]"Now blessings light on him that first invented this same sleep: it covers a man all over, thoughts and all, like a cloak; 'tis meat for the hungry, drink for the thirsty, heat for the cold, and cold for the hot." (*Don Quixote,* 2.4.68.)

——Not that I altogether disapprove of what *Montaigne* advances upon it——'tis admirable in its way.——(I quote by memory.)[2]

The world enjoys other pleasures, says he, as they do that of sleep, without tasting or feeling it as it slips and passes by ——We should study and ruminate upon it, in order to render proper thanks to him who grants it to us——for this end I cause myself to be disturbed in my sleep, that I may the better and more sensibly relish it——And yet I see few, says he again, who live with less sleep when need requires; my body is capable of a firm, but not of a violent and sudden agitation ——I evade of late all violent exercises——I am never weary with walking——but from my youth, I never liked to ride upon pavements.   I love to lie hard and alone, and even without my wife——This last word may stagger the faith of the world——but remember, "La Vraisemblance (as *Baylet* says in the affair of *Liceti*) n'est pas toujours du Côté de la Verité."[3] And so much for sleep.

CHAP. XVI.

I F my wife will but venture him——brother *Toby*, *Trismegistus* shall be dress'd and brought down to us, whilst you and I are getting our breakfasts together.——

——Go, tell *Susannah*, *Obadiah*, to step here.

She is run up stairs, answered *Obadiah*, this very instant, sobbing and crying, and wringing her hands as if her heart would break.——

We shall have a rare month of it, said my father, turning his head from *Obadiah*, and looking wistfully in my uncle *Toby*'s face for some time——we shall have a devilish month of it, brother *Toby*, said my father, setting his arms a-kimbo,

---

[2] The following passage is an olio of quotation and paraphrase from Montaigne's essay "Of Experience."

[3] "The appearance is not always on the side of the truth"; see p. 282, n. *.

and shaking his head; fire, water, women, wind——brother *Toby!*——'Tis some misfortune, quoth my uncle *Toby*—— That it is, cried my father,——to have so many jarring elements breaking loose, and riding triumph in every corner of a gentleman's house——Little boots it to the peace of a family, brother *Toby,* that you and I possess ourselves, and sit here silent and unmoved,——whilst such a storm is whistling over our heads.——

——And what's the matter, *Susannah?*   They have called the child *Tristram*——and my mistress is just got out of an hysterick fit about it——No!——'tis not my fault, said *Susannah* ——I told him it was *Tristram-gistus.*

——Make tea for yourself, brother *Toby,* said my father, taking down his hat——but how different from the sallies and agitations of voice and members which a common reader would imagine!

——For he spake in the sweetest modulation——and took down his hat with the gentlest movement of limbs, that ever affliction harmonized and attuned together.

——Go to the bowling-green for corporal *Trim,* said my uncle *Toby,* speaking to *Obadiah,* as soon as my father left the room.

CHAP. XVII.

WHEN the misfortune of my NOSE fell so heavily upon my father's head,——the reader remembers that he walked instantly up stairs, and cast himself down upon his bed; and from hence, unless he has a great insight into human nature, he will be apt to expect a rotation of the same ascending and descending movements from him, upon this misfortune of my NAME;——no.

The different weight, dear Sir,——nay even the different package of two vexations of the same weight,——makes a very wide difference in our manners of bearing and getting through with them.——It is not half an hour ago, when (in the great hurry and precipitation of a poor devil's writing for daily bread) I threw a fair sheet, which I had just finished, and carefully wrote out, slap into the fire, instead of the foul one.

Instantly I snatch'd off my wig, and threw it perpendicularly, with all imaginable violence, up to the top of the room——indeed I caught it as it fell——but there was an end of the matter; nor do I think any thing else in *Nature,* would have given such immediate ease: She, dear Goddess, by an instantaneous impulse, in all *provoking cases,* determines us to a sally of this or that member——or else she thrusts us into this or that place, or posture of body, we know not why——But mark, madam, we live amongst riddles and mysteries——the most obvious things, which come in our way, have dark sides, which the quickest sight cannot penetrate into; and even the clearest and most exalted understandings amongst us find ourselves puzzled and at a loss in almost every cranny of nature's works; so that this, like a thousand other things, falls out for us in a way, which tho' we cannot reason upon it,——yet we find the good of it, may it please your reverences and your worships——and that's enough for us.

Now, my father could not lie down with this affliction for his life——nor could he carry it up stairs like the other—— He walked composedly out with it to the fish-pond.

Had my father leaned his head upon his hand, and reasoned an hour which way to have gone——reason, with all her force, could not have directed him to any thing like it: there is something, Sir, in fish-ponds——but what it is, I leave to system builders and fish pond diggers betwixt 'em to find out ——but there is something, under the first disorderly transport of the humours, so unaccountably becalming in an orderly and a sober walk towards one of them, that I have often wondered that neither *Pythagoras,*[1] nor *Plato,* nor *Solon,* nor

---

[1] Pythagoras (c.582–c.500 B.C.) was a Greek philosopher and mathematician whose *ipse dixit* was the law of his followers and from whose teachings the ancient lawgivers of Sicily and Grecian Italy were said by Seneca (*Epistolae,* 90.6) to have derived the laws which they established. Plato (c.427–347 B.C.), the Athenian philosopher, was motivated by a zeal for human improvement, which found its most practical expression in

Licurgus, nor *Mahomet,* nor any of your noted lawgivers, ever
gave order about them.

CHAP. XVIII.

YOUR honour, said *Trim,* shutting the parlour door before
he began to speak, has heard, I imagine, of this unlucky
accident——O yes, *Trim!* said my uncle *Toby,* and it gives me
great concern——I am heartily concerned too, but I hope your
honour, replied *Trim,* will do me the justice to believe, that
it was not in the least owing to me——To thee——*Trim!*——
cried my uncle *Toby,* looking kindly in his face——'twas *Susannah's* and the curate's folly betwixt them——What business
could they have together, an' please your honour, in the garden?——In the gallery, thou meanest, replied my uncle *Toby.*

Trim found he was upon a wrong scent, and stopped short
with a low bow——Two misfortunes, quoth the corporal to
himself, are twice as many at least as are needful to be talked
over at one time,——the mischief the cow has done in breaking into the fortifications, may be told his honour hereafter
——*Trim's* casuistry and address, under the cover of his low
bow, prevented all suspicion in my uncle *Toby,* so he went on
with what he had to say to *Trim* as follows.

————For my own part, *Trim,* though I can see little or no
difference betwixt my nephew's being called *Tristram* or *Trismegistus*——yet as the thing sits so near my brother's heart,
Trim,——I would freely have given a hundred pounds rather
than it should have happened——A hundred pounds, an'
please your honour, replied *Trim,*——I would not give a
cherry-stone to boot——Nor would I, *Trim,* upon my own

dialogues on legislation and statecraft such as the *Gorgias,* the *Republic.*
the *Statesman,* and the *Laws.* Solon (c.638–c.559 B.C.) was an Athenian
statesman and lawgiver. Lycurgus (fl. c.800 B.C.) was a traditionary
Spartan legislator, the reputed founder of the laws and institutions of
Sparta. Ancient Moslem law was based largely on the Koran, as revealed to Mahomet (c.570–632), the founder of Islam, and on the de-
cisions of the prophet, who, during his lifetime, was the inspired legislator and judge of his people.

account, quoth my uncle *Toby*——but my brother, whom
there is no arguing with in this case——maintains that a great
deal more depends, *Trim,* upon christian names, than what
ignorant people imagine;——for he says there never was a
great or heroic action performed since the world began by
one called *Tristram*——nay he will have it, *Trim,* that a man
can neither be learned, or wise, or brave——'Tis all a fancy,
an' please your honour——I fought just as well, replied the
corporal, when the regiment called me *Trim,* as when they
called me *James Butler*——And for my own part, said my
uncle *Toby,* though I should blush to boast of myself, *Trim,*
——yet had my name been *Alexander,* I could have done no
more at *Namur* than my duty——Bless your honour! cried
Trim, advancing three steps as he spoke, does a man think
of his christian name when he goes upon the attack?——Or
when he stands in the trench, *Trim?* cried my uncle *Toby,*
looking firm——Or when he enters a breach? said *Trim,* pushing in between two chairs——Or forces the lines? cried my
uncle, rising up, and pushing his crutch like a pike——Or
facing a platoon, cried *Trim,* presenting his stick like a firelock——Or when he marches up the glacis, cried my uncle
Toby, looking warm and setting his foot upon his stool.——

CHAP. XIX.

MY father was returned from his walk to the fish-pond——
and opened the parlour-door in the very height of the
attack, just as my uncle *Toby* was marching up the glacis——
Trim recovered his arms——never was my uncle *Toby* caught
riding at such a desperate rate in his life! Alas! my uncle
Toby! had not a weightier matter called forth all the ready
eloquence of my father——how hadst thou then and thy poor
HOBBY-HORSE too have been insulted!

My father hung up his hat with the same air he took it
down; and after giving a slight look at the disorder of the
room, he took hold of one of the chairs which had formed

the corporal's breach, and placing it over-against my uncle *Toby,* he sat down in it, and as soon as the tea-things were taken away and the door shut, he broke out in a lamentation as follows.

My Father's Lamentation

IT is in vain longer, said my father, addressing himself as much to *Ernulphus's* curse, which was laid upon the corner of the chimney-piece,——as to my uncle *Toby* who sat under it——it is in vain longer, said my father, in the most querulous monotone imaginable, to struggle as I have done against this most uncomfortable of human persuasions——I see it plainly, that either for my own sins, brother *Toby,* or the sins and follies of the *Shandy*-family, heaven has thought fit to draw forth the heaviest of its artillery against me; and that the prosperity of my child is the point upon which the whole force of it is directed to play——Such a thing would batter the whole universe about our ears, brother *Shandy,* said my uncle *Toby,*——if it was so——Unhappy *Tristram!* child of wrath! child of decrepitude! interruption! mistake! and discontent! What one misfortune or disaster in the book of embryotic evils, that could unmechanize thy frame, or entangle thy filaments! which has not fallen upon thy head, or ever thou camest into the world——what evils in thy passage into it!——What evils since!——produced into being, in the decline of thy father's days——when the powers of his imagination and of his body were waxing feeble——when radical heat and radical moisture,[1] the elements which should have temper'd thine, were drying up; and nothing left to found thy stamina in, but negations——'tis pitiful——brother *Toby,* at the best, and called out for all the little helps that care and attention on both sides could give it. But how were we defeated! You know the event, brother *Toby,*——'tis too melancholy a one to be repeated now,——when the few animal spirits[2] I was

---

[1] Fundamental or natural heat and moisture of the body.

[2] See p. 4, n. 2.

worth in the world, and with which memory, fancy, and quick parts should have been convey'd,——were all dispersed, confused, confounded, scattered, and sent to the devil.——

Here then was the time to have put a stop to this persecution against him;——and tried an experiment at least—— whether calmness and serenity of mind in your sister, with a due attention, brother *Toby,* to her evacuations and repletions ——and the rest of her non-naturals,[3] might not, in a course of nine months gestation, have set all things to rights.——My child was bereft of these!——What a teazing life did she lead herself, and consequently her fœtus too, with that nonsensical anxiety of hers about lying in in town?   I thought my sister submitted with the greatest patience, replied my uncle *Toby* ———I never heard her utter one fretful word about it—— She fumed inwardly, cried my father; and that, let me tell you, brother, was ten times worse for the child——and then! what battles did she fight with me, and what perpetual storms about the midwife——There she gave vent, said my uncle *Toby*—— Vent! cried my father, looking up——

But what was all this, my dear *Toby,* to the injuries done us by my child's coming head foremost into the world, when all I wished in this general wreck of his frame, was to have saved this little casket unbroke, unrifled——

With all my precautions, how was my system turned topside turvy in the womb with my child! his head exposed to the hand of violence, and a pressure of 470 pounds averdupois weight acting so perpendicularly upon its apex——that at this hour 'tis ninety *per Cent.* insurance, that the fine network of the intellectual web be not rent and torn to a thousand tatters.

——Still we could have done.——Fool, coxcomb, puppy ——give him but a NOSE——Cripple, Dwarf, Driviller, Goosecap——(shape him as you will) the door of Fortune stands open——O *Licetus! Licetus!*[4] had I been blest with a fœtus five inches long and a half, like thee——fate might have done her worst.

---

[3] See p. 76, n. 8.
[4] See p. 282.

Still, brother *Toby,* there was one cast of the dye left for our child after all——O *Tristram! Tristram! Tristram!*

We will send for Mr. *Yorick,* said my uncle *Toby.*

——You may send for whom you will, replied my father.

CHAP. XX.

WHAT a rate have I gone on at, curvetting and frisking it away, two up and two down for four volumes together, without looking once behind, or even on one side of me, to see whom I trod upon!——I'll tread upon no one,—— quoth I to myself when I mounted——I'll take a good rattling gallop; but I'll not hurt the poorest jack-ass upon the road—— So off I set——up one lane——down another, through this turn-pike——over that, as if the arch-jockey of jockeys had got behind me.

Now ride at this rate with what good intention and resolution you may,——'tis a million to one you'll do some one a mischief, if not yourself——He's flung——he's off——he's lost his seat——he's down——he'll break his neck——see!——if he has not galloped full amongst the scaffolding of the undertaking[1] criticks!——he'll knock his brains out against some of their posts——he's bounced out!——look——he's now riding like a madcap full tilt through a whole crowd of painters, fiddlers, poets, biographers, physicians, lawyers, logicians, players, schoolmen, churchmen, statesmen, soldiers, casuists, connoisseurs, prelates, popes, and engineers——Don't fear, said I——I'll not hurt the poorest jack-ass upon the king's high-way——But your horse throws dirt; see you've splash'd a bishop[2]——I hope in God, 'twas only *Ernulphus,* said I—— But you have squirted full in the faces of Mess. *Le Moyne, De*

---

[1]Enterprising; used here in the derogatory sense of officious, overreaching.

[2]An allusion to William Warburton (1698–1779), Bishop of Gloucester. Whether started by Sterne or not, the report had spread in London that the pompous and pedantic Bishop was to be caricatured in *Shandy* as Tristram's tutor. When Sterne vigorously but perhaps disingenuously

Romigny, and *De Marcilly,* doctors of the Sorbonne[3]——That was last year, replied I——But you have trod this moment upon a king.——Kings have bad times on't, said I, to be trod upon by such people as me.

You have done it, replied my accuser.

I deny it, quoth I, and so have got off, and here am I standing with my bridle in one hand, and with my cap in the other, to tell my story——And what is it? You shall hear in the next chapter.

CHAP. XXI.

AS *Francis* the first of *France* was one winterly night warming himself over the embers of a wood fire, and talking with his first minister of sundry things for the good of the state*——it would not be amiss, said the king, stirring up the embers with his cane, if this good understanding betwixt ourselves and *Switzerland* was a little strengthened——There is no end, Sire, replied the minister, in giving money to these people——they would swallow up the treasury of *France*—— Poo! poo! answered the king——there are more ways, Mons.

---

denied the rumour, Warburton, apparently in gratitude for his escape, became Sterne's patron, recommending his book "to all the best company in town," pushing the subscription to his forthcoming sermons, and even presenting him with "a purse of guineas." But when he proceeded to give the successful author books to improve his style and prudish advice to regulate his personal and literary careers, Sterne declined to follow his direction, and an increasing coolness developed between the two men. See p. 610, n. 1. For Ernulphus, see p. 170.

[3]See p. 62.

*Vide Menagiana, vol. I. [Sterne's note. *Menagiana* is a collection of the oral opinions of Gilles Ménage (1613–1692), a French philologist, first published in 1693. Sterne's yarn is an elaboration of the following passage: "It is said that Francis I wished to take the Republic of Switzerland as the godmother of one of his sons; but he changed his mind when he learned that they wished to name him Shadrach, Meshach, and Abed-nego."—*Menagiana ou les bons mots et remarques critiques, historiques, morales et d'érudition, de Monsieur Menage,* 3rd ed. (Paris, 1715), 2.214. Shadrach, Meshach, and Abed-nego were the Jews who, according to Daniel, 3.12–30, survived the ordeal of the fiery furnace.]

le Premier, of bribing states, besides that of giving money——
I'll pay *Switzerland* the honour of standing godfather for my
next child——Your majesty, said the minister, in so doing,
would have all the grammarians in *Europe* upon your back;
——*Switzerland,* as a republick, being a female, can in no
construction be godfather——She may be godmother, replied
Francis, hastily——so announce my intentions by a courier
to morrow morning.

I am astonished, said *Francis* the First, (that day fortnight)
speaking to his minister as he entered the closet, that we have
had no answer from *Switzerland*——Sire, I wait upon you this
moment, said Mons. *le Premier,* to lay before you my dis-
patches upon that business.——They take it kindly? said the
king——They do, Sire, replied the minister, and have the
highest sense of the honour your majesty has done them——
but the republick, as godmother, claims her right in this case,
of naming the child.

In all reason, quoth the king——she will christen him
Francis, or *Henry,* or *Lewis,* or some name that she knows will
be agreeable to us. Your majesty is deceived, replied the
minister——I have this hour received a dispatch from our
resident, with the determination of the republick on that point
also——And what name has the republick fixed upon for the
Dauphin?——*Shadrach, Mesech,* and *Abed-nego,* replied the
minister——By saint *Peter's* girdle, I will have nothing to do
with the *Swiss,* cried *Francis* the First, pulling up his breeches
and walking hastily across the floor.

Your majesty, replied the minister calmly, cannot bring
yourself off.

We'll pay them in money——said the king.

Sire, there are not sixty thousand crowns in the treasury,
answered the minister——I'll pawn the best jewel in my
crown, quoth *Francis* the First.

Your honour stands pawn'd already in this matter, answered
Monsieur *le Premier.*

Then, Mons. *le Premier,* said the king, by——we'll go to
war with 'em.

CHAP. XXII.

ALBEIT, gentle reader, I have lusted earnestly, and endeavoured carefully (according to the measure of such slender skill as God has vouchsafed me, and as convenient leisure from other occasions of needful profit and healthful pastime have permitted) that these little books, which I here put into thy hands, might stand instead of many bigger books——yet have I carried myself towards thee in such fanciful guise of careless disport, that right sore am I ashamed now to entreat thy lenity seriously——in beseeching thee to believe it of me, that in the story of my father and his christen-names,——I had no thoughts of treading upon *Francis* the First——nor in the affair of the nose——upon *Francis* the Ninth[1]——nor in the character of my uncle *Toby*——of characterizing the militiating spirits of my country——the wound upon his groin, is a wound to every comparison of that kind,——nor by *Trim*,——that I meant the duke of *Ormond*[2]——or that my book is wrote against predestination, or free will, or taxes——If 'tis wrote against any thing,——'tis wrote, an' please your worships, against the spleen; in order, by a more frequent and a more convulsive elevation and depression of the diaphragm, and the succussations of the intercostal and abdominal muscles in laughter, to drive the *gall* and other

---

[1]There was no Francis IX, wherein (probably) lies the jest. If Sterne meant an actual king, he likely intended Francis I, who had a very long and large nose, who was said to have died of syphilis, and whose critics insisted on the physical consequences of his shamelessly licentious life. It is barely possible that Sterne may have had in mind Francis, Duke of Alençon and of Anjou (the youngest brother of Charles IX), whose tremendous nose, badly scarred by smallpox, was the object of contemporary satire; or even Francis, the powerful Duke of Guise, who at the siege of Boulogne in 1545 had received a severe wound which disfigured his nose and face.

[2]James Butler (which was, indeed, Trim's name; see p. 94), (1665–1745), second Duke of Ormonde, an Irish statesman and soldier who in 1711 replaced Marlborough as captain-general; impeached by the Whigs in 1715, however, he spent the rest of his life in Spain and France.

bitter juices from the gall bladder, liver and sweet-bread of his majesty's subjects, with all the inimicitious[3] passions which belong to them, down into their duodenums.

CHAP. XXIII.

——**B**UT can the thing be undone, *Yorick?* said my father ——for in my opinion, continued he, it cannot. I am a vile canonist, replied *Yorick*——but of all evils, holding suspense to be the most tormenting, we shall at least know the worst of this matter. I hate these great dinners——said my father——The size of the dinner is not the point, answered *Yorick*——we want, Mr. *Shandy,* to dive into the bottom of this doubt, whether the name can be changed or not——and as the beards of so many commissaries, officials, advocates, proctors, registers, and of the most able of our school-divines, and others, are all to meet in the middle of one table, and *Didius* has so pressingly invited you,——who in your distress would miss such an occasion? All that is requisite, continued *Yorick,* is to apprize *Didius,* and let him manage a conversation after dinner so as to introduce the subject——Then my brother *Toby,* cried my father, clapping his two hands together, shall go with us.

——Let my old tye wig, quoth my uncle *Toby,* and my laced regimentals, be hung to the fire all night, *Trim.*

———

[3]Inimical, unfriendly.

CHAP. XXV.

——NO doubt, Sir——there is a whole chapter wanting here——and a chasm of ten pages made in the book by it——but the book-binder is neither a fool, or a knave, or a puppy——nor is the book a jot more imperfect, (at least upon that score)——but, on the contrary, the book is more perfect and complete by wanting the chapter, than having it, as I shall demonstrate to your reverences in this manner—— I question first by the bye, whether the same experiment might not be made as successfully upon sundry other chapters—— but there is no end, an' please your reverences, in trying experiments upon chapters——we have had enough of it—— So there's an end of that matter.

But before I begin my demonstration, let me only tell you, that the chapter which I have torn out, and which otherwise you would all have been reading just now, instead of this, ——was the description of my father's, my uncle *Toby's*, *Trim's*, and *Obadiah's* setting out and journeying to the visitations[1] at ****.

We'll go in the coach, said my father——Prithee, have the arms been altered, *Obadiah*?——It would have made my story much better, to have begun with telling you, that at the time my mother's arms were added to the *Shandy's*, when the coach was repainted upon my father's marriage, it had so fallen out, that the coach-painter, whether by performing all his works with the left-hand, like *Turpilius* the *Roman*,[2] or *Hans Holbein* of *Basil*——or whether 'twas more from the blunder of

---

[1] The examinations by a bishop of the churches in his diocese; the dinner to which the Shandys are setting out is a burlesque of the visitation dinners at York.

[2] Labeo Turpillius of Venice (fl. 60 A.D.), a Roman knight and (left-handed) painter of merit, mentioned by Pliny (*Naturalis Historia*, 35.7[4]). Hans Holbein, the younger (1497–1543), a German historical and portrait painter, painted, according to tradition, with his left hand.

his head than hand——or whether, lastly, it was from the
sinister turn, which every thing relating to our family was
apt to take——It so fell out, however, to our reproach, that
instead of the *bend dexter,* which since *Harry* the Eighth's
reign was honestly our due——a *bend sinister,*[3] by some of
these fatalities, had been drawn quite across the field of the
Shandy-arms. 'Tis scarce credible that the mind of so wise
a man as my father was, could be so much incommoded with
so small a matter. The word coach——let it be whose it
would——or coach-man, or coach-horse, or coach-hire, could
never be named in the family, but he constantly complained
of carrying this vile mark of Illegitimacy upon the door of his
own; he never once was able to step into the coach, or out
of it, without turning round to take a view of the arms, and
making a vow at the same time, that it was the last time he
would ever set his foot in it again, till the *bend-sinister* was
taken out——but like the affair of the hinge, it was one of the
many things which the *Destinies* had set down in their books
——ever to be grumbled at (and in wiser families than ours)
——but never to be mended.

——Has the *bend-sinister* been brush'd out, I say? said my
father——There has been nothing brush'd out, Sir, answered
Obadiah, but the lining. We'll go o'horse-back, said my
father, turning to *Yorick*——Of all things in the world, except
politicks, the clergy know the least of heraldry, said *Yorick*
——No matter for that, cried my father——I should be sorry
to appear with a blot in my escutcheon before them——Never
mind the *bend-sinister,* said my uncle *Toby*, putting on his
tye-wig——No, indeed, said my father,——you may go with
my aunt *Dinah* to a visitation with a *bend-sinister,* if you think
fit——My poor uncle *Toby* blush'd. My father was vexed at
himself——No——my dear brother *Toby,* said my father,
changing his tone——but the damp of the coach-lining about
my loins, may give me the Sciatica again, as it did *December,*

---

[3]According to some authorities and to general usage, the bend-sinister
(a diagonal band on a shield, drawn from the sinister chief to the dexter
base) denotes bastardy.

January, and *February* last winter——so if you please you shall ride my wife's pad——and as you are to preach, *Yorick,* you had better make the best of your way before,——and leave me to take care of my brother *Toby,* and to follow at our own rates.

Now the chapter I was obliged to tear out, was the description of this cavalcade, in which Corporal *Trim* and *Obadiah,* upon two coach-horses a-breast, led the way as slow as a patrole ——whilst my uncle *Toby,* in his laced regimentals and tye-wig, kept his rank with my father, in deep roads and dissertations alternately upon the advantage of learning and arms, as each could get the start.

——But the painting of this journey, upon reviewing it, appears to be so much above the stile and manner of any thing else I have been able to paint in this book, that it could not have remained in it, without depreciating every other scene; and destroying at the same time that necessary equipoise and balance, (whether of good or bad) betwixt chapter and chapter, from whence the just proportions and harmony of the whole work results. For my own part, I am but just set up in the business, so know little about it——but, in my opinion, to write a book is for all the world like humming a song——be but in tune with yourself, madam, 'tis no matter how high or how low you take it.

——This is the reason, may it please your reverences, that some of the lowest and flattest compositions pass off very well ——(as *Yorick* told my uncle *Toby* one night) by siege—— My uncle *Toby* looked brisk at the sound of the word *siege,* but could make neither head or tail of it.

I'm to preach at court next Sunday, said *Homenas*[4]——run over my notes——so I humm'd over doctor *Homenas's* notes ——the modulation's very well——'twill do, *Homenas,* if it holds on at this rate——so on I humm'd——and a tolerable tune I thought it was; and to this hour, may it please your reverences, had never found out how low, how flat, how spirit-

[4]Homenas (homilist) was the "right reverend" Bishop of Papimany in Rabelais, 4.48–54.

less and jejune it was, but that all of a sudden, up started an
air in the middle of it, so fine, so rich, so heavenly——it
carried my soul up with it into the other world; now had I,
(as *Montaigne* complained in a parallel accident[5])——had I
found the declivity easy, or the ascent accessible——certes I
had been outwitted——Your notes, *Homenas,* I should have
said, are good notes,——but it was so perpendicular a precipice——so wholly cut off from the rest of the work, that by
the first note I humm'd, I found myself flying into the other
world, and from thence discovered the vale from whence I
came, so deep, so low, and dismal, that I shall never have
the heart to descend into it again.

☞ A dwarf who brings a standard along with him to
measure his own size——take my word, is a dwarf in more
articles than one——And so much for tearing out of chapters.

CHAP. XXVI.

——SEE if he is not cutting it all into slips, and giving
them about him to light their pipes!——'Tis abominable, answered *Didius;*[1] it should not go unnoticed, said doctor *Kysarcius*——☞ he was of the *Kysarcij* of the low
countries.

---

[5]A reference to the essay "Of the Education of Children," in which
Montaigne remarks: "I hapned the other Day upon . . . a *French* Book,
where after I had a long Time run dreaming over a great many Words,
so dull, so insipid, so void of all Wit, or common Sence, that indeed
they were only Words; after a long and tedious travel, I came at last to
meet with a piece that was lofty, rich, and elevated to the very Clouds:
of which, had I found either the Declivity easie, or the Ascent accessible,
there had been some excuse; but it was so perpendicular a Precipice,
and so wholly cut off from the rest of the Work, that by the six first
words I found my self flying into the other World, and from thence discover'd the Vale from whence I came so deep and low, that I had never
since the Heart to descend into it any more. If I should set out my
Discourses with such rich Spoils as these, the Plagiary would be too mani-
fest in his own Defects, and I should too much discover the imperfec-
tion of my own Writing."

[1]See p. 12, n. 1; for Kysarcius, see p. 194, n. 5.

Methinks, said *Didius,* half rising from his chair, in order to remove a bottle and a tall decanter, which stood in a direct line betwixt him and *Yorick*——you might have spared this sarcastick stroke, and have hit upon a more proper place, Mr. *Yorick*——or at least upon a more proper occasion to have shewn your contempt of what we have been about: If the Sermon is of no better worth than to light pipes with——'twas certainly, Sir, not good enough to be preached before so learned a body; and if 'twas good enough to be preached before so learned a body——'twas certainly, Sir, too good to light their pipes with afterwards.

——I have got him fast hung up, quoth *Didius* to himself, upon one of the two horns of my dilemma—let him get off as he can.

I have undergone such unspeakable torments, in bringing forth this sermon, quoth *Yorick,* upon this occasion,——that I declare, *Didius,* I would suffer martyrdom——and if it was possible my horse with me, a thousand times over, before I would sit down and make such another: I was delivered of it at the wrong end of me——it came from my head instead of my heart——and it is for the pain it gave me, both in the writing and preaching of it, that I revenge myself of it, in this manner.——To preach, to shew the extent of our reading, or the subtleties of our wit——to parade it in the eyes of the vulgar with the beggarly accounts of a little learning, tinseled over with a few words which glitter, but convey little light and less warmth——is a dishonest use of the poor single half hour in a week which is put into our hands——'Tis not preaching the gospel——but ourselves——For my own part, continued *Yorick,* I had rather direct five words point blank to the heart——

As *Yorick* pronounced the word *point blank,* my uncle *Toby* rose up to say something upon projectiles——when a single word, and no more, uttered from the opposite side of the table, drew every one's ears towards it——a word of all others in the dictionary the last in that place to be expected——a word I am ashamed to write——yet must be written——

must be read;——illegal——uncanonical——guess ten thousand guesses, multiplied into themselves——rack——torture
your invention for ever, you're where you was——In short,
I'll tell it in the next chapter.

CHAP. XXVII.

Z OUNDS![1]——————————————————

——————————————————————————

——————————Z——ds! cried *Phutatorius,*[2] partly to himself
——and yet high enough to be heard——and what seemed
odd, 'twas uttered in a construction of look, and in a tone of
voice, somewhat between that of a man in amazement, and of
one in bodily pain.

One or two who had very nice ears, and could distinguish
the expression and mixture of the two tones as plainly as a
third or a *fifth,* or any other chord in musick——were the
most puzzled and perplexed with it——the *concord* was good
in itself——but then 'twas quite out of the key, and no way
applicable to the subject started;——so that with all their
knowledge, they could not tell what in the world to make of it.

Others who knew nothing of musical expression, and merely
lent their ears to the plain import of the *word,* imagined that
Phutatorius, who was somewhat of a cholerick spirit, was just
going to snatch the cudgels out of *Didius's* hands, in order to
bemawl *Yorick* to some purpose——and that the desperate
monosyllable Z——ds was the exordium to an oration,
which, as they judged from the sample, presaged but a rough
kind of handling of him; so that my uncle *Toby's* good nature
felt a pang for what *Yorick* was about to undergo. But seeing *Phutatorius* stop short, without any attempt or desire to
go on——a third party began to suppose, that it was no more

[1]Abbreviation of "God's wounds," referring to the wounds of Christ
on the cross; an exclamation formerly used as an oath or as an expression
of indignation or wonder.

[2]See p. 193, n. 1.

than an involuntary respiration, casually forming itself into
the shape of a twelve-penny oath——without the sin or substance of one.

Others, and especially one or two who sat next him, looked
upon it on the contrary, as a real and substantial oath pro-
pensly formed against *Yorick,* to whom he was known to bear
no good liking——which said oath, as my father philosophized
upon it, actually lay fretting and fuming at that very time in
the upper regions of *Phutatorius's* purtenance; and so was
naturally, and according to the due course of things, first
squeezed out by the sudden influx of blood, which was driven
into the right ventricle of *Phutatorius's* heart, by the stroke of
surprize which so strange a theory of preaching had excited.

How finely we argue upon mistaken facts!

There was not a soul busied in all these various reasonings
upon the monosyllable which *Phutatorius* uttered,——who did
not take this for granted, proceeding upon it as from an axiom,
namely, that *Phutatorius's* mind was intent upon the subject of
debate which was arising between *Didius* and *Yorick;* and indeed as he looked first towards the one, and then towards the
other, with the air of a man listening to what was going forwards,——who would not have thought the same? But the
truth was, that *Phutatorius* knew not one word or one syllable
of what was passing——but his whole thoughts and attention
were taken up with a transaction which was going forwards at
that very instant within the precincts of his own *Galligaskins,*
and in a part of them, where of all others he stood most interested to watch accidents: So that notwithstanding he looked
with all the attention in the world, and had gradually skrewed
up every nerve and muscle in his face, to the utmost pitch the
instrument would bear, in order, as it was thought, to give a
sharp reply to *Yorick,* who sat over-against him——Yet I say,
was *Yorick* never once in any one domicile of *Phutatorius's*
brain——but the true cause of his exclamation lay at least a
yard below.

This I will endeavour to explain to you with all imaginable
decency.

You must be informed then, that *Gastripheres*,[3] who had taken a turn into the kitchen a little before dinner, to see how things went on——observing a wicker-basket of fine chesnuts standing upon the dresser, had ordered that a hundred or two of them might be roasted and sent in, as soon as dinner was over——*Gastripheres* inforcing his orders about them, that *Didius,* but *Phutatorius* especially, were particularly fond of 'em.

About two minutes before the time that my uncle *Toby* interrupted *Yorick*'s harangue——*Gastripheres*'s chesnuts were brought in——and as *Phutatorius*'s fondness for 'em, was uppermost in the waiter's head, he laid them directly before *Phutatorius,* wrapt up hot in a clean damask napkin.

Now whether it was physically impossible, with half a dozen hands all thrust into the napkin at a time——but that some one chesnut, of more life and rotundity than the rest, must be put in motion——it so fell out, however, that one was actually sent rolling off the table; and as *Phutatorius* sat straddling under——it fell perpendicularly into that particular aperture of *Phutatorius*'s breeches, for which, to the shame and indelicacy of our language be it spoke, there is no chaste word throughout all *Johnson*'s dictionary——let it suffice to say—— it was that particular aperture, which in all good societies, the laws of decorum do strictly require, like the temple of *Janus* (in peace at least) to be universally shut up.[4]

The neglect of this punctilio in *Phutatorius* (which by the bye should be a warning to all mankind) had opened a door to this accident.——

——Accident, I call it, in compliance to a received mode of speaking,——but in no opposition to the opinion either of *Acrites*[5] or *Mythogeras* in this matter; I know they were both prepossessed and fully persuaded of it——and are so to this

---

[3]See p. 194, n. 5.

[4]In Rome the doors of the temple of Janus, an ancient Italian deity who was god of doorways and guardian of the state during war, were closed in time of peace, ever open in time of war.

[5]One lacking in discernment. Mythogeras: Tale-bearer.

hour, That there was nothing of accident in the whole event
——but that the chesnut's taking that particular course, and
in a manner of its own accord——and then falling with all its
heat directly into that one particular place, and no other——
was a real judgment upon *Phutatorius,* for that filthy and
obscene treatise *de Concubinis retinendis,*[6] which *Phutatorius*
had published about twenty years ago——and was that identical week going to give the world a second edition of.

It is not my business to dip my pen in this controversy——
much undoubtedly may be wrote on both sides of the question
——all that concerns me as an historian, is to represent the
matter of fact, and render it credible to the reader, that the
hiatus in *Phutatorius'*s breeches was sufficiently wide to receive
the chesnut;——and that the chesnut, some how or other, did
fall perpendicularly and piping hot into it, without *Phutatorius'*s perceiving it, or any one else at that time.

The genial warmth which the chesnut imparted, was not
undelectable for the first twenty or five and twenty seconds,
——and did no more than gently solicit *Phutatorius'*s attention
towards the part:——But the heat gradually increasing, and
in a few seconds more getting beyond the point of all sober
pleasure, and then advancing with all speed into the regions of
pain,——the soul of *Phutatorius,* together with all his ideas,
his thoughts, his attention, his imagination, judgment, resolution, deliberation, ratiocination, memory, fancy, with ten
batallions of animal spirits, all tumultuously crouded down,
through different defiles and circuits, to the place in danger,
leaving all his upper regions, as you may imagine, as empty
as my purse.

With the best intelligence which all these messengers could
bring him back, *Phutatorius* was not able to dive into the
secret of what was going forwards below, nor could he make
any kind of conjecture, what the devil was the matter with it:
However, as he knew not what the true cause might turn out,
he deemed it most prudent, in the situation he was in at
present, to bear it, if possible, like a stoick; which, with the

[6]*Of Keeping Concubines.*

help of some wry faces and compursions of the mouth, he had certainly accomplished, had his imagination continued neuter ——but the sallies of the imagination are ungovernable in things of this kind——a thought instantly darted into his mind, that tho' the anguish had the sensation of glowing heat ——it might, notwithstanding that, be a bite as well as a burn; and if so, that possibly a *Newt* or an *Asker*,[7] or some such detested reptile, had crept up, and was fastening his teeth—— the horrid idea of which, with a fresh glow of pain arising that instant from the chesnut, seized *Phutatorius* with a sudden panick, and in the first terrifying disorder of the passion it threw him, as it has done the best generals upon earth, quite off his guard;——the effect of which was this, that he leapt incontinently up, uttering as he rose that interjection of surprise so much discanted upon, with the aposiopestick break after it, marked thus, Z——ds——which, though not strictly canonical, was still as little as any man could have said upon the occasion;——and which, by the bye, whether canonical or not, *Phutatorius* could no more help than he could the cause of it.

Though this has taken up some time in the narrative, it took up little more time in the transaction, than just to allow time for *Phutatorius* to draw forth the chesnut, and throw it down with violence upon the floor——and for *Yorick,* to rise from his chair, and pick the chesnut up.

It is curious to observe the triumph of slight incidents over the mind:——What incredible weight they have in forming and governing our opinions, both of men and things,——that trifles light as air, shall waft a belief into the soul, and plant it so immoveably within it,——that *Euclid's* demonstrations, could they be brought to batter it in breach, should not all have power to overthrow it.

Yorick, I said, picked up the chesnut which *Phutatorius's* wrath had flung down——the action was trifling——I am ashamed to account for it——he did it, for no reason, but that he thought the chesnut not a jot worse for the adventure—— and that he held a good chesnut worth stooping for.———But

---

[7]An ask; provincial term for a newt.

this incident, trifling as it was, wrought differently in *Phuta-torius*'s head: He considered this act of *Yorick*'s, in getting off his chair, and picking up the chesnut, as a plain acknowledg-ment in him, that the chesnut was originally his,——and in course, that it must have been the owner of the chesnut, and no one else, who could have plaid him such a prank with it: What greatly confirmed him in this opinion, was this, that the table being parallelogramical and very narrow, it afforded a fair opportunity for *Yorick,* who sat directly over-against *Phutatorius,* of slipping the chesnut in——and consequently that he did it. The look of something more than suspicion, which *Phutatorius* cast full upon *Yorick* as these thoughts arose, too evidently spoke his opinion——and as *Phutatorius* was naturally supposed to know more of the matter than any person besides, his opinion at once became the general one; ——and for a reason very different from any which have been yet given——in a little time it was put out of all manner of dispute.

When great or unexpected events fall out upon the stage of this sublunary world——the mind of man, which is an inqui-sitive kind of a substance, naturally takes a flight, behind the scenes, to see what is the cause and first spring of them—— The search was not long in this instance.

It was well known that *Yorick* had never a good opinion of the treatise which *Phutatorius* had wrote *de Concubinis re-tinendis,* as a thing which he feared had done hurt in the world——and 'twas easily found out, that there was a mystical meaning in *Yorick*'s prank——and that his chucking the ches-nut hot into *Phutatorius*'s ***-*****, was a sarcastical fling at his book——the doctrines of which, they said, had inflamed many an honest man in the same place.

This conceit awaken'd *Somnolentus*[8]——made *Agelastes* smile——and if you can recollect the precise look and air of a man's face intent in finding out a riddle——it threw *Gas-tripheres*'s into that form——and in short was thought by many to be a master-stroke of arch-wit.

------

[8]See p. 194, n. 5; for Agelastes, see p. 193, n. 1.

This, as the reader has seen from one end to the other, was as groundless as the dreams of philosophy: *Yorick,* no doubt, as *Shakespear* said of his ancestor————*"was a man of jest,"*[9] but it was temper'd with something which withheld him from that, and many other ungracious pranks, of which he as undeservedly bore the blame;————but it was his misfortune all his life long to bear the imputation of saying and doing a thousand things of which (unless my esteem blinds me) his nature was incapable. All I blame him for————or rather, all I blame and alternately like him for, was that singularity of his temper, which would never suffer him to take pains to set a story right with the world, however in his power. In every ill usage of that sort, he acted precisely as in the affair of his lean horse ————he could have explained it to his honour, but his spirit was above it; and besides he ever looked upon the inventor, the propagator and believer of an illiberal report alike so injurious to him,————he could not stoop to tell his story to them ————and so trusted to time and truth to do it for him.

This heroic cast produced him inconveniences in many respects————in the present, it was followed by the fixed resentment of *Phutatorius,* who, as *Yorick* had just made an end of his chesnut, rose up from his chair a second time, to let him know it————which indeed he did with a smile; saying only ————that he would endeavour not to forget the obligation.

But you must mark and carefully separate and distinguish these two things in your mind.

————The smile was for the company.

————The threat was for *Yorick.*

CHAP. XXVIII.

————CAN you tell me, quoth *Phutatorius,* speaking to *Gastripheres* who sat next to him,————for one would not apply to a surgeon in so foolish an affair,————can you tell me, *Gastripheres,* what is best to take out the fire?————Ask

---

[9]Shakespeare's Yorick was "a fellow of infinite jest" (*Hamlet,* 5.1.202).

Eugenius, said *Gastripheres*——That greatly depends, said *Eugenius,*[1] pretending ignorance of the adventure, upon the nature of the part——If it is a tender part, and a part which can conveniently be wrapt up——It is both the one and the other, replied *Phutatorius,* laying his hand as he spoke, with an emphatical nod of his head, upon the part in question, and lifting up his right leg at the same time to ease and ventilate it ——If that is the case, said *Eugenius,* I would advise you, *Phutatorius,* not to tamper with it by any means; but if you will send to the next printer, and trust your cure to such a simple thing as a soft sheet of paper just come off the press[2] ——you need do nothing more than twist it round——The damp paper, quoth *Yorick* (who sat next to his friend *Eugenius*) though I know it has a refreshing coolness in it—— yet I presume is no more than the vehicle——and that the oil and lamp-black with which the paper is so strongly impregnated, does the business——Right, said *Eugenius,* and is of any outward application I would venture to recommend the most anodyne and safe.

Was it my case, said *Gastripheres,* as the main thing is the oil and lamp-black, I should spread them thick upon a rag, and clap it on directly. That would make a very devil of it, replied *Yorick*——And besides, added *Eugenius,* it would not answer the intention, which is the extreame neatness and elegance of the prescription, which the faculty[3] hold to be half in half——for consider, if the type is a very small one, (which it should be) the sanative particles, which come into contact in this form, have the advantage of being spread so infinitely thin and with such a mathematical equality (fresh paragraphs and large capitals excepted) as no art or management of the spatula can come up to. It falls out very luckily, replied *Phutatorius,* that the second edition of my treatise *de Concubinis retinendis,* is at this instant in the press——You may

[1]See p. 28, n. 1.

[2]On the early hand presses, to insure evenness of impression the paper was printed damp.

[3]See p. 257, n. 20.

take any leaf of it, said *Eugenius*————No matter which————
provided, quoth *Yorick,* there is no bawdry in it————

They are just now, replied *Phutatorius,* printing off the
ninth chapter————which is the last chapter but one in the
book————Pray what is the title to that chapter, said *Yorick,*
making a respectful bow to *Phutatorius* as he spoke————I
think, answered *Phutatorius,* 'tis that, *de re concubinariâ.*[4]

For heaven's sake keep out of that chapter, quoth *Yorick.*
————By all means————added *Eugenius.*

CHAP. XXIX.

————NOW, quoth *Didius,* rising up, and laying his right-
hand with his fingers spread upon his breast————
had such a blunder about a christian-name happened before
the reformation————(It happened the day before yesterday,
quoth my uncle *Toby* to himself) and when baptism was administer'd in *Latin*————('Twas all in *English,* said my uncle)
————Many things might have coincided with it, and upon
the authority of sundry decreed cases, to have pronounced the
baptism null, with a power of giving the child a new name
————Had a priest, for instance, which was no uncommon thing,
through ignorance of the *Latin* tongue, baptized a child of
Tom-o'Stiles, *in nomino patriæ & filia & spiritum sanctos,*[1]————
the baptism was held null————I beg your pardon, replied
Kysarcius,————in that case, as the mistake was only in the *ter-
minations,* the baptism was valid————and to have rendered it
null, the blunder of the priest should have fallen upon the first
syllable of each noun————and not, as in your case, upon the
last.————

My father delighted in subtleties of this kind, and listen'd
with infinite attention.

Gastripheres, for example, continued *Kysarcius,* baptizes a

---

[4] *Of a matter pertaining to concubinage.*

[1] Incorrect rendering of the declensional endings, though not of the significant roots, of the phrase *in nomine patris et filii et spiritus sancti:* in
the name of the father and of the son and of the holy ghost.

child of *John Stradling*'s in *Gomine* gatris, &c. &c. instead of
in Nomine patris, &c.——Is this a baptism?   No,——say the
ablest canonists; inasmuch as the radix of each word is hereby
torn up, and the sense and meaning of them removed and
changed quite to another object; for *Gomine* does not signify
a name, nor *gatris* a father——What do they signify? said my
uncle *Toby*——Nothing at all——quoth *Yorick*——Ergo,
such a baptism is null, said *Kysarcius*——In course, answered
Yorick, in a tone two parts jest and one part earnest——

But in the case cited, continued *Kysarcius*, where *patriæ* is
put for *patris*, *filia* for *filij*, and so on——as it is a fault only in
the declension, and the roots of the words continue untouch'd,
the inflexions of their branches, either this way or that, does
not in any sort hinder the baptism, inasmuch as the same sense
continues in the words as before——But then, said *Didius*,
the intention of the priest's pronouncing them grammatically,
must have been proved to have gone along with it——Right,
answered *Kysarcius*; and of this, brother *Didius*, we have
an instance in a decree of the decretals of Pope *Leo* the
IIId.[2]——But my brother's child, cried my uncle *Toby*, has
nothing to do with the Pope——'tis the plain child of a
Protestant gentleman, christen'd *Tristram* against the wills and
wishes both of its father and mother, and all who are a-kin
to it——

If the wills and wishes, said *Kysarcius*, interrupting my
uncle *Toby*, of those only who stand related to Mr. *Shandy*'s
child, were to have weight in this matter, Mrs. *Shandy*, of all
people, has the least to do in it——My uncle *Toby* lay'd down

---

[2]There is an important pronouncement regarding the intention of the
priest in baptism, in a decree of Innocent III; I have been unable to discover anything of the sort in Leo III.   The famous case to which Kysarcius alludes was one in which St. Boniface doubted the validity of baptism by an ignorant Bavarian priest *In nomine patria et filia et Spiritu
Sancta*, and concerning which Pope Zachary decreed, in a letter of July 1,
744, that as long as the bad grammar resulted from ignorance and not
from heresy, the baptism was valid.   See *Corpus Iuris Canonici*, Decreti
Tertia Pars, "De Consecratione," Distinctio IV, C. 86, *De sacerdote, qui
per inpericiam linguae latinae in inuocatione Trinitatis deliquit. Item
Zacharias Papa Bonifatio Episcopo.*

his pipe, and my father drew his chair still closer to the table
to hear the conclusion of so strange an introduction.

It has not only been a question, captain *Shandy,* amongst
the * best lawyers and civilians[3] in this land, continued *Kysarcius, "Whether the mother be of kin to her child,"*——but
after much dispassionate enquiry and jactitation of the arguments on all sides,——it has been adjudged for the negative,
——namely, *"That the mother is not of kin to her child†."*
My father instantly clapp'd his hand upon my uncle *Toby's*
mouth, under colour of whispering in his ear——the truth was,
he was alarmed for *Lillabullero*——and having a great desire
to hear more of so curious an argument——he begg'd my uncle
Toby, for heaven's sake, not to disappoint him in it——My
uncle *Toby* gave a nod——resumed his pipe, and contenting
himself with whistling *Lillabullero* inwardly——*Kysarcius,
Didius,* and *Triptolemus*[4] went on with the discourse as follows.

This determination, continued *Kysarcius,* how contrary soever it may seem to run to the stream of vulgar ideas, yet had
reason strongly on its side; and has been put out of all manner of dispute from the famous case, known commonly by
the name of the Duke of *Suffolk's* case:——It is cited in
Brook, said *Triptolemus*——And taken notice of by Lord
Coke,[5] added *Didius*——And you may find it in *Swinburn* on
Testaments, said *Kysarcius.*

The case, Mr. *Shandy,* was this.

In the reign of *Edward* the Sixth, *Charles* duke of *Suffolk*

---

*Vid. Swinburn on Testaments, Part 7. §8. [Sterne's note. The ref-
erence is to Henry Swinburne (c.1560–1623), *A Treatise of Testaments
and Last Wills,* from which Sterne took almost verbatim the following account of the famous case.]

[3]Civil lawyers.

†Vid. Brook Abridg. Tit. Administr. N.47. [Sterne's note. The reference, which is to Sir Robert Broke (d. 1558), *La Graunde abridgement,*
occurs in Swinburne, *op. cit.*]

[4]See p. 193, n. 1.

[5]Sir Edward Coke (1552–1634), English jurist and legal writer. The
reference (which Sterne found in Swinburne) is to the account of "Rat-
cliff's Case" in Part 3 of his *Reports.*

having issue a son by one venter, and a daughter by another
venter, made his last will, wherein he devised goods to his
son, and died; after whose death the son died also——but
without will, without wife, and without child——his mother
and his sister by the father's side (for she was born of the
former venter) then living. The mother took the administration of her son's goods, according to the statute of the 21st
of *Harry* the Eighth,[6] whereby it is enacted, That in case any
person die intestate, the administration of his goods shall be
committed to the next of kin.

The administration being thus (surreptitiously) granted to
the mother, the sister by the father's side commenced a suit
before the Ecclesiastical Judge, alledging, 1st, That she herself
was next of kin; and 2dly, That the mother was not of kin at
all to the party deceased; and therefore pray'd the court, that
the administration granted to the mother might be revoked,
and be committed unto her, as next of kin to the deceased, by
force of the said statute.

Hereupon, as it was a great cause, and much depending
upon its issue——and many causes of great property likely to
be decided in times to come, by the precedent to be then
made——the most learned, as well in the laws of this realm,
as in the civil law, were consulted together, whether the mother
was of kin to her son, or no.——Whereunto not only the temporal lawyers——but the church-lawyers——the juris-consulti[7]
——the juris-prudentes——the civilians——the advocates——
the commissaries——the judges of the consistory and prerogative courts of *Canterbury* and *York,* with the master of the
faculties, were all unanimously of opinion, That the mother
was not of * kin to her child——

---

[6]Swinburne's note reads: "Sta.H.8.an.21.c.5"; *i.e.,* Statutes of the
twenty-first year of the reign of Henry VIII, Caput 5.

[7]Legal counselors. Juris-prudentes: persons learned in the law.

*Mater non numeratur inter consanguineos. Bald. in ult. C. de
Verb. signific. [Sterne's note. The reference, which he miscopied from
Swinburne, is to Pietro Baldi de Ubaldis (1327–1406), Italian jurist and
professor of law at Perugia, *In Sextum Codicis Commentaria, Tit. De
verborum et rerum significatione, Lex 5, §3.*]

And what said the duchess of *Suffolk* to it? said my uncle *Toby*.

The unexpectedness of my uncle *Toby*'s question, confounded *Kysarcius* more than the ablest advocate——He stopp'd a full minute, looking in my uncle *Toby*'s face without replying——and in that single minute *Triptolemus* put by him, and took the lead as follows.

'Tis a ground and principle in the law, said *Triptolemus,* that things do not ascend, but descend in it; and I make no doubt 'tis for this cause, that however true it is, that the child may be of the blood or seed of its parents——that the parents, nevertheless, are not of the blood and seed of it; inasmuch as the parents are not begot by the child, but the child by the parents——For so they write, *Liberi sunt de sanguine patris & matris, sed pater et mater non sunt de sanguine liberorum.*[8]

——But this, *Triptolemus,* cried *Didius,* proves too much—— for from this authority cited it would follow, not only what indeed is granted on all sides, that the mother is not of kin to her child——but the father likewise——It is held, said *Triptolemus,* the better opinion; because the father, the mother, and the child, though they be three persons, yet are they but (*una caro**) one flesh; and consequently no degree of kindred ——or any method of acquiring one *in nature*——There you push the argument again too far, cried *Didius*——for there is no prohibition *in nature,* though there is in the levitical law,[9] ——but that a man may beget a child upon his grandmother ——in which case, supposing the issue a daughter, she would stand in relation both of——But who ever thought, cried *Kysarcius,* of laying with his grandmother?——The young gentleman, replied *Yorick,* whom *Selden*[10] speaks of——who not only thought of it, but justified his intention to his father

---

[8]Children are of the blood of their father and mother, but the father and mother are not of the blood of their children.

*Vide Brook Abridg. tit. Administr. N.47. [Sterne's note.]

[9]See Leviticus, 18.6ff.

[10]John Selden (1584–1654), English jurist, antiquary, Orientalist, and author, relates this story in his *Table Talk.*

by the argument drawn from the law of retaliation——"You lay'd, Sir, with my mother, said the lad——why may not I lay with yours?"——'Tis the *Argumentum commune*,[11] added *Yorick*.——'Tis as good, replied *Eugenius*, taking down his hat, as they deserve.

The company broke up——

CHAP. XXX.

——A ND pray, said my uncle *Toby*, leaning upon *Yorick*, as he and my father were helping him leisurely down the stairs——don't be terrified, madam, this stair-case conversation is not so long as the last——And pray, *Yorick*, said my uncle *Toby*, which way is this said affair of *Tristram* at length settled by these learned men? Very satisfactorily, replied *Yorick*; no mortal, Sir, has any concern with it——for Mrs. *Shandy* the mother is nothing at all akin to him——and as the mother's is the surest side——Mr. *Shandy*, in course, is still less than nothing——In short, he is not as much akin to him, Sir, as I am——

——That may well be, said my father, shaking his head.

——Let the learned say what they will, there must certainly, quoth my uncle *Toby*, have been some sort of consanguinity betwixt the duchess of *Suffolk* and her son——

The vulgar are of the same opinion, quoth *Yorick*, to this hour.

CHAP. XXXI.

T HOUGH my father was hugely tickled with the subtleties of these learned discourses——'twas still but like the anointing of a broken bone——The moment he got home, the weight of his afflictions returned upon him but so much the heavier, as is ever the case when the staff we lean on slips

---

[11]Common argument; argument equally appropriate to either side of a cause.

from under us——He became pensive——walked frequently
forth to the fish-pond——let down one loop[1] of his hat——
sigh'd often——forbore to snap——and, as the hasty sparks of
temper, which occasion snapping, so much assist perspiration
and digestion, as *Hippocrates*[2] tells us——he had certainly
fallen ill with the extinction of them, had not his thoughts
been critically drawn off, and his health rescued by a fresh
train of disquietudes left him, with a legacy of a thousand
pounds by my aunt *Dinah*——

My father had scarce read the letter, when taking the thing
by the right end, he instantly begun to plague and puzzle his
head how to lay it out mostly to the honour of his family——
A hundred and fifty odd projects took possession of his brains
by turns——he would do this, and that, and t'other——He
would go to *Rome*——he would go to law——he would buy
stock——he would buy *John Hobson*'s farm——he would new
fore-front his house, and add a new wing to make it even——
There was a fine water-mill on this side, and he would build
a wind-mill on the other side of the river in full view to answer
it——But above all things in the world, he would inclose the
great *Ox-moor,* and send out my brother *Bobby* immediately
upon his travels.

But as the sum was *finite,* and consequently could not do
every thing——and in truth very few of these to any purpose,
——of all the projects which offered themselves upon this
occasion, the two last seemed to make the deepest impression;
and he would infallibly have determined upon both at once,
but for the small inconvenience hinted at above, which absolutely put him under a necessity of deciding in favour either
of the one or the other.

This was not altogether so easy to be done; for though 'tis
certain my father had long before set his heart upon this neces-

---

[1] Loops of ribbon fastened up the sides of the cocked hat.

[2] See p. 83, n. 3; the present passage appears to derive, however, from
Mackenzie (for whom see p. 83, n. 4), the *History of Health,* 2.2.6.3:
"Moderate joy and anger . . . and those passions and affections of the
mind which partake of their nature . . . invigorate the nerves, accelerate
the circulating fluids, promote perspiration, and assist digestion . . ."

sary part of my brother's education, and like a prudent man
had actually determined to carry it into execution, with the
first money that returned from the second creation of actions
in the *Missisippi*-scheme,[3] in which he was an adventurer——
yet the *Ox-moor,* which was a fine, large, whinny,[4] undrained,
unimproved common, belonging to the *Shandy*-estate, had almost as old a claim upon him: He had long and affectionately
set his heart upon turning it likewise to some account.

But having never hitherto been pressed with such a conjuncture of things, as made it necessary to settle either the
priority or justice of their claims,——like a wise man he had
refrained entering into any nice or critical examination about
them: So that upon the dismission of every other project at
this crisis,———the two old projects, the Ox-MOOR and my
BROTHER, divided him again; and so equal a match were they
for each other, as to become the occasion of no small contest
in the old gentleman's mind,——which of the two should be
set o'going first.

——People may laugh as they will——but the case was this.

It had ever been the custom of the family, and by length of
time was almost become a matter of common right, that the
eldest son of it should have free ingress, egress, and regress
into foreign parts before marriage,——not only for the sake
of bettering his own private parts, by the benefit of exercise
and change of so much air——but simply for the mere delec-
tation of his fancy, by the feather put into his cap, of having
been abroad——*tantum valet,* my father would say, *quantum
sonat.*[5]

Now as this was a reasonable, and in course a most christian
indulgence——to deprive him of it, without why or wherefore,——and thereby make an example of him, as the first
Shandy unwhirl'd about *Europe* in a post-chaise, and only be-

[3] A huge speculative scheme for paying off the national debt of France
by the profits accruing to a great maritime and colonial company, which,
started in 1717, resulted in a financial panic in 1720.

[4] Abounding in whins or gorse.

[5] It is worth as much as it sounds.

cause he was a heavy lad——would be using him ten times worse than a *Turk*.

On the other hand, the case of the *Ox-moor* was full as hard.

Exclusive of the original purchase-money, which was eight hundred pounds——it had cost the family eight hundred pounds more in a law-suit about fifteen years before——besides the Lord knows what trouble and vexation.

It had been moreover in possession of the *Shandy*-family ever since the middle of the last century; and though it lay full in view before the house, bounded on one extremity by the water-mill, and on the other by the projected wind-mill spoken of above,——and for all these reasons seemed to have the fairest title of any part of the estate to the care and protection of the family——yet by an unaccountable fatality, common to men, as well as the ground they tread on,——it had all along most shamefully been overlook'd; and to speak the truth of it, had suffered so much by it, that it would have made any man's heart have bled (*Obadiah* said) who understood the value of land, to have rode over it, and only seen the condition it was in.

However, as neither the purchasing this tract of ground—— nor indeed the placing of it where it lay, were either of them, properly speaking, of my father's doing——he had never thought himself any way concerned in the affair———till the fifteen years before, when the breaking out of that cursed law-suit mentioned above (and which had arose about its boundaries)———which being altogether my father's own act and deed, it naturally awakened every other argument in its favour; and upon summing them all up together, he saw, not merely in interest, but in honour, he was bound to do something for it——and that now or never was the time.

I think there must certainly have been a mixture of ill-luck in it, that the reasons on both sides should happen to be so equally balanced by each other; for though my father weigh'd them in all humours and conditions———spent many an anxious hour in the most profound and abstracted meditation upon what was best to be done——reading books of farming one day———books of travels another———laying aside all passion whatever———viewing the arguments on both sides in all their lights and circumstances———communing every day with my uncle *Toby*———arguing with *Yorick,* and talking over the whole affair of the *Ox-moor* with *Obadiah*———yet nothing in all that time appeared so strongly in behalf of the one, which was not either strictly applicable to the other, or at least so far counterbalanced by some consideration of equal weight, as to keep the scales even.

For to be sure, with proper helps, and in the hands of some people, tho' the *Ox-moor* would undoubtedly have made a different appearance in the world from what it did, or ever would do in the condition it lay———yet every tittle of this was true, with regard to my brother *Bobby*———let *Obadiah* say what he would.———

In point of interest———the contest, I own, at first sight, did not appear so undecisive betwixt them; for whenever my father took pen and ink in hand, and set about calculating the simple expence of paring and burning, and fencing in the *Ox-moor*, &c. &c.———with the certain profit it would bring him in return———the latter turned out so prodigiously in his way of working the account, that you would have sworn the *Ox-moor* would have carried all before it. For it was plain he should reap a hundred lasts of rape, at twenty pounds a last, the very first year———besides an excellent crop of wheat the year following———and the year after that, to speak within bounds, a hundred———but, in all likelihood, a hundred and fifty———if not two hundred quarters of pease and beans——— besides potatoes without end———But then, to think he was all this while breeding up my brother like a hog to eat them——— knocked all on the head again, and generally left the old gentleman in such a state of suspence———that, as he often declared to my uncle *Toby*———he knew no more than his heels what to do.

No body, but he who has felt it, can conceive what a plaguing thing it is to have a man's mind torn asunder by two projects of equal strength, both obstinately pulling in a contrary direction at the same time: For to say nothing of the havock, which by a certain consequence is unavoidably made by it all over the finer system of the nerves, which you know convey the animal spirits and more subtle juices from the heart to the head, and so on——It is not to be told in what a degree such a wayward kind of friction works upon the more gross and solid parts, wasting the fat and impairing the strength of a man every time as it goes backwards and forwards.

My father had certainly sunk under this evil, as certainly as he had done under that of my CHRISTIAN NAME——had he not been rescued out of it as he was out of that, by a fresh evil ——the misfortune of my brother *Bobby*'s death.

What is the life of man! Is it not to shift from side to side? ——from sorrow to sorrow?——to button up one cause of vexation!——and unbutton another!

CHAP. XXXII.

FROM this moment I am to be considered as heir-apparent to the *Shandy* family——and it is from this point properly, that the story of my LIFE and my OPINIONS sets out; with all my hurry and precipitation I have but been clearing the ground to raise the building——and such a building do I foresee it will turn out, as never was planned, and as never was executed since *Adam*. In less than five minutes I shall have thrown my pen into the fire, and the little drop of thick ink which is left remaining at the bottom of my ink-horn, after it——I have but half a score things to do in the time——I have a thing to name ——a thing to lament——a thing to hope——a thing to promise, and a thing to threaten——I have a thing to suppose——a thing to declare——a thing to conceal——a thing to chuse, and a thing to pray for.——This chapter, therefore, I *name* the chapter of THINGS——and my next chapter to it, that is, the first chapter of my next volume, if I live, shall be my

chapter upon WHISKERS, in order to keep up some sort of connection in my works.

The thing I lament is, that things have crowded in so thick
upon me, that I have not been able to get into that part of my
work, towards which, I have all the way, looked forwards,
with so much earnest desire; and that is the campaigns, but
especially the amours of my uncle *Toby,* the events of which
are of so singular a nature, and so Cervantick[1] a cast, that if
I can so manage it, as to convey but the same impressions to
every other brain, which the occurrences themselves excite in
my own——I will answer for it the book shall make its way
in the world, much better than its master has done before it
——Oh *Tristram! Tristram!* can this but be once brought
about——the credit, which will attend thee as an author, shall
counterbalance the many evils which have befallen thee as a
man——thou wilt feast upon the one——when thou hast lost
all sense and remembrance of the other!——

No wonder I itch so much as I do, to get at these amours
——They are the choicest morsel of my whole story! and
when I do get at 'em——assure yourselves, good folks,——
(nor do I value whose squeamish stomach takes offence at it)
I shall not be at all nice in the choice of my words;——and
that's the thing I have to *declare.*——I shall never get all
through in five minutes, that I fear——and the thing I *hope*
is, that your worships and reverences are not offended——if
you are, depend upon't I'll give you something, my good gentry, next year, to be offended at——that's my dear *Jenny's*
way——but who my *Jenny* is[2]——and which is the right and
which the wrong end of a woman, is the thing to be *concealed*
——it shall be told you the next chapter but one, to my chapter of button-holes,——and not one chapter before.

And now that you have just got to the end of these four
volumes——the thing I have to *ask* is, how you feel your
heads? my own akes dismally——as for your healths, I know,
they are much better——True *Shandeism,* think what you will

---

[1] Resembling the writings of Cervantes.
[2] See p. 44, n. 3.

against it, opens the heart and lungs, and like all those affections which partake of its nature, it forces the blood and other vital fluids of the body to run freely thro' its channels, and makes the wheel of life run long and chearfully round.

Was I left like *Sancho Pança,* to chuse my kingdom, it should not be maritime——or a kingdom of blacks to make a penny of[3]——no, it should be a kingdom of hearty laughing subjects: And as the bilious and more saturnine passions, by creating disorders in the blood and humours, have as bad an influence, I see, upon the body politick as body natural—— and as nothing but a habit of virtue can fully govern those passions, and subject them to reason——I should add to my prayer——that God would give my subjects grace to be as WISE as they were MERRY; and then should I be the happiest monarch, and they the happiest people under heaven——

And so, with this moral for the present, may it please your worships and your reverences, I take my leave of you till this time twelve-month, when (unless this vile cough kills me in the mean time) I'll have another pluck at your beards, and lay open a story to the world you little dream of.

FINIS.

---

[3]Sancho's frequently flagging spirits were as frequently raised by his master's solemn assurances that he should shortly become governor of an island. When at one time he thought himself about to become governor of a land of negroes, "What care I, quoth he, tho' they be blacks? Best of all; 'tis but loading a ship with 'em, and having 'em into Spain, where I shall find chapmen enow to take 'em off my hands, and pay me ready money for 'em . . ." (*Don Quixote* 1.4.2.)

THE
LIFE
AND
OPINIONS
OF
TRISTRAM SHANDY,
GENTLEMAN.

Dixero si quid fortè jocosius, hoc mihi juris
Cum venia dabis.—— HOR.

——Si quis calumnietur levius esse quam decet theo-
logum, aut mordacius quam deceat Christia-
num—non Ego, sed Democritus dixit.——
ERASMUS.

VOL. V.

LONDON:
Printed for T. BECKET and P. A. DEHONDT,
in the Strand.   M DCC LXII.

Facsimile of the title page to the first edition of Volumes V and VI.
The first quotation, from Horace's *Satires*, 1.4.104–5, as slightly changed
by Burton in "Democritus Junior to the Reader," the preface to *The*
[over]

Anatomy of Melancholy, may be translated: "If I shall say anything too facetious, you will judge me indulgently." The second quotation, from the "Letter to Sir Thomas More" prefatory to Erasmus's *Moriæ Encomium,* and likewise taken from the loose paraphrase found in "Democritus Junior to the Reader," may be translated: "If anyone should censure my writings as lighter than becomes a divine or more satirical than becomes a Christian—not I, but Democritus said it."

In the second and subsequent editions, a third quotation was added: "*Si quis Clericus, aut Monachus, verba joculatoria, risum moventia sciebat, anathema esto.*—SECOND COUNCIL OF CARTHAGE." ("If any priest or monk know jesting words, exciting laughter, let him be damned.") The records of the early councils of Carthage are confused; Sterne has apparently perverted one of the early canons ("Quartum" in J. D. Mansi, *Sacrorum Conciliorum Nova et Amplissima Collectio* [Paris, 1901], 3.893), "*De clericis scurris: Si quis clericus aut monachus verba scurrilia, joculatoria, risumque moventia loquitur, acerrime corripiatur.*" ("If any priest or monk speak words which are scurrilous, jesting, and exciting to laughter, let him be very sharply rebuked.")

VOLUME V.

To the Right Honourable

JOHN,

Lord Viscount SPENCER.

MY LORD,

I Humbly beg leave to offer you these two Volumes;[1] they are the best my talents, with such bad health as I have, could produce:——had providence granted me a larger stock of either, they had been a much more proper present to your Lordship.

I beg your Lordship will forgive me, if, at the same time I dedicate this work to you, I join Lady SPENCER, in the liberty I take of inscribing the story of *Le Fever* in the sixth volume to her name; for which I have no other motive, which my heart has informed me of, but that the story is a humane one.

I am,
My Lord,
Your Lordship's
Most devoted,
And most humble Servant,
LAUR. STERNE.

---

[1]Volumes 5 and 6, published in December, 1761. John Spencer (1734–1783), a great-grandson of the Duke of Marlborough, was a friend and great patron of Sterne.

CHAP. I.

IF it had not been for those two mettlesome tits, and that madcap of a postillion, who drove them from Stilton to Stamford, the thought had never entered my head. He flew like lightning——there was a slope of three miles and a half——we scarce touched the ground——the motion was most rapid——most impetuous——'twas communicated to my brain——my heart partook of it——By the great God of day, said I, looking towards the sun, and thrusting my arm out of the fore-window of the chaise, as I made my vow, "I will lock up my study door the moment I get home, and throw the key of it ninety feet below the surface of the earth, into the draw-well at the back of my house."[1]

The London waggon confirmed me in my resolution: it hung tottering upon the hill, scarce progressive, drag'd——drag'd up by eight *heavy beasts*——"by main strength!——quoth I, nodding——but your betters draw the same way——and something of every bodies!——O rare!"

Tell me, ye learned, shall we for ever be adding so much to the *bulk*——so little to the *stock?*

---

[1] A characteristic example of Sterne's roguishness. Having declared that he has locked his study door—*i.e.,* that he has separated himself from the authors whom he was wont to plunder—he breaks into a castigation of plagiaries in an impassioned passage which is itself cribbed from Burton! "Cribbed," however, is too strong a word. That Sterne has here, as in practically every other case of "borrowing," deftly altered and heightened (and, incidentally, miscopied) his original, and has made the passage incontestably his own, will be evident to anyone who compares the following paragraphs with their sources in the *Anatomy of Melancholy,* "Democritus Junior to the Reader" (Shilleto's edition, 1.20–21), and 1.1.1.1. Burton himself had borrowed heavily in these particular passages, and in any case Sterne expected his learned readers to recognize his source and to laugh with him at the absurdity of inveighing against plagiarism in a plagiarism.

Shall we for ever make new books, as apothecaries make new mixtures, by pouring only out of one vessel into another?

Are we for ever to be twisting, and untwisting the same rope? for ever in the same track——for ever at the same pace?

Shall we be destined to the days of eternity, on holy-days, as well as working-days, to be shewing the *relicks of learning,* as monks do the relicks of their saints——without working one ——one single miracle with them?

Who made MAN, with powers which dart him from earth to heaven in a moment——that great, that most excellent, and most noble creature of the world——the *miracle* of nature, as Zoroaster in his book περὶ φύσεως called him——the SHEKINAH of the divine presence, as Chrysostom——the *image* of God, as Moses——the *ray* of divinity, as Plato——the *marvel* of *marvels,* as Aristotle——to go sneaking on at this pitiful—— pimping——pettifogging rate?

I scorn to be as abusive as Horace[2] upon the occasion—— but if there is no catachresis in the wish, and no sin in it, I wish from my soul, that every imitator in *Great Britain, France,* and *Ireland,* had the farcy for his pains; and that there was a good farcical house, large enough to hold——aye—— and sublimate them, *shag-rag and bob-tail,* male and female, all together: and this leads me to the affair of *Whiskers*—— but, by what chain of ideas——I leave as a legacy in *mort main* to Prudes and Tartufs,[3] to enjoy and make the most of.

Upon Whiskers.

I'm sorry I made it——'twas as inconsiderate a promise as ever entered a man's head——A chapter upon whiskers! alas! the world will not bear it——'tis a delicate world——but I knew not of what mettle it was made——nor had I ever seen the underwritten fragment; otherwise, as surely as noses are

---

[2]An allusion to the *Epistolae,* 1.19.1–20, of Horace (for whom, see p. 7, n. 2), in which the poet castigates "the servile herd of imitators."

[3]Tartuffe is the sanctimonious hypocrite in the comedy of that name by Molière (1622–1673).

noses, and whiskers are whiskers still; (let the world say what it will to the contrary) so surely would I have steered clear of this dangerous chapter.

The Fragment.

*   *   *   *   *   *   *   *   *   *
*   *   *   *   *   *   *   *   *   *

*   *——You are half asleep, my good lady, said the old gentleman, taking hold of the old lady's hand and giving it a gentle squeeze, as he pronounced the word *Whiskers*——shall we change the subject? By no means, replied the old lady——I like your account of these matters: so throwing a thin gauze handkerchief over her head, and leaning it back upon the chair with her face turned towards him, and advancing her two feet as she reclined herself——I desire, continued she, you will go on.

The old gentleman went on as follows.——Whiskers! cried the queen of *Navarre*,[4] dropping her knotting-ball, as *La Fosseuse* uttered the word——Whiskers; madam, said *La Fosseuse*, pinning the ball to the queen's apron, and making a courtesy as she repeated it.

La Fosseuse's voice was naturally soft and low, yet 'twas an articulate voice: and every letter of the word *whiskers* fell distinctly upon the queen of *Navarre*'s ear——Whiskers! cried the queen, laying a greater stress upon the word, and as if she had still distrusted her ears——Whiskers; replied *La Fosseuse*, repeating the word a third time——There is not a cavalier, madam, of his age in *Navarre*, continued the maid of honour, pressing the page's interest upon the queen, that has so gallant a pair——Of what? cried *Margaret*, smiling——Of whiskers, said *La Fosseuse*, with infinite modesty.

The word whiskers still stood its ground, and continued to be made use of in most of the best companies throughout the

---

[4] An allusion to Margaret of Angoulême (1492–1549), queen of Henry of Navarre and author of the *Heptameron*. Certain of the names in Sterne's "Fragment" are those of members of her court.

little kingdom of *Navarre,* notwithstanding the indiscreet use
which *La Fosseuse* had made of it: the truth was, *La Fosseuse*
had pronounced the word, not only before the queen, but
upon sundry other occasions at court, with an accent which
always implied something of a mystery——And as the court
of *Margaret,* as all the world knows, was at that time a mixture of gallantry and devotion——and whiskers being as applicable to the one, as the other, the word naturally stood its
ground——it gain'd full as much as it lost; that is, the clergy
were for it——the laity were against it——and for the women,
——*they* were divided.——

The excellency of the figure and mien of the young Sieur
De Croix, was at that time beginning to draw the attention of
the maids of honour towards the terras[5] before the palace
gate, where the guard was mounted. The Lady *de Baussiere*
fell deeply in love with him,——*La Battarelle* did the same
——it was the finest weather for it, that ever was remembered
in *Navarre*——*La Guyol, La Maronette, La Sabatiere,* fell in
love with the Sieur *de Croix* also——*La Rebours* and *La Fosseuse* knew better——*De Croix* had failed in an attempt to
recommend himself to *La Rebours;* and *La Rebours* and *La
Fosseuse* were inseparable.

The queen of *Navarre* was sitting with her ladies in the
painted bow-window, facing the gate of the second court, as
De Croix passed through it——He is handsome, said the Lady
Baussiere.——He has a good mien, said *La Battarelle.*——He
is finely shaped, said *La Guyol.*——I never saw an officer of
the horse-guards in my life, said *La Maronette,* with two such
legs——Or who stood so well upon them, said *La Sabatiere*
——But he has no whiskers, cried *La Fosseuse*——Not a pile,
said *La Rebours.*

The queen went directly to her oratory, musing all the way,
as she walked through the gallery, upon the subject; turning
it this way and that way in her fancy——*Ave Maria* + ——
what can *La Fosseuse* mean? said she, kneeling down upon
the cushion.

—————
[5]Terrace.

La Guyol, La Battarelle, La Maronette, La Sabatiere, retired
instantly to their chambers——Whiskers! said all four of them
to themselves, as they bolted their doors on the inside.

The Lady *Carnavallette* was counting her beads with both
hands, unsuspected under her farthingal——from St. *Antony*
down to St. *Ursula* inclusive, not a saint passed through her
fingers without whiskers; St. *Francis,* St. *Dominick,* St. *Bennet,* St. *Basil,* St. *Bridget,* had all whiskers.

The Lady *Baussiere* had got into a wilderness of conceits,
with moralizing too intricately upon *La Fosseuse's* text——She
mounted her palfry, her page followed her——the host passed
by——the lady *Baussiere* rode on.

One denier, cried the order of mercy——one single denier,
in behalf of a thousand patient captives, whose eyes look
towards heaven and you for their redemption.

——The Lady *Baussiere* rode on.

Pity the unhappy, said a devout, venerable, hoary-headed
man, meekly holding up a box, begirt with iron, in his withered
hands——I beg for the unfortunate—good, my lady, 'tis for
a prison——for an hospital——'tis for an old man——a poor
man undone by shipwreck, by suretyship, by fire——I call
God and all his angels to witness——'tis to cloath the naked
——to feed the hungry——'tis to comfort the sick and the
broken hearted.

——The Lady *Baussiere* rode on.

A decayed kinsman bowed himself to the ground.

——The Lady *Baussiere* rode on.

He ran begging bare-headed on one side of her palfry, con-
juring her by the former bonds of friendship, alliance, consanguinity, *&c.*——Cousin, aunt, sister, mother——for virtue's
sake, for your own, for mine, for Christ's sake remember me
——pity me.

——The Lady *Baussiere* rode on.

Take hold of my whiskers, said the Lady *Baussiere*——The
page took hold of her palfry. She dismounted at the end of
the terrace.

There are some trains of certain ideas which leave prints of

themselves about our eyes and eye-brows; and there is a consciousness of it, somewhere about the heart, which serves but
to make these etchings the stronger——we see, spell, and put
them together without a dictionary.

Ha, ha! he, hee! cried *La Guyol* and *La Sabatiere,* looking
close at each others prints——Ho, ho! cried *La Battarelle* and
Maronette, doing the same:——Whist! cried one——st, st,
——said a second,——hush, quoth a third——poo, poo, replied
a fourth——gramercy! cried the Lady *Carnavallette;*——'twas
she who bewhisker'd St. *Bridget.*

La Fosseuse drew her bodkin from the knot of her hair, and
having traced the outline of a small whisker, with the blunt
end of it, upon one side of her upper lip, put it into *La Rebours*'s hand——*La Rebours* shook her head.

The Lady *Baussiere* cough'd thrice into the inside of her
muff——*La Guyol* smiled——Fy, said the Lady *Baussiere.*
The queen of *Navarre* touched her eye with the tip of her
fore finger——as much as to say, I understand you all.

'Twas plain to the whole court the word was ruined: *La
Fosseuse* had given it a wound, and it was not the better for
passing through all these defiles——It made a faint stand, however, for a few months; by the expiration of which, the Sieur
De Croix, finding it high time to leave *Navarre* for want of
whiskers——the word in course became indecent, and (after
a few efforts) absolutely unfit for use.

The best word, in the best language of the best world, must
have suffered under such combinations.————The curate of
d'Estella wrote a book against them, setting forth the dangers
of accessory ideas, and warning the *Navarois* against them.[6]

Does not all the world know, said the curate *d'Estella* at the
conclusion of his work, that Noses ran the same fate some
centuries ago in most parts of *Europe,* which Whiskers have
now done in the kingdom of *Navarre*——The evil indeed
spread no further then,——but have not beds and bolsters, and

---

[6]Possibly a reference to the *Rhétorique ecclésiastique, ou traité de l'art
du prédicateur* of Diego d'Estella (1524?–1578), a Franciscan teacher and
author of the village of Estella in the province of Navarre.

night-caps and chamber-pots stood upon the brink of destruction ever since? Are not trouse,[7] and placket-holes, and
pump-handles——and spigots and faucets, in danger still,
from the same association?——Chastity, by nature the gentlest
of all affections——give it but its head——'tis like a ramping
and a roaring lion.

The drift of the curate *d'Estella*'s argument was not understood.——They ran the scent the wrong way.——The world
bridled his ass at the tail.——And when the *extreams* of DELI-
CACY, and the *beginnings* of CONCUPISCENCE, hold their next
provincial chapter together, they may decree that bawdy also.

CHAP. II.

W HEN my father received the letter which brought him
the melancholy account of my brother *Bobby*'s death, he
was busy calculating the expence of his riding post from
Calais to *Paris,* and so on to *Lyons.*

'Twas a most inauspicious journey; my father having had
every foot of it to travel over again, and his calculation to begin afresh, when he had almost got to the end of it, by *Obadiah*'s opening the door to acquaint him the family was out
of yeast——and to ask whether he might not take the great
coach-horse early in the morning, and ride in search of some.
——With all my heart, *Obadiah,* said my father, (pursuing
his journey)——take the coach-horse, and welcome.——But
he wants a shoe, poor creature! said *Obadiah.*——Poor creature! said my uncle *Toby,* vibrating the note back again, like
a string in unison. Then ride the *Scotch* horse, quoth my
father hastily.——He cannot bear a saddle upon his back,
quoth *Obadiah,* for the whole world.——The devil's in that
horse; then take PATRIOT, cried my father, and shut the door.
——PATRIOT is sold, said *Obadiah.*——Here's for you! cried my

---

[7] Close-fitting, short breeches.

father, making a pause, and looking in my uncle *Toby*'s face, as if the thing had not been a matter of fact.——Your worship ordered me to sell him last *April,* said *Obadiah.*——Then go on foot for your pains, cried my father.——I had much rather walk than ride, said *Obadiah,* shutting the door.

What plagues! cried my father, going on with his calculation.——But the waters are out, said *Obadiah,*——opening the door again.

Till that moment, my father, who had a map of *Sanson's,*[1] and a book of the post roads before him, had kept his hand upon the head of his compasses, with one foot of them fixed upon *Nevers,* the last stage he had paid for——purposing to go on from that point with his journey and calculation, as soon as *Obadiah* quitted the room; but this second attack of *Obadiah's,* in opening the door and laying the whole country under water, was too much.——He let go his compasses—— or rather with a mixed motion betwixt accident and anger, he threw them upon the table; and then there was nothing for him to do, but to return back to *Calais* (like many others) as wise as he had set out.

When the letter was brought into the parlour, which contained the news of my brother's death, my father had got forwards again upon his journey to within a stride of the compasses of the very same stage of *Nevers.*——By your leave, Mons. *Sanson,* cried my father, striking the point of his compasses through *Nevers* into the table,——and nodding to my uncle *Toby,* to see what was in the letter,——twice of one night is too much for an *English* gentleman and his son, Mons. *Sanson,* to be turned back from so lousy a town as *Nevers,*—— what think'st thou, *Toby,* added my father in a sprightly tone. ——Unless it be a garrison town, said my uncle *Toby,*——for then——I shall be a fool, said my father, smiling to himself, as long as I live.——So giving a second nod——and keeping his compasses still upon *Nevers* with one hand, and holding his book of the post-roads in the other——half calculating and

---

[1]Nicolas Sanson (1600–1667), French cartographer, councillor of state, and geographer to the king.

half listening, he leaned forwards upon the table with both
elbows, as my uncle *Toby* hummed over the letter.

——— ——— ——— ——— ——— ———

——— ——— ——— ——— ——— ———

——— —— —— —— ———he's gone! said my uncle *Toby.*
——Where——Who? cried my father.——My nephew, said
my uncle *Toby.*——What——without leave——without money
——without governor? cried my father in amazement. No:
——he is dead, my dear brother, quoth my uncle *Toby.*——
Without being ill? cried my father again.——I dare say not,
said my uncle *Toby,* in a low voice, and fetching a deep sigh
from the bottom of his heart, he has been ill enough, poor
lad! I'll answer for him——for he is dead.

When *Agrippina* was told of her son's death, *Tacitus*[2] informs us, that not being able to moderate the violence of her
passions, she abruptly broke off her work——My father stuck
his compasses into *Nevers,* but so much the faster.——What
contrarieties! his, indeed, was matter of calculation——*Agrippina's* must have been quite a different affair; who else could
pretend to reason from history?

How my father went on, in my opinion, deserves a chapter
to itself.——

CHAP. III.

——— ——— And a chapter it shall have, and a devil of
a one too——so look to yourselves.

'Tis either *Plato,*[1] or *Plutarch,* or *Seneca,* or *Xenophon,* or
Epictetus, or *Theophrastus,* or *Lucian*——or some one per-

[2]For Tacitus, see p. 66, n. 4. The reference is a badly confused one
to his *Annales,* 13.16 and 3.1, but Sterne's immediate source for this
and for most of the following chapter was *The Anatomy of Melancholy,*
2.3.5.

[1]A burlesque of pedantic catalogues of authorities to prove self-evident
facts; specifically, a burlesque of a passage in the *Anatomy,* 2.3.5, wherein
Burton soberly proves that " 'tis a natural passion to weep for our
friends, an irresistible passion to lament and grieve." The actual list
of names comes, however, from Burton, 2.3.1.1.

haps of later date——either *Cardan,* or *Budæus,* or *Petrarch,*
or *Stella*——or possibly it may be some divine or father of
the church, St. *Austin,* or St. *Cyprian,* or *Barnard,* who affirms
that it is an irresistable and natural passion to weep for the
loss of our friends or children——and *Seneca*[2] (I'm positive)
tells us somewhere, that such griefs evacuate themselves best
by that particular channel.——And accordingly we find, that
David wept for his son *Absolom*[3]——*Adrian* for his *Antinous*
——*Niobe* for her children, and that *Apollodorus* and *Crito*
both shed tears for *Socrates* before his death.

My father managed his affliction otherwise; and indeed differently from most men either ancient or modern; for he
neither wept it away, as the *Hebrews* and the *Romans*——or
slept it off, as the *Laplanders*——or hang'd it, as the *English,*
or drowned it, as the *Germans*——nor did he curse it, or
damn it, or excommunicate it, or rhyme it, or lillabullero
it.——

——He got rid of it, however.

Will your worships give me leave to squeeze in a story between these two pages?

When *Tully* was bereft of his dear daughter *Tullia,* at first
he laid it to his heart,——he listened to the voice of nature,
and modulated his own unto it.——O my *Tullia!* my daughter! my child!——still, still, still,——'twas O my *Tullia!*——
my *Tullia!* Methinks I see my *Tullia,* I hear my *Tullia,* I
talk with my *Tullia.*——But as soon as he began to look into
the stores of philosophy, and consider how many excellent
things might be said upon the occasion——no body upon earth

---

[2] *Lucius Annæus Seneca* (c.54 B.C.–39 A.D.), "the elder," rhetorician,
and father of the statesman and philosopher. The reference is to his
Controversiæ, 5.30, but Sterne is "positive" on Burton's authority. The
conclusion of the paragraph echoes the *Anatomy,* 1.2.4.7, as well as 2.3.5.

[3] See 2 Samuel, 18.33–19.4. Antinous was an attendant and favourite
of the emperor Hadrian (76–138); at his suicide, the emperor was deeply
grieved and caused extravagant respect to be paid to his memory. Niobe,
in Greek mythology, wept for her slain children even after Zeus turned
her to stone. The grief of Crito, Apollodorus, and the others who were
with Socrates as he drank the poisoned cup, is related in Plato's *Phædo,*
117.

can conceive, says the great orator, how happy, how joyful it made me.[4]

My father was as proud of his eloquence as MARCUS TULLIUS CICERO could be for his life, and for aught I am convinced of to the contrary at present, with as much reason: it was indeed his strength——and his weakness too.——His strength——for he was by nature eloquent,——and his weakness—for he was hourly a dupe to it; and provided an occasion in life would but permit him to shew his talents, or say either a wise thing, a witty, or a shrewd one——(bating the case of a systematick misfortune)——he had all he wanted.——A blessing which tied up my father's tongue, and a misfortune which set it loose with a good grace, were pretty equal: sometimes, indeed, the misfortune was the better of the two; for instance, where the pleasure of the harangue was as *ten,* and the pain of the misfortune but as *five*——my father gained half in half, and consequently was as well again off, as it never had befallen him.

This clue will unravel, what otherwise would seem very inconsistent in my father's domestick character; and it is this, that in the provocations arising from the neglects and blunders of servants, or other mishaps unavoidable in a family, his anger, or rather the duration of it, eternally ran counter to all conjecture.

My father had a favourite little mare, which he had consigned over to a most beautiful Arabian horse, in order to have a pad out of her for his own riding: he was sanguine in all his projects; so talked about his pad every day with as absolute a security, as if it had been reared, broke,——and bridled and saddled at his door ready for mounting. By some neglect or other in *Obadiah,* it so fell out, that my father's expectations were answered with nothing better than a mule, and as ugly a beast of the kind as ever was produced.

My mother and my uncle *Toby* expected my father would

---

[4]An exaggeration of Cicero's account, in *Ad Atticum,* 12.14, *Tusculanæ Disputationes,* 4.29.63, and elsewhere, of the relief he received in writing his *De Consolatione.*

be the death of *Obadiah*——and that there never would be an
end of the disaster.——See here! you rascal, cried my father,
pointing to the mule, what you have done!——It was not me,
said *Obadiah*.——How do I know that? replied my father.

Triumph swam in my father's eyes, at the repartee——the
Attic salt brought water into them——and so *Obadiah* heard
no more about it.

Now let us go back to my brother's death.

Philosophy has a fine saying for every thing.——For *Death*
it has an entire set; the misery was, they all at once rushed
into my father's head, that 'twas difficult to string them together, so as to make any thing of a consistent show out of
them.——He took them as they came.[5]

" ' 'Tis an inevitable chance——the first statute in *Magnâ
Chartâ*——it is an everlasting act of parliament, my dear
brother,——*All must die.*

"If my son could not have died, it had been matter of wonder,——not that he is dead."

"Monarchs and princes dance in the same ring with us."

"——*To die,* is the great debt and tribute due unto nature:
tombs and monuments, which should perpetuate our memories, pay it themselves; and the proudest pyramid of them all,
which wealth and science have erected, has lost its apex, and
stands obtruncated in the traveller's horizon." (My father
found he got great ease, and went on)——"Kingdoms and
provinces, and towns and cities, have they not their periods?
and when those principles and powers, which at first cemented
and put them together, have performed their several evolutions, they fall back."——Brother *Shandy,* said my uncle *Toby,*
laying down his pipe at the word *evolutions*——Revolutions,
I meant, quoth my father,——by heaven! I meant revolutions, brother *Toby*——evolutions is nonsense.——'Tis not
nonsense——said my uncle *Toby.*——But is it not nonsense to
break the thread of such a discourse, upon such an occasion?
cried my father——do not——dear *Toby,* continued he, tak-

---

[5]Those which follow are still revamped from Burton's collection in the
Anatomy, 2.3.5.

ing him by the hand, do not——do not, I beseech thee, interrupt me at this crisis.——My uncle *Toby* put his pipe into his
mouth.

"Where is *Troy* and *Mycenæ,* and *Thebes* and *Delos,* and
Persepolis and *Agrigentum*"——continued my father, taking
up his book of post-roads, which he had laid down.——"What
is become, brother *Toby,* of *Nineveh* and *Babylon,* of *Cizicum*
and *Mitylenæ?* The fairest towns that ever the sun rose upon,
are now no more: the names only are left, and those (for many
of them are wrong spelt) are falling themselves by piece-meals
to decay, and in length of time will be forgotten, and involved
with every thing in a perpetual night: the world itself, brother
Toby, must——must come to an end.

"Returning out of *Asia,* when I sailed from *Ægina* towards
Megara," (*when can this have been? thought my uncle Toby*)
"I began to view the country round about. *Ægina* was behind
me, *Megara* was before, *Pyræus* on the right hand, *Corinth* on
the left.——What flourishing towns now prostrate upon the
earth! Alas! alas! said I to myself, that man should disturb
his soul for the loss of a child, when so much as this lies aw-
fully buried in his presence——Remember, said I to myself
again——remember thou art a man."——

Now my uncle *Toby* knew not that this last paragraph was
an extract of *Servius Sulpicius's* consolatory letter to *Tully.*[6]
——He had as little skill, honest man, in the fragments, as he
had in the whole pieces of antiquity.——And as my father,
whilst he was concerned in the *Turky* trade, had been three or
four different times in the *Levant,* in one of which he had
staid a whole year and an half at *Zant,* my uncle *Toby* naturally concluded, that in some one of these periods he had taken
a trip across the *Archipelago* into *Asia;* and that all this sailing affair with *Ægina* behind, and *Megara* before, and *Pyræus*
on the right hand, *&c. &c.* was nothing more than the true
course of my father's voyage and reflections.——'Twas cer-

---

[6]Servius Sulpicius Rufus (105–43 B.C.), Roman orator and jurist. The
passage is taken from Cicero's *Epistolæ ad Familiores,* 4.5, *via* Burton,
2.3.5.

tainly in his *manner,* and many an undertaking critick would have built two stories higher upon worse foundations.——And pray, brother, quoth my uncle *Toby,* laying the end of his pipe upon my father's hand in a kindly way of interruption——but waiting till he finished the account——what year of our Lord was this?——'Twas no year of our Lord, replied my father.——That's impossible, cried my uncle *Toby.*——Simpleton! said my father,——'twas forty years before Christ was born.

My uncle *Toby* had but two things for it; either to suppose his brother to be the wandering *Jew,*[7] or that his misfortunes had disordered his brain.——"May the Lord God of heaven and earth protect him and restore him," said my uncle *Toby,* praying silently for my father, and with tears in his eyes.

——My father placed the tears to a proper account, and went on with his harangue with great spirit.

"There is not such great odds, brother *Toby,* betwixt good and evil, as the world imagines"——(this way of setting off, by the bye, was not likely to cure my uncle *Toby's* suspicions.)——"Labour, sorrow, grief, sickness, want, and woe, are the sauces of life."——Much good may it do them——said my uncle *Toby* to himself.——

"My son is dead!——so much the better;——'tis a shame in such a tempest to have but one anchor."

"But he is gone for ever from us!——be it so. He is got from under the hands of his barber before he was bald——he is but risen from a feast before he was surfeited——from a banquet before he had got drunken."

"The *Thracians* wept when a child was born"——(and we were very near it, quoth my uncle *Toby*)——"and feasted and made merry when a man went out of the world; and with reason.——Death opens the gate of fame, and shuts the gate of envy after it,——it unlooses the chain of the captive, and puts the bondsman's task into another man's hands."

---

[7]The legendary Jew who, for having mistreated Christ while he was on his way to Calvary, was sentenced to wander on the earth until Christ's return.

"Shew me the man, who knows what life is, who dreads it, and I'll shew thee a prisoner who dreads his liberty."

Is it not better, my dear brother *Toby,* (for mark——our appetites are but diseases)——is it not better not to hunger at all, than to eat?——not to thirst, than to take physick to cure it?

Is it not better to be freed from cares and agues, from love and melancholy, and the other hot and cold fits of life, than like a galled traveller, who comes weary to his inn, to be bound to begin his journey afresh?

There is no terror, brother *Toby,* in its looks, but what it borrows from groans and convulsions——and the blowing of noses, and the wiping away of tears with the bottoms of curtains in a dying man's room.——Strip it of these, what is it ——'Tis better in battle than in bed, said my uncle *Toby.*—— Take away its herses, its mutes, and its mourning,——its plumes, scutcheons, and other mechanic aids——What is it? ——*Better in battle!* continued my father, smiling, for he had absolutely forgot my brother *Bobby*——'tis terrible no way ——for consider, brother *Toby,*——when we *are*——death is *not;*——and when death *is*——we are *not.* My uncle *Toby* laid down his pipe to consider the proposition; my father's eloquence was too rapid to stay for any man——away it went, ——and hurried my uncle *Toby*'s ideas along with it.——

For this reason, continued my father, 'tis worthy to recollect, how little alteration in great men, the approaches of death have made.——*Vespasian*[8] died in a jest upon his close stool——*Galba* with a sentence——*Septimius Severus* in a dis-

---

[8]Titus Flavius Vespasianus (9–79), Roman emperor, died after cynically observing, "Methinks I am becoming a god." Servius Sulpicius Galba (5 B.C.–69 A.D.), Roman emperor, addressed his assassins: "Strike, if it be for the good of the Roman people." Septimius Severus (146–211), Roman emperor, died after admonishing his attendants: "Make haste, if there is anything more for me to do"; in "conveying" this paragraph from Bacon's essay "Of Death," Sterne confusingly miscopied Bacon's "in dispatch." Tiberius Claudius Nero (42 B.C.–37 A.D.), Roman emperor, vainly attempted to conceal his approaching death by maintaining a pretence of strength and debauchery. Augustus Cæsar (63 B.C.–14 A.D.), Roman emperor, died in his wife's arms, saying, "Farewell Livia; live and forget not the days of our marriage."

patch——*Tiberius* in dissimulation, and *Cæsar Augustus* in a
compliment.——I hope, 'twas a sincere one—quoth my uncle
Toby.

——'Twas to his wife,——said my father.

CHAP. IV.

——And lastly——for of all the choice anecdotes which
history can produce of this matter, continued my father,——
this, like the gilded dome which covers in the fabrick——
crowns all.——

'Tis of *Cornelius Gallus,* the prætor[1]——which I dare say,
brother *Toby,* you have read.——I dare say I have not, replied
my uncle.——He died, said my father, as *   *   *   *   *
*   *   *   *   *   *   *   *   ——And if it was with his wife,
said my uncle *Toby*——there could be no hurt in it.——
That's more than I know——replied my father.

CHAP. V.

MY mother was going very gingerly in the dark along the
passage which led to the parlour, as my uncle *Toby* pronounced the word *wife*.——'Tis a shrill, penetrating sound of
itself, and *Obadiah* had helped it by leaving the door a little
a-jar, so that my mother heard enough of it, to imagine herself the subject of the conversation: so laying the edge of her
finger across her two lips——holding in her breath, and bend-
ing her head a little downwards, with a twist of her neck——
(not towards the door, but from it, by which means her ear
was brought to the chink)——she listened with all her powers:
——the listening slave, with the Goddess of Silence at his
back, could not have given a finer thought for an intaglio.

In this attitude I am determined to let her stand for five

---

[1]According to Pliny, *Historia Naturalis,* 7.54 [53], "Cornelius Gallus,
who had filled the office of prætor, . . . died in the venereal act."

minutes: till I bring up the affairs of the kitchen (as *Rapin*
does those of the church[1]) to the same period.

CHAP. VI.

THOUGH in one sense, our family was certainly a simple
machine, as it consisted of a few wheels; yet there was
thus much to be said for it, that these wheels were set in
motion by so many different springs, and acted one upon the
other from such a variety of strange principles and impulses,
——that though it was a simple machine, it had all the honour
and advantages of a complex one,——and a number of as odd
movements within it, as ever were beheld in the inside of a
Dutch silk-mill.

Amongst these there was one, I am going to speak of, in
which, perhaps, it was not altogether so singular, as in
many others; and it was this, that whatever motion, debate,
harangue, dialogue, project, or dissertation, was going forwards in the parlour, there was generally another at the same
time, and upon the same subject, running parallel along with
it in the kitchen.

Now to bring this about, whenever an extraordinary message, or letter, was delivered in the parlour,——or a discourse
suspended till a servant went out——or the lines of discontent were observed to hang upon the brows of my father or
mother——or, in short, when any thing was supposed to be
upon the tapis worth knowing or listening to, 'twas the rule
to leave the door, not absolutely shut, but somewhat a-jar——
as it stands just now,——which, under covert of the bad hinge,
(and that possibly might be one of the many reasons why it
was never mended) it was not difficult to manage; by which
means, in all these cases, a passage was generally left, not
indeed as wide as the *Dardanells,* but wide enough, for all that,

---

[1]It was the practice of Paul de Rapin (1661–1725), French historian, in
his great *L'Histoire d' Angleterre,* at the end of nearly every book to bring
up to date the affairs of the church in a special section.

to carry on as much of this windward trade, as was sufficient to save my father the trouble of governing his house;——my mother at this moment stands profiting by it.——*Obadiah* did the same thing, as soon as he had left the letter upon the table which brought the news of my brother's death; so that before my father had well got over his surprize, and entered upon his harangue,——had *Trim* got upon his legs, to speak his sentiments upon the subject.

A curious observer of nature, had he been worth the inventory of all *Job's* stock——though, by the bye, *your curious observers are seldom worth a groat*——would have given the half of it, to have heard Corporal *Trim* and my father, two orators so contrasted by nature and education, haranguing over the same bier.

My father a man of deep reading——prompt memory—— with *Cato*, and *Seneca*, and *Epictetus*, at his fingers ends.——

The corporal——with nothing——to remember——of no deeper reading than his muster-roll——or greater names at his finger's end, than the contents of it.

The one proceeding from period to period, by metaphor and allusion, and striking the fancy as he went along, (as men of wit and fancy do) with the entertainment and pleasantry of his pictures and images.

The other, without wit or antithesis, or point, or turn, this way or that; but leaving the images on one side, and the pictures on the other, going strait forwards as nature could lead him, to the heart. O *Trim!* would to heaven thou had'st a better historian!——would!——thy historian had a better pair of breeches!——O ye criticks! will nothing melt you?

CHAP. VII.

——My young master in *London* is dead! said *Obadiah.*——

——A green sattin night-gown of my mother's, which had been twice scoured, was the first idea which *Obadiah's*

exclamation brought into *Susannah's* head.——Well might
Locke write a chapter upon the imperfections of words.[1]——
Then, quoth *Susannah,* we must all go into mourning.——But
note a second time: the word *mourning,* notwithstanding *Susannah* made use of it herself——failed also of doing its office;
it excited not one single idea, tinged either with grey or black,
——all was green.——The green sattin night-gown hung there
still.

——O! 'twill be the death of my poor mistress, cried *Susannah.*——My mother's whole wardrobe followed.——What
a procession! her red damask,——her orange-tawny,——her
white and yellow lutestrings,——her brown taffata,——her
bone-laced caps, her bed-gowns, and comfortable under-
petticoats.——Not a rag was left behind.——*"No,——she will
never look up again,"* said *Susannah.*

We had a fat foolish scullion——my father, I think, kept
her for her simplicity;——she had been all autumn struggling
with a dropsy.——He is dead! said *Obadiah,*——he is certainly dead!——So am not I, said the foolish scullion.

——Here is sad news, *Trim!* cried *Susannah,* wiping her
eyes as *Trim* step'd into the kitchen,——master *Bobby* is
dead and *buried,*——the funeral was an interpolation of *Susannah's,*——we shall have all to go into mourning, said *Susannah.*

I hope not, said *Trim.*——You hope not! cried *Susannah*
earnestly.——The mourning ran not in *Trim's* head, whatever it did in *Susannah's.*——I hope——said *Trim,* explaining
himself, I hope in God the news is not true. I heard the letter read with my own ears, answered *Obadiah;* and we shall
have a terrible piece of work of it in stubbing the ox-moor.
——Oh! he's dead, said *Susannah.*——As sure, said the scullion, as I am alive.

I lament for him from my heart and my soul, said *Trim,*
fetching a sigh.——Poor creature!——poor boy! poor gentleman!

——He was alive last *Whitsontide,* said the coachman.——

[1] *An Essay Concerning Human Understanding,* 3.9.

Whitsontide! alas! cried *Trim,* extending his right arm, and
falling instantly into the same attitude in which he read the
sermon,——what is *Whitsontide, Jonathan,* (for that was the
coachman's name) or *Shrovetide,* or any tide or time past, to
this?   Are we not here now, continued the corporal, (striking the end of his stick perpendicularly upon the floor, so as
to give an idea of health and stability)——and are we not——
(dropping his hat upon the ground) gone! in a moment!——
'Twas infinitely striking!   *Susannah* burst into a flood of tears.
——We are not stocks and stones.——*Jonathan, Obadiah,* the
cook-maid, all melted.——The foolish fat scullion herself, who
was scouring a fish-kettle upon her knees, was rous'd with it.
——The whole kitchen crouded about the corporal.

Now as I perceive plainly, that the preservation of our constitution in church and state,——and possibly the preservation
of the whole world——or what is the same thing, the distribution and balance of its property and power, may in time to
come depend greatly upon the right understanding of this
stroke of the corporal's eloquence——I do demand your attention,——your worships and reverences, for any ten pages together, take them where you will in any other part of the
work, shall sleep for it at your ease.

I said, "we were not stocks and stones"——'tis very well.
I should have added, nor are we angels, I wish we were,——
but men cloathed with bodies, and governed by our imaginations;——and what a junketting piece of work of it there is,
betwixt these and our seven senses, especially some of them,
for my own part, I own it, I am ashamed to confess.   Let it
suffice to affirm, that of all the senses, the eye, (for I absolutely deny the touch, though most of your *Barbati,*[2] I know,
are for it) has the quickest commerce with the soul,——gives
a smarter stroke, and leaves something more inexpressible
upon the fancy, than words can either convey——or sometimes get rid of.

---

[2]"Bearded ones"; also goats and philosophers.   The Atomists believed
that sensation and thought were ultimately identical, and that touch was
the basis of all sensation.

——I've gone a little about——no matter, 'tis for health——
let us only carry it back in our mind to the mortality of *Trim's*
hat.——"Are we not here now,——and gone in a moment?"
——There was nothing in the sentence——'twas one of your
self-evident truths we have the advantage of hearing every
day; and if *Trim* had not trusted more to his hat than his head
——he had made nothing at all of it.

——"Are we not here now;"——continued the corporal,
"and are we not"——(dropping his hat plumb upon the
ground——and pausing, before he pronounced the word)——
"gone! in a moment?" The descent of the hat was as if a
heavy lump of clay had been kneaded into the crown of it.
——Nothing could have expressed the sentiment of mortality,
of which it was the type and fore-runner, like it,——his hand
seemed to vanish from under it,——it fell dead,——the corporal's eye fix'd upon it, as upon a corps,——and *Susannah*
burst into a flood of tears.

Now——Ten thousand, and ten thousand times ten thousand (for matter and motion are infinite) are the ways by
which a hat may be dropped upon the ground, without any
effect.——Had he flung it, or thrown it, or cast it, or skimmed
it, or squirted, or let it slip or fall in any possible direction
under heaven,——or in the best direction that could be given
to it,——had he dropped it like a goose——like a puppy——
like an ass——or in doing it, or even after he had done, had
he looked like a fool,——like a ninny——like a nicompoop
——it had fail'd, and the effect upon the heart had been lost.

Ye who govern this mighty world and its mighty concerns
with the *engines* of eloquence,——who heat it, and cool it, and
melt it, and mollify it,——and then harden it again to *your
purpose*——

Ye who wind and turn the passions with this great wind-
lass,——and, having done it, lead the owners of them, whither
ye think meet——

Ye, lastly, who drive——and why not, Ye also who are
driven, like turkeys to market, with a stick and a red clout——
meditate——meditate, I beseech you, upon *Trim's* hat.

CHAP. VIII.

STAY——I have a small account to settle with the reader, before *Trim* can go on with his harangue.——It shall be done in two minutes.

Amongst many other book-debts, all of which I shall discharge in due time,——I own myself a debtor to the world for two items,——a chapter upon *chamber-maids and button-holes,* which, in the former part of my work, I promised and fully intended to pay off this year: but some of your worships and reverences telling me, that the two subjects, especially so connected together, might endanger the morals of the world, ——I pray the chapter upon chamber-maids and button-holes may be forgiven me,——and that they will accept of the last chapter in lieu of it; which is nothing, an't please your reverences, but a chapter of *chamber-maids, green-gowns,*[1] *and old hats.*

Trim took his off the ground,——put it upon his head,—— and then went on with his oration upon death, in manner and form following.

CHAP. IX.

——To us, *Jonathan,* who know not what want or care is ——who live here in the service of two of the best of masters ——(bating in my own case his majesty King *William* the Third, whom I had the honour to serve both in *Ireland* and *Flanders*)——I own it, that from *Whitsontide* to within three weeks of *Christmas,*——'tis not long——'tis like nothing;—— but to those, *Jonathan,* who know what death is, and what havock and destruction he can make, before a man can well

---

[1] An allusion to the green gown of harlotry. For "old hats," see p. 549 and n. 1.

wheel about——'tis like a whole age.——O *Jonathan!* 'twould
make a good-natured man's heart bleed, to consider, continued
the corporal, (standing perpendicularly) how low many a
brave and upright fellow has been laid since that time!——
And trust me, *Susy,* added the corporal, turning to *Susannah,*
whose eyes were swimming in water,——before that time
comes round again,——many a bright eye will be dim.——
Susannah placed it to the right side of the page——she wept
——but she court'sied too.——Are we not, continued *Trim,*
looking still at *Susannah*——are we not like a flower of the
field——a tear of pride stole in betwixt every two tears of
humiliation——else no tongue could have described *Susannah's* affliction——is not all flesh grass?——'Tis clay,——'tis
dirt.——They all looked directly at the scullion,——the scullion had just been scouring a fish-kettle.——It was not
fair.——

——What is the finest face that ever man looked at!——I
could hear *Trim* talk so for ever, cried *Susannah,*——what is
it! (*Susannah* laid her hand upon *Trim's* shoulder)——but
corruption?——*Susannah* took it off.

——Now I love you for this——and 'tis this delicious mixture within you which makes you dear creatures what you are
——and he who hates you for it——all I can say of the matter, is——That he has either a pumkin for his head——or a
pippin for his heart,——and whenever he is dissected 'twill
be found so.

CHAP. X.

WHETHER *Susannah,* by taking her hand too suddenly
from off the corporal's shoulder, (by the whisking about
of her passions)——broke a little the chain of his reflections——

Or whether the corporal began to be suspicious, he had got
into the doctor's quarters, and was talking more like the
chaplain than himself——

Or whether - - - - - - - - - - - - - - -
Or whether——for in all such cases a man of invention and
parts may with pleasure fill a couple of pages with supposi-
tions——which of all these was the cause, let the curious
physiologist, or the curious any body determine——'tis certain,
at least, the corporal went on thus with his harangue.

For my own part, I declare it, that out of doors, I value not
death at all:——not this . . added the corporal, snapping his
fingers,——but with an air which no one but the corporal
could have given to the sentiment.——In battle, I value death
not this . . . and let him not take me cowardly, like poor *Joe
Gibbins,* in scouring his gun.——What is he? A pull of a
trigger——a push of a bayonet an inch this way or that——
makes the difference.——Look along the line——to the right
——see! *Jack's* down! well,——'tis worth a regiment of
horse to him.——No——'tis *Dick.* Then *Jack's* no worse.
——Never mind which,——we pass on,——in hot pursuit the
wound itself which brings him is not felt,——the best way is
to stand up to him,——the man who flies, is in ten times more
danger than the man who marches up into his jaws.——I've
look'd him, added the corporal, an hundred times in the face,
——and know what he is.——He's nothing, *Obadiah,* at all in
the field.——But he's very frightful in a house, quoth *Obadiah.*
——I never mind it myself, said *Jonathan,* upon a coach-box.
——It must, in my opinion, be most natural in bed, replied
Susannah.——And could I escape him by creeping into the
worst calf's skin that ever was made into a knapsack, I would
do it there——said *Trim*——but that is nature.

——Nature is nature, said *Jonathan.*——And that is the reason, cried *Susannah,* I so much pity my mistress.——She will
never get the better of it.——Now I pity the captain the most
of any one in the family, answered *Trim.*——Madam will get
ease of heart in weeping,——and the Squire in talking about
it,——but my poor master will keep it all in silence to himself.——I shall hear him sigh in his bed for a whole month
together, as he did for lieutenant *Le Fever.* An' please your
honour, do not sigh so piteously, I would say to him as I laid

besides him. I cannot help it, *Trim,* my master would say,
——'tis so melancholy an accident——I cannot get it off my
heart.——Your honour fears not death yourself.——I hope,
Trim, I fear nothing, he would say, but the doing a wrong
thing.——Well, he would add, whatever betides, I will take
care of *Le Fever's* boy.——And with that, like a quieting
draught, his honour would fall asleep.

I like to hear *Trim's* stories about the captain, said *Susannah.*——He is a kindly-hearted gentleman, said *Obadiah,* as
ever lived.——Aye,——and as brave a one too, said the corporal, as ever stept before a platoon.——There never was a
better officer in the king's army,——or a better man in God's
world; for he would march up to the mouth of a cannon,
though he saw the lighted match at the very touch-hole,——
and yet, for all that, he has a heart as soft as a child for other
people.——He would not hurt a chicken.——I would sooner,
quoth *Jonathan,* drive such a gentleman for seven pounds a
year——than some for eight.——Thank thee, *Jonathan!* for
thy twenty shillings,——as much, *Jonathan,* said the corporal,
shaking him by the hand, as if thou hadst put the money into
my own pocket.——I would serve him to the day of my death
out of love. He is a friend and a brother to me,——and could
I be sure my poor brother *Tom* was dead,——continued the
corporal, taking out his handkerchief,——was I worth ten
thousand pounds, I would leave every shilling of it to the
captain.——*Trim* could not refrain from tears at this testa-
mentary proof he gave of his affection to his master.——The
whole kitchen was affected.——Do tell us this story of the
poor lieutenant, said *Susannah.*——With all my heart, answered the corporal.

Susannah, the cook, *Jonathan, Obadiah,* and corporal *Trim,*
formed a circle about the fire; and as soon as the scullion had
shut the kitchen door,——the corporal begun.

CHAP. XI.

I Am a *Turk* if I had not as much forgot my mother, as if
Nature had plaistered me up, and set me down naked
upon the banks of the river *Nile,* without one.[1]——Your most
obedient servant, Madam——I've cost you a great deal of
trouble,——I wish it may answer;——but you have left a crack
in my back,——and here's a great piece fallen off here before,
——and what must I do with this foot?——I shall never reach
England with it.

For my own part I never wonder at any thing;——and so
often has my judgment deceived me in my life, that I always
suspect it, right or wrong,——at least I am seldom hot upon
cold subjects. For all this, I reverence truth as much as any
body; and when it has slipped us, if a man will but take me
by the hand, and go quietly and search for it, as for a thing we
have both lost, and can neither of us do well without,——I'll
go to the world's end with him:——But I hate disputes,——
and therefore (bating religious points, or such as touch society)
I would almost subscribe to any thing which does not choak
me in the first passage, rather than be drawn into one——
But I cannot bear suffocation,——and bad smells worst of all.
——For which reasons, I resolved from the beginning, That
if ever the army of martyrs was to be augmented,——or a new
one raised,——I would have no hand in it, one way or t'other.

CHAP. XII.

——B UT to return to my mother.

My uncle *Toby*'s opinion, Madam, "that there could be no
harm in *Cornelius Gallus,* the *Roman* prætor's lying with his

---

[1]An allusion to the ancient popular belief in the spontaneous or
"equivocal" generation of animal life from the sun-warmed mud of the
Nile.

wife;"——or rather the last word of that opinion,——(for it
was all my mother heard of it) caught hold of her by the
weak part of the whole sex:——You shall not mistake me,——
I mean her curiosity,——she instantly concluded herself the
subject of the conversation, and with that prepossession upon
her fancy, you will readily conceive every word my father
said, was accommodated either to herself, or her family concerns.

——Pray, Madam, in what street does the lady live, who
would not have done the same?

From the strange mode of *Cornelius*'s death, my father had
made a transition to that of *Socrates,* and was giving my uncle
Toby an abstract of his pleading before his judges;[1]——'twas
irresistable:——not the oration of *Socrates,*——but my father's
temptation to it.——He had wrote the * Life of *Socrates* himself the year before he left off trade, which, I fear, was the
means of hastening him out of it;——so that no one was able
to set out with so full a sail, and in so swelling a tide of heroic
loftiness upon the occasion, as my father was. Not a period
in *Socrates*'s oration, which closed with a shorter word than
transmigration, or *annihilation,*——or a worse thought in the
middle of it than *to be*——*or not to be,*——the entering upon
a new and untried state of things;——or, upon a long, a profound and peaceful sleep, without dreams, without disturbance;——*That we and our children were born to die,*——*but
neither of us born to be slaves.*——No——there I mistake;
that was part of *Eleazer*'s oration, as recorded by *Josephus* (*de
Bell. Judaic.*)——*Eleazer* owns he had it from the philosophers
of *India*;[2] in all likelihood *Alexander* the Great, in his ir-

---

[1] In Plato's *Apology;* the reference in the following chapter is to the
Apology, 34.

*This book my father would never consent to publish; 'tis in manu-
script, with some other tracts of his, in the family, all, or most of which
will be printed in due time. [Sterne's note.]

[2] On the contrary, this sentiment, which is the theme of the whole
oration, Eleazer takes as his own, though he refers with admiration to the
willing self-cremation of the Indian philosophers. See *The Wars of the
Jews,* 7.8, by Flavius Josephus (37–c.95), the celebrated Jewish historian.
In the remainder of this paragraph and in those following, Sterne

ruption into *India,* after he had over-run *Persia,* amongst the many things he stole,——stole that sentiment also; by which means it was carried, if not all the way by himself, (for we all know he died at *Babylon*) at least by some of his maroders, into *Greece,*——from *Greece* it got to *Rome,*——from *Rome* to *France,*——and from *France* to *England:*——So things come round.——

By land carriage I can conceive no other way.——

By water the sentiment might easily have come down the *Ganges* into the *Sinus Gangeticus,* or *Bay of Bengal,* and so into the *Indian Sea;* and following the course of trade, (the way from *India* by the *Cape of Good Hope* being then unknown) might be carried with other drugs and spices up the *Red Sea* to *Joddah,* the port of *Mekka,* or else to *Tor* or *Sues,* towns at the bottom of the gulf; and from thence by karrawans to *Coptos,* but three days journey distant, so down the *Nile* directly to *Alexandria,* where the SENTIMENT would be landed at the very foot of the great stair-case of the *Alexandrian* library,[3]——and from that store-house it would be fetched. ——Bless me! what a trade was driven by the learned in those days!

CHAP. XIII.

——NOW my father had a way, a little like that of *Job's* (in case there ever was such a man——if not, there's an end of the matter.——

Though, by the bye, because your learned men find some difficulty in fixing the precise æra in which so great a man lived;——whether, for instance, before or after the patriarchs, &c.——to vote, therefore, that he never lived *at all,* is a little

burlesques serious attempts (such as that of Sir William Temple in his *Reflections upon Ancient and Modern Learning,* 1692) to trace the progress of the arts and sciences from their presumed origin in the East, to western Europe.

[3]See p. 262, n. 26.

cruel,——'tis not doing as they would be done by——happen
that as it may)——My father, I say, had a way, when things
went extremely wrong with him, especially upon the first sally
of his impatience,——of wondering why he was begot,——
wishing himself dead;——sometimes worse:——And when
the provocation ran high, and grief touched his lips with
more than ordinary powers,——Sir, you scarce could have distinguished him from *Socrates* himself.——Every word would
breathe the sentiments of a soul disdaining life, and careless
about all its issues; for which reason, though my mother was
a woman of no deep reading, yet the abstract of *Socrates*'s
oration, which my father was giving my uncle *Toby,* was not
altogether new to her.——She listened to it with composed
intelligence, and would have done so to the end of the chapter, had not my father plunged (which he had no occasion to
have done) into that part of the pleading where the great
philosopher reckons up his connections, his alliances, and
children; but renounces a security to be so won by working
upon the passions of his judges.——"I have friends——I have
relations,——I have three desolate children,"——says
Socrates.——

——Then, cried my mother, opening the door,——you have
one more, Mr. *Shandy,* than I know of.

By heaven! I have one less,——said my father, getting up
and walking out of the room.

CHAP. XIV.

——They are *Socrates*'s children, said my uncle *Toby*. He
has been dead a hundred years ago, replied my mother.

My uncle *Toby* was no chronologer——so not caring to advance a step but upon safe ground, he laid down his pipe
deliberately upon the table, and rising up, and taking my
mother most kindly by the hand, without saying another word,
either good or bad, to her, he led her out after my father, that
he might finish the ecclaircissment himself.

CHAP. XV.

HAD this volume been a farce, which, unless every one's
life and opinions are to be looked upon as a farce as
well as mine, I see no reason to suppose—the last chapter, Sir,
had finished the first act of it, and then this chapter must
have set off thus.

Ptr..r..r..ing——twing——twang——prut——trut——'tis a
cursed bad fiddle.——Do you know whether my fiddle's in
tune or no?——trut..prut..——They should be *fifths*.——'Tis
wickedly strung——tr...a.e.i.o.u.-twang.——The bridge is a
mile too high, and the sound-post absolutely down,——else
——trut . . prut——hark! 'tis not so bad a tone.——Diddle
diddle, diddle diddle, diddle diddle, dum. There is nothing
in playing before good judges,——but there's a man there——
no——not him with the bundle under his arm——the grave
man in black.——'Sdeath! not the gentleman with the sword
on.——Sir, I had rather play a *Caprichio*[1] to *Calliope* herself,
than draw my bow across my fiddle before that very man; and
yet, I'll stake my *Cremona* to a *Jew*'s trump,[2] which is the
greatest musical odds that ever were laid, that I will this
moment stop three hundred and fifty leagues out of tune upon
my fiddle, without punishing one single nerve that belongs
to him.——Twaddle diddle, tweddle diddle,——twiddle diddle,——twoddle diddle,——twuddle diddle,——prut-trut——
krish——krash——krush.——I've undone you, Sir,——but
you see he is no worse,——and was *Apollo* to take his fiddle
after me, he can make him no better.

Diddle diddle, diddle diddle, diddle diddle——hum——
dum——drum.

——Your worships and your reverences love musick——and

---

[1]A musical composition in a free, sometimes capricious style. Calliope,
in Greek mythology, was the muse or goddess of epic poetry, the chief of
the muses.

[2]Jew's-harp.

God has made you all with good ears——and some of you play delightfully yourselves——trut-prut,——prut-trut.

O! there is——whom I could sit and hear whole days,—— whose talents lie in making what he fiddles to be felt,—— who inspires me with his joys and hopes, and puts the most hidden springs of my heart into motion.——If you would borrow five guineas of me, Sir,——which is generally ten guineas more than I have to spare——or you, Messrs. Apothecary and Taylor, want your bills paying,——that's your time.

CHAP. XVI.

THE first thing which entered my father's head, after affairs were a little settled in the family, and *Susannah* had got possession of my mother's green sattin night-gown, ——was to sit down coolly, after the example of *Xenophon,*[1] and write a TRISTRA-*pœdia,* or system of education for me; collecting first for that purpose his own scattered thoughts, counsels, and notions; and binding them together, so as to form an INSTITUTE for the government of my childhood and adolescence.   I was my father's last stake——he had lost my brother *Bobby* entirely,——he had lost, by his own computation, full three fourths of me——that is, he had been unfortunate in his three first great casts for me——my geniture, nose, and name,——there was but this one left; and accordingly my father gave himself up to it with as much devotion as ever my uncle *Toby* had done to his doctrine of projectils.——The difference between them was, that my uncle *Toby* drew his whole knowledge of projectils from *Nicholas Tartaglia*[2]—— My father spun his, every thread of it, out of his own brain, ——or reeled and cross-twisted what all other spinners and

---

[1] Xenophon (c.444–355 B.C.), a Greek historian and essayist whose romance, the *Cyropædia,* describes among other things the boyhood and training of Cyrus, the founder of the Persian empire, and contains Xenophon's own ideas on the training and educating of youth.

[2] See p. 89, n. 6.

spinsters had spun before him, that 'twas pretty near the same torture to him.

In about three years, or something more, my father had got advanced almost into the middle of his work.——Like all other writers, he met with disappointments.——He imagined he should be able to bring whatever he had to say, into so small a compass, that when it was finished and bound, it might be rolled up in my mother's hussive.[3]——Matter grows under our hands.——Let no man say,——"Come——I'll write a *duodecimo*."

My father gave himself up to it, however, with the most painful diligence, proceeding step by step in every line, with the same kind of caution and circumspection (though I cannot say upon quite so religious a principle) as was used by *John de la Casse,* the lord archbishop of *Benevento,*[4] in compassing his *Galateo;* in which his Grace of *Benevento* spent near forty years of his life; and when the thing came out, it was not of above half the size or the thickness of a *Rider*'s Almanack.——How the holy man managed the affair, unless he spent the greatest part of his time in combing his whiskers, or playing at *primero* with his chaplain,——would pose any mortal not let into the true secret;——and therefore 'tis worth explaining to the world, was it only for the encouragement of those few in it, who write not so much to be fed——as to be famous.

I own had *John de la Casse,* the archbishop of *Benevento,* for whose memory (notwithstanding his *Galateo*) I retain the highest veneration,——had he been, Sir, a slender clerk——of dull wit——slow parts——costive head, and so forth,——he and his *Galateo* might have jogged on together to the age of *Methusalah* for me,——the phænomenon had not been worth a parenthesis.——

---

[3]Hussif, housewife; a case for scissors, needle, thread, etc.

[4]Giovanni della Casa (1503–1556) was an accomplished Italian poet and ecclesiastic: his *Galateo* (for which, see p. 618, n. 3.) was actually composed between 1551 and 1554.   Rider's *Almanack* was issued in small octavo and duodecimo forms: the *Galateo* runs to sligl.tly over a hundred tiny pages.

But the reverse of this was the truth: *John de la Casse* was a genius of fine parts and fertile fancy; and yet with all these great advantages of nature, which should have pricked him forwards with his *Galateo,* he lay under an impuissance at the same time of advancing above a line and an half in the compass of a whole summer's day: this disability in his Grace arose from an opinion he was afflicted with,——which opinion was this,——*viz.* that whenever a Christian was writing a book (not for his private amusement, but) where his intent and purpose was *bonâ fide,*[5] to print and publish it to the world, his first thoughts were always the temptations of the evil one. ——This was the state of ordinary writers: but when a personage of venerable character and high station, either in church or state, once turned author,——he maintained, that from the very moment he took pen in hand——all the devils in hell broke out of their holes to cajole him.——'Twas Termtime with them,——every thought, first and last, was captious;——how specious and good soever,——'twas all one; ——in whatever form or colour it presented itself to the imagination,——'twas still a stroke of one or other of 'em levelled at him, and was to be fenced off.——So that the life of a writer, whatever he might fancy to the contrary, was not so much a state of *composition,* as a state of *warfare;* and his probation in it, precisely that of any other man militant upon earth,——both depending alike, not half so much upon the degrees of his WIT——as his RESISTANCE.

My father was hugely pleased with this theory of *John de la Casse,* archbishop of *Benevento;* and (had it not cramped him a little in his creed) I believe would have given ten of the best acres in the *Shandy* estate, to have been the broacher of it. ——How far my father actually believed in the devil, will be seen, when I come to speak of my father's religious notions, in the progress of this work: 'tis enough to say here, as he could not have the honour of it, in the literal sense of the doctrine——he took up with the allegory of it;——and would often say, especially when his pen was a little retrograde, there

---

[5]In good faith.

was as much good meaning, truth, and knowledge, couched under the veil of *John de la Casse*'s parabolical representation, ——as was to be found in any one poetic fiction, or mystick record of antiquity.——Prejudice of education, he would say, *is the devil*,——and the multitudes of them which we suck in with our mother's milk——*are the devil and all*.——We are haunted with them, brother *Toby*, in all our lucubrations and researches; and was a man fool enough to submit tamely to what they obtruded upon him,——what would his book be? Nothing,——he would add, throwing his pen away with a vengeance,——nothing but a farrago of the clack of nurses, and of the nonsense of the old women (of both sexes) through-out the kingdom.

This is the best account I am determined to give of the slow progress my father made in his *Tristra-pædia;* at which (as I said) he was three years and something more, indefatigably at work, and at last, had scarce compleated, by his own reckon-ing, one half of his undertaking: the misfortune was, that I was all that time totally neglected and abandoned to my mother; and what was almost as bad, by the very delay, the first part of the work, upon which my father had spent the most of his pains, was rendered entirely useless,——every day a page or two became of no consequence.——

——Certainly it was ordained as a scourge upon the pride of human wisdom, That the wisest of us all, should thus out-wit ourselves, and eternally forego our purposes in the intem-perate act of pursuing them.

In short, my father was so long in all his acts of resistance, ——or in other words,——he advanced so very slow with his work, and I began to live and get forwards at such a rate, that if an event had not happened,——which, when we get to it, if it can be told with decency, shall not be concealed a mo-ment from the reader——I verily believe, I had put by my father, and left him drawing a sun-dial, for no better purpose than to be buried under ground.

CHAP. XVII.

———'TWAS nothing,——I did not lose two drops of blood by it——'twas not worth calling in a surgeon, had he lived next door to us——thousands suffer by choice, what I did by accident.——Doctor *Slop* made ten times more of it, than there was occasion:——some men rise, by the art of hanging great weights upon small wires,——and I am this day (*August* the 10th, 1761) paying part of the price of this man's reputation.——O 'twould provoke a stone, to see how things are carried on in this world!——The chamber-maid had left no ******* *** under the bed:——Cannot you contrive, master, quoth *Susannah,* lifting up the sash with one hand, as she spoke, and helping me up into the window seat with the other,——cannot you manage, my dear, for a single time to **** *** ** *** ******?

I was five years old.——*Susannah* did not consider that nothing was well hung in our family,——so slap came the sash down like lightening upon us;——Nothing is left,——cried *Susannah,*——nothing is left——for me, but to run[1] my country.——

My uncle *Toby*'s house was a much kinder sanctuary; and so *Susannah* fled to it.

CHAP. XVIII.

WHEN *Susannah* told the corporal the misadventure of the sash, with all the circumstances which attended the *murder* of me,——(as she called it)——the blood forsook his cheeks;——all accessaries in murder, being principals,—— *Trim*'s conscience told him he was as much to blame as *Susannah,*——and if the doctrine had been true, my uncle *Toby* had as much of the blood-shed to answer for to heaven, as either of

———
[1]Flee from.

'em;——so that neither reason or instinct, separate or together, could possibly have guided *Susannah's* steps to so proper an asylum. It is in vain to leave this to the Reader's imagination: ——to form any kind of hypothesis that will render these propositions feasible, he must cudgel his brains sore,——and to do it without,——he must have such brains as no reader ever had before him.——Why should I put them either to tryal or to torture? 'Tis my own affair: I'll explain it myself.

CHAP. XIX

'TIS a pity, *Trim,* said my uncle *Toby,* resting with his hand upon the corporal's shoulder, as they both stood surveying their works,——that we have not a couple of field pieces to mount in the gorge of that new redoubt;——'twould secure the lines all along there, and make the attack on that side quite complete:——get me a couple cast, *Trim.*

Your honour shall have them, replied *Trim,* before to-morrow morning.

It was the joy of *Trim's* heart,——nor was his fertile head ever at a loss for expedients in doing it, to supply my uncle *Toby* in his campaigns, with whatever his fancy called for; had it been his last crown, he would have sate down and hammered it into a paderero[1] to have prevented a single wish in his Master. The corporal had already,——what with cutting off the ends of my uncle *Toby's* spouts——hacking and chiseling up the sides of his leaden gutters,——melting down his pewter shaving bason,——and going at last, like *Lewis* the fourteenth, on to the top of the church,[2] for spare ends, &c.——he had that very campaign brought no less than eight new battering cannons, besides three demi-culverins[3] into the field; my

---

[1] Pedrero, a form of cannon.

[2] To finance his long and expensive campaigns, Louis XIV frequently resorted to forced loans from the clergy.

[3] Cannon having 4½ inch bore and throwing 9½ pound shot.

uncle *Toby*'s demand for two more pieces for the redoubt, had set the corporal at work again; and no better resource offering, he had taken the two leaden weights from the nursery window: and as the sash pullies, when the lead was gone, were of no kind of use, he had taken them away also, to make a couple of wheels for one of their carriages.

He had dismantled every sash window in my uncle *Toby*'s house long before, in the very same way,——though not always in the same order; for sometimes the pullies had been wanted, and not the lead,——so then he began with the pullies, ——and the pullies being picked out, then the lead became useless,——and so the lead went to pot too.

——A great MORAL might be picked handsomly out of this, but I have not time——'tis enough to say, wherever the demolition began, 'twas equally fatal to the sash window.

CHAP. XX.

THE corporal had not taken his measures so badly in this stroke of artilleryship, but that he might have kept the matter entirely to himself, and left *Susannah* to have sustained the whole weight of the attack, as she could;——true courage is not content with coming off so.——The corporal, whether as general or comptroller of the train,——'twas no .matter, ——had done that, without which, as he imagined, the misfortune could never have happened,——*at least in* Susannah's *hands;*——How would your honours have behaved?——He determined at once, not to take shelter behind *Susannah,*—— but to give it; and with this resolution upon his mind, he marched upright into the parlour, to lay the whole *manœuvre* before my uncle *Toby*.

My uncle *Toby* had just then been giving *Yorick* an account of the Battle of *Steenkirk,* and of the strange conduct of count *Solmes*[1] in ordering the foot to halt, and the horse to march

---

[1]Heinrich Maastricht, Count Solms (1636–1693), commanded the allied

where it could not act; which was directly contrary to the king's commands, and proved the loss of the day.

There are incidents in some families so pat to the purpose of what is going to follow,——they are scarce exceeded by the invention of a dramatic writer;——I mean of ancient days.——

Trim, by the help of his forefinger, laid flat upon the table, and the edge of his hand striking a-cross it at right angles, made a shift to tell his story so, that priests and virgins might have listened to it;——and the story being told,——the dialogue went on as follows.

CHAP. XXI.

——I would be picquetted[1] to death, cried the corporal, as he concluded *Susannah's* story, before I would suffer the woman to come to any harm,——'twas my fault, an please your honour,——not hers.

Corporal *Trim,* replied my uncle *Toby,* putting on his hat which lay upon the table,——if any thing can be said to be a fault, when the service absolutely requires it should be done, ——'tis I certainly who deserve the blame,——you obeyed your orders.

Had count *Solmes, Trim,* done the same at the battle of *Steenkirk,* said *Yorick,* drolling a little upon the corporal, who had been run over by a dragoon in the retreat,——he had saved thee;——Saved! cried *Trim,* interrupting *Yorick,* and finishing the sentence for him after his own fashion,——he had saved five battalions, an please your reverence, every soul of them:——there was *Cutts's*——continued the corporal, clapping the forefinger of his right hand upon the thumb of his

---

main body in its luckless attack on the French at Steinkirk during the latter part of July, 1692.

[1]Picketed, tortured by standing on pickets or stakes.

left, and counting round his hand,——there was *Cutts's*[2]——
Mackay's,——*Angus's*,——*Graham's*——and *Leven's*, all cut
to pieces;——and so had the *English* life-guards too, had it not
been for some regiments upon the right, who marched up
boldly to their relief, and received the enemy's fire in their
faces, before any one of their own platoons discharged a musket,——they'll go to heaven for it,——added *Trim*.——*Trim*
is right, said my uncle *Toby,* nodding to *Yorick,*——he's perfectly right. What signified his marching the horse, continued
the corporal, where the ground was so strait, and the *French*
had such a nation of hedges, and copses, and ditches, and
fell'd trees laid this way and that to cover them; (as they always have.)——Count *Solmes* should have sent us,——we
would have fired muzzle to muzzle with them for their lives.
——There was nothing to be done for the horse:——he had
his foot shot off however for his pains, continued the corporal,
the very next campaign at *Landen*.——Poor *Trim* got his
wound there, quoth my uncle *Toby*.——'Twas owing, an
please your honour, entirely to count *Solmes,*——had we
drub'd them soundly at *Steenkirk,* they would not have
fought us at *Landen*.——Possibly not,——*Trim,* said my uncle
Toby;——though if they have the advantage of a wood, or you
give them a moment's time to intrench themselves, they are a
nation which will pop and pop for ever at you.——There is no
way but to march coolly up to them,——receive their fire, and
fall in upon them, pell-mell——Ding dong, added *Trim*.——
Horse and foot, said my uncle *Toby*.——Helter skelter, said
Trim.——Right and left, cried my uncle *Toby*.——Blood an'
ounds,[3] shouted the corporal;——the battle raged,——*Yorick*

---

[2]Baron John Cutts of Gowran (1661–1707) commanded a brigade of
Mackay's division which was almost destroyed at Steinkirk; Hugh
Mackay (1640?–1692) with the rank of lieutenant-general commanded
the British division of the allied army at Steinkirk, where he met his
death; James Hamilton, Earl of Angus, a colonel of the Cameronians,
was likewise killed in the battle of Steinkirk; Sir Charles Graham commanded a regiment at Steinkirk; David Melville, third Earl of Leven
(1660–1728), also commanded a regiment at Steinkirk.

[3]Wounds; an exclamation formerly used as an oath.

drew his chair a little to one side for safety, and after a moment's pause, my uncle *Toby* sinking his voice a note,——resumed the discourse as follows.

CHAP. XXII.

KING *William*, said my uncle *Toby*, addressing himself to *Yorick*, was so terribly provoked at count *Solmes* for disobeying his orders, that he would not suffer him to come into his presence for many months after.——I fear, answered *Yorick*, the squire will be as much provoked at the corporal, as the King at the count.——But 'twould be singularly hard in this case, continued he, if corporal *Trim*, who has behaved so diametrically opposite to count *Solmes*, should have the fate to be rewarded with the same disgrace;——too oft in this world, do things take that train.——I would spring a mine, cried my uncle *Toby*, rising up,——and blow up my fortifications, and my house with them, and we would perish under their ruins, ere I would stand by and see it.——*Trim* directed a slight,——but a grateful bow towards his master,——and so the chapter ends.

CHAP. XXIII.

——Then, *Yorick*, replied my uncle *Toby*, you and I will lead the way abreast,——and do you, corporal, follow a few paces behind us.——And *Susannah*, an' please your honour, said *Trim*, shall be put in the rear.——'Twas an excellent disposition,——and in this order, without either drums beating, or colours flying, they marched slowly from my uncle *Toby*'s house to *Shandy-hall*.

——I wish, said *Trim*, as they entered the door,——instead of the sash-weights, I had cut off the church-spout, as I once thought to have done.——You have cut off spouts enow, replied *Yorick*.——

CHAP. XXIV.

A S many pictures as have been given of my father, how like him soever in different airs and attitudes,——not one, or all of them, can ever help the reader to any kind of preconception of how my father would think, speak, or act, upon any untried occasion or occurrence of life.——There was that infinitude of oddities in him, and of chances along with it, by which handle he would take a thing,——it baffled, Sir, all calculations.——The truth was, his road lay so very far on one side, from that wherein most men travelled,——that every object before him presented a face and section of itself to his eye, altogether different from the plan and elevation of it seen by the rest of mankind.——In other words, 'twas a different object,——and in course was differently considered:

This is the true reason, that my dear *Jenny* and I, as well as all the world besides us, have such eternal squabbles about nothing.——She looks at her outside,——I, at her in——. How is it possible we should agree about her value?

CHAP. XXV.

'T IS a point settled,——and I mention it for the comfort of * *Confucius,* who is apt to get entangled in telling a plain story——that provided he keeps along the line of his story,——he may go backwards and forwards as he will,—— 'tis still held to be no digression.

This being premised, I take the benefit of the *act of going backwards* myself.

----

*Mr. *Shandy* is supposed to mean ***** *** ***, Esq; member for ******,——and not the *Chinese* Legislator. [Sterne's note.]

CHAP. XXVI.

FIFTY thousand pannier loads of devils——(not of the Archbishop of *Benevento's*,——I mean of *Rabelais's* devils[1]) with their tails chopped off by their rumps, could not have made so diabolical a scream of it, as I did——when the accident befell me: it summoned up my mother instantly into the nursery,——so that *Susannah* had but just time to make her escape down the back stairs, as my mother came up the fore.

Now, though I was old enough to have told the story myself,——and young enough, I hope, to have done it without malignity; yet *Susannah,* in passing by the kitchen, for fear of accidents, had left it in short-hand with the cook——the cook had told it with a commentary to *Jonathan,* and *Jonathan* to *Obadiah;* so that by the time my father had rung the bell half a dozen times, to know what was the matter above,——was *Obadiah* enabled to give him a particular account of it, just as it had happened.——I thought as much, said my father, tucking up his night-gown;——and so walked up stairs.

One would imagine from this——(though for my own part I somewhat question it)——that my father before that time, had actually wrote that remarkable chapter in the *Tristrapædia,* which to me is the most original and entertaining one in the whole book;——and that is the *chapter upon sash-windows,* with a bitter *Philippick* at the end of it, upon the forgetfulness of chamber-maids.——I have but two reasons for thinking otherwise.

First, Had the matter been taken into consideration, before the event happened, my father certainly would have nailed up the sash-window for good an' all;——which, considering with what difficulty he composed books,——he might have done

---

[1]In the Prologue to his Second Book, Rabelais gives himself "to a hundred thousand panniers full of devils" if he lies "so much as one single word in this whole history"; similarly phrased references to vast numbers of devils are frequent throughout the book.

with ten times less trouble, than he could have wrote the
chapter: this argument I foresee holds good against his writing the chapter, even after the event; but 'tis obviated under
the second reason, which I have the honour to offer to the
world in support of my opinion, that my father did not write
the chapter upon sash-windows and chamber-pots, at the time
supposed,——and it is this.

——That, in order to render the *Tristrapædia* complete,
——I wrote the chapter myself.

CHAP. XXVII.

MY father put on his spectacles——looked,——took them
off,——put them into the case——all in less than a
statutable minute; and without opening his lips, turned about,
and walked precipitately down stairs: my mother imagined he
had stepped down for lint and basilicon; but seeing him return with a couple of folios under his arm, and *Obadiah* following him with a large reading desk, she took it for granted
'twas an herbal, and so drew him a chair to the bed side, that
he might consult upon the case at his ease.

——If it be but right done,——said my father, turning to
the *Section*——*de sede vel subjecto circumcisionis*,——for he
had brought up *Spencer de Legibus Hebræorum Ritualibus*[1]
——and *Maimonides,* in order to confront and examine us altogether.——

——If it be but right done, quoth he:——Only tell us, cried
my mother, interrupting him, what herbs.——For that, replied
my father, you must send for Dr. *Slop.*

---

[1]John Spencer (1630–1695), Dean of Ely, from whose *De Legibus
Hebræorum Ritualibus* (*Concerning the Ritual Laws of the Hebrews*),
1.5.3–4, Sterne's material concerning circumcision is taken. The section
De Sede vel Subjecto Circumcisionis (*Concerning the Foundation or
rather the Subject of Circumcision*) is 1.5.3. Rabbi Moses ben Maimon
(1135–1204), the most celebrated Jewish Talmudist, philosopher, scientist, and writer of the Middle Ages, sets forth the reasons for circumcision in his *Moreh Nebuchim,* 3.49.

My mother went down, and my father went on, reading the section as follows.

* * * * * * * * * * * * * * *
* * * * * * * * * * * * * * *
* * * * * * *——Very well,——said my father,
* * * * * * * * * * * * * * *
* * * * * * * * * * * * * * *

* * *——nay, if it has that convenience——and so without stopping a moment to settle it first in his mind, whether the *Jews* had it from the *Egyptians,* or the *Egyptians* from the *Jews*,[2]——he rose up, and rubbing his forehead two or three times across with the palm of his hand, in the manner we rub out the footsteps of care, when evil has trod lighter upon us than we foreboded,——he shut the book, and walked down stairs.——Nay, said he, mentioning the name of a different great nation upon every step as he set his foot upon it——if the EGYPTIANS,——the SYRIANS,——the PHOENICIANS,——the ARABIANS,——the CAPADOCIANS,[3]——if the COLCHI, and TROGLODYTES did it——if SOLON and PYTHAGORAS submitted,—— what is TRISTRAM?——Who am I, that I should fret or fume one moment about the matter?

CHAP. XXVIII.

DEAR *Yorick,* said my father smiling, (for *Yorick* had broke his rank with my uncle *Toby* in coming through the narrow entry, and so had stept first into the parlour)—— this *Tristram* of ours, I find, comes very hardly by all his religious rites.——Never was the son of *Jew, Christian, Turk,* or *Infidel* initiated into them in so oblique and slovenly a man-

---

[2] A question argued at length in Spencer, 1.5.4.

[3] Ancient inhabitants of an extensive inland district of Asia Minor. Colchi: Inhabitants of an ancient district of Asia Minor. Troglodytes: "Cave-dwellers"; a name given in antiquity to various tribes but most commonly, as here, to certain inhabitants of the coast of the Red Sea. Pythagoras was said to have submitted to circumcision by the Egyptians that he might be admitted into their most secret places and learn their mystical philosophy.

ner.——But he is no worse, I trust, said *Yorick*.——There
has been certainly, continued my father, the duce and all to
do in some part or other of the ecliptic, when this offspring
of mine was formed.——That, you are a better judge of than
I, replied *Yorick*.——Astrologers, quoth my father, know better than us both:——the trine and sextil aspects have jumped
awry,——or the opposite of their ascendents have not hit it,
as they should,——or the lords of the genitures (as they call
them) have been at *bo-peep*,[1]——or something has been wrong
above, or below with us.

'Tis possible, answered *Yorick*.——But is the child, cried
my uncle *Toby*, the worse?——The *Troglodytes* say not, replied my father.——And your theologists, *Yorick*, tell us——
Theologically? said *Yorick*,——or speaking after the manner
of * apothecaries?—— † statesmen?——or ‡ washer-women?

——I'm not sure, replied my father,——but they tell us,
brother *Toby*, he's the better for it.——Provided, said *Yorick*,
you travel him into *Egypt*.——Of that, answered my father, he
will have the advantage, when he sees the *Pyramids*.——

Now every word of this, quoth my uncle *Toby*, is *Arabick*
to me.——I wish, said *Yorick*, 'twas so, to half the world.

——** ILUS, continued my father, circumcised his whole

---

[1]Authentic astrological terms used to describe an impossible or monstrous situation in the heavens—the trine and sextil aspects cannot jump
awry, nor can the lords of geniture play bo-peep. A burlesque of a passage in Burton's *Anatomy of Melancholy*, 3.1.2.2.

*Χαλεπῆς νόσου, καὶ δυσιάτου ἀπαλλαγή, ἥν ἄνθρακα καλοῦσιν.——PHILO.
[Sterne's note. This passage, taken (by Spencer) from Philo Judæus
(c.20 B.C.–c.40 A.D.), a Hellenistic Jewish philosopher of Alexandria, *De
Circumcisione,* may be translated: "A release from a terrible disease, and
hard to cure, which they call anthrax."]

†Τὰ τεμνόμενα τῶν ἐθνῶν πολυγονώτατα, καὶ πολυανθρωπότατα εἶναι.
[Sterne's note. This passage, also from Philo, may be translated: "Circumcised races are most prolific and most populous."]

‡Καθαριότητος εἵνεκεν.——BOCHART. [Sterne's note. Sterne has miscopied from Spencer the source of this passage, which is the *History* of
Herodotus (c.484–c.424 B.C.), the Greek historian, 2.37. The phrase
means: "For the sake of cleanliness."]

**'Ο Ιλος, τὰ αἰδοῖα περιτέμνεται, τἀυτὸ ποιῆσαι καὶ τοὺς ἀμ' αὑτῶ συμμά-
χους καταναγκάσας.——SANCHUNIATHO. [Sterne's note. Sanchuniathon
was an alleged ancient Phœnician writer, whose works Philo Byblius

army one morning.——Not without a court martial? cried my
uncle *Toby*.——Though the learned, continued he, taking no
notice of my uncle *Toby's* remark, but turning to *Yorick*,——
are greatly divided still who *Ilus* was;——some say *Saturn;*
——some the supream Being;——others, no more than a
brigadier general under *Pharoah-neco*.——Let him be who he
will, said my uncle *Toby,* I know not by what article of war he
could justify it.

The controvertists, answered my father, assign two and
twenty different reasons for it:——others indeed, who have
drawn their pens on the opposite side of the question, have
shewn the world the futility of the greatest part of them.——
But then again, our best polemic divines——I wish there was
not a polemic divine, said *Yorick,* in the kingdom;——one
ounce of practical divinity——is worth a painted ship load of
all their reverences have imported these fifty years.——Pray,
Mr. *Yorick,* quoth my uncle *Toby,*——do tell me what a
polemic divine is.——The best description, captain *Shandy,* I
have ever read, is a couple of 'em, replied *Yorick,* in the account of the battle fought single hands betwixt *Gymnast* and
captain *Tripet;* which I have in my pocket.——I beg I may hear
it, quoth my uncle *Toby* earnestly.——You shall, said *Yorick*.
——And as the corporal is waiting for me at the door,——and
I know the description of a battle, will do the poor fellow
more good than his supper,——I beg, brother, you'll give him
leave to come in.——With all my soul, said my father.——
Trim came in, erect and happy as an emperour; and having
shut the door, *Yorick* took a book from his right-hand coat
pocket, and read, or pretended to read, as follows.[2]

CHAP. XXIX.

——"which words being heard by all the soldiers which
were there, divers of them being inwardly terrified, did shrink

(fl.100 A.D.), a Phœnician grammarian, pretended to have translated.
This passage may be translated: "Ilus is circumcised and compels the
allies with him to do the same thing."]

[2]The quoted passage is a fairly close transcription from *Rabelais,* 1.35.

back and make room for the assailant: all this did *Gymnast* very well remark and consider; and therefore, making as if he would have alighted from off his horse, as he was poising himself on the mounting side, he most nimbly (with his short sword by his thigh) shifting his feet in the stirrup and performing the stirrup-leather feat, whereby, after the inclining of his body downwards, he forthwith launched himself aloft into the air, and placed both his feet together upon the saddle, standing upright, with his back turned towards his horse's head,——Now (said he) my case goes forward. Then suddenly in the same posture wherein he was, he fetched a gambol upon one foot, and turning to the left-hand, failed not to carry his body perfectly round, just into his former position, without missing one jot.——Ha! said *Tripet,* I will not do that at this time,——and not without cause. Well, said *Gymnast,* I have failed,——I will undo this leap; then with a marvellous strength and agility, turning towards the right-hand, he fetched another frisking gambol as before; which done, he set his right-hand thumb upon the bow of the saddle, raised himself up, and sprung into the air, poising and upholding his whole weight upon the muscle and nerve of the said thumb, and so turned and whirled himself about three times: at the fourth, reversing his body and overturning it upside-down, and foreside back, without *touching any thing,* he brought himself betwixt the horse's two ears, and then giving himself a jerking swing, he seated himself upon the crupper——"

(This can't be fighting, said my uncle *Toby.*——The corporal shook his head at it.——Have patience, said *Yorick.*)

"Then (*Tripet*) pass'd his right leg over his saddle, and placed himself *en croup.*[1]——But, said he, 'twere better for me to get into the saddle; then putting the thumbs of both hands upon the crupper before him, and thereupon leaning himself, as upon the only supporters of his body, he incontinently turned heels over head in the air, and straight found himself betwixt the bow of the saddle in a tolerable seat; then springing into the air with a summerset, he turned him about like a

[1]On the rump of the horse, behind the saddle.

wind-mill, and made above a hundred frisks, turns and demi-pommadas."[2]——Good God! cried *Trim,* losing all patience, ——one home thrust of a bayonet is worth it all.——I think so too, replied *Yorick.*——

——I am of a contrary opinion, quoth my father.

CHAP. XXX.

——No,——I think I have advanced nothing, replied my father, making answer to a question which *Yorick* had taken the liberty to put to him,——I have advanced nothing in the *Tristrapædia,* but what is as clear as any one proposition in *Euclid.*——Reach me, *Trim,* that book from off the scrutoir:[1] it has oft times been in my mind, continued my father, to have read it over both to you, *Yorick,* and to my brother *Toby,* and I think it a little unfriendly in myself, in not having done it long ago:——shall we have a short chapter or two now,—— and a chapter or two hereafter, as occasions serve; and so on, till we get through the whole? My uncle *Toby* and *Yorick* made the obeisance which was proper; and the corporal, though he was not included in the compliment, laid his hand upon his breast, and made his bow at the same time.——The company smiled. *Trim,* quoth my father, has paid the full price for staying out the *entertainment.*——He did not seem to relish the play, replied *Yorick.*——'Twas a Tom-fool-battle, an' please your reverence, of captain *Tripet's* and that other officer, making so many summersets, as they advanced;——the *French* come on capering now and then in that way,——but not quite so much.

My uncle *Toby* never felt the consciousness of his existence with more complacency than what the corporal's, and his own reflections, made him do at that moment;——he lighted his

---

[2]Pomada; a trick of vaulting upon or over a horse by laying one hand on the pommel of the saddle.

[1]Escritoire, writing-desk.

pipe,——*Yorick* drew his chair closer to the table,——*Trim* snuff'd the candle,——my father stir'd up the fire,——took up the book,——cough'd twice, and begun.

CHAP. XXXI.

THE first thirty pages, said my father, turning over the leaves,——are a little dry; and as they are not closely connected with the subject,——for the present we'll pass them by: 'tis a prefatory introduction, continued my father, or an introductory preface (for I am not determined which name to give it) upon political or civil government; the foundation of which being laid in the first conjunction betwixt male and female, for procreation of the species——I was insensibly led into it. ——'Twas natural, said *Yorick*.

The original of society, continued my father, I'm satisfied is, what *Politian*[1] tells us, *i.e.* merely conjugal; and nothing more than the getting together of one man and one woman;——to which, (according to *Hesiod*[2]) the philosopher adds a servant: ——but supposing in the first beginning there were no men servants born——he lays the foundation of it, in a man,——a woman——and a bull.——I believe 'tis an ox, quoth *Yorick,* quoting the passage (οἶκον μὲν πρώτιστα, γυναῖκά τε, βοῦν τ' ἀροτῆρα.[3])——A bull must have given more trouble than his head was worth.——But there is a better reason still, said my father, (dipping his pen into his ink) for, the ox being the most patient of animals, and the most useful withal in tilling the ground for their nourishment,——was the properest instrument, and emblem too, for the new joined couple, that the creation could have associated with them.——And there is a stronger reason, added my uncle *Toby,* than them all

---

[1]Angelo Poliziano (1454–1494), Florentine humanist and poet.

[2]Hesiod (fl. c.735 B.C.), a Greek poet. The reference is to his *Works and Days,* 405–09.

[3]First of all a house, a woman, and a ploughing ox.

for the ox.——My father had not power to take his pen out of his ink-horn, till he had heard my uncle *Toby*'s reason.—— For when the ground was tilled, said my uncle *Toby,* and made worth inclosing, then they began to secure it by walls and ditches, which was the origin of fortification.——True, true; dear *Toby,* cried my father, striking out the bull, and putting the ox in his place.

My father gave *Trim* a nod, to snuff the candle, and re- sumed his discourse.

——I enter upon this speculation, said my father carelessly, and half shutting the book, as he went on,——merely to shew the foundation of the natural relation between a father and his child; the right and jurisdiction over whom he acquires these several ways——

1st, by marriage.

2d, by adoption.

3d, by legitimation.

And 4th, by procreation; all which I consider in their order.

I lay a slight stress upon one of them; replied *Yorick*——the act, especially where it ends there, in my opinion lays as little obligation upon the child, as it conveys power to the father. ——You are wrong,——said my father argutely,[4] and for this plain reason   *   *   *   *   *   *   *   *   *   *   *
*   *   *   *   *   *   *   *   *   *   *   *   *   *
*   *   *   *   *   *   *   *   *   *   *   .   ——I own, added my father, that the offspring, upon this account, is not so under the power and jurisdiction of the *mother.*——But the reason, replied *Yorick,* equally holds good for her.——She is under authority herself, said my father:——and besides, con- tinued my father, nodding his head and laying his finger upon the side of his nose, as he assigned his reason,——*she is not the principal agent,* Yorick.——In what? quoth my uncle *Toby,* stopping his pipe.——Though by all means, added my father (not attending to my uncle *Toby*) *"The son ought to pay her respect,"* as you may read, *Yorick,* at large in the first book of the Institutes of *Justinian,* at the eleventh title and the

---

[4]Sharply, shrewdly.

tenth section.[5]——I can read it as well, replied *Yorick,* in the Catechism.

CHAP. XXXII.

*T*RIM can repeat every word of it by heart, quoth my uncle
  Toby.——Pugh! said my father, not caring to be interrupted with *Trim's* saying his Catechism. He can upon my honour, replied my uncle *Toby.*——Ask him, Mr. *Yorick,* any question you please.——

——The fifth Commandment, *Trim*——said *Yorick,* speaking mildly, and with a gentle nod, as to a modest Catechumen. The corporal stood silent.——You don't ask him right, said my uncle *Toby,* raising his voice, and giving it rapidly like the word of command;——The fifth—— ——cried my uncle *Toby.*——I must begin with the first, an' please your honour, said the corporal.——

——*Yorick* could not forbear smiling.——Your reverence does not consider, said the corporal, shouldering his stick like a musket, and marching into the middle of the room, to illustrate his position,——that 'tis exactly the same thing, as doing one's exercise in the field.——

"Join your right hand to your firelock," cried the corporal, giving the word of command, and performing the motion.——

"Poise your firelock," cried the corporal, doing the duty still of both adjutant and private man.

"Rest your firelock;"——one motion, an' please your reverence, you see leads into another.——If his honour will begin but with the *first*——

THE FIRST——cried my uncle *Toby,* setting his hand upon his side—— *   *   *   *   *   *   *   *   *   *   *
*   *   *   *   *   *   *   *   *   *   *

THE SECOND——cried my uncle *Toby,* waving his tobacco-pipe, as he would have done his sword at the head of a regiment.

---

[5]No; it is the preceding principle, that children are not subject to the power of their mothers, that is laid down in the *Institutes,* 1.11.10.

——The corporal went through his *manual* with exactness; and having *honoured his father and mother,* made a low bow, and fell back to the side of the room.

Every thing in this world, said my father, is big with jest, ——and has wit in it, and instruction too,——if we can but find it out.

——Here is the *scaffold work* of INSTRUCTION, its true point of folly, without the BUILDING behind it.——

——Here is the glass[1] for pedagogues, preceptors, tutors, governours, gerund-grinders and bear-leaders[2] to view themselves in, in their true dimensions.——

Oh! there is a husk and shell, *Yorick,* which grows up with learning, which their unskilfulness knows not how to fling away!

——SCIENCES MAY BE LEARNED BY ROTE, BUT WISDOM NOT.

Yorick thought my father inspired.——I will enter into obligations this moment, said my father, to lay out all my aunt *Dinah's* legacy, in charitable uses (of which, by the bye, my father had no high opinion) if the corporal has any one determinate idea annexed to any one word he has repeated.—— Prythee, *Trim,* quoth my father, turning round to him,—— What do'st thou mean, by *"honouring thy father and mother?"*

Allowing them, an' please your honour, three halfpence a day out of my pay, when they grew old.——And didst thou do that, *Trim?* said *Yorick.*——He did indeed, replied my uncle *Toby.*——Then, *Trim,* said *Yorick,* springing out of his chair, and taking the corporal by the hand, thou art the best commentator upon that part of the *Decalogue;* and I honour thee more for it, corporal *Trim,* than if thou hadst had a hand in the *Talmud*[3] itself.

---

[1]Looking-glass, mirror.

[2]Tutors in charge of youth at the university or on travels.

[3]The book which contains the body of Jewish traditional civil and ceremonial law additional to the Pentateuch, and the later commentary thereupon.

CHAP. XXXIII.

O Blessed health! cried my father, making an exclamation, as he turned over the leaves to the next chapter,——thou art above all gold and treasure; 'tis thou who enlargest the soul,——and openest all it's powers to receive instruction and to relish virtue.——He that has thee, has little more to wish for;——and he that is so wretched as to want thee,——wants every thing with thee.

I have concentrated all that can be said upon this important head, said my father, into a very little room, therefore we'll read the chapter quite thro'.

My father read as follows.

"The whole secret of health depending upon the due contention for mastery betwixt the radical heat and the radical moisture"[1]——You have proved that matter of fact, I suppose, above, said *Yorick*.   Sufficiently, replied my father.

In saying this, my father shut the book,——not as if he resolved to read no more of it, for he kept his forefinger in the chapter:——nor pettishly,——for he shut the book slowly; his thumb resting, when he had done it, upon the upper-side of the cover, as his three fingers supported the lower-side of it, without the least compressive violence.——

I have demonstrated the truth of that point, quoth my father, nodding to *Yorick,* most sufficiently in the preceding chapter.

Now could the man in the moon be told, that a man in the earth had wrote a chapter, sufficiently demonstrating, That the secret of all health depended upon the due contention for mastery betwixt the *radical heat* and the *radical moisture,*—— and that he had managed the point so well, that there was not one single word wet or dry upon radical heat or radical moisture, throughout the whole chapter,——or a single syllable in it, *pro* or *con,* directly or indirectly, upon the contention be-

[1]See p. 296, n. 1.

twixt these two powers in any part of the animal œconomy——
"O thou eternal maker of all beings!"——he would cry,
striking his breast with his right hand, (in case he had one)
——"Thou whose power and goodness can enlarge the faculties of thy creatures to this infinite degree of excellence and
perfection,——What have we Moonites done?"

CHAP. XXXIV.

WITH two strokes, the one at *Hippocrates*,[1] the other at
Lord *Verulam*,[2] did my father atchieve it.

The stroke at the prince of physicians, with which he began,
was no more than a short insult upon his sorrowful complaint
of the *Ars longa*,——and *Vita brevis*.[3]——Life short, cried my
father,——and the art of healing tedious! And who are we to
thank for both, the one and the other, but the ignorance of
quacks themselves,——and the stage-loads of chymical nos-
trums, and peripatetic lumber, with which in all ages, they
have first flatter'd the world, and at last deceived it.

——O my lord *Verulam!* cried my father, turning from *Hippocrates,* and making his second stroke at him, as the principal of nostrum-mongers, and the fittest to be made an example of to the rest,——What shall I say to thee, my great
lord *Verulam?* What shall I say to thy internal spirit,——thy
opium,——thy salt-petre,——thy greasy unctions,——thy daily
purges,——thy nightly glisters,[4] and succedaneums?

——My father was never at a loss what to say to any man,
upon any subject; and had the least occasion for the exordium
of any man breathing: how he dealt with his lordship's

---

[1]See p. 83, n. 3.

[2]Francis Bacon, Baron Verulam and Viscount St. Albans (1561–1626),
the English philosopher, statesman, scientist, and essayist.

[3]"Art is long, and life is short," the first of the *Aphorisms* of Hippocrates.

[4]Enemas. Succedaneums: substitutes; drugs, frequently of inferior ef-
ficacy, substituted for others.

opinion,——you shall see;——but when——I know not:——
we must first see what his lordship's opinion was.

CHAP. XXXV.

"THE two great causes, which conspire with each other
to shorten life, says lord *Verulam,* are first——

"The internal spirit, which like a gentle flame, wastes the
body down to death:——And secondly, the external air, that
parches the body up to ashes:——which two enemies attacking us on both sides of our bodies together, at length destroy
our organs, and render them unfit to carry on the functions of
life."[1]

This being the state of the case; the road to Longevity was
plain; nothing more being required, says his lordship, but to
repair the waste committed by the internal spirit, by making
the substance of it more thick and dense, by a regular course
of opiates on one side, and by refrigerating the heat of it on
the other, by three grains and a half of salt-petre every morning before you got up.——

Still this frame of ours was left exposed to the inimical
assaults of the air without;——but this was fenced off again
by a course of greasy unctions, which so fully saturated the
pores of the skin, that no spicula[2] could enter;——nor could
any one get out.——This put a stop to all perspiration, sensible and insensible, which being the cause of so many scurvy
distempers——a course of glisters was requisite to carry off
redundant humours,[3]——and render the system compleat.

What my father had to say to my lord of *Verulam's* opiates,
his salt-petre, and greasy unctions and glisters, you shall read,

---

[1]The quotation is a translation of a sentence in the Introduction to
Bacon's *Historia Vitæ et Mortis;* the following paragraphs are a résumé
of the first two of the ten "operations" contributing toward longevity,
which form the central portion of the *Historia.*

[2]Spicule; small, splinter-like body.

[3]See p. 4, n. 1.

——but not to day—or to morrow: time presses upon me,——
my reader is impatient——I must get forwards.——You shall
read the chapter at your leisure, (if you chuse it) as soon as
ever the *Tristrapædia* is published.——

Sufficeth it at present, to say, my father levelled the hypothesis with the ground, and in doing that, the learned know,
he built up and established his own.——

CHAP. XXXVI.

THE whole secret of health, said my father, beginning the
sentence again, depending evidently upon the due contention betwixt the radical heat and radical moisture within us;
——the least imaginable skill had been sufficient to have maintained it, had not the schoolmen confounded the task, merely
(as *Van Helmont,* the famous chymist,[1] has proved) by all
along mistaking the radical moisture for the tallow and fat of
animal bodies.

Now the radical moisture is not the tallow or fat of animals,
but an oily and balsamous substance; for the fat and tallow,
as also the phlegm or watery parts are cold; whereas the oily
and balsamous parts are of a lively heat and spirit, which
accounts for the observation of *Aristotle,* "*Quod omne animal
post coitum est* triste."[2]

Now it is certain, that the radical heat lives in the radical
moisture, but whether *vice versâ,* is a doubt: however, when
the one decays, the other decays also; and then is produced,
either an unnatural heat, which causes an unnatural dryness
——or an unnatural moisture, which causes dropsies.——So

[1] Jean-Baptiste van Helmont (1577–1644) was a Flemish physician and
chemist; the reference is to his essay, "Humidum Radicale," in the
Supplementum to his chief work, the *Ortus Medicinæ* (ed. Lyons, 1655,
pp. 438–441).

[2] After coition, every creature is dejected. This apophthegm, sometimes followed by facetious exceptions to the rule, has been traditionally
assigned to Aristotle. It is a paraphrase of passages found in his *Of the
Generation of Animals,* 1.18 (725b), and *Problems,* 4.6 (877a), 4.12
(877b), 4.21 (879a), and 30.1 (955a).

that if a child, as he grows up, can but be taught to avoid running into fire or water, as either of 'em threaten his destruction,——'twill be all that is needful to be done upon that head.——

CHAP. XXXVII.

THE description of the siege of *Jerico* itself, could not have engaged the attention of my uncle *Toby* more powerfully than the last chapter;——his eyes were fixed upon my father, throughout it;——he never mentioned radical heat and radical moisture, but my uncle *Toby* took his pipe out of his mouth, and shook his head; and as soon as the chapter was finished, he beckoned to the corporal to come close to his chair, to ask him the following question,——*aside.*—— *   *   *   *   *
*   *   *   *   *   *   *   *   *   *   * . It was at the siege of *Limerick,*[1] an' please your honour, replied the corporal, making a bow.

The poor fellow and I, quoth my uncle *Toby,* addressing himself to my father, were scarce able to crawl out of our tents, at the time the siege of *Limerick* was raised, upon the very account you mention.——Now what can have got into that precious noddle of thine, my dear brother *Toby?* cried my father, mentally.——By Heaven! continued he, communing still with himself, it would puzzle an *Œdipus*[2] to bring it in point.——

I believe, an' please your honour, quoth the corporal, that if it had not been for the quantity of brandy we set fire to every night, and the claret and cinnamon with which I plyed your honour off;——And the geneva, *Trim,* added my uncle *Toby,* which did us more good than all——I verily believe, continued the corporal, we had both, an' please your honour, left our lives in the trenches, and been buried in them too.——

---

[1]Limerick was besieged in 1690 by William III, who was forced to raise the siege August 30 because of the heavy rains.

[2]In Greek legend, Œdipus solved the famous riddle of the Sphinx; hence, anyone with unusual skill at solving riddles.

The noblest grave, corporal! cried my uncle *Toby*, his eyes sparkling as he spoke, that a soldier could wish to lie down in.——But a pitiful death for him! an' please your honour, replied the corporal.

All this was as much *Arabick* to my father, as the rites of the *Colchi* and *Troglodites* had been before to my uncle *Toby*; my father could not determine whether he was to frown or smile.——

My uncle *Toby*, turning to *Yorick*, resumed the case at *Limerick*, more intelligibly than he had begun it,——and so settled the point for my father at once.

CHAP. XXXVIII.

IT was undoubtedly, said my uncle *Toby*, a great happiness for myself and the corporal, that we had all along a burning fever, attended with a most raging thirst, during the whole five and twenty days the flux was upon us in the camp; otherwise what my brother calls the radical moisture, must, as I conceive it, inevitably have got the better.——My father drew in his lungs top-full of air, and looking up, blew it forth again, as slowly as he possibly could.——

——It was heaven's mercy to us, continued my uncle *Toby*, which put it into the corporal's head to maintain that due contention betwixt the radical heat and the radical moisture, by reinforcing the fever, as he did all along, with hot wine and spices; whereby the corporal kept up (as it were) a continual firing, so that the radical heat stood its ground from the beginning to the end, and was a fair match for the moisture, terrible as it was.——Upon my honour, added my uncle *Toby*, you might have heard the contention within our bodies, brother *Shandy*, twenty toises.[1]——If there was no firing, said *Yorick*.

Well——said my father, with a full aspiration, and pausing a while after the word——Was I a judge, and the laws of the

----
[1] See p. 83, n. 5.

country which made me one permitted it, I would condemn some of the worst malefactors, provided they had had their clergy —— —— —— —— —— ——

——*Yorick* foreseeing the sentence was likely to end with no sort of mercy, laid his hand upon my father's breast, and begged he would respite it for a few minutes, till he asked the corporal a question.——Prithee, *Trim,* said *Yorick,* without staying for my father's leave,——tell us honestly——what is thy opinion concerning this self-same radical heat and radical moisture?

With humble submission to his honour's better judgment, quoth the corporal, making a bow to my uncle *Toby*——Speak thy opinion freely, corporal, said my uncle *Toby.*——The poor fellow is my servant,——not my slave,——added my uncle *Toby,* turning to my father.——

The corporal put his hat under his left arm, and with his stick hanging upon the wrist of it, by a black thong split into a tassel about the knot, he marched up to the ground where he had performed his catechism; then touching his under jaw with the thumb and fingers of his right hand before he opened his mouth,——he delivered his notion thus.

CHAP. XXXIX.

JUST as the corporal was humming, to begin——in waddled Dr. *Slop.*——'Tis not two-pence matter——the corporal shall go on in the next chapter, let who will come in.——

Well, my good doctor, cried my father sportively, for the transitions of his passions were unaccountably sudden,——and what has this whelp of mine to say to the matter?——

Had my father been asking after the amputation of the tail of a puppy-dog——he could not have done it in a more careless air: the system which Dr. *Slop* had laid down, to treat the accident by, no way allowed of such a mode of enquiry. ——He sat down.

Pray, Sir, quoth my uncle *Toby,* in a manner which could

not go unanswered,——in what condition is the boy?——
'Twill end in a *phimosis*,[1] replied Dr. *Slop*.

I am no wiser than I was, quoth my uncle *Toby*,——returning his pipe into his mouth.——Then let the corporal go on,
said my father, with his medical lecture.——The corporal
made a bow to his old friend, Dr. *Slop,* and then delivered his
opinion concerning radical heat and radical moisture, in the
following words.

CHAP. XL.

THE city of *Limerick,* the siege of which was begun under
his majesty king *William* himself, the year after I went
into the army——lies, an' please your honours, in the middle
of a devilish wet, swampy country.——'Tis quite surrounded,
said my uncle *Toby,* with the *Shannon,* and is, by its situation,
one of the strongest fortified places in *Ireland.*——

I think this is a new fashion, quoth Dr. *Slop,* of beginning a
medical lecture.——'Tis all true, answered *Trim.*——Then I
wish the faculty[1] would follow the cut of it, said *Yorick.*——
'Tis all cut through, an' please your reverence, said the corporal, with drains and bogs; and besides, there was such a
quantity of rain fell during the siege, the whole country was
like a puddle,——'twas that, and nothing else, which brought
on the flux, and which had like to have killed both his honour
and myself; now there was no such thing, after the first ten
days, continued the corporal, for a soldier to lie dry in his
tent, without cutting a ditch round it, to draw off the water;
——nor was that enough, for those who could afford it, as his
honour could, without setting fire every night to a pewter dish
full of brandy, which took off the damp of the air, and made
the inside of the tent as warm as a stove.——

And what conclusion dost thou draw, Corporal *Trim,* cried
my father, from all these premises?

---

[1] A narrowing of the preputial orifice.
[1] See p. 257, n. 20.

I infer, an' please your worship, replied *Trim,* that the radical moisture is nothing in the world but ditch-water——and that the radical heat, of those who can go to the expence of it, is burnt brandy——the radical heat and moisture of a private man, an' please your honours, is nothing but ditch-water—— and a dram of geneva——and give us but enough of it, with a pipe of tobacco, to give us spirits, and drive away the vapours[2] ——we know not what it is to fear death.

I am at a loss, Captain *Shandy,* quoth Doctor *Slop,* to determine in which branch of learning your servant shines most, whether in physiology, or divinity.——*Slop* had not forgot *Trim's* comment upon the sermon.——

It is but an hour ago, replied *Yorick,* since the corporal was examined in the latter, and pass'd muster with great honour.——

The radical heat and moisture, quoth Doctor *Slop,* turning to my father, you must know, is the basis and foundation of our being,——as the root of a tree is the source and principle of its vegetation.——It is inherent in the seeds of all animals, and may be preserved sundry ways, but principally in my opinion by *consubstantials,*[3] *impriments,* and *occludents.*—— Now this poor fellow, continued Dr. *Slop,* pointing to the corporal, has had the misfortune to have heard some superficial emperic discourse upon this nice point.——That he has,—— said my father.——Very likely, said my uncle.——I'm sure of it——quoth *Yorick.*——

CHAP. XLI.

DOCTOR *Slop* being called out to look at a cataplasm he had ordered, it gave my father an opportunity of going on with another chapter in the *Tristra-pœdia.*——Come! chear

---

[2]Moisture in the air; also, depression of spirit, hypochondria.

[3]Medicaments of like or fortifying nature. Impriments: "something that impresses or imprints" (O.E.D.). Occludents: medicaments of closing or retaining nature. The phrase is taken from Bacon's *Historia Vitæ et Mortis,* Canon 26.

up, my lads; I'll shew you land——for when we have tugged through that chapter, the book shall not be opened again this twelve-month.——Huzza!——

CHAP. XLII.

——FIVE years with a bib under his chin;
         Four years in travelling from Christ-cross-row[1] to *Malachi;*
A year and a half in learning to write his own name;
Seven long years and more τύπτω-ing[2] it, at Greek and Latin;
Four years at his *probations* and his *negations*——the fine statue still lying in the middle of the marble block,——and nothing done, but his tools sharpened to hew it out!——'Tis a piteous delay!——Was not the great *Julius Scaliger*[3] within an ace of never getting his tools sharpened at all?——Forty-four years old was he before he could manage his Greek;—— and *Peter Damianus,*[4] lord bishop of *Ostia,* as all the world knows, could not so much as read, when he was of man's estate.——And *Baldus*[5] himself, as eminent as he turned out after, entered upon the law so late in life, that every body

---

[1] The alphabet; so called from the figure of a cross prefixed to it in horn-books. The Old Testament, of which Malachi is the last book, was in the old schools the text book of the highest class in reading.

[2] Pounding, slogging away; this word was formerly used as a paradigm of the Greek verb. Probations and negations: study of logic.

[3] Julius Cæsar Scaliger (1484–1558) was a distinguished Italian humanist, philosopher, and scientist who, although he did not commence serious study until he was nearly forty years of age, had attained at his death the highest scientific and literary reputation of any man in Europe.

[4] St. Pietro Damiani (c.1007–1072), cardinal and reformer, entered a religious life after a neglected youth spent in privation and ignorance.

[5] Petrus Baldus (1327–1406) was an eminent Italian jurist (see p. 329, n. *). But the story that he began to study law at the age of forty and that his master said to him, "You come late, Baldus; you will be an advocate in the other world," is apocryphal; actually, he was admitted to the degree of Doctor of Civil Law at the early age of seventeen.

imagined he intended to be an advocate in the other world: no wonder, when *Eudamidas*,[6] the son of *Archidamas,* heard *Xenocrates* at seventy-five disputing about *wisdom,* that he asked gravely,——*If the old man be yet disputing and enquiring concerning wisdom,——what time will he have to make use of it?*

Yorick listened to my father with great attention; there was a seasoning of wisdom unaccountably mixed up with his strangest whims, and he had sometimes such illuminations in the darkest of his eclipses, as almost attoned for them:——be wary, Sir, when you imitate him.

I am convinced, *Yorick,* continued my father, half reading and half discoursing, that there is a North-west passage[7] to the intellectual world; and that the soul of man has shorter ways of going to work, in furnishing itself with knowledge and instruction, than we generally take with it.——But alack! all fields have not a river or a spring running besides them;—— every child, *Yorick!* has not a parent to point it out.

——The whole entirely depends, added my father, in a low voice, upon the *auxiliary verbs,* Mr. *Yorick.*

Had *Yorick* trod upon *Virgil's* snake,[8] he could not have looked more surprised.——I am surprised too, cried my father, observing it,——and I reckon it as one of the greatest calamities which ever befell the republick of letters, That those who have been entrusted with the education of our children, and whose business it was to open their minds, and stock them early with ideas, in order to set the imagination loose upon them, have made so little use of the auxiliary verbs in doing

---

[6]Eudamidas I (fl. c.330 B.C.), King of Sparta, son of Archidamus III. Xenocrates (396–314) was an eminent Greek philosopher and head of the Platonic Academy at Athens. The story is found in Plutarch's *Apophthegmata.*

[7]An allusion to the long-sought passage from the Atlantic to the Pacific by the northern coast of America; figuratively, a short-cut.

[8]An allusion to the *Culex,* generally attributed to Virgil and thought by some critics to have been autobiographical; the poem tells how a gnat, stinging the sleeping speaker, awakened him just in time to escape the sting of an approaching snake.

it, as they have done——So that, except *Raymond Lullius,*[9] and the elder *Pelegrini,* the last of which arrived to such perfection in the use of 'em, with his topics, that in a few lessons, he could teach a young gentleman to discourse with plausibility upon any subject, *pro* and *con,* and to say and write all that could be spoken or written concerning it, without blotting a word, to the admiration of all who beheld him.——I should be glad, said *Yorick,* interrupting my father, to be made to comprehend this matter. You shall, said my father.

The highest stretch of improvement a single word is capable of, is a high metaphor,——for which, in my opinion, the idea is generally the worse, and not the better;——but be that as it may,——when the mind has done that with it——there is an end,——the mind and the idea are at rest,——until a second idea enters;——and so on.

Now the use of the *Auxiliaries* is, at once to set the soul a going by herself upon the materials as they are brought her; and by the versability of this great engine, round which they are twisted, to open new tracks of enquiry, and make every idea engender millions.

You excite my curiosity greatly, said *Yorick.*

For my own part, quoth my uncle *Toby,* I have given it up. ——The *Danes,* an' please your honour, quoth the corporal, who were on the left at the siege of *Limerick,* were all auxiliaries.——And very good ones, said my uncle *Toby.*——But the auxiliaries, *Trim,* my brother is talking about,——I conceive to be different things.——

——You do? said my father, rising up.

---

[9]Raimon Lull (c.1235–1315) was a Spanish mystic and missionary whose philosophical treatises contain incoherent formulæ to which, he declared, every demonstration in science may be reduced. Matteo Pellegrini (d.1652) was an Italian humanist, the author of *I Fonti dell' ingegno ridotti ad arte;* he developed a system of predication (which, as it was reported and recommended by Obadiah Walker (1616–1699), master of University College, Oxford, in his *Of Education,* 1.11, is burlesqued in the following pages) by which a gentleman "arrived to such a perfection, as to be able in a short time to write, without defacing one word, many pages concerning any the meanest subject proposed to him; to the great admiration of as many as knew him."

CHAP. XLIII.

MY father took a single turn across the room, then sat down and finished the chapter.

The verbs auxiliary we are concerned in here, continued my father, are, *am; was; have; had; do; did; make; made; suffer; shall; should; will; would; can; could; owe; ought; used; or is wont.*——And these varied with tenses, *present, past, future,* and conjugated with the verb *see,*——or with these questions added to them;——*Is it? Was it? Will it be? Would it be? May it be? Might it be?* And these again put negatively, *Is it not? Was it not? Ought it not?*——Or affirmatively,——*It is; It was; It ought to be.* Or chronologically,——*Has it been always? Lately? How long ago?*——Or hypothetically,——*If it was; If it was not?* What would follow?——If the *French* should beat the *English?* If the *Sun* go out of the *Zodiac?*

Now, by the right use and application of these, continued my father, in which a child's memory should be exercised, there is no one idea can enter his brain how barren soever, but a magazine[1] of conceptions and conclusions may be drawn forth from it.——Did'st thou ever see a white bear? cried my father, turning his head round to *Trim,* who stood at the back of his chair:——No, an' please your honour, replied the corporal.——But thou could'st discourse about one, *Trim,* said my father, in case of need?——How is it possible, brother, quoth my uncle *Toby,* if the corporal never saw one?——'Tis the fact I want; replied my father,——and the possibility of it, is as follows.

A WHITE BEAR! Very well. Have I ever seen one? Might I ever have seen one? Am I ever to see one? Ought I ever to have seen one? Or can I ever see one?

Would I had seen a white bear! (for how can I imagine it?)

---

[1]Storehouse.

If I should see a white bear, what should I say?   If I should
never see a white bear, what then?

If I never have, can, must or shall see a white bear alive;
have I ever seen the skin of one?   Did I ever see one painted?
—described?   Have I never dreamed of one?

Did my father, mother, uncle, aunt, brothers or sisters, ever
see a white bear?   What would they give?   How would they
behave?   How would the white bear have behaved?   Is he
wild?   Tame?   Terrible?   Rough?   Smooth?

——Is the white bear worth seeing?——

——Is there no sin in it?——

Is it better than a BLACK ONE?

 END of the FIFTH VOLUME.

VOLUME VI.[1]

CHAP. I.

——WE'LL not stop two moments, my dear Sir,——only, as we have got thro' these five volumes, (do, Sir, sit down upon a set——they are better than nothing) let us just look back upon the country we have pass'd through.——

——What a wilderness has it been! and what a mercy that we have not both of us been lost, or devoured by wild beasts in it.

Did you think the world itself, Sir, had contained such a number of Jack Asses?[2]——How they view'd and review'd us as we passed over the rivulet at the bottom of that little valley!——and when we climbed over that hill, and were just getting out of sight——good God! what a braying did they all set up together!

——Prithee, shepherd! who keeps all those Jack Asses? * * *

——Heaven be their comforter——What! are they never curried?——Are they never taken in in winter?——Bray bray ——bray. Bray on,——the world is deeply your debtor;—— louder still——that's nothing;——in good sooth, you are ill-used:——Was I a Jack Asse, I solemnly declare, I would bray in G-sol-re-ut[3] from morning, even unto night.

---

[1]Published, with Volume 5, in December, 1761.

[2]A conventional epithet for unfavorable literary critics, applied here to those who had deprecated the third and fourth volumes of *Shandy*.

[3]The upper G of the bass; an expression occasionally used to suggest a high, strident cry.

CHAP. II.

WHEN my father had danced his white bear backwards and forwards through half a dozen pages, he closed the book for good an' all,——and in a kind of triumph redelivered it into *Trim*'s hand, with a nod to lay it upon the 'scrutoire where he found it.——*Tristram, said he, shall be made to conjugate every word in the dictionary, backwards and forwards the same way;——every word, *Yorick*, by this means, you see, is converted into a thesis or an hypothesis;——every thesis and hypothesis have an offspring of propositions;—— and each proposition has its own consequences and conclusions; every one of which leads the mind on again, into fresh tracks of enquiries and doubtings.——The force of this engine, added my father, is incredible, in opening a child's head. ——'Tis enough, brother *Shandy*, cried my uncle *Toby*, to burst it into a thousand splinters.——

I presume, said *Yorick*, smiling,——it must be owing to this, ——(for let logicians say what they will, it is not to be accounted for sufficiently from the bare use of the ten predicaments[1])——That the famous *Vincent Quirino*,[2] amongst the many other astonishing feats of his childhood, of which the Cardinal *Bembo* has given the world so exact a story,—— should be able to paste up in the publick schools at *Rome,* so early as in the eighth year of his age, no less than four thousand, five hundred, and sixty different theses, upon the most abstruse points of the most abstruse theology;——and to defend and maintain them in such sort, as to cramp and dumb-

---

[1]The ten predicaments or categories of Aristotle, the ultimate conceptions to which all knowledge can be reduced, are: substance, quantity, quality, relation, place, time, position, possession, activity, and passivity.

[2]Vincenzo Quirino (1479–c.1514), a noble Venetian humanist, philosopher, and diplomat, of whose precocity, as related by his friend Cardinal Pietro Bembo (1470–1547), Italian scholar and historian of Venice, in his *De Culice Virgilii,* Sterne found an account in Baillet, *Des Enfans celebres.*

found his opponents.——What is that, cried my father, to
what is told us of *Alphonsus Tostatus*,[3] who, almost in his
nurse's arms, learned all the sciences and liberal arts without
being taught any one of them?——What shall we say of the
great *Piereskius*?[4]——That's the very man, cried my uncle
Toby, I once told you of, brother *Shandy*, who walked a matter of five hundred miles, reckoning from *Paris* to *Schevling*,
and from *Schevling* back again, merely to see *Stevinus*'s flying
chariot.——He was a very great man! added my uncle *Toby*;
(meaning *Stevinus*)——He was so; brother *Toby*, said my
father, (meaning *Piereskius*)——and had multiplied his ideas
so fast, and increased his knowledge to such a prodigious
stock, that, if we may give credit to an anecdote concerning
him, 'which we cannot withhold here, without shaking the
authority of all anecdotes whatever——at seven years of age,
his father committed entirely to his care the education of his
younger brother, a boy of five years old,——with the sole management of all his concerns.——Was the father as wise as the
son? quoth my uncle *Toby*:——I should think not, said
Yorick:——But what are these, continued my father——
(breaking out in a kind of enthusiasm)——what are these,
to those prodigies of childhood in *Grotius*,[5] *Scioppius, Hein-*

---

[3]Alfonso Tostado (c.1400–1455) was an eminent Spanish theologian and
author of many works and commentaries who by the age of twenty-two
had received his doctorate and was said to have mastered the whole circle
of human knowledge.

[4]Peiresc (for whom, see p. 117, n. 3), an unusually attentive child, was
at the age of seven sent to school at San Maximitan College at Brinonia,
whither he was accompanied by his five-year-old brother Palamede (afterwards called Valavesius) whom he had persuaded his father to commit
to his care as overseer of his studies.

[5]Hugo Grotius (1583–1645), the Dutch statesman, jurist, theologian,
and poet, founder of the science of international law, wrote good
Latin verses at nine, entered the university at twelve, at fifteen edited
the encyclopædic work of Martianus Capella, and at sixteen took the degree of doctor of law and entered on practice as an advocate. Schoppe
(for whom, see p. 52, n. 7) was renowned for his youthful genius and
learning, and before he was twenty-four years of age had published half
a score of critical and other works. Both Daniel Heinsius (1580–1655)
and his son Nikolaes (1620–1681), Dutch classical philologists, were
remarkable for their youthful attainments; this reference is probably

sius, Politian, Pascal, Joseph Scaliger, Ferdinand de Cordouè,
and others——some of which left off their *substantial forms* at
nine years old, or sooner, and went on reasoning without
them;——others went through their classics at seven;——
wrote tragedies at eight;——*Ferdinand de Cordouè* was so
wise at nine,——'twas thought the Devil was in him;——and
at *Venice* gave such proofs of his knowledge and goodness,
that the monks imagined he was *Antichrist*, or nothing.——
Others were masters of fourteen languages at ten,——finished
the course of their rhetoric, poetry, logic, and ethics at eleven,
——put forth their commentaries upon *Servius*[6] and *Martianus
Capella* at twelve,——and at thirteen received their degrees
in philosophy, laws, and divinity:——But you forget the great
Lipsius,[7] quoth *Yorick,* who composed a work * the day he

---

to the father (who, along with most of the other prodigies in this list, is
noted in Baillet, *op. cit.*), who at the age of ten was renowned for a
Latin elegy, and at fourteen entered the university of Leyden where at
twenty he began to explicate the classics and at twenty-five he held the
chair of history and politics. Angelo Poliziano (for whom see p. 390,
n. 1) at the age of thirteen circulated Latin letters, at sixteen translated
four books of the *Iliad* into Latin hexameters, at seventeen sent forth
essays in Greek versification, and at eighteen published an edition of
Catullus. Blaise Pascal (1623–1662), the French religious philosopher
and mathematician, was so zealous a student that although books were
denied him for a while he continued his speculations unaided, invented
geometry anew at the age of twelve, and achieved fame at the age of
seventeen with his treatise on conic sections. Joseph Justus Scaliger
(1540–1609), the son of Julius Cæsar Scaliger (for whom, see p. 403,
n. 3), was famous for his precocity in Latin and Greek. Ferdinand of
Cordova (1422–c.1480), a Spanish theologian, physician, and scholar, was
celebrated at an early age for his prodigious memory and wisdom.

[6]Marius Servius Honoratus (fl. 400 A.D.) was a Roman grammarian and
writer of a commentary on Virgil which was itself the subject of numerous
commentaries. Martianus Capella (fl. 5th C.) was a Latin writer whose
De Nuptiis Philologiæ et Mercurii et de Septem Artibus Liberalibus, an
encyclopædia of the liberal culture of his time, was highly reputed and
frequently commented upon during the Middle Ages.

[7]Justus Lipsius (1547–1606), a Flemish philologist and critic.

*Nous aurions quelque interêt, says *Baillet,* de montrer qu'il n' a rien
de ridicule s'il étoit véritable, au moins dans le sense énigmatique que
Nicius Erythræus a tâché de lui donner. Cet auteur dit que pour com-
prendre comme *Lipse,* a pû composer un ouvrage le premier jour de sa
vie, il faut s'imaginer, que ce premier jour n'est pas celui de sa naissance
charnelle, mais celui au quel il a commencé d'user de la raison; il veut que

was born;——They should have wiped it up, said my uncle
Toby, and said no more about it.

CHAP. III.

WHEN the cataplasm was ready, a scruple of *decorum*
had unseasonably rose up in *Susannah's* conscience
about holding the candle, whilst *Slop* tied it on; *Slop* had not
treated *Susannah's* distemper with anodines,——and so a quarrel had ensued betwixt them.

——Oh! oh!——said *Slop,* casting a glance of undue freedom in *Susannah's* face, as she declined the office;——then, I
think I know you, madam——You know me, Sir! cried *Susannah* fastidiously, and with a toss of her head, levelled evidently,
not at his profession, but at the doctor himself,——you know
me! cried *Susannah* again.——Dr. *Slop* clapped his finger and
his thumb instantly upon his nostrils;——*Susannah's* spleen
was ready to burst at it;——'Tis false, said *Susannah.*——
Come, come, Mrs. Modesty, said *Slop,* not a little elated with
the success of his last thrust,——if you won't hold the candle,
and look——you may hold it and shut your eyes:——That's
one of your popish shifts, cried *Susannah:*——'Tis better, said
Slop, with a nod, than no shift at all, young woman;——I
defy you, sir, cried *Susannah,* pulling her shift sleeve below
her elbow.

It was almost impossible for two persons to assist each
other in a surgical case with a more splenetic cordiality.

çait été à l'age de *neuf* ans; et il nous veut persuader que ce fut en cet
âge, que *Lipse* fit un poème.——Le tour est ingenieux, &c. &c. [Sterne's
note. This passage, taken with slight variations from Baillet, *op. cit.,*
may be translated as follows: "We should have some interest, says Baillet,
in showing that there is nothing ridiculous, if it was true, at least in
the enigmatic sense which Nicius Erythræus has attempted to give it.
This author says that to understand how Lipsius may have composed a
work the first day of his life it is necessary to imagine that the first day is
not that of his birth in the flesh, but that on which he commenced to use
his reason; he maintains that it was at the age of nine years, and he wishes
to persuade us that it was at that age that Lipsius wrote a poem.——
The attempt is ingenious, etc. etc."]

Slop snatched up the cataplasm,——*Susannah* snatched up the candle;——a little this way, said *Slop; Susannah* looking one way, and rowing another, instantly set fire to *Slop's* wig, which being somewhat bushy and unctuous withal, was burnt out before it was well kindled.——You impudent whore! cried *Slop,*——(for what is passion, but a wild beast)——you impudent whore, cried *Slop,* getting upright, with the cataplasm in his hand;——I never was the destruction of any body's nose,[1] said *Susannah,*——which is more than you can say:——Is it? cried *Slop,* throwing the cataplasm in her face; ——Yes, it is, cried *Susannah,* returning the compliment with what was left in the pan.——

CHAP. IV.

DOCTOR *Slop* and *Susannah* filed cross-bills against each other in the parlour; which done, as the cataplasm had failed, they retired into the kitchen to prepare a fomentation for me;——and whilst that was doing, my father determined the point as you will read.

CHAP. V.

YOU see 'tis high time, said my father, addressing himself equally to my uncle *Toby* and *Yorick,* to take this young creature out of these women's hands, and put him into those of a private governor. *Marcus Antoninus*[1] provided fourteen governors all at once to superintend his son *Commodus's* education,——and in six weeks he cashiered five of them;——I know very well, continued my father, that *Commodus's* mother was in love with a gladiator at the time of her concep-

---

[1]An allusion to the characteristic ravage of the "French disease."

[1]Although Marcus Aurelius Antoninus (121–180), Roman emperor and Stoic philosopher, carefully educated his son, Commodus (161–192) displayed as emperor a cruel and detestable character.

tion, which accounts for a great many of *Commodus's* cruel-
ties when he became emperor;——but still I am of opinion,
that those five whom *Antoninus* dismissed, did *Commodus's*
temper in that short time, more hurt than the other nine were
able to rectify all their lives long.

Now as I consider the person who is to be about my son, as
the mirror in which he is to view himself from morning to
night, and by which he is to adjust his looks, his carriage, and
perhaps the inmost sentiments of his heart;——I would have
one, *Yorick,* if possible, polished at all points, fit for my child
to look into.——This is very good sense, quoth my uncle
Toby to himself.

——There is, continued my father, a certain mien and motion of the body and all its parts, both in acting and speaking,
which argues a man *well within;* and I am not at all surprized
that *Gregory* of *Nazianzum,*[2] upon observing the hasty and
untoward gestures of *Julian,* should foretel he would one day
become an apostate;——or that St. *Ambrose*[3] should turn his
Amanuensis out of doors, because of an indecent motion of his
head, which went backwards and forwards like a flail;——or
that *Democritus*[4] should conceive *Protagoras* to be a scholar,
from seeing him bind up a faggot, and thrusting, as he did it,
the small twigs inwards.——There are a thousand unnoticed
openings, continued my father, which let a penetrating eye at
once into a man's soul; and I maintain it, added he, that a

---

[2]St. Gregory of Nazianzus (c.325–c.389), one of the fathers of the Eastern Church, and Bishop of Constantinople, had been during his youth a
fellow-student at Athens of Julian (Flavius Claudius Julianus (331–363),
the Roman Emperor), and wrote, about 361, two *Invectivæ* against him.
Sterne's reference is to his *Oratio V* ("Secunda in Julianum Imperatorem
Invectiva"), 23.

[3]Apparently an allusion to the *De Officiis Ministrorum,* 1.72, of St.
Ambrose (c.340–397), one of the fathers of the Latin Church, and
Bishop of Milan.

[4]See p. 483, n. 2. Protagoras (c.481–c.411 B.C.) was a Greek Sophist,
born at Abdera and said, though doubtfully, to have been a pupil of
Democritus. The story, probably apocryphal, is that Protagoras was
originally a poor porter whose skill in fastening together and poising upon
his shoulders a large bundle of wood attracted the attention of Democritus who, taking a liking to him, cared for and instructed him

man of sense does not lay down his hat in coming into a room,
——or take it up in going out of it, but something escapes,
which discovers him.

It is for these reasons, continued my father, that the governor I make choice of shall neither * lisp, or squint, or wink, or
talk loud, or look fierce, or foolish;——or bite his lips, or
grind his teeth, or speak through his nose, or pick it, or blow
it with his fingers.——

He shall neither walk fast,——or slow, or fold his arms,——
for that is laziness;——or hang them down,——for that is folly;
or hide them in his pocket, for that is nonsense.——

He shall neither strike, or pinch, or tickle,——or bite, or
cut his nails, or hawk, or spit, or snift, or drum with his feet
or fingers in company;——nor (according to *Erasmus*[5]) shall
he speak to any one in making water,——nor shall he point to
carrion or excrement.——Now this is all nonsense again, quoth
my uncle *Toby* to himself.——

I will have him, continued my father, cheerful, faceté,[6] jovial;
at the same time, prudent, attentive to business, vigilant,
acute, argute, inventive, quick in resolving doubts and speculative questions;——he shall be wise and judicious, and
learned:——And why not humble, and moderate, and gentle
tempered, and good? said *Yorick:*——And why not, cried my
uncle *Toby,* free, and generous, and bountiful, and brave?——
He shall, my dear *Toby,* replied my father, getting up and
shaking him by his hand.——Then, brother *Shandy,* answered
my uncle *Toby,* raising himself off the chair, and laying down
his pipe to take hold of my father's other hand,——I humbly
beg I may recommend poor *Le Fever's* son to you;——a tear
of joy of the first water sparkled in my uncle *Toby's* eye,——
and another, the fellow to it, in the corporal's, as the proposition was made;——you will see why when you read *Le Fever's*
story:——fool that I was! nor can I recollect, (nor perhaps

---

*Vid. *Pellegrina.* [Sterne's note. See p. 405, n. 9.]

[5]In his *Colloquia,* "In Primo Congressu"; the original reads: "*Sed
incivilius etiam eum salutare, qui reddit urinam, aut alvum exonerat.*"

[6]Facetious, pleasant.

you) without turning back to the place, what it was that hindered me from letting the corporal tell it in his own words; ——but the occasion is lost,——I must tell it now in my own.

CHAP. VI.

The Story of LE FEVER.

IT was some time in the summer of that year[1] in which *Dendermond* was taken by the allies,——which was about seven years before my father came into the country,——and about as many, after the time, that my uncle *Toby* and *Trim* had privately decamped from my father's house in town, in order to lay some of the finest sieges to some of the finest fortified cities in *Europe*——when my uncle *Toby* was one evening getting his supper, with *Trim* sitting behind him at a small sideboard,——I say, sitting——for in consideration of the corporal's lame knee (which sometimes gave him exquisite pain) ——when my uncle *Toby* dined or supped alone, he would never suffer the corporal to stand; and the poor fellow's veneration for his master was such, that, with a proper artillery, my uncle *Toby* could have taken *Dendermond* itself, with less trouble than he was able to gain this point over him; for many a time when my uncle *Toby* supposed the corporal's leg was at rest, he would look back, and detect him standing behind him with the most dutiful respect: this bred more little squabbles betwixt them, than all other causes for five and twenty years together——But this is neither here nor there——why do I mention it?——Ask my pen,——it governs me,——I govern not it.

He was one evening sitting thus at his supper, when the landlord of a little inn in the village came into the parlour with an empty phial in his hand, to beg a glass or two of sack; 'Tis for a poor gentleman,——I think, of the army, said the landlord, who has been taken ill at my house four days ago,

---

[1]1706.

and has never held up his head since, or had a desire to taste
any thing, till just now, that he has a fancy for a glass of sack
and a thin toast,——*I think,* says he, taking his hand from his
forehead, *it would comfort me.*——

——If I could neither beg, borrow, or buy such a thing,
——added the landlord,——I would almost steal it for the poor
gentleman, he is so ill.——I hope in God he will still mend,
continued he ——we are all of us concerned for him.

Thou art a good natured soul, I will answer for thee, cried
my uncle *Toby;* and thou shalt drink the poor gentleman's
health in a glass of sack thyself,——and take a couple of bottles with my service, and tell him he is heartily welcome to
them, and to a dozen more if they will do him good.

Though I am persuaded, said my uncle *Toby,* as the landlord shut the door, he is a very compassionate fellow——
Trim,——yet I cannot help entertaining a high opinion of his
guest too; there must be something more than common in him,
that in so short a time should win so much upon the affections
of his host;——And of his whole family, added the corporal,
for they are all concerned for him.——Step after him, said my
uncle *Toby,*——do *Trim,*——and ask if he knows his name.

——I have quite forgot it, truly, said the landlord, coming
back into the parlour with the corporal,——but I can ask his
son again:——Has he a son with him then? said my uncle
Toby.——A boy, replied the landlord, of about eleven or twelve
years of age;——but the poor creature has tasted almost as
little as his father; he does nothing but mourn and lament for
him night and day:——He has not stirred from the bedside
these two days.

My uncle *Toby* laid down his knife and fork, and thrust his
plate from before him, as the landlord gave him the account;
and *Trim,* without being ordered, took away without saying
one word, and in a few minutes after brought him his pipe and
tobacco.

——Stay in the room a little, said my uncle *Toby.*——

Trim!——said my uncle *Toby,* after he lighted his pipe, and
smoak'd about a dozen whiffs.——*Trim* came in front of his

master and made his bow;——my uncle *Toby* smoak'd on, and said no more.——Corporal! said my uncle *Toby*——the corporal made his bow.——My uncle *Toby* proceeded no farther, but finished his pipe.

Trim! said my uncle *Toby,* I have a project in my head, as it is a bad night, of wrapping myself up warm in my roquelaure, and paying a visit to this poor gentleman.——Your honour's roquelaure, replied the corporal, has not once been had on, since the night before your honour received your wound, when we mounted guard in the trenches before the gate of St. *Nicholas;*——and besides it is so cold and rainy a night, that what with the roquelaure, and what with the weather, 'twill be enough to give your honour your death, and bring on your honour's torment in your groin. I fear so; replied my uncle *Toby,* but I am not at rest in my mind, *Trim,* since the account the landlord has given me.——I wish I had not known so much of this affair,——added my uncle *Toby,*——or that I had known more of it:——How shall we manage it? Leave it, an't please your honour, to me, quoth the corporal;——I'll take my hat and stick and go to the house and reconnoitre, and act accordingly; and I will bring your honour a full account in an hour.——Thou shalt go, *Trim,* said my uncle *Toby,* and here's a shilling for thee to drink with his servant. ——I shall get it all out of him, said the corporal, shutting the door.

My uncle *Toby* filled his second pipe; and had it not been, that he now and then wandered from the point, with considering whether it was not full as well to have the curtain of the tennaile[2] a straight line, as a crooked one,——he might be said to have thought of nothing else but poor *Le Fever* and his boy the whole time he smoaked it.

---

[2]An outwork of two faces forming a re-entering angle, located in the main ditch in front of the curtain and between two bastions.

CHAP. VII.

The Story of LE FEVER *continued.*

IT was not till my uncle *Toby* had knocked the ashes out of
his third pipe, that corporal *Trim* returned from the inn,
and gave him the following account.

I despaired at first, said the corporal, of being able to bring
back your honour any kind of intelligence concerning the poor
sick lieutenant——Is he in the army then? said my uncle
Toby——He is: said the corporal——And in what regiment?
said my uncle *Toby*——I'll tell your honour, replied the corporal, every thing straight forwards, as I learnt it.——Then,
Trim, I'll fill another pipe, said my uncle *Toby,* and not interrupt thee till thou hast done; so sit down at thy ease, *Trim,* in
the window seat, and begin thy story again. The corporal
made his old bow, which generally spoke as plain as a bow
could speak it——*Your honour is good:*——And having done
that, he sat down, as he was ordered,——and begun the story
to my uncle *Toby* over again in pretty near the same words.

I despaired at first, said the corporal, of being able to bring
back any intelligence to your honour, about the lieutenant and
his son; for when I asked where his servant was, from whom
I made myself sure of knowing every thing which was proper
to be asked,——That's a right distinction, *Trim,* said my uncle
Toby——I was answered, an' please your honour, that he had
no servant with him;——that he had come to the inn with
hired horses, which, upon finding himself unable to proceed,
(to join, I suppose, the regiment) he had dismissed the morning after he came.——If I get better, my dear, said he, as he
gave his purse to his son to pay the man,——we can hire
horses from hence.——But alas! the poor gentleman will never
get from hence, said the landlady to me,——for I heard the
death-watch[1] all night long;——and when he dies, the youth,

---

[1] A beetle whose ticking sound is supposed to portend death.

his son, will certainly die with him; for he is broken hearted already.

I was hearing this account, continued the corporal, when the youth came into the kitchen, to order the thin toast the land-lord spoke of;——but I will do it for my father myself, said the youth.——Pray let me save you the trouble, young gentle-man, said I, taking up a fork for the purpose, and offering him my chair to sit down upon by the fire, whilst I did it.——I believe, Sir, said he, very modestly, I can please him best my-self.——I am sure, said I, his honour will not like the toast the worse for being toasted by an old soldier.——The youth took hold of my hand, and instantly burst into tears.——Poor youth! said my uncle *Toby*,——he has been bred up from an infant in the army, and the name of a soldier, *Trim*, sounded in his ears like the name of a friend;——I wish I had him here.

——I never in the longest march, said the corporal, had so great a mind to my dinner, as I had to cry with him for com-pany:——What could be the matter with me, an' please your honour? Nothing in the world, *Trim*, said my uncle *Toby*, blowing his nose,——but that thou art a good natured fellow.

When I gave him the toast, continued the corporal, I thought it was proper to tell him I was Captain *Shandy's* servant, and that your honour (though a stranger) was ex-tremely concerned for his father;——and that if there was any thing in your house or cellar——(And thou might'st have added my purse too, said my uncle *Toby*)——he was heartily welcome to it:——He made a very low bow, (which was meant to your honour) but no answer,——for his heart was full——so he went up stairs with the toast;——I warrant you, my dear, said I, as I opened the kitchen door, your father will be well again.——Mr. *Yorick's* curate was smoking a pipe by the kitchen fire,——but said not a word good or bad to com-fort the youth.——I thought it wrong; added the corporal—— I think so too, said my uncle *Toby*.

When the lieutenant had taken his glass of sack and toast, he felt himself a little revived, and sent down into the kitchen, to let me know, that in about ten minutes he should be glad if

I would step up stairs.——I believe, said the landlord, he is
going to say his prayers,——for there was a book laid upon
the chair by his bedside, and as I shut the door, I saw his son
take up a cushion.——

I thought, said the curate, that you gentlemen of the army,
Mr. *Trim,* never said your prayers at all.——I heard the poor
gentleman say his prayers last night, said the landlady, very
devoutly, and with my own ears, or I could not have believed
it.——Are you sure of it? replied the curate.——A soldier, an'
please your reverence, said I, prays as often (of his own accord) as a parson;——and when he is fighting for his king,
and for his own life, and for his honour too, he has the most
reason to pray to God, of any one in the whole world——
'Twas well said of thee, *Trim,* said my uncle *Toby.*——But
when a soldier, said I, an' please your reverence, has been
standing for twelve hours together in the trenches, up to his
knees in cold water,——or engaged, said I, for months together in long and dangerous marches;——harrassed, perhaps,
in his rear to-day;——harrassing others to-morrow;——detached here;——countermanded there;——resting this night
out upon his arms;——beat up in his shirt the next;——be-
numbed in his joints;——perhaps without straw in his tent to
kneel on;——must say his prayers *how* and *when* he can.——
I believe, said I,——for I was piqued, quoth the corporal, for
the reputation of the army,——I believe, an' please your reverence, said I, that when a soldier gets time to pray,——he
prays as heartily as a parson,——though not with all his fuss
and hypocrisy.——Thou shouldst not have said that, *Trim,*
said my uncle *Toby,*——for God only knows who is a hypocrite, and who is not:——At the great and general review of
us all, corporal, at the day of judgment, (and not till then)——
it will be seen who has done their duties in this world,——
and who has not; and we shall be advanced, *Trim,* accordingly.——I hope we shall, said *Trim.*——It is in the Scripture,
said my uncle *Toby;* and I will shew it thee to-morrow:——
In the mean time we may depend upon it, *Trim,* for our comfort, said my uncle *Toby,* that God Almighty is so good and

just a governor of the world, that if we have but done our duties in it,——it will never be enquired into, whether we have done them in a red coat or a black one:——I hope not; said the corporal——But go on, *Trim,* said my uncle *Toby,* with thy story.

When I went up, continued the corporal, into the lieutenant's room, which I did not do till the expiration of the ten minutes,——he was lying in his bed with his head raised upon his hand, with his elbow upon the pillow, and a clean white cambrick handkerchief beside it:——The youth was just stooping down to take up the cushion, upon which I supposed he had been kneeling,——the book was laid upon the bed,—— and as he rose, in taking up the cushion with one hand, he reached out his other to take it away at the same time.——Let it remain there, my dear, said the lieutenant.

He did not offer to speak to me, till I had walked up close to his bed-side:——If you are Captain *Shandy*'s servant, said he, you must present my thanks to your master, with my little boy's thanks along with them, for his courtesy to me;——if he was of *Levens's*[2]——said the lieutenant.——I told him your honour was——Then, said he, I served three campaigns with him in *Flanders,* and remember him,——but 'tis most likely, as I had not the honour of any acquaintance with him, that he knows nothing of me.——You will tell him, however, that the person his good nature has laid under obligations to him, is one *Le Fever,* a lieutenant in *Angus's*——but he knows me not,——said he, a second time, musing;——possibly he may my story——added he——pray tell the captain, I was the ensign at *Breda,*[3] whose wife was most unfortunately killed with a musket shot, as she lay in my arms in my tent.——I remember the story, an't please your honour, said I, very well. ——Do you so? said he, wiping his eyes with his handkerchief,——then well may I.——In saying this, he drew a little ring out of his bosom, which seemed tied with a black ribband about his neck, and kiss'd it twice——Here, *Billy,* said

---

[2] For Leven's and Angus's, see p. 380, n. 2.

[3] A town in the Netherlands frequently used for winter quarters.

he,——the boy flew across the room to the bed-side,——and
falling down upon his knee, took the ring in his hand, and
kissed it too,——then kissed his father, and sat down upon
the bed and wept.

I wish, said my uncle *Toby,* with a deep sigh,——I wish,
Trim, I was asleep.

Your honour, replied the corporal, is too much concerned;
——shall I pour your honour out a glass of sack to your pipe?
——Do, *Trim,* said my uncle *Toby.*

I remember, said my uncle *Toby,* sighing again, the story of
the ensign and his wife, with a circumstance his modesty
omitted;——and particularly well that he, as well as she, upon
some account or other, (I forget what) was universally pitied
by the whole regiment;——but finish the story thou art upon:
——'Tis finished already, said the corporal,——for I could
stay no longer,——so wished his honour a good night; young
Le Fever rose from off the bed, and saw me to the bottom of
the stairs; and as we went down together, told me, they had
come from *Ireland,* and were on their route to join the regiment in *Flanders.*——But alas! said the corporal,——the lieutenant's last day's march is over.——Then what is to become
of his poor boy? cried my uncle *Toby.*

CHAP. VIII.

The Story of LE FEVER continued.

IT was to my uncle *Toby's* eternal honour,——though I tell
it only for the sake of those, who, when coop'd in betwixt
a natural and a positive law, know not for their souls, which
way in the world to turn themselves——That notwithstanding my uncle *Toby* was warmly engaged at that time in carrying on the siege of *Dendermond,* parallel with the allies, who
pressed theirs on so vigorously, that they scarce allowed him
time to get his dinner——that nevertheless he gave up *Dendermond,* though he had already made a lodgment upon the

counterscarp;——and bent his whole thoughts towards the private distresses at the inn; and, except that he ordered the garden gate to be bolted up, by which he might be said to have turned the siege of *Dendermond* into a blockade,——he left *Dendermond* to itself,——to be relieved or not by the *French* king, as the *French* king thought good; and only considered how he himself should relieve the poor lieutenant and his son.

——That kind Being, who is a friend to the friendless, shall recompence thee for this.

Thou hast left this matter short, said my uncle *Toby* to the corporal, as he was putting him to bed,——and I will tell thee in what, *Trim*.——In the first place, when thou madest an offer of my services to *Le Fever*,——as sickness and travelling are both expensive, and thou knowest he was but a poor lieutenant, with a son to subsist as well as himself, out of his pay, ——that thou didst not make an offer to him of my purse; because, had he stood in need, thou knowest, *Trim,* he had been as welcome to it as myself.——Your honour knows, said the corporal, I had no orders;——True, quoth my uncle *Toby*,—— thou didst very right, *Trim,* as a soldier,——but certainly very wrong as a man.

In the second place, for which, indeed, thou hast the same excuse, continued my uncle *Toby*,——when thou offeredst him whatever was in my house,——thou shouldst have offered him my house too:——A sick brother officer should have the best quarters, *Trim,* and if we had him with us,——we could tend and look to him:——Thou art an excellent nurse thyself, *Trim,*——and what with thy care of him, and the old woman's, and his boy's, and mine together, we might recruit him again at once, and set him upon his legs.——

——In a fortnight or three weeks, added my uncle *Toby*, smiling,——he might march.——He will never march, an' please your honour, in this world, said the corporal:——He will march; said my uncle *Toby*, rising up from the side of the bed, with one shoe off:——An' please your honour, said the corporal, he will never march, but to his grave:——He shall

march, cried my uncle *Toby,* marching the foot which had a
shoe on, though without advancing an inch,——he shall march
to his regiment.——He cannot stand it, said the corporal;——
He shall be supported, said my uncle *Toby;*——He'll drop at
last, said the corporal, and what will become of his boy?——
He shall not drop, said my uncle *Toby,* firmly.——A-well-o'-
day,——do what we can for him, said *Trim,* maintaining his
point,——the poor soul will die:——He shall not die, by
G—, cried my uncle *Toby.*

——The ACCUSING SPIRIT which flew up to heaven's chancery
with the oath, blush'd as he gave it in;——and the RECORDING
ANGEL as he wrote it down, dropp'd a tear upon the word, and
blotted it out for ever.

CHAP. IX.

——MY uncle *Toby* went to his bureau,——put his purse
into his breeches pocket, and having ordered the
corporal to go early in the morning for a physician,——he
went to bed, and fell asleep.

CHAP. X.

The Story of LE FEVER *concluded.*

THE sun looked bright the morning after, to every eye in
the village but *Le Fever's* and his afflicted son's; the hand
of death press'd heavy upon his eye-lids,——and hardly could
the wheel at the cistern turn round its circle,——when my
uncle *Toby,* who had rose up an hour before his wonted time,
entered the lieutenant's room, and without preface or apology,
sat himself down upon the chair by the bed-side, and inde-
pendantly of all modes and customs, opened the curtain in
the manner an old friend and brother officer would have done
it, and asked him how he did,——how he had rested in the

night,——what was his complaint,——where was his pain,
——and what he could do to help him:——and without giving
him time to answer any one of the enquiries, went on and
told him of the little plan which he had been concerting with
the corporal the night before for him.——

——You shall go home directly, *Le Fever,* said my uncle
Toby, to my house,——and we'll send for a doctor to see what's
the matter,——and we'll have an apothecary,——and the corporal shall be your nurse;——and I'll be your servant, *Le Fever.*

There was a frankness in my uncle *Toby,*——not the *effect*
of familiarity,——but the *cause* of it,——which let you at once
into his soul, and shewed you the goodness of his nature; to
this, there was something in his looks, and voice, and manner,
superadded, which eternally beckoned to the unfortunate to
come and take shelter under him; so that before my uncle
Toby had half finished the kind offers he was making to the
father, had the son insensibly pressed up close to his knees,
and had taken hold of the breast of his coat, and was pulling
it towards him.——The blood and spirits of *Le Fever,* which
were waxing cold and slow within him, and were retreating
to their last citadel, the heart,——rallied back,——the film
forsook his eyes for a moment,——he looked up wishfully in
my uncle *Toby's* face,——then cast a look upon his boy,——
and that *ligament,* fine as it was,——was never broken.——

Nature instantly ebb'd again,——the film returned to its
place,——the pulse fluttered——stopp'd——went on——
throb'd——stopp'd again——moved——stopp'd——shall I go
on?——No.

CHAP. XI.

I Am so impatient to return to my own story, that what
remains of young *Le Fever's,* that is, from this turn of his
fortune, to the time my uncle *Toby* recommended him for my
preceptor, shall be told in a very few words, in the next chapter.——All that is necessary to be added to this chapter is as
follows.——

That my uncle *Toby,* with young *Le Fever* in his hand, attended the poor lieutenant, as chief mourners, to his grave.

That the governor of *Dendermond* paid his obsequies all military honours,——and that *Yorick,* not to be behind hand ——paid him all ecclesiastic——for he buried him in his chancel:——And it appears likewise, he preached a funeral sermon over him——I say it *appears,*——for it was *Yorick's* custom, which I suppose a general one with those of his profession, on the first leaf of every sermon which he composed, to chronicle down the time, the place, and the occasion of its being preached: to this, he was ever wont to add some short comment or stricture upon the sermon itself, seldom, indeed, much to its credit:——For instance, *This sermon upon the jewish dispensation*——*I don't like it at all;*——*Though I own there is a world of* WATER-LANDISH[1] *knowledge in it,*——*but 'tis all tritical, and most tritically put together.*——*This is but a flimsy kind of a composition; what was in my head when I made it?*

——N. B. *The excellency of this text is, that it will suit any sermon,*——*and of this sermon,*——*that it will suit any text.*——

——*For this sermon I shall be hanged,*——*for I have stolen the greatest part of it. Doctor* Paidagunes[2] *found me out.* ☞*Set a thief to catch a thief.*——

On the back of half a dozen I find written, *So, so,* and no more——and upon a couple *Moderato;* by which, as far as one may gather from *Altieri's Italian* dictionary,——but mostly from the authority of a piece of green whipcord, which seemed to have been the unravelling of *Yorick's* whip-lash, with which he has left us the two sermons marked *Moderato,* and the half dozen of *So, so,* tied fast together in one bundle by themselves, ——one may safely suppose he meant pretty near the same thing.

---

[1] An allusion to Dr. Daniel Waterland (1683–1740), from whose sermons Sterne sometimes took hints and materials for his own. Tritical: trite.

[2] "Doctor Pedagogue," a pedant; probably a sneer at one of Sterne's fellow clergymen.

There is but one difficulty in the way of this conjecture, which is this, that the *moderato*'s are five times better than the *so, so*'s;——shew ten times more knowledge of the human heart;——have seventy times more wit and spirit in them; ——(and, to rise properly in my climax)——discover a thousand times more genius;——and to crown all, are infinitely more entertaining than those tied up with them;——for which reason, whene'er *Yorick*'s *dramatic* sermons are offered to the world, though I shall admit but one out of the whole number of the *so, so*'s, I shall, nevertheless, adventure to print the two *moderato*'s without any sort of scruple.

What *Yorick* could mean by the words *lentamente*,[3]—— *tenutè*,——*grave*,——and sometimes *adagio*,——as applied to theological compositions, and with which he has characterized some of these sermons, I dare not venture to guess.——I am more puzzled still upon finding *a l'octava alta!* upon one;—— *Con strepito* upon the back of another;——*Siciliana* upon a third;——*Alla capella* upon a fourth;——*Con l'arco* upon this; ——*Senza l'arco* upon that.——All I know is, that they are musical terms, and have a meaning;——and as he was a musical man, I will make no doubt, but that by some quaint application of such metaphors to the compositions in hand, they impressed very distinct ideas of their several characters upon his fancy,——whatever they may do upon that of others.

Amongst these, there is that particular sermon which has unaccountably led me into this digression——The funeral sermon upon poor *Le Fever,* wrote out very fairly, as if from a hasty copy.——I take notice of it the more, because it seems to have been his favourite composition——It is upon mortality; and is tied length-ways and cross-ways with a yarn thrum, and then rolled up and twisted round with a half sheet of dirty blue paper, which seems to have been once the cast cover of a general review, which to this day smells hor-

---

[3]Slowly. *Tenutè*: sustained, held to its full value. *Grave*: slow, solemn. *Adagio*: slowly, gracefully. *A l'octava alta*: in the high octave. *Con strepito*: uproariously. *Siciliana*: slow (as for a Sicilian dance). *Alla capella*: for a chapel. *Con l'arco*: with the bow (as opposed to pizzicato). *Senza l'arco*: without the bow, pizzicato.

ribly of horse-drugs.[4]——Whether these marks of humiliation
were designed,——I something doubt;——because at the end
of the sermon, (and not at the beginning of it)——very different from his way of treating the rest, he had wrote——

Bravo!

——Though not very offensively,——for it is at two inches,
at least, and a half's distance from, and below the concluding
line of the sermon, at the very extremity of the page, and in
that right hand corner of it, which, you know, is generally covered with your thumb; and, to do it justice, it is wrote besides
with a crow's quill so faintly in a small *Italian* hand, as scarce
to sollicit the eye towards the place, whether your thumb is
there or not,——so that from the *manner of it,* it stands half
excused; and being wrote moreover with very pale ink, diluted
almost to nothing,——'tis more like a *ritratto*[5] of the shadow
of vanity, than of VANITY herself——of the two; resembling
rather a faint thought of transient applause, secretly stirring
up in the heart of the composer, than a gross mark of it,
coarsely obtruded upon the world.

With all these extenuations, I am aware, that in publishing
this, I do no service to *Yorick*'s character as a modest man;
——but all men have their failings! and what lessens this still
farther, and almost wipes it away, is this; that the word was
struck through sometime afterwards (as appears from a different tint of the ink) with a line quite across it in this manner, ~~BRAVO~~—— as if he had retracted, or was ashamed of
the opinion he had once entertained of it.

These short characters of his sermons were always written,
excepting in this one instance, upon the first leaf of his sermon, which served as a cover to it; and usually upon the inside
of it, which was turned towards the text;——but at the end of
his discourse, where, perhaps, he had five or six pages, and
sometimes, perhaps, a whole score to turn himself in,——he

---

[4]Probably a sly jab at the blue-covered *Critical Review,* which had given
Sterne unfavorable reviews, and at its contentious editor, Tobias Smollett,
M.D., who had taken up literary and journalistic work only after failing
as a practicing physician. See p. 628, n. 2.

[5]Portrait.

took a larger circuit, and, indeed, a much more mettlesome one;——as if he had snatched the occasion of unlacing himself with a few more frolicksome strokes at vice, than the straitness of the pulpit allowed.——These, though hussar-like, they skirmish lightly and out of all order, are still auxiliaries on the side of virtue——; tell me then, Mynheer Vander Blonederdondergewdenstronke,[6] why they should not be printed together?

CHAP. XII.

WHEN my uncle *Toby* had turned every thing into money, and settled all accounts betwixt the agent of the regiment and *Le Fever,* and betwixt *Le Fever* and all mankind,——there remained nothing more in my uncle *Toby's* hands, than an old regimental coat and a sword; so that my uncle *Toby* found little or no opposition from the world in taking administration. The coat my uncle *Toby* gave the corporal;——Wear it, *Trim,* said my uncle *Toby,* as long as it will hold together, for the sake of the poor lieutenant——And this,——said my uncle *Toby,* taking up the sword in his hand, and drawing it out of the scabbard as he spoke——and this, *Le Fever,* I'll save for thee,——'tis all the fortune, continued my uncle *Toby,* hanging it up upon a crook, and pointing to it,——'tis all the fortune, my dear *Le Fever,* which God has left thee; but if he has given thee a heart to fight thy way with it in the world,——and thou doest it like a man of honour, ——'tis enough for us.

As soon as my uncle *Toby* had laid a foundation, and taught him to inscribe a regular polygon in a circle, he sent him to a public school, where, excepting *Whitsontide* and *Christmas,* at which times the corporal was punctually dispatched for him,

---

[6]This monstrous name Sterne has invented to suggest the ponderous and myopic dullness with which Dutch commentators had long been identified. It is probably a nonsense-word; if it means anything, the suggestion of the individual elements would add up to something like "Super-dull-dunderhead."

——he remained to the spring of the year, seventeen; when the stories of the emperor's sending his army into *Hungary* against the *Turks,* kindling a spark of fire in his bosom, he left his *Greek* and *Latin* without leave, and throwing himself upon his knees before my uncle *Toby,* begged his father's sword, and my uncle *Toby's* leave along with it, to go and try his fortune under *Eugene.*[1]——Twice did my uncle *Toby* forget his wound, and cry out, *Le Fever!* I will go with thee, and thou shalt fight beside me——And twice he laid his hand upon his groin, and hung down his head in sorrow and disconsolation.——

My uncle *Toby* took down the sword from the crook, where it had hung untouched ever since the lieutenant's death, and delivered it to the corporal to brighten up;——and having detained *Le Fever* a single fortnight to equip him, and contract for his passage to *Leghorn,*——he put the sword into his hand,——If thou art brave, *Le Fever,* said my uncle *Toby,* this will not fail thee,——but Fortune, said he, (musing a little) ——Fortune may——And if she does,——added my uncle *Toby,* embracing him, come back again to me, *Le Fever,* and we will shape thee another course.

The greatest injury could not have oppressed the heart of *Le Fever* more than my uncle *Toby's* paternal kindness;—— he parted from my uncle *Toby,* as the best of sons from the best of fathers——both dropped tears——and as my uncle *Toby* gave him his last kiss, he slipped sixty guineas, tied up in an old purse of his father's, in which was his mother's ring, into his hand,——and bid God bless him.

CHAP. XIII.

L E *Fever* got up to the Imperial army just time enough to try what metal his sword was made of, at the defeat of the *Turks* before *Belgrade;* but a series of unmerited mis-

[1]Prince François Eugène of Savoie-Carignano (1663–1736), a celebrated Austrian general who in 1716–1718 led the forces of Charles VI, who was allied with Venice, against the Turks.

chances had pursued him from that moment, and trod close upon his heels for four years together after: he had withstood these buffetings to the last, till sickness overtook him at *Marseilles,* from whence he wrote my uncle *Toby* word, he had lost his time, his services, his health, and, in short, every thing but his sword;——and was waiting for the first ship to return back to him.

As this letter came to hand about six weeks before *Susannah's* accident, *Le Fever* was hourly expected; and was uppermost in my uncle *Toby's* mind all the time my father was giving him and *Yorick* a description of what kind of a person he would chuse for a preceptor to me: but as my uncle *Toby* thought my father at first somewhat fanciful in the accomplishments he required, he forebore mentioning *Le Fever's* name,——till the character, by *Yorick's* interposition, ending unexpectedly, in one, who should be gentle tempered, and generous, and good, it impressed the image of *Le Fever,* and his interest upon my uncle *Toby* so forceably, he rose instantly off his chair; and laying down his pipe, in order to take hold of both my father's hands——I beg, brother *Shandy,* said my uncle *Toby,* I may recommend poor *Le Fever's* son to you—— I beseech you, do, added *Yorick*——He has a good heart, said my uncle *Toby*——And a brave one too, an' please your honour, said the corporal.

——The best hearts, *Trim,* are ever the bravest, replied my uncle *Toby.*——And the greatest cowards, an' please your honour, in our regiment, were the greatest rascals in it.—— There was serjeant *Kumbur,* and ensign——

——We'll talk of them, said my father, another time.

CHAP. XIV.

WHAT a jovial and a merry world would this be, may it please your worships, but for that inextricable labyrinth of debts, cares, woes, want, grief, discontent, melancholy, large jointures, impositions, and lies!

Doctor *Slop,* like a son of a w——, as my father called him
for it,——to exalt himself,——debased me to death,——and
made ten thousand times more of *Susannah's* accident, than
there was any grounds for; so that in a week's time, or less, it
was in every body's mouth, *That poor Master Shandy* * * *
* * * * * * * * * * * entirely.——
And FAME, who loves to double every thing,——in three days
more, had sworn positively she saw it,——and all the world, as
usual, gave credit to her evidence——"That the nursery
window had not only * * * * * * * * * *
* * * * * * * * * * * * * * *
* * * * ;——but that * * * * * * * *
* * * * * * * * * * * * * * *
* * * * * *'s also."
Could the world have been sued like a BODY-CORPORATE,——
my father had brought an action upon the case, and trounced
it sufficiently; but to fall foul of individuals about it——as
every soul who had mentioned the affair, did it with the greatest pity imaginable;——'twas like flying in the very face of his
best friends:——And yet to acquiesce under the report, in
silence——was to acknowledge it openly,——at least in the
opinion of one half of the world; and to make a bustle again,
in contradicting it,——was to confirm it as strongly in the
opinion of the other half.——

——Was ever poor devil of a country gentleman so ham-
pered? said my father.

I would shew him publickly, said my uncle *Toby,* at the
market cross.

——'Twill have no effect, said my father.

CHAP. XV.

——I'll put him, however, into breeches said my father,——
let the world say what it will.

CHAP. XVI.

THERE are a thousand resolutions, Sir, both in church and
state, as well as in matters, Madam, of a more private concern;——which, though they have carried all the appearance
in the world of being taken, and entered upon in a hasty, hare-
brained, and unadvised manner, were, notwithstanding this,
(and could you or I have got into the cabinet, or stood behind
the curtain, we should have found it was so) weighed, poized,
and perpended——argued upon——canvassed through——
entered into, and examined on all sides with so much coolness, that the GODDESS of COOLNESS herself (I do not take upon
me to prove her existence) could neither have wished it, or
done it better.

Of the number of these was my father's resolution of putting me into breeches; which, though determined at once,
——in a kind of huff, and a defiance of all mankind, had,
nevertheless, been *pro'd* and *conn'd,* and judicially talked over
betwixt him and my mother about a month before, in two
several *beds of justice,* which my father had held for that purpose. I shall explain the nature of these beds of justice in my
next chapter; and in the chapter following that, you shall step
with me, Madam, behind the curtain, only to hear in what
kind of manner my father and my mother debated between
themselves, this affair of the breeches,——from which you
may form an idea, how they debated all lesser matters.

CHAP. XVII.

THE ancient *Goths* of *Germany,* who (the learned *Clu-
verius*[1] is positive) were first seated in the country between the *Vistula* and the *Oder,* and who afterwards incor-

---

[1]Philip Cluwer (1580–1623), German geographer and historian; the
reference is to his great *Germania Antiqua,* but the following account of

porated the *Herculi,* the *Bugians,* and some other *Vandallick*
clans to 'em,——had all of them a wise custom of debating
every thing of importance to their state, twice; that is,——once
drunk, and once sober:——Drunk——that their counsels
might not want vigour;——and sober——that they might not
want discretion.

Now my father being entirely a water-drinker,——was a
long time gravelled almost to death, in turning this as much
to his advantage, as he did every other thing, which the
ancients did or said; and it was not till the seventh year of his
marriage, after a thousand fruitless experiments and devices,
that he hit upon an expedient which answered the purpose;
——and that was when any difficult and momentous point was
to be settled in the family, which required great sobriety, and
great spirit too, in its determination,——he fixed and set apart
the first *Sunday* night in the month, and the *Saturday* night
which immediately preceded it, to argue it over, in bed with
my mother: By which contrivance, if you consider, Sir, with
yourself,   *   *   *   *   *   *   *   *   *   *   *   *
*   *   *   *   *   *   *   *   *   *   *   *   *   *
*   *   *   *   *   *   *   *   *   *   *   *   *   *
*   *   *   *   *   *   *   *   *   *   *   *   *   *
*   *   *   *   *   *   *   *

These my father, humourously enough, called his *beds of
justice;*[2]——for from the two different counsels taken in these
two different humours, a middle one was generally found out,
which touched the point of wisdom as well, as if he had got
drunk and sober a hundred times.

It must not be made a secret of to the world, that this answers full as well in literary discussions, as either in military or
conjugal; but it is not every author that can try the experiment

---

the double counsels Sterne probably paraphrased from a passage in Sir
William Temple's *Observations upon the United Provinces of the Netherlands.* (*Works* (2 vols., London, 1740), 1.51.)

[2] The bed of justice (*lit de justice*) was the throne on which the king of
France sat when he attended parliament; hence the term came to imply
a formal visit of the king to the parliament, and, latterly, an attempt to
compel that body to accede to his will.

as the *Goths* and *Vandals* did it——or if he can, may it be always for his body's health; and to do it, as my father did it, ——am I sure it would be always for his soul's.——

My way is this:——

In all nice and ticklish discussions,——(of which, heaven knows, there are but too many in my book)——where I find I cannot take a step without the danger of having either their worships or their reverences upon my back——I write one half *full*,——and t'other *fasting*;——or write it all full,——and correct it fasting;——or write it fasting,——and correct it full, for they all come to the same thing:——So that with a less variation from my father's plan, than my father's from the *Gothick*——I feel myself upon a par with him in his first bed of justice,——and no way inferior to him in his second.—— These different and almost irreconcileable effects, flow uniformly from the wise and wonderful mechanism of nature, ——of which,——be her's the honour.——All that we can do, is to turn and work the machine to the improvement and better manufactury of the arts and sciences.——

Now, when I write full,——I write as if I was never to write fasting again as long as I live;——that is, I write free from the cares, as well as the terrors of the world.——I count not the number of my scars,——nor does my fancy go forth into dark entries and bye corners to antedate my stabs.——In a word, my pen takes its course; and I write on as much from the fullness of my heart, as my stomach.——

But when, an' please your honours, I indite fasting, 'tis a different history.——I pay the world all possible attention and respect,——and have as great a share (whilst it lasts) of that understrapping virtue of discretion, as the best of you.—— So that betwixt both, I write a careless kind of a civil, nonsensical, good humoured *Shandean* book, which will do all your hearts good——

——And all your heads too,——provided you understand it.

CHAP. XVIII.

WE should begin, said my father, turning himself half round in bed, and shifting his pillow a little towards my mother's, as he opened the debate——We should begin to think, Mrs. *Shandy,* of putting this boy into breeches.——

We should so,——said my mother.——We defer it, my dear, quoth my father, shamefully.——

I think we do, Mr. *Shandy,*——said my mother.

——Not but the child looks extremely well, said my father, in his vests and tunicks.——

——He does look very well in them,——replied my mother.——

——And for that reason it would be almost a sin, added my father, to take him out of 'em.——

——It would so,——said my mother:——But indeed he is growing a very tall lad,——rejoin'd my father.

——He is very tall for his age, indeed,——said my mother.——

——I can not (making two syllables of it) imagine, quoth my father, who the duce he takes after.——

I cannot conceive, for my life,——said my mother.——

Humph!——said my father.

(The dialogue ceased for a moment.)

——I am very short myself,——continued my father, gravely.

You are very short, Mr. *Shandy,*——said my mother.

Humph! quoth my father to himself, a second time: in muttering which, he plucked his pillow a little further from my mother's,——and turning about again, there was an end of the debate for three minutes and a half.

——When he gets these breeches made, cried my father in a higher tone, he'll look like a beast in 'em.

He will be very aukward in them at first, replied my mother.——

——And 'twill be lucky, if that's the worst on't, added my father.

It will be very lucky, answered my mother.

I suppose, replied my father,——making some pause first, ——he'll be exactly like other people's children.——

Exactly, said my mother.——

——Though I should be sorry for that, added my father: and so the debate stopped again.

——They should be of leather, said my father, turning him about again.——

They will last him, said my mother, the longest.

But he can have no linings to 'em, replied my father.——

He cannot, said my mother.

'Twere better to have them of fustian, quoth my father.

Nothing can be better, quoth my mother.——

——Except dimity,——replied my father:——'Tis best of all,——replied my mother.

——One must not give him his death, however,——interrupted my father.

By no means, said my mother:——and so the dialogue stood still again.

I am resolved, however, quoth my father, breaking silence the fourth time, he shall have no pockets in them.——

——There is no occasion for any, said my mother.——

I mean in his coat and waistcoat,——cried my father.

——I mean so too,——replied my mother.

——Though if he gets a gig[1] or a top——Poor souls! it is a crown and a scepter to them,——they should have where to secure it.——

Order it as you please, Mr. *Shandy,* replied my mother.——

——But don't you think it right? added my father, pressing the point home to her.

Perfectly, said my mother, if it pleases you, Mr. *Shandy.*——

——There's for you! cried my father, losing temper—— Pleases me!——You never will distinguish, Mrs. *Shandy,* nor shall I ever teach you to do it, betwixt a point of pleasure and

---

[1]Whirligig.

a point of convenience.——This was on the *Sunday* night;
——and further this chapter sayeth not.

CHAP. XIX.

AFTER my father had debated the affair of the breeches with
my mother,——he consulted *Albertus Rubenius*[1] upon it;
and *Albertus Rubenius* used my father ten times worse in the
consultation (if possible) than even my father had used my
mother: For as *Rubenius* had wrote a quarto *express, De re
Vestiaria Veterum,*——it was *Rubenius's* business to have
given my father some lights.——On the contrary, my father
might as well have thought of extracting the seven cardinal
virtues out of a long beard,——as of extracting a single word
out of *Rubenius* upon the subject.

Upon every other article of ancient dress, *Rubenius* was
very communicative to my father;——gave him a full and satisfactory account of

> The Toga, or loose gown.
> The Chlamys.[2]
> The Ephod.
> The Tunica, or Jacket.
> The Synthesis.
> The Pænula.

---

[1]Albert Rubens (1614–1657), the eldest son of the painter and Isabella
Brant, was an archaeologist and writer of some note. In his *De Re
Vestiaria Veterum, Præcipue de Lato Clavo (Of the Clothing of the
Ancients, Particularly of the Latus Clavus)*, from which Sterne took the
following lists of articles of clothing and of authorities, Rubenius devoted
nearly two hundred quarto pages to pedantic speculations on the details
of ancient costume and the conflicting arguments of learned men thereupon.

[2]A broad woolen cloak or mantle worn by the Greeks. Ephod: a garment worn by the priest at Hebrew religious celebrations. Synthesis: a
set of wearing-apparel, also a loose dressing-gown. Pænula: a woolen
cloak or mantle covering the whole body. Lacema: probably a misprint
for *lacerna*, a military cloak. Cucullus: a cap or hood fastened to a garment. Paludamentum: a military cloak. Prætexta: a purple-bordered
outer garment worn by Roman magistrates and free-born children.
Trabea: a Roman robe of state.

The Lacema, with its Cucullus.

The Paludamentum.

The Prætexta.

The Sagum, or soldier's jerkin.

The Trabea: of which, according to *Suetonius*,[3] there were three kinds.——

——But what are all these to the breeches? said my father. *Rubenius* threw him down upon the counter all kinds of shoes which had been in fashion with the *Romans*.——— There was,

> The open shoe.
>
> The close shoe.
>
> The slip shoe.
>
> The wooden shoe.
>
> The soc.[4]
>
> The buskin.

And The military shoe with hobnails in it, which *Juvenal*[5] takes notice of.

There were, The clogs.

> The patins.[6]
>
> The pantoufles.
>
> The brogues.
>
> The sandals, with latchets to them.

There was, The felt shoe.

> The linen shoe.
>
> The laced shoe.
>
> The braided shoe.
>
> The calceus incisus.

And The calceus rostratus.

---

[3]Caius Suetonius Tranquillus (fl. first part of 2nd C., A.D.), Roman biographer and historian. The reference, to his *De Genere Vestium,* is taken from Rubenius.

[4]Sock; light, low shoe.

[5]Decimus Junius Juvenalis (c.60–c.127), Roman satirist. The reference is to the *Satiræ,* 16.24–25.

[6]Pattens, overshoes with wooden soles raised above iron rings. Pantoufles: pantofles, slippers. Calceus incisus: a cutwork shoe. Calceus rostratus: a beaked or pointed shoe.

Rubenius shewed my father how well they all fitted,——in what manner they laced on,——with what points, straps, thongs, lachets, ribands, jaggs, and ends.——

——But I want to be informed about the breeches, said my father.

Albertus Rubenius informed my father that the *Romans* manufactured stuffs of various fabricks,——some plain,—— some striped,——others diapered throughout the whole con- texture of the wool, with silk and gold——That linen did not begin to be in common use, till towards the declension of the empire, when the *Egyptians* coming to settle amongst them, brought it into vogue.

——That persons of quality and fortune distinguished them- selves by the fineness and whiteness of their cloaths; which colour (next to purple, which was appropriated to the great offices) they most affected and wore on their birth-days and public rejoicings.——That it appeared from the best historians of those times, that they frequently sent their cloaths to the fuller, to be cleaned and whitened;——but that the inferior people, to avoid that expence, generally wore brown cloaths, and of a something coarser texture,——till towards the begin- ning of *Augustus*'s reign, when the slave dressed like his mas- ter, and almost every distinction of habiliment was lost, but the *Latus Clavus.*

And what was the *Latus Clavus?*[7] said my father.

Rubenius told him, that the point was still litigating amongst the learned:——That *Egnatius,*[8] *Sigonius, Bossius Ticinensis, Bayfius, Budæus, Salmasius, Lipsius, Lazius, Isaac Casaubon,*

---

[7]Literally, a broad nail; by metonymy the name was applied to the broad purple stripe worn on the tunic by Roman patricians.

[8]Baptista Egnatius (c.1475–1553) was a humanist of Venice; Carlo Sigonio (c.1520–1584) was an Italian historian and antiquary; Bossius Ticinensis: probably Matthew Bossus (1428–1502), a canon of the Lateran; Lazare de Baïf (1496?–1547) was a French scholar and diplomat; Guil- laume Budé (1467–1540) was a French scholar and antiquarian; Claudius Salmasius (1588–1653) was a noted French classical scholar; for Lipsius, see p. 411, n. 7.   Wolfgang Lazius (1514–1565) was a German antiquary and physician; Isaac Casaubon (1559–1614) was a famous classical scholar and Protestant theologian; for Scaliger, see p. 411, n. 5.

and *Joseph Scaliger,* all differed from each other,——and he from them: That some took it to be the button,——some the coat itself,——others only the colour of it:——That the great *Bayfius,* in his Wardrobe of the ancients, chap. 12.——honestly said, he knew not what it was,——whether a tibula,[9]——a stud,——a button,——a loop,——a buckle,——or clasps and keepers.——

——My father lost the horse, but not the saddle——They are *hooks and eyes,* said my father——and with hooks and eyes he ordered my breeches to be made.

CHAP. XX.

WE are now going to enter upon a new scene of events.——

——Leave we then the breeches in the taylor's hands, with my father standing over him with his cane, reading him as he sat at work a lecture upon the *latus clavus,* and pointing to the precise part of the waistband, where he was determined to have it sewed on.——

Leave we my mother——(truest of all the *Poco-curante's*[1] of her sex!)——careless about it, as about every thing else in the world which concerned her;——that is,——indifferent whether it was done this way or that,——provided it was but done at all.——

Leave we *Slop* likewise to the full profits of all my dishon-ours.——

Leave we poor *Le Fever* to recover, and get home from *Marseilles* as he can.——And last of all,——because the hard-est of all——

Let us leave, if possible, *myself:*——But 'tis impossible,—— I must go along with you to the end of the work.

---

[9]Probably a misprint for *fibula,* a brooch or clasp.
[1]Indifferent, apathetic persons.

CHAP. XXI.

IF the reader has not a clear conception of the rood and the
half of ground which lay at the bottom of my uncle *Toby's*
kitchen garden, and which was the scene of so many of his
delicious hours,——the fault is not in me,——but in his
imagination;——for I am sure I gave him so minute a description, I was almost ashamed of it.

When FATE was looking forwards one afternoon, into the
great transactions of future times,——and recollected for
what purposes, this little plot, by a decree fast bound down in
iron, had been destined,——she gave a nod to NATURE——
'twas enough——Nature threw half a spade full of her kindliest compost upon it, with just so *much* clay in it, as to retain
the forms of angles and indentings,——and so *little* of it too,
as not to cling to the spade, and render works of so much
glory, nasty in foul weather.

My uncle *Toby* came down, as the reader has been informed,
with plans along with him, of almost every fortified town in
Italy and *Flanders;* so let the Duke of *Marlborough*,[1] or the
allies,[2] have set down before what town they pleased, my
uncle *Toby* was prepared for them.

His way, which was the simplest one in the world, was this;
as soon as ever a town was invested——(but sooner when the
design was known) to take the plan of it, (let it be what town
it would) and enlarge it upon a scale to the exact size of his
bowling-green; upon the surface of which, by means of a large
role of packthread, and a number of small piquets driven into
the ground, at the several angles and redans,[3] he transferred

---

[1]John Churchill (1650–1722), first Duke of Marlborough, the great
English general and statesman, was commander-in-chief of the British
forces under William III and Anne.

[2]See p. 97, n. 9.

[3]A simple form of field fortification having two faces which form a
salient angle with its apex toward the enemy and its rear unprotected.
Banquets: banquettes, raised ways behind ramparts from which riflemen
fire.

the lines from his paper; then taking the profile of the place, with its works, to determine the depths and slopes of the ditches,——the talus of the glacis, and the precise height of the several banquets, parapets, &c.——he set the corporal to work——and sweetly went it on:——The nature of the soil, ——the nature of the work itself,——and above all, the good nature of my uncle *Toby* sitting by from morning to night, and chatting kindly with the corporal upon past-done deeds, ——left LABOUR little else but the ceremony of the name.

When the place was finished in this manner, and put into a proper posture of defence,——it was invested,——and my uncle *Toby* and the corporal began to run their first parallel.[4] ——I beg I may not be interrupted in my story, by being told, *That the first parallel should be at least three hundred toises distant from the main body of the place,——and that I have not left a single inch for it;*——for my uncle *Toby* took the liberty of incroaching upon his kitchen garden, for the sake of enlarging his works on the bowling green, and for that reason generally ran his first and second parallels betwixt two rows of his cabbages and his collyflowers; the conveniences and inconveniences of which will be considered at large in the history of my uncle *Toby*'s and the corporal's campaigns, of which, this I'm now writing is but a sketch, and will be finished, if I conjecture right, in three pages (but there is no guessing)——The campaigns themselves will take up as many books; and therefore I apprehend it would be hanging too great a weight of one kind of matter in so flimsy a performance as this, to rhapsodize them, as I once intended, into the body of the work——surely they had better be printed apart, ——we'll consider the affair——so take the following sketch of them in the mean time.

[4]Trench before and parallel to a fortification for the protection of the besiegers. For *toises,* see p. 83, n. 5.

CHAP. XXII.

WHEN the town, with its works, was finished, my uncle
Toby and the corporal began to run their first parallel
——not at random, or any how——but from the same points
and distances the allies had begun to run theirs; and regulating
their approaches and attacks, by the accounts my uncle *Toby*
received from the daily papers,——they went on, during the
whole siege, step by step with the allies.

When the duke of *Marlborough* made a lodgment,——my
uncle *Toby* made a lodgment too.——And when the face of a
bastion was battered down, or a defence ruined,——the corporal took his mattock and did as much,——and so on;——
gaining ground, and making themselves masters of the works
one after another, till the town fell into their hands.

To one who took pleasure in the happy state of others,——
there could not have been a greater sight in the world, than,
on a post-morning, in which a practicable breach had been
made by the duke of *Marlborough,* in the main body of the
place,——to have stood behind the horn-beam hedge, and
observed the spirit with which my uncle *Toby,* with *Trim*
behind him, sallied forth;——the one with the *Gazette*[1] in his
hand,——the other with a spade on his shoulder to execute the
contents.——What an honest triumph in my uncle *Toby*'s
looks as he marched up to the ramparts! What intense pleasure swimming in his eye as he stood over the corporal, reading
the paragraph ten times over to him, as he was at work, lest,
peradventure, he should make the breach an inch too wide,
——or leave it an inch too narrow——But when the *chamade*[2]
was beat, and the corporal helped my uncle up it, and followed with the colours in his hand, to fix them upon the ramparts——Heaven! Earth! Sea!——but what avails apostro-
phes?——with all your elements, wet or dry, ye never compounded so intoxicating a draught.

---

[1] The official court newspaper, which reported all national affairs.

[2] A signal, by drum or trumpet, for retreat or parley.

In this track of happiness for many years, without one interruption to it, except now and then when the wind continued to blow due west for a week or ten days together,
which detained the *Flanders* mail, and kept them so long in
torture,——but still 'twas the torture of the happy——In this
track, I say, did my uncle *Toby* and *Trim* move for many years,
every year of which, and sometimes every month, from the invention of either the one or the other of them, adding some
new conceit or quirk of improvement to their operations, which
always opened fresh springs of delight in carrying them on.

The first year's campaign was carried on from beginning to
end, in the plain and simple method I've related.

In the second year, in which my uncle *Toby* took *Liege* and
Ruremond,[3] he thought he might afford the expence of four
handsome draw-bridges, of two of which I have given an exact
description, in the former part of my work.

At the latter end of the same year he added a couple of gates
with portcullises:——These last were converted afterwards
into orgues,[4] as the better thing; and during the winter of the
same year, my uncle *Toby,* instead of a new suit of cloaths,
which he always had at *Christmas,* treated himself with a
handsome sentry-box, to stand at the corner of the bowling-
green, betwixt which point and the foot of the glacis, there
was left a little kind of an esplanade for him and the corporal
to confer and hold councils of war upon.

——The sentry-box was in case of rain.

All these were painted white three times over the ensuing
spring, which enabled my uncle *Toby* to take the field with
great splendour.

My father would often say to *Yorick,* that if any mortal in
the whole universe had done such a thing, except his brother
Toby, it would have been looked upon by the world as one of
the most refined satyrs upon the parade and prancing manner, in which *Lewis* XIV. from the beginning of the war, but

---

[3]These battles were fought in 1702.
[4]Weapons composed of several small cannon mounted together on a
gun carriage.

particularly that very year, had taken the field[5]——But 'tis not
my brother *Toby*'s nature, kind soul! my father would add, to
insult any one.

——But let us go on.

CHAP. XXIII.

I Must observe, that although in the first year's campaign,
the word *town* is often mentioned,——yet there was no
town at that time within the polygon; that addition was not
made till the summer following the spring in which the bridges
and sentry-box were painted, which was the third year of my
uncle *Toby*'s campaigns,——when upon his taking *Amberg,
Bonn,* and *Rhinberg,* and *Huy* and *Limbourg,*[1] one after another, a thought came into the corporal's head, that to talk of
taking so many towns, *without one* TOWN *to show for it,*——
was a very nonsensical way of going to work, and so proposed
to my uncle *Toby,* that they should have a little model of a
town built for them,——to be run up together of slit deals,
and then painted, and clapped within the interior polygon to
serve for all.

My uncle *Toby* felt the good of the project instantly, and
instantly agreed to it, but with the addition of two singular
improvements, of which he was almost as proud, as if he had
been the original inventor of the project itself.

The one was to have the town built exactly in the stile of
those, of which it was most likely to be the representative:
——with grated windows, and the gable ends of the houses,
facing the streets, &c. &c.——as those in *Ghent* and *Bruges,*
and the rest of the towns in *Brabant* and *Flanders.*

The other was, not to have the houses run up together, as
the corporal proposed, but to have every house independant,
to hook on, or off, so as to form into the plan of whatever

[5]Something of the brilliance for which his court was famous attached
itself to Louis's confident opening of hostilities. He always prided himself on being the first in the field, and conducted his sieges with much
pomp.

[1]These cities were taken in 1703.

town they pleased. This was put directly into hand, and many and many a look of mutual congratulation was exchanged between my uncle *Toby* and the corporal, as the carpenter did the work.

——It answered prodigiously the next summer——the town was a perfect *Proteus*[2]——It was *Landen*,[3] and *Trerebach,* and *Santvliet,* and *Drusen,* and *Hagenau,*——and then it was *Ostend* and *Menin,* and *Aeth* and *Dendermond.*

——Surely never did any TOWN act so many parts, since *Sodom* and *Gomorrah,*[4] as my uncle *Toby's* town did.

In the fourth year, my uncle *Toby* thinking a town looked foolishly without a church, added a very fine one with a steeple.——*Trim* was for having bells in it;——my uncle *Toby* said, the mettle had better be cast into cannon.

This led the way the next campaign for half a dozen brass field pieces,——to be planted three and three on each side of my uncle *Toby's* sentry-box; and in a short time, these led the way for a train of somewhat larger,——and so on——(as must always be the case in hobby-horsical affairs) from pieces of half an inch bore, till it came at last to my father's jack boots.

The next year,[5] which was that in which *Lisle* was besieged, and at the close of which both *Ghent* and *Bruges* fell into our hands,——my uncle *Toby* was sadly put to it for *proper* ammunition;——I say proper ammunition——because his great artillery would not bear powder; and 'twas well for the *Shandy* family they would not——For so full were the papers, from the beginning to the end of the siege, of the incessant firings kept up by the besiegers,——and so heated was my uncle

---

[2] A sea god, in classical mythology, who had the power of assuming different shapes; hence, anything which readily changes its form.

[3] The battle of Landen, in which Trim had been wounded, had been fought in 1693; this reference is probably to Marlborough's dramatic march to the old battle-ground in 1705. The battle of Trerebach was fought in 1704; those of Santvliet, Drusen, and Hagenau, in 1705; those of Ostend, Menin, Aeth, and Dendermond, in 1706.

[4] Cities which for their wickedness were destroyed by the Lord (Genesis, 19); their names have since been accepted as epithets designating any wicked city.

[5] 1708.

Toby's imagination with the accounts of them, that he had infallibly shot away all his estate.

SOMETHING therefore was wanting, as a *succedaneum,*[6] especially in one or two of the more violent paroxysms of the siege, to keep up something like a continual firing in the imagination,——and this *something,* the corporal, whose principal strength lay in invention, supplied by an entire new system of battering of his own,——without which, this had been objected to by military critics, to the end of the world, as one of the great *desiderata*[7] of my uncle*Toby*'s apparatus.

This will not be explained the worse, for setting off, as I generally do, at a little distance from the subject.

CHAP. XXIV.

WITH two or three other trinkets, small in themselves, but of great regard, which poor *Tom,* the corporal's unfortunate brother, had sent him over, with the account of his marriage with the *Jew*'s widow——there was

A *Montero*-cap[1] and two *Turkish* tobacco pipes.

The *Montero*-cap I shall describe by and bye.——The *Turkish* tobacco pipes had nothing particular in them, they were fitted up and ornamented as usual, with flexible tubes of *Morocco* leather and gold wire, and mounted at their ends, the one of them with ivory,——the other with black ebony, tipp'd with silver.

My father, who saw all things in lights different from the rest of the world, would say to the corporal, that he ought to look upon these two presents more as tokens of his brother's nicety, than his affection.——*Tom* did not care, *Trim,* he would say, to put on the cap, or to smoak in the tobacco-pipe of a *Jew*.——God bless your honour, the corporal would say,

---

[6]Substitute.

[7]Things desired.

[1]Spanish horseman's or hunter's cap, having a round crown and flaps capable of being drawn down over the ears.

(giving a strong reason to the contrary)——how can that be?——

The Montero-cap was scarlet, of a superfine *Spanish* cloth, died in grain, and mounted all round with furr, except about four inches in the front, which was faced with a light blue, slightly embroidered,——and seemed to have been the property of a *Portuguese* quartermaster, not of foot, but of horse, as the word denotes.

The corporal was not a little proud of it, as well for its own sake, as the sake of the giver, so seldom or never put it on but upon GALA-days; and yet never was a Montero-cap put to so many uses; for in all controverted points, whether military or culinary, provided the corporal was sure he was in the right, ——it was either his *oath*,——his *wager*,——or his *gift*.

——'Twas his gift in the present case.

I'll be bound, said the corporal, speaking to himself, to *give* away my Montero-cap to the first beggar who comes to the door, if I do not manage this matter to his honour's satisfaction.

The completion was no further off, than the very next morning; which was that of the storm of the counterscarp[2] betwixt the *Lower Deule,* to the right, and the gate St. *Andrew,*—— on the left, between St. *Magdalen's* and the river.

As this was the most memorable attack in the whole war, ——the most gallant and obstinate on both sides,——and I must add the most bloody too, for it cost the allies themselves that morning above eleven hundred men,——my uncle *Toby* prepared himself for it with a more than ordinary solemnity.

The eve which preceded, as my uncle *Toby* went to bed, he ordered his ramallie wig,[3] which had laid inside out for many years in the corner of an old campaigning trunk, which stood by his bedside, to be taken out and laid upon the lid of it, ready for the morning;——and the very first thing he did in

---

[2]*I.e.,* in the siege of Lille.

[3]A wig having a long, gradually diminishing plait, with a large bow at the top and a smaller at the bottom, so called in commemoration of Marlborough's victory over the French in 1706 at Ramillies.

his shirt, when he had stepped out of bed, my uncle *Toby,*
after he had turned the rough side outwards,——put it on:
——This done, he proceeded next to his breeches, and having
buttoned the waist-band, he forthwith buckled on his sword
belt, and had got his sword half way in,——when he considered he should want shaving, and that it would be very
inconvenient doing it with his sword on,——so took it off:
——In assaying to put on his regimental coat and waistcoat,
my uncle *Toby* found the same objection in his wig,——so
that went off too:——So that what with one thing, and what
with another, as always falls out when a man is in the most
haste,——'twas ten o'clock, which was half an hour later than
his usual time, before my uncle *Toby* sallied out.

CHAP. XXV.

MY uncle *Toby* had scarce turned the corner of his yew
hedge, which separated his kitchen garden from his
bowling green, when he perceived the corporal had began the
attack without him.——

Let me stop and give you a picture of the corporal's apparatus; and of the corporal himself in the height of this attack
just as it struck my uncle *Toby,* as he turned towards the sentry
box, where the corporal was at work,——for in nature there is
not such another,——nor can any combination of all that is
grotesque and whimsical in her works produce its equal.

The corporal——

——Tread lightly on his ashes, ye men of genius,——for he
was your kinsman:

Weed his grave clean, ye men of goodness,——for he was
your brother.——Oh corporal! had I thee, but now,——now,
that I am able to give thee a dinner and protection,——how
would I cherish thee! thou should'st wear thy Montero-cap
every hour of the day, and every day of the week,——and
when it was worn out, I would purchase thee a couple like it:
——But alas! alas! alas! now that I can do this, in spight of

their reverences——the occasion is lost——for thou art gone; ——thy genius fled up to the stars from whence it came;—— and that warm heart of thine, with all its generous and open vessels, compressed into a *clod of the valley!*

——But what——what is this, to that future and dreaded page, where I look towards the velvet pall, decorated with the military ensigns of thy master——the first——the foremost of created beings;——where, I shall see thee, faithful servant! laying his sword and scabbard with a trembling hand across his coffin, and then returning pale as ashes to the door, to take his mourning horse by the bridle, to follow his hearse, as he directed thee;——where——all my father's systems shall be baffled by his sorrows; and, in spight of his philosophy, I shall behold him, as he inspects the lackered plate, twice taking his spectacles from off his nose, to wipe away the dew which nature has shed upon them——When I see him cast in the rosemary with an air of disconsolation, which cries through my ears,——O *Toby!* in what corner of the world shall I seek thy fellow?

——Gracious powers! which erst have opened the lips of the dumb in his distress, and made the tongue of the stammerer speak plain——when I shall arrive at this dreaded page, deal not with me, then, with a stinted hand.

CHAP. XXVI.

THE corporal, who the night before had resolved in his mind, to supply the grand *desideratum,* of keeping up something like an incessant firing upon the enemy during the heat of the attack,——had no further idea in his fancy at that time, than a contrivance of smoking tobacco against the town, out of one of my uncle *Toby's* six field pieces, which were planted on each side of his sentry-box; the means of effecting which occurring to his fancy at the same time, though he had pledged his cap, he thought it in no danger from the miscarriage of his projects.

Upon turning it this way, and that, a little in his mind, he soon began to find out, that by means of his two *Turkish* tobacco-pipes, with the supplement of three smaller tubes of wash-leather at each of their lower ends, to be tagg'd by the same number of tin pipes fitted to the touch holes, and sealed with clay next the cannon, and then tied hermetically with waxed silk at their several insertions into the *Morocco* tube,——he should be able to fire the six field pieces all together, and with the same ease as to fire one.——

——Let no man say from what taggs and jaggs hints may not be cut out for the advancement of human knowledge. Let no man who has read my father's first and second *beds of justice,* ever rise up and say again, from collision of what kinds of bodies, light may, or may not be struck out, to carry the arts and sciences up to perfection.——Heaven! thou knowest how I love them;——thou knowest the secrets of my heart, and that I would this moment give my shirt——Thou art a fool, *Shandy,* says *Eugenius,*——for thou hast but . dozen in the world,——and 'twill break thy set.——

No matter for that, *Eugenius;* I would give the shirt off my back to be burnt into tinder, were it only to satisfy one feverish enquirer, how many sparks at one good stroke, a good flint and steel could strike into the tail of it.——Think ye not that in striking these *in,*——he might, peradventure, strike something *out?* as sure as a gun.——

——But this project, by the bye.

The corporal sat up the best part of the night in bringing *his* to perfection; and having made a sufficient proof of his cannon, with charging them to the top with tobacco,——he went with contentment to bed.

CHAP. XXVII.

THE corporal had slipped out about ten minutes before my uncle *Toby,* in order to fix his apparatus, and just give the enemy a shot or two before my uncle *Toby* came.

He had drawn the six field-pieces for this end, all close up together in front of my uncle *Toby*'s sentry-box, leaving only an interval of about a yard and a half betwixt the three, on the right and left, for the convenience of charging, &c.——and the sake possibly of two batteries, which he might think double the honour of one.

In the rear, and facing this opening, with his back to the door of the sentry-box, for fear of being flanked, had the corporal wisely taken his post:——He held the ivory pipe, appertaining to the battery on the right, betwixt the finger and thumb of his right hand,——and the ebony pipe tipp'd with silver, which appertained to the battery on the left, betwixt the finger and thumb of the other——and with his right knee fixed firm upon the ground, as if in the front rank of his platoon, was the corporal, with his montero-cap upon his head, furiously playing off his two cross batteries at the same time against the counterguard, which faced the counterscarp, where the attack was to be made that morning. His first intention, as I said, was no more than giving the enemy a single puff or two;——but the pleasure of the *puffs,* as well as the *puffing,* had insensibly got hold of the corporal, and drawn him on from puff to puff, into the very height of the attack, by the time my uncle *Toby* joined him.

'Twas well for my father, that my uncle *Toby* had not his will to make that day.

CHAP. XXVIII.

M Y uncle *Toby* took the ivory pipe out of the corporal's hand,——looked at it for half a minute, and returned it.

In less than two minutes my uncle *Toby* took the pipe from the corporal again, and raised it half way to his mouth—— then hastily gave it back a second time.

The corporal redoubled the attack,——my uncle *Toby* smiled,——then looked grave,——then smiled for a moment,

——then looked serious for a long time;——Give me hold of the ivory pipe, *Trim,* said my uncle *Toby*——my uncle *Toby* put it to his lips,——drew it back directly,——gave a peep over the horn-beam hedge;——never did my uncle *Toby's* mouth water so much for a pipe in his life.——My uncle *Toby* retired into the sentry-box with the pipe in his hand.——

——Dear uncle *Toby!* don't go into the sentry-box with the pipe,——there's no trusting a man's self with such a thing in such a corner.

CHAP. XXIX.

I Beg the reader will assist me here, to wheel off my uncle *Toby's* ordnance behind the scenes,——to remove his sentry-box, and clear the theatre, *if possible,* of horn-works and half moons, and get the rest of his military apparatus out of the way;——that done, my dear friend *Garrick,*[1] we'll snuff the candles bright,——sweep the stage with a new broom,——draw up the curtain, and exhibit my uncle *Toby* dressed in a new character, throughout which the world can have no idea how he will act: and yet, if pity be akin to love, ——and bravery no alien to it, you have seen enough of my uncle *Toby* in these, to trace these family likenesses, betwixt the two passions (in case there is one) to your heart's content.

Vain science! thou assists us in no case of this kind——and thou puzzlest us in every one.

There was, Madam, in my uncle *Toby,* a singleness of heart which misled him so far out of the little serpentine tracks in which things of this nature usually go on; you can——you can have no conception of it: with this, there was a plainness and simplicity of thinking, with such an unmistrusting ignorance of the plies and foldings of the heart of woman;——and so naked and defenceless did he stand before you, (when a siege was out of his head) that you might have stood behind any one of your serpentine walks, and shot my uncle *Toby* ten

[1]See p. 180, n. 1.

times in a day, through his liver,[2] if nine times in a day, Madam, had not served your purpose.

With all this, Madam,——and what confounded every thing as much on the other hand, my uncle *Toby* had that unparalleled modesty of nature I once told you of, and which, by the bye, stood eternal sentry upon his feelings, that you might as soon——But where am I going? these reflections croud in upon me ten pages at least too soon, and take up that time, which I ought to bestow upon facts.

CHAP. XXX.

O F the few legitimate sons of *Adam,* whose breasts never felt what the sting of love was,——(maintaining first, all mysogynists to be bastards)——the greatest heroes of ancient and modern story have carried off amongst them, nine parts in ten of the honour; and I wish for their sakes I had the key of my study out of my draw-well,[1] only for five minutes, to tell you their names——recollect them I cannot——so be content to accept of these, for the present, in their stead.——

There was the great king *Aldrovandus,*[2] and *Bosphorus,* and

---

[2]This organ was formerly regarded as the seat of amorous passion.

[1]See p. 342.

[2]The following jumble of names is probably Sterne's fun. If he had the key to his study, he says, he could tell us the names of mysogynists; but since he cannot recollect them he gives us this list "in their stead." Aldrovandus (Ulisse Aldrovandi (1522–1605), a noble and celebrated Italian naturalist) he probably remembered from Burton, who frequently cites his works. Capadocius, Pontus, and Asius may echo the "Cappadocia, in Pontus, and Asia" of Acts, 2.9. Bosphorus, Babylonicus, Mediterraneus, Persicus, and Prusicus appear likewise to be based on geographical names. Yet most of these names have been borne by actual men: Bosphore (360–406) was a bishop of Colonia (Cappadocia); and of various Pontuses one, Pontus de Thiard (1521–1605), the French poet, became bishop of Châlons-sur-Saône, and another, Louis de Ponte (1554–1624), a Spanish Jesuit, was famous for his pious writings and ascetic life. Dardanus may refer to the mythical founder of Dardanus on the Hellespont; or to the philosopher (fl. 110 B.C.) who was a leader of the Stoics at Athens; or to others of the same name. There were many

Capadocius, and *Dardanus,* and *Pontus,* and *Asius,*——to say nothing of the iron-hearted *Charles* the XIIth, whom the Countess of K***** herself could make nothing of.——There was *Babylonicus,* and *Mediterraneus,* and *Polixenes,* and *Persicus,* and *Prusicus,* not one of whom (except *Capadocius* and *Pontus,* who were both a little suspected) ever once bowed down his breast to the goddess——The truth is, they had all of them something else to do——and so had my uncle *Toby* ——till Fate——till Fate I say, envying his name the glory of being handed down to posterity with *Aldrovandus's* and the rest,——she basely patched up the peace of *Utrecht.*[3]

——Believe me, Sirs, 'twas the worst deed she did that year.

CHAP. XXXI.

AMONGST the many ill consequences of the treaty of *Utrecht,* it was within a point of giving my uncle *Toby* a surfeit of sieges; and though he recovered his appetite afterwards, yet *Calais* itself left not a deeper scar in *Mary's* heart,[1] than *Utrecht* upon my uncle *Toby's.* To the end of his life he never could hear *Utrecht* mentioned upon any account whatever,——or so much as read an article of news extracted

---

Polixeneses in mythology and history; perhaps Sterne remembered the "good Polixenes" in *The Winter's Tale* who was no mysogynist although his friendship for Hermione was chaste. Persicus may possibly be a slip for Persius (Aulus Persius Flaccus) (34–62), the Roman satirical poet, who, according to Bayle, a favorite authority of Sterne, "was very chaste . . . sober, as meek as a lamb, and as modest as a young virgin." Charles XII (1682–1718), King of Sweden, however, was an authentic and famed mysogynist. He never married, and he lived so austere a life that when the Countess of Königsmark, a celebrated wit and beauty who had become the mistress of Augustus the Strong, King of Poland, was sent to him by her lover to sue for peace, neither her charms nor her artifices were able to persuade him to treat with her.

[3]The treaty (1713) which concluded the War of the Spanish Succession.

[1]Mary (1516–1558), Queen of England, so grieved over the loss, in 1558, of Calais, the last English foothold on foreign soil, that she declared, according to Holinshed's *Chronicles,* "When I am dead and opened you shall find Calais lying upon my heart."

out of the *Utrecht Gazette,* without fetching a sigh, as if his heart would break in twain.

My father, who was a great MOTIVE-MONGER, and consequently a very dangerous person for a man to sit by, either laughing or crying,——for he generally knew your motive for doing both, much better than you knew it yourself—— would always console my uncle *Toby* upon these occasions, in a way, which shewed plainly, he imagined my uncle *Toby* grieved for nothing in the whole affair, so much as the loss of his *hobby-horse.*——Never mind, brother *Toby,* he would say,——by God's blessing we shall have another war break out again some of these days; and when it does,——the belligerent powers, if they would hang themselves, cannot keep us out of play.——I defy 'em, my dear *Toby,* he would add, to take countries without taking towns,——or towns without sieges.

My uncle *Toby* never took this back-stroke of my father's at his hobby horse kindly.——He thought the stroke ungenerous; and the more so, because in striking the horse, he hit the rider too, and in the most dishonourable part a blow could fall; so that upon these occasions, he always laid down his pipe upon the table with more fire to defend himself than common.

I told the reader, this time two years, that my uncle *Toby* was not eloquent; and in the very same page gave an instance to the contrary:——I repeat the observation, and a fact which contradicts it again.——He was not eloquent,——it was not easy to my uncle *Toby* to make long harangues,——and he hated florid ones; but there were occasions where the stream overflowed the man, and ran so counter to its usual course, that in some parts my uncle *Toby,* for a time, was at least equal to *Tertullus*[2]——but in others, in my own opinion, infinitely above him.

---

[2] "A certain orator named Tertullus" informed Felix against Paul, in Acts, 24.1–8. Considering the nature of my uncle Toby's argument, however, it is possible that Sterne was thinking of Tertullianus (c.155– c.222), the first great writer of Latin Christianity, whose chief work, *Apologeticus adversus Gentes pro Christianis,* an expertly argued vindication of the Christian church against false accusations, was the weightiest apologia for Christianity produced during the first two centuries.

My father was so highly pleased with one of these apologetical orations of my uncle *Toby*'s, which he had delivered one evening before him and *Yorick,* that he wrote it down before he went to bed.

I have had the good fortune to meet with it amongst my father's papers, with here and there an insertion of his own, betwixt two crooks, thus [   ], and is endorsed,

My brother TOBY'*s justification of his own principles and conduct in wishing to continue the war.*

I may safely say, I have read over this apologetical oration of my uncle *Toby*'s a hundred times, and think it so fine a model of defence,——and shews so sweet a temperament of gallantry and good principles in him, that I give it the world, word for word, (interlineations and all) as I find it.

CHAP. XXXII.

My uncle TOBY'*s apologetical oration.*

I Am not insensible, brother *Shandy,* that when a man, whose profession is arms, wishes, as I have done, for war,——it has an ill aspect to the world;——and that, how just and right soever his motives and intentions may be,——he stands in an uneasy posture in vindicating himself from private views in doing it.

For this cause, if a soldier is a prudent man, which he may be, without being a jot the less brave, he will be sure not to utter his wish in the hearing of an enemy; for say what he will, an enemy will not believe him.——He will be cautious of doing it even to a friend,——lest he may suffer in his esteem: ——But if his heart is overcharged, and a secret sigh for arms must have its vent, he will reserve it for the ear of a brother, who knows his character to the bottom, and what his true notions, dispositions, and principles of honour are: What, I *hope,* I have been in all these, brother *Shandy,* would be unbecoming in me to say:——much worse, I know, have I been than I ought,——and something worse, perhaps, than I think: But such as I am, you, my dear brother *Shandy,* who have sucked the same breasts with me,——and with whom I have been brought up from my cradle,——and from whose knowledge, from the first hours of our boyish pastimes, down to this, I have concealed no one action of my life, and scarce a thought in it——Such as I am, brother, you must by this time know me, with all my vices, and with all my weaknesses too, whether of my age, my temper, my passions, or my understanding.

Tell me then, my dear brother *Shandy,* upon which of them it is, that when I condemned the peace of *Utrecht,* and grieved the war was not carried on with vigour a little longer, you should think your brother did it upon unworthy views; or that in wishing for war, he should be bad enough to wish more of his fellow creatures slain,——more slaves made, and more families driven from their peaceful habitations, merely for his own pleasure:——Tell me, brother *Shandy,* upon what one deed of mine do you ground it? [*The devil a deed do I know of, dear* Toby, *but one for a hundred pounds, which I lent thee to carry on these cursed sieges.*]

If, when I was a school-boy, I could not hear a drum beat, but my heart beat with it——was it my fault?——Did I plant the propensity there?——did I sound the alarm within, or Nature?

When *Guy,* Earl of *Warwick,*[1] and *Parismus* and *Paris-*

---

[1] A legendary hero of English romance, whose popular exploits have been retold in many forms since the twelfth century. The school-boy's copy was probably one of the ballads or chap-books popular during the seventeenth and eighteenth centuries. The histories of Parismus, Prince of Bohemia, and of his son, Parismenos, were very popular imitations of the Spanish chivalric romances. *Valentine and Orson* was a romance of the Charlemagne cycle, popular in many languages and versions since the fifteenth century. The *Seven Champions* may be a slip for *The Seven Champions of Christendom,* the name given in many popular medieval tales to the seven national saints (George of England, Denis of France, James of Spain, Anthony of Italy, Andrew of Scotland, Patrick of Ireland, and David of Wales), whose exploits have been celebrated in countless romances, ballads, and plays.

menus, and *Valentine* and *Orson,* and the *Seven Champions of England* were handed around the school,——were they not all purchased with my own pocket money?   Was that selfish, brother *Shandy?*   When we read over the siege of *Troy,* which lasted ten years and eight months,——though with such a train of artillery as we had at *Namur,* the town might have been carried in a week——was I not as much concerned for the destruction of the *Greeks* and *Trojans* as any boy of the whole school?   Had I not three strokes of a ferula given me, two on my right hand and one on my left, for calling *Helena*[2] a bitch for it?   Did any one of you shed more tears for *Hector?*   And when king *Priam* came to the camp to beg his body, and returned weeping back to *Troy* without it,[3]——you know, brother, I could not eat my dinner.——

——Did that bespeak me cruel?   Or because, brother *Shandy,* my blood flew out into the camp, and my heart panted for war,——was it a proof it could not ache for the distresses of war too?

O brother! 'tis one thing for a soldier to gather laurels,—— and 'tis another to scatter cypress.——[*Who told thee, my dear* Toby, *that cypress was used by the ancients on mournful occasions?*]

——'Tis one thing, brother *Shandy,* for a soldier to hazard his own life——to leap first down into the trench, where he is sure to be cut in pieces:——'Tis one thing, from public spirit and a thirst of glory, to enter the breach the first man,——to stand in the foremost rank, and march bravely on with drums and trumpets, and colours flying about his ears:——'Tis one thing, I say, brother *Shandy,* to do this——and 'tis another thing to reflect on the miseries of war;——to view the desolations of whole countries, and consider the intolerable fatigues and hardships which the soldier himself, the instrument who works them, is forced (for six-pence a day, if he can get it) to undergo.

---

[2]Helen of Troy.

[3]According to traditional accounts, Priam's attempt to recover the body of Hector from Achilles, who had slain him, was successful.

Need I be told, dear *Yorick,* as I was by you, in *Le Fever's* funeral sermon, *That so soft and gentle a creature, born to love, to mercy, and kindness, as man is, was not shaped for this?*——But why did you not add, *Yorick,*——if not by NA-TURE——that he is so by NECESSITY?——For what is war? what is it, *Yorick,* when fought as ours has been, upon principles of *liberty,* and upon principles of *honour*——what is it, but the getting together of quiet and harmless people, with their swords in their hands, to keep the ambitious and the turbulent within bounds? And heaven is my witness, brother *Shandy,* that the pleasure I have taken in these things,——and that infinite delight, in particular, which has attended my sieges in my bowling green, has arose within me, and I hope in the corporal too, from the consciousness we both had, that in carrying them on, we were answering the great ends of our creation.

CHAP. XXXIII.

I Told the Christian reader——I say *Christian*——hoping he is one——and if he is not, I am sorry for it——and only beg he will consider the matter with himself, and not lay the blame entirely upon this book,——

I told him, Sir——for in good truth, when a man is telling a story in the strange way I do mine, he is obliged continually to be going backwards and forwards to keep all tight together in the reader's fancy——which, for my own part, if I did not take heed to do more than at first, there is so much unfixed and equivocal matter starting up, with so many breaks and gaps in it,——and so little service do the stars afford, which, nevertheless, I hang up in some of the darkest passages, knowing that the world is apt to lose its way, with all the lights the sun itself at noon day can give it——and now, you see, I am lost myself!——

——But 'tis my father's fault; and whenever my brains come to be dissected, you will perceive, without spectacles, that he

has left a large uneven thread, as you sometimes see in an un-
saleable piece of cambrick, running along the whole length
of the web, and so untowardly, you cannot so much as cut
out a * *, (here I hang up a couple of lights again)——or a
fillet, or a thumb-stall, but it is seen or felt.————

Quanto id diligentius in liberis procreandis cavendum,[1]
sayeth *Cardan*. All which being considered, and that you see
'tis morally impracticable for me to wind this round to where
I set out————

I begin the chapter over again.

CHAP. XXXIV.

I Told the Christian reader in the beginning of the chapter
which preceded my uncle *Toby's* apologetical oration,——
though in a different trope from what I shall make use of
now, That the peace of *Utrecht* was within an ace of creating
the same shyness betwixt my uncle *Toby* and his hobby-horse,
as it did betwixt the queen and the rest of the confederating
powers.

There is an indignant way in which a man sometimes dis-
mounts his horse, which as good as says to him, "I'll go afoot,
Sir, all the days of my life, before I would ride a single mile
upon your back again." Now my uncle *Toby* could not be
said to dismount his horse in this manner; for in strictness of
language, he could not be said to dismount his horse at all——
his horse rather flung him——and somewhat *viciously*, which
made my uncle *Toby* take it ten times more unkindly. Let
this matter be settled by state jockies as they like.——It
created, I say, a sort of shyness betwixt my uncle *Toby* and his
hobby-horse.——He had no occasion for him from the month
of *March* to *November*, which was the summer after the

---

[1]How much more careful should we be in begetting our children.
Girolamo Cardan (1501–1576) was an Italian mathematician, physician,
and astrologer. I have been unable to find this passage in his works;
Sterne may have adapted it from the *Anatomy of Melancholy*, 1.2.1.6.

articles were signed, except it was now and then to take a
short ride out, just to see that the fortifications and harbour
of *Dunkirk* were demolished, according to stipulation.[1]

The *French* were so backwards all that summer in setting
about that affair, and Monsieur *Tugghe,* the deputy from the
magistrates of *Dunkirk,* presented so many affecting petitions
to the queen,——beseeching her majesty to cause only her
thunderbolts to fall upon the martial works, which might
have incurred her displeasure,——but to spare——to spare
the mole, for the mole's sake; which, in its naked situation,
could be no more than an object of pity——and the queen
(who was but a woman) being of a pitiful disposition,——
and her ministers also, they not wishing in their hearts to have
the town dismantled, for these private reasons,   *   *   *   *
*   *   *   *   *   *   *   *   *   *   *   *   *   *   *   *
*   *   *   *   *   *   *   *   *————
   *   *   *   *   *   *   *   *   *   *   *   *   *   *
*   *   *   *   *   *   *   *   *   *   *   *   *   *   *
*   *   *   *   *; so that the whole went heavily on with my
uncle *Toby;* insomuch, that it was not within three full
months, after he and the corporal had constructed the town,
and put it in a condition to be destroyed, that the several
commandants, commissaries, deputies, negotiators, and in-
tendants, would permit him to set about it.——Fatal interval
of inactivity!

The corporal was for beginning the demolition, by making
a breach in the ramparts, or main fortifications of the town
——No,——that will never do, corporal, said my uncle *Toby,*
for in going that way to work with the town, the *English* garrison will not be safe in it an hour; because if the *French* are
treacherous——They are as treacherous as devils, an' please
your honour, said the corporal——It gives me concern always
when I hear it, *Trim,* said my uncle *Toby,*——for they don't
want personal bravery; and if a breach is made in the ramparts, they may enter it, and make themselves masters of the
place when they please:——Let them enter it, said the cor-

─────────────
[1]See p. 208, n. 1.

poral, lifting up his pioneer's spade in both his hands, as if he
was going to lay about him with it,——let them enter, an'
please your honour, if they dare.——In cases like this, corporal, said my uncle *Toby,* slipping his right hand down to
the middle of his cane, and holding it afterwards truncheon-
wise, with his forefinger extended,——'tis no part of the consideration of a commandant, what the enemy dare,——or what
they dare not do; he must act with prudence. We will begin
with the outworks both towards the sea and the land, and
particularly with fort *Louis,* the most distant of them all, and
demolish it first,——and the rest, one by one, both on our
right and left, as we retreat towards the town;——then we'll
demolish the mole,——next fill up the harbour,——then retire into the citadel, and blow it up into the air; and having
done that, corporal, we'll embark for *England.*——We are
there, quoth the corporal, recollecting himself——Very true,
said my uncle *Toby*——looking at the church.

CHAP. XXXV.

A Delusive, delicious consultation or two of this kind, betwixt my uncle *Toby* and *Trim,* upon the demolition of
Dunkirk,——for a moment rallied back the ideas of those
pleasures, which were slipping from under him:——still——
still all went on heavily——the magic left the mind the weaker
——Stillness, with Silence at her back, entered the solitary
parlour, and drew their gauzy mantle over my uncle *Toby*'s
head;——and Listlessness, with her lax fibre and undirected
eye, sat quietly down beside him in his arm chair.——No
longer *Amberg,* and *Rhinberg,* and *Limbourg,* and *Huy,* and
Bonn, in one year,[1]——and the prospect of *Landen,* and *Trerebach,* and *Drusen,* and *Dendermond,* the next,[2]——hurried on
the blood:——No longer did saps, and mines, and blinds, and
gabions, and palisadoes, keep out this fair enemy of man's

---

[1]1703.

[2]See p. 448, n. 3.

repose:——No more could my uncle *Toby,* after passing the *French* lines, as he eat his egg at supper, from thence break into the heart of *France,*——cross over the *Oyes,* and with all *Picardie* open behind him, march up to the gates of *Paris,* and fall asleep with nothing but ideas of glory:——No more was he to dream, he had fixed the royal standard upon the tower of the *Bastile,* and awake with it streaming in his head.

——Softer visions,——gentler vibrations stole sweetly in upon his slumbers;——the trumpet of war fell out of his hands,——he took up the lute, sweet instrument! of all others the most delicate! the most difficult!——how wilt thou touch it, my dear uncle *Toby?*

CHAP. XXXVI.

NOW, because I have once or twice said, in my inconsiderate way of talking, That I was confident the following memoirs of my uncle *Toby*'s courtship of widow *Wadman,* whenever I got time to write them, would turn out one of the most compleat systems, both of the elementary and practical part of love and love-making, that ever was addressed to the world——are you to imagine from thence, that I shall set out with a description of *what love is?* whether part God and part Devil, as *Plotinus*[1] will have it——

——Or by a more critical equation, and supposing the whole of love to be as ten——to determine, with *Ficinus,*[2] *"How many parts of it*——*the one,*——*and how many the other;"*—or whether it is *all of it one great Devil,* from head

---

[1]Plotinus (204–270), a celebrated Greek Neoplatonist, declared in his *Enneades,* 3.5, that love is twofold, the higher love being a god, the lower a daemon or guardian spirit. "Devil," in the traditional Christian sense of the word, is a mistranslation. Here, and possibly in the following reference to Ficinus, Sterne's immediate source was the *Anatomy of Melancholy,* 3.1.1.2.

[2]Marsilio Ficini (1433–1499), an Italian physician, Platonic philosopher, and commentator on Plato and Plotinus, to whose elaborate *Commentaria* on Plato's *Convivio,* 6.8, Sterne here alludes loosely—or in burlesque.

to tail, as *Plato*[3] has taken upon him to pronounce; concerning which conceit of his, I shall not offer my opinion:——but my opinion of *Plato* is this; that he appears, from this instance, to have been a man of much the same temper and way of reasoning with doctor *Baynard,* who being a great enemy to blisters, as imagining that half a dozen of 'em on at once, would draw a man as surely to his grave, as a herse and six ——rashly concluded, that the Devil himself was nothing in the world, but one great bouncing *Cantharidis.*[4]——

I have nothing to say to people who allow themselves this monstrous liberty in arguing, but what *Nazianzen*[5] cried out (*that is polemically*) to *Philagrius*——

"Ἐυγε!" *O rare! 'tis fine reasoning, Sir, indeed!*——"ὅτι φιλοσοφεῖς ἐν Πάθεσι."——*and most nobly do you aim at truth, when you philosophize about it in your moods and passions.*

Nor is it to be imagined, for the same reason, I should stop to enquire, whether love is a disease,——or embroil myself

----

[3]Plato (for whom, see p. 293, n. 1) made Diotima assert that love is a great spirit or daemon who mediates between gods and men (*Symposium,* 202); Sterne's immediate source, however, is Burton, *ibid.*

[4]Edward Baynard (fl. 1719), an English physician and poet, wrote in *The History of Cold-Bathing* (by Sir John Floyer and Baynard): "How many Men has intempestive and over Blistering destroy'd, . . . by mixing the venomous and corrosive Effluvium's of the *Cantharides* with the Blood, actuating the *Pulse,* besides bringing *Stranguries* and other Mischiefs on the *Bladder?* insomuch that I believe the Devil himself, old *Beelzebub,* to be nothing but a great *Cantharid,* the Prince of *Flies,* they act so according to his Nature, to plague Mankind where-ever they are applied. . . . And here I cannot omit a Story of an Apothecary's Man, in *Fleetstreet,* whose Master died in a few Days Sickness of a *Fever,* which his Doctors quickly made malignant. *Quoth he,* I wonder that my Master should die so soon, for he had a Dozen *Blisters* on, and they all drew very strong: That is true, *quoth one standing by,* thou art in the right on't, for in Four Days Time (together with the help of a Team of Doctors) he was drawn out of his Bed into the Vault over the way there, pointing at St. *Dunstan's* Church" (ed. London, 1702, Part 2, pp. 199–200). Cantharides is a medicinal preparation of Spanish flies, used for blistering.

[5]St. Gregory Nazianzen (for whom, see p. 414, n. 2). Philagrius (fl. 370) was a friend and correspondent of Gregory. The passage in Greek, which may be translated, "Bravo! that you philosophize in your sufferings," is taken from Gregory's *Epistola 32,* "Philagrio," where it is not intended ironically.

with *Rhasis*[6] and *Dioscorides,* whether the seat of it is in the
brain or liver;——because this would lead me on, to an examination of the two very opposite manners, in which patients
have been treated——the one, of *Aætius,*[7] who always begun
with a cooling glyster of hempseed and bruised cucumbers;
——and followed on with thin potations of water lillies and
purslane——to which he added a pinch of snuff, of the herb
Hanea;——and where *Aætius* durst venture it,——his topaz-
ring.

——The other, that of *Gordonius,*[8] who (in his cap. 15. *de
Amore*) directs they should be thrashed, *"ad putorem usque,"*
——till they stink again.

These are disquisitions, which my father, who had laid in
a great stock of knowledge of this kind, will be very busy
with, in the progress of my uncle *Toby*'s affairs: I must anticipate thus much, That from his theories of love, (with which,
by the way, he contrived to crucify my uncle *Toby*'s mind,
almost as much as his amours themselves)——he took a single
step into practice;——and by means of a camphorated cere-
cloth,[9] which he found means to impose upon the taylor for

---

[6]Rhazes (fl. 925 A.D.) was an Arabian physician and author of many
works on medicine. Pedanius Dioscorides (fl. 75 A.D.) was a Greek
physician and author of a great *Materia Medica,* the most important
work on plants and drugs extant until the seventeenth century.

[7]Amidenus Aëtius (fl. 540) was a Greek physician and medical writer
of importance. The following herbs. whose properties are discussed in
Aëtius's *Tetrabiblos,* 1.1, 1.2, 3.3, *et passim,* were standard refrigerants.
"Hanea" Sterne found in *The Anatomy of Melancholy,* 3.2.5.1, which is
the source of the present passage; it is apparently Burton's mistrans-
literation of ἄγνος, the *agnus castus,* an aromatic shrub or tree sup-
posedly powerful to preserve chastity. According to medieval lapidaries,
the topaz had a tranquillizing effect on all the passions, but was particularly valuable as a cure for sensuality.

[8]This appears to be a paraphrase of Bernard de Gordon (fl. 1285–
1305), a highly esteemed French physician, *Lilium Medicinæ,* 2.20, *De
Amore qui hereos dicitur: "Frequenter et fortiter flagelletur donec totus
incipiat fetere."* A closer paraphrase is found in Burton, *ibid.*

[9]Cloth saturated with wax to which medicaments were sometimes
added for use as a bandage. The old herbals listed camphor, among
other refrigerants, as preventing the formation of semen. In Burton,
ibid., Sterne had read: "*Camphora pudendis alligata, et in bracâ gestata
. . . membrum flaccidum reddit.*"

buckram, whilst he was making my uncle *Toby* a new pair of breeches, he produced *Gordonius's* effect upon my uncle *Toby* without the disgrace.

What changes this produced, will be read in its proper place: all that is needful to be added to the anecdote, is this,——That whatever effect it had upon my uncle *Toby*,——it had a vile effect upon the house;——and if my uncle *Toby* had not smoaked it down as he did, it might have had a vile effect upon my father too.

CHAP. XXXVII.

——'TWILL come out of itself by and bye.——All I contend for is, that I am not *obliged* to set out with a definition of what love is; and so long as I can go on with my story intelligibly, with the help of the word itself, without any other idea to it, than what I have in common with the rest of the world, why should I differ from it a moment before the time?——When I can get on no further,——and find myself entangled on all sides of this mystick labyrinth,——my Opinion will then come in, in course,——and lead me out.

At present, I hope I shall be sufficiently understood, in telling the reader, my uncle *Toby fell in love:*

——Not that the phrase is at all to my liking: for to say a man is *fallen* in love,——or that he is *deeply* in love,——or up to the ears in love,——and sometimes even *over head and ears in it,*——carries an idiomatical kind of implication, that love is a thing *below* a man:——this is recurring again to *Plato's* opinion, which, with all his divinityship,——I hold to be damnable and heretical;——and so much for that.

Let love therefore be what it will,——my uncle *Toby* fell into it.

——And possibly, gentle reader, with such a temptation—— so wouldst thou: For never did thy eyes behold, or thy concupiscence covet any thing in this world, more concupiscible than widow *Wadman.*

CHAP. XXXVIII.

TO conceive this right,——call for pen and ink——here's
paper ready to your hand.——Sit down, Sir, paint her to
your own mind——as like your mistress as you can——as
unlike your wife as your conscience will let you——'tis all
one to me——please but your own fancy in it.

——Was ever any thing in Nature so sweet!——so exquisite!

——Then, dear Sir, how could my uncle *Toby* resist it?

Thrice happy book! thou wilt have one page, at least, within thy covers, which MALICE will not blacken, and which IGNORANCE cannot misrepresent.

CHAP. XXXIX.

AS *Susannah* was informed by an express from Mrs. *Bridget,* of my uncle *Toby*'s falling in love with her mistress, fifteen days before it happened,——the contents of which express, *Susannah* communicated to my mother the next day, ——it has just given me an opportunity of entering upon my uncle *Toby*'s amours a fortnight before their existence.

I have an article of news to tell you, Mr. *Shandy,* quoth my mother, which will surprise you greatly.——

Now my father was then holding one of his second beds of justice, and was musing within himself about the hardships of matrimony, as my mother broke silence.——

"——My brother *Toby,* quoth she, is going to be married to Mrs. *Wadman.*"

——Then he will never, quoth my father, be able to lie *diagonally* in his bed again as long as he lives.

It was a consuming vexation to my father, that my mother never asked the meaning of a thing she did not understand.

——That she is not a woman of science, my father would say——is her misfortune—but she might ask a question.——

My mother never did.——In short, she went out of the world at last without knowing whether it turned *round,* or stood *still.*——My father had officiously told her above a thousand times which way it was,——but she always forgot.

For these reasons a discourse seldom went on much further betwixt them, than a proposition,——a reply, and a rejoinder; at the end of which, it generally took breath for a few minutes, (as in the affair of the breeches) and then went on again.

If he marries, 'twill be the worse for us,——quoth my mother.

Not a cherry-stone, said my father,——he may as well batter away his means upon that, as any thing else.

——To be sure, said my mother: so here ended the proposition,——the reply,——and the rejoinder, I told you of.

It will be some amusement to him, too,——said my father.

A very great one, answered my mother, if he should have
children.——

——Lord have mercy upon me,——said my father to himself—— * * * * * * * * * * * * * * * *
* * * * * * * * * * * * * * * * *
* * * * * * * * * * * * * * * * *
* * * * * * * * * * * * * * * * *
* * * * * * * * * * *

CHAP. XL.

I Am now beginning to get fairly into my work; and by the
help of a vegitable diet, with a few of the cold seeds,[1] I
make no doubt but I shall be able to go on with my uncle
Toby's story, and my own, in a tolerable straight line. Now,

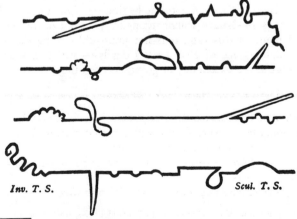

Inv. T. S.　　　　　　　　　　　　　*Scul. T. S.*

---

[1]The seeds of the cucumber, gourd, pumpkin, etc. Such a diet was
thought to cool the blood and compose the passions.

These were the four lines I moved in through my first, second, third, and fourth volumes.——In the fifth volume I have been very good,——the precise line I have described in it being this:

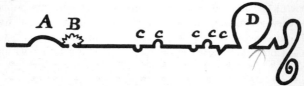

By which it appears, that except at the curve, marked A. where I took a trip to *Navarre,*——and the indented curve *B.* which is the short airing when I was there with the Lady *Baussiere* and her page,——I have not taken the least frisk of a digression, till *John de la Casse*'s devils led me the round you see marked D.——for as for *c c c c* they are nothing but parentheses, and the common *ins* and *outs* incident to the lives of the greatest ministers of state; and when compared with what men have done,——or with my own transgressions at the letters A B D——they vanish into nothing.

In this last volume I have done better still——for from the end of *Le Fever*'s episode, to the beginning of my uncle *Toby*'s campaigns,——I have scarce stepped a yard out of my way.

If I mend at this rate, it is not impossible——by the good leave of his grace of *Benevento*'s devils——but I may arrive hereafter at the excellency of going on even thus;

———

which is a line drawn as straight as I could draw it, by a writing-master's ruler, (borrowed for that purpose) turning neither to the right hand or to the left.

This *right line,*——the path-way for Christians to walk in! say divines[2]——

——The emblem of moral rectitude! says *Cicero*[3]——

[2]An allusion to the "straight paths" of Hebrews, 12.13, or to some similar counsel.

[3]A not infrequent figure in Cicero's writings.

——The *best line!* say cabbage-planters——is the shortest line, says *Archimedes,*[4] which can be drawn from one given point to another.——

I wish your ladyships would lay this matter to heart in your next birth-day suits![5]

——What a journey!

Pray can you tell me,——that is, without anger, before I write my chapter upon straight lines——by what mistake—— who told them so——or how it has come to pass, that your men of wit and genius have all along confounded this line, with the line of GRAVITATION?

END of the SIXTH VOLUME.

---

[4]"Of all lines which have the same extremities the straight line is the least."—Archimedes (for whom, see p. 50, n. 2), *On the Sphere and Cylinder,* 1, Assumption 1.

[5]Clothes worn at a birthday celebration.

THE
LIFE
AND
OPINIONS

OF

TRISTRAM SHANDY,
GENTLEMAN.

Non enim excurſus hic ejus, ſed opus ipſum eſt.
PLIN, Lib. quintus Epiſtola ſexta,

VOL. VII.

LONDON:
Printed for T. BECKET and P. A. DEHONT,
in the Strand.   MDCCLXV.

Facsimile of the title page to the first edition of Volumes VII and VIII.
The motto, which glances at the unexpected subject matter of Volume VII,
is from the *Epistles,* 5.6.44, of Pliny the Younger (c.62–c.114), the Roman
author and orator, and may be translated: "For this is not an excursion
from it, but is the work itself."

VOLUME VII.

CHAP. I.

NO——I think, I said, I would write two volumes every year, provided the vile cough which then tormented me, and which to this hour I dread worse than the devil, would but give me leave——and in another place——(but where, I can't recollect now) speaking of my book as a *machine,* and laying my pen and ruler down cross-wise upon the table, in order to gain the greater credit to it——I swore it should be kept a going at that rate these forty years if it pleased but the fountain of life to bless me so long with health and good spirits.

Now as for my spirits, little have I to lay to their charge—— nay so very little (unless the mounting me upon a long stick, and playing the fool with me nineteen hours out of the twenty-four, be accusations) that on the contrary, I have much—— much to thank 'em for: cheerily have ye made me tread the path of life with all the burdens of it (except its cares) upon my back; in no one moment of my existence, that I remember, have ye once deserted me, or tinged the objects which came in my way, either with sable, or with a sickly green; in dangers ye gilded my horizon with hope, and when DEATH himself knocked at my door——ye bad him come again; and in so gay a tone of careless indifference, did ye do it, that he doubted of his commission——

"——There must certainly be some mistake in this matter," quoth he.

Now there is nothing in this world I abominate worse, than to be interrupted in a story——and I was that moment telling *Eugenius*[1] a most tawdry one in my way, of a nun who fancied

[1]See p. 28, n. 1.

herself a shell-fish, and of a monk damn'd for eating a muscle,[2] and was shewing him the grounds and justice of the procedure——

"——Did ever so grave a personage get into so vile a scrape?" quoth Death. Thou hast had a narrow escape, *Tristram,* said *Eugenius,* taking hold of my hand as I finish'd my story——

But there is no *living, Eugenius,* replied I, at this rate; for as this *son of a whore* has found out my lodgings——

——You call him rightly, said *Eugenius,*——for by sin, we are told, he enter'd the world——I care not which way he enter'd, quoth I, provided he be not in such a hurry to take me out with him——for I have forty volumes to write, and forty thousand things to say and do, which no body in the world will say and do for me, except thyself; and as thou seest he has got me by the throat (for *Eugenius* could scarce hear me speak across the table) and that I am no match for him in the open field, had I not better, whilst these few scatter'd spirits remain, and these two spider legs of mine (holding one of them up to him) are able to support me——had I not better, *Eugenius,* fly for my life? 'tis my advice, my dear *Tristram,* said *Eugenius*——then by heaven! I will lead him a dance he little thinks of——for I will gallop, quoth I, without looking once behind me to the banks of the *Garonne;* and if I hear him clattering at my heels——I'll scamper away to mount *Vesuvius*——from thence to *Joppa,* and from *Joppa* to the world's end, where, if he follows me, I pray God he may break his neck——

——He runs more risk *there,* said *Eugenius,* than thou.

Eugenius's wit and affection brought blood into the cheek from whence it had been some months banish'd——'twas a vile moment to bid adieu in; he led me to my chaise—— *Allons!*[3] said I; the post boy gave a crack with his whip——off I went like a cannon, and in half a dozen bounds got into *Dover.*

---

[2]Mussel. The story was probably suggested by a reference in *The Anatomy of Melancholy,* 1.1.3.2.

[3]Let's go!

CHAP. II.

NOW hang it! quoth I, as I look'd towards the *French* coast——a man should know something of his own country too, before he goes abroad——and I never gave a peep into *Rochester* church, or took notice of the dock of *Chatham,* or visited St. *Thomas* at *Canterbury,*[1] though they all three laid in my way——

——But mine, indeed, is a particular case——

So without arguing the matter further with *Thomas o' Becket,* or any one else——I skip'd into the boat, and in five minutes we got under sail and scudded away like the wind.

Pray captain, quoth I, as I was going down into the cabin, is a man never overtaken by *Death* in this passage?

Why, there is not time for a man to be sick in it, replied he ——What a cursed lyar! for I am sick as a horse, quoth I, already——what a brain!——upside down!——hey dey! the cells are broke loose one into another, and the blood, and the lymph, and the nervous juices, with the fix'd and volatile salts, are all jumbled into one mass——good g—! every thing turns round in it like a thousand whirlpools——I'd give a shilling to know if I shan't write the clearer for it——

Sick! sick! sick! sick!——

——When shall we get to land? captain——they have hearts like stones——O I am deadly sick!——reach me that thing, boy——'tis the most discomfiting sickness——I wish I was at the bottom——Madam! how is it with you? Undone! undone! un—— O! undone! sir——What the first time?——No, 'tis the second, third, sixth, tenth time, sir,——hey-day—— what a trampling over head!——hollo! cabin boy! what's the matter——

The wind chopp'd about! s'Death!——then I shall meet him full in the face.

----

[1] *I.e.,* the scene of Thomas à Becket's murder and the site of his shrine in Canterbury cathedral.

What luck!——'tis chopp'd about again, master——O the devil chop it——

Captain, quoth she, for heaven's sake, let us get ashore.

CHAP. III.

IT is a great inconvenience to a man in a haste, that there are three distinct roads between *Calais* and *Paris*, in behalf of which there is so much to be said by the several deputies from the towns which lie along them, that half a day is easily lost in settling which you'll take.

First, the road by *Lisle* and *Arras*, which is the most about ——but most interesting, and instructing.

The second that by *Amiens*, which you may go, if you would see *Chantilly*——

And that by *Beauvais*, which you may go, if you will.

For this reason a great many chuse to go by *Beauvais*.

CHAP. IV.

"NOW before I quit *Calais*," a travel-writer would say, "it would not be amiss to give some account of it."—— Now I think it very much amiss——that a man cannot go quietly through a town, and let it alone, when it does not meddle with him, but that he must be turning about and drawing his pen at every kennel he crosses over, merely, o' my conscience, for the sake of drawing it; because, if we may judge from what has been wrote of these things, by all who have *wrote and gallop'd*——or who have *gallop'd and wrote*, which is a different way still; or who for more expedition than the rest, have *wrote-galloping*, which is the way I do at present ——from the great *Addison*[1] who did it with his satchel of school-books hanging at his a—— and galling his beast's crupper

---

[1] An allusion to Addison's *Remarks on Several Parts of Italy*, in the Preface to which he had written: "I have taken care particularly to consider the several passages of the ancient Poets, which have any

at every stroke——there is not a galloper of us all who might
not have gone on ambling quietly in his own ground (in case
he had any) and have wrote all he had to write, dry shod, as
well as not.

For my own part, as heaven is my judge, and to which I shall
ever make my last appeal——I know no more of *Calais,* (except the little my barber told me of it, as he was whetting
his razor) than I do this moment of *Grand Cairo;* for it was
dusky in the evening when I landed, and dark as pitch in the
morning when I set out, and yet by merely knowing what is
what, and by drawing this from that in one part of the town,
and by spelling and putting this and that together in another
——I would lay any travelling odds, that I this moment write
a chapter upon *Calais* as long as my arm; and with so distinct
and satisfactory a detail of every item, which is worth a
stranger's curiosity in the town——that you would take me for
the town clerk of *Calais* itself——and where, sir, would be the
wonder? was not *Democritus,*[2] who laughed ten times more
than I——town-clerk of *Abdera?* and was not (I forget his
name) who had more discretion than us both, town-clerk of
Ephesus?[3]——it should be penn'd moreover, Sir, with so much
knowledge and good sense, and truth, and precision——

——Nay——if you don't believe me, you may read the chapter for your pains.

relation to the Places and Curiosities that I met with; For before I
entered on my voyage I took care to refresh my memory among the
Classic Authors, and to make such collections out of them as I might
afterwards have occasion for. I must confess it was not one of the least
entertainments that I met with in travelling, to examine these several
Descriptions, as it were, upon the spot, and to compare the natural face
of the country with the Landskips that the Poets have given us of it."

[2]Democritus (c.460–c.357 B.C.), one of the greatest of the Greek physical philosophers, was an inhabitant of Abdera, in Thrace; according to
one tradition, his fellow-citizens contributed toward the alleviation of his
poverty. Because he chose not to weep at the spectacle of human life,
he received the absurd epithet, "the laughing philosopher."

[3]A reference to Heraclitus (c.540–c.475 B.C.), a celebrated Greek philosopher who quitted his magistracy in Ephesus, which was hereditary in his
family, to apply himself to philosophic speculation. From his lonely
life, philosophic profundity, and contempt for mankind he was hyper-
bolically called, in contrast to Democritus, "the weeping philosopher."

CHAP. V.

CALAIS, *Calatium, Calusium, Calesium.*[1]
This town, if we may trust its archives, the authority of which I see no reason to call in question in this place——was *once* no more than a small village belonging to one of the first Counts *de Guines;* and as it boasts at present of no less than fourteen thousand inhabitants, exclusive of four hundred and twenty distinct families in the *basse ville,*[2] or suburbs——it must have grown up by little and little, I suppose, to it's present size.

Though there are four convents, there is but one parochial church in the whole town; I had not an opportunity of taking its exact dimensions, but it is pretty easy to make a tolerable conjecture of 'em——for as there are fourteen thousand inhabitants in the town, if the church holds them all, it must be considerably large——and if it will not——'tis a very great pity they have not another——it is built in form of a cross, and dedicated to the Virgin *Mary;* the steeple which has a spire to it, is placed in the middle of the church, and stands upon four pillars elegant and light enough, but sufficiently strong at the same time——it is decorated with eleven altars, most of which are rather fine than beautiful. The great altar is a masterpiece in its kind; 'tis of white marble, and as I was told near sixty feet high——had it been much higher, it had been as high as mount *Calvary* itself——therefore, I suppose it must be high enough in all conscience.

There was nothing struck me more than the great *Square;* tho' I cannot say 'tis either well paved or well built; but 'tis in the heart of the town, and most of the streets, especially those in that quarter, all terminate in it; could there have been a fountain in all *Calais,* which it seems there cannot, as such

---

[1] Former spellings of the word *Calais;* an appropriate introduction to the following burlesque of pedantic guide-books.

[2] The lower town; that portion lying outside the fortifications.

an object would have been a great ornament, it is not to be doubted, but that the inhabitants would have had it in the very centre of this square,——not that it is properly a square,——because 'tis forty feet longer from east to west, than from north to south; so that the *French* in general have more reason on their side in calling them *Places* than *Squares,* which strictly speaking, to be sure they are not.

The town-house seems to be but a sorry building, and not to be kept in the best repair; otherwise it had been a second great ornament to this place; it answers however its destination, and serves very well for the reception of the magistrates, who assemble in it from time to time; so that 'tis presumable, justice is regularly distributed.

I have heard much of it, but there is nothing at all curious in the *Courgain;* 'tis a distinct quarter of the town inhabited solely by sailors and fishermen; it consists of a number of small streets, neatly built and mostly of brick; 'tis extremely populous, but as that may be accounted for, from the principles of their diet,——there is nothing curious in that neither.—— A traveller may see it to satisfy himself——he must not omit however taking notice of *La Tour de Guet,*[3] upon any account; 'tis so called from its particular destination, because in war it serves to discover and give notice of the enemies which approach the place, either by sea or land;——but 'tis monstrous high, and catches the eye so continually, you cannot avoid taking notice of it, if you would.

It was a singular disappointment to me, that I could not have permission to take an exact survey of the fortifications, which are the strongest in the world, and which, from first to last, that is, from the time they were set about by *Philip* of *France* Count of *Bologne,* to the present war, wherein many reparations were made, have cost (as I learned afterwards from an engineer in *Gascony*)——above a hundred millions of livres. It is very remarkable that at the *Tête de Gravelenes,* and where the town is naturally the weakest, they have expended the most money; so that the outworks stretch a great

---

[3]Watch-tower.

way into the campaign,[4] and consequently occupy a large tract of ground.——However, after all that is *said* and *done,* it must be acknowledged that *Calais* was never upon any account so considerable from itself, as from its situation, and that easy enterance which it gave our ancestors upon all occasions into *France:* it was not without its inconveniences also; being no less troublesome to the *English* in those times, than *Dunkirk* has been to us, in ours; so that it was deservedly looked upon as the key to both kingdoms, which no doubt is the reason that there have arisen so many contentions who should keep it: of these, the siege of *Calais,* or rather the blockade (for it was shut up both by land and sea) was the most memorable, as it withstood the efforts of *Edward* the third a whole year, and was not terminated at last but by famine and extream misery; the gallantry of *Eustace de St. Pierre,*[5] who first offered himself a victim for his fellow citizens, has rank'd his name with heroes. As it will not take up above fifty pages, it would be injustice to the reader, not to give him a minute account of that romantic transaction, as well as of the siege itself, in *Rapin'*s[6] own words:

CHAP. VI.

——**B**UT courage! gentle reader!——I scorn it——'tis enough to have thee in my power——but to make use of the advantage which the fortune of the pen has now gained over thee, would be too much——No——! by that all powerful fire which warms the visionary brain, and lights the spirits through unworldly tracts! ere I would force a helpless creature upon this hard service, and make thee pay, poor soul!

[4] Open country.

[5] The wealthiest burgher of Calais; according to Froissart, he was the foremost of the six citizens who, to save their city after the battle of Crécy in 1346, presented themselves to the conquering Edward III "with bare heads and feet, with ropes round their necks, and the keys of the town and castle in their hands."

[6] In his *L'Histoire d'Angleterre,* Rapin (for whom, see p. 358, n. 1) treats briefly the siege of Calais, including the story of Eustace de St. Pierre, basing his account on Froissart.

for fifty pages which I have no right to sell thee,——naked as
I am, I would browse upon the mountains, and smile that the
north wind brought me neither my tent or my supper.

——So put on, my brave boy! and make the best of thy way
to *Boulogne.*

CHAP. VII.

——BOULOGNE!——hah!——so we are all got together
——debtors and sinners before heaven; a jolly set
of us——but I can't stay and quaff it off with you——I'm pursued myself like a hundred devils, and shall be overtaken before I can well change horses:——for heaven's sake, make
haste——'Tis for high treason, quoth a very little man, whispering as low as he could to a very tall man that stood next
him——Or else for murder; quoth the tall man——Well
thrown *Size-ace!*[1] quoth I.   No; quoth a third, the gentleman
has been committing —— ——.

Ah! ma chere fille![2] said I, as she tripp'd by, from her matins
——you look as rosy as the morning (for the sun was rising,
and it made the compliment the more gracious)——No; it
can't be that, quoth a fourth——(she made a curt'sy to me
——I kiss'd my hand) 'tis debt; continued he: 'Tis certainly
for debt; quoth a fifth; I would not pay that gentleman's
debts, quoth *Ace,* for a thousand pounds; Nor would I, quoth
Size, for six times the sum——Well thrown, *Size-Ace,* again!
quoth I;——but I have no debt but the debt of NATURE, and I
want but patience of her, and I will pay her every farthing I
owe her————How can you be so hard-hearted, MADAM, to
arrest a poor traveller going along without molestation to any
one, upon his lawful occasions? do stop that death-looking,
long-striding scoundrel of a scare-sinner, who is posting after
me——he never would have followed me but for you——if it

---

[1]Size: sice, six.   The tall and short men, who are hazarding opinions,
are designated by this gamester's term for a throw of two dice which
turns up a six and a one.

[2]Ah! my dear girl!

be but for a stage, or two, just to give me start of him, I beseech you, madam————do, dear lady——

————Now, in troth, 'tis a great pity, quoth mine *Irish* host,
that all this good courtship should be lost; for the young
gentlewoman has been after going out of hearing of it all
along——.

————Simpleton! quoth I.

————So you have nothing *else* in *Boulogne* worth seeing?

————By Jasus! there is the finest SEMINARY for the HUMANI-
TIES——.

————There cannot be a finer; quoth I.

CHAP. VIII.

WHEN the precipitancy of a man's wishes hurries on his
ideas ninety times faster than the vehicle he rides in
——woe be to truth! and woe be to the vehicle and its tackling
(let 'em be made of what stuff you will) upon which he
breathes forth the disappointment of his soul!

As I never give general characters either of men or things in
choler, *"the most haste, the worst speed;"* was all the reflection
I made upon the affair, the first time it happen'd;——the
second, third, fourth, and fifth time, I confined it respectively
to those times, and accordingly blamed only the second, third,
fourth, and fifth post-boy for it, without carrying my reflections further; but the event continuing to befall me from the
fifth, to the sixth, seventh, eighth, ninth, and tenth time, and
without one exception, I then could not avoid making a national reflection of it, which I do in these words;

*That something is always wrong in a French post-chaise
upon first setting out.*

Or the proposition may stand thus.

*A French postilion has always to alight before he has got
three hundred yards out of town.*

What's wrong now?——Diable![1]——a rope's broke!——a

---

[1] The deuce!

knot has slipt!——a staple's drawn!——a bolt's to whittle!——
a tag, a rag, a jag, a strap, a buckle, or a buckle's tongue, want
altering.——

Now true as all this is, I never think myself impower'd to
excommunicate thereupon either the post-chaise, or its driver
——nor do I take it into my head to swear by the living
G—, I would rather go a foot ten thousand times——or that
I will be damn'd if ever I get into another——but I take the
matter coolly before me, and consider, that some tag, or rag,
or jag, or bolt, or buckle, or buckle's tongue, will ever be a
wanting, or want altering, travel where I will——so I never
chaff, but take the good and the bad as they fall in my road,
and get on:——Do so, my lad! said I; he had lost five minutes
already, in alighting in order to get at a luncheon of black
bread which he had cramm'd into the chaise-pocket, and was
remounted and going leisurely on, to relish it the better——
Get on, my lad, said I, briskly——but in the most persuasive
tone imaginable, for I jingled a four and twenty sous piece
against the glass, taking care to hold the flat side towards him,
as he look'd back: the dog grinn'd intelligence from his right
ear to his left, and behind his sooty muzzle discover'd such a
pearly row of teeth, that *Sovereignty* would have pawn'd her
jewels for them.——

Just heaven! { What masticators!——
             { What bread!——

and so, as he finish'd the last mouthful of it, we enter'd the
town of *Montreuil*.

CHAP. IX.

THERE is not a town in all *France,* which in my opinion,
looks better in the map, than MONTREUIL;——I own, it
does not look so well in the book of post roads; but when you
come to see it——to be sure it looks most pitifully.

There is one thing however in it at present very handsome; and that is the inn-keeper's daughter: She has been

eighteen months at *Amiens,* and six at *Paris,* in going through her classes; so knits, and sews, and dances, and does the little coquetries very well.——

——A slut! in running them over within these five minutes that I have stood looking at her, she has let fall at least a dozen loops in a white thread stocking——Yes, yes——I see, you cunning gipsy!——'tis long, and taper——you need not pin it to your knee——and that 'tis your own——and fits you exactly.——

——That Nature should have told this creature a word about a *statue's thumb!*——

——But as this sample is worth all their thumbs——besides I have her thumbs and fingers in at the bargain if they can be any guide to me,——and as *Janatone* withal (for that is her name) stands so well for a drawing——may I never draw more, or rather may I draw like a draught-horse, by main strength all the days of my life,——if I do not draw her in all her proportions, and with as determin'd a pencil, as if I had her in the wettest drapery.——

——But your worships chuse rather that I give you the length, breadth, and perpendicular height of the great parish church, or a drawing of the façade of the abbey of Saint *Austreberte* which has been transported from *Artois* hither ——every thing is just I suppose as the masons and carpenters left them,——and if the belief in *Christ* continues so long, will be so these fifty years to come——so your worships and reverences, may all measure them at your leisures——but he who measures thee, *Janatone,* must do it now——thou carriest the principles of change within thy frame; and considering the chances of a transitory life, I would not answer for thee a moment; e'er twice twelve months are pass'd and gone, thou mayest grow out like a pumkin, and lose thy shapes——or, thou mayest go off like a flower, and lose thy beauty——nay, thou mayest go off like a hussy——and lose thyself.——I would not answer for my aunt *Dinah,* was she alive——'faith, scarce for her picture——were it but painted by *Reynolds*[1]——

[1]See p. 159, n. 1.

——But if I go on with my drawing, after naming that son of *Apollo*, I'll be shot——

So you must e'en be content with the original; which if the evening is fine in passing thro' *Montreuil*, you will see at your chaise door, as you change horses: but unless you have as bad a reason for haste as I have——you had better stop:——She has a little of the *devote:*[2] but that, sir, is a terce to a nine[3] in your favour——

——L—— help me! I could not count a single point: so had been piqued, and repiqued, and capotted[4] to the devil.

CHAP. X.

ALL which being considered, and that Death moreover might be much nearer me than I imagined——I wish I was at *Abbeville*, quoth I, were it only to see how they card and spin——so off we set.
de Montreuil à Nampont - poste et demi[1]
de Nampont à *Bernay* - - - poste
de *Bernay* à *Nouvion* - - - poste
de *Nouvion* à *Abbeville*   poste
——but the carders and spinners were all gone to bed.

CHAP. XI.

WHAT a vast advantage is travelling! only it heats one; but there is a remedy for that, which you may pick out of the next chapter.

---

[2]Devotee.

[3]In piquet, a tierce minor; a term indicating a slight advantage.

[4]Terms from piquet signifying complete defeat.

*Vid. Book of French post-roads, page 36. edition of 1762. [Sterne's note. The reference is to the *Liste générale des postes de France,* an official guide or set of tables of the post-roads of France, published annually in Paris, from 1708 to 1779, by successive members of the Jaillot family.]

[1]From Montreuil to Nampont—a post and a half. A post was a distance of six miles.

CHAP. XII.

WAS I in a condition to stipulate with death, as I am this moment with my apothecary, how and where I will take his glister[1]——I should certainly declare against submitting to it before my friends; and therefore, I never seriously think upon the mode and manner of this great catastrophe, which generally takes up and torments my thoughts as much as the catastrophe itself, but I constantly draw the curtain across it with this wish, that the Disposer of all things may so order it, that it happen not to me in my own house——but rather in some decent inn——at home, I know it,——the concern of my friends, and the last services of wiping my brows and smoothing my pillow, which the quivering hand of pale affection shall pay me, will so crucify my soul, that I shall die of a distemper which my physician is not aware of: but in an inn, the few cold offices I wanted, would be purchased with a few guineas, and paid me with an undisturbed, but punctual attention—— but mark. This inn, should not be the inn at *Abbeville*——if there was not another inn in the universe, I would strike that inn out of the capitulation: so

Let the horses be in the chaise exactly by four in the morning——Yes, by four, Sir,——or by *Genevieve!*[2] I'll raise a clatter in the house, shall wake the dead.

CHAP. XIII.

" *MAKE them like unto a wheel*,"[1] is a bitter sarcasm, as all the learned know, against the *grand tour,* and that restless spirit for making it, which *David* prophetically foresaw would haunt the children of men in the latter days; and

[1]Enema.
[2]Patron saint of Paris.
[1]Psalms, 83.13.

therefore, as thinketh the great bishop *Hall*,[2] 'tis one of the
severest imprecations which *David* ever utter'd against the
enemies of the Lord——and, as if he had said, "I wish them
no worse luck than always to be rolling about"——So much
motion, continues he, (for he was very corpulent)——is so
much unquietness; and so much of rest, by the same analogy,
is so much of heaven.

Now, I (being very thin) think differently; and that so
much of motion, is so much of life, and so much of joy——
and that to stand still, or get on but slowly, is death and the
devil——

Hollo! Ho!——the whole world's asleep!——bring out the
horses——grease the wheels——tie on the mail——and drive
a nail into that moulding——I'll not lose a moment——

Now the wheel we are talking of, and *whereinto* (but not
whereunto, for that would make an Ixion's wheel[3] of it) he
curseth his enemies, according to the bishop's habit of body,
should certainly be a post-chaise wheel, whether they were
set up in *Palestine* at that time or not——and my wheel, for
the contrary reasons, must as certainly be a cart-wheel groan-
ing round its revolution once in an age; and of which sort,
were I to turn commentator, I should make no scruple to
affirm, they had great store in that hilly country.

I love the Pythagoreans[4] (much more than ever I dare tell
my dear *Jenny*) for their "χωρισμὸν ἀπὸ τοῦ Σώματος, εἰς τὸ
καλῶς φιλοσοφεῖν"——[their] *"getting out of the body, in
order to think well."* No man thinks right whilst he is in it;
blinded as he must be, with his congenial[5] humours, and

---

[2]See p. 72, n. 1. The following passage paraphrases portions of
Hall's *Occasional Meditations,* 140, and *Self-Conferences,* 80.

[3]Ixion, in Greek mythology, was punished for impious ingratitude by
being chained to an ever-rolling wheel.

[4]Pythagoras (for whom, see p. 293, n. 1), who viewed the body as the
tomb of the soul, held that truth could be attained only by a mind puri-
fied and superior to the passions and weaknesses of the body, and taught
his disciples to follow a life of silence and contemplation as a means of
emancipating themselves from the evils of the flesh.

[5]Native.

drawn differently aside, as the bishop and myself have been, with too lax or too tense a fibre——Reason is, half of it, Sense; and the measure of heaven itself is but the measure of our present appetites and concoctions——

——But which of the two, in the present case, do you think to be mostly in the wrong?

You, certainly: quoth she, to disturb a whole family so early.

CHAP. XIV.

——But she did not know I was under a vow not to shave my beard till I got to *Paris;*——yet I hate to make mysteries of nothing;——'tis the cold cautiousness of one of those little souls from which *Lessius*[1] (*lib.* 13. *de moribus divinis, cap.* 24.) hath made his estimate, wherein he setteth forth, That one *Dutch* mile, cubically multiplied, will allow room enough, and to spare, for eight hundred thousand millions, which he supposes to be as great a number of souls (counting from the fall of *Adam*) as can possibly be damn'd to the end of the world.

From what he has made this second estimate——unless from the parental goodness of God——I don't know—I am much more at a loss what could be in *Franciscus Ribbera's*[2] head, who pretends that no less a space than one of two hundred *Italian* miles multiplied into itself, will be sufficient to hold the like number——he certainly must have gone upon some of the old *Roman* souls, of which he had read, without reflecting how much, by a gradual and most tabid[3] decline, in a course of eighteen hundred years, they must unavoidably

---

[1]Leonardus Lessius (1554–1623), a Jesuit theologian; this passage from his *De Perfectionibus Moribusque Divinis,* 13.24, Sterne probably took from Burton, 2.2.3. A Dutch mile is about 4.4 English miles.

[2]Francisco Ribera (1537–1591), a Spanish Jesuit, commentator, and devotional writer; this passage from his *Apocalypsis,* 14.20, Sterne probably took from Burton, *ibid.* An Italian mile is about .9 of an English mile.

[3]Slowly wasting.

have shrunk, so as to have come, when he wrote, almost to nothing.

In *Lessius's* time, who seems the cooler man, they were as little as can be imagined——

——We find them less *now*——

And next winter we shall find them less again; so that if we go on from little to less, and from less to nothing, I hesitate not one moment to affirm, that in half a century, at this rate, we shall have no souls at all; which being the period beyond which I doubt likewise of the existence of the Christian faith, 'twill be one advantage that both of 'em will be exactly worn out together.

Blessed *Jupiter!* and blessed every other heathen god and goddess! for now ye will all come into play again, and with *Priapus*[4] at your tails——what jovial times!——but where am I? and into what a delicious riot of things am I rushing?   I ——I who must be cut short in the midst of my days, and taste no more of 'em than what I borrow from my imagination ——peace to thee, generous fool! and let me go on.

CHAP. XV.

——"So hating, I say, to make mysteries of *nothing*"——I intrusted it with the post-boy, as soon as ever I got off the stones; he gave a crack with his whip to balance the compliment; and with the thill-horse trotting, and a sort of an up and a down of the other, we danced it along to *Ailly au clochers,* famed in days of yore for the finest chimes in the world; but we danced through it without music——the chimes being greatly out of order——(as in truth they were through all *France*).

And so making all possible speed, from
Ailly au clochers, I got to *Hixcourt,*
from *Hixcourt,* I got to *Pequignay,* and

---

[4] In Greek mythology, Priapus, the son of Dionysus and Aphrodite, was the god of male generative power.

from *Pequignay,* I got to Amiens,
concerning which town I have nothing to inform you, but
what I have informed you once before——and that was——
that *Janatone* went there to school.

CHAP. XVI.

IN the whole catalogue of those whiffling vexations which
come puffing across a man's canvass, there is not one of a
more teasing and tormenting nature, than this particular one
which I am going to describe——and for which, (unless you
travel with an avance-courier,[1] which numbers do in order to
prevent it)——there is no help: and it is this.

That be you in never so kindly a propensity to sleep——
tho' you are passing perhaps through the finest country——
upon the best roads,——and in the easiest carriage for doing
it in the world——nay was you sure you could sleep fifty
miles straight forwards, without once opening your eyes——
nay what is more, was you as demonstratively satisfied as you
can be of any truth in *Euclid,* that you should upon all accounts be full as well asleep as awake——nay perhaps better
——Yet the incessant returns of paying for the horses at every
stage,——with the necessity thereupon of putting your hand
into your pocket, and counting out from thence, three livres
fifteen sous (sous by sous) puts an end to so much of the
project, that you cannot execute above six miles of it (or supposing it is a post and a half, that is but nine)——were it to
save your soul from destruction.

——I'll be even with 'em, quoth I, for I'll put the precise
sum into a piece of paper, and hold it ready in my hand all
the way: "Now I shall have nothing to do" said I (composing
myself to rest) "but to drop this gently into the post-boy's hat,
and not say a word."——Then there wants two sous more to
drink——or there is a twelve sous piece of *Louis* XIV. which

---

[1]Advance-courier.

will not pass[2]——or livre and some odd liards to be brought
over from the last stage, which Monsieur had forgot; which
altercations (as a man cannot dispute very well asleep) rouse
him: still is sweet sleep retrievable; and still might the flesh
weigh down the spirit, and recover itself of these blows——
but then, by heaven! you have paid but for a single post——
whereas 'tis a post and a half; and this obliges you to pull out
your book of post-roads, the print of which is so very small, it
forces you to open your eyes, whether you will or no: then
Monsieur *le Curé*[3] offers you a pinch of snuff——or a poor
soldier shews you his leg——or a shaveling[4] his box——or the
priestesse of the cistern will water your wheels——they do not
want it——but she swears by her *priesthood* (throwing it
back) that they do:——then you have all these points to
argue, or consider over in your mind; in doing of which, the
rational powers get so thoroughly awakened——you may get
'em to sleep again as you can.

It was entirely owing to one of these misfortunes, or I had
pass'd clean by the stables of *Chantilly*[5]——

——But the postillion first affirming, and then persisting in
it to my face, that there was no mark upon the two sous piece,
I open'd my eyes to be convinced——and seeing the mark
upon it, as plain as my nose——I leap'd out of the chaise in a
passion, and so saw every thing at *Chantilly* in spite.——I tried
it but for three posts and a half, but believe 'tis the best principle in the world to travel speedily upon; for as few objects
look very inviting in that mood——you have little or nothing
to stop you; by which means it was that I pass'd through St.

---

[2]There had been a general recoinage of sous, under Louis XV, in 1738.
A livre was an old French coin about equal in value to and later converted into the franc.   A sou was about one-twentieth of a livre; a liard
was one-fourth of a sou.

[3]The parish priest.

[4]A shaven person; an opprobrious term for a friar.   The box is that in
which he carries whatever money he has begged for his order.

[5]Great stables built (1719-1735) near the course where are held the
great annual races of the French Jockey Club, by Louis-Henri, duke of
Bourbon.

Dennis, without turning my head so much as on side towards the Abby——

——Richness of their treasury! stuff and nonsense!——bating their jewels, which are all false, I would not give three sous for any one thing in it, but *Jaidas's lantern*[6]——nor for that either, only as it grows dark, it might be of use.

CHAP. XVII.

CRACK, crack——crack, crack——crack, crack——so this is *Paris!* quoth I (continuing in the same mood)——and this is *Paris!*——humph!——*Paris!* cried I, repeating the name the third time——

The first, the finest, the most brilliant——

——The streets however are nasty;

But it looks, I suppose, better than it smells——crack, crack ——crack, crack——What a fuss thou makest!——as if it concern'd the good people to be inform'd, That a man with pale face, and clad in black, had the honour to be driven into *Paris* at nine o'clock at night, by a postilion in a tawny yellow jerkin turned up with red calamanco——crack, crack——crack, crack——crack, crack——I wish thy whip——

——But 'tis the spirit of thy nation; so crack——crack on.

Ha!——and no one gives the wall![1]——but in the SCHOOL of URBANITY herself, if the walls are besh-t——how can you do otherwise?

And prithee when do they light the lamps? What?—— never in the summer months!——Ho! 'tis the time of sallads.

----

[6] The lantern and cup used by Judas Iscariot were said to be preserved in the treasury of the Abbey at St. Denis.

[1] The privilege of passing next the wall when meeting others was valued in old-fashioned streets with narrow or no sidewalks, as giving a safer and (usually) cleaner passage than the middle of the cobblestoned or mud streets which were frequently little better than open sewers. In the *Journal of a Tour to the Hebrides* for September 20, Boswell quotes Johnson as saying that "in the last age, when his mother lived in London, there were two sets of people, those who gave the wall and those who took it; the peaceable and the quarrelsome."

——O rare! sallad and soup——soup and sallad——sallad and soup, *encore*——

——'Tis *too much* for sinners.

Now I cannot bear the barbarity of it; how can that unconscionable coachman talk so much bawdy to that lean horse? don't you see, friend, the streets are so villainously narrow, that there is not room in all *Paris* to turn a wheel-barrow? In the grandest city of the whole world, it would not have been amiss, if they had been left a thought wider; nay were it only so much in every single street, as that a man might know (was it only for satisfaction) on which side of it he was walking.

One——two——three——four——five——six——seven—— eight——nine——ten.——Ten cook's shops! and twice the number of barber's! and all within three minutes driving! one would think that all the cooks in the world on some great merry-meeting with the barbers, by joint consent had said—— Come, let us all go live at *Paris:* the *French* love good eating ——they are all *gourmands*——we shall rank high; if their god is their belly——their cooks must be gentlemen: and forasmuch as *the periwig maketh the man,* and the periwig-maker maketh the periwig——*ergo,* would the barbers say, we shall rank higher still——we shall be above you all——we shall be * *Capitouls* at least——*pardi!*[2] we shall all wear swords——

——And so, one would swear, (that is by candle-light,—— but there is no depending upon it) they continue to do, to this day.

CHAP. XVIII.

THE *French* are certainly misunderstood:——but whether the fault is theirs, in not sufficiently explaining themselves; or speaking with that exact limitation and precision which one would expect on a point of such importance, and which

*Chief Magistrate in Toulouse, &c. &c. &c.   [Sterne's note.]

[2]Literally, *by God!* but lacking the profanity and force of the English translation.   About the equivalent of *indeed!*

moreover, is so likely to be contested by us——or whether the fault may not be altogether on our side, in not understanding their language always so critically as to know "what they would be at"——I shall not decide; but 'tis evident to me, when they affirm, *"That they who have seen* Paris, *have seen every thing,"* they must mean to speak of those who have seen it by day-light.

As for candle-light——I give it up——I have said before, there was no depending upon it——and I repeat it again; but not because the lights and shades are too sharp——or the tints confounded——or that there is neither beauty or keeping, &c. . . . for that's not truth——but it is an uncertain light in this respect, That in all the five hundred grand Hôtels, which they number up to you in *Paris*——and the five hundred good things, at a modest computation (for 'tis only allowing one good thing to a Hôtel) which by candle-light are best to be *seen, felt, heard and understood* (which, by the bye is a quotation from *Lilly*[1])——the devil a one of us out of fifty, can get our heads fairly thrust in amongst them.

This is no part of the *French* computation: 'tis simply this.

That by the last survey taken in the year one thousand seven hundred and sixteen, since which time there have been considerable augmentations, *Paris* doth contain nine hundred streets; (viz.)

In the quarter called the *City*——there are fifty three streets.

In St. *James* of the Shambles, fifty five streets.

In St. *Oportune*, thirty four streets.

In the quarter of the *Louvre*, twenty five streets.

In the *Palace Royal*, or St. *Honorius*, forty nine streets.

In *Mont. Martyr*, forty one streets.

In St. *Eustace*, twenty nine streets.

In the *Halles*, twenty seven streets.

In St. *Dennis*, fifty five streets.

In St. *Martin*, fifty four streets.

In St. *Paul*, or the *Mortellerie*, twenty seven streets.

---

[1]Apparently an allusion to the rule for verbs of "seeing, feeling, hearing, understanding, etc." in William Lily's or some other grammar.

The *Greve,* thirty eight streets.

In St. *Avoy,* or the *Verrerie,* nineteen streets.

In the *Marais,* or the *Temple,* fifty two streets.

In St. *Antony*'s, sixty eight streets.

In the *Place Maubert,* eighty one streets.

In St. *Bennet,* sixty streets.

In St. *Andrews de Arcs,* fifty one streets.

In the quarter of the *Luxembourg,* sixty two streets.

And in that of St. Germain, fifty five streets, into any of which you may walk; and that when you have seen them with all that belongs to them, fairly by day-light——their gates, their bridges, their squares, their statues - - - - and have crusaded it moreover through all their parish churches, by no means omitting St. *Roche* and *Sulpice*[2] - - - and to crown all, have taken a walk to the four palaces, which you may see either with or without the statues and pictures, just as you chuse——

——Then you will have seen——

——but, 'tis what no one needeth to tell you, for you will read it yourself upon the portico of the *Louvre,* in these words,

* EARTH NO SUCH FOLKS!——NO FOLKS E'ER SUCH A TOWN
   AS PARIS IS!——SING, DERRY, DERRY, DOWN.

The *French* have a *gay* way of treating every thing that is Great; and that is all can be said upon it.

CHAP. XIX.

IN mentioning the word *gay* (as in the close of the last chapter) it puts one (*i.e.* an author) in mind of the word *spleen* ——especially if he has any thing to say upon it: not that by

[2]St. Roch, completed in 1740, and St. Sulpice, the imposing façade of which was completed in 1745, are outstanding examples of the baroque "classical" style of architecture which was held in high regard during the eighteenth century.

*Non Orbis gentem, non urbem gens habet ullam
                   ———————ulla parem.
[Sterne's note. The passage may be translated: The earth has no other such a people, nor has any people such a city.]

any analysis——or that from any table of interest or genealogy, there appears much more ground of alliance betwixt them, than betwixt light and darkness, or any two of the most unfriendly opposites in nature——only 'tis an undercraft of authors to keep up a good understanding amongst words, as politicians do amongst men——not knowing how near they may be under a necessity of placing them to each other—— which point being now gain'd, and that I may place mine exactly to my mind, I write it down here——

SPLEEN.

This, upon leaving *Chantilly,* I declared to be the best principle in the world to travel speedily upon; but I gave it only as matter of opinion, I still continue in the same sentiments ——only I had not then experience enough of its working to add this, that though you do get on at a tearing rate, yet you get on but uneasily to yourself at the same time; for which reason I here quit it entirely, and for ever, and 'tis heartily at any one's service——it has spoiled me the digestion of a good supper, and brought on a bilious diarrhæa, which has brought me back again to my first principle on which I set out——and with which I shall now scamper it away to the banks of the *Garonne*——

——No;——I cannot stop a moment to give you the character of the people——their genius——their manners——their customs——their laws——their religion——their government ——their manufactures——their commerce——their finances, with all the resources and hidden springs which sustain them: qualified as I may be, by spending three days and two nights amongst them, and during all that time, making these things the entire subject of my enquiries and reflections——

Still——still I must away——the roads are paved——the posts are short——the days are long——'tis no more than noon——I shall be at *Fontainbleau* before the king——

——Was he going there? not that I know——

CHAP. XX.

NOW I hate to hear a person, especially if he be a traveller, complain that we do not get on so fast in *France* as we do in *England;* whereas we get on much faster, *consideratis considerandis;*[1] thereby always meaning, that if you weigh their vehicles with the mountains of baggage which you lay both before and behind upon them——and then consider their puny horses, with the very little they give them——'tis a wonder they get on at all: their suffering is most unchristian, and 'tis evident thereupon to me, that a *French* post-horse would not know what in the world to do, was it not for the two words ****** and ****** in which there is as much sustenance, as if you gave him a peck of corn: now as these words cost nothing, I long from my soul to tell the reader what they are; but here is the question——they must be told him plainly, and with the most distinct articulation, or it will answer no end——and yet to do it in that plain way——though their reverences may laugh at it in the bed-chamber——full well I wot, they will abuse it in the parlour: for which cause, I have been volving[2] and revolving in my fancy some time, but to no purpose, by what clean device or facete contrivance I might so modulate them, that whilst I satisfy *that ear* which the reader chuses to *lend* me——I might not dissatisfy the other which he keeps to himself.

——My ink burns my finger to try——and when I have—— 'twill have a worse consequence——it will burn (I fear) my paper.

——No;——I dare not——

But if you wish to know how the *abbess* of *Andoüillets*,[3] and

---

[1] Considering the circumstances.

[2] Turning over in mind, considering.   Facete: facetious.

[3] Considering the nature of the following story, it seems possible that Sterne chose Andoüillets because of its similarity to *andouille* (sausage; *andouillettes:* little sausages), a word frequently used by Rabelais (4.35ff.) with erotic innuendo.

a novice of her convent got over the difficulty (only first wishing myself all imaginable success)——I'll tell you without the
least scruple.

CHAP. XXI.

THE abbess of *Andoüillets,* which if you look into the large
set of provincial maps now publishing at *Paris,* you will
find situated amongst the hills which divide *Burgundy* from
Savoy, being in danger of an *Anchylosis* or stiff joint (the
sinovia[1] of her knee becoming hard by long matins) and having tried every remedy——first, prayers and thanksgiving;
then invocations to all the saints in heaven promiscuously——
then particularly to every saint who had ever had a stiff leg
before her——then touching it with all the reliques of the
convent, principally with the thigh-bone of the man of *Lystra,*
who had been impotent from his youth[2]——then wrapping
it up in her veil when she went to bed——then cross-wise her
rosary——then bringing in to her aid the secular arm, and
anointing it with oils and hot fat of animals——then treating
it with emollient and resolving fomentations———then with
poultices of marsh-mallows, mallows, bonus Henricus,[3] white
lillies and fenugreek——then taking the woods, I mean the
smoak of 'em, holding her scapulary across her lap——then
decoctions of wild chicory, water cresses, chervil, sweet cecily
and cochlearia——and nothing all this while answering, was
prevailed on at last to try the hot baths of *Bourbon*——so having first obtain'd leave of the visitor-general to take care of her
existence——she ordered all to be got ready for her journey:

---

[1] Synovia; the lubricating fluid secreted by the lining membranes of the
joints.

[2] The man of Lystra, who was "impotent in his feet," was healed by
Paul; the account is given in Acts, 14.8–10.

[3] Good-king-Henry; a plant with a mucilaginous, saline taste. Scapulary: scapular; a short, working cloak worn by certain monastic orders.
Cochlearia: an antiscorbutic herb. Whitloe: whitlow, an inflammatory
tumour on the finger.

a novice of the convent of about seventeen, who had been troubled with a whitloe in her middle finger, by sticking it constantly into the abbess's cast poultices, &c.——had gained such an interest, that overlooking a sciatical old nun, who might have been set up for ever by the hot baths of *Bourbon, Margarita,* the little novice, was elected as the companion of the journey.

An old calesh,[4] belonging to the abbesse, lined with green frize, was ordered to be drawn out into the sun——the gardener of the convent being chosen muleteer, led out the two old mules to clip the hair from the rump-ends of their tails, whilst a couple of lay-sisters were busied, the one in darning the lining, and the other in sewing on the shreds of yellow binding, which the teeth of time had unravelled——the under-gardener dress'd the muleteer's hat in hot wine-lees——and a taylor sat musically at it, in a shed overagainst the convent, in assorting four dozen of bells for the harness, whistling to each bell as he tied it on with a thong——

——The carpenter and the smith of *Andoüillets* held a council of wheels; and by seven, the morning after, all look'd spruce, and was ready at the gate of the convent for the hot-baths of *Bourbon*——two rows of the unfortunate stood ready there an hour before.

The abbess of *Andoüillets,* supported by *Margarita* the novice, advanced slowly to the calesh, both clad in white, with their black rosaries hanging at their breasts——

——There was a simple solemnity in the contrast: they entered the calesh; and nuns in the same uniform, sweet emblem of innocence, each occupied a window, and as the abbess and *Margarita* look'd up——each (the sciatical poor nun excepted)——each stream'd out the end of her veil in the air ——then kiss'd the lilly hand which let it go: the good abbess and *Margarita* laid their hands saint-wise upon their breasts ——look'd up to heaven——then to them——and look'd "God bless you, dear sisters."

---

[4]Calash; a low, light carriage with a folding top. Frize: frieze, coarse woolen cloth.

I declare I am interested in this story, and wish I had been there.

The gardener, who I shall now call the muleteer, was a little, hearty, broad-set, good natured, chattering, toping kind of a fellow, who troubled his head very little with the *hows* and *whens* of life; so had mortgaged a month of his conventical wages in a borrachio, or leathern cask of wine, which he had disposed behind the calesh, with a large russet coloured riding coat over it, to guard it from the sun; and as the weather was hot, and he, not a niggard of his labours, walking ten times more than he rode——he found more occasions than those of nature, to fall back to the rear of his carriage; till by frequent coming and going, it had so happen'd, that all his wine had leak'd out at the *legal* vent of the borrachio, before one half of the journey was finish'd.

Man is a creature born to habitudes. The day had been sultry——the evening was delicious——the wine was generous——the *Burgundian* hill on which it grew was steep——a little tempting bush[5] over the door of a cool cottage at the foot of it, hung vibrating in full harmony with the passions——a gentle air rustled distinctly through the leaves——"Come—— come, thirsty muleteer——come in."

——The muleteer was a son of *Adam*. I need not say one word more. He gave the mules, each of 'em, a sound lash, and looking in the abbess's and *Margarita's* faces (as he did it)——as much as to say, "here I am"——he gave a second good crack——as much as to say to his mules, "get on"——so slinking behind, he enter'd the little inn at the foot of the hill.

The muleteer, as I told you, was a little, joyous, chirping fellow, who thought not of to-morrow, nor of what had gone before, or what was to follow it, provided he got but his scantling of Burgundy, and a little chit-chat along with it; so entering into a long conversation, as how he was chief gardener to the convent of *Andoüillets, &c. &c.* and out of friendship for the abbess and Mademoiselle *Margarita,* who was only in her noviciate, he had come along with them from the confines

---

[5]Branch of a tree, formerly used as a tavern sign.

of *Savoy, &c.* - - *&c.* - - and as how she had got a white swelling by her devotions——and what a nation of herbs he had
procured to mollify her humours, *&c. &c.* and that if the
waters of *Bourbon* did not mend that leg——she might as
well be lame of both——*&c. &c. &c.*——He so contrived his
story as absolutely to forget the heroine of it——and with her,
the little novice, and what was a more ticklish point to be
forgot than both——the two mules; who being creatures that
take advantage of the world, inasmuch as their parents took
it of them——and they not being in a condition to return the
obligation *downwards* (as men and women and beasts are)
——they do it side-ways, and long-ways, and back-ways——
and up hill, and down hill, and which way they can.——
Philosophers, with all their ethics, have never considered this
rightly——how should the poor muleteer then, in his cups,
consider it at all? he did not in the least——'tis time we do;
let us leave him then in the vortex of his element, the happiest
and most thoughtless of mortal men——and for a moment let
us look after the mules, the abbess, and *Margarita.*

By virtue of the muleteer's two last strokes, the mules had
gone quietly on, following their own consciences up the hill,
till they had conquer'd about one half of it; when the elder of
them, a shrewd crafty old devil, at the turn of an angle, giving a side glance, and no muleteer behind them——

By my fig! said she, swearing, I'll go no further——And if
I do, replied the other——they shall make a drum of my
hide.——

And so with one consent they stopp'd thus——

CHAP. XXII.

——Get on with you, said the abbess.
——Wh - - - - ysh——ysh——cried *Margarita.*
Sh - - - a——shu - u——shu - - u——sh - - aw——shaw'd the
abbess.

——Whu — v — w —— whew — w — w —— whuv'd *Margarita,* pursing up her sweet lips betwixt a hoot and a whistle.

Thump——thump——thump——obstreperated the abbess
of *Andoüillets* with the end of her gold-headed cane against
the bottom of the calesh——

——The old mule let a f——

CHAP. XXIII.

WE are ruin'd and undone, my child, said the abbess to
Margarita——we shall be here all night——we shall be
plunder'd——we shall be ravish'd——

——We shall be ravish'd, said *Margarita,* as sure as a gun.

Sancta Maria! cried the abbess (forgetting the *O!*)——why
was I govern'd by this wicked stiff joint? why did I leave the
convent of *Andoüillets?* and why didst thou not suffer thy
servant to go unpolluted to her tomb?

O my finger! my finger! cried the novice, catching fire at
the word *servant*——why was I not content to put it here, or
there, any where rather than be in this strait?

——Strait! said the abbess.

Strait——said the novice; for terrour had struck their understandings——the one knew not what she said——the other
what she answer'd.

O my virginity! virginity! cried the abbess.

——inity!——inity! said the novice, sobbing.

CHAP. XXIV.

MY dear mother, quoth the novice, coming a little to herself,——there are two certain words, which I have been
told will force any horse, or ass, or mule, to go up a hill
whether he will or no; be he never so obstinate or ill-will'd,
the moment he hears them utter'd, he obeys. They are words
magic! cried the abbess, in the utmost horrour——No; re-

plied *Margarita* calmly——but they are words sinful——What
are they? quoth the abbess, interrupting her: They are sinful
in the first degree, answered *Margarita,*——they are mortal
——and if we are ravish'd and die unabsolved of them, we
shall both——but you may pronounce them to me, quoth the
abbess of *Andoüillets*——They cannot, my dear mother, said
the novice, be pronounced at all; they will make all the blood
in one's body fly up into one's face——But you may whisper
them in my ear, quoth the abbess.

Heaven! hadst thou no guardian angel to delegate to the
inn at the bottom of the hill? was there no generous and
friendly spirit unemploy'd——no agent in nature, by some
monitory shivering, creeping along the artery which led to his
heart, to rouze the muleteer from his banquet?——no sweet
minstrelsy to bring back the fair idea of the abbess and *Margarita,* with their black rosaries!

Rouse! rouse!——but 'tis too late——the horrid words are
pronounced this moment——

——and how to tell them——Ye, who can speak of every
thing existing, with unpolluted lips——instruct me——guide
me——

CHAP. XXV.

ALL sins whatever, quoth the abbess, turning casuist in the
distress they were under, are held by the confessor of
our convent to be either mortal or venial: there is no further
division. Now a venial sin being the slightest and least of
all sins,——being halved——by taking, either only the half of
it, and leaving the rest——or, by taking it all, and amicably
halving it betwixt yourself and another person——in course
becomes diluted into no sin at all.

Now I see no sin in saying, *bou, bou, bou, bou, bou,* a hundred times together; nor is there any turpitude in pronouncing the syllable *ger, ger, ger, ger, ger,* were it from our matins
to our vespers: Therefore, my dear daughter, continued the
abbess of *Andouillets*——I will say *bou,* and thou shalt say

ger; and then alternately, as there is no more sin in *fou* then in *bou*——Thou shalt say *fou*——and I will come in (like fa, sol, la, re, mi, ut, at our complines) with *ter*.[1]   And accordingly the abbess, giving the pitch note, set off thus:

Abbess,   } Bou - - bou - - bou - -
Margarita, } ——ger, - - ger, - - ger
Margarita, } Fou - - fou - - fou - -
Abbess,   } ——ter, - - ter, - - ter.

The two mules acknowledged the notes by a mutual lash of their tails; but it went no further.——'Twill answer by an' by, said the novice.

Abbess,   } Bou- bou- bou- bou- bou- bou-
Margarita, } ——ger, ger, ger, ger, ger, ger.

Quicker still, cried *Margarita.*

Fou, fou, fou, fou, fou, fou, fou, fou, fou.

Quicker still, cried *Margarita.*

Bou, bou, bou, bou, bou, bou, bou, bou, bou.

Quicker still——God preserve me! said the abbess——They do not understand us, cried *Margarita*——But the Devil does, said the abbess of *Andouillets.*

CHAP. XXVI.

WHAT a tract of country have I run!——how many degrees nearer to the warm sun am I advanced, and how many fair and goodly cities have I seen, during the time you have been reading, and reflecting, Madam, upon this story! There's FONTAINBLEAU, and SENS, and JOIGNY, and AUXERRE, and DIJON the capital of *Burgundy,* and CHALLON, and *Mâcon* the capital of the *Mâconese,* and a score more upon the road to LYONS——and now I have run them over——I might as well talk to you of so many market-towns in the moon, as tell you one word about them: it will be this chapter at the least, if not both this and the next entirely lost, do what I will——

---

[1]The verb *bouger,* to move, budge, was not in polite usage during the eighteenth century; *fouter (foutre):* to shove, bugger, copulate.

——Why, 'tis a strange story! *Tristram*.

——————Alas! Madam, had it been upon some melancholy lecture of the cross——the peace of meekness, or the contentment of resignation——I had not been incommoded: or had I thought of writing it upon the purer abstractions of the soul, and that food of wisdom, and holiness, and contemplation, upon which the spirit of man (when separated from the body) is to subsist for ever——You would have come with a better appetite from it——

——I wish I never had wrote it: but as I never blot any thing out——let us use some honest means to get it out of our heads directly.

——Pray reach me my fool's cap——I fear you sit upon it, Madam——'tis under the cushion——I'll put it on——

Bless me! you have had it upon your head this half hour. ——There then let it stay, with a

Fa-ra diddle di
and a fa-ri diddle d
and a high-dum——dye-dum
    fiddle - - - dumb - c.

And now, Madam, we may venture, I hope, a little to go on.

CHAP. XXVII.

——All you need say of *Fontainbleau* (in case you are ask'd) is, that it stands about forty miles (south *something*) from *Paris,* in the middle of a large forest——That there is some‧thing great in it——That the king goes there once, every two or three years, with his whole court, for the pleasure of the chase——and that during that carnival of sporting, any *English* gentleman of fashion (you need not forget yourself) may be accommodated with a nag or two, to partake of the sport, taking care only not to out-gallop the king——

Though there are two reasons why you need not talk loud of this to every one.

First, Because 'twill make the said nags the harder to be got; and

Secondly, 'Tis not a word of it true.——*Allons!*[1]

As for SENS——you may dispatch it in a word————*" 'Tis an archiepiscopal see."*

For JOIGNY——the less, I think, one says of it, the better.

But for AUXERRE——I could go on for ever: for in my *grand tour* through *Europe,* in which, after all, my father (not caring to trust me with any one) attended me himself, with my uncle *Toby,* and *Trim,* and *Obadiah,* and indeed most of the family, except my mother, who being taken up with a project of knitting my father a pair of large worsted breeches——(the thing is common sense)——and she not caring to be put out of her way, she staid at home at SHANDY HALL, to keep things right during the expedition; in which, I say, my father stopping us two days at *Auxerre,* and his researches being ever of such a nature, that they would have found fruit even in a desert——he has left me enough to say upon AUXERRE: in short, wherever my father went——but 'twas more remarkably so, in this journey through *France* and *Italy,* than in any other stages of his life——his road seemed to lie so much on one side of that, wherein all other travellers had gone before him ——he saw kings and courts and silks of all colours, in such strange lights——and his remarks and reasonings upon the characters, the manners and customs of the countries we pass'd over, were so opposite to those of all other mortal men, particularly those of my uncle *Toby* and *Trim*——(to say nothing of myself)——and to crown all——the occurrences and scrapes which we were perpetually meeting and getting into, in consequence of his systems and opiniatry——they were of so odd, so mixed and tragicomical a contexture——That the whole put together, it appears of so different a shade and tint from any tour of *Europe,* which was ever executed——That I will venture to pronounce——the fault must be mine and mine only——if it be not read by all travellers and travel-readers, till travelling is no more,——or which comes to the

---

[1]Let's go on!

same point——till the world, finally, takes it into its head to stand still.——

——But this rich bale is not to be open'd now; except a small thread or two of it, merely to unravel the mystery of my father's stay at AUXERRE.

——As I have mentioned it——'tis too slight to be kept suspended; and when 'tis wove in, there's an end of it.

We'll go, brother *Toby,* said my father, whilst dinner is cod-dling[2]——to the abby of Saint *Germain,* if it be only to see these bodies, of which monsieur *Seguier*[3] has given such a recommendation.——I'll go see any body; quoth my uncle *Toby;* for he was all compliance thro' every step of the jour-ney——Defend me! said my father——they are all mummies ——Then one need not shave; quoth my uncle *Toby*—— Shave! no——cried my father——'twill be more like relations to go with our beards on——So out we sallied, the corporal lending his master his arm, and bringing up the rear, to the abby of Saint *Germain.*

Every thing is very fine, and very rich, and very superb, and very magnificent, said my father, addressing himself to the sacristan, who was a young brother of the order of *Bene-dictines*——but our curiosity has led us to see the bodies, of which monsieur *Seguier* has given the world so exact a descrip-tion.——The sacristan made a bow, and lighting a torch first, which he had always in the vestry ready for the purpose; he led us into the tomb of St. *Heribald*——This, said the sacris-tan, laying his hand upon the tomb, was a renowned prince of the house of *Bavaria,* who under the successive reigns of *Charlemagne, Louis le Debonair,* and *Charles the Bald,* bore a great sway in the government, and had a principal hand in bringing every thing into order and discipline——

Then he has been as great, said my uncle, in the field, as in

---

[2]Stewing.

[3]Dominique Séguier (1593–1659), bishop of Auxerre, in 1636 opened the tombs in the crypt of the abbey of St. Germain d'Auxerre and made an official report on the condition in which he found the bodies of the saints buried there. Germain, Héribalde, and Optatus were bishops of Auxerre in the fifth, ninth, and sixth centuries.

the cabinet——I dare say he has been a gallant soldier——He was a monk——said the sacristan.

My uncle *Toby* and *Trim* sought comfort in each others faces——but found it not: my father clapp'd both his hands upon his cod-piece, which was a way he had when any thing hugely tickled him; for though he hated a monk and the very smell of a monk worse than all the devils in hell——Yet the shot hitting my uncle *Toby* and *Trim* so much harder than him, 'twas a relative triumph; and put him into the gayest humour in the world.

——And pray what do you call this gentleman? quoth my father, rather sportingly: This tomb, said the young *Benedictine,* looking downwards, contains the bones of Saint MAXIMA, who came from *Ravenna* on purpose to touch the body——

——Of Saint MAXIMUS,[4] said my father, popping in with his saint before him——they were two of the greatest saints in the whole martyrology, added my father——Excuse me, said the sacristan————'twas to touch the bones of Saint *Germain* the builder of the abby——And what did she get by it? said my uncle *Toby*——What does any woman get by it? said my father——MARTYRDOME; replied the young *Benedictine,* making a bow down to the ground, and uttering the word with so humble, but decisive a cadence, it disarmed my father for a moment. 'Tis supposed, continued the *Benedictine,* that St. *Maxima* has lain in this tomb four hundred years, and two hundred before her canonization——'Tis but a slow rise, brother *Toby,* quoth my father, in this self same army of martyrs.——A desperate slow one, an' please your honour, said *Trim,* unless one could purchase——I should rather sell out entirely, quoth my uncle *Toby*——I am pretty much of your opinion, brother *Toby,* said my father.

——Poor St. *Maxima!* said my uncle *Toby* low to himself, as we turn'd from her tomb: She was one of the fairest and

---

[4]My father is playing upon the Latin signification of *maxima* and *maximus,* which are the feminine and masculine forms of the word meaning *greatest.*

most beautiful ladies either of *Italy* or *France,* continued the sacristan——But who the duce has got lain down here, besides her, quoth my father, pointing with his cane to a large tomb as we walked on——It is Saint *Optat,* Sir, answered the sacristan——And properly is Saint *Optat* plac'd! said my father: And what is Saint *Optat's* story? continued he. Saint *Optat,* replied the sacristan, was a bishop——

——I thought so, by heaven! cried my father, interrupting him——Saint *Optat!*——how should Saint *Optat* fail? so snatching out his pocket-book, and the young *Benedictine* holding him the torch as he wrote, he set it down as a new prop to his system of christian names,[5] and I will be bold to say, so disinterested was he in the search of truth, that had he found a treasure in St. *Optat's* tomb, it would not have made him half so rich: 'Twas as successful a short visit as ever was paid to the dead; and so highly was his fancy pleas'd with all that had passed in it,——that he determined at once to stay another day in *Auxerre.*

——I'll see the rest of these good gentry to-morrow, said my father, as we cross'd over the square——And while you are paying that visit, brother *Shandy,* quoth my uncle *Toby*—— the corporal and I will mount the ramparts.

CHAP. XXVIII.

——NOW this is the most puzzled skein of all——for in this last chapter, as far at least as it has help'd me through *Auxerre,* I have been getting forwards in two different journies together, and with the same dash of the pen—— for I have got entirely out of *Auxerre* in this journey which I am writing now, and I am got half way out of *Auxerre* in that which I shall write hereafter——There is but a certain degree of perfection in every thing; and by pushing at something beyond that, I have brought myself into such a situation, as no

[5] Latin *optatus* means *desired, dear.*

traveller ever stood before me; for I am this moment walking
across the market-place of *Auxerre* with my father and my
uncle *Toby,* in our way back to dinner——and I am this moment also entering *Lyons* with my post-chaise broke into a
thousand pieces——and I am moreover this moment in a
handsome pavillion built by *Pringello**, upon the banks of the
Garonne, which Mons. *Sligniac*[1] has lent me, and where I now
sit rhapsodizing all these affairs.

——Let me collect myself, and pursue my journey.

CHAP. XXIX.

I Am glad of it, said I, settling the account with myself as I
walk'd into *Lyons*——my chaise being all laid higgledy-
piggledy with my baggage in a cart, which was moving slowly
before me——I am heartily glad, said I, that 'tis all broke to
pieces; for now I can go directly by water to *Avignon,* which
will carry me on a hundred and twenty miles of my journey,
and not cost me seven livres——and from thence, continued
I, bringing forwards the account, I can hire a couple of mules
——or asses, if I like, (for no body knows me) and cross the
plains of *Languedoc,* for almost nothing——I shall gain four

---

*The same Don *Pringello,* the celebrated *Spanish* architect, of whom
my cousin *Antony* has made such honourable mention in a scholium to
the Tale inscribed to his name. Vid. p. 129, small edit. [Sterne's note.
"Antony" was the name by which Sterne's friend Hall-Stevenson (for
whom, see the Introduction) was known to his intimates. Alluding probably to the saint, the name may have been chosen from certain humorous
parallels and antitheses in the men's careers. St. Antony, the founder of
Christian asceticism, retired from the society of men to a ruined
castle, and eventually his sanctity attracted numerous disciples; Hall-
Stevenson, hardly an ascetic, retired to his castle, which from its ruinous
condition he called "Crazy Castle," where his bibulous hospitality
attracted a Rabelaisian group of men who, in imitation of the "Monks"
of Medmenham Abbey, called themselves Demoniacs, and to whom
Sterne referred as "the household of faith." "Don Pringello" was the
name given by Hall-Stevenson to an architect to whom, as one of the
Demoniacs, he had ascribed one of his *Crazy Tales.*]

[1]Presumably Sterne's landlord at Toulouse.

hundred livres by the misfortune clear into my purse; and pleasure! worth——worth double the money by it.   With what velocity, continued I, clapping my two hands together, shall I fly down the rapid *Rhone,* with the Vivares on my right-hand, and Dauphiny on my left, scarce seeing the ancient cities of Vienne, *Valence,* and *Vivieres.*   What a flame will it rekindle in the lamp, to snatch a blushing grape from the *Hermitage* and *Côte rôtie,*[1] as I shoot by the foot of them? and what a fresh spring in the blood! to behold upon the banks advancing and retiring, the castles of romance, whence courteous knights have whilome rescued the distress'd——and see vertiginous, the rocks, the mountains, the cataracts, and all the hurry which Nature is in with all her great works about her——

As I went on thus, methought my chaise, the wreck of which look'd stately enough at the first, insensibly grew less and less in its size; the freshness of the painting was no more——the gilding lost its lustre——and the whole affair appeared so poor in my eyes——so sorry!——so contemptible! and, in a word, so much worse than the abbess of *Andoüillets'* itself——that I was just opening my mouth to give it to the devil——when a pert vamping chaise-undertaker, stepping nimbly across the street, demanded if Monsieur would have his chaise refitted ——No, no, said I, shaking my head sideways——Would Monsieur chuse to sell it? rejoin'd the undertaker——With all my soul, said I——the iron work is worth forty livres——and the glasses worth forty more——and the leather you may take to live on.

——What a mine of wealth, quoth I, as he counted me the money, has this post chaise brought me in?   And this is my usual method of book-keeping, at least with the disasters of life——making a penny of every one of 'em as they happen to me——

——Do, my dear *Jenny,* tell the world for me, how I behaved under one, the most oppressive of its kind which could befall me as a man, proud, as he ought to be, of his manhood——

'Tis enough, said'st thou, coming close up to me, as I stood

---

[1] Famous vineyards near Tain and Ampuis.

with my garters in my hand, reflecting upon what had *not* pass'd——'Tis enough, *Tristram,* and I am satisfied, said'st thou, whispering these words in my ear, **** ** **** *** ******;____**** ** ****——any other man would have sunk down to the center——

——Every thing is good for something, quoth I.

——I'll go into *Wales* for six weeks, and drink goat's-whey ——and I'll gain seven years longer life for the accident. For which reason I think myself inexcusable, for blaming Fortune so often as I have done, for pelting me all my life long, like an ungracious duchess, as I call'd her, with so many small evils: surely if I have any cause to be angry with her, 'tis that she has not sent me great ones——a score of good cursed, bouncing losses, would have been as good as a pension to me.

——One of a hundred a year, or so, is all I wish——I would not be at the plague of paying land tax for a larger.

CHAP. XXX.

TO those who call vexations, VEXATIONS, as knowing what they are, there could not be a greater, than to be the best part of a day in *Lyons,* the most opulent and flourishing city in *France,* enriched with the most fragments of antiquity——and not be able to see it.   To be withheld upon *any* account, must be a vexation; but to be withheld *by* a vexation——must certainly be, what philosophy justly calls

VEXATION

upon

VEXATION.

I had got my two dishes of milk coffee (which by the bye is excellently good for a consumption, but you must boil the milk and coffee together——otherwise 'tis only coffee and milk) ——and as it was no more than eight in the morning, and the

boat did not go off till noon, I had time to see enough of
Lyons to tire the patience of all the friends I had in the world
with it.   I will take a walk to the cathedral, said I, looking at
my list, and see the wonderful mechanism of this great clock[1]
of *Lippius* of *Basil,* in the first place——

Now, of all things in the world, I understand the least of
mechanism——I have neither genius, or taste, or fancy——and
have a brain so entirely unapt for every thing of that kind, that
I solemnly declare I was never yet able to comprehend the
principles of motion of a squirrel cage, or a common knife-
grinder's wheel——tho' I have many an hour of my life look'd
up with great devotion at the one——and stood by with as
much patience as any christian ever could do, at the other——

I'll go see the surprising movements of this great clock, said
I, the very first thing I do: and then I will pay a visit to the
great library of the Jesuits, and procure, if possible, a sight of
the thirty volumes of the general history of *China,*[2] wrote (not
in the *Tartarian*) but in the *Chinese* language, and in the
Chinese character too.

Now I almost know as little of the *Chinese* language, as I do
of the mechanism of *Lippius*'s clock-work; so, why these should
have jostled themselves into the two first articles of my list——
I leave to the curious as a problem of Nature.   I own it looks
like one of her ladyship's obliquities; and they who court her,
are interested in finding out her humour as much as I.

When these curiosities are seen, quoth I, half addressing
myself to my *valet de place*,[3] who stood behind me——'twill
be no hurt if we go to the church of St. *Ireneus,* and see the

---

[1]According to the *Recherche des antiquités et curiosités de la ville de
Lyon* of Jacob Spon (1647–1685), a French antiquary and physician
whom Sterne names in the following chapter as one of his authorities,
this famous clock, with its amazingly complicated mechanism, was next
to that of Strasburg the finest in the world.   (*Op. cit.* (Lyon, 1857),
pp. 24–25.)

[2]This set of books was said by Piganiol de la Force (1673–1753),
French geographer and historian from whose *Nouveau voyage de France*
Sterne took considerable material for this seventh volume, to be unique
in France.   (*Op. cit.* (Paris, 1755), 1.252.)

[3]Courier, guide.

pillar to which *Christ* was tied[4]——and after that, the house
where *Pontius Pilate* lived[5]——'Twas at the next town, said
the *valet de place*——at *Vienne;* I am glad of it, said I, rising
briskly from my chair, and walking across the room with
strides twice as long as my usual pace——"for so much the
sooner shall I be at the *Tomb of the two lovers."*[6]

What was the cause of this movement, and why I took such
long strides in uttering this——I might leave to the curious
too; but as no principle of clock-work is concern'd in it——
'twill be as well for the reader if I explain it myself.

CHAP. XXXI.

O! There is a sweet æra in the life of man, when, (the brain
being tender and fibrillous, and more like pap than any
thing else)——a story read of two fond lovers, separated from
each other by cruel parents, and by still more cruel destiny——

Amandus——He
Amanda——She——

each ignorant of the other's course,

He——east
She——west

Amandus taken captive by the *Turks,* and carried to the
emperor of *Morocco's* court, where the princess of *Morocco*
falling in love with him, keeps him twenty years in prison, for
the love of his *Amanda*——

---

[4]A portion of a marble column to which, according to Piganiol de la
Force, *op. cit.,* 1.250, Christ was supposed to have been bound while he
was beaten; Spon, *op. cit.,* p. 71., records merely that Christian martyrs
were said to have been tied to it while they were tortured.

[5]In his *Recherches curieuses d'antiquité* (Lyon, 1683), p. 168, Spon explains that "the name of an Italian, Humbert Pilati, Secretary to the last
Dauphin Humbert, has given rise to all those idle dreams of calling a
tower at Vienne near the Rhone the Tower of Pilate; a country-house
near Saint Vallier, the House of Pilate; and the church of Notre Dame
de la Vie, the Prætorium of Pilate."

[6]An ancient tomb, of disputed origin, which formerly stood outside the
gate of Lyons in the Faubourg de Vaise. It is discussed in Spon's
Recherche des . . . Lyon, p.133ff.

She——(*Amanda*) all the time wandering barefoot, and with dishevell'd hair, o'er rocks and mountains enquiring for *Amandus*——*Amandus! Amandus!*——making every hill and vally to echo back his name——

Amandus! Amandus!

at every town and city sitting down forlorn at the gate—— Has *Amandus!*——has my *Amandus* enter'd?——till,——going round, and round, and round the world——chance unexpected bringing them at the same moment of the night, though by different ways, to the gate of *Lyons* their native city, and each in well known accents calling out aloud,

Is *Amandus* } still alive?
Is my *Amanda* }

they fly into each others arms, and both drop down dead for joy.

There is a soft æra in every gentle mortal's life, where such a story affords more *pabulum* to the brain, than all the *Frusts*,[1] and *Crusts,* and *Rusts* of antiquity, which travellers can cook up for it.

——'Twas all that stuck on the right side of the cullender in my own, of what *Spon* and others, in their accounts of *Lyons,* had *strained* into it; and finding, moreover, in some Itinerary, but in what God knows——That sacred to the fidelity of *Amandus* and *Amanda,* a tomb was built without the gates, where to this hour, lovers call'd upon them to attest their truths,——I never could get into a scrape of that kind in my life, but this *tomb of the lovers,* would some how or other, come in at the close——nay such a kind of empire had it establish'd over me, that I could seldom think or speak of *Lyons* ——and sometimes not so much as see even a *Lyons-waistcoat,* but this remnant of antiquity would present itself to my fancy; and I have often said in my wild way of running on——tho' I fear with some irreverence——"I thought this shrine (neglected as it was) as valuable as that of *Mecca,*[2] and so little short, ex-

---

[1] Bits.

[2] The great holy city of Islam, the birthplace of Mohammed and the site of the Kaaba; the most sacred of all Mohammedan shrines. The Santa

cept in wealth, of the *Santa Casa* itself, that some time or other, I would go a pilgrimage (though I had no other business at *Lyons*) on purpose to pay it a visit."

In my list, therefore, of *Videnda*[3] at *Lyons,* this, tho' *last*——was not, you see, *least;* so taking a dozen or two of longer strides than usual across my room, just whilst it passed my brain, I walked down calmly into the *Basse Cour,*[4] in order to sally forth; and having called for my bill——as it was uncertain whether I should return to my inn, I had paid it——had moreover given the maid ten sous, and was just receiving the dernier compliments of Monsieur *Le Blanc,* for a pleasant voyage down the *Rhône*——when I was stopped at the gate——

CHAP. XXXII.

——'TWAS by a poor ass who had just turned in with a couple of large panniers upon his back, to collect eleemosunary turnip tops and cabbage-leaves; and stood dubious, with his two forefeet on the inside of the threshold, and with his two hinder feet towards the street, as not knowing very well whether he was to go in, or no.

Now, 'tis an animal (be in what hurry I may) I cannot bear to strike——there is a patient endurance of sufferings, wrote so unaffectedly in his looks and carriage, which pleads so mightily for him, that it always disarms me; and to that degree, that I do not like to speak unkindly to him: on the contrary, meet him where I will——whether in town or country——in cart or under panniers——whether in liberty or bondage——I have ever something civil to say to him on my part; and as one

Casa, or Holy House, is a stone building in Loreto, Italy, said to have been the home of the virgin Mary in Nazareth whence it was aerially transported to Loreto by angels. It is a celebrated objective of Roman Catholic pilgrimages, and in Sterne's day its treasury contained a large number of rich and curious votive offerings.

[3]Things to see.

[4]Lower court, stable-yard.

word begets another (if he has as little to do as I)——I generally fall into conversation with him; and surely never is my
imagination so busy as in framing his responses from the etchings of his countenance——and where those carry me not
deep enough——in flying from my own heart into his, and seeing what is natural for an ass to think——as well as a man,
upon the occasion. In truth, it is the only creature of all the
classes of beings below me, with whom I can do this: for par-
rots, jackdaws, &c.——I never exchange a word with them
——nor with the apes, &c. for pretty near the same reason;
they act by rote, as the others speak by it, and equally make
me silent: nay my dog and my cat, though I value them both
——(and for my dog he would speak if he could)——yet some
how or other, they neither of them possess the talents for conversation——I can make nothing of a discourse with them,
beyond the *proposition,* the *reply,* and *rejoinder,* which terminated my father's and my mother's conversations, in his beds
of justice——and those utter'd——there's an end of the dialogue——

——But with an ass, I can commune for ever.

Come *Honesty!* said I,——seeing it was impracticable to
pass betwixt him and the gate——art thou for coming in, or
going out?

The ass twisted his head round to look up the street——

Well——replied I——we'll wait a minute for thy driver:

——He turned his head thoughtful about, and looked wistfully the opposite way——

I understand thee perfectly; answered I——if thou takest a
wrong step in this affair, he will cudgel thee to death——
Well! a minute is but a minute, and if it saves a fellow creature a drubbing, it shall not be set down as ill-spent.

He was eating the stem of an artichoke as this discourse
went on, and in the little peevish contentions of nature betwixt hunger and unsavouriness, had dropt it out of his mouth
half a dozen times, and pick'd it up again——God help thee,
Jack! said I, thou hast a bitter breakfast on't——and many a
bitter day's labour——and many a bitter blow, I fear, for its

wages——'tis all——all bitterness to thee, whatever life is to others.——And now thy mouth, if one knew the truth of it, is as bitter, I dare say, as soot——(for he had cast aside the stem) and thou hast not a friend perhaps in all this world, that will give thee a macaroon.——In saying this, I pull'd out a paper of 'em, which I had just purchased, and gave him one ——and at this moment that I am telling it, my heart smites me, that there was more of pleasantry in the conceit, of seeing *how* an ass would eat a macaroon——than of benevolence in giving him one, which presided in the act.

When the ass had eaten his macaroon, I press'd him to come in——the poor beast was heavy loaded——his legs seem'd to tremble under him——he hung rather backwards, and as I pull'd at his halter, it broke short in my hand——he look'd up pensive in my face——"Don't thrash me with it——but if you will, you may"——If I do, said I, I'll be d——d.

The word was but one half of it pronounced, like the abbess of *Andoüillets'*——(so there was no sin in it)——when a person coming in, let fall a thundering bastinado upon the poor devil's crupper, which put an end to the ceremony.

    Out upon it!

cried I——but the interjection was equivocal——and, I think, wrong placed too——for the end of an osier which had started out from the contexture of the ass's pannier, had caught hold of my breeches pocket as he rush'd by me, and rent it in the most disastrous direction you can imagine——so that the

Out upon it! in my opinion, should have come in here——— but this I leave to be settled by

The

REVIEWERS

of

MY BREECHES.

which I have brought over along with me for that purpose.

CHAP. XXXIII.

WHEN all was set to rights, I came down stairs again into
the *basse cour* with my valet de place, in order to sally
out towards the tomb of the two lovers, &c.——and was a
second time stopp'd at the gate——not by the ass——but by
the person who struck him; and who, by that time, had taken
possession (as is not uncommon after a defeat) of the very
spot of ground where the ass stood.

It was a commissary sent to me from the post-office, with a
rescript in his hand for the payment of some six livres odd
sous.

Upon what account? said I.——'Tis upon the part of the
king, replied the commissary, heaving up both his shoulders——

——My good friend, quoth I——as sure as I am I——and
you are you——

——And who are you? said he.—— ——Don't puzzle me;
said I.

CHAP. XXXIV.

——But it is an indubitable verity, continued I, addressing
myself to the commissary, changing only the form of my as-
severation——that I owe the king of *France* nothing but my
good-will; for he is a very honest man, and I wish him all
health and pastime in the world——

Pardonnez moi[1]——replied the commissary, you are indebted to him six livres four sous, for the next post from
hence to St. *Fons,* in your rout to *Avignion*——which being a
post royal, you pay double for the horses and postillion——
otherwise 'twould have amounted to no more than three livres,
two sous——

---

[1]Pardon me.

——But I don't go by land; said I.

——You may if you please; replied the commissary——

Your most obedient servant——said I, making him a low bow——

The commissary, with all the sincerity of grave good breeding——made me one, as low again.——I never was more disconcerted with a bow in my life.

——The devil take the serious character of these people! quoth I——(aside) they understand no more of IRONY than this——

The comparison was standing close by with his panniers——but something seal'd up my lips——I could not pronounce the name——

Sir, said I, collecting myself——it is not my intention to take post——

——But you may——said he, persisting in his first reply——you may take post if you chuse——

——And I may take salt to my pickled herring, said I, if I chuse——

——But I do not chuse——

——But you must pay for it, whether you do or no——

Aye! for the salt; said I (I know)——

——And for the post too; added he. Defend me; cried I——

I travel by water——I am going down the *Rhône* this very afternoon——my baggage is in the boat——and I have actually paid nine livres for my passage——

C'est tout egal[2]——'tis all one; said he.

Bon Dieu![3] what, pay for the way I go! and for the way I do *not* go!

——*C'est tout egal;* replied the commissary——

——The devil it is! said I——but I will go to ten thousand Bastiles first——

O *England! England!* thou land of liberty, and climate of

---

[2] It's all the same.

[3] Literally, *good God!,* but lacking the profanity of the English; about the equivalent of *good heavens!*

good sense, thou tenderest of mothers——and gentlest of
nurses, cried I, kneeling upon one knee, as I was beginning my
apostrophe——

When the director of Madam *Le Blanc*'s conscience coming
in at that instant, and seeing a person in black, with a face as
pale as ashes, at his devotions——looking still paler by the
contrast and distress of his drapery——ask'd, if I stood in want
of the aids of the church——

I go by WATER——said I——and here's another will be for
making me pay for going by OYL.[4]

CHAP. XXXV.

AS I perceived the commissary of the post-office would have
his six livres four sous, I had nothing else for it, but to
say some smart thing upon the occasion, worth the money:

And so I set off thus——

——And pray Mr. commissary, by what law of courtesy is
a defenceless stranger to be used just the reverse from what
you use a *Frenchman* in this matter?

By no means; said he.

Excuse me; said I——for you have begun, sir, with first
tearing off my breeches——and now you want my pocket——

Whereas——had you first taken my pocket, as you do with
your own people——and then left me bare a—'d after——
I had been a beast to have complain'd——

As it is——

——'Tis contrary to the *law of nature*.

——'Tis contrary to *reason*.

——'Tis contrary to the GOSPEL.

But not to this——said he——putting a printed paper into
my hand.

---

[4] *I.e.*, "I go by water down the Rhone; this priest, who seems to think
me dying, wishes to administer extreme unction." In the Church of
England, priests do not follow the Roman custom of anointing the sick
with oil.

PAR LE ROY.[1]

—— ——'Tis a pithy prolegomenon, quoth I——and so read
on —— —— —— —— —— —— —— —— —— —— —— ——
—— —— —— —— —— —— —— —— —— ——
—— —— —— —— —— —— —— —— —— ——
—— —— —— —— —— —— —— —— —— ——
—— —— —— —— —— —— —— —— —— ——

——By all which it appears, quoth I, having read it over,
a little too rapidly, that if a man sets out in a post-chaise from
Paris——he must go on travelling in one, all the days of his
life——or pay for it.——Excuse me, said the commissary, the
spirit of the ordinance is this——That if you set out with an
intention of running post from *Paris* to *Avignon*, *&c.* you
shall not change that intention or mode of travelling, without
first satisfying the fermiers[2] for two posts further than the place
you repent at——and 'tis founded, continued he, upon this,
that the REVENUES are not to fall short through your *fickleness*——

——O by heavens! cried I——if fickleness is taxable in
France——we have nothing to do but to make the best peace
with you we can——

AND SO THE PEACE WAS MADE;

——And if it is a bad one——as *Tristram Shandy* laid the
corner stone of it——nobody but *Tristram Shandy* ought to be
hanged.

CHAP. XXXVI.

THOUGH I was sensible I had said as many clever things
to the commissary as came to six livres four sous, yet I
was determined to note down the imposition amongst my remarks before I retir'd from the place; so putting my hand into
my coat pocket for my remarks——(which by the bye, may be

[1]By [Command of] the King.
[2]Farmers (of taxes).

a caution to travellers to take a little more care of *their* remarks for the future) "my remarks were *stolen*"————Never
did sorry traveller make such a pother and racket about his
remarks as I did about mine, upon the occasion.

Heaven! earth! sea! fire! cried I, calling in every thing to my
aid but what I should————My remarks are stolen!————what
shall I do?————Mr. commissary! pray did I drop any remarks
as I stood besides you?————

You dropp'd a good many very singular ones; replied he
————Pugh! said I, those were but a few, not worth above six
livres two sous————but these are a large parcel————He shook
his head————Monsieur *Le Blanc!* Madam *Le Blanc!* did you see
any papers of mine?————you maid of the house! run up stairs
————*François!* run up after her————

————I must have my remarks————they were the best remarks,
cried I, that ever were made————the wisest————the wittiest————
What shall I do?————which way shall I turn myself?

Sancho Pança, when he lost his ass's FURNITURE, did not ex-
claim more bitterly.[1]

CHAP. XXXVII.

WHEN the first transport was over, and the registers of
the brain were beginning to get a little out of the confusion into which this jumble of cross accidents had cast them
————it then presently occurr'd to me, that I had left my remarks in the pocket of the chaise————and that in selling my
chaise, I had sold my remarks along with it, to the chaise-
vamper.   I
leave this void space that the reader may swear into it, any
oath that he is most accustomed to————For my own part, if
ever I swore a *whole* oath into a vacancy in my life, I think it
was into that————*** **** **, said I————and so my remarks
through *France,* which were as full of wit, as an egg is full of

---

[1] It was upon the loss of ass and all that Sancho "broke out into the
most pitiful and sad lamentations in the world; insomuch that he wak'd
Don Quixote with his moans." (*Don Quixote,* 1.3.9.)

meat, and as well worth four hundred guineas, as the said egg
is worth a penny——Have I been selling here to a chaise-
vamper——for four *Louis d'Ors*[1]——and giving him a post-
chaise (by heaven) worth six into the bargain; had it been to
Dodsley, or *Becket,*[2] or any creditable bookseller, who was
either leaving off business, and wanted a post-chaise——or
who was beginning it——and wanted my remarks, and two
or three guineas along with them——I could have borne it
——but to a chaise-vamper!——shew me to him this moment
François,——said I——the valet de place put on his hat, and
led the way——and I pull'd off mine, as I pass'd the commissary, and followed him.

CHAP. XXXVIII.

WHEN we arrived at the chaise-vamper's house, both the
house and the shop were shut up; it was the eighth of
September, the nativity of the blessed Virgin *Mary,* mother of
God——

——Tantarra - ra - tan - tivi——the whole world was going
out a May-poling——frisking here——capering there——no
body cared a button for me or my remarks; so I sat me down
upon a bench by the door, philosophating upon my condition:
by a better fate than usually attends me, I had not waited half
an hour, when the mistress came in, to take the papilliotes[1]
from off her hair, before she went to the May-poles——

The *French* women, by the bye, love May-poles, *à la folie*[2]
——that is, as much as their matins——give 'em but a May-
pole, whether in *May, June, July,* or *September*——they never
count the times——down it goes——'tis meat, drink, washing,
and lodging to 'em——and had we but the policy, an' please

---

[1] A gold coin having the value of twenty francs.

[2] Sterne's booksellers.   Volumes 1–4 of *Shandy* were published and sold
by the brothers Robert and James Dodsley, volumes 5–9 by Thomas
Becket and P. A. Dehondt.

[1] Papillotes, curl-papers.

[2] To the point of folly.

your worships (as wood is a little scarce in *France*) to send them but plenty of May-poles——

The women would set them up; and when they had done, they would dance round them (and the men for company) till they were all blind.

The wife of the chaise-vamper step'd in, I told you, to take the papilliotes from off her hair——the toilet stands still for no man——so she jerk'd off her cap, to begin with them as she open'd the door, in doing which, one of them fell upon the ground——I instantly saw it was my own writing——

——O Seigneur! cried I——you have got all my remarks upon your head, Madam!——*J'en suis bien mortifiée*,[3] said she ——'tis well, thinks I, they have stuck there—for could they have gone deeper, they would have made such confusion in a *French* woman's noddle——She had better have gone with it unfrizled, to the day of eternity.

Tenez[4]——said she——so without any idea of the nature of my suffering, she took them from her curls, and put them gravely one by one into my hat——one was twisted this way ——another twisted that——ay! by my faith; and when they are published, quoth I,——

They will be worse twisted still.

CHAP. XXXIX.

AND now for *Lippius*'s clock! said I, with the air of a man, who had got thro' all his difficulties——nothing can prevent us seeing that, and the *Chinese* history, &c. except the time, said *François*——for 'tis almost eleven——then we must speed the faster, said I, striding it away to the cathedral.

I cannot say, in my heart, that it gave me any concern in being told by one of the minor canons, as I was entering the west door,——That *Lippius*'s great clock was all out of joints, and had not gone for some years——It will give me the more

[3] I am quite mortified.
[4] Here, take them!

time, thought I, to peruse the *Chinese* history; and besides I
shall be able to give the world a better account of the clock in
it's decay, than I could have done in its flourishing condition——

——And so away I posted to the college of the Jesuits.

Now it is with the project of getting a peep at the history of
China in *Chinese* characters——as with many others I could
mention, which strike the fancy only at a distance; for as I
came nearer and nearer to the point——my blood cool'd——
the freak gradually went off, till, at length I would not have
given a cherry-stone to have it gratified——The truth was,
my time was short, and my heart was at the Tomb of the
Lovers——I wish to God, said I, as I got the rapper in my
hand, that the key of the library may be but lost; it fell out as
well——

For all the JESUITS *had got the cholic*——and to that degree,
as never was known in the memory of the oldest practitioner.[1]

CHAP. XL.

AS I knew the geography of the Tomb of the Lovers, as well
as if I had lived twenty years in *Lyons,* namely, that it
was upon the turning of my right hand, just without the gate,
leading to the *Fauxbourg de Vaise*——I dispatch'd *François*
to the boat, that I might pay the homage I so long ow'd it,
without a witness of my weakness.——I walk'd with all
imaginable joy towards the place——when I saw the gate
which intercepted the tomb, my heart glowed within me——

——Tender and faithful spirits! cried I, addressing myself
to *Amandus* and *Amanda*——long——long have I tarried to
drop this tear upon your tomb——I come——I come——

When I came——there was no tomb to drop it upon.

What would I have given for my uncle *Toby* to have
whistled, Lillo bullero!

---

[1] An allusion to the battle over the legality of the constitution of the
Jesuits, which resulted in the suppression of the order in France in 1764.

CHAP. XLI.

NO matter how, or in what mood——but I flew from the tomb of the lovers——or rather I did not fly *from* it—— (for there was no such thing existing) and just got time enough to the boat to save my passage;——and e'er I had sailed a hundred yards, the *Rhône* and the *Saôn* met together, and carried me down merrily betwixt them.

But I have described this voyage down the *Rhône,* before I made it——

——So now I am at *Avignion*—and as there is nothing to see but the old house, in which the duke of *Ormond*[1] resided, and nothing to stop me but a short remark upon the place, in three minutes you will see me crossing the bridge upon a mule, with *François* upon a horse with my portmanteau behind him, and the owner of both, striding the way before us with a long gun upon his shoulder, and a sword under his arm, least peradventure we should run away with his cattle. Had you seen my breeches in entering *Avignon,*——Though you'd have seen them better, I think, as I mounted——you would not have thought the precaution amiss, or found in your heart to have taken it, in dudgeon: for my own part, I took it most kindly; and determined to make him a present of them, when we got to the end of our journey, for the trouble they had put him to, of arming himself at all points against them.

Before I go further, let me get rid of my remark upon *Avignon,* which is this; That I think it wrong, merely because a man's hat has been blown off his head by chance the first night he comes to *Avignion,*——that he should therefore say, "*Avignion* is more subject to high winds than any town in all *France:*" for which reason I laid no stress upon the accident till I had inquired of the master of the inn about it, who telling

---

[1] See p. 30, n. 2. "Nothing to see" may be one of Sterne's characteristic slaps at Catholicism, for the sight for which Avignon has been famous since the fourteenth century is its great papal palace.

me seriously it was so——and hearing moreover, the windy-
ness of *Avignion* spoke of in the country about as a proverb
——I set it down, merely to ask the learned what can be the
cause——the consequence I saw——for they are all Dukes,
Marquisses, and Counts, there——the duce a Baron, in all
Avignion——so that there is scarce any talking to them, on a
windy day.

Prithee friend, said I, take hold of my mule for a moment
——for I wanted to pull off one of my jack-boots, which hurt
my heel——the man was standing quite idle at the door of the
inn, and as I had taken it into my head, he was someway concerned about the house or stable, I put the bridle into his
hand——so begun with my boot:——when I had finished the
affair, I turned about to take the mule from the man, and
thank him——

——But *Monsieur le Marquis* had walked in——

CHAP. XLII.

I Had now the whole south of *France,* from the banks of the
Rhône to those of the *Garonne* to traverse upon my mule at
my own leisure——*at my own leisure*——for I had left Death,
the lord knows——and He only——how far behind me——"I
have followed many a man thro' *France,* quoth he——but
never at this mettlesome rate"——Still he followed,——and
still I fled him——but I fled him chearfully——still he pursued——but like one who pursued his prey without hope——
as he lag'd, every step he lost, softened his looks——why
should I fly him at this rate?

So notwithstanding all the commissary of the post-office had
said, I changed the *mode* of my travelling once more; and after
so precipitate and rattling a course as I had run, I flattered my
fancy with thinking of my mule, and that I should traverse the
rich plains of *Languedoc* upon his back, as slowly as foot could
fall.

There is nothing more pleasing to a traveller——or more

terrible to travel-writers, than a large rich plain; especially if
it is without great rivers or bridges; and presents nothing to
the eye, but one unvaried picture of plenty: for after they have
once told you that 'tis delicious! or delightful! (as the case
happens)——that the soil was grateful, and that nature pours
out all her abundance, &c. . . . they have then a large plain
upon their hands, which they know not what to do with——
and which is of little or no use to them but to carry them to
some town; and that town, perhaps of little more, but a new
place to start from to the next plain——and so on.

——This is most terrible work; judge if I don't manage my
plains better.

CHAP. XLIII.

I Had not gone above two leagues and a half, before the man
with his gun, began to look at his priming.

I had three several times loiter'd *terribly* behind; half a mile
at least every time: once, in deep conference with a drum-
maker, who was making drums for the fairs of *Baucaira* and
Tarascone——I did not understand the principles——

The second time, I cannot so properly say, I stopp'd——for
meeting a couple of *Franciscans*[1] straiten'd more for time than
myself, and not being able to get to the bottom of what I was
about——I had turn'd back with them——

The third, was an affair of trade with a gossip, for a hand
basket of *Provence* figs for four sous; this would have been
transacted at once; but for a case of conscience at the close of
it; for when the figs were paid for, it turn'd out, that there
were two dozen of eggs cover'd over with vine-leaves at the
bottom of the basket——as I had no intention of buying eggs
——I made no sort of claim of them——as for the space they
had occupied——what signified it? I had figs enow for my
money——

——But it was my intention to have the basket——it was

---

[1]Members of an order of mendicant friars founded in the thirteenth
century by Saint Francis of Assisi.

the gossip's intention to keep it, without which, she could do nothing with her eggs——and unless I had the basket, I could do as little with my figs, which were too ripe already, and most of 'em burst at the side: this brought on a short conten-tion, which terminated in sundry proposals, what we should both do——

——How we disposed of our eggs and figs, I defy you, or the Devil himself, had he not been there (which I am per-suaded he was) to form the least probable conjecture: You will read the whole of it——not this year, for I am hastening to the story of my uncle *Toby*'s amours——but you will read it in the collection of those which have arose out of the journey across this plain——and which, therefore, I call my

PLAIN STORIES.

How far my pen has been fatigued like those of other travellers, in this journey of it, over so barren a track——the world must judge——but the traces of it, which are now all set o' vibrating together this moment, tell me 'tis the most fruitful and busy period of my life; for as I had made no convention with my man with the gun as to time——by stopping and talking to every soul I met who was not in a full trot——join-ing all parties before me——waiting for every soul behind—— hailing all those who were coming through cross roads—— arresting all kinds of beggars, pilgrims, fiddlers, fryars——not passing by a woman in a mulberry-tree without commending her legs, and tempting her into conversation with a pinch of snuff——In short, by seizing every handle, of what size or shape soever, which chance held out to me in this journey—— I turned my *plain* into a *city*——I was always in company, and with great variety too; and as my mule loved society as much as myself, and had some proposals always on his part to offer to every beast he met——I am confident we could have passed through *Pall-Mall* or St. *James*'s-Street for a month together, with fewer adventures——and seen less of human nature.

O! there is that sprightly frankness which at once unpins every plait of a *Languedocian*'s dress——that whatever is beneath it, it looks so like the simplicity which poets sing of in better days——I will delude my fancy, and believe it is so.

'Twas in the road betwixt *Nismes* and *Lunel,* where there is the best *Muscatto* wine in all *France,* and which by the bye belongs to the honest canons of MONTPELLIER——and foul befall the man who has drank it at their table, who grudges them a drop of it.

——The sun was set——they had done their work; the nymphs had tied up their hair afresh——and the swains were preparing for a carousal——My mule made a dead point—— 'Tis the fife and tabourin, said I——I'm frighten'd to death, quoth he——They are running at the ring of pleasure, said I, giving him a prick——By saint *Boogar,*[2] and all the saints at the backside of the door of purgatory, said he——(making the same resolution with the abbesse of *Andoüillets*) I'll not go a step further———'Tis very well, sir, said I——I never will argue a point with one of your family, as long as I live; so leaping off his back, and kicking off one boot into this ditch, and t'other into that——I'll take a dance, said I——so stay you here.

A sun-burnt daughter of Labour rose up from the groupe to meet me as I advanced towards them; her hair, which was a dark chestnut, approaching rather to a black, was tied up in a knot, all but a single tress.

We want a cavalier, said she, holding out both her hands, as if to offer them——And a cavalier ye shall have; said I, taking hold of both of them.

Hadst thou, *Nannette,* been array'd like a dutchesse!

——But that cursed slit in thy petticoat!

Nannette cared not for it.

We could not have done without you, said she, letting go one hand, with self-taught politeness, leading me up with the other.

A lame youth, whom *Apollo* had recompenced with a pipe, and to which he had added a tabourin of his own accord, ran sweetly over the prelude, as he sat upon the bank——Tie

---

[2]A phonetic coinage from the French *bougre* or English *bugger.*

me up this tress instantly, said *Nannette,* putting a piece of string into my hand——It taught me to forget I was a stranger ——The whole knot fell down——We had been seven years acquainted.

The youth struck the note upon the tabourin——his pipe followed, and off we bounded——"the duce take that slit!"

The sister of the youth who had stolen her voice from heaven, sung alternately with her brother——'twas a *Gascoigne* roundelay.

Viva la joia!
Fidon la tristessa![3]

The nymphs join'd in unison, and their swains an octave below them——

I would have given a crown to have it sew'd up——*Nannette* would not have given a sous——*Viva la joia!* was in her lips——*Viva la joia!* was in her eyes. A transient spark of amity shot across the space betwixt us——She look'd amiable! ——Why could I not live and end my days thus? Just disposer of our joys and sorrows, cried I, why could not a man sit down in the lap of content here——and dance, and sing, and say his prayers, and go to heaven with this nut brown maid? Capriciously did she bend her head on one side, and dance up insiduous——Then 'tis time to dance off, quoth I; so changing only partners and tunes, I danced it away from *Lunel* to *Montpellier*——from thence to *Pesçnas, Beziers*——I danced it along through *Narbonne, Carcasson,* and *Castle Naudairy,* till at last I danced myself into *Perdrillo's*[4] pavillion, where pulling a paper of black lines, that I might go on straight forwards, without digression or parenthesis, in my uncle *Toby's* amours——

I begun thus——

END of the SEVENTH VOLUME.

---

[3]Long live joy! Fie on sadness! *Fidon=fi-donc;* this is apparently Provençal as Sterne's ears heard it.

[4]Apparently a misprint for Pringello; see p. 516, n. *.

VOLUME VIII.[1]

CHAP. I.

——BUT softly——for in these sportive plains, and under this genial sun, where at this instant all flesh is running out piping, fiddling, and dancing to the vintage, and every step that's taken, the judgment is surprised by the imagination, I defy, notwithstanding all that has been said upon *straight lines* * in sundry pages of my book——I defy the best cabbage planter that ever existed, whether he plants backwards or forwards, it makes little difference in the account (except that he will have more to answer for in the one case than in the other)——I defy him to go on coolly, critically, and canonically, planting his cabbages one by one, in straight lines, and stoical distances, especially if slits in petticoats are unsew'd up——without ever and anon straddling out, or sidling into some bastardly digression——In *Freeze-land, Fog-land* and some other lands I wot of——it may be done——

But in this clear climate of fantasy and perspiration, where every idea, sensible and insensible, gets vent——in this land, my dear *Eugenius*——in this fertile land of chivalry and romance, where I now sit, unskrewing my ink-horn to write my uncle *Toby*'s amours, and with all the meanders of JULIA's track in quest of her DIEGO, in full view of my study window ——if thou comest not and takest me by the hand——

What a work is it likely to turn out!

Let us begin it.

---

[1]Published, with Volume VII, in January, 1765.
*Vid. Vol. VI. p. 152.   [Sterne's note; p. 473 in this edition.]

CHAP. II.

IT is with LOVE as with CUCKOLDOM[1]——
——But now I am talking of beginning a book, and have
long had a thing upon my mind to be imparted to the reader,
which if not imparted now, can never be imparted to him as
long as I live (whereas the COMPARISON may be imparted to
him any hour in the day)——I'll just mention it, and begin in
good earnest.

The thing is this.

That of all the several ways of beginning a book which are
now in practice throughout the known world, I am confident
my own way of doing it is the best——I'm sure it is the most
religious——for I begin with writing the first sentence——and
trusting to Almighty God for the second.

'Twould cure an author for ever of the fuss and folly of
opening his street-door, and calling in his neighbours and
friends, and kinsfolk, with the devil and all his imps, with
their hammers and engines, &c. only to observe how one sentence of mine follows another, and how the plan follows the
whole.

I wish you saw me half starting out of my chair, with what
confidence, as I grasp the elbow of it, I look up——catching
the idea, even sometimes before it half way reaches me——

I believe in my conscience I intercept many a thought which
heaven intended for another man.

Pope and his Portrait* are fools to me[2]——no martyr is ever

---

[1]The state of being a cuckold, a dishonoured husband.

*Vid. *Pope*'s Portrait.   [Sterne's note.]

[2]*I.e.,* Pope and his portrait are as nothing compared to me.   Sterne is
probably referring to one of the several allegorical engravings of Alexander Pope receiving inspiration from the classic gods, muses, and poets.
In Warburton's edition of Pope, with which Sterne was familiar, *Windsor
Forest* is prefaced by an engraving of Pope, laurel-crowned, with pen
poised, taking dictation from Flora; the *Satires* are preceded by an engraving of the poet similarly seated, receiving inspiration from Mercury
and Apollo; another engraving in the same volume graphically illus-

so full of faith or fire——I wish I could say of good works too
——but I have no

Zeal or Anger——or

Anger or Zeal——

And till gods and men agree together to call it by the same
name——the errantest TARTUFFE,[3] in science——in politics
——or in religion, shall never kindle a spark within me, or
have a worse word, or a more unkind greeting, than what he
will read in the next chapter.

CHAP. III.

——Bon jour!——good-morrow!——so you have got your
cloak on betimes!——but 'tis a cold morning, and you judge
the matter rightly——'tis better to be well mounted, than go
o'foot——and obstructions in the glands are dangerous——
And how goes it with thy concubine——thy wife——and thy
little ones o'both sides? and when did you hear from the old
gentleman and lady——your sister, aunt, uncle and cousins
——I hope they have got better of their colds, coughs, claps,
tooth-aches, fevers, stranguries, sciaticas, swellings, and sore-
eyes.——What a devil of an apothecary! to take so much blood
——give such a vile purge——puke——poultice——plaister
——night-draught——glister[1]——blister?——And   why   so
many grains of calomel? santa Maria! and such a dose of
opium! periclitating,[2] pardi! the whole family of ye, from
head to tail——By my great aunt *Dinah's* old black velvet
mask! I think there was no occasion for it.

---

trates the lines from the *Epilogue* to the *Satires,* Dialogue 2, apostrophiz-
ing his pen:

O sacred weapon! left for Truth's defence,
Sole Dread of Folly, Vice, and Insolence!
To all but Heav'n-directed hands deny'd,
The Muse may give thee, but the Gods must guide.

[3]See p. 343, n. 3.
[1]Clyster, enema.
[2]Endangering.

Now this being a little bald about the chin, by frequently putting off and on, *before* she was got with child by the coach-man——not one of our family would wear it after. To cover the MASK afresh, was more than the mask was worth——and to wear a mask which was bald, or which could be half seen through, was as bad as having no mask at all——

This is the reason, may it please your reverences, that in all our numerous family, for these four generations, we count no more than one archbishop, a *Welch* judge, some three or four aldermen, and a single mountebank——

In the sixteenth century, we boast of no less than a dozen alchymists.

CHAP. IV.

"IT is with Love as with Cuckoldom"——the suffering party is at least the *third,* but generally the last in the house who knows any thing about the matter: this comes, as all the world knows, from having half a dozen words for one thing; and so long, as what in this vessel of the human frame, is *Love*——may be *Hatred,* in that——*Sentiment* half a yard higher——and *Nonsense*————no, Madam,——not there ——I mean at the part I am now pointing to with my fore-finger——how can we help ourselves?

Of all mortal, and immortal men too, if you please, who ever soliloquized upon this mystic subject, my uncle *Toby* was the worst fitted, to have push'd his researches, thro' such a contention of feelings; and he had infallibly let them all run on, as we do worse matters, to see what they would turn out ——had not *Bridget's* pre-notification of them to *Susannah,* and *Susannah's* repeated manifesto's thereupon to all the world, made it necessary for my uncle *Toby* to look into the affair.

CHAP. V.

WHY weavers, gardeners, and gladiators——or a man with a pined leg (proceeding from some ailment in the *foot*)——should ever have had some tender nymph breaking her heart in secret for them, are points well and duely settled and accounted for, by ancient and modern physiologists.

A water-drinker, provided he is a profess'd one, and does it without fraud or covin, is precisely in the same predicament: not that, at first sight, there is any consequence, or shew of logic in it, "That a rill of cold water dribbling through my inward parts, should light up a torch in my *Jenny's*——"

——The proposition does not strike one; on the contrary it seems to run opposite to the natural workings of causes and effects——

But it shews the weakness and imbecility of human reason.

——"And in perfect good health with it?"

——The most perfect——Madam, that friendship herself could wish me——

——"And drink nothing!——nothing but water?"

——Impetuous fluid! the moment thou pressest against the flood-gates of the brain——see how they give way!——

In swims CURIOSITY, beckoning to her damsels to follow—— they dive into the centre of the current——

FANCY sits musing upon the bank, and with her eyes following the stream, turns straws and bulrushes into masts and bowsprits——And DESIRE, with vest held up to the knee in one hand, snatches at them, as they swim by her, with the other——

O ye water-drinkers! is it then by this delusive fountain, that ye have so often governed and turn'd this world about like a mill-wheel——grinding the faces of the impotent——be-powdering their ribs——be-peppering their noses, and changing sometimes even the very frame and face of nature——

——If I was you, quoth *Yorick,* I would drink more water,

Eugenius.——And, if I was you, *Yorick,* replied *Eugenius,* so would I.

Which shews they had both read *Longinus*[1]——

For my own part, I am resolved never to read any book but my own, as long as I live.

CHAP. VI.

I Wish my uncle *Toby* had been a water-drinker; for then the thing had been accounted for, That the first moment Widow *Wadman* saw him, she felt something stirring within her in his favour——Something!——something.

——Something perhaps more than friendship——less than love——something——no matter what——no matter where ——I would not give a single hair off my mule's tail, and be obliged to pluck it off myself (indeed the villain has not many to spare, and is not a little vicious into the bargain) to be let by your worships into the secret——

But the truth is, my uncle *Toby* was not a water-drinker; he drank it neither pure nor mix'd, or any how, or any where, except fortuitously upon some advanced posts, where better liquor was not to be had——or during the time he was under cure; when the surgeon telling him it would extend the fibres, and bring them sooner into contact——my uncle *Toby* drank it for quietness sake.

Now as all the world knows, that no effect in nature can be produced without a cause and as it is as well known, that my uncle *Toby* was neither a weaver——a gardener, or a gladiator ——unless as a captain, you will needs have him one——but then he was only a captain of foot——and besides the whole is an equivocation——There is nothing left for us to suppose,

---

[1] In a lost portion of *On the Sublime,* Longinus (for whom, see p. 52, n. 7) refers to a conversation reputed to have taken place between Alexander the Great and Parmenio, his counsellor. According to the version recorded by Arrian in the *Anabasis,* 2.25.2, when the latter urged Alexander to accept overtures of peace from Darius, saying that if he were Alexander he should readily embrace them, "So would I," replied Alexander, "if I were Parmenio."

but that my uncle *Toby*'s leg——but that will avail us little in the present hypothesis, unless it had proceeded from some ailment *in the foot*——whereas his leg was not emaciated from any disorder in his foot——for my uncle *Toby*'s leg was not emaciated at all. It was a little stiff and awkward, from a total disuse of it, for the three years he lay confined at my father's house in town; but it was plump and muscular, and in all other respects as good and promising a leg as the other.

I declare, I do not recollect any one opinion or passage of my life, where my understanding was more at a loss to make ends meet, and torture the chapter I had been writing, to the service of the chapter following it, than in the present case: one would think I took a pleasure in running into difficulties of this kind, merely to make fresh experiments of getting out of 'em——Inconsiderate soul that thou art! What! are not the unavoidable distresses with which, as an author and a man, thou art hemm'd in on every side of thee——are they, *Tristram,* not sufficient, but thou must entangle thyself still more?

Is it not enough that thou art in debt, and that thou hast ten cart-loads of thy fifth and sixth volumes still——still unsold, and art almost at thy wit's ends, how to get them off thy hands.

To this hour art thou not tormented with the vile asthma thou gattest in skating against the wind in *Flanders?* and is it but two months ago, that in a fit of laughter, on seeing a cardinal make water like a quirister[1] (with both hands) thou brakest a vessel in thy lungs, whereby, in two hours, thou lost as many quarts of blood; and hadst thou lost as much more, did not the faculty tell thee——it would have amounted to a gallon?——

CHAP. VII.

——But for heaven's sake, let us not talk of quarts or gallons——let us take the story straight before us; it is so nice

[1] A choir boy.

and intricate a one, it will scarce bear the transposition of a single tittle; and some how or other, you have got me thrust almost into the middle of it——

——I beg we may take more care.

CHAP. VIII.

MY uncle *Toby* and the corporal had posted down with so much heat and precipitation, to take possession of the spot of ground we have so often spoke of, in order to open their campaign as early as the rest of the allies; that they had forgot one of the most necessary articles of the whole affair; it was neither a pioneer's spade, a pick-ax, or a shovel——

——It was a bed to lie on: so that as *Shandy Hall* was at that time unfurnished; and the little inn where poor *Le Fever* died, not yet built; my uncle *Toby* was constrained to accept of a bed at Mrs. *Wadman's*, for a night or two, till corporal *Trim* (who to the character of an excellent valet, groom, cook, sempster,[1] surgeon and engineer, superadded that of an excellent upholsterer too) with the help of a carpenter and a couple of taylors, constructed one in my uncle *Toby's* house.

A daughter of *Eve,* for such was widow *Wadman,* and 'tis all the character I intend to give of her——

——*"That she was a perfect woman;"*
had better be fifty leagues off——or in her warm bed——or playing with a case-knife——or any thing you please——than make a man the object of her attention, when the house and all the furniture is her own.

There is nothing in it out of doors and in broad day-light, where a woman has a power, physically speaking, of viewing a man in more lights than one——but here, for her soul, she can see him in no light without mixing something of her own goods and chattels along with him——till by reiterated acts of such combinations, he gets foisted into her inventory——

——And then good night.

[1] Seamster.

But this is not matter of SYSTEM; for I have delivered that above———nor is it matter of BREVIARY———for I make no man's creed but my own———nor matter of FACT———at least that I know of; but 'tis matter copulative and introductory to what follows.

CHAP. IX.

I Do not speak it with regard to the coarseness or clean-ness of them———or the strength of their gussets———but pray do not night-shifts[1] differ from day-shifts as much in this particular, as in any thing else in the world; That they so far exceed the others in length, that when you are laid down in them, they fall almost as much below the feet, as the day-shifts fall short of them?

Widow *Wadman's* night-shifts (as was the mode I suppose in King *William's* and Queen *Anne's* reigns) were cut how-ever after this fashion; and if the fashion is changed, (for in *Italy* they are come to nothing)———so much the worse for the public; they were two *Flemish* ells[2] and a half in length; so that allowing a moderate woman two ells, she had half an ell to spare, to do what she would with.

Now from one little indulgence gain'd after another, in the many bleak and decemberly nights of a seven years widow-hood, things had insensibly come to this pass, and for the two last years had got establish'd into one of the ordinances of the bed-chamber———That as soon as Mrs. *Wadman* was put to bed, and had got her legs stretched down to the bottom of it, of which she always gave *Bridget* notice———*Bridget* with all suitable decorum, having first open'd the bed-cloaths at the feet, took hold of the half ell of cloath we are speaking of, and having gently, and with both her hands, drawn it downwards to its furthest extension, and then contracted it again side long by four or five even plaits, she took a large corking pin[3]

---

[1] Shirts.

[2] The variable Flemish ell averaged 27.4 inches.

[3] A pin of largest size.

out of her sleeve, and with the point directed towards her, pin'd the plaits all fast together a little above the hem; which done she tuck'd all in tight at the feet, and wish'd her mistress a good night.

This was constant, and without any other variation than this; that on shivering and tempestuous nights, when *Bridget* untuck'd the feet of the bed, *&c.* to do this——she consulted no thermometer but that of her own passions; and so performed it standing——kneeling——or squatting, according to the different degrees of faith, hope, and charity, she was in, and bore towards her mistress that night. In every other respect the *etiquette* was sacred, and might have vied with the most mechanical one of the most inflexible bed-chamber in *Christendom.*

The first night, as soon as the corporal had conducted my uncle *Toby* up stairs, which was about ten——Mrs. *Wadman* threw herself into her arm chair, and crossing her left knee with her right, which formed a resting-place for her elbow, she reclin'd her cheek upon the palm of her hand, and leaning forwards, ruminated till midnight upon both sides of the question.

The second night she went to her bureau, and having ordered *Bridget* to bring her up a couple of fresh candles and leave them upon the table, she took out her marriage-settlement, and read it over with great devotion: and the third night (which was the last of my uncle *Toby's* stay) when *Bridget* had pull'd down the night-shift, and was assaying to stick in the corking pin——

——With a kick of both heels at once, but at the same time the most natural kick that could be kick'd in her situation—— for supposing * * * * * * * * * to be the sun in its meridian, it was a north-east kick——she kick'd the pin out of her fingers——the *etiquette* which hung upon it, down—— down it fell to the ground, and was shivered into a thousand atoms.

From all which it was plain that widow *Wadman* was in love with my uncle *Toby.*

CHAP. X.

MY uncle *Toby's* head at that time was full of other matters, so that it was not till the demolition of *Dunkirk,*
when all the other civilities of *Europe* were settled, that he
found leisure to return this.

This made an armistice (that is speaking with regard to my
uncle *Toby*——but with respect to Mrs. *Wadman,* a vacancy)
——of almost eleven years. But in all cases of this nature, as
it is the second blow, happen at what distance of time it will,
which makes the fray——I chuse for that reason to call these
the amours of my uncle *Toby* with Mrs. *Wadman,* rather than
the amours of Mrs. *Wadman* with my uncle *Toby.*

This is not a distinction without a difference.

It is not like the affair of *an old hat cock'd*——and *a cock'd
old hat,*[1] about which your reverences have so often been at
odds with one another——but there is a difference here in the
nature of things——

And let me tell you, gentry, a wide one too.

CHAP. XI.

NOW as widow *Wadman* did love my uncle *Toby*——and
my uncle *Toby* did not love widow *Wadman,* there was
nothing for widow *Wadman* to do, but to go on and love
my uncle *Toby*——or let it alone.

Widow *Wadman* would do neither the one or the other——
——Gracious heaven!——but I forget I am a little of her
temper myself; for whenever it so falls out, which it sometimes does about the equinoxes, that an earthly goddess is so
much this, and that, and t'other, that I cannot eat my breakfast for her——and that she careth not three halfpence whether
I eat my breakfast or no——

[1] "Old hat": cant term for the female sex organs.

——Curse on her! and so I send her to *Tartary,* and from *Tartary* to *Terra del Fuogo,* and so on to the devil: in short there is not an infernal nitch where I do not take her divinity-ship and stick it.

But as the heart is tender, and the passions in these tides ebb and flow ten times in a minute, I instantly bring her back again; and as I do all things in extremes, I place her in the very centre of the milky-way——

Brightest of stars! thou wilt shed thy influence upon some one———

——The duce take her and her influence too——for at that word I lose all patience——much good may it do him!——By all that is hirsute and gashly![1] I cry, taking off my furr'd cap, and twisting it round my finger——I would not give sixpence for a dozen such!

——But 'tis an excellent cap too (putting it upon my head, and pressing it close to my ears)——and warm——and soft; especially if you stroke it the right way——but alas! that will never be my luck——(so here my philosophy is shipwreck'd again)

——No; I shall never have a finger in the pye (so here I break my metaphor)——

Crust and crumb

Inside and out

Top and bottom——I detest it, I hate it, I repudiate it——I'm sick at the sight of it——

'Tis all pepper,

       garlick,

       staragen,[2]

       salt, and

       devil's dung——by the great arch cook of cooks, who does nothing, I think, from morning to night, but sit down by the fire-side and invent inflammatory dishes for us, I would not touch it for the world——

O *Tristram! Tristram!* cried *Jenny.*

---

[1]Ghastly; but a *double entendre* may be suspected.

[2]Tarragon.

O *Jenny! Jenny!* replied I, and so went on with the twelfth chapter.

CHAP. XII.

——"Not touch it for the world" did I say——
Lord, how I have heated my imagination with this metaphor!

CHAP. XIII.

WHICH shews, let your reverences and worships say what you will of it (for as for *thinking*——all who *do* think ——think pretty much alike, both upon it and other matters) ——Love is certainly, at least alphabetically speaking, one of the most

A gitating
B ewitching
C onfounded
D evilish affairs of life——the most
E xtravagant
F utilitous[1]
G alligaskinish
H andy-dandyish
I racundulous (there is no K to it) and
L yrical of all human passions: at the same time, the most
M isgiving
N innyhammering
O bstipating
P ragmatical
S tridulous
R idiculous——though by the bye the R should have gone

[1]Futile. Galligaskinish: pertaining to galligaskins, a humorous term for loose breeches. Iracundulous: irascible. Obstipating: stopping-up, constipating.   Stridulous: having a thin, squeaky sound.

first——But in short 'tis of such a nature, as my father once told my uncle *Toby* upon the close of a long dissertation upon the subject——"You can scarce," said he, "combine two ideas together upon it, brother *Toby,* without an hypallage"—— What's that? cried my uncle *Toby.*

The cart before the horse, replied my father——

——And what has he to do there? cried my uncle *Toby*—— Nothing, quoth my father, but to get in——or let it alone.

Now widow *Wadman,* as I told you before, would do neither the one or the other.

She stood however ready harnessed and caparisoned at all points to watch accidents.

CHAP. XIV.

THE Fates, who certainly all foreknew of these amours of widow *Wadman* and my uncle *Toby,* had, from the first creation of matter and motion (and with more courtesy than they usually do things of this kind) established such a chain of causes and effects hanging so fast to one another, that it was scarce possible for my uncle *Toby* to have dwelt in any other house in the world, or to have occupied any other garden in *Christendom,* but the very house and garden which join'd and laid parallel to Mrs. *Wadman*'s; this, with the advantage of a thickset arbour in Mrs. *Wadman*'s garden, but planted in the hedge-row of my uncle *Toby*'s, put all the occasions into her hands which Love-militancy wanted; she could observe my uncle *Toby*'s motions, and was mistress likewise of his councils of war; and as his unsuspecting heart had given leave to the corporal, through the mediation of *Bridget,* to make her a wicker gate of communication to enlarge her walks, it enabled her to carry on her approaches to the very door of the sentry-box; and sometimes out of gratitude, to make the attack, and endeavour to blow my uncle *Toby* up in the very sentry-box itself.

CHAP. XV.

I T is a great pity——but 'tis certain from every day's observation of man, that he may be set on fire like a candle, at
either end——provided there is a sufficient wick standing
out; if there is not——there's an end of the affair; and if there
is——by lighting it at the bottom, as the flame in that case has
the misfortune generally to put out itself——there's an end of
the affair again.

For my part, could I always have the ordering of it which
way I would be burnt myself——for I cannot bear the thoughts
of being burnt like a beast——I would oblige a housewife constantly to light me at the top; for then I should burn down
decently to the socket; that is, from my head to my heart,
from my heart to my liver, from my liver to my bowels, and
so on by the meseraick veins and arteries, through all the turns
and lateral insertions of the intestines and their tunicles to
the blind gut[1]——

——I beseech you, doctor *Slop*, quoth my uncle *Toby*, interrupting him as he mentioned the *blind gut*, in a discourse
with my father the night my mother was brought to bed of
me——I beseech you, quoth my uncle *Toby*, to tell me which
is the blind gut; for, old as I am, I vow I do not know to this
day where it lies.

The *blind gut*, answered doctor *Slop*, lies betwixt the *Illion*[2]
and *Colon*——

——In a man? said my father.

——'Tis precisely the same, cried doctor *Slop*, in a
woman——

That's more than I know; quoth my father.[3]

---

[1] The Caecum, the blind pouch which is the beginning of the colon.

[2] Ileum, the terminal portion of the small intestine.

[3] My father has apparently understood "caecum" in its basic sense of
"any tube with a closed end."

CHAP. XVI.

——And so to make sure of both systems, Mrs. *Wadman* predetermined to light my uncle *Toby* neither at this end or that; but like a prodigal's candle, to light him, if possible, at both ends at once.

Now, through all the lumber rooms of military furniture, including both of horse and foot, from the great arsenal of *Venice* to the *Tower* of *London* (exclusive) if Mrs. *Wadman* had been rummaging for seven years together, and with *Bridget* to help her, she could not have found any one *blind* or *mantelet*[1] so fit for her purpose, as that which the expediency of my uncle *Toby*'s affairs had fix'd up ready to her hands.

I believe I have not told you——but I don't know——possibly I have——be it as it will, 'tis one of the number of those many things, which a man had better do over again, than dispute about it——That whatever town or fortress the corporal was at work upon, during the course of their campaign, my uncle *Toby* always took care on the inside of his sentry-box, which was towards his left hand, to have a plan of the place, fasten'd up with two or three pins at the top, but loose at the bottom, for the conveniency of holding it up to the eye, &c. . . . as occasions required; so that when an attack was resolved upon, Mrs. *Wadman* had nothing more to do, when she had got advanced to the door of the sentry-box, but to extend her right hand; and edging in her left foot at the same movement, to take hold of the map or plan, or upright, or whatever it was, and with out-stretched neck meeting it half way, ——to advance it towards her; on which my uncle *Toby*'s passions were sure to catch fire——for he would instantly take hold of the other corner of the map in his left hand, and with the end of his pipe, in the other, begin an explanation.

When the attack was advanced to this point;——the world will naturally enter into the reasons of Mrs. *Wadman*'s next

---

[1] A movable shelter used to protect besiegers in their attacks.

stroke of generalship——which was, to take my uncle *Toby*'s
tobacco-pipe out of his hand as soon as she possibly could;
which, under one pretence or other, but generally that of
pointing more distinctly at some redoubt or breast-work in
the map, she would effect before my uncle *Toby* (poor soul!)
had well march'd above half a dozen toises[2] with it.

——It obliged my uncle *Toby* to make use of his forefinger.

The difference it made in the attack was this; That in going upon it, as in the first case, with the end of her forefinger
against the end of my uncle *Toby*'s tobacco-pipe, she might
have travelled with it, along the lines, from *Dan* to *Beersheba,*
had my uncle *Toby*'s lines reach'd so far, without any effect:
For as there was no arterial or vital heat in the end of the
tobacco-pipe, it could excite no sentiment——it could neither
give fire by pulsation——or receive it by sympathy——'twas
nothing but smoak.

Whereas, in following my uncle *Toby*'s forefinger with hers,
close thro' all the little turns and indentings of his works—
pressing sometimes against the side of it——then treading
upon it's nail——then tripping it up——then touching it here
——then there, and so on——it set something at least in motion.

This, tho' slight skirmishing, and at a distance from the
main body, yet drew on the rest; for here, the map usually
falling with the back of it, close to the side of the sentry-box,
my uncle *Toby,* in the simplicity of his soul, would lay his
hand flat upon it, in order to go on with his explanation; and
Mrs. *Wadman,* by a manœuvre as quick as thought, would as
certainly place her's close besides it; this at once opened a
communication, large enough for any sentiment to pass or re-
pass, which a person skill'd in the elementary and practical
part of love-making, has occasion for——

By bringing up her forefinger parallel (as before) to my
uncle *Toby*'s——it unavoidably brought the thumb into action
——and the forefinger and thumb being once engaged, as
naturally brought in the whole hand. Thine, dear uncle

[2]See p. 83, n. 5.

Toby! was never now in it's right place——Mrs. *Wadman* had it ever to take up, or, with the gentlest pushings, protrusions, and equivocal compressions, that a hand to be removed is capable of receiving——to get it press'd a hair breadth of one side out of her way.

Whilst this was doing, how could she forget to make him sensible, that it was her leg (and no one's else) at the bottom of the sentry-box, which slightly press'd against the calf of his ——So that my uncle *Toby* being thus attacked and sore push'd on both his wings——was it a wonder, if now and then, it put his centre into disorder?——

——The duce take it! said my uncle *Toby.*

CHAP. XVII.

THESE attacks of Mrs. *Wadman,* you will readily conceive to be of different kinds; varying from each other, like the attacks which history is full of, and from the same reasons. A general looker on, would scarce allow them to be attacks at all——or if he did, would confound them all together—— but I write not to them: it will be time enough to be a little more exact in my descriptions of them, as I come up to them, which will not be for some chapters; having nothing more to add in this, but that in a bundle of original papers and draw- ings which my father took care to roll up by themselves, there is a plan of *Bouchain* in perfect preservation (and shall be kept so, whilst I have power to preserve any thing) upon the lower corner of which, on the right hand side, there is still remain- ing the marks of a snuffy finger and thumb, which there is all the reason in the world to imagine, were Mrs. *Wadman's;* for the opposite side of the margin, which I suppose to have been my uncle *Toby's,* is absolutely clean: This seems an authenticated record of one of these attacks; for there are vestigia of the two punctures partly grown up, but still visible on the opposite corner of the map, which are unquestionably

the very holes, through which it has been pricked up in the
sentry-box——

By all that is priestly! I value this precious relick, with it's
stigmata and *pricks,* more than all the relicks of the *Romish*
church——always excepting, when I am writing upon these
matters, the pricks which enter'd the flesh of St. *Radagunda*[1]
in the desert, which in your road from FESSE to CLUNY, the
nuns of that name will shew you for love.

CHAP. XVIII.

I Think, an' please your honour, quoth *Trim,* the fortifications are quite destroyed——and the bason[1] is upon a level
with the mole——I think so too; replied my uncle *Toby* with
a sigh half suppress'd——but step into the parlour, *Trim,* for
the stipulation——it lies upon the table.

It has lain there these six weeks, replied the corporal, till
this very morning that the old woman kindled the fire with
it——

——Then, said my uncle *Toby,* there is no further occasion
for our services. The more, an' please your honour, the pity,
said the corporal; in uttering which he cast his spade into the
wheel-barrow, which was beside him, with an air the most expressive of disconsolation that can be imagined, and was
heavily turning about to look for his pick-ax, his pioneer's
shovel, his picquets and other little military stores, in order
to carry them off the field——when a heigh ho! from the
sentry-box, which, being made of thin slit deal, reverberated
the sound more sorrowfully to his ear, forbad him.

——No; said the corporal to himself, I'll do it before his
honour rises to-morrow morning; so taking his spade out of
the wheel-barrow again, with a little earth in it, as if to level

---

[1]Noted for her austerities, Saint Radegunde (for whom, see p. 251,
n. 6) is said to have mortified her flesh by applying to it a heated metal
cross "armed with sharp points."

[1]Basin, harbour.

something at the foot of the glacis——but with a real intent
to approach nearer to his master, in order to divert him——
he loosen'd a sod or two——pared their edges with his spade,
and having given them a gentle blow or two with the back of
it, he sat himself down close by my uncle *Toby*'s feet, and
began as follows.

CHAP. XIX.

IT was a thousand pities——though I believe, an' please your
honour, I am going to say but a foolish kind of a thing for
a soldier——

A soldier, cried my uncle *Toby,* interrupting the corporal, is
no more exempt from saying a foolish thing, *Trim,* than a
man of letters——But not so often, an' please your honour,
replied the corporal——My uncle *Toby* gave a nod.

It was a thousand pities then, said the corporal, casting his
eye upon *Dunkirk,* and the mole, as *Servius Sulpicius,* in returning out of *Asia* (when he sailed from *Ægina* towards
Megara) did upon *Corinth* and *Pyreus*[1]——

——"It was a thousand pities, an' please your honour, to
destroy these works——and a thousand pities to have let them
stood."——

——Thou art right, *Trim,* in both cases; said my uncle *Toby*
——This, continued the corporal, is the reason, that from the
beginning of their demolition to the end——I have never once
whistled, or sung, or laugh'd, or cry'd, or talk'd of pass'd done
deeds, or told your honour one story good or bad——

——Thou hast many excellencies, *Trim,* said my uncle *Toby,*
and I hold it not the least of them, as thou happenest to be a
story-teller, that of the number thou hast told me, either to
amuse me in my painful hours, or divert me in my grave ones
——thou hast seldom told me a bad one——

——Because, an' please your honour, except one of a *King*

[1]See p. 354.

of Bohemia and his seven castles,——they are all true; for they are about myself——

I do not like the subject the worse, *Trim,* said my uncle *Toby,* on that score: But prithee what is this story? thou hast excited my curiosity.

I'll tell it your honour, quoth the corporal directly——Provided, said my uncle *Toby,* looking earnestly towards *Dunkirk* and the mole again——provided it is not a merry one; to such, *Trim,* a man should ever bring one half of the entertainment along with him; and the disposition I am in at present would wrong both thee, *Trim,* and thy story——It is not a merry one by any means, replied the corporal——Nor would I have it altogether a grave one, added my uncle *Toby*——It is neither the one nor the other, replied the corporal, but will suit your honour exactly——Then I'll thank thee for it with all my heart, cried my uncle *Toby,* so prithee begin it, *Trim.*

The corporal made his reverence; and though it is not so easy a matter as the world imagines, to pull off a lank montero cap with grace——or a whit less difficult, in my conceptions, when a man is sitting squat upon the ground, to make a bow so teeming with respect as the corporal was wont, yet by suffering the palm of his right hand, which was towards his master, to slip backward upon the grass, a little beyond his body, in order to allow it the greater sweep——and by an unforced compression, at the same time, of his cap with the thumb and the two forefingers of his left, by which the diameter of the cap became reduced, so that it might be said, rather to be insensibly squeez'd——than pull'd off with a flatus——the corporal acquitted himself of both, in a better manner than the posture of his affairs promised; and having hemmed twice, to find in what key his story would best go, and best suit his master's humour——he exchanged a single look of kindness with him, and set off thus.

The Story of the king of Bohemia
and his seven castles.

THERE was a certain king of Bo - - he————

As the corporal was entering the confines of *Bohemia,*
my uncle *Toby* obliged him to halt for a single moment; he
had set out bare-headed, having since he pull'd off his Montero-
cap in the latter end of the last chapter, left it lying beside him
on the ground.

————The eye of Goodness espieth all things————so that before the corporal had well got through the first five words of
his story, had my uncle *Toby* twice touch'd his Montero-cap
with the end of his cane, interrogatively————as much as to say,
Why don't you put it on, *Trim?* *Trim* took it up with the
most respectful slowness, and casting a glance of humiliation
as he did it, upon the embroidery of the fore-part, which being
dismally tarnish'd and fray'd moreover in some of the principal leaves and boldest parts of the pattern, he lay'd it down
again betwixt his two feet, in order to moralize upon the
subject.

————'Tis every word of it but too true, cried my uncle *Toby,*
that thou art about to observe————

"Nothing in this world, Trim, is made to last for ever." .

————But when tokens, dear *Tom,* of thy love and remembrance wear out, said *Trim,* what shall we say?

There is no occasion, *Trim,* quoth my uncle *Toby,* to say any
thing else; and was a man to puzzle his brains till Doom's
day, I believe, *Trim,* it would be impossible.

The corporal perceiving my uncle *Toby* was in the right,
and that it would be in vain for the wit of man to think of extracting a purer moral from his cap, without further attempting it, he put it on; and passing his hand across his forehead
to rub out a pensive wrinkle, which the text and the doctrine
between them had engender'd, he return'd, with the same look

and tone of voice, to his story of the king of *Bohemia* and his
seven castles.

The story of the king of Bohemia and
his seven castles, continued.

THERE was a certain king of *Bohemia,* but in whose reign,
except his own, I am not able to inform your honour——
I do not desire it of thee, *Trim,* by any means, cried my uncle
Toby.

——It was a little before the time, an' please your honour,
when giants were beginning to leave off breeding;——but in
what year of our Lord that was——

——I would not give a half-penny to know, said my uncle
Toby.

——Only, an' please your honour, it makes a story look the
better in the face——

——'Tis thy own, *Trim,* so ornament it after thy own fashion; and take any date, continued my uncle *Toby,* looking
pleasantly upon him——take any date in the whole world thou
choosest, and put it to——thou art heartily welcome——

The corporal bowed; for of every century, and of every year
of that century, from the first creation of the world down to
Noah's flood; and from *Noah's* flood to the birth of *Abraham;*
through all the pilgrimages of the patriarchs, to the departure
of the *Israelites* out of *Egypt*——and throughout all the Dynas-
ties, Olympiads, Urbecondita's,[2] and other memorable epochas
of the different nations of the world, down to the coming of
Christ, and from thence to the very moment in which the
corporal was telling his story——had my uncle *Toby* subjected
this vast empire of time and all its abysses at his feet; but as
MODESTY scarce touches with a finger what LIBERALITY offers her
with both hands open——the corporal contented himself with
the very *worst year* of the whole bunch; which, to prevent

---

[2] By the founding of cities—as events were dated before and after the
foundation of Rome.

your honours of the Majority and Minority from tearing the very flesh off your bones in contestation, 'Whether that year is not always the last cast-year[3] of the last cast-almanack'—— I tell you plainly it was; but from a different reason than you wot of——

——It was the year next him——which being the year of our Lord seventeen hundred and twelve, when the duke of *Ormond* was playing the devil in *Flanders*——the corporal took it, and set out with it afresh on his expedition to *Bohemia*.

The story of the king of Bohemia and his seven castles, continued.

IN the year of our Lord one thousand seven hundred and twelve, there was, an' please your honour——

——To tell thee truly, *Trim,* quoth my uncle *Toby,* any other date would have pleased me much better, not only on account of the sad stain upon our history that year, in marching off our troops, and refusing to cover the siege of *Quesnoi,* though *Fagel* was carrying on the works with such incredible vigour ——but likewise on the score, *Trim,* of thy own story; because if there are——and which, from what thou hast dropt, I partly suspect to be the fact——if there are giants in it——

There is but one, an' please your honour——

——'Tis as bad as twenty, replied my uncle *Toby*——thou should'st have carried him back some seven or eight hundred years out of harm's way, both of criticks and other people; and therefore I would advise thee, if ever thou tellest it again——

——If I live, an' please your honour, but once to get through it, I will never tell it again, quoth *Trim,* either to man, woman, or child——Poo——poo! said my uncle *Toby*——but with accents of such sweet encouragement did he utter it, that the corporal went on with his story with more alacrity than ever.

---

[3]Cast: discarded.

The story of the king of Bohemia and
his seven castles, continued.

THERE was, an' please your honour, said the corporal, raising his voice and rubbing the palms of his two hands
cheerily together as he begun, a certain king of *Bohemia*——
——Leave out the date entirely, *Trim,* quoth my uncle *Toby,*
leaning forwards, and laying his hand gently upon the corporal's shoulder to temper the interruption——leave it out
entirely, *Trim;* a story passes very well without these niceties,
unless one is pretty sure of 'em——Sure of 'em! said the corporal, shaking his head——

Right; answered my uncle *Toby,* it is not easy, *Trim,* for
one, bred up as thou and I have been to arms, who seldom
looks further forward than to the end of his musket, or backwards beyond his knapsack, to know much about this matter
——God bless your honour! said the corporal, won by the
manner of my uncle *Toby*'s reasoning, as much as by the reasoning itself, he has something else to do; if not on action, or
a march, or upon duty in his garrison——he has his firelock,
an' please your honour, to furbish——his accoutrements to take
care of——his regimentals to mend——himself to shave and
keep clean, so as to appear always like what he is upon the
parade; what business, added the corporal triumphantly, has
a soldier, an' please your honour, to know any thing at all of
geography?

——Thou would'st have said *chronology, Trim,* said my
uncle *Toby;* for as for geography, 'tis of absolute use to him;
he must be acquainted intimately with every country and its
boundaries where his profession carries him; he should know
every town and city, and village and hamlet, with the canals,
the roads, and hollow ways which lead up to them; there is
not a river or a rivulet he passes, *Trim,* but he should be able
at first sight to tell thee what is its name——in what mountains it takes its rise——what is its course——how far it is

navigable——where fordable——where not; he should know
the fertility of every valley, as well as the hind who ploughs
it; and be able to describe, or, if it is required, to give thee
an exact map of all the plains and defiles, the forts, the acclivi-
ties, the woods and morasses, thro' and by which his army is
to march; he should know their produce, their plants, their
minerals, their waters, their animals, their seasons, their climates, their heats and cold, their inhabitants, their customs,
their language, their policy, and even their religion.

Is it else to be conceived, corporal, continued my uncle
Toby, rising up in his sentry-box, as he began to warm in this
part of his discourse——how *Marlborough* could have marched
his army from the banks of the *Maes* to *Belburg;* from *Belburg*
to *Kerpenord*——(here the corporal could sit no longer) from
Kerpenord, Trim, to *Kalsaken;* from *Kalsaken* to *Newdorf;*
from *Newdorf* to *Landenbourg;* from *Landenbourg* to *Mildenheim;* from *Mildenheim* to *Elchingen;* from *Elchingen* to *Gingen;* from *Gingen* to *Balmerchoffen;* from *Balmerchoffen* to
Skellenburg, where he broke in upon the enemy's works;
forced his passage over the *Danube;* cross'd the *Lech*——
pushed on his troops into the heart of the empire, marching at
the head of them through *Friburg, Hokenwert,* and *Schone-
velt,* to the plains of *Blenheim* and *Hochstet?*——Great as he
was, corporal, he could not have advanced a step, or made one
single day's march without the aids of *Geography*——As for
Chronology, I own, *Trim,* continued my uncle *Toby,* sitting
down again coolly in his sentry-box, that of all others, it seems
a science which the soldier might best spare, was it not for the
lights which that science must one day give him, in determining the invention of powder; the furious execution of which,
renversing every thing like thunder before it, has become a
new æra to us of military improvements, changing so totally
the nature of attacks and defences both by sea and land, and
awakening so much art and skill in doing it, that the world
cannot be too exact in ascertaining the precise time of its discovery, or too inquisitive in knowing what great man was
the discoverer, and what occasions gave birth to it.

I am far from controverting, continued my uncle *Toby,*
what historians agree in, that in the year of our Lord 1380, under
the reign of *Wenceslaus,* son of *Charles* the fourth——a certain
priest, whose name was *Schwartz,*[4] shew'd the use of powder
to the *Venetians,* in their wars against the *Genoese;* but 'tis
certain he was not the first; because if we are to believe Don
Pedro the bishop of *Leon*[5]——How came priests and bishops,
an' please your honour, to trouble their heads so much about
gun-powder?——God knows, said my uncle *Toby*——his providence brings good out of every thing——and he avers, in his
chronicle of King *Alphonsus,* who reduced *Toledo,* That in
the year 1343, which was full thirty seven years before that
time, the secret of powder was well known, and employed with
success, both by Moors and Christians, not only in their sea-
combats, at that period, but in many of their most memorable
sieges in *Spain* and *Barbary*——And all the world knows, that
Friar *Bacon*[6] had wrote expressly about it, and had generously given the world a receipt to make it by, above a hundred and fifty years before even *Schwartz* was born——And
that the *Chinese,* added my uncle *Toby,* embarass us, and all
accounts of it still more, by boasting of the invention some
hundreds of years even before him——

——They are a pack of liars, I believe, cried *Trim*——

——They are some how or other deceived, said my uncle
Toby, in this matter, as is plain to me from the present miserable state of military architecture amongst them; which consists of nothing more than a fossé with a brick wall without
flanks——and for what they give us as a bastion at each angle

---

[4]Berthold Schwartz, a German monk, is said to have been the inventor of fire-arms, and perhaps of gunpowder, about 1330; Wenceslaus
(1361–1419) became Holy Roman Emperor in 1378.

[5]The chronicler Pedro, bishop of Leon, died in 1112. Sterne was led
astray by misreading his source for this passage, "Gunpowder," in
Ephraim Chambers's *Cyclopædia,* in which Peter Mexia is cited as the
authority for the use of powder by the Moors in 1343, and Don Pedro as
authority for a yet earlier use of fire-arms.

[6]In his *De Mirabili Potestate Artis et Naturæ,* Roger Bacon (c.1214–
c.1294), English philosopher and scientist, revealed considerable knowledge of explosive powders.

of it, 'tis so barbarously constructed, that it looks for all the world—— —— Like one of my seven castles, an' please your honour, quoth *Trim*.

My uncle *Toby*, tho' in the utmost distress for a comparison, most courteously refused *Trim*'s offer——till *Trim* telling him, he had half a dozen more in *Bohemia*, which he knew not how to get off his hands——my uncle *Toby* was so touch'd with the pleasantry of heart of the corporal——that he discontinued his dissertation upon gunpowder——and begged the corporal forthwith to go on with his story of the King of *Bohemia* and his seven castles.

The story of the king of Bohemia and his seven castles, continued.

THIS *unfortunate* King of *Bohemia*, said *Trim*——Was he unfortunate then? cried my uncle *Toby*, for he had been so wrapt up in his dissertation upon gun-powder and other military affairs, that tho' he had desired the corporal to go on, yet the many interruptions he had given, dwelt not so strong upon his fancy, as to account for the epithet——Was he *unfortunate* then, *Trim?* said my uncle *Toby*, pathetically——The corporal, wishing first the *word* and all its synonimas at the devil, forthwith began to run back in his mind, the principal events in the King of *Bohemia*'s story; from every one of which, it appearing that he was the most fortunate man that ever existed in the world——it put the corporal to a stand: for not caring to retract his epithet——and less, to explain it ——and least of all, to twist his tale (like men of lore) to serve a system——he looked up in my uncle *Toby*'s face for assistance——but seeing it was the very thing, my uncle *Toby* sat in expectation of himself——after a hum and a haw, he went on——

The King of *Bohemia*, an' please your honour, replied the corporal, was *unfortunate*, as thus——That taking great pleasure and delight in navigation and all sort of sea-affairs——

and there *happening* throughout the whole kingdom of *Bohemia,* to be no sea-port town whatever——

How the duce should there——*Trim?* cried my uncle *Toby;* for *Bohemia* being totally inland, it could have happen'd no otherwise——It might; said *Trim,* if it had pleased God——

My uncle *Toby* never spoke of the being and natural attributes of God, but with diffidence and hesitation——

——I believe not, replied my uncle *Toby,* after some pause ——for being inland, as I said, and having *Silesia* and *Moravia* to the east; *Lusatia* and *Upper Saxony* to the north; *Franconia* to the west; and *Bavaria* to the south: *Bohemia* could not have been propell'd to the sea, without ceasing to be *Bohemia*—— nor could the sea, on the other hand, have come up to *Bohemia,* without overflowing a great part of *Germany,* and destroying millions of unfortunate inhabitants who could make no defence against it——Scandalous! cried *Trim*——Which would bespeak, added my uncle *Toby,* mildly, such a want of compassion in him who is the father of it——that, I think, *Trim* ——the thing could have happen'd no way.

The corporal made the bow of unfeigned conviction; and went on.

Now the King of *Bohemia* with his queen and courtiers *happening* one fine summer's evening to walk out——Aye! there the word *happening* is right, *Trim,* cried my uncle *Toby;* for the King of *Bohemia* and his queen might have walk'd out, or let it alone;——'twas a matter of contingency, which might happen, or not, just as chance ordered it.

King *William* was of an opinion, an' please your honour, quoth *Trim,* that every thing was predestined for us in this world; insomuch, that he would often say to his soldiers, that "every ball had it's billet." He was a great man, said my uncle *Toby*——And I believe, continued *Trim,* to this day, that the shot which disabled me at the battle of *Landen,* was pointed at my knee for no other purpose, but to take me out of his service, and place me in your honour's, where I should be taken so much better care of in my old age——It shall never, *Trim,* be construed otherwise, said my uncle *Toby.*

The heart, both of the master and the man, were alike subject to sudden overflowings;——a short silence ensued.

Besides, said the corporal, resuming the discourse——but in a gayer accent——if it had not been for that single shot, I had never, an' please your honour, been in love——

So, thou wast once in love, *Trim!* said my uncle *Toby,* smiling——

Souse! replied the corporal——over head and ears! an' please your honour. Prithee when? where?——and how came it to pass?——I never heard one word of it before; quoth my uncle *Toby:*——I dare say, answered *Trim,* that every drummer and serjeant's son in the regiment knew of it——Its high time I should——said my uncle *Toby.*

Your honour remembers with concern, said the corporal, the total rout and confusion of our camp and army at the affair of *Landen;* every one was left to shift for himself; and if it had not been for the regiments of *Wyndham, Lumley,* and *Galway,* which covered the retreat over the bridge of *Neerspeeken,* the king himself could scarce have gain'd it——he was press'd hard, as your honour knows, on every side of him——

Gallant mortal! cried my uncle *Toby,* caught up with enthusiasm——this moment, now that all is lost, I see him galloping across me, corporal, to the left, to bring up the remains of the English horse along with him to support the right, and tear the laurel from *Luxembourg's* brows, if yet 'tis possible ——I see him with the knot of his scarfe just shot off, infusing fresh spirits into poor *Galway's* regiment——riding along the line——then wheeling about, and charging *Conti* at the head of it——Brave! brave by heaven! cried my uncle *Toby*——he deserves a crown——As richly, as a thief a halter; shouted *Trim.*

My uncle *Toby* knew the corporal's loyalty;——otherwise the comparison was not at all to his mind——it did not altogether strike the corporal's fancy when he had made it—— but it could not be recall'd——so he had nothing to do, but proceed.

As the number of wounded was prodigious, and no one had time to think of any thing, but his own safety——Though *Talmash,* said my uncle *Toby,* brought off the foot with great prudence——But I was left upon the field, said the corporal. Thou wast so; poor fellow! replied my uncle *Toby*——So that it was noon the next day, continued the corporal, before I was exchanged, and put into a cart with thirteen or fourteen more, in order to be convey'd to our hospital.

There is no part of the body, an' please your honour, where a wound occasions more intolerable anguish than upon the knee——

Except the groin; said my uncle *Toby.* An' please your honour, replied the corporal, the knee, in my opinion, must certainly be the most acute, there being so many tendons and what-d'ye-call-'ems all about it.

It is for that reason, quoth my uncle *Toby,* that the groin is infinitely more sensible——there being not only as many tendons and what-d'ye-call-'ems (for I know their names as little as thou do'st)——about it——but moreover * * *——

Mrs. *Wadman,* who had been all the time in her arbour——instantly stopp'd her breath——unpinn'd her mob at the chin, and stood up upon one leg——

The dispute was maintained with amicable and equal force betwixt my uncle *Toby* and *Trim* for some time; till *Trim* at length recollecting that he had often cried at his master's sufferings, but never shed a tear at his own——was for giving up the point, which my uncle *Toby* would not allow——'Tis a proof of nothing, *Trim,* said he, but the generosity of thy temper——

So that whether the pain of a wound in the groin (cæteris paribus[7]) is greater than the pain of a wound in the knee——or

Whether the pain of a wound in the knee is not greater than the pain of a wound in the groin——are points which to this day remain unsettled.

---

[7]Other things being equal.

CHAP. XX.

THE anguish of my knee, continued the corporal, was excessive in itself; and the uneasiness of the cart, with the roughness of the roads which were terribly cut up——making bad still worse——every step was death to me: so that with the loss of blood, and the want of care-taking of me, and a fever I felt coming on besides——(Poor soul! said my uncle *Toby*) all together, an' please your honour, was more than I could sustain.

I was telling my sufferings to a young woman at a peasant's house, where our cart, which was the last of the line, had halted; they had help'd me in, and the young woman had taken a cordial out of her pocket and dropp'd it upon some sugar, and seeing it had cheer'd me, she had given it me a second and a third time——So I was telling her, an' please your honour, the anguish I was in, and was saying it was so intolerable to me, that I had much rather lie down upon the bed, turning my face towards one which was in the corner of the room——and die, than go on——when, upon her attempting to lead me to it, I fainted away in her arms. She was a good soul! as your honour, said the corporal, wiping his eyes, will hear.

I thought *love* had been a joyous thing, quoth my uncle *Toby*.

'Tis the most serious thing, an' please your honour (sometimes) that is in the world.

By the persuasion of the young woman, continued the corporal, the cart with the wounded men set off without me: she had assured them I should expire immediately if I was put into the cart. So when I came to myself——I found myself in a still quiet cottage, with no one but the young woman, and the peasant and his wife. I was laid across the bed in the corner of the room, with my wounded leg upon a chair, and the young woman beside me, holding the corner of her handkerchief dipp'd in vinegar to my nose with one hand, and rubbing my temples with the other.

I took her at first for the daughter of the peasant (for it was no inn)——so had offer'd her a little purse with eighteen florins, which my poor brother *Tom* (here *Trim* wip'd his eyes) had sent me as a token, by a recruit, just before he set out for *Lisbon*——

——I never told your honour that piteous story yet——here *Trim* wiped his eyes a third time.

The young woman call'd the old man and his wife into the room, to shew them the money, in order to gain me credit for a bed and what little necessaries I should want, till I should be in a condition to be got to the hospital——Come then! said she, tying up the little purse——I'll be your banker——but as that office alone will not keep me employ'd, I'll be your nurse too.

I thought by her manner of speaking this, as well as by her dress, which I then began to consider more attentively——that the young woman could not be the daughter of the peasant.

She was in black down to her toes, with her hair conceal'd under a cambrick border, laid close to her forehead: she was one of those kind of nuns, an' please your honour, of which, your honour knows, there are a good many in *Flanders* which they let go loose——By thy description, *Trim,* said my uncle *Toby,* I dare say she was a young *Beguine,*[1] of which there are none to be found any where but in the *Spanish Netherlands* ——except at *Amsterdam*——they differ from nuns in this, that they can quit their cloister if they choose to marry; they visit and take care of the sick by profession——I had rather, for my own part, they did it out of good-nature.

——She often told me, quoth *Trim,* she did it for the love of Christ——I did not like it.——I believe, *Trim,* we are both wrong, said my uncle *Toby*——we'll ask Mr. *Yorick* about it to-night at my brother *Shandy's*——so put me in mind; added my uncle *Toby.*

The young *Beguine,* continued the corporal, had scarce given herself time to tell me "she would be my nurse," when she

---

[1]See p. 265, n. 30.

hastily turned about to begin the office of one, and prepare something for me——and in a short time——though I thought it a long one——she came back with flannels, &c. &c. and having fomented my knee soundly for a couple of hours, &c. and made me a thin basin of gruel for my supper——she wish'd me rest, and promised to be with me early in the morning.——She wish'd me, an' please your honour, what was not to be had. My fever ran very high that night——her figure made sad disturbance within me——I was every moment cutting the world in two——to give her half of it——and every moment was I crying, That I had nothing but a knapsack and eighteen florins to share with her——The whole night long was the fair *Beguine,* like an angel, close by my bedside, holding back my curtain and offering me cordials——and I was only awakened from my dream by her coming there at the hour promised, and giving them in reality. In truth, she was scarce ever from me, and so accustomed was I to receive life from her hands, that my heart sickened, and I lost colour when she left the room: and yet, continued the corporal (making one of the strangest reflections upon it in the world)——

——*"It was not love"*——for during the three weeks she was almost constantly with me, fomenting my knee with her hand, night and day——I can honestly say, an' please your honour ——that *   *   *   *   *   *   *   *   *   *
*   *   *   *   *   *   *   once.

That was very odd, *Trim,* quoth my uncle *Toby*——
I think so too——said Mrs. *Wadman.*
It never did, said the corporal.

CHAP. XXI.

——But 'tis no marvel, continued the corporal——seeing my uncle *Toby* musing upon it——for Love, an' please your honour, is exactly like war, in this; that a soldier, though he has escaped three weeks compleat o'*Saturday*-night,——may nevertheless be shot through his heart on *Sunday* morning——*It happened so here,* an' please your honour, with this difference only——that it was on *Sunday* in the afternoon, when I fell in love all at once with a sisserara[1]——it burst upon me, an' please your honour, like a bomb——scarce giving me time to say, "God bless me."

I thought, *Trim,* said my uncle *Toby,* a man never fell in love so very suddenly.

Yes, an' please your honour, if he is in the way of it—— replied *Trim.*

I prithee, quoth my uncle *Toby,* inform me how this matter happened.

——With all pleasure, said the corporal, making a bow.

CHAP. XXII.

I Had escaped, continued the corporal, all that time from falling in love, and had gone on to the end of the chapter, had it not been predestined otherwise——there is no resisting our fate.

It was on a *Sunday,* in the afternoon, as I told your honour——

The old man and his wife had walked out——

Every thing was still and hush as midnight about the house——

There was not so much as a duck or a duckling about the yard——

——When the fair *Beguine* came in to see me.

My wound was then in a fair way of doing well——the inflammation had been gone off for some time, but it was succeeded with an itching both above and below my knee, so insufferable, that I had not shut my eyes the whole night for it.

Let me see it, said she, kneeling down upon the ground parallel to my knee, and laying her hand upon the part below it——It only wants rubbing a little, said the *Beguine;* so cov-

---

[1] Siserary, any effective action. With a siserary: with suddenness or violence.

ering it with the bed cloaths, she began with the forefinger of her right-hand to rub under my knee, guiding her fore-finger backwards and forwards by the edge of the flannel which kept on the dressing.

In five or six minutes I felt slightly the end of her second finger——and presently it was laid flat with the other, and she continued rubbing in that way round and round for a good while; it then came into my head, that I should fall in love ——I blush'd when I saw how white a hand she had——I shall never, an' please your honour, behold another hand so white whilst I live——

——Not in that place: said my uncle *Toby*——

Though it was the most serious despair in nature to the corporal——he could not forbear smiling.

The young *Beguine,* continued the corporal, perceiving it was of great service to me——from rubbing, for some time, with two fingers——proceeded to rub at length, with three ——till by little and little she brought down the fourth, and then rubb'd with her whole hand: I will never say another word, an' please your honour, upon hands again——but it was softer than satin——

——Prithee, *Trim,* commend it as much as thou wilt, said my uncle *Toby;* I shall hear thy story with the more delight ——The corporal thank'd his master most unfeignedly; but having nothing to say upon the *Beguine's* hand, but the same over again——he proceeded to the effects of it.

The fair *Beguine,* said the corporal, continued rubbing with her whole hand under my knee——till I fear'd her zeal would weary her——"I would do a thousand times more," said she, "for the love of Christ"——In saying which she pass'd her hand across the flannel, to the part above my knee, which I had equally complained of, and rubb'd it also.

I perceived, then, I was beginning to be in love——

As she continued rub-rub-rubbing——I felt it spread from under her hand, an' please your honour, to every part of my frame——

The more she rubb'd, and the longer strokes she took——

the more the fire kindled in my veins——till at length, by two
or three strokes longer than the rest——my passion rose to the
highest pitch——I seiz'd her hand——

——And then, thou clapped'st it to thy lips, *Trim,* said my
uncle *Toby*——and madest a speech.

Whether the corporal's amour terminated precisely in the
way my uncle *Toby* described it, is not material; it is enough
that it contain'd in it the essence of all the love-romances
which ever have been wrote since the beginning of the world.

CHAP. XXIII.

A S soon as the corporal had finished the story of his amour
——or rather my uncle *Toby* for him——Mrs. *Wadman*
silently sallied forth from her arbour, replaced the pin in her
mob, pass'd the wicker gate, and advanced slowly towards my
uncle *Toby*'s sentry-box: the disposition which *Trim* had made
in my uncle *Toby*'s mind, was too favourable a crisis to be let
slipp'd——

——The attack was determin'd upon: it was facilitated still
more by my uncle *Toby*'s having ordered the corporal to wheel
off the pioneer's shovel, the spade, the pick-axe, the picquets,
and other military stores which lay scatter'd upon the ground
where *Dunkirk* stood——The corporal had march'd——the
field was clear.

Now consider, sir, what nonsense it is, either in fighting, or
writing, or any thing else (whether in rhyme to it, or not)
which a man has occasion to do——to act by plan: for if ever
Plan, independent of all circumstances, deserved registering
in letters of gold (I mean in the archives of *Gotham*[1])——it
was certainly the PLAN of Mrs *Wadman*'s attack of my uncle
Toby in his sentry-box, BY PLAN——Now the Plan hanging up
in it at this juncture, being the Plan of *Dunkirk*——and the
tale of *Dunkirk* a tale of relaxation, it opposed every impres-

---

[1]An allusion to the apparent simplicity, which served to conceal the
real shrewdness, of the "wise men" of Gotham.

sion she could make: and besides, could she have gone upon it——the manœuvre of fingers and hands in the attack of the sentry-box, was so outdone by that of the fair *Beguine*'s in *Trim*'s story——that just then, that particular attack, however successful before——became the most heartless attack that could be made——

O! let woman alone for this. Mrs. *Wadman* had scarce open'd the wicker-gate, when her genius sported with the change of circumstances.

——She formed a new attack in a moment.

CHAP. XXIV.

——I am half distracted, captain *Shandy,* said Mrs. *Wadman,* holding up her cambrick handkerchief to her left eye, as she approach'd the door of my uncle *Toby*'s sentry-box——a mote ——or sand——or something——I know not what, has got into this eye of mine——do look into it——it is not in the white——

In saying which, Mrs. *Wadman* edged herself close in beside my uncle *Toby,* and squeezing herself down upon the corner of his bench, she gave him an opportunity of doing it without rising up————Do look into it——said she.

Honest soul! thou didst look into it with as much innocency of heart, as ever child look'd into a raree-shew-box;[1] and 'twere as much a sin to have hurt thee.

——If a man will be peeping of his own accord into things of that nature——I've nothing to say to it——

My uncle *Toby* never did: and I will answer for him, that he would have sat quietly upon a sopha from *June* to *January,* (which, you know, takes in both the hot and cold months) with an eye as fine as the *Thracian* * *Rodope*'s besides him, without being able to tell, whether it was a black or a blue one.

---

[1] A portable box containing a peep-show.

*Rodope Thracia tam inevitabili fascino instructa, tam exacte oculis intuens attraxit, ut si in illam quis incidesset, fieri non posset, quin

The difficulty was to get my uncle *Toby,* to look at one, at all.

'Tis surmounted. And

I see him yonder with his pipe pendulous in his hand, and the ashes falling out of it——looking——and looking——then rubbing his eyes——and looking again, with twice the good nature that ever *Gallileo* look'd for a spot in the sun.[2]

——In vain! for by all the powers which animate the organ ——Widow *Wadman's* left eye shines this moment as lucid as her right——there is neither mote, or sand, or dust, or chaff, or speck, or particle of opake matter floating in it——There is nothing, my dear paternal uncle! but one lambent delicious fire, furtively shooting out from every part of it, in all directions, into thine——

——If thou lookest, uncle *Toby,* in search of this mote one moment longer——thou art undone.

CHAP. XXV.

AN eye is for all the world exactly like a cannon, in this respect; That it is not so much the eye or the cannon, in themselves, as it is the carriage of the eye——and the carriage of the cannon, by which both the one and the other are enabled to do so much execution.   I don't think the comparison a bad one: However, as 'tis made and placed at the head of the chapter, as much for use as ornament, all I desire in return, is, that whenever I speak of Mrs. *Wadman's* eyes (except once in the next period) that you keep it in your fancy.

---

caperetur.——I know not who. [Sterne's note. Rhodopis of Thrace was a celebrated Greek courtesan of the sixth century, B.C. The Latin, taken from Heliodorus's *An Æthiopian History,* 2.25, via *The Anatomy of Melancholy,* 3.2.2.3, may be translated: Rhodopis of Thrace was provided with such inevitable fascination, and attracted so perfectly with her eyes when looking at anyone, that if anyone fell in with her it was impossible but that he would be captivated.]

[2]Galileo (for whom, see p. 90, n. 7) discovered the spots on the sun in 1610; his important letters on the subject were published three years later.

I protest, Madam, said my uncle *Toby,* I can see nothing whatever in your eye.

It is not in the white; said Mrs. *Wadman:* my uncle *Toby* look'd with might and main into the pupil——

Now of all the eyes, which ever were created——from your own, Madam, up to those of *Venus* herself, which certainly were as venereal a pair of eyes as ever stood in a head—— there never was an eye of them all, so fitted to rob my uncle *Toby* of his repose, as the very eye, at which he was looking ——it was not, Madam, a rolling eye——a romping or a wanton one——nor was it an eye sparkling——petulant or imperious——of high claims and terrifying exactions, which would have curdled at once that milk of human nature, of which my uncle *Toby* was made up——but 'twas an eye full of gentle salutations——and soft responses——speaking——not like the trumpet stop of some ill-made organ, in which many an eye I talk to, holds coarse converse——but whispering soft ——like the last low accents of an expiring saint——"How can you live comfortless, captain *Shandy,* and alone, without a bosom to lean your head on——or trust your cares to?"

It was an eye——

But I shall be in love with it myself, if I say another word about it.

——It did my uncle *Toby'*s business.

CHAP. XXVI.

THERE is nothing shews the characters of my father and my uncle *Toby,* in a more entertaining light, than their different manner of deportment, under the same accident—— for I call not love a misfortune, from a persuasion, that a man's heart is ever the better for it——Great God! what must my uncle *Toby'*s have been, when 'twas all benignity without it.

My father, as appears from many of his papers, was very subject to this passion, before he married——but from a little subacid kind of drollish impatience in his nature, whenever it

befell him, he would never submit to it like a christian; but
would pish, and huff, and bounce, and kick, and play the
Devil, and write the bitterest Philippicks against the eye that
ever man wrote——there is one in verse upon some body's eye
or other, that for two or three nights together, had put him by
his rest; which in his first transport of resentment against it,
he begins thus:

> "A Devil 'tis——and mischief such doth work
> As never yet did *Pagan, Jew,* or *Turk.*"*

In short during the whole paroxism, my father was all abuse
and foul language, approaching rather towards malediction
——only he did not do it with as much method as *Ernulphus*[1]
——he was too impetuous; nor with *Ernulphus's* policy——for
tho' my father, with the most intolerant spirit, would curse
both this and that, and every thing under heaven, which was
either aiding or abetting to his love——yet never concluded
his chapter of curses upon it, without cursing himself in at the
bargain, as one of the most egregious fools and coxcombs, he
would say, that ever was let loose in the world.

My uncle *Toby,* on the contrary, took it like a lamb——sat
still and let the poison work in his veins without resistance
——in the sharpest exacerbations of his wound (like that on
his groin) he never dropt one fretful or discontented word
——he blamed neither heaven nor earth——or thought or
spoke an injurious thing of any body, or any part of it; he sat
solitary and pensive with his pipe——looking at his lame leg
——then whiffing out a sentimental heigh ho! which mixing
with the smoak, incommoded no one mortal.

He took it like a lamb——I say.

In truth he had mistook it at first; for having taken a ride
with my father, that very morning, to save if possible a beautiful wood, which the dean and chapter were hewing down to

---

*This will be printed with my father's life of *Socrates, &c. &c.*
[Sterne's note. The couplet is lifted from Burton (who credits it to
R[obert] T[ofte]), 3.2.4.1.]

[1]See p. 170.

give to the poor*; which said wood being in full view of my
uncle *Toby*'s house, and of singular service to him in his
description of the battle of *Wynnendale*——by trotting on too
hastily to save it——upon an uneasy saddle——worse horse,
&c. &c. . . it had so happened, that the serous part of the
blood had got betwixt the two skins, in the nethermost part
of my uncle *Toby*——the first shootings of which (as my uncle
Toby had no experience of love) he had taken for a part of the
passion——till the blister breaking in the one case——and the
other remaining——my uncle *Toby* was presently convinced,
that his wound was not a skin-deep-wound——but that it had
gone to his heart.

CHAP. XXVII.

THE world is ashamed of being virtuous——My uncle
Toby knew little of the world; and therefore when he felt
he was in love with widow *Wadman,* he had no conception
that the thing was any more to be made a mystery of, than if
Mrs. *Wadman,* had given him a cut with a gap'd¹ knife across
his finger: Had it been otherwise——yet as he ever look'd
upon *Trim* as a humble friend; and saw fresh reasons every
day of his life, to treat him as such——it would have made no
variation in the manner in which he informed him of the
affair.

"I am in love, corporal!" quoth my uncle *Toby*.

CHAP. XXVIII.

IN love!——said the corporal——your honour was very well
the day before yesterday, when I was telling your honour
the story of the King of *Bohemia*——*Bohemia!* said my uncle

---

*Mr. *Shandy* must mean the poor *in spirit;* inasmuch as they divided
the money amongst themselves.   [Sterne's note.]

¹Opened.

Toby - - - - musing a long time - - - What became of that story, *Trim?*

——We lost it, an' please your honour, somehow betwixt us ——but your honour was as free from love then, as I am—— 'twas, just whilst thou went'st off with the wheel-barrow—— with Mrs. *Wadman,* quoth my uncle *Toby*——She has left a ball here——added my uncle *Toby*——pointing to his breast——

——She can no more, an' please your honour, stand a siege, than she can fly——cried the corporal——

——But as we are neighbours, *Trim,*——the best way I think is to let her know it civilly first——quoth my uncle *Toby.*

Now if I might presume, said the corporal, to differ from your honour——

——Why else, do I talk to thee *Trim:* said my uncle *Toby,* mildly——

——Then I would begin, an' please your honour, with making a good thundering attack upon her, in return——and telling her civilly afterwards——for if she knows any thing of your honour's being in love, before hand——L—d help her! ——she knows no more at present of it, *Trim,* said my uncle *Toby*——than the child unborn——

Precious souls!——

Mrs. *Wadman* had told it with all its circumstances, to Mrs. *Bridget* twenty-four hours before; and was at that very moment sitting in council with her, touching some slight misgivings with regard to the issue of the affair, which the Devil, who never lies dead in a ditch, had put into her head—— before he would allow half time, to get quietly through her *te Deum*[1]——

I am terribly afraid, said widow *Wadman,* in case I should marry him, *Bridget*——that the poor captain will not enjoy his health, with the monstrous wound upon his groin——

It may not, Madam, be so very large, replied *Bridget,* as you

---

[1]See p. 48, n. 7.

think——and I believe besides, added she——that 'tis dried
up——

——I could like to know—merely for his sake, said Mrs.
Wadman——

——We'll know the long and the broad of it, in ten days——
answered Mrs. *Bridget,* for whilst the captain is paying his
addresses to you——I'm confident Mr. *Trim* will be for making love to me——and I'll let him as much as he will——added
Bridget——to get it all out of him——

The measures were taken at once——and my uncle *Toby*
and the corporal went on with theirs.

Now, quoth the corporal, setting his left hand a kimbo, and
giving such a flourish with his right, as just promised success
——and no more——if your honour will give me leave to lay
down the plan of this attack——

——Thou wilt please me by it, *Trim,* said my uncle *Toby,*
exceedingly——and as I foresee thou must act in it as my *aid
de camp,* here's a crown, corporal, to begin with, to steep[2] thy
commission.

Then, an' please your honour, said the corporal (making a
bow first for his commission)——we will begin with getting
your honour's laced cloaths out of the great campaign-trunk,
to be well-air'd, and have the blue and gold taken up at the
sleeves——and I'll put your white ramallie-wig[3] fresh into
pipes——and send for a taylor, to have your honour's thin
scarlet breeches turn'd——

——I had better take the red plush ones, quoth my uncle
Toby——They will be too clumsy——said the corporal.

CHAP. XXIX.

——Thou wilt get a brush and a little chalk[1] to my sword
——'Twill be only in your honour's way, replied *Trim.*

---

[2] Wet; *i.e.,* to initiate or celebrate by a drink.
[3] See p. 450, n. 3. The pipes were clay cylinders used in curling wigs.
[1] Powdered chalk, used as a metal polish.

CHAP. XXX.

——But your honour's two razors shall be new set[1]——and
I will get my Montero cap furbish'd up, and put on poor lieutenant *Le Fever's* regimental coat, which your honour gave me
to wear for his sake——and as soon as your honour is clean
shaved——and has got your clean shirt on, with your blue and
gold, or your fine scarlet——sometimes one and sometimes
t'other——and every thing is ready for the attack——we'll
march up boldly, as if 'twas to the face of a bastion; and whilst
your honour engages Mrs. *Wadman* in the parlour, to the right
——I'll attack Mrs. *Bridget* in the kitchen, to the left; and
having seiz'd that pass, I'll answer for it, said the corporal,
snapping his fingers over his head——that the day is our own.

I wish I may but manage it right; said my uncle *Toby*——
but I declare, corporal I had rather march up to the very edge
of a trench——

——A woman is quite a different thing——said the corporal.

——I suppose so, quoth my uncle *Toby*.

CHAP. XXXI.

IF any thing in this world, which my father said, could have
provoked my uncle *Toby,* during the time he was in love, it
was the perverse use my father was always making of an expression of *Hilarion* the hermit;[1] who, in speaking of his absti-
nence, his watchings, flagellations, and other instrumental
parts of his religion——would say——tho' with more faceti-

---

[1]Sharpened.

[1]Saint Hilarion (291–371), who introduced the monastic system into
Palestine.   The incident which follows is related in St. Jerome's *Vita S.
Hilarionis Eremitæ,* 3, and is mentioned in *The Anatomy of Melancholy,*
3.2.5.1.

ousness than became an hermit——"That they were the means
he used, to make his *ass* (meaning his body) leave off kicking."

It pleased my father well; it was not only a laconick way of
expressing——but of libelling, at the same time, the desires
and appetites of the lower part of us; so that for many years of
my father's life, 'twas his constant mode of expression——he
never used the word *passions* once——but *ass* always instead
of them——So ihat he might be said truly, to have been upon
the bones, or the back of his own ass, or else of some other
man's, during all that time.

I must here observe to you, the difference betwixt

     My father's ass

     and my hobby-horse——in order to keep characters as
separate as may be, in our fancies as we go along.

For my hobby-horse, if you recollect a little, is no way a
vicious beast; he has scarce one hair or lineament of the ass
about him——'Tis the sporting little filly-folly which carries
you out for the present hour——a maggot, a butterfly, a picture, a fiddle-stick——an uncle *Toby's* siege——or an *any
thing,* which a man makes a shift to get a stride on, to canter
it away from the cares and solicitudes of life——'Tis as useful
a beast as is in the whole creation——nor do I really see how
the world could do without it——

——But for my father's ass———oh! mount him——mount
him——mount him——(that's three times, is it not?)——
mount him not:——'tis a beast concupiscent——and foul befall the man, who does not hinder him from kicking.

CHAP. XXXII.

WELL! dear brother *Toby,* said my father, upon his first
seeing him after he fell in love——and how goes it with
your Asse?

Now my uncle *Toby* thinking more of the *part* where he had
had the blister, than of *Hilarion's* metaphor——and our pre-
conceptions having (you know) as great a power over the

sounds of words as the shapes of things, he had imagined, that
my father, who was not very ceremonious in his choice of
words, had enquired after the part by its proper name; so notwithstanding my mother, doctor *Slop,* and Mr. *Yorick,* were
sitting in the parlour, he thought it rather civil to conform to
the term my father had made use of than not.   When a man is
hemm'd in by two indecorums, and must commit one of 'em
——I always observe——let him choose which he will, the
world will blame him——so I should not be astonished if it
blames my uncle *Toby.*

My A—e, quoth my uncle *Toby,* is much better——
brother *Shandy*——My father had formed great expectations
from his Asse in this onset; and would have brought him on
again; but doctor *Slop* setting up an intemperate laugh——
and my mother crying out L— bless us!——it drove my
father's Asse off the field——and the laugh then becoming
general——there was no bringing him back to the charge, for
some time——

And so the discourse went on without him.

Every body, said my mother, says you are in love, brother
Toby——and we hope it is true.

I am as much in love, sister, I believe, replied my uncle
Toby, as any man usually is——Humph! said my father——
and when did you know it? quoth my mother——

——When the blister broke; replied my uncle *Toby.*

My uncle *Toby*'s reply put my father into good temper——
so he charged o'foot.

CHAP. XXXIII.

AS the antients agree, brother *Toby,* said my father, that
there are two different and distinct kinds of *love,* according to the different parts which are affected by it——the Brain
or Liver——I think when a man is in love, it behoves him a
little to consider which of the two he is fallen into.

What signifies it, brother *Shandy,* replied my uncle *Toby,* which of the two it is, provided it will but make a man marry, and love his wife, and get a few children.

——A few children! cried my father, rising out of his chair, and looking full in my mother's face, as he forced his way betwixt her's and doctor *Slop's*——a few children! cried my father, repeating my uncle *Toby's* words as he walk'd to and fro'——

——Not, my dear brother *Toby*, cried my father, recovering himself all at once, and coming close up to the back of my uncle *Toby's* chair——not that I should be sorry had'st thou a score——on the contrary I should rejoice——and be as kind, *Toby*, to every one of them as a father——

My uncle *Toby* stole his hand unperceived behind his chair, to give my father's a squeeze——

——Nay, moreover, continued he, keeping hold of my uncle *Toby's* hand——so much do'st thou possess, my dear *Toby*, of the milk of human nature, and so little of its asperities——'tis piteous the world is not peopled by creatures which resemble thee; and was I an *Asiatick* monarch, added my father, heating himself with his new project——I would oblige thee, provided it would not impair thy strength——or dry up thy radical moisture too fast——or weaken thy memory or fancy, brother *Toby*, which these gymnicks inordinately taken, are apt to do——else, dear *Toby*, I would procure thee the most beautiful women in my empire, and I would oblige thee, *nolens, volens*,[1] to beget for me one subject every *month*——

As my father pronounced the last word of the sentence—— my mother took a pinch of snuff.

Now I would not, quoth my uncle *Toby*, get a child, *nolens, volens*, that is, whether I would or no, to please the greatest prince upon earth——

——And 'twould be cruel in me, brother *Toby*, to compell thee; said my father——but 'tis a case put to shew thee, that it is not thy begetting a child——in case thou should'st be able ——but the system of Love and marriage thou goest upon, which I would set thee right in——

---

[1] Unwilling or willing.

There is at least, said *Yorick,* a great deal of reason and plain sense in captain *Shandy's* opinion of love; and 'tis amongst the ill spent hours of my life which I have to answer for, that I have read so many flourishing poets and rhetoricians in my time, from whom I never could extract so much——

I wish, *Yorick,* said my father, you had read *Plato;*[2] for there you would have learnt that there are two LOVES——I know there were two RELIGIONS, replied *Yorick,* amongst the ancients ——one——for the vulgar, and another for the learned; but I think ONE LOVE might have served both of them very well——

It could not; replied my father——and for the same reasons: for of these Loves, according to *Ficinus's*[3] comment upon *Valesius,* the one is *rational*——

——the other is *natural*——

the first ancient——without mother——where *Venus* had nothing to do: the second, begotten of *Jupiter* and *Dione*——

——Pray brother, quoth my uncle *Toby,* what has a man who believes in God to do with this? My father could not stop to answer, for fear of breaking the thread of his discourse——

This latter, continued he, partakes wholly of the nature of *Venus.*

The first, which is the golden chain let down from heaven, excites to love heroic, which comprehends in it, and excites to the desire of philosophy and truth——the second, excites to *desire,* simply——

---

[2]In the *Symposium,* 180, Plato makes Pausanias say: "And am I not right in asserting that there are two goddesses [of love]? The elder one, having no mother, who is called the heavenly Aphrodite—she is the daughter of Uranus; the younger, who is the daughter of Zeus and Dione —her we call common; and the Love who is her fellow-worker is rightly named common, as the other love is called heavenly." Sterne's immediate source for the following passage, however, is *The Anatomy of Melancholy,* 3.1.1.2.

[3]See p. 466, n. 2. Francisco Valles de Covarrubias (fl. 16th C.) was a Spanish medical writer, physician to Philip II. This passage is a confused paraphrase of the *Anatomy of Melancholy,* 3.1.1.2, wherein Burton cites Valesius's and Ficinus's commentaries on Plato; the reference to Valesius is to his *Controversiarum Medicarum et Philosophicarum,* and that to Ficinus is to his *Commentaria* on the *Convivio,* 6.7, 8.

——I think the procreation of children as beneficial to the world, said *Yorick,* as the finding out the longitude[4]——

——To be sure, said my mother, *love* keeps peace in the world——

——In the *house*——my dear, I own——

——It replenishes the earth; said my mother——

But it keeps heaven empty——my dear; replied my father.

——'Tis Virginity, cried *Slop,* triumphantly, which fills paradise.

Well push'd nun! quoth my father.

CHAP. XXXIV.

M Y father had such a skirmishing, cutting kind of a slash-ing way with him in his disputations, thrusting and rip-ping, and giving every one a stroke to remember him by in his turn——that if there were twenty people in company—— in less than half an hour he was sure to have every one of 'em against him.

What did not a little contribute to leave him thus without an ally, was, that if there was any one post more untenable than the rest, he would be sure to throw himself into it; and to do him justice, when he was once there, he would defend it so gallantly, that 'twould have been a concern, either to a brave man, or a good-natured one, to have seen him driven out.

Yorick, for this reason, though he would often attack him ——yet could never bear to do it with all his force.

Doctor *Slop's* Virginity, in the close of the last chapter, had got him for once on the right side of the rampart; and he was

---

[4]As early as 1713 an act of Parliament had offered rewards up to £20,000 for methods of determining the longitude at sea; at the time Sterne was writing this volume considerable sums were being paid to John Harrison of Foulby (1693–1776) for his chronometer, for which he eventually received the full reward. Burton's translation of Ficinus (*idem,* 6.8) reads, ". . . procreation of children is as necessary as . . . finding out of truth . . ." (*Anatomy,* 3.1.1.2).

beginning to blow up all the convents in *Christendom* about *Slop*'s ears, when corporal *Trim* came into the parlour to inform my uncle *Toby,* that his thin scarlet breeches, in which the attack was to be made upon Mrs. *Wadman,* would not do; for, that the taylor, in ripping them up, in order to turn them, had found they had been turn'd before——Then turn them again, brother, said my father rapidly, for there will be many a turning of 'em yet before all's done in the affair——They are as rotten as dirt, said the corporal——Then by all means, said my father, bespeak a new pair, brother——for though I know, continued my father, turning himself to the company, that widow *Wadman* has been deeply in love with my brother *Toby* for many years, and has used every art and circumvention of woman to outwit him into the same passion, yet now that she has caught him——her fever will be pass'd it's height——

——She has gain'd her point.

In this case, continued my father, which *Plato,* I am persuaded, never thought of——Love, you see, is not so much a SENTIMENT as a SITUATION, into which a man enters, as my brother *Toby* would do, into a *corps*——no matter whether he loves the service or no——being once in it——he acts as if he did; and takes every step to shew himself a man of prowesse.

The hypothesis, like the rest of my father's, was plausible enough, and my uncle *Toby* had but a single word to object to it——in which *Trim* stood ready to second him——but my father had not drawn his conclusion——

For this reason, continued my father (stating the case over again) notwithstanding all the world knows, that Mrs. *Wadman affects* my brother *Toby*——and my brother *Toby* contrariwise *affects* Mrs. *Wadman,* and no obstacle in nature to forbid the music striking up this very night, yet will I answer for it, that this self-same tune will not be play'd this twelvemonth.

We have taken our measures badly, quoth my uncle *Toby,* looking up interrogatively in *Trim*'s face.

I would lay my Montero cap, said *Trim*——Now *Trim's*
Montero-cap, as I once told you, was his constant wager; and
having furbish'd it up that very night, in order to go upon the
attack——it made the odds look more considerable——I
would lay, an' please your honour, my Montero-cap to a shilling——was it proper, continued *Trim* (making a bow) to offer
a wager before your honours——

——There is nothing improper in it, said my father——'tis
a mode of expression; for in saying thou would'st lay thy Montero-cap to a shilling——all thou meanest is this——that thou
believest——

——Now, What do'st thou believe?

That widow *Wadman,* an' please your worship, cannot hold
it out ten days——

And whence, cried *Slop,* jeeringly, hast thou all this knowledge of woman, friend?

By falling in love with a popish clergy-woman; said *Trim.*

'Twas a *Beguine,* said my uncle *Toby.*

Doctor *Slop* was too much in wrath to listen to the distinction; and my father taking that very crisis to fall in helter-
skelter upon the whole order of Nuns and *Beguines,* a set of
silly, fusty baggages——*Slop* could not stand it——and my
uncle *Toby* having some measures to take about his breeches
——and *Yorick* about his fourth general division[1]——in order
for their several attacks next day——the company broke up:
and my father being left alone, and having half an hour upon
his hands betwixt that and bed-time; he called for pen, ink,
and paper, and wrote my uncle *Toby* the following letter of
instructions.

My dear brother *Toby,*

WHAT I am going to say to thee, is upon the nature of
women, and of love-making to them; and perhaps it is
as well for thee——tho' not so well for me——that thou hast

[1] Of his sermon.

occasion for a letter of instructions upon that head, and that I am able to write it to thee.

Had it been the good pleasure of him who disposes of our lots——and thou no sufferer by the knowledge, I had been well content that thou should'st have dipp'd the pen this moment into the ink, instead of myself; but that not being the case————Mrs. *Shandy* being now close besides me, preparing for bed——I have thrown together without order, and just as they have come into my mind, such hints and documents as I deem may be of use to thee; intending, in this, to give thee a token of my love; not doubting, my dear *Toby,* of the manner in which it will be accepted.

In the first place, with regard to all which concerns religion in the affair——though I perceive from a glow in my cheek, that I blush as I begin to speak to thee upon the subject, as well knowing, notwithstanding thy unaffected secrecy, how few of its offices thou neglectest——yet I would remind thee of one (during the continuance of thy courtship) in a particular manner, which I would not have omitted; and that is, never to go forth upon the enterprize, whether it be in the morning or the afternoon, without first recommending thyself to the protection of Almighty God, that he may defend thee from the evil one.

Shave the whole top of thy crown clean, once at least every four or five days, but oftner if convenient; lest in taking off thy wig before her, thro' absence of mind, she should be able to discover how much has been cut away by Time——how much by *Trim.*

——'Twere better to keep ideas of baldness out of her fancy.

Always carry it in thy mind, and act upon it, as a sure maxim, *Toby*——

"*That women are timid:*" And 'tis well they are——else there would be no dealing with them.

Let not thy breeches be too tight, or hang too loose about thy thighs, like the trunk-hose of our ancestors.

——A just medium prevents all conclusions.

Whatever thou hast to say, be it more or less, forget not to utter it in a low soft tone of voice. Silence, and whatever approaches it, weaves dreams of midnight secrecy into the brain: For this cause, if thou canst help it, never throw down the tongs and poker.

Avoid all kinds of pleasantry and facetiousness in thy discourse with her, and do whatever lies in thy power at the same time, to keep from her all books and writings which tend thereto: there are, some devotional tracts, which if thou canst entice her to read over——it will be well: but suffer her not to look into *Rabelais,* or *Scarron,*[2] or *Don Quixote*——

——They are all books which excite laughter; and thou knowest, dear *Toby,* that there is no passion so serious, as lust.

Stick a pin in the bosom of thy shirt, before thou enterest her parlour.

And if thou art permitted to sit upon the same sopha with her, and she gives thee occasion to lay thy hand upon hers ——beware of taking it——thou can'st not lay thy hand on hers, but she will feel the temper of thine. Leave that and as many other things as thou canst, quite undetermined; by so doing, thou wilt have her curiosity on thy side; and if she is not conquer'd by that, and thy ASSE continues still kicking, which there is great reason to suppose——Thou must begin, with first losing a few ounces of blood below the ears, according to the practice of the ancient *Scythians,* who cured the most intemperate fits of the appetite by that means.

Avicenna,[3] after this, is for having the part anointed with the syrrup of hellebore, using proper evacuations and purges ——and I believe rightly. But thou must eat little or no goat's flesh, nor red deer——nor even foal's flesh by any means; and carefully abstain——that is, as much as thou canst, from peacocks, cranes, coots, didappers, and water-hens——

As for thy drink——I need not tell thee, it must be the in-

---

[2]Paul Scarron (1610–1660) was a French burlesque poet, dramatist, and novelist, whose chief work, the *Roman comique,* had considerable influence upon Sterne.

[3]See p. 282, n. 2. The source of this and the preceding and following paragraphs is *The Anatomy of Melancholy,* 3.2.5.1.

fusion of VERVAIN,[4] and the herb HANEA, of which *Ælian*[5] relates such effects——but if thy stomach palls with it——discontinue it from time to time, taking cucumbers, melons, purslane, water-lillies, woodbine, and lettice, in the stead of them.

There is nothing further for thee, which occurs to me at present——

——Unless the breaking out of a fresh war——So wishing every thing, dear *Toby,* for the best,

I rest thy affectionate brother,

WALTER SHANDY.

CHAP. XXXV.

WHILST my father was writing his letter of instructions, my uncle *Toby* and the corporal were busy in preparing every thing for the attack. As the turning of the thin scarlet breeches was laid aside (at least for the present) there was nothing which should put it off beyond the next morning; so accordingly it was resolv'd upon, for eleven o'clock.

Come, my dear, said my father to my mother——'twill be but like a brother and sister, if you and I take a walk down to my brother *Toby*'s——to countenance him in this attack of his.

My uncle *Toby* and the corporal had been accoutred both some time, when my father and mother enter'd, and the clock striking eleven, were that moment in motion to sally forth—— but the account of this is worth more, than to be wove into the fag end of the eighth volume of such a work as this.——My father had no time but to put the letter of instructions into my uncle *Toby*'s coat-pocket——and join with my mother in wishing his attack prosperous.

---

[4] A plant of the genus *Verbena* having a bitter and astringent taste, formerly used as a cooling remedy. For hanea, see p. 468, n. 7.

[5] Claudius Ælianus (fl. c.200) was a Roman author and teacher of rhetoric; the reference is to his *De Natura Animalium,* 9.26, *via* Burton, *ibid.*

I could like, said my mother, to look through the key-hole out of *curiosity*——Call it by it's right name, my dear, quoth my father——

And look through the key-hole as long as you will.

END of the EIGHTH VOLUME.

THE
LIFE
AND
OPINIONS
OF
TRISTRAM SHANDY,
GENTLEMAN.

*Si quid urbaniuſculè luſum a nobis, per Muſas et Cha-
ritas et omnium poetarum Numina, Oro te, ne me
malè capias.*

VOL. IX.

LONDON:
Printed for T. BECKET and P. A. DEHONDT,
in the Strand.   MDCCLXVII.

Facsimile of the title page to the first edition of Volume IX.   The
motto, a plea of Julius Caesar Scaliger to Cardan as quoted by Burton in
The Anatomy of Melancholy, 3.1.1.1., may be translated: "If we have
sported with anything too facetiously, by the Muses and the Graces and
the divine will of all the poets, I pray you, do not take me badly."

VOLUME IX.

A

DEDICATION

TO A

GREAT MAN.[1]

HAVING, *a priori,* intended to dedicate *The Amours of my uncle Toby* to Mr. ***——I see more reasons, *a posteriori,*[2] for doing it to Lord *******.

I should lament from my soul, if this exposed me to the jealousy of their Reverences; because, *a posteriori,* in Court-latin, signifies, the kissing hands for preferment——or any thing else——in order to get it.

My opinion of Lord ******* is neither better nor worse, than it was of Mr. ***. Honours, like impressions upon coin, may give an ideal and local value to a bit of base metal; but Gold and Silver will pass all the world over without any other recommendation than their own weight.

The same good will that made me think of offering up half an hour's amusement to Mr. *** when out of place—operates more forcibly at present, as half an hour's amusement will be more serviceable and refreshing after labour and sorrow, than after a philosophical repast.

Nothing is so perfectly *Amusement* as a total change of ideas; no ideas are so totally different as those of Ministers,

---

[1]In this dedication to Pitt, to whom the opening volumes of *Shandy* had been dedicated seven years before, Sterne gracefully alludes to the Great Commoner's absence from office between 1761 and 1766, and to his becoming in 1766 premier, Viscount Pitt, and Earl of Chatham.

[2]See p. 141, n. 17. In the following paragraph Sterne plays upon other meanings of *posterior:* subsequent in place, lower in position, posteriors.

and innocent Lovers: for which reason, when I come to talk of
Statesmen and Patriots, and set such marks upon them as will
prevent confusion and mistakes concerning them for the future
——I propose to dedicate that Volume to some gentle Shepherd,

> Whose Thoughts proud Science never taught to stray,
> Far as the Statesman's walk or Patriot-way;
> Yet *simple Nature* to his hopes had given
> Out of a cloud-capp'd head a humbler heaven;
> Some *untam'd* World in depth of woods embraced——
> Some happier Island in the watry-waste——
> And where admitted to that equal sky,
> His *faithful Dogs* should bear him company.

In a word, by thus introducing an entire new set of objects
to his Imagination, I shall unavoidably give a *Diversion* to his
passionate and love-sick Contemplations. In the mean time,

I am

The AUTHOR.

CHAP. I.

I CALL all the powers of time and chance, which severally check us in our careers in this world, to bear me witness, that I could never yet get fairly to my uncle *Toby*'s amours, till this very moment, that my mother's *curiosity,* as she stated the affair,——or a different impulse in her, as my father would have it——wished her to take a peep at them through the key-hole.

"Call it, my dear, by its right name, quoth my father, and look through the key-hole as long as you will."

Nothing but the fermentation of that little subacid humour, which I have often spoken of, in my father's habit, could have vented such an insinuation——he was however frank and generous in his nature, and at all times open to conviction; so that he had scarce got to the last word of this ungracious retort, when his conscience smote him.

My mother was then conjugally swinging with her left arm twisted under his right, in such wise, that the inside of her hand rested upon the back of his——she raised her fingers, and let them fall——it could scarce be call'd a tap; or if it was a tap——'twould have puzzled a casuist to say, whether 'twas a tap of remonstrance, or a tap of confession: my father, who was all sensibilities from head to foot, class'd it right——Conscience redoubled her blow——he turn'd his face suddenly the other way, and my mother supposing his body was about to turn with it in order to move homewards, by a cross movement of her right leg, keeping her left as its centre, brought herself so far in front, that as he turned his head, he met her eye———Confusion again! he saw a thousand reasons to wipe out the reproach, and as many to reproach himself——a thin, blue, chill, pellucid chrystal with all its humours so at rest, the least mote or speck of desire might have been seen at the bottom of it, had it existed——it did not——and how I happen to be so lewd myself, particularly a little before the vernal and autumnal equinoxes——Heaven above knows——My mother——madam——was so at no time, either by nature, by institution, or example.

A temperate current of blood ran orderly through her veins in all months of the year, and in all critical moments both of the day and night alike; nor did she superinduce the least heat into her humours from the manual effervescencies of devotional tracts, which having little or no meaning in them, nature is oft times obliged to find one——And as for my father's example! 'twas so far from being either aiding or abetting thereunto, that 'twas the whole business of his life to keep all fancies of that kind out of her head——Nature had done her part, to have spared him this trouble; and what was not a little inconsistent, my father knew it——And here am I sitting, this 12th day of *August,* 1766, in a purple jerkin and yellow pair of slippers, without either wig or cap on, a most tragicomical completion of his prediction, "That I should neither think, nor act like any other man's child, upon that very account."

The mistake of my father, was in attacking my mother's motive, instead of the act itself: for certainly key-holes were made for other purposes; and considering the act, as an act which interfered with a true proposition, and denied a key-hole to be what it was——it became a violation of nature; and was so far, you see, criminal.

It is for this reason, an' please your Reverences, That key-holes are the occasions of more sin and wickedness, than all other holes in this world put together.

——which leads me to my uncle *Toby's* amours.

CHAP. II.

THOUGH the Corporal had been as good as his word in
putting my uncle *Toby*'s great ramallie-wig into pipes, yet
the time was too short to produce any great effects from it:
it had lain many years squeezed up in the corner of his old
campaign trunk; and as bad forms are not so easy to be got
the better of, and the use of candle-ends not so well understood, it was not so pliable a business as one would have
wished. The Corporal with cheary eye and both arms extended, had fallen back perpendicular from it a score times,
to inspire it, if possible, with a better air——had SPLEEN given
a look at it, 'twould have cost her ladyship a smile——it
curl'd every where but where the Corporal would have it; and
where a buckle or two, in his opinion, would have done it
honour, he could as soon have raised the dead.

Such it was——or rather such would it have seem'd upon
any other brow; but the sweet look of goodness which sat
upon my uncle *Toby*'s, assimilated every thing around it so
sovereignly to itself, and Nature had moreover wrote GENTLE-
MAN with so fair a hand in every line of his countenance, that
even his tarnish'd gold-laced hat and huge cockade of flimsy
taffeta became him; and though not worth a button in themselves, yet the moment my uncle *Toby* put them on, they became serious objects, and altogether seem'd to have been
picked up by the hand of Science to set him off to advantage.

Nothing in this world could have co-operated more powerfully towards this, than my uncle *Toby*'s blue and gold——
had not Quantity in some measure been necessary to Grace: in
a period of fifteen or sixteen years since they had been made,
by a total inactivity in my uncle *Toby*'s life, for he seldom
went further than the bowling-green——his blue and gold had
become so miserably too strait for him, that it was with the
utmost difficulty the Corporal was able to get him into them:
the taking them up at the sleeves, was of no advantage.——

They were laced however down the back, and at the seams of the sides, &c. in the mode of King *William's* reign; and to shorten all description, they shone so bright against the sun that morning, and had so metallick, and doughty an air with them, that had my uncle *Toby* thought of attacking in armour, nothing could have so well imposed upon his imagination.

As for the thin scarlet breeches, they had been unripp'd by the taylor between the legs, and left at *sixes and sevens*——

——Yes, Madam,——but let us govern our fancies. It is enough they were held impracticable the night before, and as there was no alternative in my uncle *Toby's* wardrobe, he sallied forth in the red plush.

The Corporal had array'd himself in poor *Le Fevre's* regimental coat; and with his hair tuck'd up under his Montero cap, which he had furbish'd up for the occasion, march'd three paces distant from his master: a whiff of military pride had puff'd out his shirt at the wrist; and upon that in a black leather thong clipp'd into a tassel beyond the knot, hung the Corporal's stick——My uncle *Toby* carried his cane like a pike.

——It looks well at least; quoth my father to himself.

CHAP. III.

MY uncle *Toby* turn'd his head more than once behind him, to see how he was supported by the Corporal; and the Corporal as oft as he did it, gave a slight flourish with his stick——but not vapouringly; and with the sweetest accent of most respectful encouragement, bid his honour "never fear."

Now my uncle *Toby* did fear; and grievously too: he knew not (as my father had reproach'd him) so much as the right end of a Woman from the wrong, and therefore was never altogether at his ease near any one of them——unless in sor-

row or distress; then infinite was his pity; nor would the most
courteous knight of romance have gone further, at least upon
one leg, to have wiped away a tear from a woman's eye; and
yet excepting once that he was beguiled into it by Mrs. *Wadman*, he had never looked stedfastly into one; and would often
tell my father in the simplicity of his heart, that it was almost
(if not alout[1]) as bad as talking bawdy.———

———And suppose it is? my father would say.

CHAP. IV.

S HE cannot, quoth my uncle *Toby,* halting, when they had
march'd up to within twenty paces of Mrs. *Wadman*'s door
———she cannot, Corporal, take it amiss.———

———She will take it, an' please your honour, said the Corporal, just as the *Jew*'s widow at *Lisbon* took it of my brother
Tom.———

———And how was that? quoth my uncle *Toby,* facing quite
about to the Corporal.

Your honour, replied the Corporal, knows of *Tom*'s misfortunes; but this affair has nothing to do with them any further
than this, That if *Tom* had not married the widow———or had
it pleased God after their marriage, that they had but put pork
into their sausages, the honest soul had never been taken out
of his warm bed, and dragg'd to the inquisition———'Tis a
cursed place———added the Corporal, shaking his head,———
when once a poor creature is in, he is in, an' please your honour, for ever.

'Tis very true; said my uncle *Toby* looking gravely at Mrs.
Wadman's house, as he spoke.

Nothing, continued the Corporal, can be so sad as confinement for life———or so sweet, an' please your honour, as liberty.

Nothing, *Trim*———said my uncle *Toby,* musing———

----
[1]All out; fully.

Whilst a man is free——cried the Corporal, giving a flourish
with his stick thus——

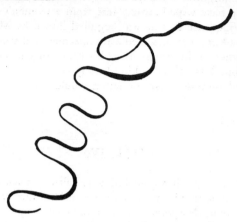

A thousand of my father's most subtle syllogisms could not
have said more for celibacy.

My uncle *Toby* look'd earnestly towards his cottage and his
bowling green.

The Corporal had unwarily conjured up the Spirit of calculation with his wand; and he had nothing to do, but to con-
jure him down again with his story, and in this form of Exor-
cism, most un-ecclesiastically did the Corporal do it.

CHAP. V.

AS *Tom*'s place, an' please your honour, was easy——and the
weather warm——it put him upon thinking seriously of
settling himself in the world; and as it fell out about that time,
that a *Jew* who kept a sausage shop in the same street, had
the ill luck to die of a strangury, and leave his widow in possession of a rousing trade——*Tom* thought (as every body in
Lisbon was doing the best he could devise for himself) there

could be no harm in offering her his service to carry it on: so
without any introduction to the widow, except that of buying
a pound of sausages at her shop——*Tom* set out——counting
the matter thus within himself, as he walk'd along; that let the
worst come of it that could, he should at least get a pound of
sausages for their worth——but, if things went well, he should
be set up; inasmuch as he should get not only a pound of sausages——but a wife——and a sausage-shop, an' please your
honour, into the bargain.

Every servant in the family, from high to low, wish'd *Tom*
success; and I can fancy, an' please your honour, I see him this
moment with his white dimity waistcoat and breeches, and
hat a little o' one side, passing jollily along the street, swinging
his stick, with a smile and a chearful word for every body he
met:——But alas! *Tom!* thou smilest no more, cried the Corporal, looking on one side of him upon the ground, as if he
apostrophized him in his dungeon.

Poor fellow! said my uncle *Toby,* feelingly.

He was an honest, light-hearted lad, an' please your honour,
as ever blood warm'd——

——Then he resembled thee, *Trim,* said my uncle *Toby,*
rapidly.

The Corporal blush'd down to his fingers ends——a tear of
sentimental bashfulness——another of gratitude to my uncle
Toby——and a tear of sorrow for his brother's misfortunes,
started into his eye and ran sweetly down his cheek together;
my uncle *Toby*'s kindled as one lamp does at another; and
taking hold of the breast of *Trim*'s coat (which had been that
of *Le Fevre*'s) as if to ease his lame leg, but in reality to gratify
a finer feeling——he stood silent for a minute and a half; at
the end of which he took his hand away, and the Corporal
making a bow, went on with his story of his brother and the
Jew's widow.

CHAP. VI.

WHEN *Tom,* an' please your honour, got to the shop, there was nobody in it, but a poor negro girl, with a bunch of white feathers slightly tied to the end of a long cane, flapping away flies——not killing them.——'Tis a pretty picture! said my uncle *Toby*——she had suffered persecution, *Trim,* and had learnt mercy——

——She was good, an' please your honour, from nature as well as from hardships; and there are circumstances in the story of that poor friendless slut that would melt a heart of stone, said *Trim;* and some dismal winter's evening, when your honour is in the humour, they shall be told you with the rest of *Tom's* story, for it makes a part of it——

Then do not forget, *Trim,* said my uncle *Toby.*

A Negro has a soul? an' please your honour, said the Corporal (doubtingly).

I am not much versed, Corporal, quoth my uncle *Toby,* in things of that kind; but I suppose, God would not leave him without one, any more than thee or me——

——It would be putting one sadly over the head of another, quoth the Corporal.

It would so; said my uncle *Toby.* Why then, an' please your honour, is a black wench to be used worse than a white one?

I can give no reason, said my uncle *Toby*——

——Only, cried the Corporal, shaking his head, because she has no one to stand up for her——

——'Tis that very thing, *Trim,* quoth my uncle *Toby,*—— which recommends her to protection——and her brethren with her; 'tis the fortune of war which has put the whip into our hands *now*——where it may be hereafter, heaven knows! ——but be it where it will, the brave, *Trim!* will not use it unkindly.

——God forbid, said the Corporal.

Amen, responded my uncle *Toby,* laying his hand upon his heart.[1]

The Corporal returned to his story, and went on——but with an embarrassment in doing it, which here and there a reader in this world will not be able to comprehend; for by the many sudden transitions all along, from one kind and cordial passion to another, in getting thus far on his way, he had lost the sportable key of his voice which gave sense and spirit to his tale: he attempted twice to resume it, but could not please himself; so giving a stout hem! to rally back the re-treating spirits, and aiding Nature at the same time with his left arm a-kimbo on one side, and with his right a little ex-tended, supporting her on the other——the Corporal got as near the note as he could; and in that attitude, continued his story.

[1]On July 21, 1766, Ignatius Sancho, a negro who had been born a slave and who was then butler to the fourth Earl of Cardigan, wrote Sterne an effusive letter praising his philanthropy and "zealously intreat-ing" him to "give half an hours attention to slavery . . . that subject handled in your own manner, would ease the Yoke of many, perhaps occasion a reformation throughout our Islands . . ." Six days later Sterne replied, in part, as follows:

"There is a strange coincidence, Sancho, in the little events, as well as the great ones of this world; for I had been writing a tender tale of the sorrows of a friendless poor negro girl, and my eyes had scarse done smarting, When your Letter of recommendation in behalf of so many of her brethren and Sisters came to me—but why, *her brethren?*—or yours? Sancho,—any more than mine: it is by the finest tints and most insensible gradations that nature descends from the fairest face about St. James's, to the sootyest complexion in Africa: at which tint of these, is it, Sancho, that the ties of blood & nature cease? and how many tones must we descend lower still in the scale, 'ere Mercy is to vanish with them? but tis no uncommon thing my good Sancho, for one half of the world to use the other half of it like brutes, and then en-deavour to make 'em so.

"For my own part, I never look westward, (when I am in a pensive mood at least) but I think of the burdens which our brethren are there carrying; and could I take one ounce from the Shoulders of a few of 'em who are the heaviest loaden'd, I would go a Pilgrimage to Mecca for their Sakes . . .

"If I can weave the Tale I have wrote, into what I am about, tis at the service of the afflicted; and a much greater matter: for in honest truth, it casts, a great Shade upon the world, that so great a part of it, are, and have been so long bound down in chains of darkness & in chains of misery . . ."

CHAP. VII.

AS *Tom,* an' please your honour, had no business at that time with the *Moorish* girl, he passed on into the room beyond to talk to the *Jew*'s widow about love——and his pound of sausages; and being, as I have told your honour, an open, cheary hearted lad, with his character wrote in his looks and carriage, he took a chair, and without much apology, but with great civility at the same time, placed it close to her at the table, and sat down.

There is nothing so awkward, as courting a woman, an' please your honour, whilst she is making sausages——So *Tom* began a discourse upon them; first gravely,——"as how they were made——with what meats, herbs and spices"——Then a little gayly——as, "With what skins——and if they never burst——Whether the largest were not the best"——and so on ——taking care only as he went along, to season what he had to say upon sausages, rather under, than over;——that he might have room to act in——

It was owing to the neglect of that very precaution, said my uncle *Toby,* laying his hand upon *Trim*'s shoulder, That Count *de la Motte* lost the battle of *Wynendale:* he pressed too speedily into the wood; which if he had not done, *Lisle* had not fallen into our hands, nor *Ghent* and *Bruges,* which both followed her example; it was so late in the year, continued my uncle *Toby,* and so terrible a season came on, that if things had not fallen out as they did, our troops must have perished in the open field.——

——Why therefore, may not battles, an' please your honour, as well as marriages, be made in heaven?——My uncle *Toby* mused.——

Religion inclined him to say one thing, and his high idea of military skill tempted him to say another; so not being able to frame a reply exactly to his mind——my uncle *Toby* said nothing at all; and the Corporal finished his story.

As *Tom* perceived, an' please your honour, that he gained ground, and that all he had said upon the subject of sausages was kindly taken, he went on to help her a little in making them.——First, by taking hold of the ring of the sausage whilst she stroked the forced meat down with her hand—— then by cutting the strings into proper lengths, and holding them in his hand, whilst she took them out one by one—— then, by putting them across her mouth, that she might take them out as she wanted them——and so on from little to more, till at last he adventured to tie the sausage himself, whilst she held the snout.——

——Now a widow, an' please your honour, always chuses a second husband as unlike the first as she can: so the affair was more than half settled in her mind before *Tom* mentioned it.

She made a feint however of defending herself, by snatching up a sausage:——*Tom* instantly laid hold of another——

But seeing *Tom*'s had more gristle in it——

She signed the capitulation——and *Tom* sealed it; and there was an end of the matter.

CHAP. VIII.

ALL womankind, continued *Trim,* (commenting upon his story) from the highest to the lowest, an' please your honour, love jokes; the difficulty is to know how they chuse to have them cut; and there is no knowing that, but by trying as we do with our artillery in the field, by raising or letting down their breeches, till we hit the mark.——

——I like the comparison, said my uncle *Toby,* better than the thing itself——

——Because your honour, quoth the Corporal, loves glory, more than pleasure.

I hope, *Trim,* answered my uncle *Toby,* I love mankind more than either; and as the knowledge of arms tends so apparently to the good and quiet of the world——and particularly that branch of it which we have practised together in our bowling-green, has no object but to shorten the strides of AMBITION, and intrench the lives and fortunes of the *few,* from the plunderings of the *many*——whenever that drum beats in our ears, I trust, Corporal, we shall neither of us want so much humanity and fellow-feeling as to face about and march.

In pronouncing this, my uncle *Toby* faced about, and march'd firmly as at the head of his company——and the faithful Corporal, shouldering his stick, and striking his hand upon his coat-skirt as he took his first step——march'd close behind him down the avenue.

——Now what can their two noddles be about? cried my father to my mother——by all that's strange, they are besieging Mrs. *Wadman* in form, and are marching round her house to mark out the lines of circumvallation.

I dare say, quoth my mother——————But stop, dear Sir ——for what my mother dared to say upon the occasion—— and what my father did say upon it——with her replies and his rejoinders, shall be read, perused, paraphrased, commented and discanted upon——or to say it all in a word, shall be thumb'd over by Posterity in a chapter apart——I say, by Posterity——and care not, if I repeat the word again——for what has this book done more than the Legation of Moses,[1] or the Tale of a Tub, that it may not swim down the gutter of Time along with them?

I will not argue the matter: Time wastes too fast: every letter I trace tells me with what rapidity Life follows my pen; the days and hours of it, more precious, my dear *Jenny!*[2] than the rubies about thy neck, are flying over our heads like light clouds of a windy day, never to return more——every thing

---

[1]Another thrust at Bishop Warburton (for whom, see p. 298, n. 2), who was not amused at this irreverent coupling of *The Divine Legation of Moses Demonstrated on the Principles of a Religious Deist,* his most important theological publication, with the works, in very different keys, of Swift and Sterne. *A Tale of a Tub* had been facetiously dedicated to "Prince Posterity."

[2]See p. 44, n. 3.

presses on——whilst thou art twisting that lock,——see! it
grows grey; and every time I kiss thy hand to bid adieu, and
every absence which follows it, are preludes to that eternal
separation which we are shortly to make.——

——Heaven have mercy upon us both!

CHAP. IX.

NOW, for what the world thinks of that ejaculation——I
would not give a groat.

CHAP. X.

MY mother had gone with her left arm twisted in my
father's right, till they had got to the fatal angle of the
old garden wall, where Doctor *Slop* was overthrown by *Obadiah* on the coach-horse: as this was directly opposite to the
front of Mrs. *Wadman's* house, when my father came to it, he
gave a look across; and seeing my uncle *Toby* and the Corporal within ten paces of the door, he turn'd about——"Let
us just stop a moment, quoth my father, and see with what
ceremonies my brother *Toby* and his man *Trim* make their
first entry——it will not detain us, added my father, a single
minute:"——No matter, if it be ten minutes, quoth my
mother.

——It will not detain us half a one; said my father.

The Corporal was just then setting in with the story of his
brother *Tom* and the *Jew's* widow: the story went on——and
on——it had episodes in it——it came back, and went on——
and on again; there was no end of it——the reader found it
very long——

——G— help my father! he pish'd fifty times at every new
attitude, and gave the corporal's stick, with all its flourishings
and danglings, to as many devils as chose to accept of them.

When issues of events like these my father is waiting for,

are hanging in the scales of fate, the mind has the advantage of changing the principle of expectation three times, without which it would not have power to see it out.

Curiosity governs the *first moment;* and the second moment is all œconomy to justify the expence of the first——and for the third, fourth, fifth, and sixth moments, and so on to the day of judgment——'tis a point of HONOUR.

I need not be told, that the ethic writers have assigned this all to Patience; but that VIRTUE methinks, has extent of dominion sufficient of her own, and enough to do in it, without invading the few dismantled castles which HONOUR has left him upon the earth.

My father stood it out as well as he could with these three auxiliaries to the end of *Trim's* story; and from thence to the end of my uncle *Toby's* panegyrick upon arms, in the chapter following it; when seeing, that instead of marching up to Mrs. *Wadman's* door, they both faced about and march'd down the avenue diametrically opposite to his expectation——he broke out at once with that little subacid soreness of humour which, in certain situations, distinguished his character from that of all other men.

CHAP. XI.

——"NOW what can their two noddles be about?" cried my father - - &c. - - - -

I dare say, said my mother, they are making fortifications——

——Not on Mrs. *Wadman's* premises! cried my father, stepping back——

I suppose not: quoth my mother.

I wish, said my father, raising his voice, the whole science of fortification at the devil, with all its trumpery of saps, mines, blinds, gabions, fausse-brays[1] and cuvetts——

——They are foolish things——said my mother.

---

[1]Small mounds of earth thrown up about a rampart. Cuvetts: trenches dug in the middle of a large ditch.

Now she had a way, which by the bye, I would this moment give away my purple jerkin, and my yellow slippers into the bargain, if some of your reverences would imitate——and that was never to refuse her assent and consent to any proposition my father laid before her, merely because she did not understand it, or had[2] no ideas to the principal word or term of art, upon which the tenet or proposition rolled. She contented herself with doing all that her godfathers and godmothers promised for her——but no more; and so would go on using a hard word twenty years together——and replying to it too, if it was a verb, in all its moods and tenses, without giving herself any trouble to enquire about it.

This was an eternal source of misery to my father, and broke the neck, at the first setting out, of more good dialogues between them, than could have done the most petulant contradiction——the few which survived were the better for the *cuvetts*——

——"They are foolish things;" said my mother.

——Particularly the *cuvetts;* replied my father.

'Twas enough——he tasted the sweet of triumph——and went on.

——Not that they are, properly speaking, Mrs. *Wadman*'s premises, said my father, partly correcting himself——because she is but tenant for life——

——That makes a great difference——said my mother——

——In a fool's head, replied my father——

Unless she should happen to have a child——said my mother——

——But she must persuade my brother *Toby* first to get her one——

——To be sure, Mr. *Shandy,* quoth my mother.

——Though if it comes to persuasion——said my father ——Lord have mercy upon them.

Amen: said my mother, *piano*.

Amen: cried my father, *fortissimè*.

Amen: said my mother again——but with such a sighing

---

[2]*I.e.*, associated, connected.

cadence of personal pity at the end of it, as discomfited every fibre about my father——he instantly took out his almanack; but before he could untie it, *Yorick*'s congregation coming out of church, became a full answer to one half of his business with it——and my mother telling him it was a sacrament day[3]—— left him as little in doubt, as to the other part——He put his almanack into his pocket.

The first Lord of the Treasury thinking of *ways and means,* could not have returned home, with a more embarrassed look.

CHAP. XII.

UPON looking back from the end of the last chapter and surveying the texture of what has been wrote, it is necessary, that upon this page and the five following, a good quantity of heterogeneous matter be inserted, to keep up that just balance betwixt wisdom and folly, without which a book would not hold together a single year: nor is it a poor creeping digression (which but for the name of, a man might continue as well going on in the king's highway) which will do the business——no; if it is to be a digression, it must be a good frisky one, and upon a frisky subject too, where neither the horse or his rider are to be caught, but by rebound.

The only difficulty, is raising powers suitable to the nature of the service: FANCY is capricious——WIT must not be searched for——and PLEASANTRY (good-natured slut as she is) will not come in at a call, was an empire to be laid at her feet.

——The best way for a man, is to say his prayers——

Only if it puts him in mind of his infirmities and defects as well ghostly as bodily——for that purpose, he will find himself rather worse after he has said them than before——for other purposes, better.

---

[3]Although local customs varied in Sterne's day, the sacrament was usually administered monthly, frequently on the first Sunday of each month. Here is probably a sly reference to Mr. Shandy's habit of taking care of "some other little family concernments" the first Sunday night of each month (for which, see p. 8).

For my own part there is not a way either moral or mechanical under heaven that I could think of, which I have not taken with myself in this case: sometimes by addressing myself directly to the soul herself, and arguing the point over and over again with her upon the extent of her own faculties——

——I never could make them an inch the wider——

Then by changing my system, and trying what could be made of it upon the body, by temperance, soberness and chastity: These are good, quoth I, in themselves——they are good, absolutely;——they are good, relatively;——they are good for health——they are good for happiness in this world ——they are good for happiness in the next——

In short, they were good for every thing but the thing wanted; and there they were good for nothing, but to leave the soul just as heaven made it: as for the theological virtues of faith and hope, they give it courage; but then that sniveling virtue of Meekness (as my father would always call it) takes it quite away again, so you are exactly where you started.

Now in all common and ordinary cases, there is nothing which I have found to answer so well as this——

——Certainly, if there is any dependence upon Logic, and that I am not blinded by self-love, there must be something of true genius about me, merely upon this symptom of it, that I do not know what envy is: for never do I hit upon any invention or device which tendeth to the furtherance of good writing, but I instantly make it public; willing that all mankind should write as well as myself.

——Which they certainly will, when they think as little.

CHAP. XIII.

NOW in ordinary cases, that is, when I am only stupid, and the thoughts rise heavily and pass gummous through my pen——

Or that I am got, I know not how, into a cold unmetaphorical vein of infamous writing, and cannot take a plumb-lift out of it *for my soul;* so must be obliged to go on writing like a *Dutch* commentator[1] to the end of the chapter, unless something be done——

——I never stand conferring with pen and ink one moment; for if a pinch of snuff or a stride or two across the room will not do the business for me——I take a razor at once; and having tried the edge of it upon the palm of my hand, without further ceremony, except that of first lathering my beard, I shave it off; taking care only if I do leave a hair, that it be not a grey one: this done, I change my shirt——put on a better coat——send for my last wig——put my topaz ring[2] upon my finger; and in a word, dress myself from one end to the other of me, after my best fashion.

Now the devil in hell must be in it, if this does not do: for consider, Sir, as every man chuses to be present at the shaving of his own beard (though there is no rule without an exception) and unavoidably sits overagainst himself the whole time it is doing, in case he has a hand in it——the Situation, like all others, has notions of her own to put into the brain.——

——I maintain it, the conceits of a rough-bearded man, are seven years more terse and juvenile for one single operation; and if they did not run a risk of being quite shaved away, might be carried up by continual shavings, to the highest pitch of sublimity——How *Homer* could write with so long a beard, I don't know——and as it makes against my hypothesis, I as little care——But let us return to the Toilet.

Ludovicus Sorbonensis makes this entirely an affair of the body (ἐξωτερικὴ πρᾶξις[3]) as he calls it——but he is deceived: the soul and body are joint-sharers in every thing they get: A man cannot dress, but his ideas get cloath'd at the same time; and if he dresses like a gentleman, every one of them stands

---

[1]Dutch commentators were supposed to be even duller than others; see p. 430, n. 6.

[2]See p. 468, n. 7.

[3]An external matter. I have not been able to identify Ludovicus Sorbonensis.

presented to his imagination, genteelized along with him——
so that he has nothing to do, but take his pen, and write like
himself.

For this cause, when your honours and reverences would
know whether I writ clean and fit to be read, you will be able
to judge full as well by looking into my Laundress's bill, as my
book: there was one single month in which I can make it appear, that I dirtied one and thirty shirts with clean writing;
and after all, was more abus'd, curs'd, criticis'd and confounded, and had more mystic heads shaken at me, for what
I had wrote in that one month, than in all the other months
of that year put together.

——But their honours and reverences had not seen my
bills.

CHAP. XIV.

AS I never had any intention of beginning the Digression, I
am making all this preparation for, till I come to the 15th
chapter——I have this chapter to put to whatever use I think
proper——I have twenty this moment ready for it——I could
write my chapter of Button-holes in it——

Or my chapter of *Pishes,* which should follow them——

Or my chapter of *Knots,*[1] in case their reverences have done
with them——they might lead me into mischief: the safest
way is to follow the tract of the learned, and raise objections
against what I have been writing, tho' I declare beforehand, I
know no more than my heels how to answer them.

And first, it may be said, there is a pelting kind of *thersitical* satire, as black as the very ink 'tis wrote with——(and by
the bye, whoever says so, is indebted to the muster-master
general of the *Grecian* army, for suffering the name of so ugly
and foul-mouth'd a man as *Thersites*[2] to continue upon his

---

[1] An allusion to the marital "knot," or coition.

[2] In the *Iliad*, Thersites was the most scurrilous and impudent talker
among the Greeks. Thersitical: grossly abusive, foul-mouthed.

roll——for it has furnished him with an epithet)——in these
productions he will urge, all the personal washings and scrub-
bings upon earth do a sinking genius no sort of good——but
just the contrary, inasmuch as the dirtier the fellow is, the better generally he succeeds in it.

To this, I have no other answer——at least ready——but
that the Archbishop of *Benevento* wrote his *nasty* Romance
of the *Galateo*,[3] as all the world knows, in a purple coat, waistcoat, and purple pair of breeches; and that the penance set him
of writing a commentary upon the book of the *Revelations,* as
severe as it was look'd upon by one part of the world, was
far from being deem'd so, by the other, upon the single account of that *Investment.*

Another objection, to all this remedy, is its want of univer-
sality; forasmuch as the shaving part of it, upon which so
much stress is laid, by an unalterable law of nature excludes
one half of the species entirely from its use: all I can say is,
that female writers, whether of *England,* or of *France,* must
e'en go without it——

As for the *Spanish* ladies——I am in no sort of distress——

CHAP. XV.

THE fifteenth chapter is come at last; and brings nothing
with it but a sad signature of "How our pleasures slip
from under us in this world;"

For in talking of my digression——I declare before heaven
I have made it!   What a strange creature is mortal man! said
she.

'Tis very true, said I——but 'twere better to get all these
things out of our heads, and return to my uncle *Toby.*

---

[3]The *Galateo* of Giovanni della Casa (see p. 373, n. 4) is a prose
treatise on polite manners and refined conversation; Sterne is evidently
thinking of della Casa's *Capitolo del forno,* a lascivious *jeu d'esprit* which
the archbishop later regretted having written. "Purple" alludes to the
amaranth-red costume of a bishop of the Church of Rome.

CHAP. XVI.

WHEN my uncle *Toby* and the Corporal had marched down to the bottom of the avenue, they recollected their business lay the other way; so they faced about and marched up streight to Mrs. *Wadman*'s door.

I warrant your honour; said the Corporal, touching his Montero-cap with his hand, as he passed him in order to give a knock at the door——My uncle *Toby,* contrary to his invariable way of treating his faithful servant, said nothing good or bad: the truth was, he had not altogether marshal'd his ideas; he wish'd for another conference, and as the Corporal was mounting up the three steps before the door——he hem'd twice——a portion of my uncle *Toby*'s most modest spirits fled, at each expulsion, towards the Corporal; he stood with the rapper of the door suspended for a full minute in his hand, he scarce knew why. *Bridget* stood perdue within, with her finger and her thumb upon the latch, benumb'd with expectation; and Mrs. *Wadman,* with an eye ready to be deflowered again, sat breathless behind the window-curtain of her bedchamber, watching their approach.

Trim! said my uncle *Toby*——but as he articulated the word, the minute expired, and *Trim* let fall the rapper.

My uncle *Toby* perceiving that all hopes of a conference were knock'd on the head by it——whistled Lillabullero.

CHAP. XVII.

AS Mrs. *Bridget*'s finger and thumb were upon the latch, the Corporal did not knock as oft as perchance your honour's taylor——I might have taken my example something nearer home; for I owe mine, some five and twenty pounds at least, and wonder at the man's patience——

——But this is nothing at all to the world: only 'tis a cursed thing to be in debt; and there seems to be a fatality in the exchequers of some poor princes, particularly those of our house, which no Economy can bind down in irons: for my own part, I'm persuaded there is not any one prince, prelate, pope, or potentate, great or small upon earth, more desirous in his heart of keeping streight with the world than I am——or who takes more likely means for it. I never give above half a guinea——or walk with boots——or cheapen tooth-picks—— or lay out a shilling upon a band-box the year round; and for the six months I'm in the country, I'm upon so small a scale, that with all the good temper in the world, I out-do *Rousseau*,[1] a bar length——for I keep neither man or boy, or horse, or cow, or dog, or cat, or any thing that can eat or drink, except a thin poor piece of a Vestal[2] (to keep my fire in) and who has generally as bad an appetite as myself——but if you think this makes a philosopher of me——I would not, my good people! give a rush for your judgments.

True philosophy——but there is no treating the subject whilst my uncle is whistling Lillabullero.

——Let us go into the house.

---

[1]At the time Sterne was writing this, in the autumn of 1766, Jean Jacques Rousseau (1712–1778), the French philosopher, who had developed the paradox that a state of savagery is superior to one of civilization and who urged mankind to return to a simple, "natural" mode of life, was himself living simply in exile, though hardly with philosophic content, in a house procured for him in Derbyshire by his and Sterne's friend David Hume.

[2]A play upon the secondary meaning of *vestal:* a virgin, and the primary meaning: a virgin consecrated to the task of keeping the sacred fire of Vesta, the goddess of the hearth, perpetually burning upon her altar.

CHAP. XVIII.

CHAP. XIX.

CHAP. XX.

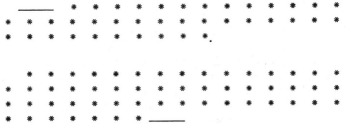

——You shall see the very place, Madam; said my uncle *Toby*.

Mrs. *Wadman* blush'd——look'd towards the door——turn'd pale——blush'd slightly again——recovered her natural colour——blush'd worse than ever; which for the sake of the unlearned reader, I translate thus——

"L—d! I cannot look at it——
What would the world say if I look'd at it?
I should drop down, if I look'd at it——
I wish I could look at it——
There can be no sin in looking at it.
——I will look at it."

Whilst all this was running through Mrs. *Wadman's* imagination, my uncle *Toby* had risen from the sopha, and got to the other side of the parlour-door, to give *Trim* an order about it in the passage——

* * * * * * * * * * * * * *
* * * * * ——I believe it is in the garret, said my uncle *Toby*——I saw it there, an' please your honour, this morning, answered *Trim*——Then prithee, step directly for it, *Trim,* said my uncle *Toby,* and bring it into the parlour.

The Corporal did not approve of the orders, but most chearfully obey'd them. The first was not an act of his will——the second was; so he put on his Montero cap, and went as fast as

his lame knee would let him.   My uncle *Toby* returned into
the parlour, and sat himself down again upon the sopha.

——You shall lay your finger upon the place——said my
uncle *Toby*.——I will not touch it, however, quoth Mrs. *Wadman* to herself.

This requires a second translation:——it shews what little
knowledge is got by mere words——we must go up to the
first springs.

Now in order to clear up the mist which hangs upon these
three pages, I must endeavour to be as clear as possible myself.

Rub your hands thrice across your foreheads——blow your
noses——cleanse your emunctories——sneeze, my good people!——God bless you——

Now give me all the help you can.

CHAP. XXI.

AS there are fifty different ends (counting all ends in——as
well civil as religious) for which a woman takes a husband, she first sets about and carefully weighs, then separates
and distinguishes in her mind, which of all that number of
ends, is hers: then by discourse, enquiry, argumentation and
inference, she investigates and finds out whether she has got
hold of the right one——and if she has——then, by pulling it
gently this way and that way, she further forms a judgment,
whether it will not break in the drawing.

The imagery under which *Slawkenbergius* impresses this
upon his reader's fancy, in the beginning of his third Decad,
is so ludicrous, that the honour I bear the sex, will not suffer
me to quote it——otherwise 'tis not destitute of humour.

"She first, saith *Slawkenbergius,* stops the asse, and holding
his halter in her left hand (lest he should get away) she
thrusts her right hand into the very bottom of his pannier to
search for it——For what?——you'll not know the sooner,
quoth *Slawkenbergius,* for interrupting me——

"I have nothing, good Lady, but empty bottles;" says the asse.

"I'm loaded with tripes;" says the second.

——And thou art little better, quoth she to the third; for nothing is there in thy panniers but trunk-hose and pantofles ——and so to the fourth and fifth, going on one by one through the whole string, till coming to the asse which carries it, she turns the pannier upside down, looks at it—— considers it——samples it——measures it——stretches it ——wets it——dries it——then takes her teeth both to the warp and weft of it——

——Of what? for the love of Christ!

I am determined, answered *Slawkenbergius,* that all the powers upon earth shall never wring that secret from my breast.

CHAP. XXII.

WE live in a world beset on all sides with mysteries and riddles——and so 'tis no matter——else it seems strange, that Nature, who makes every thing so well to answer its destination, and seldom or never errs, unless for pastime, in giving such forms and aptitudes to whatever passes through her hands, that whether she designs for the plough, the caravan, the cart——or whatever other creature she models, be it but an asse's foal, you are sure to have the thing you wanted; and yet at the same time should so eternally bungle it as she does, in making so simple a thing as a married man.

Whether it is in the choice of the clay——or that it is frequently spoiled in the baking; by an excess of which a husband may turn out too crusty (you know) on one hand——or not enough so, through defect of heat, on the other——or whether this great Artificer is not so attentive to the little Platonic exigencies *of that part* of the species, for whose use she is fabricating *this*——or that her Ladyship sometimes scarce knows what sort of a husband will do——I know not: we will discourse about it after supper.

It is enough, that neither the observation itself, or the reasoning upon it, are at all to the purpose——but rather against it; since with regard to my uncle *Toby's* fitness for the marriage state, nothing was ever better: she had formed him of the best and kindliest clay——had temper'd it with her own milk, and breathed into it the sweetest spirit——she had made him all gentle, generous and humane——she had fill'd his heart with trust and confidence, and disposed every passage which led to it, for the communication of the tenderest offices ——she had moreover considered the other causes for which matrimony was ordained——

And accordingly   *   *   *   *   *   *   *   *   *   *
*   *   *   *   *   *   *   *   *   *   *   *   *   *   *
*   *   *   *   *   *   *   *   *   *   *   *   *   *   *
*   *   *   *.

The DONATION was not defended by my uncle *Toby's* wound.

Now this last article was somewhat apocryphal; and the Devil, who is the great disturber of our faiths in this world, had raised scruples in Mrs. *Wadman's* brain about it; and like a true devil as he was, had done his own work at the same time, by turning my uncle *Toby's* Virtue thereupon into nothing but *empty bottles, tripes, trunk-hose,* and *pantofles.*

CHAP. XXIII.

MRS. *Bridget* had pawn'd all the little stock of honour a poor chambermaid was worth in the world, that she would get to the bottom of the affair in ten days; and it was built upon one of the most concessible *postulata*[1] in nature: namely, that whilst my uncle *Toby* was making love to her mistress, the Corporal could find nothing better to do, than

---

[1]Postulations.

make love to her——"*And I'll let him as much as he will,*" said *Bridget*, "*to get it out of him.*"

Friendship has two garments; an outer, and an under one. *Bridget* was serving her mistress's interests in the one——and doing the thing which most pleased herself in the other; so had as many stakes depending upon my uncle *Toby*'s wound, as the Devil himself——Mrs. *Wadman* had but one——and as it possibly might be her last (without discouraging Mrs. *Bridget*, or discrediting her talents) was determined to play her cards herself.

She wanted not encouragement: a child might have look'd into his hand——there was such a plainness and simplicity in his playing out what trumps he had——with such an unmistrusting ignorance of the *ten-ace*——and so naked and defenceless did he sit upon the same sopha with widow *Wadman*, that a generous heart would have wept to have won the game of him.

Let us drop the metaphor.

CHAP. XXIV.

——AND the story too——if you please: for though I have all along been hastening towards this part of it, with so much earnest desire, as well knowing it to be the choicest morsel of what I had to offer to the world, yet now that I am got to it, any one is welcome to take my pen, and go on with the story for me that will——I see the difficulties of the descriptions I'm going to give——and feel my want of powers.

It is one comfort at least to me, that I lost some fourscore ounces of blood this week in a most uncritical fever which attacked me at the beginning of this chapter; so that I have still some hopes remaining, it may be more in the serous or globular parts of the blood, than in the subtile *aura* of the brain——be it which it will——an Invocation can do no hurt

——and I leave the affair entirely to the *invoked,* to inspire or to inject me according as he sees good.

THE INVOCATION.

GENTLE Spirit of sweetest humour, who erst didst sit upon the easy pen of my beloved CERVANTES; Thou who glided'st daily through his lattice, and turned'st the twilight of his prison into noon-day brightness by thy presence—— tinged'st his little urn of water with heaven-sent Nectar, and all the time he wrote of *Sancho* and his master, didst cast thy mystic mantle o'er his wither'd * stump, and wide extended it to all the evils of his life——

——Turn in hither, I beseech thee!——behold these breeches!——they are all I have in the world——that piteous rent was given them at *Lyons*——

My shirts! see what a deadly schism has happen'd amongst 'em——for the laps are in *Lombardy,* and the rest of 'em here ——I never had but six, and a cunning gypsey of a laundress at *Milan* cut me off the *fore*-laps of five——To do her justice, she did it with some consideration——for I was returning *out* of *Italy.*

And yet, notwithstanding all this, and a pistol tinder-box which was moreover filch'd from me at *Sienna,* and twice that I pay'd five Pauls[1] for two hard eggs, once at *Raddicoffini,* and a second time at *Capua*——I do not think a journey through *France* and *Italy,* provided a man keeps his temper all the way, so bad a thing as some people[2] would make you

---

*He lost his hand at the battle of *Lepanto.* [Sterne's note. From his remark in the Preface to *Don Quixote,* "You may suppose it the child of disturbance, engendred in some dismal prison, where wretchedness keeps its residence, and every dismal sound its habitation," it has been thought that Cervantes conceived and perhaps began writing his master-piece during one of his terms of imprisonment at Seville between 1597 and 1602.]

[1]The paolo is an obsolete Italian coin worth about ten cents.

[2]An allusion to the vivid but splenetic *Travels through France and Italy* published in 1766 by Tobias Smollett (for whom, see p. 429, n. 4). In

believe: there must be *ups* and *downs,* or how the duce should
we get into vallies where Nature spreads so many tables of
entertainment.——'Tis nonsense to imagine they will lend
you their voitures³ to be shaken to pieces for nothing; and
unless you pay twelve sous for greasing your wheels, how
should the poor peasant get butter to his bread?——We really
expect too much——and for the livre or two above par for
your suppers and bed——at the most they are but one shilling
and ninepence halfpenny——who would embroil their philosophy for it? for heaven's and for your own sake, pay it
——pay it with both hands open, rather than leave *Disappointment* sitting drooping upon the eye of your fair Hostess
and her Damsels in the gate-way, at your departure——and
besides, my dear Sir, you get a sisterly kiss of each of 'em
worth a pound——at least I did——

——For my uncle *Toby's* amours running all the way in my
head, they had the same effect upon me as if they had been
my own——I was in the most perfect state of bounty and
good will; and felt the kindliest harmony vibrating within me,
with every oscillation of the chaise alike; so that whether the
roads were rough or smooth, it made no difference; every
thing I saw, or had to do with, touch'd upon some secret spring
either of sentiment or rapture.

——They were the sweetest notes I ever heard; and I instantly let down the fore-glass to hear them more distinctly

---

A Sentimental Journey, Sterne further assailed the ill-tempered physician:
    "The learned SMELFUNGUS travelled from Boulogne to Paris—from Paris
to Rome—and so on—but he set out with the spleen and jaundice, and
every object he pass'd by was discoloured or distorted—He wrote an
account of them, but 't was nothing but the account of his miserable
feelings. . . .
    "I popp'd upon Smelfungus again at Turin, in his return home; and
a sad tale of sorrowful adventures he had to tell, 'wherein he spoke
of moving accidents by flood and field, and of the cannibals which each
other eat: the Anthropophagi'—he had been flay'd alive, and bedevil'd,
and used worse than St Bartholomew, at every stage he had come at——
    "—I'll tell it, cried Smelfungus, to the world. You had better tell
it, said I, to your physician."   ("In the Street—Calais.")
    ³Carriages.

——'Tis *Maria;* said the postilion, observing I was listening ——Poor *Maria,* continued he, (leaning his body on one side to let me see her, for he was in a line betwixt us) is sitting upon a bank playing her vespers upon her pipe, with her little goat beside her.

The young fellow utter'd this with an accent and a look so perfectly in tune to a feeling heart, that I instantly made a vow, I would give him a four and twenty sous piece, when I got to *Moulins*——

——And who is *poor Maria?* said I.

The love and pity of all the villages around us; said the postillion——it is but three years ago, that the sun did not. shine upon so fair, so quick-witted and amiable a maid; and better fate did *Maria* deserve, than to have her Banns forbid, by the intrigues of the curate of the parish who published them——

He was going on, when *Maria,* who had made a short pause, put the pipe to her mouth and began the air again——they were the same notes;——yet were ten times sweeter: It is the evening service to the Virgin, said the young man——but who has taught her to play it——or how she came by her pipe, no one knows; we think that Heaven has assisted her in both; for ever since she has been unsettled in her mind, it seems her only consolation——she has never once had the pipe out of her hand, but plays that *service* upon it almost night and day.

The postillion delivered this with so much discretion and natural eloquence, that I could not help decyphering some-thing in his face above his condition, and should have sifted out his history, had not poor *Maria's* taken such full posses-sion of me.

We had got up by this time almost to the bank where *Maria* was sitting: she was in a thin white jacket with her hair, all but two tresses, drawn up into a silk net, with a few olive leaves twisted a little fantastically on one side——she was beautiful; and if ever I felt the full force of an honest heart-ache, it was the moment I saw her——

——God help her! poor damsel! above a hundred masses,

said the postillion, have been said in the several parish churches and convents around, for her,——but without effect; we have still hopes, as she is sensible for short intervals, that the Virgin at last will restore her to herself; but her parents, who know her best, are hopeless upon that score, and think her senses are lost for ever.

As the postillion spoke this, MARIA made a cadence so melancholy, so tender and querulous, that I sprung out of the chaise to help her, and found myself sitting betwixt her and her goat before I relapsed from my enthusiasm.

MARIA look'd wistfully for some time at me, and then at her goat——and then at me——and then at her goat again, and so on, alternately——

——Well, *Maria,* said I softly——What resemblance do you find?

I do intreat the candid reader to believe me, that it was from the humblest conviction of what a *Beast* man is,——that I ask'd the question; and that I would not have let fallen an unseasonable pleasantry in the venerable presence of Misery, to be entitled to all the wit that ever *Rabelais* scatter'd—— and yet I own my heart smote me, and that I so smarted at the very idea of it, that I swore I would set up for Wisdom and utter grave sentences the rest of my days——and never—— never attempt again to commit mirth with man, woman, or child, the longest day I had to live.

As for writing nonsense to them——I believe, there was a reserve——but that I leave to the world.

Adieu, *Maria!*——adieu, poor hapless damsel!——some time, but not *now,* I may hear thy sorrows from thy own lips—— but I was deceived; for that moment she took her pipe and told me such a tale of woe with it, that I rose up, and with broken and irregular steps walk'd softly to my chaise.

——What an excellent inn at *Moulins!*

CHAP. XXV.

WHEN we have got to the end of this chapter (but not before) we must all turn back to the two blank chapters, on the account of which my honour has lain bleeding this half hour——I stop it, by pulling off one of my yellow slippers and throwing it with all my violence to the opposite side of my room, with a declaration at the heel of it——

——That whatever resemblance it may bear to half the chapters which are written in the world, or, for aught I know, may be now writing in it——that it was as casual as the foam of *Zeuxis* his horse:[1] besides, I look upon a chapter which has, *only nothing in it,* with respect; and considering what worse things there are in the world——That it is no way a proper subject for satire——

——Why then was it left so?   And here, without staying for my reply, shall I be call'd as many blockheads, numsculs, doddypoles, dunderheads, ninny-hammers, goosecaps, jolt-heads, nicompoops, and sh--t-a-beds——and other unsavory appellations, as ever the cake-bakers of *Lerné,* cast in the teeth of King *Gargantua'*s shepherds[2]——And I'll let them do it, as *Bridget* said, as much as they please; for how was it possible

---

[1]Sterne is perhaps confusing Zeuxis (fl. 400 B.C.), the celebrated Greek painter, with Nealces (fl. 245 B.C.), a Greek painter who, according to Pliny (*Naturalis Historia,* 35.36[10]), succeeded in painting the foam at a horse's mouth by throwing his sponge at the picture.

[2]In Rabelais, 1.25, the cake-bakers "did injure [the shepherds] most outrageously, calling them prating gabblers, lickerish gluttons, freckled bittors, mangy rascals, shite-a-bed scoundrels, drunken roisterers, sly knaves, drowsy loiterers, slapsauce fellows, slabberdegullion druggles, lubberly louts, cozening foxes, ruffian rogues, paltry customers, sycophant varlets, drawlatch hoydens, flouting milk-sops, jeering companions, staring clowns, forlorn snakes, ninny lobcocks, scurvy sneaksbies, fondling fops, base loons, saucy coxcombs, idle lusks, scoffing braggarts, noddy meacocks, blockish grutnols, doddypoll joltheads, jobbernowl goosecaps, foolish loggerheads, slutch calf-lollies, grout-head gnatsnappers, lobdotterels, gaping changelings, codshead loobies, woodcock slangams, ninnyhammer flycatchers, noddypeak simpletons, turdy gut, shitten shepherds, and other such defamatory epithets . . ."

they should foresee the necessity I was under of writing the 25th chapter of my book, before the 18th, &c.?

——So I don't take it amiss——All I wish is, that it may be a lesson to the world, *"to let people tell their stories their own way."*

The Eighteenth Chapter.

AS Mrs. *Bridget* open'd the door before the Corporal had well given the rap, the interval betwixt that and my uncle *Toby*'s introduction into the parlour, was so short, that Mrs. *Wadman* had but just time to get from behind the curtain——lay a Bible upon the table, and advance a step or two towards the door to receive him.

My uncle *Toby* saluted Mrs. *Wadman,* after the manner in which women were saluted by men in the year of our Lord God one thousand seven hundred and thirteen——then facing about, he march'd up abreast with her to the sopha, and in three plain words——though not before he was sat down—— nor after he was sat down——but as he was sitting down, told her, *"he was in love"*——so that my uncle *Toby* strained himself more in the declaration than he needed.

Mrs. *Wadman* naturally looked down, upon a slit she had been darning up in her apron, in expectation every moment, that my uncle *Toby* would go on; but having no talents for amplification, and Love moreover of all others being a subject of which he was the least a master——When he had told Mrs. *Wadman* once that he loved her, he let it alone, and left the matter to work after its own way.

My father was always in raptures with this system of my uncle *Toby*'s, as he falsely called it, and would often say, that could his brother *Toby* to his processe have added but a pipe of tobacco——he had wherewithal to have found his way, if there was faith in a *Spanish* proverb,[1] towards the hearts of half the women upon the globe.

---

[1] Various Spanish proverbs enforce Lope de Vega's "Brief words are a sign of love" (*La Dama Melindrosa,* 2.4).

My uncle *Toby* never understood what my father meant; nor will I presume to extract more from it, than a condemnation of an error which the bulk of the world lie under——but the *French,* every one of 'em to a man, who believe in it, almost as much as the REAL PRESENCE,[2] *"That talking of love, is making it."*

——I would as soon set about making a black-pudding by the same receipt.

Let us go on: Mrs. *Wadman* sat in expectation my uncle *Toby* would do so, to almost the first pulsation of that minute, wherein silence on one side or the other, generally becomes indecent: so edging herself a little more towards him, and raising up her eyes, sub-blushing, as she did it——she took up the gauntlet——or the discourse (if you like it better) and communed with my uncle *Toby,* thus.

The cares and disquietudes of the marriage state, quoth Mrs. *Wadman,* are very great. I suppose so——said my uncle *Toby:* and therefore when a person, continued Mrs. *Wadman,* is so much at his ease as you are——so happy, captain *Shandy,* in yourself, your friends and your amusements——I wonder, what reasons can incline you to the state——

——They are written, quoth my uncle *Toby,* in the Common-Prayer Book.[3]

Thus far my uncle *Toby* went on warily, and kept within his depth, leaving Mrs. *Wadman* to sail upon the gulph as she pleased.

——As for children——said Mrs. *Wadman*——though a principal end perhaps of the institution, and the natural wish, I suppose, of every parent——yet do not we all find, they are

---

[2]The doctrine that the body and blood of Christ "truly, really, and substantially" exist in the eucharist.

[3]According to the Book of Common Prayer, matrimony "was ordained for the procreation of children, to be brought up in the fear and nurture of the Lord, and to the praise of his holy Name . . . for a remedy against sin, and to avoid fornication; that such persons as have not the gift of continency might marry, and keep themselves undefiled members of Christ's body . . . for the mutual society, help, and comfort, that the one ought to have of the other, both in prosperity and adversity."

certain sorrows, and very uncertain comforts? and what is there, dear sir, to pay one for the heart-aches——what compensation for the many tender and disquieting apprehensions of a suffering and defenceless mother who brings them into life? I declare, said my uncle *Toby*, smit with pity, I know of none; unless it be the pleasure which it has pleased God——

A fiddlestick! quoth she.

Chapter the Nineteenth.

NOW there are such an infinitude of notes, tunes, cants, chants, airs, looks, and accents with which the word *fiddlestick* may be pronounced in all such causes as this, every one of 'em impressing a sense and meaning as different from the other, as *dirt* from *cleanliness*——That Casuists) for it is an affair of conscience on that score) reckon up no less than fourteen thousand in which you may do either right or wrong.

Mrs. *Wadman* hit upon the *fiddlestick,* which summoned up all my uncle *Toby's* modest blood into his cheeks——so feeling within himself that he had somehow or other got beyond his depth, he stopt short; and without entering further either into the pains or pleasures of matrimony, he laid his hand upon his heart, and made an offer to take them as they were, and share them along with her.

When my uncle *Toby* had said this, he did not care to say it again; so casting his eye upon the Bible which Mrs. *Wadman* had laid upon the table, he took it up; and popping, dear soul! upon a passage in it, of all others the most interesting to him ——which was the siege of *Jericho*——he set himself to read it over——leaving his proposal of marriage, as he had done his declaration of love, to work with her after its own way. Now it wrought neither as an astringent or a loosener; nor like opium, or bark, or mercury, or buckthorn,[1] or any one drug which nature had bestowed upon the world——in short, it work'd not at all in her; and the cause of that was, that there

----

[1] A hedge-plant formerly used as a cathartic.

was something working there before——Babbler that I am! I have anticipated what it was a dozen times; but there is fire still in the subject——allons.

CHAP. XXVI.

IT is natural for a perfect stranger who is going from *London* to *Edinburgh,* to enquire before he sets out, how many miles to *York;* which is about the half way——nor does any body wonder, if he goes on and asks about the Corporation, &c. - -

It was just as natural for Mrs. *Wadman,* whose first husband was all his time afflicted with a Sciatica,[1] to wish to know how far from the hip to the groin; and how far she was likely to suffer more or less in her feelings, in the one case than in the other.

She had accordingly read *Drake*'s[2] anatomy from one end to the other.   She had peeped into *Wharton*[3] upon the brain, and borrowed * *Graaf* upon the bones and muscles; but could make nothing of it.

She had reason'd likewise from her own powers——laid down theorems——drawn consequences, and come to no conclusion.

To clear up all, she had twice asked Doctor *Slop,* "if poor captain *Shandy* was ever likely to recover of his wound ——?"

---

[1]See p. 9, n. 4.

[2]James Drake (1667–1707), physician and political writer, was author of a popular medical treatise called *Anthropologia Nova, or a New System of Anatomy.*

[3]Thomas Wharton (1614–1673), a noted anatomist, discussed the nature of the brain in his *Adenographia; sive Glandularum Totius Corporis Descriptio.*

*This must be a mistake in Mr. *Shandy;* for *Graaf* wrote upon the pancreatick juice, and the parts of generation. [Sterne's note. Regnier de Graaf (1641–1673), a celebrated Dutch physician, was the author of works on each of these subjects; Mrs. Wadman probably examined his *De Virorum Organis Generationi Inservientibus.*]

——He is recovered, Doctor *Slop* would say——

What! quite?

——Quite: madam——

But what do you mean by a recovery? Mrs. *Wadman* would say.

Doctor *Slop* was the worst man alive at definitions; and so Mrs. *Wadman* could get no knowledge: in short, there was no way to extract it, but from my uncle *Toby* himself.

There is an accent of humanity in an enquiry of this kind which lulls SUSPICION to rest——and I am half persuaded the serpent got pretty near it, in his discourse with Eve; for the propensity in the sex to be deceived could not be so great, that she should have boldness to hold chat with the devil, without it——But there is an accent of humanity——how shall I describe it?——'tis an accent which covers the part with a garment, and gives the enquirer a right to be as particular with it, as your body-surgeon.

"——Was it without remission?——

"——Was it more tolerable in bed?

"——Could he lie on both sides alike with it?

"——Was he able to mount a horse?

"——Was motion bad for it?" et cætera, were so tenderly spoke to, and so directed towards my uncle *Toby*'s heart, that every item of them sunk ten times deeper into it than the evils themselves——but when Mrs. *Wadman* went round about by *Namur* to get at my uncle *Toby*'s groin; and engaged him to attack the point of the advanced counterscarp, and *pêle mêle*[4] with the *Dutch* to take the counterguard of St. *Roch* sword in hand——and then with tender notes playing upon his ear, led him all bleeding by the hand out of the trench, wiping her eye, as he was carried to his tent—— Heaven! Earth! Sea!——all was lifted up——the springs of nature rose above their levels——an angel of mercy sat besides him on the sopha——his heart glow'd with fire——and had he been worth a thousand, he had lost every heart of them to Mrs. *Wadman*.

---

[4] Pell-mell, jumbled together.

——And whereabouts, dear Sir, quoth Mrs. *Wadman,* a little categorically, did you receive this sad blow?——In asking this question, Mrs. *Wadman* gave a slight glance towards the waistband of my uncle *Toby*'s red plush breeches, expecting naturally, as the shortest reply to it, that my uncle *Toby* would lay his fore-finger upon the place——It fell out otherwise—— for my uncle *Toby* having got his wound before the gate of St. *Nicolas,* in one of the traverses of the trench, opposite to the salient angle of the demi-bastion of St. *Roch;* he could at any time stick a pin upon the identical spot of ground where he was standing when the stone struck him: this struck instantly upon my uncle *Toby*'s sensorium——and with it, struck his large map of the town and citadel of *Namur* and its environs, which he had purchased and pasted down upon a board by the Corporal's aid, during his long illness——it had lain with other military lumber in the garret ever since, and accordingly the Corporal was detached into the garret to fetch it.

My uncle *Toby* measured off thirty toises, with Mrs. *Wadman*'s scissars, from the returning angle before the gate of St. *Nicolas;* and with such a virgin modesty laid her finger upon the place, that the goddess of Decency, if then in being—— if not, 'twas her shade——shook her head, and with a finger wavering across her eyes——forbid her to explain the mistake.

Unhappy Mrs. *Wadman!*——

——For nothing can make this chapter go off with spirit but an apostrophe to. thee——but my heart tells me, that in such a crisis an apostrophe is but an insult in disguise, and ere I would offer one to a woman in distress——let the chapter go to the devil; provided any damn'd critick *in keeping*[5] will be but at the trouble to take it with him.

CHAP. XXVII.

M Y uncle *Toby*'s Map is carried down into the kitchen.

[5]*I.e.,* "kept" and hence controlled by his publisher.

CHAP. XXVIII.

—— AND here is the *Maes*——and this is the *Sambre;* said
the Corporal, pointing with his right hand extended
a little towards the map, and his left upon Mrs. *Bridget*'s shoulder——but not the shoulder next him——and this, said he, is
the town of *Namur*——and this the citadel——and there lay
the *French*——and here lay his honour and myself——and in
this cursed trench, Mrs. *Bridget,* quoth the Corporal, taking
her by the hand, did he receive the wound which crush'd him
so miserably *here*——In pronouncing which he slightly press'd
the back of her hand towards the part he felt for——and let it
fall.

We thought, Mr. *Trim,* it had been more in the middle——
said Mrs. *Bridget*——

That would have undone us for ever——said the Corporal.

——And left my poor mistress undone too——said *Bridget*.
The Corporal made no reply to the repartee, but by giving
Mrs. *Bridget* a kiss.

Come——come——said *Bridget*——holding the palm of her
left-hand parallel to the plane of the horizon, and sliding
the fingers of the other over it, in a way which could not have
been done, had there been the least wart or protuberance——
'Tis every syllable of it false, cried the Corporal, before she
had half finished the sentence——

——I know it to be fact, said *Bridget,* from credible witnesses.

————Upon my honour, said the Corporal, laying his hand
upon his heart, and blushing as he spoke with honest resentment——'tis a story, Mrs. *Bridget,* as false as hell——Not, said
Bridget, interrupting him, that either I or my mistress care a
halfpenny about it, whether 'tis so or no——only that when
one is married, one would chuse to have such a thing by one
at least——

It was somewhat unfortunate for Mrs. *Bridget,* that she had

begun the attack with her manual exercise; for the Corporal
instantly   *   *   *   *   *   *   *   *   *   *   *   *
*   *   *   *   *   *   *   *   *   *   *   *   *   *
*   *   *   *   *   *   *   *   *   *   *   *   *   *
*   *   *   *.

CHAP. XXIX.

IT was like the momentary contest in the moist eye-lids of an
April morning, "Whether *Bridget* should laugh or cry."

She snatch'd up a rolling-pin——'twas ten to one, she had
laugh'd——

She laid it down——she cried; and had one single tear of
'em but tasted of bitterness, full sorrowful would the Corporal's heart have been that he had used the argument; but
the Corporal understood the sex, a *quart major*[1] *to a terce* at
least, better than my uncle *Toby,* and accordingly he assailed
Mrs. *Bridget* after this manner.

I know, Mrs. *Bridget,* said the Corporal, giving her a most
respectful kiss, that thou art good and modest by nature, and
art withal so generous a girl in thyself, that if I know thee
rightly, thou wouldst not wound an insect, much less the honour of so gallant and worthy a soul as my master, wast thou
sure to be made a countess of——but thou hast been set on,
and deluded, dear *Bridget,* as is often a woman's case, "to
please others more than themselves——"

Bridget's eyes poured down at the sensations the Corporal
excited.

——Tell me——tell me then, my dear *Bridget,* continued the
Corporal, taking hold of her hand, which hung down dead by
her side,——and giving a second kiss——whose suspicion has
misled thee?

Bridget sobb'd a sob or two——then open'd her eyes——
the Corporal wiped 'em with the bottom of her apron——she
then open'd her heart and told him all.

---

[1]A sequence of the four highest cards in any suit. Terce: tierce, a sequence of three cards.

CHAP. XXX.

MY uncle *Toby* and the Corporal had gone on separately with their operations the greatest part of the campaign, and as effectually cut off from all communication of what either the one or the other had been doing, as if they had been separated from each other by the *Maes* or the *Sambre*.

My uncle *Toby*, on his side, had presented himself every afternoon in his red and silver, and blue and gold alternately, and sustained an infinity of attacks in them, without knowing them to be attacks——and so had nothing to communicate——

The Corporal, on his side, in taking *Bridget,* by it had gain'd considerable advantages——and consequently had much to communicate——but what were the advantages——as well, as what was the manner by which he had seiz'd them, required so nice an historian that the Corporal durst not venture upon it; and as sensible as he was of glory, would rather have been contented to have gone bareheaded and without laurels for ever, than torture his master's modesty for a single moment——

——Best of honest and gallant servants!——But I have apostrophiz'd thee, *Trim!* once before——and could I apotheosize thee also (that is to say) with good company——I would do it *without ceremony* in the very next page.

CHAP. XXXI.

NOW my uncle *Toby* had one evening laid down his pipe upon the table, and was counting over to himself upon his finger ends, (beginning at his thumb) all Mrs. *Wadman's* perfections one by one; and happening two or three times together, either by omitting some, or counting others twice over to puzzle himself sadly before he could get beyond his middle finger——Prithee, *Trim!* said he, taking up his pipe again,——bring me a pen and ink: *Trim* brought paper also.

Take a full sheet——*Trim!* said my uncle *Toby,* making a sign with his pipe at the same time to take a chair and sit down close by him at the table. The Corporal obeyed—— placed the paper directly before him——took a pen and dip'd it in the ink.

——She has a thousand virtues, *Trim!* said my uncle *Toby*——

Am I to set them down, an' please your honour? quoth the Corporal.

——But they must be taken in their ranks, replied my uncle *Toby;* for of them all, *Trim,* that which wins me most, and which is a security for all the rest, is the compassionate turn and singular humanity of her character——I protest, added my uncle *Toby,* looking up, as he protested it, towards the top of the ceiling——That was I her brother, *Trim,* a thousand fold, she could not make more constant or more tender enquiries after my sufferings——though now no more.

The Corporal made no reply to my uncle *Toby's* protestation, but by a short cough——he dip'd the pen a second time into the inkhorn; and my uncle *Toby,* pointing with the end of his pipe as close to the top of the sheet at the left hand corner of it, as he could get it——the Corporal wrote down the word

HUMANITY - - - - - - - - - - - - - - - thus.

Prithee, Corporal, said my uncle *Toby,* as soon as *Trim* had done it——how often does Mrs. *Bridget* enquire after the wound on the cap of thy knee, which thou received'st at the battle of *Landen?*

She never, an' please your honour, enquires after it at all.

That, Corporal, said my uncle *Toby,* with all the triumph the goodness of his nature would permit——That shews the difference in the character of the mistress and maid——had the fortune of war allotted the same mischance to me, Mrs. *Wadman* would have enquired into every circumstance relating to it a hundred times——She would have enquired, an' please

your honour, ten times as often about your honour's groin——
The pain, *Trim,* is equally excruciating,——and Compassion
has as much to do with the one as the other——

——God bless your honour! cried the Corporal——what
has a woman's compassion to do with a wound upon the cap of
a man's knee? had your honour's been shot into ten thousand
splinters at the affair of *Landen,* Mrs. *Wadman* would have
troubled her head as little about it as *Bridget;* because, added
the Corporal, lowering his voice and speaking very distinctly,
as he assigned his reason——

"The knee is such a distance from the main body——
whereas the groin, your honour knows, is upon the very *curtin*
of the *place.*"

My uncle *Toby* gave a long whistle——but in a note which
could scarce be heard across the table.

The Corporal had advanced too far to retire——in three
words he told the rest——

My uncle *Toby* laid down his pipe as gently upon the fender, as if it had been spun from the unravellings of a spider's
web——

——Let us go to my brother *Shandy's,* said he.

CHAP. XXXII.

THERE will be just time, whilst my uncle *Toby* and *Trim*
are walking to my father's, to inform you, that Mrs. *Wadman* had, some moons before this, made a confident of my
mother; and that Mrs. *Bridget,* who had the burden of her
own, as well as her mistress's secret to carry, had got happily
delivered of both to *Susannah* behind the garden-wall.

As for my mother, she saw nothing at all in it, to make the
least bustle about——but *Susannah* was sufficient by herself for
all the ends and purposes you could possibly have, in exporting
a family secret; for she instantly imparted it by signs to *Jonathan*——and *Jonathan* by tokens to the cook, as she was bast-

ing a loin of mutton; the cook sold it with some kitchen-fat to the postillion for a groat, who truck'd it with the dairy maid for something of about the same value——and though whisper'd in the hay-loft, FAME caught the notes with her brazen trumpet and sounded them upon the house-top——In a word, not an old woman in the village or five miles round, who did not understand the difficulties of my uncle *Toby*'s siege, and what were the secret articles which had delay'd the surrender.——

My father, whose way was to force every event in nature into an hypothesis, by which means never man crucified TRUTH at the rate he did——had but just heard of the report as my uncle *Toby* set out; and catching fire suddenly at the trespass done his brother by it, was demonstrating to *Yorick,* notwithstanding my mother was sitting by——not only, "That the devil was in women, and that the whole of the affair was lust;" but that every evil and disorder in the world, of what kind or nature soever, from the first fall of *Adam,* down to my uncle *Toby*'s (inclusive) was owing one way or other to the same unruly appetite.

Yorick was just bringing my father's hypothesis to some temper, when my uncle *Toby* entering the room with marks of infinite benevolence and forgiveness in his looks, my father's eloquence rekindled against the passion——and as he was not very nice in the choice of his words when he was wroth—— as soon as my uncle *Toby* was seated by the fire, and had filled his pipe, my father broke out in this manner.

CHAP. XXXIII.

——THAT provision should be made for continuing the race of so great, so exalted and godlike a Being as man——I am far from denying——but philosophy speaks freely of every thing; and therefore I still think and do maintain it to be a pity, that it should be done by means of a passion which bends down the faculties, and turns all the wisdom, contemplations, and operations of the soul backwards——a passion, my dear, continued my father, addressing himself to my mother, which couples and equals wise men with fools, and makes us come out of caverns and hiding-places more like satyrs and four-footed beasts than men.

I know it will be said, continued my father (availing himself of the *Prolepsis*) that in itself, and simply taken——like hunger, or thirst, or sleep——'tis an affair neither good or bad ——or shameful or otherwise.——Why then did the delicacy of *Diogenes* and *Plato* so recalcitrate against it?[1] and wherefore, when we go about to make and plant a man, do we put out the candle? and for what reason is it, that all the parts thereof——the congredients——the preparations——the instruments, and whatever serves thereto, are so held as to be conveyed to a cleanly mind by no language, translation, or periphrasis whatever?

——The act of killing and destroying a man, continued my father raising his voice——and turning to my uncle *Toby*—— you see, is glorious——and the weapons by which we do it are honourable——We march with them upon our shoulders—— We strut with them by our sides——We gild them——We carve them——We in-lay them——We enrich them——Nay, if it be but a *scoundril* cannon, we cast an ornament upon the breech of it.——

——My uncle *Toby* laid down his pipe to intercede for a better epithet——and *Yorick* was rising up to batter the whole hypothesis to pieces——

——When *Obadiah* broke into the middle of the room with a complaint, which cried out for an immediate hearing.

---

[1]Diogenes the Cynic (for whom, see p. 78, n. 1) is said to have "recalcitrated"—though certainly not for delicacy's sake—against the inconvenience and expense and loss of independence to which men were subjected who were dependent upon women for their sexual gratification. In the *Laws* (6.783) Plato (for whom, see p. 293, n. 1) makes the Athenian inveigh against "the third and greatest and sharpest want and desire . . . the fire of sexual lust, which kindles in men every species of wantonness and madness"; and throughout his *Dialogues* he deprecates the "mad and furious master," sensual passion.

The case was this:

My father, whether by ancient custom of the manor, or as impropriator of the great tythes,[2] was obliged to keep a Bull for the service of the Parish, and *Obadiah* had led his cow upon a *pop-visit* to him one day or other the preceeding summer——— I say, one day or other———because as chance would have it, it was the day on which he was married to my father's house-maid———so one was a reckoning to the other. Therefore when *Obadiah's* wife was brought to bed———*Obadiah* thanked God———

———Now, said *Obadiah,* I shall have a calf: so *Obadiah* went daily to visit his cow.

She'll calve on Monday———on Tuesday———on Wednesday at the farthest———

The cow did not calve———no———she'll not calve till next week———the cow put it off terribly———till at the end of the sixth week *Obadiah's* suspicions (like a good man's) fell upon the Bull.

Now the parish being very large, my father's Bull, to speak the truth of him, was no way equal to the department; he had, however, got himself, somehow or other, thrust into employment———and as he went through the business with a grave face, my father had a high opinion of him.

———Most of the townsmen, an' please your worship, quoth *Obadiah,* believe that 'tis all the Bull's fault———

———But may not a cow be barren? replied my father, turning to Doctor *Slop.*

It never happens: said Dr. *Slop,* but the man's wife may have come before her time naturally enough———Prithee has the child hair upon his head?———added Dr. *Slop*———

———It is as hairy as I am; said *Obadiah.*———*Obadiah* had not been shaved for three weeks———Wheu - - u - - - - u - - - - - - - - cried my father; beginning the sentence with an exclamatory whistle———and so, brother *Toby,* this poor Bull of mine, who is as good a Bull as ever p–ss'd, and might

---

[2] A layman who cares for and disburses church revenues paid in the form of grain, hay, and wood.

have done for *Europa*[3] herself in purer times——had he but
two legs less, might have been driven into Doctors Commons[4]
and lost his character——which to a Town Bull, brother *Toby,*
is the very same thing as his life——

L - - d! said my mother, what is all this story about?——

A COCK and a BULL, said *Yorick*——And one of the best
of its kind, I ever heard.

The End of the Ninth Volume.[5]

---

[3]A Phœnician princess whose beauty charmed Zeus who, assuming the
form of a bull, carried her off to Crete where she became by him the
mother of Minos, Rhadamanthus, and Sarpedon.

[4]The College of Doctors of Civil Law in London, where divorces,
among other civil business, were transacted.

[5]Sterne did not live to continue the book.